THE SHORT STORY

50 MASTERPIECES

THE SHORT STORY

50 MASTERPIECES

St. Martin's Press

New York

Library of Congress Catalog Card Number: 82–60462

Manufactured in the United States of America
9 8 7 6 5
o n m l k
For information, write St. Martin's Press, Inc.
175 Fifth Avenue, New York, NY 10010

cover design: Darby Downey

cover illustration: *Incoming Tide: Scarboro, Maine;* Winslow Homer; National Gallery of Art, Washington; Gift of Ruth K. Henschel in memory of her husband, Charles R. Henschel.

ISBN: 0–312–72216–8

Acknowledgments

Acknowledgments and copyrights continue at the back of the book, on pages 788–792, which constitute an extension of the copyright page.

Publisher's Foreword

Our aim in publishing this anthology may be stated simply: to offer a rich but not extravagantly large selection of works of short fiction, all of which are widely regarded as literary masterpieces and also have proved accessible and exciting in the classroom—and to make these stories available in a book of high quality and inviting format at a low price.

Represented here are fifty masters of the genre, spanning a century and a half from Hawthorne and Poe to García Márquez, Barthelme, and Oates. The collection is wide ranging not only in its chronological span but in its representation of literary masters of both sexes and of diverse cultural and ethnic backgrounds. In addition to shorter works, two short novels—Conrad's *The Secret Sharer* and Tolstoy's *The Death of Ivan Ilych*—are included. We have chosen to give the available space to stories rather than use it for critical discussions, suggested topics for papers, and other such materials that many instructors prefer to provide themselves. However, we believe that students will appreciate brief biographical notes on the authors, and those appear on pages 760 to 787.

In making the selections we have been guided by the suggestions of hundreds of instructors who have let us know, in one way or another, what stories they and their students have found most rewarding. The many comments from instructors who have used *The Short Story: 25 Masterpieces,* the predecessor of this volume, have been particularly valuable in guiding our selection. *The Short Story: 25 Masterpieces* will continue to be available for instructors who prefer a briefer book.

The comments of instructors and students on the present volume will be welcomed and will be taken carefully into account in the preparation of future editions.

Ellen C. Wynn
College Division, St. Martin's Press

Contents

Young Goodman Brown

NATHANIEL HAWTHORNE

[1804–1864]

Young Goodman Brown came forth at sunset into the street of Salem village; but put his head back, after crossing the threshold, to exchange a parting kiss with his young wife. And Faith, as the wife was aptly named, thrust her own pretty head into the street, letting the wind play with the pink ribbons of her cap while she called to Goodman Brown.

"Dearest heart," whispered she, softly and rather sadly, when her lips were close to his ear, "prithee put off your journey until sunrise and sleep in your own bed to-night. A lone woman is troubled with dreams and such thoughts that she's afeared of herself sometimes. Pray tarry with me this night, dear husband, of all nights in the year."

"My love and my Faith," replied young Goodman Brown, "of all nights in the year, this one night must I tarry away from thee. My journey, as thou callest it, forth and back again, must needs be done 'twixt now and sunrise. What, my sweet, pretty wife, dost thou doubt me already, and we but three months married?"

"Then God bless you!" said Faith, with the pink ribbons; "and may you find all well when you come back."

"Amen!" cried Goodman Brown. "Say thy prayers, dear Faith, and go to bed at dusk, and no harm will come to thee."

So they parted; and the young man pursued his way until, being about to turn the corner by the meeting-house, he looked back and saw the head of Faith still peeping after him with a melancholy air, in spite of her pink ribbons.

"Poor little Faith!" thought he, for his heart smote him. "What a wretch am I to leave her on such an errand! She talks of dreams, too. Methought as she spoke there was trouble in her face, as if a dream had warned her what work is to be done tonight. But no, no; 't would kill her to think it. Well, she's a blessed angel on earth; and after this one night I'll cling to her skirts and follow her to heaven."

With this excellent resolve for the future, Goodman Brown felt himself justified in making more haste on his present evil purpose. He had taken a dreary road, darkened by all the gloomiest trees of the forest, which barely stood aside to let the narrow path creep through, and closed immediately behind. It was all as lonely as could be; and there is this peculiarity in such a solitude, that the traveller knows not who may be concealed by the innumerable trunks and the thick boughs overhead; so that with lonely footsteps he may yet be passing through an unseen multitude.

"There may be a devilish Indian behind every tree," said Goodman Brown to himself; and he glanced fearfully behind him as he added, "What if the devil himself should be at my very elbow!"

His head turned back, he passed a crook of the road, and, looking forward again, beheld the figure of a man, in grave and decent attire, seated at the foot of an old tree. He arose at Goodman Brown's approach and walked onward side by side with him.

"You are late, Goodman Brown," said he. "The clock of the Old South was striking as I came through Boston, and that is full fifteen minutes agone."

"Faith kept me back a while," replied the young man, with a tremor in his voice, caused by the sudden appearance of his companion, though not wholly unexpected.

It was now deep dusk in the forest, and deepest in that part of it where these two were journeying. As nearly as could be discerned, the second traveller was about fifty years old, apparently in the same rank of life as Goodman Brown, and bearing a considerable resemblance to him, though perhaps more in expression than features. Still they might have been taken for father and son. And yet, though the elder person was as simply clad as the younger, and as simple in manner too, he had an indescribable air of one who knew the world, and who would not have felt abashed at the governor's dinner table or in King William's court, were it possible that his affairs should call him thither. But the only thing about him that could be fixed upon as remarkable was his staff, which bore the likeness of a great black snake, so curiously wrought that it might almost be seen to twist and wriggle itself like a living serpent. This, of course, must have been an ocular deception, assisted by the uncertain light.

"Come, Goodman Brown," cried his fellow-traveller, "this is a dull pace for the beginning of a journey. Take my staff, if you are so soon weary."

"Friend," said the other, exchanging his slow pace for a full stop, "having kept covenant by meeting thee here, it is my purpose now to return whence I came. I have scruples touching the matter thou wot'st of."

"Sayest thou so?" replied he of the serpent, smiling apart. "Let us walk on, nevertheless, reasoning as we go; and if I convince thee not thou shalt turn back. We are but a little way in the forest yet."

"Too far! too far!" exclaimed the goodman, unconsciously resuming his walk. "My father never went into the woods on such an errand, nor his father before him. We have been a race of honest men and good Christians since the days of the martyrs; and shall I be the first of the name of Brown that ever took this path and kept —"

"Such company, thou wouldst say," observed the elder person, interpreting his pause. "Well said, Goodman Brown! I have been as well acquainted with your family as with ever a one among the Puritans; and that's no trifle to say. I helped your grandfather, the constable, when he lashed the Quaker woman so smartly through the streets of Salem; and it was I that brought your father a pitch-pine knot, kindled at my own hearth, to set fire to an Indian village, in King Philip's war. They were my good friends, both; and many a pleasant walk have we had along this path, returned merrily after midnight. I would fain be friends with you for their sake."

"If it be as thou sayest," replied Goodman Brown, "I marvel they never spoke of these matters; or, verily, I marvel not, seeing that the least rumor of the sort would have driven them from New England. We are a people of prayer, and good works to boot, and abide no such wickedness."

"Wickedness or not," said the traveller with the twisted staff, "I have a very general acquaintance here in New England. The deacons of many a church have drunk the communion wine with me; the selectmen of divers towns make me their chairman; and a majority of the Great and General Court are firm supporters of my interest. The governor and I, too—But these are state secrets."

"Can this be so?" cried Goodman Brown, with a stare of amazement at his undisturbed companion. "Howbeit, I have nothing to do with the governor and council; they have their own ways, and are no rule for a simple husbandman like me. But, were I to go on with thee, how should I meet the eye of that good old man, our minister, at Salem village? Oh, his voice would make me tremble both Sabbath day and lecture day."

Thus far the elder traveller had listened with due gravity; but now burst into a fit of irrepressible mirth, shaking himself so violently that his snakelike staff actually seemed to wriggle in sympathy.

"Ha! ha! ha!" shouted he again and again; then composing himself, "Well, go on, Goodman Brown, go on; but, prithee, don't kill me with laughing."

"Well, then, to end the matter at once," said Goodman Brown, considerably nettled, "there is my wife, Faith. It would break her dear little heart; and I'd rather break my own."

"Nay, if that be the case," answered the other, "e'en go thy ways, Goodman Brown. I would not for twenty old women like the one hobbling before us that Faith should come to any harm."

As he spoke he pointed his staff at a female figure on the path, in whom Goodman Brown recognized a very pious and exemplary dame, who had taught him his catechism in youth, and was still his moral and spiritual adviser, jointly with the minister and Deacon Gookin.

"A marvel, truly, that Goody Cloyse should be so far in the wilderness at nightfall," said he. "But with your leave, friend, I shall take a cut through the woods until we have left this Christian woman behind. Being a stranger to you, she might ask whom I was consorting with and whither I was going."

"Be it so," said his fellow-traveller. "Betake you to the woods, and let me keep the path."

Accordingly the young man turned aside, but took care to watch his companion, who advanced softly along the road until he had come within a staff's length of the old dame. She, meanwhile, was making the best of her way, with singular speed for so aged a woman, and mumbling some indistinct words—a prayer, doubtless—as she went. The traveller put forth his staff and touched her withered neck with what seemed the serpent's tail.

"The devil!" screamed the pious old lady.

"Then Goody Cloyse knows her old friend?" observed the traveller, confronting her and leaning on his writhing stick.

"Ah, forsooth, and is it your worship indeed?" cried the good dame. "Yea, truly is it, and in the very image of my old gossip, Goodman Brown, the grandfather of the silly fellow that now is. But—would your worship believe it?—my broomstick hath strangely disappeared, stolen, as I suspect, by that unhanged witch, Goody Cory, and that, too, when I was all anointed with the juice of smallage, and cinquefoil, and wolf's bane—"

"Mingled with fine wheat and the fat of a new-born babe," said the shape of old Goodman Brown.

"Ah, your worship knows the recipe," cried the old lady, cackling aloud. "So, as I was saying, being all ready for the meeting, and no horse to ride on, I made up my mind to foot it; for they tell me there is a nice young man to be taken into communion to-night. But now your good worship will lend me your arm, and we shall be there in a twinkling."

"That can hardly be," answered her friend. "I may not spare you my arm, Goody Cloyse; but here is my staff, if you will."

So saying, he threw it down at her feet, where, perhaps, it assumed life, being one of the rods which its owner had formerly lent to the Egyptian magi. Of this fact, however, Goodman Brown could not take cognizance. He had cast up his eyes in astonishment, and, looking down again, beheld neither Goody Cloyse nor the serpentine staff, but his fellow-traveller alone, who waited for him as calmly as if nothing had happened.

"That old woman taught me my catechism," said the young man; and there was a world of meaning in this simple comment.

They continued to walk onward, while the elder traveller exhorted his companion to make good speed and persevere in the path, discoursing so aptly that his arguments seemed rather to spring up in the bosom of his auditor than to be suggested by himself. As they went, he plucked a branch of maple to serve for a walking stick, and began to strip it of the twigs and little boughs, which were wet with evening dew. The moment his fingers touched them they became strangely withered and dried up as with a week's sunshine. Thus the pair proceeded, at a good free pace, until suddenly, in a gloomy hollow of the road, Goodman Brown sat himself down on the stump of a tree and refused to go any farther.

"Friend," said he, stubbornly, "my mind is made up. Not another step will I budge on this errand. What if a wretched old woman do choose to go to the devil when I thought she was going to heaven: is that any reason why I should quit my dear Faith and go after her?"

"You will think better of this by and by," said his acquaintance, composedly. "Sit here and rest yourself a while; and when you feel like moving again, there is my staff to help you along."

Without more words, he threw his companion the maple stick, and was as speedily out of sight as if he had vanished into the deepening gloom. The young man sat a few moments by the roadside, applauding himself greatly, and thinking with how clear a conscience he should meet the minister in his morning walk, nor shrink from the eye of good old Deacon Gookin. And what calm sleep would be his that very night, which was to have been spent so wickedly, but so purely and sweetly now, in the arms of Faith! Amidst these pleasant and praiseworthy meditations, Goodman Brown heard the tramp of horses along the road, and deemed it advisable to conceal himself within the verge of the forest, conscious of the guilty purpose that had brought him thither, though now so happily turned from it.

On came the hoof tramps and the voices of the riders, two grave old voices, conversing soberly as they drew near. These mingled sounds appeared to pass along the road, within a few yards of the young man's hiding-place; but, owing doubtless to the depth of the gloom at that particular spot, neither the travellers nor their steeds were visible. Though their figures brushed the small boughs by the wayside, it could not be seen that they intercepted, even for a moment, the faint gleam from the strip of bright sky athwart which they must have passed. Goodman Brown alternately crouched and stood on tiptoe, pulling aside the branches and thrusting forth his head as far as he durst without discerning so much as a shadow. It vexed him the more, because he could have sworn, were such a thing possible, that he recognized the voices of the minister and Deacon Gookin, jogging along quietly, as they were wont to do, when bound to some ordination or ecclesiastical council. While yet within hearing, one of the riders stopped to pluck a switch.

"Of the two, reverend sir," said the voice like the deacon's, "I had rather miss an ordination dinner than to-night's meeting. They tell me that some of our community are to be here from Falmouth and beyond, and others from Connecticut and Rhode Island, besides several of the Indian powwows, who, after their fashion, know almost as much deviltry as the best of us. Moreover, there is a goodly young woman to be taken into communion."

"Mighty well, Deacon Gookin!" replied the solemn old tones of the minister. "Spur up, or we shall be late. Nothing can be done, you know, until I get on the ground."

The hoofs clattered again; and the voices, talking so strangely in the empty air, passed on through the forest, where no church had ever been gathered or solitary Christian prayed. Whither, then, could these holy men be journeying so deep into the heathen wilderness? Young Goodman Brown caught hold of a tree for support, being ready to sink down on the ground, faint and overburdened with the heavy sickness of his heart. He looked up to the sky, doubting whether there really was a heaven above him. Yet there was the blue arch, and the stars brightening in it.

"With heaven above and Faith below, I will yet stand firm against the devil!" cried Goodman Brown.

While he still gazed upward into the deep arch of the firmament and had lifted his hands to pray, a cloud, though no wind was stirring, hurried across the zenith and hid the brightening stars. The blue sky was still visible, except directly overhead, where this black mass of cloud was sweeping swiftly northward. Aloft in the air, as if from the depths of the cloud, came a confused and doubtful sound of voices. Once the listener fancied that he could distinguish the accents of towns-people of his own, men and women, both pious and ungodly, many of whom he had met at the communion table, and had seen others rioting at the tavern. The next moment, so indistinct were the sounds, he doubted whether he had heard aught but the murmur of the old forest, whispering without a wind. Then came a stronger swell of those familiar tones, heard daily in the sunshine at Salem village, but never until now from a cloud of night. There was one voice of a young woman, uttering lamentations, yet with an uncertain sorrow, and entreating for some favor, which, perhaps, it would grieve her to obtain; and all the unseen multitude, both saints and sinners, seemed to encourage her onward.

"Faith!" shouted Goodman Brown, in a voice of agony and desperation; and the echoes of the forest mocked him, crying, "Faith! Faith!" as if bewildered wretches were seeking her all through the wilderness.

The cry of grief, rage, and terror was yet piercing the night, when the unhappy husband held his breath for a response. There was a scream, drowned immediately in a louder murmur of voices, fading into far-off laughter, as the dark cloud swept away, leaving the clear and silent sky above Goodman Brown. But something fluttered lightly down through the air and caught on the branch of a tree. The young man seized it, and beheld a pink ribbon.

"My Faith is gone!" cried he, after one stupefied moment. "There is no good on earth; and sin is but a name. Come, devil; for to thee is this world given."

And, maddened with despair, so that he laughed loud and long, did Goodman Brown grasp his staff and set forth again, at such a rate that he seemed to fly along the forest path rather than to walk or run. The road grew wilder and drearier and more faintly traced, and vanished at length, leaving him in the heart of the dark wilderness, still rushing onward with the instinct that guides mortal men to evil. The whole forest was peopled with frightful sounds—the creaking of the trees, the howling of wild beasts, and the yell of Indians; while sometimes the wind tolled like a distant church bell, and sometimes gave a broad roar around the traveller, as if all Nature were laughing him to scorn. But he was himself the chief horror of the scene, and shrank not from its other horrors.

"Ha! ha! ha!" roared Goodman Brown when the wind laughed at him. "Let us hear which will laugh loudest. Think not to frighten me with your deviltry. Come witch, come wizard, come Indian powwow, come devil himself, and here comes Goodman Brown. You may as well fear him as he fear you."

In truth, all through the haunted forest there could be nothing more frightful than the figure of Goodman Brown. On he flew among the black pines, brandishing his staff with frenzied gestures, now giving vent to an inspiration of horrid blasphemy, and now shouting forth such laughter as set all the echoes of the forest laughing like demons around him. The fiend in his own shape is less hideous than when he rages in the breast of man. Thus sped the demoniac on his course, until, quivering among the trees, he saw a red light before him, as when the felled trunks and branches of a clearing have been set on fire, and throw up their lurid blaze against the sky, at the hour of midnight. He paused, in a lull of the tempest that had driven him onward, and heard the swell of what seemed a hymn, rolling solemnly from a distance with the weight of many voices. He knew the tune; it was a familiar one in the choir of the village meeting-house. The verse died heavily away, and was lengthened by a chorus, not of human voices, but of all the sounds of the benighted wilderness pealing in awful harmony together. Goodman Brown cried out, and his cry was lost to his own ear by its unison with the cry of the desert.

In the interval of silence he stole forward until the light glared full upon his eyes. At one extremity of an open space, hemmed in by the dark wall of the forest, arose a rock, bearing some rude, natural resemblance either to an altar or a pulpit, and surrounded by four blazing pines, their tops aflame, their stems untouched, like candles at an evening meeting. The mass of foliage that had overgrown the summit of the rock was all on fire, blazing high into the night and fitfully illuminating the whole field. Each pendent twig and leafy festoon was in a blaze. As the red light arose and fell, a numerous congregation alternately shone forth, then disappeared in shadow, and again grew, as it were, out of the darkness, peopling the heart of the solitary woods at once.

"A grave and dark-clad company," quoth Goodman Brown.

In truth they were such. Among them, quivering to and fro between gloom and splendor, appeared faces that would be seen next day at the council board of the province, and others which, Sabbath after Sabbath, looked devoutly heavenward, and benignantly over the crowded pews, from the holiest pulpits in the land. Some affirm that the lady of the governor was there. At least there were high dames well known to her, and wives of honored husbands, and widows, a great multitude, and ancient maidens, all of excellent repute, and fair young girls, who trembled lest their mothers should espy them. Either the sudden gleams of light flashing over the obscure field bedazzled Goodman Brown, or he recognized a score of the church members of Salem village famous for their especial sanctity. Good old Deacon Gookin had arrived, and waited at the skirts of that venerable saint, his revered pastor. But, irreverently consorting with these grave, reputable, and pious people, these elders of the church, these chaste dames and dewy virgins, there were men of dissolute lives and women of spotted fame, wretches given over to all mean and filthy vice, and suspected even of horrid crimes. It was strange to see that the good shrank not from the wicked, nor were the sinners abashed by the saints. Scattered also among their pale-faced enemies were the Indian priests, or powwows, who had often scared their native forest with more hideous incantations than any known to English witchcraft.

"But where is Faith?" thought Goodman Brown; and, as hope came into his heart, he trembled.

Another verse of the hymn arose, a slow and mournful strain, such as the pious love, but joined to words which expressed all that our nature can conceive of sin, and darkly hinted at far more. Unfathomable to mere mortals is the lore of fiends. Verse after verse was sung; and still the chorus of the desert swelled between like the deepest tone of a mighty organ; and with the final peal of that dreadful anthem there came a sound, as if the roaring wind, the rushing streams, the howling beasts, and every other voice of the unconcerted wilderness were mingling and according with the voice of guilty man in homage to the prince of all. The four blazing pines threw up a loftier flame, and obscurely discovered shapes and visages of horror on the smoke wreaths above the impious assembly. At the same moment the fire on the rock shot redly forth and formed a glowing arch above its base, where now appeared a figure. With reverence be it spoken, the figure bore no slight similitude, both in garb and manner, to some grave divine of the New England churches.

"Bring forth the converts!" cried a voice that echoed through the field and rolled into the forest.

At the word, Goodman Brown stepped forth from the shadow of the trees and approached the congregation, with whom he felt a loathful brotherhood by the sympathy of all that was wicked in his heart. He could have well-nigh sworn that the shape of his own dead father beckoned him to advance, looking downward from a smoke wreath, while a woman, with dim features of despair, threw out her hand to warn him back. Was it his mother? But he had no power to retreat one step, nor to resist, even in thought, when the minister and good old Deacon Gookin seized his arms and led him to the blazing rock. Thither came also the slender form of a veiled female, led between Goody Cloyse, that pious teacher of the catechism, and Martha Carrier, who had received the devil's promise to be queen of hell. A rampant hag was she. And there stood the proselytes beneath the canopy of fire.

"Welcome, my children," said the dark figure, "to the communion of your race. Ye have found thus young your nature and your destiny. My children, look behind you!"

They turned; and flashing forth, as it were, in a sheet of flame, the fiend worshippers were seen; the smile of welcome gleamed darkly on every visage.

"There," resumed the sable form, "are all whom ye have reverenced from youth. Ye deemed them holier than yourselves, and shrank from your own sin, contrasting it with their lives of righteousness and prayerful aspirations heavenward. Yet here are they all in my worshipping assembly. This night it shall be granted you to know their secret deeds; how hoary-bearded elders of the church have whispered wanton words to the young maids of their households; how many a woman, eager for widows' weeds, has given her husband a drink at bedtime and let him sleep his last sleep in her bosom; how beardless youths have made haste to inherit their fathers' wealth; and how fair damsels—blush not, sweet ones—have dug little graves in the garden, and bidden me, the sole guest, to an infant's funeral. By the sympathy of your human hearts for sin ye shall scent out all the places—whether in church, bedchamber, street, field, or forest—where crime has been committed, and shall exult to behold the whole earth one stain of guilt, one mighty blood spot. Far more than this. It shall be yours to penetrate, in every bosom, the deep mystery of sin, the fountain of all wicked arts, and which inexhaustibly supplies more evil impulses than human power—than my power at its utmost—can make manifest in deeds. And now, my children, look upon each other."

They did so; and, by the blaze of the hell-kindled torches, the wretched man beheld his Faith, and the wife her husband, trembling before that unhallowed altar.

"Lo, there ye stand, my children," said the figure, in a deep and solemn tone, almost sad with its despairing awfulness, as if his once angelic nature could yet mourn for our miserable race. "Depending upon one another's hearts, ye had still hoped that virtue were not all a dream. Now are ye undeceived. Evil is the nature of mankind. Evil must be your only happiness. Welcome again, my children, to the communion of your race."

"Welcome," repeated the fiend worshippers, in one cry of despair and triumph.

And there they stood, the only pair, as it seemed, who were yet hesitating on the verge of wickedness in this dark world. A basin was hollowed, naturally, in the rock. Did it contain water, reddened by the lurid light? or was it blood? or, perchance, a liquid flame? Herein did the shape of evil dip his hand and prepare to lay the mark of baptism upon their foreheads, that they might be partakers of the mystery of sin, more conscious of the secret guilt of others, both in deed and thought, than they could now be of their own. The husband cast one look at his pale wife, and Faith at him. What polluted wretches would the next glance show them to each other, shuddering alike at what they disclosed and what they saw!

"Faith! Faith!" cried the husband, "look up to heaven, and resist the wicked one."

Whether Faith obeyed he knew not. Hardly had he spoken when he found himself amid calm night and solitude, listening to a roar of the wind which died heavily away through the forest. He staggered against the rock, and felt it chill and damp; while a hanging twig, that had been all on fire, besprinkled his cheek with the coldest dew.

The next morning young Goodman Brown came slowly into the street of Salem village, staring around him like a bewildered man. The good old minister was taking a walk along the graveyard to get an appetite for breakfast and meditate his sermon, and bestowed a blessing, as he passed, on Goodman Brown. He shrank from the venerable saint as if to avoid an anathema. Old Deacon Gookin was at domestic worship, and the holy words of his prayer were heard through the open window. "What God doth the wizard pray to?" quoth Goodman Brown. Goody Cloyse, that excellent old Christian, stood in the early sunshine at her own lattice, catechizing a little girl who had brought her a pint of morning's milk. Goodman Brown snatched away the child as from the grasp of the fiend himself. Turning the corner by the meeting-house, he spied the head of Faith, with the pink ribbons, gazing anxiously forth, and bursting into such joy at sight of him that she skipped along the street and almost kissed her husband before the whole village. But Goodman Brown looked sternly and sadly into her face, and passed on without a greeting.

Had Goodman Brown fallen asleep in the forest and only dreamed a wild dream of a witch-meeting?

Be it so if you will; but, alas! it was a dream of evil omen for young Goodman Brown. A stern, a sad, a darkly meditative, a distrustful, if not a desperate man did he become from the night of that fearful dream. On the Sabbath day, when the congregation were singing a holy psalm, he could not listen because an anthem of sin rushed loudly upon his ear and drowned all the blessed strain. When the minister spoke from the pulpit with power and fervid eloquence, and, with his hand on the open Bible, of the sacred truths of our religion, and of saint-like lives and triumphant deaths, and of future bliss or misery unutterable, then did Goodman Brown turn pale, dreading lest the roof should thunder down upon the gray blasphemer and his hearers. Often, waking suddenly at midnight, he shrank from the bosom of Faith; and at morning or eventide, when the family knelt down at prayer, he scowled and muttered to himself, and gazed sternly at his wife, and turned away. And when he had lived long, and was borne to his grave a hoary corpse, followed by Faith, an aged woman, and children and grandchildren, a goodly procession, besides neighbors not a few, they carved no hopeful verse upon his tombstone, for his dying hour was gloom.

1835

The Fall of the House of Usher

EDGAR ALLAN POE

[1809–1849]

Son coeur est un luth suspendu;
Sitôt qu'on le touche il résonne.
De Béranger

During the whole of a dull, dark, and soundless day in the autumn of the year, when the clouds hung oppressively low in the heavens, I had been passing alone, on horseback, through a singularly dreary tract of country; and at length found myself, as the shades of the evening drew on, within view of the melancholy House of Usher. I knew not how it was—but, with the first glimpse of the building, a sense of insufferable gloom pervaded my spirit. I say insufferable; for the feeling was unrelieved by any of that half-pleasurable, because poetic, sentiment with which the mind usually receives even the sternest natural images of the desolate or terrible. I looked upon the scene before me—upon the mere house, and the simple landscape features of the domain, upon the bleak walls, upon the vacant eye-like windows, upon a few rank sedges, and upon a few white trunks of decayed trees—with an utter depression of soul which I can compare to no earthly sensation more properly than to the afterdream of the reveler upon opium; the bitter lapse into everyday life, the hideous dropping off of the veil. There was an iciness, a sinking, a sickening of the heart, an unredeemed dreariness of thought which no goading of the imagination could torture into aught of the sublime. What was it—I paused to think—what was it that so unnerved me in the contemplation of the House of Usher? It was a mystery all insoluble; nor could I grapple with the shadowy fancies that crowded upon me as I pondered. I was forced to fall back upon the unsatisfactory conclusion, that while, beyond doubt, there *are* combinations of very simple natural objects which have the power of thus affecting us, still the analysis of this power lies among considerations beyond our depth. It was possible, I reflected, that a mere different arrangement of the particulars of the scene, of the details of the picture, would be sufficient to modify, or perhaps to annihilate, its capacity for sorrowful impression; and, acting upon this idea, I reined my horse to the precipitous brink of a black and lurid tarn that lay in unruffled luster by the dwelling, and gazed down—but with a shudder even more thrilling than before—upon the remodeled and inverted images of the gray sedge, and the ghastly tree stems, and the vacant and eye-like windows.

Nevertheless, in this mansion of gloom I now proposed to myself a sojourn of some weeks. Its proprietor, Roderick Usher, had been one of my boon companions in boyhood; but many years had elapsed since our last meeting. A letter, however, had lately reached me in a distant part of the country—a letter from him—which in its wildly importunate nature had admitted of no other than a personal reply. The MS. gave evidence of nervous agitation. The writer spoke of acute bodily illness, of a mental disorder which oppressed him, and of an earnest desire to see me, as his best and indeed his only personal friend, with a view of attempting, by the cheerfulness of my society, some alleviation of his malady. It was the manner in which all this, and much more, was said—it was the apparent *heart* that went with his request—which allowed me no room for hesitation; and I accordingly obeyed forthwith what I still considered a very singular summons.

Although as boys we had been even intimate associates, yet I really knew little of my friend. His reserve had been always excessive and habitual. I was aware, however, that his very ancient family had been noted, time out of mind, for a peculiar sensibility of temperament, displaying itself, through long ages, in many works of exalted art, and manifested of late in repeated deeds of munificent yet unobtrusive charity, as well as in a passionate devotion of the intricacies, perhaps even more than to the orthodox and easily recognizable beauties, of musical science. I had learned, too, the very remarkable fact that the stem of the Usher race, all time-honored as it was, had put forth at no period any enduring branch;

in other words, that the entire family lay in the direct line of descent, and had always, with very trifling and very temporary variation, so lain. It was this deficiency, I considered, while running over in thought the perfect keeping of the character of the premises with the accredited character of the people, and while speculating upon the possible influence which the one, in the long lapse of centuries, might have exercised upon the other—it was this deficiency, perhaps, of collateral issue, and the consequent undeviating transmission from sire to son of the patrimony with the name, which had, at length, so identified the two as to merge the original title of the estate in the quaint and equivocal appellation of the "House of Usher"—an appellation which seemed to include, in the minds of the peasantry who used it, both the family and the family mansion.

I have said that the sole effect of my somewhat childish experiment, that of looking down within the tarn, had been to deepen the first singular impression. There can be no doubt that the consciousness of the rapid increase of my superstition—for why should I not so term it?—served mainly to accelerate the increase itself. Such, I have long known, is the paradoxical law of all sentiments having terror as a basis. And it might have been for this reason only, that, when I again uplifted my eyes to the house itself, from its image in the pool, there grew in my mind a strange fancy—a fancy so ridiculous, indeed, that I but mention it to show the vivid force of the sensations which oppressed me. I had so worked upon my imagination as really to believe that about the whole mansion and domain there hung an atmosphere peculiar to themselves and their immediate vicinity: an atmosphere which had no affinity with the air of heaven, but which had reeked up from the decayed trees, and the gray wall, and the silent tarn: a pestilent and mystic vapor, dull, sluggish, faintly discernible, and leaden-hued.

Shaking off from my spirit what *must* have been a dream, I scanned more narrowly the real aspect of the building. Its principal feature seemed to be that of an excessive antiquity. The discoloration of ages had been great. Minute fungi overspread the whole exterior, hanging in a fine tangled webwork from the eaves. Yet all this was apart from any extraordinary dilapidation. No portion of the masonry had fallen; and there appeared to be a wild inconsistency between its still perfect adaptation of parts and the crumbling condition of the individual stones. In this there was much that reminded me of the specious totality of old woodwork which has rotted for long years in some neglected vault, with no disturbance from the breath of the external air. Beyond this indication of excessive decay, however, the fabric gave little token of instability. Perhaps the eye of a scrutinizing observer might have discovered a barely perceptible fissure, which, extending from the roof of the building in front, made its way down the wall in a zigzag direction, until it became lost in the sullen waters of the tarn.

Noticing these things, I rode over a short causeway to the house. A servant in waiting took my horse, and I entered the Gothic archway of the hall. A valet, of stealthy step, thence conducted me, in silence, through many dark and intricate passages in my progress to the studio of his master. Much that I encountered on the way contributed, I know not how, to heighten the vague sentiments of which I have already spoken. While the objects around me—while the carvings of the ceilings, the somber tapestries of the walls, the ebon blackness of the floors, and the phantasmagoric armorial trophies which rattled as I strode, were but matters to which, or to such as which, I had been accustomed from my infancy—while I hesitated not to acknowledge how familiar was all this—I still wondered to find how unfamiliar were the fancies which ordinary images were stirring up. On one of the staircases, I met the physician of the family. His countenance, I thought, wore a mingled expression of low cunning and perplexity. He accosted me with trepidation and passed on. The valet now threw open a door and ushered me into the presence of his master.

The room in which I found myself was very large and lofty. The windows were long, narrow, and pointed, and at so vast a distance from the black oaken floor as to be altogether inaccessible from within. Feeble gleams of encrimsoned light made their way through the trellised panes, and served to render sufficiently distinct the more prominent objects around; the eye, however, struggled in vain to reach the remoter angles of the chamber, or the recesses of the vaulted and fretted ceiling. Dark draperies hung upon the walls. The general furniture was profuse, comfortless, antique, and tattered. Many books and musical instruments lay scattered about, but failed to give any vitality to the scene. I felt that I breathed an atmosphere of sorrow. An air of stern, deep, and irredeemable gloom hung over and pervaded all.

Upon my entrance, Usher arose from a sofa on which he had been lying at full length, and greeted me with a vivacious warmth which had much in it, I at first thought, of an overdone cordiality—of the constrained effort of the *ennuyé* man of the world. A glance, however, at his countenance, convinced me of his perfect sincerity. We sat down; and for some moments, while he spoke not, I gazed upon him with a feeling half of pity, half of awe. Surely man had never before so terribly altered in so brief a period as had Roderick Usher! It was with difficulty that I could bring myself to admit the identity of the wan being before me with the companion of my boyhood. Yet the character of his face had been at all times remarkable. A cadaverousness of complexion; an eye large, liquid, and luminous beyond comparison; lips somewhat thin and very pallid, but of a surpassingly beautiful curve; a nose of a delicate Hebrew model, but with a breadth of nostril unusual in similar formations; a finely molded chin, speaking, in its want of prominence, of a want of moral energy; hair of a more than weblike softness and tenuity; these features, with an inordinate expansion above the regions of the temple, made up altogether a countenance not easily to be forgotten. And now in the mere exaggeration of the prevailing character of these features, and of the expression they were wont to convey, lay so much of change that I doubted to whom I spoke. The now ghostly pallor of the skin, and the now miraculous luster of the eye, above all things startled and even awed me. The silken hair, too, had been suffered to grow all unheeded, and as, in its wild gossamer texture, it floated rather than fell about the face, I could not, even with effort, connect its arabesque expression with any idea of simple humanity.

In the manner of my friend I was at once struck with an incoherence, an inconsistency; and I soon found this to arise from a series of feeble and futile struggles to overcome an habitual trepidancy, an excessive nervous agitation. For something of this nature I had indeed been prepared, no less by his letter than by reminiscences of certain boyish traits, and by conclusions deduced from his peculiar physical conformation and temperament. His action was alternatively vivacious and sullen. His voice varied rapidly from a tremulous indecision (when the animal spirits seemed utterly in abeyance) to that species of energetic concision—that abrupt, weighty, unhurried, and hollow-sounding enunciation—that leaden, self-balanced and perfectly modulated guttural utterance—which may be observed in the lost drunkard, or the irreclaimable eater of opium, during the periods of his most intense excitement.

It was thus that he spoke of the object of my visit, of his earnest desire to see me, and of the solace he expected me to afford him. He entered, at some length, into what he conceived to be the nature of his malady. It was, he said, a constitutional and a family evil, and one for which he despaired to find a remedy—a mere nervous affection, he immediately added, which would undoubtedly soon pass off. It displayed itself in a host of unnatural sensations. Some of these, as he detailed them, interested and bewildered me: although, perhaps, the terms and the general manner of the narration had their weight. He suffered much from a morbid acuteness of the senses; the most insipid food was alone endurable; he could wear only garments of a certain texture; the odors of all flowers were oppressive; his eyes were tortured by even a faint light; and there were but peculiar sounds, and these from stringed instruments, which did not inspire him with horror.

To an anomalous species of terror I found him a bounden slave. "I shall perish," said he, "I *must* perish in this deplorable folly. Thus, thus, and not otherwise, shall I be lost. I dread the events of the future, not in themselves, but in their results. I shudder at the thought of any, even the most trivial, incident, which may operate upon this intolerable agitation of soul. I have, indeed, no abhorrence of danger, except in its absolute effect—in terror. In this unnerved—in this pitiable condition—I feel that the period will sooner or later arrive when I must abandon life and reason together, in some struggle with the grim phantasm, FEAR."

I learned moreover at intervals, and through broken and equivocal hints, another singular feature of his mental condition. He was enchained by certain superstitious impressions in regard to the dwelling which he tenanted, and whence, for many years, he had never ventured forth—in regard to an influence whose suppositious force was conveyed in terms too shadowy here to be restated—an influence which some peculiarities in the mere form and substance of his family mansion, had, by dint of long sufferance, he said, obtained over his spirit—an effect which the physique of the gray walls and turrets, and of the dim tarn into which they all looked down, had, at length, brought about upon the morale of his existence.

He admitted, however, although with hesitation, that much of the peculiar gloom which thus afflicted him could be traced to a more natural and far more palpable origin—to the severe and long-continued illness, indeed to the evidently approaching dissolution, of a tenderly beloved sister—his sole companion for long years, his last and only relative on earth. "Her decease," he said, with a bitterness which I can never forget, "would leave him (him the hopeless and the frail) the last of the ancient race of the Ushers." While he spoke, the lady Madeline (for so was she called) passed slowly through a remote portion of the apartment, and, without having noticed my presence, disappeared. I regarded her with an utter astonishment not unmingled with dread, and yet I found it impossible to account for such feelings. A sensation of stupor oppressed me, as my eyes followed her retreating steps. When a door, at length, closed upon her, my glance sought instinctively and eagerly the countenance of the brother, but he had buried his face in his hands, and I could only perceive that a far more than ordinary wanness had overspread the emaciated fingers through which trickled many passionate tears.

The disease of the lady Madeline had long baffled the skill of her physicians. A settled apathy, a gradual wasting away of the person, and frequent although transient affections of a partially cataleptical character, were the unusual diagnosis. Hitherto she had steadily borne up against the pressure of her malady, and had not betaken herself finally to bed; but, on the closing in of the evening of my arrival at the house, she succumbed (as her brother told me at night with inexpressible agitation) to the prostrating power of the destroyer; and I learned that the glimpse I had obtained of her person would thus probably be the last I should obtain—that the lady, at least while living, would be seen by me no more.

For several days ensuing, her name was unmentioned by either Usher or myself; and during this period I was busied in earnest endeavors to alleviate the melancholy of my friend. We painted and read together; or I listened, as if in a dream, to the wild improvisation of his speaking guitar. And thus, as a closer and still closer intimacy admitted me more unreservedly into the recesses of his spirit, the more bitterly did I perceive the futility of all attempt at cheering a mind from which darkness, as if an inherent positive quality, poured forth upon all objects of the moral and physical universe, in one unceasing radiation of gloom.

I shall ever bear about me a memory of the many solemn hours I thus spent alone with the master of the House of Usher. Yet I should fail in any attempt to convey an idea of the exact character of the studies, or of the occupations, in which he involved me, or led me the way. An excited and highly distempered ideality threw a sulphurous luster over all. His long improvised dirges will ring forever in my ears. Among other things, I hold painfully in mind a certain singular perversion and amplification of the wild air of the last waltz of Von Weber. From the paintings over which his elaborate fancy brooded, and which grew, touch by touch, into vagueness at which I shuddered the more thrillingly because I shuddered knowing not why;—from these paintings (vivid as their images now are before me) I would in vain endeavor to educe more than a small portion which should lie within the compass of merely written words. By the utter simplicity, by the nakedness of his designs, he arrested and overawed attention. If ever mortal painted an idea, that mortal was Roderick Usher. For me at least, in the circumstances then surrounding me, there arose, out of the pure abstractions which the hypochondriac contrived to throw upon his canvas, an intensity of intolerable awe, no shadow of which felt I ever yet in the contemplation of the certainly glowing yet too concrete reveries of Fuseli.

One of the phantasmagoric conceptions of my friend, partaking not so rigidly of the spirit of abstraction, may be shadowed forth, although feebly, in words. A small picture presented the interior of an immensely long and rectangular vault or tunnel, with low walls, smooth, white, and without interruption or device. Certain accessory points of the design served well to convey the idea that this excavation lay at an exceeding depth below the surface of the earth. No outlet was observed in any portion of its vast extent, and no torch or other artificial source of light was discernible; yet a flood of intense rays rolled throughout, and bathed the whole in a ghastly and inappropriate splendor.

I have just spoken of that morbid condition of the auditory nerve which rendered all music intolerable to the sufferer, with the exception of certain effects of stringed instruments. It was, perhaps, the narrow limits to which he thus confined himself upon the guitar, which gave birth, in great measure, to the fantastic character of his performances. But the fervid *facility* of his *impromptus* could not be so accounted for. They must have been, and were, in the notes, as well as in the words of his wild fantasias (for he not unfrequently accompanied himself with rhymed verbal improvisations), the result of that intense mental collectedness and concentration to which I have previously alluded as observable only in particular moments of the highest artificial excitement. The words of one of these rhapsodies I have easily remembered. I was, perhaps, the more forcibly impressed with it, as he gave it, because, in the under or mystic current of its meaning, I fancied that I perceived, and for the first time, a full consciousness, on the part of Usher, of the tottering of his lofty reason upon her throne. The verses, which were entitled "The Haunted Palace," ran very nearly, if not accurately, thus:

I

In the greenest of our valleys,
By good angels tenanted,
Once a fair and stately palace—
Radiant palace—reared its head.
In the monarch Thought's dominion,
It stood there!
Never seraph spread a pinion
Over fabric half so fair.

II

Banners yellow, glorious, golden,
On its roof did float and flow,
(This—all this—was in the olden
Time long ago)
And every gentle air that dallied,
In that sweet day,
Along the ramparts plumed and pallid,
A wingèd odor went away.

III

Wanderers in that happy valley
Through two luminous windows saw

Spirits moving musically
To a lute's well-tunèd law,
Round about a throne where, sitting,
(Porphyrogene!)
In state his glory well befitting,
The ruler of the realm was seen.

IV

And all with pearl and ruby glowing
Was the fair palace door,
Through which came flowing, flowing, flowing,
And sparkling evermore,
A troop of Echoes whose sweet duty
Was but to sing.
In voices of surpassing beauty,
The wit and wisdom of their king.

V

But evil things, in robes of sorrow,
Assailed the monarch's high estate;
(Ah, let us mourn, for never morrow
Shall dawn upon him, desolate!)
And round about his home the glory
That blushed and bloomed
Is but a dim-remembered story
Of the old time entombed.

VI

And travellers now within that valley
Through the red-litten windows see
Vast forms that move fantastically
To a discordant melody;
While, like a rapid ghastly river,
Through the pale door,
A hideous throng rush out forever,
And laugh—but smile no more.

I well remember that suggestions arising from this ballad led us into a train of thought, wherein there became manifest an opinion of Usher's which I mention not so much on account of its novelty (for other men have thought thus) as on account of the pertinacity with which he maintained it. This opinion, in its general form, was that of the sentience of all vegetable things. But in his disordered fancy the idea had assumed a more daring character, and trespassed, under certain conditions, upon the kingdom of inorganization. I lack words to express the full extent, or the earnest *abandon* of his persuasion. The belief, however, was connected (as I have previously hinted) with the gray stones of the home of his forefathers. The conditions of the sentience had been here, he imagined, fulfilled in the method of collocation of these stones—in the order of their arrangement, as well as in that of the many fungi which overspread them, and of the decayed trees which stood around—above all, in the long undisturbed endurance of this arrangement, and in its reduplication in the still waters of the tarn. Its evidence—the evidence of the sentience—was to be seen, he said (and I here started as he spoke), in the gradual yet certain condensation of an atmosphere of their own about the waters and the walls. The result was discoverable, he added, in that silent, yet importunate and terrible influence which for centuries had molded the destinies of his family, and which made *him* what I now saw him—what he was. Such opinions need no comment, and I will make none.

Our books—the books which, for years, had formed no small portion of the mental existence of the invalid—were, as might be supposed, in strict keeping with this character of phantasm. We pored together over such works as the Ververt and Chartreuse of Gresset; the Belphegor of Machiavelli; the Heaven and Hell of Swedenborg; the Subterranean Voyage of Nicholas Klimm by Holberg; the Chiromancy of Robert Flud, of Jean D'Indaginé, and of De la Chambre; the Journey into the Blue Distance of Tieck; and the City of the Sun of Campanella. One favorite volume was a small octavo edition of the *Directorium Inquisitorium,* by the Dominican Eymeric de Gironne; and there were passages in Pomponius Mela, about the old African Satyrs and Ægipans, over which Usher would sit dreaming for hours. His chief delight, however, was found in the perusal of an exceedingly rare and curious book in quarto Gothic —the manual of a forgotten church—the *Vigiliæ Mortuorum Secundum Chorum Ecclesiæ Maguntinæ.*

I could not help thinking of the wild ritual of this work, and of its probable influence upon the hypochondriac, when one evening, having informed me abruptly that the lady Madeline was no more, he stated his intention of preserving her corpse for a fortnight (previously to its final interment) in one of the numerous vaults within the main walls of the building. The worldly reason, however, assigned for this singular proceeding was one which I did not feel at liberty to dispute. The brother had been led to his resolution (so he told me) by consideration of the unusual character of the malady of the deceased, of certain obtrusive and eager inquiries on the part of her medical men, and of the remote and exposed situation of the burialground of the family. I will not deny that when I called to mind the sinister countenance of the person whom I met upon the staircase, on the day of my arrival at the house, I had no desire to oppose what I regarded as at best but a harmless, and by no means an unnatural, precaution.

At the request of Usher, I personally aided him in the arrangements for the temporary entombment. The body having been encoffined, we two alone bore it to its rest. The vault in which we placed it (and which had been so long unopened that our torches, half smothered in its oppressive atmosphere, gave us little opportunity for investigation) was small, damp, and entirely without means of admission for light; lying, at great depth, immediately beneath that portion of the building in which was my own sleeping apartment. It had been used, apparently, in remote feudal times, for the worst purposes of a donjon-keep, and in later days as a place of deposit for powder, or some other highly combustible substance, as a portion of its floor, and the whole interior of a long archway through which we reached it, were carefully sheathed with copper. The door, of massive iron, had been also similarly protected. Its immense weight caused an unusually sharp grating sound, as it moved upon its hinges.

Having deposited our mournful burden upon trestles within this region of horror, we partially turned aside the yet unscrewed lid of the coffin, and looked upon the face of the tenant. A striking similitude between the brother and sister now first arrested my attention; and Usher divining, perhaps, my thoughts, murmured out some few words from which I learned that the deceased and himself had been twins, and that sympathies of a scarcely intelligible nature had always existed between them. Our glances, however, rested not long upon the dead—for we could not regard her unawed. The disease which had thus entombed the lady in the maturity of youth, had left, as usual in all maladies of a strictly cataleptical character, the mockery of a faint blush upon the bosom and the face, and that suspiciously lingering smile upon the lip which is so terrible in death. We replaced and screwed down the lid, and, having secured the door of iron, made our way, with toil, into the scarcely less gloomy apartments of the upper portion of the house.

And now, some days of bitter grief having elapsed, an observable change came over the features of the mental disorder of my friend. His ordinary manner had vanished. His ordinary occupations were neglected or forgotten. He roamed from chamber to chamber with hurried, unequal, and objectless step. The pallor of his countenance had assumed, if possible, a more ghastly hue—but the luminousness of his eye had utterly gone out. The once occasional huskiness of his tone was heard no more; and a tremulous quaver, as if of extreme terror, habitually characterized his utterance. There were times, indeed, when I thought his unceasingly agitated mind was laboring with some oppressive secret, to divulge which he struggled for the necessary courage. At times, again, I was obliged to resolve all into the mere inexplicable vagaries of madness, for I beheld him gazing upon vacancy for long hours, in an attitude of the profoundest attention, as if listening to some imaginary sound. It was no wonder that his condition terrified—that it infected me. I felt creeping upon me, by slow yet certain degrees, the wild influences of his own fantastic yet impressive superstitions.

It was, especially, upon retiring to bed late in the night of the seventh or eighth day after the placing of the lady Madeline within the donjon, that I experienced the full power of such feelings. Sleep came not near my couch, while the hours waned and waned away. I struggled to reason off the nervousness which had dominion over me. I endeavored to believe that much, if not all, of what I felt was due to the bewildering influence of the gloomy furniture of the room—of the dark and tattered draperies which, tortured into motion by the breath of a rising tempest, swayed fitfully to and fro upon the walls, and rustled uneasily about the decorations of the bed. But my efforts were fruitless. An irrepressible tremor gradually pervaded my frame; and at length there sat upon my very heart an incubus of utterly causeless alarm. Shaking this off with a gasp and a struggle, I uplifted myself upon the pillows, and, peering earnestly within the intense darkness of the chamber, hearkened—I know not why, except that an instinctive spirit prompted me—to certain low and indefinite sounds which came, through the pauses of the storm, at long intervals, I knew not whence. Overpowered by an intense sentiment of horror, unaccountable yet unendurable, I threw on my clothes with haste (for I felt that I should sleep no more during the night) and endeavored to arouse myself from the pitiable condition into which I had fallen, by pacing rapidly to and fro through the apartment.

I had taken but few turns in this manner, when a light step on an adjoining staircase arrested my attention. I presently recognized it as that of Usher. In an instant afterward he rapped with a gentle touch at my door, and entered, bearing a lamp. His countenance was, as usual, cadaverously wan—but, moreover, there was a species of mad hilarity in his eyes—an evidently restrained *hysteria* in his whole demeanor. His air appalled me—but anything was preferable to the solitude which I had so long endured, and I even welcomed his presence as a relief.

"And you have not seen it?" he said abruptly, after having stared about him for some moments in silence—"you have not then seen it?—but, stay! you shall." Thus speaking, and having carefully shaded his lamp, he hurried to one of the casements, and threw it freely open to the storm.

The impetuous fury of the entering gust nearly lifted us from our feet. It was, indeed, a tempestuous yet sternly beautiful night, and one wildly singular in its terror and its beauty. A whirlwind had apparently collected its force in our vicinity; for there were frequent and violent alterations in the direction of the wind; and the exceeding density of the clouds (which hung so low as to press upon the turrets of the house) did not prevent our perceiving the lifelike velocity with which they flew careening from all points against each other, without passing away into the distance. I say that even their exceeding density did not prevent our perceiving this; yet we had no glimpse of the moon or stars, nor was there any flashing forth of the lightning. But the under surfaces of the huge masses of agitated vapor, as well as all terrestrial objects immediately around us, were glowing in the unnatural light of a faintly luminous and distinctly visible gaseous exhalation which hung about and enshrouded the mansion.

"You must not—you shall not behold this!" said I, shudderingly, to Usher, as I led him with a gentle violence from the window to a seat. "These appearances, which bewilder you, are merely electrical phenomena not uncommon—or it may be that they have their ghastly origin in the rank miasma of the tarn. Let us close this casement; the air is chilling and dangerous to your frame. Here is one of your favorite romances. I will read, and you shall listen;—and so we will pass away this terrible night together."

The antique volume which I had taken up was the *Mad Trist* of Sir Launcelot Canning; but I had called it a favorite of Usher's more in sad jest than in earnest; for, in truth, there is little in its uncouth and unimaginative prolixity which could have had interest for the lofty and spiritual ideality of my friend. It was, however, the only book immediately at hand; and I indulged a vague hope that the excitement which now agitated the hypochondriac might find relief (for the history of mental disorder is full of similar anomalies) even in the extremeness of the folly which I should read. Could I have judged, indeed, by the wild overstrained air of vivacity with which he hearkened, or apparently hearkened, to the words of the tale, I might well have congratulated myself upon the success of my design.

I had arrived at that well-known portion of the story where Ethelred, the hero of the Trist, having sought in vain for peaceable admission into the dwelling of the hermit, proceeds to make good an entrance by force. Here, it will be remembered, the words of the narrative run thus:

> "And Ethelred, who was by nature of a doughty heart, and who was now mighty withal, on account of the powerfulness of the wine which he had drunken, waited no longer to hold parley with the hermit, who, in sooth, was of an obstinate and maliceful turn, but, feeling the rain upon his shoulders, and fearing the rising of the tempest, uplifted his mace outright, and, with blows, made quickly room in the plankings of the door for his gauntleted hand; and now pulling therewith sturdily, he so cracked, and ripped, and tore all asunder, that the noise of the dry and hollow-sounding wood alarummed and reverberated throughout the forest."

At the termination of this sentence I started, and for a moment paused; for it appeared to me (although I at once concluded that my excited fancy had deceived me)—it appeared to me that from some very remote portion of the mansion there came, indistinctly, to my ears, what might have been, in its exact similarity of character, the echo (but a stifled and dull one certainly) of the very cracking and ripping sound which Sir Launcelot had so particularly described. It was, beyond doubt, the coincidence alone which had arrested my attention; for, amid the rattling of the sashes of the casements, and the ordinary commingled noises of the still increasing storm, the sound, in itself, had nothing, surely, which should have interested or disturbed me. I continued the story:

> "But the good champion Ethelred, now entering within the door, was sore enraged and amazed to perceive no signal of the maliceful hermit; but, in the stead thereof, a dragon of a scaly and prodigious demeanor, and of a fiery tongue, which sate in guard before a palace of gold, with a floor of silver; and upon the wall there hung a shield of shining brass with this legend enwritten—
>
> Who entereth herein, a conqueror hath bin;
> Who slayeth the dragon, the shield he shall win
>
> And Ethelred uplifted his mace, and struck upon the head of the dragon, which fell before him, and gave up his pesty breath, with a shriek so horrid and harsh, and withal so piercing, that Ethelred had fain to close his ears with his hands against the dreadful noise of it, the like whereof was never before heard."

Here again I paused abruptly, and now with a feeling of wild amazement; for there could be no doubt whatever that, in this instance, I did actually hear (although from what direction it proceeded I found it impossible to say) a low and apparently distant, but harsh, protracted, and most unusual screaming or grating sound —the exact counterpart of what my fancy had already conjured up for the dragon's unnatural shriek as described by the romancer.

Oppressed, as I certainly was, upon the occurrence of this second and most extraordinary coincidence, by a thousand conflicting sensations, in which wonder and extreme terror were predominant, I still retained sufficient presence of mind to avoid exciting, by any observation, the sensitive nervousness of my companion. I was by no means certain that he had noticed the sounds in question; although, assuredly, a strange alteration had during the last few minutes taken place in his demeanor. From a position fronting my own, he had gradually brought round his chair, so as to sit with his face to the door of the chamber; and thus I could but partially perceive his features, although I saw that his lips trembled as if he were murmuring inaudibly. His head had dropped upon his breast—yet I knew that he was not asleep, from the wide and rigid opening of the eye as I caught a glance of it in profile. The motion of his body, too, was at variance with this idea—for he rocked from side to side with a gentle yet constant and uniform sway. Having rapidly taken notice of all this, I resumed the narrative of Sir Launcelot, which thus proceeded:

> "And now, the champion having escaped from the terrible fury of the dragon, bethinking himself of the brazen shield, and of the breaking up of the enchantment which was upon it, removed the carcass from out of the way before him, and approached valorously over the silver pavement of the castle to where the shield was upon the wall; which in sooth tarried not for his full coming, but fell down at his feet upon the silver floor, with a mighty great and terrible ringing sound."

No sooner had these syllables passed my lips, than—as if a shield of brass had indeed, at the moment, fallen heavily upon a floor of silver—I became aware of a distinct, hollow, metallic and clangorous, yet apparently muffled reverberation. Completely unnerved, I leaped to my feet; but the measured rocking movement of Usher was undisturbed. I rushed to the chair in which he sat. His eyes were bent fixedly before him, and throughout his whole countenance there reigned a stony rigidity. But, as I placed my hand upon his shoulder, there came a strong shudder over his whole person; a sickly smile quivered about his lips; and I saw that he spoke in a low, hurried, and gibbering murmur, as if unconscious of my presence. Bending closely over him, I at length drank in the hideous import of his words.

"Not hear it?—yes, I hear it, and *have* heard it. Long—long—long—many minutes, many hours, many days, have I heard it—yet I dared not—oh, pity me, miserable wretch that I am!—I dared not

—I dared not speak! We have put her living in the tomb! Said I not that my senses were acute? I *now* tell you that I heard her first feeble movements in the hollow coffin. I heard them—many, many days ago—yet I dared not—*I dared not speak!* And now—tonight—Ethelred—ha! ha!—the breaking of the hermit's door, and the death-cry of the dragon, and the clangor of the shield!—say, rather, the rending of her coffin, and the grating of the iron hinges of her prison, and her struggles within the coppered archway of the vault! Oh, whither shall I fly? Will she not be here anon? Is she not hurrying to upbraid me for my haste? Have I not heard her footsteps on the stair? Do I not distinguish that heavy and horrible beating of her heart? Madman!"—here he sprang furiously to his feet, and shrieked out his syllables, as if in the effort he were giving up his soul—*"Madman! I tell you that she now stands without the door!"*

As if in the superhuman energy of his utterance there had been found the potency of a spell, the huge antique panels to which the speaker pointed drew slowly back, upon the instant, their ponderous and ebony jaws. It was the work of the rushing gust—but then without the doors there *did* stand the lofty and enshrouded figure of the lady Madeline of Usher. There was blood upon her white robes, and the evidence of some bitter struggle upon every portion of her emaciated frame. For a moment she remained trembling and reeling to and fro upon the threshold—then, with a low moaning cry, fell heavily inward upon the person of her brother, and, in her violent and now final death-agonies, bore him to the floor a corpse, and a victim to the terrors he had anticipated.

From that chamber, and from that mansion, I fled aghast. The storm was still abroad in all its wrath as I found myself crossing the old causeway. Suddenly there shot along the path a wild light, and I turned to see whence a gleam so unusual could have issued; for the vast house and its shadows were alone behind me. The radiance was that of the full, setting, and blood-red moon, which now shone vividly through that once barely discernible fissure, of which I have before spoken as extending from the roof of the building, in a zigzag direction, to the base. While I gazed, this fissure rapidly widened—there came a fierce breath of the whirlwind—the entire orb of the satellite burst at once upon my sight—my brain reeled as I saw the mighty walls rushing asunder—there was a long tumultuous shouting sound like the voice of a thousand waters—and the deep and dank tarn at my feet closed sullenly and silently over the fragments of the House of Usher.

1839

Bartleby the Scrivener
A Story of Wall Street

HERMAN MELVILLE

[1819–1891]

I am a rather elderly man. The nature of my avocations, for the last thirty years, has brought me into more than ordinary contact with what would seem an interesting and somewhat singular set of men, of whom, as yet, nothing, that I know of, has ever been written—I mean, the law-copyists, or scriveners. I have known very many of them, professionally and privately, and, if I pleased, could relate divers histories, at which good-natured gentlemen might smile, and sentimental souls might weep. But I waive the biographies of all other scriveners, for a few passages in the life of Bartleby, who was a scrivener, the strangest I ever saw, or heard of. While, of other law-copyists, I might write the complete life, of Bartleby nothing of that sort can be done. I believe that no materials exist for a full and satisfactory biography of this man. It is an irreparable loss to literature. Bartleby was one of those beings of whom nothing is ascertainable, except from the original sources, and, in his case, those are very small. What my own astonished eyes saw of Bartleby, *that* is all I know of him, except, indeed, one vague report, which will appear in the sequel.

Ere introducing the scrivener, as he first appeared to me, it is fit I make some mention of myself, my employees, my business, my chambers, and general surroundings; because some such description is indispensable to an adequate understanding of the chief character about to be presented. Imprimis: I am a man who, from his youth upwards, has been filled with a profound conviction that the easiest way of life is the best. Hence, though I belong to a profession proverbially energetic and nervous, even to turbulence, at times, yet nothing of that sort have I ever suffered to invade my peace. I am one of those unambitious lawyers who never addresses a jury, or in any way draws down public applause; but, in the cool tranquillity of a snug retreat, do a snug business among rich men's bonds, and mortgages, and title-deeds. All who know me, consider me an eminently *safe* man. The late John Jacob Astor, a personage little given to poetic enthusiasm, had no hesitation in pronouncing my first grand point to be prudence; my next, method. I do not speak it in vanity, but simply record the fact, that I was not unemployed in my profession by the late John Jacob Astor; a name which, I admit, I love to repeat; for it hath a rounded and orbicular sound to it, and rings like unto bullion. I will freely add, that I was not insensible to the late John Jacob Astor's good opinion.

Some time prior to the period at which this little history begins, my avocations had been largely increased. The good old office, now extinct in the State of New York, of a Master in Chancery, had been conferred upon me. It was not a very arduous office, but very pleasantly remunerative. I seldom lose my temper; much more seldom indulge in dangerous indignation at wrongs and outrages; but, I must be permitted to be rash here, and declare that I consider the sudden and violent abrogation of the office of Master in Chancery, by the new Constitution, as a—premature act; inasmuch as I had counted upon a life-lease of the profits, whereas I only received those of a few short years. But this is by the way.

My chambers were up stairs, at No.____ Wall Street. At one end, they looked upon the white wall of the interior of a spacious skylight shaft, penetrating the building from top to bottom.

This view might have been considered rather tame than otherwise, deficient in what landscape painters call "life." But, if so, the view from the other end of my chambers offered, at least, a contrast, if nothing more. In that direction, my windows commanded an unobstructed view of a lofty brick wall, black by age and everlasting shade; which wall required no spyglass to bring out its lurking beauties, but, for the benefit of all near-sighted spectators, was pushed up to within ten feet of my window panes. Owing to the great height of the surrounding buildings, and my chambers being on the second floor, the interval between this wall and mine not a little resembled a huge square cistern.

At the period just preceding the advent of Bartleby, I had two persons as copyists in my employment, and a promising lad as an office-boy. First, Turkey; second, Nippers; third, Ginger Nut. These may seem names, the like of which are not usually found in the Directory. In truth, they were nicknames, mutually conferred upon each other by my three clerks, and were deemed expressive of their respective persons or characters. Turkey was a short, pursy Englishman, of about my own age—that is, somewhere not far from sixty. In the morning, one might say, his face was of a fine florid hue, but after twelve o'clock, meridian—his dinner hour—it blazed like a grate full of Christmas coals; and continued blazing—but, as it were, with a gradual wane—till six o'clock P.M., or thereabouts; after which, I saw no more of the proprietor of the face, which, gaining its meridian with the sun, seemed to set with it, to rise, culminate, and decline the following day, with the like regularity and undiminished glory. There are many singular coincidences I have known in the course of my life, not the least among which was the fact, that, exactly when Turkey displayed his fullest beams from his red and radiant countenance, just then, too, at that critical moment, began the daily period when I considered his business capacities as seriously disturbed for the remainder of the twenty-four hours. Not that he was absolutely idle, or averse to business, then; far from it. The difficulty was, he was apt to be altogether too energetic. There was a strange, inflamed, flurried, flighty recklessness of activity about him. He would be incautious in dipping his pen into his inkstand. All his blots upon my documents were dropped there after twelve o'clock meridian. Indeed, not only would he be reckless, and sadly given to making blots in the afternoon, but, some days, he went further, and was rather noisy. At such times, too, his face flamed with augmented blazonry, as if cannel coal had been heaped on anthracite. He made an unpleasant racket with his chair; spilled his sand-box; in mending his pens, impatiently split them all to pieces, and threw them on the floor in a sudden passion; stood up, and leaned over his table, boxing his papers about in a most indecorous manner, very sad to behold in an elderly man like him. Nevertheless, as he was in many ways a most valuable person to me, and all the time before twelve o'clock meridian, was the quickest, steadiest creature, too, accomplishing a great deal of work in a style not easily to be matched—for these reasons, I was willing to overlook his eccentricities, though, indeed, occasionally, I remonstrated with him. I did this very gently, however, because, though the civilest, nay, the blandest and most reverential of men in the morning, yet, in the afternoon, he was disposed, upon provocation, to be slightly rash with his tongue—in fact, insolent. Now, valuing his morning services as I did, and resolved not to lose them—yet, at the same time, made uncomfortable by his inflamed ways after twelve o'clock—and being a man of peace, unwilling by my admonitions to call forth unseemly retorts from him, I took upon me, one Saturday noon (he was always worse on Saturdays) to hint to him, very kindly, that, perhaps, now that he was growing old, it might be well to abridge his labors; in short, he need not come to my chambers after twelve o'clock, but, dinner over, had best go home to his lodgings, and rest himself till tea-time. But no; he insisted upon his afternoon devotions. His countenance became intolerably fervid, as he oratorically assured me—gesticulating with a long ruler at the other end of the room—that if his services in the morning were useful, how indispensable, then, in the afternoon?

"With submission, sir," said Turkey, on this occasion, "I consider myself your right-hand man. In the morning I but marshal and deploy my columns; but in the afternoon I put myself at their head, and gallantly charge the foe, thus"—and he made a violent thrust with the ruler.

"But the blots, Turkey," intimated I.

"True; but, with submission, sir, behold these hairs! I am getting old. Surely, sir, a blot or two of a warm afternoon is not to be severely urged against gray hairs. Old age—even if it blot the page —is honorable. With submission, sir, we *both* are getting old."

This appeal to my fellow-feeling was hardly to be resisted. At all events, I saw that go he would not. So, I made up my mind to let him stay, resolving, nevertheless, to see to it that, during the afternoon, he had to do with my less important papers.

Nippers, the second on my list, was a whiskered, sallow, and, upon the whole, rather piratical-looking young man, of about five and twenty. I always deemed him the victim of two evil powers—ambition and indigestion. The ambition was evinced by a certain impatience of the duties of a mere copyist, an unwarrantable usurpation of strictly professional affairs, such as the original drawing up of legal documents. The indigestion seemed betokened in an occasional nervous testiness and grinning irritability, causing the teeth to audibly grind together over mistakes committed in copying; unnecessary maledictions, hissed, rather than spoken, in the heat of business; and especially by a continual discontent with the height of the table where he worked. Though of a very ingenious, mechanical turn, Nippers could never get this table to suit him. He put chips under it, blocks of various sorts, bits of pasteboard, and at last went so far as to attempt an exquisite adjustment, by final pieces of folded blotting-paper. But no invention would answer. If, for the sake of easing his back, he brought the table lid at a sharp angle well up towards his chin, and wrote there like a man using the steep roof of a Dutch house for his desk, then he declared that it stopped the circulation in his arms. If now he lowered the table to his waistbands, and stooped over it in writing, then there was a sore aching in his back. In short, the truth of the matter was, Nippers knew not what he wanted. Or, if he wanted anything, it was to be rid of a scrivener's table altogether. Among the manifestations of his diseased ambition was a fondness he had for receiving visits from certain ambiguous-looking fellows in seedy coats, whom he called his clients. Indeed, I was aware that not only was he, at times, considerable of a ward-politician, but he occasionally did a little business at the Justices' courts, and was not unknown on the steps of the Tombs. I have good reason to believe, however, that one individual who called upon him at my chambers, and who, with a grand air, he insisted was his client, was no other than a dun, and the alleged title-deed, a bill. But, with all his failings, and the annoyances he caused me, Nippers, like his compatriot Turkey, was a very useful man to me; wrote a neat, swift hand; and, when he chose, was not deficient in a gentlemanly sort of deportment. Added to this, he always dressed in a gentlemanly sort of way; and so, incidentally, reflected credit upon my chambers. Whereas, with respect to Turkey, I had much ado to keep him from being a reproach to me. His clothes were apt to look oily, and smell of eating-houses. He wore his pantaloons very loose and baggy in summer. His coats were execrable; his hat not to be handled. But while the hat was a thing of indifference to me, inasmuch as his natural civility and deference, as a dependent Englishman, always led him to doff it the moment he entered the room, yet his coat was another matter. Concerning his coats, I reasoned with him; but with no effect. The truth was, I suppose, that a man with so small an income could not afford to sport such a lustrous face and a lustrous coat at one and the same time. As Nippers once observed, Turkey's money went chiefly for red ink. One winter day, I presented Turkey with a highly respectable-looking coat of my own—a padded gray coat, of a most comfortable warmth, and which buttoned straight up from the knee to the neck. I thought Turkey would appreciate the favor, and abate his rashness and obstreperousness of afternoons. But no; I verily believe that buttoning himself up in so downy and blanket-like a coat had a pernicious effect upon him—upon the same principle that too much oats are bad for horses. In fact, precisely as a rash, restive horse is said to feel his oats, so Turkey felt his coat. It made him insolent. He was a man whom prosperity harmed.

Though, concerning the self-indulgent habits of Turkey, I had my own private surmises, yet, touching Nippers, I was well persuaded that, whatever might be his faults in other respects, he was, at least, a temperate young man. But, indeed, nature herself seemed to have been his vintner, and, at his birth, charged him so thoroughly with an irritable, brandy-like disposition, that all subsequent potations were needless. When I consider how, amid the stillness of my chambers, Nippers would sometimes impatiently rise from his seat, and stooping over his table, spread his arms wide apart, seize the whole desk, and move it, and jerk it, with a grim, grinding motion on the floor, as if the table were a perverse voluntary agent and vexing him, I plainly perceive that, for Nippers, brandy-and-water were altogether superfluous.

It was fortunate for me that, owing to its peculiar cause—indigestion—the irritability and consequent nervousness of Nippers were mainly observable in the morning, while in the afternoon he was comparatively mild. So that, Turkey's paroxysms only coming on about twelve o'clock, I never had to do with their eccentricities at one time. Their fits relieved each other, like guards. When Nipper's was on, Turkey's was off; and *vice versa.* This was a good natural arrangement, under the circumstances.

Ginger Nut, the third on my list, was a lad, some twelve years old. His father was a car-man, ambitious of seeing his son on the bench instead of a cart, before he died. So he sent him to my office, as student at law, errand-boy, cleaner and sweeper, at the rate of one dollar a week. He had a little desk to himself; but he did not use it much. Upon inspection, the drawer exhibited a great array of the shells of various sorts of nuts. Indeed, to this quick-witted youth, the whole noble science of the law was contained in a nutshell. Not the least among the employments of Ginger Nut, as well as one which he discharged with the most alacrity, was his duty as cake and apple purveyor for Turkey and Nippers. Copying law-papers being proverbially a dry, husky sort of business, my two scriveners were fain to moisten their mouths very often with Spitzenbergs, to be had at the numerous stalls nigh the Custom House and Post Office. Also, they sent Ginger Nut very frequently for that peculiar cake—small, flat, round, and very spicy—after which he had been named by them. Of a cold morning, when business was but dull, Turkey would gobble up scores of these cakes, as if they were mere wafers—indeed, they sell them at the rate of six or eight for a penny —the scrape of his pen blending with the crunching of the crisp particles in his mouth. Rashest of all the fiery afternoon blunders and flurried rashnesses of Turkey, was his once moistening a ginger-cake between his lips, and clapping it on to a mortgage, for a seal. I came within an ace of dismissing him then. But he mollified me by making an oriental bow, and saying—

"With submission, sir, it was generous of me to find you in stationery on my own account."

Now my original business—that of a conveyancer and title hunter, and drawer-up of recondite documents of all sorts—was considerably increased by receiving the master's office. There was now great work for scriveners. Not only must I push the clerks already with me, but I must have additional help.

In answer to my advertisement, a motionless young man one morning stood upon my office threshold, the door being open, for it was summer. I can see that figure now—pallidly neat, pitiably respectable, incurably forlorn! It was Bartleby.

After a few words touching his qualifications, I engaged him, glad to have among my corps of copyists a man of so singularly sedate an aspect, which I thought might operate beneficially upon the flighty temper of Turkey, and the fiery one of Nippers.

I should have stated before that ground glass folding-doors divided my premises into two parts, one of which was occupied by my scriveners, the other by myself. According to my humor, I threw open these doors, or closed them. I resolved to assign Bartleby a corner by the folding-doors, but on my side of them, so as to have this quiet man within easy call, in case any trifling thing was to be done. I placed his desk close up to a small side-window in that part of the room, a window which originally had afforded a lateral view of certain grimy backyards and bricks, but which, owing to subsequent erections, commanded at present no view at all, though it gave some light. Within three feet of the panes was a wall, and the light came down from far above, between two lofty buildings, as from a very small opening in a dome. Still further to a satisfactory arrangement, I procured a high green folding screen, which might entirely isolate Bartleby from my sight, though not remove him from my voice. And thus, in a manner, privacy and society were conjoined.

At first, Bartleby did an extraordinary quantity of writing. As if long famishing for something to copy, he seemed to gorge himself on my documents. There was no pause for digestion. He ran a day and night line, copying by sun-light and by candle-light. I should have been quite delighted with his application, had he been cheerfully industrious. But he wrote on silently, palely, mechanically.

It is, of course, an indispensable part of a scrivener's business to verify the accuracy of his copy, word by word. Where there are two or more scriveners in an office, they assist each other in this examination, one reading from the copy, the other holding the original. It is a very dull, wearisome, and lethargic affair. I can readily imagine that, to some sanguine temperaments, it would be altogether intolerable. For example, I cannot credit that the mettlesome poet, Byron, would have contentedly sat down with Bartleby to examine a law document of, say five hundred pages, closely written in a crimpy hand.

Now and then, in the haste of business, it had been my habit to assist in comparing some brief document myself, calling Turkey or Nippers for this purpose. One object I had, in placing Bartleby so handy to me behind the screen, was to avail myself of his services on such trivial occasions. It was on the third day, I think, of his being with me, and before any necessity had arisen for having his own writing examined, that, being much hurried to complete a small affair I had in hand, I abruptly called to Bartleby. In my haste and natural expectancy of instant compliance, I sat with my head bent over the original on my desk, and my right hand sideways, and somewhat nervously extended with the copy, so that, immediately upon emerging from his retreat, Bartleby might snatch it and proceed to business without the least delay.

In this very attitude did I sit when I called to him, rapidly stating what it was I wanted him to do—namely, to examine a small paper with me. Imagine my surprise, nay, my consternation, when, without moving from his privacy, Bartleby, in a singularly mild, firm voice, replied, "I would prefer not to."

I sat awhile in perfect silence, rallying my stunned faculties. Immediately it occurred to me that my ears had deceived me, or Bartleby had entirely misunderstood my meaning. I repeated my request in the clearest tone I could assume; but in quite as clear a one came the previous reply, "I would prefer not to."

"Prefer not to," echoed I, rising in high excitement, and crossing the room with a stride. "What do you mean? Are you moon-struck? I want you to help me compare this sheet here—take it," and I thrust it towards him.

"I would prefer not to," said he.

I looked at him steadfastly. His face was leanly composed; his gray eye dimly calm. Not a wrinkle of agitation rippled him. Had there been the least uneasiness, anger, impatience, or impertinence in his manner; in other words, had there been any thing ordinarily human about him, doubtless I should have violently dismissed him from the premises. But as it was, I should have as soon thought of turning my pale plaster-of-paris bust of Cicero out of doors. I stood gazing at him awhile, as he went on with his own writing, and then reseated myself at my desk. This is very strange, thought I. What had one best do? But my business hurried me. I concluded to forget the matter for the present, reserving it for my future leisure. So calling Nippers from the other room, the paper was speedily examined.

A few days after this, Bartleby concluded four lengthy documents, being quadruplicates of a week's testimony taken before me in my High Court of Chancery. It became necessary to examine them. It was an important suit, and great accuracy was imperative. Having all things arranged, I called Turkey, Nippers, and Ginger Nut from the next room, meaning to place the four copies in the hands of my four clerks, while I should read from the original.

Accordingly, Turkey, Nippers, and Ginger Nut had taken their seats in a row, each with his document in his hand, when I called to Bartleby to join this interesting group.

"Bartleby! quick, I am waiting."

I heard a slow scrape of his chair legs on the uncarpeted floor, and soon he appeared standing at the entrance of his hermitage.

"What is wanted?" said he, mildly.

"The copies, the copies," said I, hurriedly. "We are going to examine them. There—" and I held towards him the fourth quadruplicate.

"I would prefer not to," he said, and gently disappeared behind the screen.

For a few moments I was turned into a pillar of salt, standing at the head of my seated column of clerks. Recovering myself, I advanced towards the screen, and demanded the reason for such extraordinary conduct.

"*Why* do you refuse?"

"I would prefer not to."

With any other man I should have flown outright into a dreadful passion, scorned all further words, and thrust him ignominiously from my presence. But there was something about Bartleby that not only strangely disarmed me, but in a wonderful manner, touched and disconcerted me. I began to reason with him.

"These are your own copies we are about to examine. It is labor saving to you, because one examination will answer for your four papers. It is common usage. Every copyist is bound to help examine his copy. Is it not so? Will you not speak? Answer!"

"I prefer not to," he replied in a flutelike tone. It seemed to me that, while I had been addressing him, he carefully revolved every statement that I made; fully comprehended the meaning; could not gainsay the irresistible conclusion; but, at the same time, some paramount consideration prevailed with him to reply as he did.

"You are decided, then, not to comply with my request—a request made according to common usage and common sense?"

He briefly gave me to understand, that on that point my judgment was sound. Yes: his decision was irreversible.

It is not seldom the case that, when a man is browbeaten in some unprecedented and violently unreasonable way, he begins to stagger in his own plainest faith. He begins, as it were, vaguely to surmise that, wonderful as it may be, all the justice and all the reason is on the other side. Accordingly, if any disinterested persons are present, he turns to them for some reinforcement of his own faltering mind.

"Turkey," said I, "what do you think of this? Am I not right?"

"With submission, sir," said Turkey, in his blandest tone, "I think that you are."

"Nippers," said I, "what do *you* think of it?"

"I think I should kick him out of the office."

(The reader, of nice perceptions, will here perceive that, it being morning, Turkey's answer is couched in polite and tranquil terms, but Nippers replies in ill-tempered ones. Or, to repeat a previous sentence, Nippers's ugly mood was on duty, and Turkey's off.)

"Ginger Nut," said I, willing to enlist the smallest suffrage in my behalf, "what do *you* think of it?"

"I think, sir, he's a little *luny,*" replied Ginger Nut, with a grin.

"You hear what they say," said I, turning towards the screen, "come forth and do your duty."

But he vouchsafed no reply. I pondered a moment in sore perplexity. But once more business hurried me. I determined again to postpone the consideration of this dilemma to my future leisure. With a little trouble we made out to examine the papers without Bartleby, though at every page or two Turkey deferentially dropped his opinion, that this proceeding was quite out of the common; while Nippers, twitching in his chair with a dyspeptic nervousness, ground out, between his set teeth, occasional hissing maledictions against the stubborn oaf behind the screen. And for his (Nippers's) part, this was the first and the last time he would do another man's business without pay.

Meanwhile Bartleby sat in his hermitage, oblivious to everything but his own peculiar business there.

Some days passed, the scrivener being employed upon another lengthy work. His late remarkable conduct led me to regard his ways narrowly. I observed that he never went to dinner; indeed, that he never went anywhere. As yet I had never, of my personal knowledge, known him to be outside of my office. He was a perpetual sentry in the corner. At about eleven o'clock though, in the morning, I noticed that Ginger Nut would advance toward the opening in Bartleby's screen, as if silently beckoned thither by a gesture invisible to me where I sat. The boy would then leave the office, jingling a few pence, and reappear with a handful of ginger-nuts, which he delivered in the hermitage, receiving two of the cakes for his trouble.

He lives, then, on ginger-nuts, thought I; never eats a dinner, properly speaking; he must be a vegetarian, then; but no; he never eats even vegetables; he eats nothing but ginger-nuts. My mind then ran on in reveries concerning the probable effects upon the human constitution of living entirely on ginger-nuts. Ginger-nuts are so called, because they contain ginger as one of their peculiar constituents, and the final flavoring one. Now, what was ginger? A hot, spicy thing. Was Bartleby hot and spicy? Not at all. Ginger, then, had no effect upon Bartleby. Probably he preferred it should have none.

Nothing so aggravates an earnest person as a passive resistance. If the individual so resisted be of a not inhumane temper, and the resisting one perfectly harmless in his passivity, then, in the better moods of the former, he will endeavor charitably to construe to his imagination what proves impossible to be solved by his judgment. Even so, for the most part, I regarded Bartleby and his ways. Poor fellow! thought I, he means no mischief; it is plain he intends no insolence; his aspect sufficiently evinces that his eccentricities are involuntary. He is useful to me. I can get along with him. If I turn him away, the chances are he will fall in with some less-indulgent employer, and then he will be rudely treated, and perhaps driven forth miserably to starve. Yes. Here I can cheaply purchase a delicious self-approval. To befriend Bartleby; to humor him in his strange willfulness, will cost me little or nothing, while I lay up in my soul what will eventually prove a sweet morsel for my conscience. But this mood was not invariable with me. The passiveness of Bartleby sometimes irritated me. I felt strangely goaded on to encounter him in new opposition—to elicit some angry spark from him answerable to my own. But, indeed, I might as well have essayed to strike fire with my knuckles against a bit of Windsor soap. But one afternoon the evil impulse in me mastered me, and the following little scene ensued:

"Bartleby," said I, "when those papers are all copied, I will compare them with you."

"I would prefer not to."

"How? Surely you do not mean to persist in that mulish vagary?"

No answer.

I threw open the folding-doors near by, and, turning upon Turkey and Nippers, exclaimed:

"Bartleby a second time says, he won't examine his papers. What do you think of it, Turkey?"

It was afternoon, be it remembered. Turkey sat glowing like a brass boiler; his bald head steaming; his hands reeling among his blotted papers.

"Think of it?" roared Turkey; "I think I'll just step behind his screen, and black his eyes for him!"

So saying, Turkey rose to his feet and threw his arms into a pugilistic position. He was hurrying away to make good his promise, when I detained him, alarmed at the effect of incautiously rousing Turkey's combativeness after dinner.

"Sit down, Turkey," said I, "and hear what Nippers has to say. What do you think of it, Nippers? Would I not be justified in immediately dismissing Bartleby?"

"Excuse me, that is for you to decide, sir. I think his conduct quite unusual, and, indeed, unjust, as regards Turkey and myself. But it may only be a passing whim."

"Ah," exclaimed I, "you have strangely changed your mind, then—you speak very gently of him now."

"All beer," cried Turkey; "gentleness is effects of beer—Nippers and I dined together to-day. You see how gentle *I* am, sir. Shall I go and black his eyes?"

"You refer to Bartleby, I suppose. No, not to-day, Turkey," I replied; "pray, put up your fists."

I closed the doors, and again advanced towards Bartleby. I felt additional incentives tempting me to my fate. I burned to be rebelled against again. I remembered that Bartleby never left the office.

"Bartleby," said I, "Ginger Nut is away; just step around to the Post Office, won't you? (it was but a three minutes' walk), and see if there is anything for me."

"I would prefer not to."

"You *will* not?"

"I *prefer* not."

I staggered to my desk, and sat there in a deep study. My blind inveteracy returned. Was there any other thing in which I could procure myself to be ignominiously repulsed by this lean, penniless wight?—my hired clerk? What added thing is there, perfectly reasonable, that he will be sure to refuse to do? "Bartleby!"

No answer.

"Bartleby," in a louder tone.

No answer.

"Bartleby," I roared.

Like a very ghost, agreeably to the laws of magical invocation, at the third summons, he appeared at the entrance of his hermitage.

"Go to the next room, and tell Nippers to come to me."

"I prefer not to," he respectfully and slowly said and mildly disappeared.

"Very good, Bartleby," said I, in a quiet sort of serenely-severe, self-possessed tone, intimating the unalterable purpose of some terrible retribution very close at hand. At the moment I half intended something of the kind. But upon the whole, as it was drawing towards my dinner-hour, I thought it best to put on my hat and walk home for the day, suffering much from perplexity and distress of mind.

Shall I acknowledge it? The conclusion of this whole business was, that it soon became a fixed fact of my chambers, that a pale young scrivener, by the name of Bartleby, had a desk there; that he copied for me at the usual rate of four cents a folio (one hundred words); but he was permanently exempt from examining the work done by him, that duty being transferred to Turkey and Nippers, out of compliment, doubtless, to their superior acuteness; moreover, said Bartleby was never, on any account, to be dispatched on the most trivial errand of any sort; and that even if entreated to take upon him such a matter, it was generally understood that he would "prefer not to"—in other words, that he would refuse point-blank.

As days passed on, I became considerably reconciled to Bartleby. His steadiness, his freedom from all dissipation, his incessant industry (except when he chose to throw himself into a standing revery behind his screen), his great stillness, his unalterableness of demeanor under all circumstances, made him a valuable acquisition. One prime thing was this—*he was always there*—first in the morning, continually through the day, and the last at night. I had a singular confidence in his honesty. I felt my most precious papers perfectly safe in his hands. Sometimes, to be sure, I could not, for the very soul of me, avoid falling into sudden spasmodic passions with him. For it was exceeding difficult to bear in mind all the time those strange peculiarities, privileges, and unheard of exemptions, forming the tacit stipulations on Bartleby's part under which he remained in my office. Now and then, in the eagerness of dispatching pressing business, I would inadvertently summon Bartleby, in a short, rapid tone, to put his finger, say, on the incipient tie of a bit of red tape with which I was about compressing some papers. Of course, from behind the screen the usual answer, "I prefer not to," was sure to come; and then, how could a human creature, with the common infirmities of our nature, refrain from bitterly exclaiming upon such perverseness—such unreasonableness. However, every added repulse of this sort which I received only tended to lessen the probability of my repeating the inadvertence.

Here it must be said, that according to the custom of most legal gentlemen occupying chambers in densely-populated law buildings, there were several keys to my door. One was kept by a woman residing in the attic, which person weekly scrubbed and daily swept and dusted my apartments. Another was kept by Turkey for convenience sake. The third I sometimes carried in my own pocket. The fourth I knew not who had.

Now, one Sunday morning I happened to go to Trinity Church, to hear a celebrated preacher, and finding myself rather early on the ground I thought I would walk around to my chambers for a while. Luckily I had my key with me; but upon applying it to the lock, I found it resisted by something inserted from the inside. Quite surprised, I called out; when to my consternation a key was turned from within; and thrusting his lean visage at me, and holding the door ajar, the apparition of Bartleby appeared, in his shirt sleeves, and otherwise in a strangely tattered *déshabillé,* saying quietly that he was sorry, but he was deeply engaged just then, and—preferred not admitting me at present. In a brief word or two, he moreover added, that perhaps I had better walk around the block two or three times, and by that time he would probably have concluded his affairs.

Now, the utterly unsurmised appearance of Bartleby, tenanting my law-chambers of a Sunday morning, with his cadaverously gentlemanly *nonchalance,* yet withal firm and self-possessed, had such a strange effect upon me, that incontinently I slunk away from my own door, and did as desired. But not without sundry twinges of impotent rebellion against the mild effrontery of this unaccountable scrivener. Indeed, it was his wonderful mildness chiefly, which not only disarmed me, but unmanned me as it were. For I consider that one, for the time, is somehow unmanned when he tranquilly permits his hired clerk to dictate to him, and order him away from his own premises. Furthermore, I was full of uneasiness as to what Bartleby could possibly be doing in my office in his shirt sleeves, and in an otherwise dismantled condition of a Sunday morning. Was anything amiss going on? Nay, that was out of the question. It was not to be thought of for a moment that Bartleby was an immoral person. But what could he be doing there?—copying? Nay again, whatever might be his eccentricities, Bartleby was an eminently decorous person. He would be the last man to sit down to his desk in any state approaching to nudity. Besides, it was Sunday; and there was something about Bartleby that forbade the supposition that he would by any secular occupation violate the proprieties of the day.

Nevertheless, my mind was not pacified; and full of a restless curiosity, at last I returned to the door. Without hindrance I inserted my key, opened it, and entered. Bartleby was not to be seen. I looked round anxiously, peeped behind his screen; but it was very plain that he was gone. Upon more closely examining the place, I surmised that for an indefinite period Bartleby must have eaten, dressed, and slept in my office, and that, too, without plate, mirror, or bed. The cushioned seat of a rickety old sofa in one corner bore the faint impress of a lean, reclining form. Rolled away under his desk, I found a blanket; under the empty grate, a blacking box and brush; on a chair, a tin basin, with soap and a ragged towel; in a newspaper a few crumbs of ginger-nuts and a morsel of cheese. Yes, thought I, it is evident enough that Bartleby has been making his home here, keeping bachelor's hall all by himself. Immediately then the thought came sweeping across me, what miserable friendlessness and loneliness are here revealed! His poverty is great; but his solitude, how horrible! Think of it. Of a Sunday, Wall Street is deserted as Petra, and every night of every day it is an emptiness. This building, too, which of week-days hums with industry and life, at nightfall echoes with sheer vacancy, and all through Sunday is forlorn. And here Bartleby makes his home; sole spectator of a solitude which he has seen all populous—a sort of innocent and transformed Marius brooding among the ruins of Carthage!

For the first time in my life a feeling of over-powering stinging melancholy seized me. Before, I had never experienced aught but a not unpleasing sadness. The bond of a common humanity now drew me irresistibly to gloom. A fraternal melancholy! For both I and Bartleby were sons of Adam. I remembered the bright silks and sparkling faces I had seen that day, in gala trim, swan-like sailing down the Mississippi of Broadway; and I contrasted them with the pallid copyist, and thought to myself, Ah, happiness courts the light, so we deem the world is gay; but misery hides aloof, so we deem that misery there is none. These sad fancyings—chimeras, doubtless, of a sick and silly brain—led on to other and more special thoughts, concerning the eccentricities of Bartleby. Presentiments of strange discoveries hovered round me. The scrivener's pale form appeared to me laid out, among uncaring strangers, in its shivering winding sheet.

Suddenly I was attracted by Bartleby's closed desk, the key in open sight left in the lock.

I mean no mischief, seek the gratification of no heartless curiosity, thought I; besides, the desk is mine, and its contents, too, so I will make bold to look within. Everything was methodically arranged, the papers smoothly placed. The pigeon holes were deep, and removing the files of documents, I groped into their recesses. Presently I felt something there, and dragged it out. It was an old bandanna handkerchief, heavy and knotted. I opened it, and saw it was a savings bank.

I now recalled all the quiet mysteries which I had noted in the man. I remembered that he never spoke but to answer; that, though at intervals he had considerable time to himself, yet I had never seen him reading—no, not even a newspaper; that for long periods he would stand looking out, at his pale window behind the screen, upon the dead brick wall; I was quite sure he never visited any refectory or eating house; while his pale face clearly indicated that he never drank beer like Turkey, or tea and coffee even, like other men; that he never went anywhere in particular that I could learn; never went out for a walk, unless, indeed, that was the case at present; that he had declined telling who he was, or whence he came, or whether he had any relatives in the world; that though so thin and pale, he never complained of ill health. And more than all, I remembered a certain unconscious air of pallid—how shall I call it?—of pallid haughtiness, say, or rather an austere reserve about him, which had positively awed me into my tame compliance with his eccentricities, when I had feared to ask him to do the slightest incidental thing for me, even though I might know, from his long-continued motionlessness, that behind his screen he must be standing in one of those dead-wall reveries of his.

Revolving all these things, and coupling them with the recently discovered fact, that he made my office his constant abiding place and home, and not forgetful of his morbid moodiness; revolving all these things, a prudential feeling began to steal over me. My first emotions had been those of pure melancholy and sincerest pity; but just in proportion as the forlornness of Bartleby grew and grew to my imagination, did that same melancholy merge into fear, that pity into repulsion. So true it is, and so terrible, too, that up to a certain point the thought or sight of misery enlists our best affections; but, in certain special cases, beyond that point it does not. They err who would assert that invariably this is owing to the inherent selfishness of the human heart. It rather proceeds from a certain hopelessness of remedying excessive and organic ill. To a sensitive being, pity is not seldom pain. And when at last it is perceived that such pity cannot lead to effectual succor, common sense bids the soul be rid of it. What I saw that morning persuaded me that the scrivener was the victim of innate and incurable disorder. I might give alms to his body; but his body did not pain him; it was his soul that suffered, and his soul I could not reach.

I did not accomplish the purpose of going to Trinity Church that morning. Somehow, the things I had seen disqualified me for the time from churchgoing. I walked homeward, thinking what I would do with Bartleby. Finally, I resolved upon this—I would put certain calm questions to him the next morning, touching his history, etc., and if he declined to answer them openly and unreservedly (and I supposed he would prefer not), then to give him a twenty dollar bill over and above whatever I might owe him, and tell him his services were no longer required; but that if in any other way I could assist him, I would be happy to do so, especially if he desired to return to his native place, wherever that might be, I would willingly help to defray the expenses. Moreover, if, after reaching home, he found himself at any time in want of aid, a letter from him would be sure of a reply.

The next morning came.

"Bartleby," said I, gently calling to him behind his screen.

No reply.

"Bartleby," said I, in a still gentler tone, "come here; I am not going to ask you to do anything you would prefer not to do—I simply wish to speak to you."

Upon this he noiselessly slid into view.

"Will you tell me, Bartleby, where you were born?"

"I would prefer not to."

"Will you tell me *anything* about yourself?"

"I would prefer not to."

"But what reasonable objection can you have to speak to me? I feel friendly towards you."

He did not look at me while I spoke, but kept his glance fixed upon my bust of Cicero, which, as I then sat, was directly behind me, some six inches above my head.

"What is your answer, Bartleby," said I, after waiting a considerable time for a reply, during which his countenance remained immovable, only there was the faintest conceivable tremor of the white attenuated mouth.

"At present I prefer to give no answer," he said, and retired into his hermitage.

It was rather weak in me I confess, but his manner, on this occasion, nettled me. Not only did there seem to lurk in it a certain calm disdain, but his perverseness seemed ungrateful, considering the undeniable good usage and indulgence he had received from me.

Again I sat ruminating what I should do. Mortified as I was at his behavior, and resolved as I had been to dismiss him when I entered my office, nevertheless I strangely felt something superstitious knocking at my heart, and forbidding me to carry out my purpose, and denouncing me for a villain if I dared to breathe one bitter word against this forlornest of mankind. At last, familiarly drawing my chair behind his screen, I sat down and said: "Bartleby, never mind, then, about revealing your history; but let me entreat you, as a friend, to comply as far as may be with the usages of this office. Say now, you will help to examine papers to-morrow or next day: in short, say now, that in a day or two you will begin to be a little reasonable:—say so, Bartleby."

"At present I would prefer not to be a little reasonable," was his mildly cadaverous reply.

Just then the folding-doors opened, and Nippers approached. He seemed suffering from an unusually bad night's rest, induced by severer indigestion than common. He overheard those final words of Bartleby.

"Prefer not, eh?" gritted Nippers—"I'd *prefer* him, if I were you, sir," addressing me—"I'd *prefer* him; I'd give him preferences, the stubborn mule! What is it, sir, pray, that he *prefers* not to do now?"

Bartleby moved not a limb.

"Mr. Nippers," said I, "I'd prefer that you would withdraw for the present."

Somehow, of late, I had got into the way of involuntarily using this word "prefer" upon all sorts of not exactly suitable occasions. And I trembled to think that my contact with the scrivener had already and seriously affected me in a mental way. And what further and deeper aberration might it not yet produce? This apprehension had not been without efficacy in determining me to summary measures.

As Nippers, looking very sour and sulky, was departing, Turkey blandly and deferentially approached.

"With submission, sir," said he, "yesterday I was thinking about Bartleby here, and I think that if he would but prefer to take a quart of good ale every day, it would do much towards mending him, and enabling him to assist in examining his papers."

"So you have got the word, too," said I, slightly excited.

"With submission, what word, sir," asked Turkey, respectfully crowding himself into the contracted space behind the screen, and by so doing, making me jostle the scrivener. "What word, sir?"

"I would prefer to be left alone here," said Bartleby, as if offended at being mobbed in his privacy.

"That's the word, Turkey," said I—*"that's* it."

"Oh, *prefer?* oh yes—queer word. I never use it myself. But, sir, as I was saying, if he would but prefer—"

"Turkey," interrupted I, "you will please withdraw."

"Oh certainly, sir, if you prefer that I should."

As he opened the folding-door to retire, Nippers at his desk caught a glimpse of me, and asked whether I would prefer to have a certain paper copied on blue paper or white. He did not in the least roguishly accent the word prefer. It was plain that it involuntarily rolled from his tongue. I thought to myself, surely I must get rid of a demented man, who already has in some degree turned the tongues, if not the heads of myself and clerks. But I thought it prudent not to break the dismission at once.

The next day I noticed that Bartleby did nothing but stand at his window in his dead-wall revery. Upon asking him why he did not write, he said that he had decided upon doing no more writing.

"Why, how now? what next?" exclaimed I, "do no more writing?"

"No more."

"And what is the reason?"

"Do you not see the reason for yourself," he indifferently replied.

I looked steadfastly at him, and perceived that his eyes looked dull and glazed. Instantly it occurred to me, that his unexampled diligence in copying by his dim window for the first few weeks of his stay with me might have temporarily impaired his vision.

I was touched. I said something in condolence with him. I hinted that of course he did wisely in abstaining from writing for a while; and urged him to embrace that opportunity of taking wholesome exercise in the open air. This, however, he did not do. A few days after this, my other clerks being absent, and being in a great hurry to dispatch certain letters by the mail, I thought that, having nothing else earthly to do, Bartleby would surely be less inflexible than usual, and carry these letters to the post-office. But he blankly declined. So, much to my inconvenience, I went myself.

Still added days went by. Whether Bartleby's eyes improved or not, I could not say. To all appearance I thought they did. But when I asked him if they did, he vouchsafed no answer. At all events, he would do no copying. At last, in reply to my urgings, he informed me that he had permanently given up copying.

"What!" exclaimed I; "suppose your eyes should get entirely well —better than ever before—would you not copy then?"

"I have given up copying," he answered, and slid aside.

He remained as ever, a fixture in my chamber. Nay—if that were possible—he became still more of a fixture than before. What was to be done? He would do nothing in the office; why should he stay there? In plain fact, he had now become a millstone to me, not only useless as a necklace, but afflictive to bear. Yet I was sorry for him. I speak less than truth when I say that, on his own account, he occasioned me uneasiness. If he would but have named a single relative or friend, I would instantly have written, and urged their taking the poor fellow away to some convenient retreat. But he seemed alone, absolutely alone in the universe. A bit of wreck in the mid Atlantic. At length, necessities connected with my business tyrannized over all other considerations. Decently as I could, I told Bartleby that in six days time he must unconditionally leave the office. I warned him to take measures, in the interval, for procuring some other abode. I offered to assist him in his endeavor, if he himself would but take the first step towards a removal. "And when you finally quit me, Bartleby," added I, "I shall see that you go not away entirely unprovided. Six days from this hour, remember."

At the expiration of that period, I peeped behind the screen, and lo! Bartleby was there.

I buttoned up my coat, balanced myself; advanced slowly towards him, touched his shoulder, and said, "The time has come; you must quit this place; I am sorry for you; here is money; but you must go."

"I would prefer not," he replied, with his back still towards me.

"You *must.*"

He remained silent.

Now I had an unbounded confidence in this man's common honesty. He had frequently restored to me sixpences and shillings carelessly dropped upon the floor, for I am apt to be very reckless in such shirt-button affairs. The proceeding, then, which followed will not be deemed extraordinary.

"Bartleby," said I, "I owe you twelve dollars on account; here are thirty-two; the odd twenty are yours—Will you take it?" and I handed the bills towards him.

But he made no motion.

"I will leave them here, then," putting them under a weight on the table. Then taking my hat and cane and going to the door, I tranquilly turned and added—"After you have removed your things from these offices, Bartleby, you will of course lock the door—since every one is now gone for the day but you—and if you please, slip your key underneath the mat, so that I may have it in the morning. I shall not see you again; so good-by to you. If, hereafter, in your new place of abode, I can be of any service to you, do not fail to advise me by letter. Good-by, Bartleby, and fare you well."

But he answered not a word; like the last column of some ruined temple, he remained standing mute and solitary in the middle of the otherwise deserted room.

As I walked home in a pensive mood, my vanity got the better of my pity. I could not but highly plume myself on my masterly management in getting rid of Bartleby. Masterly I call it, and such it must appear to any dispassionate thinker. The beauty of my procedure seemed to consist in its perfect quietness. There was no vulgar bullying, no bravado of any sort, no choleric hectoring, and striding to and fro across the apartment, jerking out vehement commands for Bartleby to bundle himself off with his beggarly traps. Nothing of the kind. Without loudly bidding Bartleby depart—as an inferior genius might have done—I *assumed* the ground that depart he must; and upon that assumption built all I had to say. The more I thought over my procedure, the more I was charmed with it. Nevertheless, next morning, upon awakening, I had my doubts—I had somehow slept off the fumes of vanity. One of the coolest and wisest hours a man has, is just after he awakes in the morning. My procedure seemed as sagacious as ever—but only in theory. How it would prove in practice—there was the rub. It was truly a beautiful thought to have assumed Bartleby's departure; but, after all, that assumption was simply my own, and none of Bartleby's. The great point was, not whether I had assumed that he would quit me, but whether he would prefer so to do. He was more a man of preferences than assumptions.

After breakfast, I walked down town, arguing the probabilities *pro* and *con.* One moment I thought it would prove a miserable failure, and Bartleby would be found all alive at my office as usual; the next moment it seemed certain that I should find his chair empty. And so I kept veering about. At the corner of Broadway and Canal Street, I saw quite an excited group of people standing in earnest conversation.

"I'll take odds he doesn't," said a voice as I passed.

"Doesn't go?—done!" said I; "put up your money."

I was instinctively putting my hand in my pocket to produce my own, when I remembered that this was an election day. The words I had overheard bore no reference to Bartleby, but to the success or non-success of some candidate for the mayoralty. In my intent frame of mind, I had, as it were, imagined that all Broadway shared in my excitement, and were debating the same question with me. I passed on, very thankful that the uproar of the street screened my momentary absent-mindedness.

As I had intended, I was earlier than usual at my office door. I stood listening for a moment. All was still. He must be gone. I tried the knob. The door was locked. Yes, my procedure had worked to a charm; he indeed must be vanished. Yet a certain melancholy mixed with this: I was almost sorry for my brilliant success. I was fumbling under the door mat for the key, which Bartleby was to have left there for me, when accidentally my knee knocked against a panel, producing a summoning sound, and in response a voice came to me from within—"Not yet; I am occupied."

It was Bartleby.

I was thunderstruck. For an instant I stood like the man who, pipe in mouth, was killed one cloudless afternoon long ago in Virginia, by summer lightning; at his own warm open window he was killed, and remained leaning out there upon the dreamy afternoon, till some one touched him, when he fell.

"Not gone!" I murmured at last. But again obeying that wondrous ascendancy which the inscrutable scrivener had over me, and from which ascendancy, for all my chafing, I could not completely escape, I slowly went down stairs and out into the street, and while walking round the block, considered what I should next do in this unheard-of perplexity. Turn the man out by an actual thrusting I could not; to drive him away by calling him hard names would not do; calling in the police was an unpleasant idea; and yet, permit him to enjoy his cadaverous triumph over me—this, too, I could not think of. What was to be done? or, if nothing could be done, was there anything further that I could *assume* in the matter? Yes, as before I had prospectively assumed that Bartleby would depart, so now I might retrospectively assume that departed he was. In the legitimate carrying out of this assumption, I might enter my office in a great hurry, and pretending not to see Bartleby at all, walk straight against him as if he were air. Such a proceeding would in a singular degree have the appearance of a home-thrust. It was hardly possible that Bartleby could withstand such an application of the doctrine of assumptions. But upon second thoughts the success of the plan seemed rather dubious. I resolved to argue the matter over with him again.

"Bartleby," said I, entering the office, with a quietly severe expression, "I am seriously displeased. I am pained, Bartleby. I had thought better of you. I had imagined you of such a gentlemanly organization, that in any delicate dilemma a slight hint would suffice—in short, an assumption. But it appears I am deceived. Why," I added, unaffectedly starting, "you have not even touched that money yet," pointing to it, just where I had left it the evening previous.

He answered nothing.

"Will you, or will you not, quit me?" I now demanded in a sudden passion, advancing close to him.

"I would prefer *not* to quit you," he replied, gently emphasizing the *not*.

"What earthly right have you to stay here? Do you pay any rent? Do you pay my taxes? Or is this property yours?"

He answered nothing.

"Are you ready to go on and write now? Are your eyes recovered? Could you copy a small paper for me this morning? or help examine a few lines? or step round to the post-office? In a word, will you do anything at all, to give a coloring to your refusal to depart the premises?"

He silently retired into his hermitage.

I was now in such a state of nervous resentment that I thought it but prudent to check myself at present from further demonstrations. Bartleby and I were alone. I remembered the tragedy of the unfortunate Adams and the still more unfortunate Colt in the solitary office of the latter; and how poor Colt, being dreadfully incensed by Adams, and imprudently permitting himself to get wildly excited, was at unawares hurried into his fatal act—an act which certainly no man could possibly deplore more than the actor himself. Often it had occurred to me in my ponderings upon the subject, that had that altercation taken place in the public street, or at a private residence, it would not have terminated as it did. It was the circumstance of being alone in a solitary office, up stairs, of a building entirely unhallowed by humanizing domestic associations—an uncarpeted office, doubtless, of a dusty, haggard sort of appearance —this it must have been, which greatly helped to enhance the irritable desperation of the hapless Colt.

But when this old Adam of resentment rose in me and tempted me concerning Bartleby, I grappled him and threw him. How? Why, simply by recalling the divine injunction: "A new commandment give I unto you, that ye love one another." Yes, this it was that saved me. Aside from higher considerations, charity often operates as a vastly wise and prudent principle—a great safeguard to its possessor. Men have committed murder for jealousy's sake, and anger's sake, and hatred's sake, and selfishness' sake, and spiritual pride's sake; but no man, that ever I heard of, ever committed a diabolical murder for sweet charity's sake. Mere self-interest, then, if no better motive can be enlisted, should, especially with high-tempered men, prompt all beings to charity and philanthropy. At any rate, upon the occasion in question, I strove to drown my exasperated feelings towards the scrivener by benevolently construing his conduct. Poor fellow, poor fellow! thought I, he don't mean anything; and besides, he has seen hard times, and ought to be indulged.

I endeavored, also, immediately to occupy myself, and at the same time to comfort my despondency. I tried to fancy, that in the course of the morning, at such time as might prove agreeable to him, Bartleby, of his own free accord, would emerge from his hermitage and take up some decided line of march in the direction of the door. But no. Half-past twelve o'clock came; Turkey began to glow in the face, overturn his inkstand, and become generally obstreperous; Nippers abated down into quietude and courtesy; Ginger Nut munched his noon apple; and Bartleby remained standing at his window in one of his profoundest dead-wall reveries. Will it be credited? Ought I to acknowledge it? That afternoon I left the office without saying one further word to him.

Some days now passed, during which, at leisure intervals I looked a little into "Edwards on the Will," and "Priestley on Necessity." Under the circumstances, those books induced a salutary feeling. Gradually I slid into the persuasion that these troubles of mine, touching the scrivener, had been all predestinated from eternity, and Bartleby was billeted upon me for some mysterious purpose of an all-wise Providence, which it was not for a mere mortal like me to fathom. Yes, Bartleby, stay there behind your screen, thought I; I shall persecute you no more; you are harmless and noiseless as any of these old chairs; in short, I never feel so private as when I know you are here. At last I see it, I feel it; I penetrate to the predestinated purpose of my life. I am content. Others may have loftier parts to enact; but my mission in this world, Bartleby, is to furnish you with office-room for such period as you may see fit to remain.

I believe that this wise and blessed frame of mind would have continued with me, had it not been for the unsolicited and uncharitable remarks obtruded upon me by my professional friends who visited the rooms. But thus it often is, that the constant friction of illiberal minds wears out at last the best resolves of the more generous. Though to be sure, when I reflected upon it, it was not strange that people entering my office should be struck by the peculiar aspect of the unaccountable Bartleby, and so be tempted to throw out some sinister observations concerning him. Sometimes an attorney, having business with me, and calling at my office, and finding no one but the scrivener there, would undertake to obtain some sort of precise information from him touching my whereabouts; but without heeding his idle talk, Bartleby would remain standing immovable in the middle of the room. So after contemplating him in that position for a time, the attorney would depart, no wiser than he came.

Also, when a reference was going on, and the room full of lawyers and witnesses, and business driving fast, some deeply-occupied legal gentleman present, seeing Bartleby wholly unemployed, would request him to run round to his (the legal gentleman's) office and fetch some papers for him. Thereupon, Bartleby would tranquilly decline, and yet remain idle as before. Then the lawyer would give a great stare, and turn to me. And what could I say? At last I was made aware that all through the circle of my professional acquaintance, a whisper of wonder was running round, having reference to the strange creature I kept at my office. This worried me very much. And as the idea came upon me of his possibly turning out a long-lived man, and keep occupying my chambers, and denying my authority; and perplexing my visitors; and scandalizing my professional reputation; and casting a general gloom over the premises; keeping soul and body together to the last upon his savings (for doubtless he spent but half a dime a day), and in the end perhaps outlive me, and claim possession of my office by right of his perpetual occupancy: as all these dark anticipations crowded upon me more and more, and my friends continually intruded their relentless remarks upon the apparition in my room; a great change was wrought in me. I resolved to gather all my faculties together, and forever rid me of this intolerable incubus.

Ere revolving any complicated project, however, adapted to this end, I first simply suggested to Bartleby the propriety of his permanent departure. In a calm and serious tone, I commended the idea to his careful and mature consideration. But, having taken three days to meditate upon it, he apprised me, that his original determination remained the same; in short, that he still preferred to abide with me.

What shall I do? I now said to myself, buttoning up my coat to the last button. What shall I do? what ought I to do? what does conscience say I *should* do with this man, or, rather, ghost. Rid myself of him, I must; go, he shall. But how? You will not thrust him, the poor, pale, passive mortal—you will not thrust such a helpless creature out of your door? you will not dishonor yourself by such cruelty? No, I will not, I cannot do that. Rather would I let him live and die here, and then mason up his remains in the wall. What, then, will you do? For all your coaxing, he will not budge. Bribes he leaves under your own paper-weight on your table; in short, it is quite plain that he prefers to cling to you.

Then something severe, something unusual must be done. What! surely you will not have him collared by a constable, and commit his innocent pallor to the common jail? And upon what ground could you procure such a thing to be done?—a vagrant, is he? What! he a vagrant, a wanderer, who refuses to budge? It is because he will *not* be a vagrant, then, that you seek to count him *as* a vagrant. This is too absurd. No visible means of support: there I have him. Wrong again: for indubitably he *does* support himself, and that is the only unanswerable proof that any man can show of his possessing the means so to do. No more, then. Since he will not quit me, I must quit him. I will change my offices; I will move elsewhere, and give him fair notice, that if I find him on my new premises I will then proceed against him as a common trespasser.

Acting accordingly, next day I thus addressed him: "I find these chambers too far from the City Hall; the air is unwholesome. In a word, I propose to remove my offices next week, and shall no longer require your services. I tell you this now, in order that you may seek another place."

He made no reply; and nothing more was said.

On the appointed day I engaged carts and men, proceeded to my chambers, and, having but little furniture, everything was removed in a few hours. Throughout, the scrivener remained standing behind the screen, which I directed to be removed the last thing. It was withdrawn; and, being folded up like a huge folio, left him the motionless occupant of a naked room. I stood in the entry watching him a moment, while something from within me upbraided me.

I re-entered, with my hand in my pocket—and—and my heart in my mouth.

"Good-by, Bartleby; I am going—good-by, and God some way bless you; and take that," slipping something in his hand. But it dropped upon the floor, and then—strange to say—I tore myself from him whom I had so longed to be rid of.

Established in my new quarters, for a day or two I kept the door locked, and started at every footfall in the passages. When I returned to my rooms, after any little absence, I would pause at the threshold for an instant, and attentively listen, ere applying my key. But these fears were needless. Bartleby never came nigh me.

I thought all was going well, when a perturbed-looking stranger visited me, inquiring whether I was the person who had recently occupied rooms at No.____ Wall Street.

Full of forebodings, I replied that I was.

"Then, sir," said the stranger, who proved a lawyer, "you are responsible for the man you left there. He refuses to do any copying; he refuses to do anything; he says he prefers not to; and he refuses to quit the premises."

"I am very sorry, sir," said I, with assumed tranquillity, but an inward tremor, "but, really, the man you allude to is nothing to me—he is no relation or apprentice of mine, that you should hold me responsible for him."

"In mercy's name, who is he?"

"I certainly cannot inform you. I know nothing about him. Formerly I employed him as a copyist; but he has done nothing for me now for some time past."

"I shall settle him, then—good morning, sir."

Several days passed, and I heard nothing more; and, though I often felt a charitable prompting to call at the place and see poor Bartleby, yet a certain squeamishness, of I know not what, withheld me.

All is over with him, by this time, thought I, at last, when, through another week, no further intelligence reached me. But, coming to my room the day after, I found several persons waiting at my door in a high state of nervous excitement.

"That's the man—here he comes," cried the foremost one, whom I recognized as the lawyer who had previously called upon me alone.

"You must take him away, sir, at once," cried a portly person among them, advancing upon me, and whom I knew to be the landlord of No.____ Wall Street. "These gentlemen, my tenants, cannot stand it any longer; Mr. B—," pointing to the lawyer, "has turned him out of his room, and he now persists in haunting the building generally, sitting upon the banisters of the stairs by day, and sleeping in the entry by night. Everybody is concerned; clients are leaving the offices; some fears are entertained of a mob; something you must do, and that without delay."

Aghast at this torrent, I fell back before it, and would fain have locked myself in my new quarters. In vain I persisted that Bartleby was nothing to me—no more than to any one else. In vain—I was the last person known to have anything to do with him, and they held me to the terrible account. Fearful, then, of being exposed in the papers (as one person present obscurely threatened), I considered the matter, and, at length, said, that if the lawyer would give me a confidential interview with the scrivener, in his (the lawyer's) own room, I would, that afternoon, strive my best to rid them of the nuisance they complained of.

Going up stairs to my old haunt, there was Bartleby silently sitting upon the banister at the landing.

"What are you doing here, Bartleby?" said I.

"Sitting upon the banister," he mildly replied.

I motioned him into the lawyer's room, who then left us.

"Bartleby," said I, "are you aware that you are the cause of great tribulation to me, by persisting in occupying the entry after being dismissed from the office?"

No answer.

"Now one of two things must take place. Either you must do something, or something must be done to you. Now what sort of business would you like to engage in? Would you like to re-engage in copying for some one?"

"No; I would prefer not to make any change."

"Would you like a clerkship in a dry-goods store?"

"There is too much confinement about that. No, I would not like a clerkship; but I am not particular."

"Too much confinement," I cried, "why you keep yourself confined all the time!"

"I would prefer not to take a clerkship," he rejoined, as if to settle that little item at once.

"How would a bar-tender's business suit you? There is no trying of the eye-sight in that."

"I would not like it at all; though, as I said before, I am not particular."

His unwonted wordiness inspirited me. I returned to the charge.

"Well, then, would you like to travel through the country collecting bills for the merchants? That would improve your health."

"No, I would prefer to be doing something else."

"How, then, would going as a companion to Europe, to entertain some young gentleman with your conversation—how would that suit you?"

"Not at all. It does not strike me that there is anything definite about that. I like to be stationary. But I am not particular."

"Stationary you shall be, then," I cried, now losing all patience, and, for the first time in all my exasperating connection with him, fairly flying into a passion. "If you do not go away from these premises before night, I shall feel bound—indeed, I *am* bound—to—to—to quit the premises myself!" I rather absurdly concluded, knowing not with what possible threat to try to frighten his immobility into compliance. Despairing of all further efforts, I was precipitately leaving him, when a final thought occurred to me—one which had not been wholly unindulged before.

"Bartleby," said I, in the kindest tone I could assume under such exciting circumstances, "will you go home with me now—not to my office, but my dwelling—and remain there till we can conclude upon some convenient arrangement for you at our leisure? Come, let us start now, right away."

"No: at present I would prefer not to make any change at all."

I answered nothing; but, effectually dodging every one by the suddenness and rapidity of my flight, rushed from the building, ran up Wall Street towards Broadway, and, jumping into the first omnibus, was soon removed from pursuit. As soon as tranquillity returned, I distinctly perceived that I had now done all that I possibly could, both in respect to the demands of the landlord and his tenants, and with regard to my own desire and sense of duty, to benefit Bartleby, and shield him from rude persecution. I now strove to be entirely care-free and quiescent; and my conscience justified me in the attempt; though, indeed, it was not so successful as I could have wished. So fearful was I of being again hunted out by the incensed landlord and his exasperated tenants, that, surrendering my business to Nippers, for a few days, I drove about the upper part of the town and through the suburbs, in my rockaway; crossed over to Jersey City and Hoboken, and paid fugitive visits to Manhattanville and Astoria. In fact, I almost lived in my rockaway for the time.

When again I entered my office, lo, a note from the landlord lay upon the desk. I opened it with trembling hands. It informed me that the writer had sent to the police, and had Bartleby removed to the Tombs as a vagrant. Moreover, since I knew more about him than any one else, he wished me to appear at that place, and make a suitable statement of the facts. These tidings had a conflicting effect upon me. At first I was indignant; but, at last, almost approved. The landlord's energetic, summary disposition, had led him to adopt a procedure which I do not think I would have decided upon myself; and yet, as a last resort, under such peculiar circumstances, it seemed the only plan.

As I afterwards learned, the poor scrivener, when told that he must be conducted to the Tombs, offered not the slightest obstacle, but, in his pale, unmoving way, silently acquiesced.

Some of the compassionate and curious bystanders joined the party; and headed by one of the constables arm in arm with Bartleby, the silent procession filed its way through all the noise, and heat, and joy of the roaring thoroughfares at noon.

The same day I received the note, I went to the Tombs, or, to speak more properly, the Halls of Justice. Seeking the right officer, I stated the purpose of my call, and was informed that the individual I described was, indeed, within. I then assured the functionary that Bartleby was a perfectly honest man, and greatly to be compassionated, however unaccountably eccentric. I narrated all I knew, and closed by suggesting the idea of letting him remain in as indulgent confinement as possible, till something less harsh might be done—though, indeed, I hardly knew what. At all events, if nothing else could be decided upon, the alms-house must receive him. I then begged to have an interview.

Being under no disgraceful charge, and quite serene and harmless in all his ways, they had permitted him freely to wander about the prison, and, especially, in the inclosed grass-platted yards thereof. And so I found him there, standing all alone in the quietest of the yards, his face towards a high wall, while all around, from the narrow slits of the jail windows, I thought I saw peering out upon him the eyes of murderers and thieves.

"Bartleby!"

"I know you," he said, without looking round—"and I want nothing to say to you."

"It was not I that brought you here, Bartleby," said I, keenly pained at his implied suspicion. "And to you, this should not be so vile a place. Nothing reproachful attaches to you by being here. And see, it is not so sad a place as one might think. Look, there is the sky, and here is the grass."

"I know where I am," he replied, but would say nothing more, and so I left him.

As I entered the corridor again, a broad meat-like man, in an apron, accosted me, and, jerking his thumb over his shoulder, said —"Is that your friend?"

"Yes."

"Does he want to starve? If he does, let him live on the prison fare, that's all."

"Who are you?" asked I, not knowing what to make of such an unofficially speaking person in such a place.

"I am the grub-man. Such gentlemen as have friends here, hire me to provide them with something good to eat."

"Is this so?" said I, turning to the turnkey.

He said it was.

"Well, then," said I, slipping some silver into the grub-man's hands (for so they called him), "I want you to give particular attention to my friend there; let him have the best dinner you can get. And you must be as polite to him as possible."

"Introduce me, will you?" said the grub-man, looking at me with an expression which seemed to say he was all impatience for an opportunity to give a specimen of his breeding.

Thinking it would prove of benefit to the scrivener, I acquiesced; and, asking the grub-man his name, went up with him to Bartleby.

"Bartleby, this is a friend; you will find him very useful to you."

"Your sarvant, sir, your sarvant," said the grub-man, making a low salutation behind his apron. "Hope you find it pleasant here, sir; nice grounds—cool apartments—hope you'll stay with us sometime—try to make it agreeable. What will you have for dinner to-day?"

"I prefer not to dine to-day," said Bartleby, turning away. "It would disagree with me; I am unused to dinners." So saying, he slowly moved to the other side of the inclosure, and took up a position fronting the dead-wall.

"How's this?" said the grub-man, addressing me with a stare of astonishment. "He's odd, ain't he?"

"I think he is a little deranged," said I, sadly.

"Deranged? deranged is it? Well, now, upon my word, I thought that friend of yourn was a gentleman forger; they are always pale and genteel-like, them forgers. I can't help pity 'em—can't help it, sir. Did you know Monroe Edwards?" he added, touchingly, and paused. Then, laying his hand piteously on my shoulder, sighed, "He died of consumption at Sing-Sing. So you weren't acquainted with Monroe?"

"No, I was never socially acquainted with any forgers. But I cannot stop longer. Look to my friend yonder. You will not lose by it. I will see you again."

Some few days after this, I again obtained admission to the Tombs, and went through the corridors in quest of Bartleby; but without finding him.

"I saw him coming from his cell not long ago," said a turnkey, "may be he's gone to loiter in the yards."

So I went in that direction.

"Are you looking for the silent man?" said another turnkey, passing me. "Yonder he lies—sleeping in the yard there. 'Tis not twenty minutes since I saw him lie down."

The yard was entirely quiet. It was not accessible to the common prisoners. The surrounding walls of amazing thickness, kept off all sounds behind them. The Egyptian character of the masonry weighed upon me with its gloom. But a soft imprisoned turf grew under foot. The heart of the eternal pyramids, it seemed, wherein, by some strange magic, through the clefts, grass-seed, dropped by birds, had sprung.

Strangely huddled at the base of the wall, his knees drawn up, and lying on his side, his head touching the cold stones, I saw the wasted Bartleby. But nothing stirred. I paused; then went close up to him; stooped over, and saw that his dim eyes were open; otherwise he seemed profoundly sleeping. Something prompted me to touch him. I felt his hand, when a tingling shiver ran up my arm and down my spine to my feet.

The round face of the grub-man peered upon me now. "His dinner is ready. Won't he dine to-day, either? Or does he live without dining?"

"Lives without dining," said I, and closed the eyes.

"Eh!—He's asleep, ain't he?"

"With kings and counselors," murmured I.

There would seem little need for proceeding further in this history. Imagination will readily supply the meagre recital of poor Bartleby's interment. But, ere parting with the reader, let me say, that if this little narrative has sufficiently interested him, to awaken curiosity as to who Bartleby was, and what manner of life he led prior to the present narrator's making his acquaintance, I can only reply, that in such curiosity I fully share, but am wholly unable to gratify it. Yet here I hardly know whether I should divulge one little item of rumor, which came to my ear a few months after the scrivener's decease. Upon what basis it rested, I could never ascertain; and hence, how true it is I cannot now tell. But, inasmuch as this vague report has not been without a certain suggestive interest to me, however said, it may prove the same with some others; and so I will briefly mention it. The report was this: that Bartleby had been a subordinate clerk in the Dead Letter Office at Washington, from which he had been suddenly removed by a change in the administration. When I think over this rumor, hardly can I express the emotions which seize me. Dead letters! does it not sound like dead men? Conceive a man by nature and misfortune prone to a pallid hopelessness, can any business seem more fitted to heighten it than that of continually handling these dead letters, and assorting them for the flames? For by the cart-load they are annually burned. Some times from out the folded paper the pale clerk takes a ring—the finger it was meant for, perhaps, moulders in the grave; a bank-note sent in swiftest charity—he whom it would relieve, nor eats nor hungers any more; pardon for those who died despairing; hope for those who died unhoping; good tidings for those who died stifled by unrelieved calamities. On errands of life, these letters speed to death.

Ah, Bartleby! Ah, humanity!

1853

The Death of Ivan Ilych

LEO TOLSTOY

[1828–1910]

1

During an interval in the Melvinski trial in the large building of the Law Courts, the members and public prosecutor met in Ivan Egorovich Shebek's private room, where the conversation turned on the celebrated Krasovski case. Fëdor Vasilievich warmly maintained that it was not subject to their jurisdiction, Ivan Egorovich maintained the contrary, while Peter Ivanovich, not having entered into the discussion at the start, took no part in it but looked through the *Gazette* which had just been handed in.

"Gentlemen," he said, "Ivan Ilych has died!"

"You don't say so!"

"Here, read it yourself," replied Peter Ivanovich, handing Fëdor Vasilievich the paper still damp from the press. Surrounded by a black border were the words: "Praskovya Fëdorovna Golovina, with profound sorrow, informs relatives and friends of the demise of her beloved husband Ivan Ilych Golovin, Member of the Court of Justice, which occurred on February the 4th of this year 1882. The funeral will take place on Friday at one o'clock in the afternoon."

Ivan Ilych had been a colleague of the gentlemen present and was liked by them all. He had been ill for some weeks with an illness said to be incurable. His post had been kept open for him, but there had been conjectures that in the case of his death Alexeev might receive his appointment, and that either Vinnikov or Shtabel would succeed Alexeev. So on receiving the news of Ivan Ilych's death the first thought of each of the gentlemen in that private room was of the changes and promotions it might occasion among themselves or their acquaintances.

"I shall be sure to get Shtabel's place or Vinnikov's," thought

Fëdor Vasilievich. "I was promised that long ago, and the promotion means an extra eight hundred rubles a year for me beside the allowance."

"Now I must apply for my brother-in-law's transfer from Kaluga," thought Peter Ivanovich. "My wife will be very glad, and then she won't be able to say that I never do anything for her relations."

"I thought he would never leave his bed again," said Peter Ivanovich aloud. "It's very sad."

"But what really was the matter with him?"

"The doctors couldn't say—at least they could, but each of them said something different. When last I saw him I thought he was getting better."

"And I haven't been to see him since the holidays. I always meant to go."

"Had he any property?"

"I think his wife had a little—but something quite trifling."

"We shall have to go to see her, but they live so terribly far away."

"Far away from you, you mean. Everything's far away from your place."

"You see, he never can forgive my living on the other side of the river," said Peter Ivanovich, smiling at Shebek. Then, still talking of the distances between different parts of the city, they returned to the Court.

Besides considerations as to the possible transfers and promotions likely to result from Ivan Ilych's death, the mere fact of the death of a near acquaintance aroused, as usual, in all who heard of it the complacent feeling that, "it is he who is dead and not I."

Each one thought or felt, "Well, he's dead but I'm alive!" But the more intimate of Ivan Ilych's acquaintances, his so-called friends, could not help thinking also that they would now have to fulfil the very tiresome demands of propriety by attending the funeral service and paying a visit of condolence to the widow.

Fëdor Vasilievich and Peter Ivanovich had been his nearest acquaintances. Peter Ivanovich had studied law with Ivan Ilych and had considered himself to be under obligations to him.

Having told his wife at dinner-time of Ivan Ilych's death and of his conjecture that it might be possible to get her brother transferred to their circuit, Peter Ivanovich sacrificed his usual nap, put on his evening clothes, and drove to Ivan Ilych's house.

At the entrance stood a carriage and two cabs. Leaning against the wall in the hall downstairs near the cloak-stand was a coffin-lid covered with cloth of gold, ornamented with gold cord and tassels, that had been polished up with metal powder. Two ladies in black were taking off their fur cloaks. Peter Ivanovich recognized one of them as Ivan Ilych's sister, but the other was a stranger to him. His colleague Schwartz was just coming downstairs, but on seeing Peter Ivanovich enter he stopped and winked at him, as if to say: "Ivan Ilych has made a mess of things—not like you and me."

Schwartz's face, with his Piccadilly whiskers and his slim figure in evening dress, had as usual an air of elegant solemnity which contrasted with the playfulness of his character and had a special piquancy here, or so it seemed to Peter Ivanovich.

Peter Ivanovich allowed the ladies to precede him and slowly followed them upstairs. Schwartz did not come down but remained where he was, and Peter Ivanovich understood that he wanted to arrange where they should play bridge that evening. The ladies went upstairs to the widow's room, and Schwartz, with seriously compressed lips but a playful look in his eyes, indicated by a twist of his eyebrows the room to the right where the body lay.

Peter Ivanovich, like everyone else on such occasions, entered feeling uncertain what he would have to do. All he knew was that at such times it is always safe to cross oneself. But he was not quite sure whether one should make obeisances while doing so. He therefore adopted a middle course. On entering the room he began crossing himself and made a slight movement resembling a bow. At the same time, as far as the motion of his head and arm allowed, he surveyed the room. Two young men—apparently nephews, one of whom was a high-school pupil—were leaving the room, crossing themselves as they did so. An old woman was standing motionless, and a lady with strangely arched eyebrows was saying something to her in a whisper. A vigorous, resolute Church Reader, in a frock-coat, was reading something in a loud voice with an expression that precluded any contradiction. The butler's assistant, Gerasim, stepping lightly in front of Peter Ivanovich, was strewing something on the floor. Noticing this, Peter Ivanovich was immediately aware of a faint odour of a decomposing body.

The last time he had called on Ivan Ilych, Peter Ivanovich had seen Gerasim in the study. Ivan Ilych had been particularly fond of him and he was performing the duty of a sick nurse.

Peter Ivanovich continued to make the sign of the cross, slightly inclining his head in an intermediate direction between the coffin, the Reader, and the icons on the table in a corner of the room. Afterwards, when it seemed to him that this movement of his arm in crossing himself had gone on too long, he stopped and began to look at the corpse.

The dead man lay, as dead men always lie, in a specially heavy way, his rigid limbs sunk in the soft cushions of the coffin, with the head forever bowed on the pillow. His yellow waxen brow with bald patches over his sunken temples was thrust up in the way peculiar to the dead, the protruding nose seeming to press on the upper lip. He was much changed and had grown even thinner since Peter Ivanovich had last seen him, but, as is always the case with the dead, his face was handsomer and above all more dignified than when he was alive. The expression on the face said that what was necessary had been accomplished, and accomplished rightly. Besides this there was in that expression a reproach and a warning to the living. This warning seemed to Peter Ivanovich out of place, or at least not applicable to him. He felt a certain discomfort and so he hurriedly crossed himself once more and turned and went out of the door—too hurriedly and too regardless of propriety, as he himself was aware.

Schwartz was waiting for him in the adjoining room with legs spread wide apart and both hands toying with his top-hat behind his back. The mere sight of that playful, well-groomed, and elegant figure refreshed Peter Ivanovich. He felt that Schwartz was above all these happenings and would not surrender to any depressing influences. His very look said that this incident of a church service for Ivan Ilych could not be sufficient reason for infringing the order of the session—in other words, that it would certainly not prevent his unwrapping a new pack of cards and shuffling them that evening while a footman placed four fresh candles on the table: in fact, that there was no reason for supposing that this incident would hinder their spending the evening agreeably. Indeed he said this in a whisper as Peter Ivanovich passed him, proposing that they should meet for a game at Fëdor Vasilievich's. But apparently Peter Ivanovich was not destined to play bridge that evening. Praskovya Fëdorovna (a short, fat woman who despite all efforts to the contrary had continued to broaden steadily from her shoulders downwards and who had the same extraordinary arched eyebrows as the lady who had been standing by the coffin), dressed all in black, her head covered with lace, came out of her own room with some other ladies, conducted them to the room where the dead body lay, and said: "The service will begin immediately. Please go in."

Schwartz, making an indefinite bow, stood still, evidently neither accepting nor declining this invitation. Praskovya Fëdorovna, recognizing Peter Ivanovich, sighed, went close to him, took his hand, and said: "I know you were a true friend to Ivan Ilych . . ." and looked at him awaiting some suitable response. And Peter Ivanovich knew that, just as it had been the right thing to cross himself in that room, so what he had to do here was to press her hand, sigh, and say, "Believe me. . . ." So he did all this and as he did it felt that the desired result had been achieved: that both he and she were touched.

"Come with me. I want to speak to you before it begins," said the widow. "Give me your arm."

Peter Ivanovich gave her his arm and they went to the inner rooms, passing Schwartz, who winked at Peter Ivanovich compassionately.

"That does for our bridge! Don't object if we find another player. Perhaps you can cut in when you do escape," said his playful look.

Peter Ivanovich sighed still more deeply and despondently, and Praskovya Fëdorovna pressed his arm gratefully. When they reached the drawing-room, upholstered in pink cretonne and lighted by a dim lamp, they sat down at the table—she on a sofa and Peter Ivanovich on a low pouffe, the springs of which yielded spasmodically under his weight. Praskovya Fëdorovna had been on the point of warning him to take another seat, but felt that such a warning was out of keeping with her present condition and so changed her mind. As he sat down on the pouffe Peter Ivanovich recalled how Ivan Ilych had arranged this room and had consulted him regarding this pink cretonne with green leaves. The whole room was full of furniture and knick-knacks, and on her way to the sofa the lace of the window's black shawl caught on the carved edge of the table. Peter Ivanovich rose to detach it, and the springs of the pouffe, relieved of his weight, rose also and gave him a push. The widow began detaching her shawl herself, and Peter Ivanovich again sat down, suppressing the rebellious springs of the pouffe under him. But the widow had not quite freed herself and Peter Ivanovich got up again, and again the pouffe rebelled and even creaked. When this was all over she took out a clean cambric handkerchief and began to weep. The episode with the shawl and the struggle with the pouffe had cooled Peter Ivanovich's emotions and he sat there with a sullen look on his face. This awkward situation was interrupted by Sokolov, Ivan Ilych's butler, who came to report that the plot in the cemetery that Praskovya Fëdorovna had chosen would cost two hundred rubles. She stopped weeping and, looking at Peter Ivanovich with the air of a victim, remarked in French that it was very hard for her. Peter Ivanovich made a silent gesture signifying his full conviction that it must indeed be so.

"Please smoke," she said in a magnanimous yet crushed voice, and turned to discuss with Sokolov the price of the plot for the grave.

Peter Ivanovich while lighting his cigarette heard her inquiring very circumstantially into the prices of different plots in the cemetery and finally decide which she would take. When that was done she gave instructions about engaging the choir. Sokolov then left the room.

"I look after everything myself," she told Peter Ivanovich, shifting the albums that lay on the table; and noticing that the table was endangered by his cigarette-ash, she immediately passed him an ash-tray, saying as she did so: "I consider it an affectation to say that my grief prevents my attending to practical affairs. On the contrary, if anything can—I won't say console me, but—distract me, it is seeing to everything concerning him." She again took out her handkerchief as if preparing to cry, but suddenly, as if mastering her feeling, she shook herself and began to speak calmly. "But there is something I want to talk to you about."

Peter Ivanovich bowed, keeping control of the springs of the pouffe, which immediately began quivering under him.

"He suffered terribly the last few days."

"Did he?" said Peter Ivanovich.

"Oh, terribly! He screamed unceasingly, not for minutes but for hours. For the last three days he screamed incessantly. It was unendurable. I cannot understand how I bore it; you could hear him three rooms off. Oh, what I have suffered!"

"Is it possible that he was conscious all that time?" asked Peter Ivanovich.

"Yes," she whispered. "To the last moment. He took leave of us a quarter of an hour before he died, and asked us to take Volodya away."

The thought of the sufferings of this man he had known so intimately, first as a merry little boy, then as a school-mate, and later as a grown-up colleague, suddenly struck Peter Ivanovich with horror, despite an unpleasant consciousness of his own and this woman's dissimulation. He again saw that brow, and that nose pressing down on the lip, and felt afraid for himself.

"Three days of frightful suffering and then death! Why, that might suddenly, at any time, happen to me," he thought, and for a moment felt terrified. But—he did not himself know how—the customary reflection at once occurred to him that this had happened to Ivan Ilych and not to him, and that it should not and could not happen to him, and to think that it could would be yielding to depression, which he ought not to do, as Schwartz's expression plainly showed. After which reflection Peter Ivanovich felt reassured, and began to ask with interest about the details of Ivan Ilych's death, as though death was an accident natural to Ivan Ilych but certainly not to himself.

After many details of the really dreadful physical sufferings Ivan Ilych had endured (which details he learnt only from the effect those sufferings had produced on Praskovya Fëdorovna's nerves) the widow apparently found it necessary to get to business.

"Oh, Peter Ivanovich, how hard it is! How terribly, terribly hard!" and she again began to weep.

Peter Ivanovich sighed and waited for her to finish blowing her nose. When she had done so he said, "Believe me . . ." and she again began talking and brought out what was evidently her chief concern with him—namely, to question him as to how she could obtain a grant of money from the government on the occasion of her husband's death. She made it appear that she was asking Peter Ivanovich's advice about her pension, but he soon saw that she already knew about that to the minutest detail, more even than he did himself. She knew how much could be got out of the government in consequence of her husband's death, but wanted to find out whether she could not possibly extract something more. Peter Ivanovich tried to think of some means of doing so, but after reflecting for a while and, out of propriety, condemning the government for its niggardliness, he said he thought that nothing more could be got. Then she sighed and evidently began to devise means of getting rid of her visitor. Noticing this, he put out his cigarette, rose, pressed her hand, and went out into the anteroom.

In the dining-room where the clock stood that Ivan Ilych had liked so much and had bought at an antique shop, Peter Ivanovich met a priest and a few acquaintances who had come to attend the service, and he recognized Ivan Ilych's daughter, a handsome young woman. She was in black and her slim figure appeared slimmer than ever. She had a gloomy, determined, almost angry expression, and bowed to Peter Ivanovich as though he were in some way to blame. Behind her, with the same offended look, stood a wealthy young man, an examining magistrate, whom Peter Ivanovich also knew and who was her fiancé, as he had heard. He bowed mournfully to them and was about to pass into the death-chamber, when from under the stairs appeared the figure of Ivan Ilych's schoolboy son, who was extremely like his father. He seemed a little like Ivan Ilych, such as Peter Ivanovich remembered when they studied law together. His tear-stained eyes had in them the look that is seen in the eyes of boys thirteen or fourteen who are not pure-minded. When he saw Peter Ivanovich he scowled morosely and shamefacedly. Peter Ivanovich nodded to him and entered the death-chamber. The service began: candles, groans, incense, tears, and sobs. Peter Ivanovich stood looking gloomily down at his feet. He did not look once at the dead man, did not yield to any depressing influence, and was one of the first to leave the room. There was no one in the anteroom, but Gerasim darted out of the dead man's room, rummaged with his strong hands among the fur coats to find Peter Ivanovich's and helped him on with it.

"Well, friend Gerasim," said Peter Ivanovich, so as to say something. "It's a sad affair, isn't it?"

"It's God's will. We shall all come to it some day," said Gerasim, displaying his teeth—the even, white teeth of a healthy peasant—and, like a man in the thick of urgent work, he briskly opened the front door, called the coachman, helped Peter Ivanovich into the sledge, and sprang back to the porch as if in readiness for what he had to do next.

Peter Ivanovich found the fresh air particularly pleasant after the smell of incense, the dead body, and carbolic acid.

"Where to, sir?" asked the coachman.

"It's not too late even now. . . . I'll call round on Fëdor Vasilievich."

He accordingly drove there and found them just finishing the first rubber, so that it was quite convenient for him to cut in.

2

Ivan Ilych's life had been most simple and most ordinary and therefore most terrible.

He had been a member of the Court of Justice, and died at the age of forty-five. His father had been an official who after serving in various ministries and departments in Petersburg had made the sort of career which brings men to positions from which by reason of their long service they cannot be dismissed, though they are obviously unfit to hold any responsible position, and for whom therefore posts are especially created, which though fictitious carry salaries of from six to ten thousand rubles that are not fictitious, and in receipt of which they live on to a great age.

Such was the Privy Councillor and superfluous member of various superfluous institutions, Ilya Epimovich Golovin.

He had three sons, of whom Ivan Ilych was second. The eldest son was following in his father's footsteps only in another department, and was already approaching that stage in the service at which a similar sinecure would be reached. The third son was a failure. He had ruined his prospects in a number of positions and was now serving in the railway department. His father and brothers, and still more their wives, not merely disliked meeting him, but avoided remembering his existence unless compelled to do so. His sister had married Baron Greff, a Petersburg official of her father's type. Ivan Ilych was *le phénix de la famille* as people said. He was neither as cold and formal as his elder brother nor as wild as the younger, but was a happy mean between them—an intelligent, polished, lively and agreeable man. He had studied with his younger brother at the School of Law, but the latter had failed to complete the course and was expelled when he was in the fifth class. Ivan Ilych finished the course well. Even when he was at the School of Law he was just what he remained for the rest of his life: a capable, cheerful, good-natured, and sociable man, though strict in the fulfilment of what he considered to be his duty: and he considered his duty to be what was so considered by those in authority. Neither as a boy nor as a man was he a toady, but from early youth was by nature attracted to people of high station as a fly is drawn to the light, assimilating their ways and views of life and establishing friendly relations with them. All the enthusiasms of childhood and youth passed without leaving much trace on him; he succumbed to sensuality, to vanity, and latterly among the highest classes to liberalism, but always within limits which his instinct unfailingly indicated to him as correct.

At school he had done things which had formerly seemed to him very horrid and made him feel disgusted with himself when he did them; but when later on he saw that such actions were done by people of good position and that they did not regard them as wrong, he was able not exactly to regard them as right, but to forget about them entirely or not be at all troubled at remembering them.

Having graduated from the School of Law and qualified for the tenth rank of the civil service, and having received money from his father for his equipment, Ivan Ilych ordered himself clothes at Scharmer's, the fashionable tailor, hung a medallion inscribed *respice finem* * on his watch-chain, took leave of his professor and the prince who was patron of the school, had a farewell dinner with his comrades at Donon's first-class restaurant, and with his new and fashionable portmanteau, linen, clothes, shaving and other toilet appliances, and a travelling rug, all purchased at the best shops, he set off for one of the provinces where, through his father's influence, he had been attached to the Governor as an official for special service.

In the province Ivan Ilych soon arranged as easy and agreeable a position for himself as he had had at the School of Law. He performed his official tasks, made his career, and at the same time amused himself pleasantly and decorously. Occasionally he paid official visits to country districts, where he behaved with dignity

**respice finem:* look to the end.

both to his superiors and inferiors, and performed the duties entrusted to him, which related chiefly to the sectarians, with an exactness and incorruptible honesty of which he could not but feel proud.

In official matters, despite his youth and taste for frivolous gaiety, he was exceedingly reserved, punctilious, and even severe; but in society he was often amusing and witty, and always good-natured, correct in his manner, and *bon enfant,** as the governor and his wife—with whom he was like one of the family—used to say of him.

In the province he had an affair with a lady who made advances to the elegant young lawyer, and there was also a milliner; and there were carousals with aides-de-camp who visited the district, and after-supper visits to a certain outlying street of doubtful reputation; and there was too some obsequiousness to his chief and even to his chief's wife, but all this was done with such a tone of good breeding that no hard names could be applied to it. It all came under the heading of the French saying: *"Il faut que jeunesse se passe."*† It was all done with clean hands, in clean linen, with French phrases, and above all among people of the best society and consequently with the approval of people of rank.

So Ivan Ilych served for five years and then came a change in his official life. The new and reformed judicial institutions were introduced, and new men were needed. Ivan Ilych became such a new man. He was offered the post of examining magistrate, and he accepted it though the post was in another province and obliged him to give up the connexions he had formed and to make new ones. His friends met to give him a send-off; they had a group- photograph taken and presented him with a silver cigarette-case, and he set off to his new post.

As examining magistrate Ivan Ilych was just as *comme il faut* and decorous a man, inspiring general respect and capable of separating his official duties from his private life, as he had been when acting as an official on special service. His duties now as examining magistrate were far more interesting and attractive than before. In his for-

**bon enfant:* a good child.

†*Il faut . . . passe:* You're only young once.

mer position it had been pleasant to wear an undress uniform made by Scharmer, and to pass through the crowd of petitioners and officials who were timorously awaiting an audience with the governor, and who envied him as with free and easy gait he went straight into his chief's private room to have a cup of tea and a cigarette with him. But not many people had then been directly dependent on him—only police officials and the sectarians when he went on special missions—and he liked to treat them politely, almost as comrades, as if he were letting them feel that he who had the power to crush them was treating them in this simple, friendly way. There were then but few such people. But now, as an examining magistrate, Ivan Ilych felt that everyone without exception, even the most important and self-satisfied, was in his power, and that he need only write a few words on a sheet of paper with a certain heading, and this or that important, self-satisfied person would be brought before him in the role of an accused person or a witness, and if he did not choose to allow him to sit down, would have to stand before him and answer his questions. Ivan Ilych never abused his power; he tried on the contrary to soften its expression, but the consciousness of it and of the possibility of softening its effect, supplied the chief interest and attraction of his office. In his work itself, especially in his examinations, he very soon acquired a method of eliminating all considerations irrelevant to the legal aspect of the case, and reducing even the most complicated case to a form in which it would be presented on paper only in its externals, completely excluding his personal opinion of the matter, while above all observing every prescribed formality. The work was new and Ivan Ilych was one of the first men to apply the new Code of 1864.

On taking up the post of examining magistrate in a new town, he made new acquaintances and connexions, placed himself on a new footing, and assumed a somewhat different tone. He took up an attitude of rather dignified aloofness towards the provincial authorities, but picked out the best circle of legal gentlemen and wealthy gentry living in the town and assumed a tone of slight dissatisfaction with the government, of moderate liberalism, and of enlightened citizenship. At the same time, without at all altering the elegance of his toilet, he ceased shaving his chin and allowed his beard to grow as it pleased.

Ivan Ilych settled down very pleasantly in this new town. The society there, which inclined towards opposition to the Governor, was friendly, his salary was larger, and he began to play *vint,* which he found added not a little to the pleasure of life, for he had a capacity for cards, played good-humouredly, and calculated rapidly and astutely, so that he usually won.

After living there for two years he met his future wife, Praskovya Fëdorovna Mikhel, who was the most attractive, clever, and brilliant girl of the set in which he moved, and among other amusements and relaxations from his labours as examining magistrate, Ivan Ilych established light and playful relations with her.

While he had been an official on special service he had been accustomed to dance, but now as an examining magistrate it was exceptional for him to do so. If he danced now, he did it as if to show that though he served under the reformed order of things, and had reached the fifth official rank, yet when it came to dancing he could do it better than most people. So at the end of an evening he sometimes danced with Praskovya Fëdorovna, and it was chiefly during these dances that he captivated her. She fell in love with him. Ivan Ilych had at first no definite intention of marrying, but when the girl fell in love with him he said to himself: "Really, why shouldn't I marry?"

Praskovya Fëdorovna came of a good family, was not bad looking, and had some little property. Ivan Ilych might have aspired to a more brilliant match, but even this was good. He had his salary, and she, he hoped, would have an equal income. She was well connected, and was a sweet, pretty, and thoroughly correct young woman. To say that Ivan Ilych married because he fell in love with Praskovya Fëdorovna and found that she sympathized with his views of life would be as incorrect as to say that he married because his social circle approved of the match. He was swayed by both these considerations: the marriage gave him personal satisfaction, and at the same time it was considered the right thing by the most highly placed of his associates.

So Ivan Ilych got married.

The preparations for marriage and the beginning of married life, with its conjugal caresses, the new furniture, new crockery, and new linen, were very pleasant until his wife became pregnant—so that Ivan Ilych had begun to think that marriage would not impair the easy, agreeable, gay and always decorous character of his life, approved of by society and regarded by himself as natural, but would even improve it. But from the first months of his wife's pregnancy, something new, unpleasant, depressing, and unseemly, and from which there was no way of escape, unexpectedly showed itself.

His wife, without any reason—*de gaieté de coeur** as Ivan Ilych expressed it to himself—began to disturb the pleasure and propriety of their life. She began to be jealous without any cause, expected him to devote his whole attention to her, found fault with everything, and made coarse and ill-mannered scenes.

At first Ivan Ilych hoped to escape from the unpleasantness of this state of affairs by the same easy and decorous relation to life that had served him heretofore: he tried to ignore his wife's disagreeable moods, continued to live in his usual easy and pleasant way, invited friends to his house for a game of cards, and also tried going out to his club or spending his evenings with friends. But one day his wife began upbraiding him so vigorously, using such coarse words, and continued to abuse him every time he did not fulfill her demands, so resolutely and with such evident determination not to give way till he submitted—that is, till he stayed at home and was bored just as she was—that he became alarmed. He now realized that matrimony—at any rate with Praskovya Fëdorovna—was not always conducive to the pleasures and amenities of life, but on the contrary often infringed both comfort and propriety, and that he must therefore entrench himself against such infringement. And Ivan Ilych began to seek for means of doing so. His official duties were the one thing that imposed upon Praskovya Fëdorovna, and by means of his official work and the duties attached to it he began struggling with his wife to secure his own independence.

With the birth of their child, the attempts to feed it and the various failures in doing so, and with the real and imaginary illnesses of mother and child, in which Ivan Ilych's sympathy was demanded but about which he understood nothing, the need for securing for himself an existence outside his family life became still more imperative.

As his wife grew more irritable and exacting and Ivan Ilych transferred the centre of gravity of his life more and more to his official

**de gaieté de coeur:* out of sheer wantonness.

work, so did he grow to like his work better and became more ambitious than before.

Very soon, within a year of his wedding, Ivan Ilych had realized that marriage, though it may add some comforts to life, is in fact a very intricate and difficult affair towards which in order to perform one's duty, that is, to lead a decorous life approved of by society, one must adopt a definite attitude just as towards one's official duties.

And Ivan Ilych evolved such an attitude towards married life. He only required of it those conveniences—dinner at home, housewife, and bed—which it could give him, and above all that propriety of external forms required by public opinion. For the rest he looked for light-hearted pleasure and propriety, and was very thankful when he found them, but if he met with antagonism and querulousness he at once retired into his separate fenced-off world of official duties, where he found satisfaction.

Ivan Ilych was esteemed a good official, and after three years was made Assistant Public Prosecutor. His new duties, their importance, the possibility of indicting and imprisoning anyone he chose, the publicity his speeches received, and the success he had in all these things, made his work still more attractive.

More children came. His wife became more and more querulous and ill-tempered, but the attitude Ivan Ilych had adopted towards his home life rendered him almost impervious to her grumbling.

After seven years' service in that town he was transferred to another province as Public Prosecutor. They moved, but were short of money and his wife did not like the place they moved to. Though the salary was higher the cost of living was greater, besides which two of their children died and family life became still more unpleasant for him.

Praskovya Fëdorovna blamed her husband for every inconvenience they encountered in their new home. Most of the conversations between husband and wife, especially as to the children's education, led to topics which recalled former disputes, and those disputes were apt to flare up again at any moment. There remained only those rare periods of amorousness which still came to them at times but did not last long. These were islets at which they anchored for a while and then again set out upon that ocean of veiled hostility which showed itself in their aloofness from one another.

This aloofness might have grieved Ivan Ilych had he considered that it ought not to exist, but he now regarded the position as normal, and even made it the goal at which he aimed in family life. His aim was to free himself more and more from those unpleasantnesses and to give them a semblance of harmlessness and propriety. He attained this by spending less and less time with his family, and when obliged to be at home he tried to safeguard his position by the presence of outsiders. The chief thing however was that he had his official duties. The whole interest of his life now centred in the official world and that interest absorbed him. The consciousness of his power, being able to ruin anybody he wished to ruin, the importance, even the external dignity of his entry into court, or meetings with his subordinates, his success with superiors and inferiors, and above all his masterly handling of cases, of which he was conscious—all this gave him pleasure and filled his life, together with chats with his colleagues, dinners, and bridge. So that on the whole Ivan Ilych's life continued to flow as he considered it should do—pleasantly and properly.

So things continued for another seven years. His eldest daughter was already sixteen, another child had died, and only one son was left, a schoolboy and a subject of dissension. Ivan Ilych wanted to put him in the School of Law, but to spite him Praskovya Fëdorovna entered him at the High School. The daughter had been educated at home and had turned out well: the boy did not learn badly either.

3

So Ivan Ilych lived for seventeen years after his marriage. He was already a Public Prosecutor of long standing, and had declined several proposed transfers while awaiting a more desirable post, when an unanticipated and unpleasant occurrence quite upset the peaceful course of his life. He was expecting to be offered the post of presiding judge in a University town, but Happe somehow came to the front and obtained the appointment instead. Ivan Ilych became irritable, reproached Happe, and quarrelled both with him and with his immediate superiors—who became colder to him and again passed him over when other appointments were made.

This was in 1880, the hardest year of Ivan Ilych's life. It was then that it became evident on the one hand that his salary was insufficient for them to live on, and on the other that he had been forgotten, and not only this, but that what was for him the greatest and most cruel injustice appeared to others a quite ordinary occurrence. Even his father did not consider it his duty to help him. Ivan Ilych felt himself abandoned by everyone, and that they regarded his position with a salary of 3,500 rubles as quite normal and even fortunate. He alone knew that with the consciousness of the injustices done him, with his wife's incessant nagging, and with the debts he had contracted by living beyond his means, his position was far from normal.

In order to save money that summer he obtained leave of absence and went with his wife to live in the country at her brother's place.

In the country, without his work, he experienced *ennui* for the first time in his life, and not only *ennui* but intolerable depression, and he decided that it was impossible to go on living like that, and that it was necessary to take energetic measures.

Having passed a sleepless night pacing up and down the veranda, he decided to go to Petersburg and bestir himself, in order to punish those who had failed to appreciate him and to get transferred to another ministry.

Next day, despite many protests from his wife and her brother, he started for Petersburg with the sole subject of obtaining a post with a salary of five thousand rubles a year. He was no longer bent on any particular department, or tendency, or kind of activity. All he now wanted was an appointment to another post with a salary of five thousand rubles, either in the administration, in the banks, with the railways, in one of the Empress Marya's Institutions, or even in the customs—but it had to carry with it a salary of five thousand rubles and be in a ministry other than that in which they had failed to appreciate him.

And this quest of Ivan Ilych's was crowned with remarkable and unexpected success. At Kursk an acquaintance of his, F. I. Ilyin, got into the first-class carriage, sat down beside Ivan Ilych, and told him of a telegram just received by the Governor of Kursk announcing that a change was about to take place in the ministry: Peter Ivanovich was to be superseded by Ivan Semënovich.

The proposed change, apart from its significance for Russia, had a special significance for Ivan Ilych, because by bringing forward a new man, Peter Petrovich, and consequently his friend Zachar

Ivanovich, it was highly favourable for Ivan Ilych, since Zachar Ivanovich was a friend and colleague of his.

In Moscow this news was confirmed, and on reaching Petersburg Ivan Ilych found Zachar Ivanovich and received a definite promise of an appointment in his former department of Justice.

A week later he telegraphed to his wife: "Zachar in Miller's place. I shall receive appointment on presentation of report."

Thanks to this change of personnel, Ivan Ilych had unexpectedly obtained an appointment in his former ministry which placed him two stages above his former colleagues besides giving him five thousand rubles salary and three thousand five hundred rubles for expenses connected with his removal. All his ill humour towards his former enemies and the whole department vanished, and Ivan Ilych was completely happy.

He returned to the country more cheerful and contented than he had been for a long time. Praskovya Fëdorovna also cheered up and a truce was arranged between them. Ivan Ilych told of how he had been fêted by everybody in Petersburg, how all those who had been his enemies were put to shame and now fawned on him, how envious they were of his appointment, and how much everybody in Petersburg had liked him.

Praskovya Fëdorovna listened to all this and appeared to believe it. She did not contradict anything, but only made plans for their life in the town to which they were going. Ivan Ilych saw with delight that these plans were his plans, that he and his wife agreed, and that, after a stumble, his life was regaining its due and natural character of pleasant lightheartedness and decorum.

Ivan Ilych had come back for a short time only, for he had to take up his new duties on the 10th of September. Moreover, he needed time to settle into the new place, to move all his belongings from the province, and to buy and order many additional things: in a word, to make such arrangements as he had resolved on, which were almost exactly what Praskovya Fëdorovna too had decided on.

Now that everything had happened so fortunately, and that he and his wife were at one in their aims and moreover saw so little of one another, they got on together better than they had done since the first years of marriage. Ivan Ilych had thought of taking his family away with him at once, but the insistence of his wife's brother and her sister-in-law, who had suddenly become particularly amiable and friendly to him and his family, induced him to depart alone.

So he departed, and the cheerful state of mind induced by his success and by the harmony between his wife and himself, the one intensifying the other, did not leave him. He found a delightful house, just the thing both he and his wife had dreamt of. Spacious, lofty reception rooms in the old style, a convenient and dignified study, rooms for his wife and daughter, a study for his son—it might have been specially built for them. Ivan Ilych himself superintended the arrangements, chose the wallpapers, supplemented the furniture (preferably with antiques which he considered particularly *comme il faut*), and supervised the upholstering. Everything progressed and progressed and approached the ideal he had set himself: even when things were only half completed they exceeded his expectations. He saw what a refined and elegant character, free from vulgarity, it would all have when it was ready. On falling asleep he pictured to himself how the reception-room would look. Looking at the yet unfinished drawing-room he could see the fireplace, the screen, the what-not, the little chairs dotted here and there, the dishes and plates on the walls, and the bronzes, as they would be when everything was in place. He was pleased by the thought of how his wife and daughter, who shared his taste in this matter, would be impressed by it. They were certainly not expecting as much. He had been particularly successful in finding, and buying cheaply, antiques which gave a particularly aristocratic character to the whole place. But in his letters he intentionally understated everything in order to be able to surprise them. All this so absorbed him that his new duties—though he liked his official work—interested him less than he had expected. Sometimes he even had moments of absent-mindedness during the Court Sessions, and would consider whether he should have straight or curved cornices for his curtains. He was so interested in it all that he often did things himself, rearranging the furniture, or rehanging the curtains. Once when mounting a step-ladder to show the upholsterer, who did not understand, how he wanted the hangings draped, he made a false step and slipped, but being a strong and agile man he clung on and only knocked his side against the knob of the window frame. The bruised place was painful but the pain soon passed, and he felt particularly bright and well just then. He wrote: "I feel fifteen years younger." He thought he would have everything ready by September, but it dragged on till mid-October. But the result was charming not only in his eyes but to everyone who saw it.

In reality it was just what is usually seen in the houses of people of moderate means who want to appear rich, and therefore succeed only in resembling others like themselves: there were damasks, dark wood, plants, rugs, and dull and polished bronzes—all the things people of a certain class have in order to resemble other people of that class. His house was so like the others that it would never have been noticed, but to him it all seemed to be quite exceptional. He was very happy when he met his family at the station and brought them to the newly furnished house all lit up, where a footman in a white tie opened the door into the hall decorated with plants, and when they went on into the drawing-room and the study uttering exclamations of delight. He conducted them everywhere, drank in their praises eagerly, and beamed with pleasure. At tea that evening, when Praskovya Fëdorovna among other things asked him about his fall, he laughed and showed them how he had gone flying and frightened the upholsterer.

"It's a good thing I'm a bit of an athlete. Another man might have been killed, but I merely knocked myself, just here; it hurts when touched, but it's passing off already—it's only a bruise."

So they began living in their new home—in which, as always happens, when they got thoroughly settled in they found they were just one room short—and with the increased income, which as always was just a little (some five hundred rubles) too little, but it was all very nice.

Things went particularly well at first, before everything was finally arranged and while something had still to be done: this thing bought, that thing ordered, another thing moved, and something else adjusted. Though there were some disputes between husband and wife, they were both so well satisfied and had so much to do that it all passed off without any serious quarrels. When nothing was left to arrange it became rather dull and something seemed to be lacking, but they were then making acquaintances, forming habits, and life was growing fuller.

Ivan Ilych spent his mornings at the law court and came home to dinner, and at first he was generally in a good humour, though he occasionally became irritable just on account of his house. (Every spot on the tablecloth or the upholstery, and every broken window-blind string, irritated him. He had devoted so much trouble to arranging it all that every disturbance of it distressed him.) But on the whole his life ran its course as he believed life should do: easily, pleasantly, and decorously.

He got up at nine, drank his coffee, read the paper, and then put on his undress uniform and went to the law courts. There the harness in which he worked had already been stretched to fit him and he donned it without a hitch: petitioners, inquiries at the chancery, the chancery itself, and the sittings public and administrative. In all this the thing was to exclude everything fresh and vital, which always disturbs the regular course of official business, and to admit only official relations with people, and then only on official grounds. A man would come, for instance, wanting some information. Ivan Ilych, as one in whose sphere the matter did not lie, would have nothing to do with him: but if the man had some business with him in his official capacity, something that could be expressed on officially stamped paper, he would do everything, positively everything he could within the limits of such relations, and in doing so would maintain the semblance of friendly human relations, that is, would observe the courtesies of life. As soon as the official relations ended, so did everything else. Ivan Ilych possessed this capacity to separate his real life from the official side of affairs and not mix the two, in the highest degree, and by long practice and natural aptitude had brought it to such a pitch that sometimes, in the manner of a virtuoso, he would even allow himself to let the human and official relations mingle. He let himself do this just because he felt that he could at any time he chose resume the strictly official attitude again and drop the human relation. And he did it all easily, pleasantly, correctly, and even artistically. In the intervals between the sessions he smoked, drank tea, chatted a little about politics, a little about general topics, a little about cards, but most of all about official appointments. Tired, but with the feelings of a virtuoso—one of the first violins who has played his part in an orchestra with precision—he would return home to find that his wife and daughter had been out paying calls, or had a visitor, and that his son had been to school, had done his homework with his tutor, and was duly learning what is taught at High Schools. Everything was as it should be. After dinner, if they had no visitors, Ivan Ilych sometimes read a book that was being much discussed at the time, and in the evening settled down to work, that is, read official papers, compared the depositions of witnesses, and noted paragraphs of the Code applying to them. This was neither dull nor amusing. It was dull when he might have been playing bridge, but if no bridge was available it was at any rate better than doing nothing or sitting with his wife. Ivan Ilych's chief pleasure was giving little dinners to which he invited men and women of good social position, and just as his drawing-room resembled all other drawing-rooms so did his enjoyable little parties resemble all other such parties.

Once they even gave a dance. Ivan Ilych enjoyed it and everything went off well, except that it led to a violent quarrel with his wife about the cakes and sweets. Praskovya Fëdorovna had made her own plans, but Ivan Ilych insisted on getting everything from an expensive confectioner and ordered too many cakes, and the quarrel occurred because some of those cakes were left over and the confectioner's bill came to forty-five rubles. It was a great and disagreeable quarrel. Praskovya Fëdorovna called him "a fool and an imbecile," and he clutched at his head and made angry allusions to divorce.

But the dance itself had been enjoyable. The best people were there, and Ivan Ilych had danced with Princess Trufonova, a sister of the distinguished founder of the Society "Bear my Burden."

The pleasures connected with his work were pleasures of ambition; his social pleasures were those of vanity; but Ivan Ilych's greatest pleasure was playing bridge. He acknowledged that whatever disagreeable incident happened in his life, the pleasure that beamed like a ray of light above everything else was to sit down to bridge with good players, not noisy partners, and of course to four-handed bridge (with five players it was annoying to have to stand out, though one pretended not to mind), to play a clever and serious game (when the cards allowed it) and then to have supper and drink a glass of wine. After a game of bridge, especially if he had won a little (to win a large sum was unpleasant), Ivan Ilych went to bed in specially good humour.

So they lived. They formed a circle of acquaintances among the best people and were visited by people of importance and by young folk. In their views as to their acquaintances, husband, wife and daughter were entirely agreed, and tacitly and unanimously kept at arm's length and shook off the shabby friends and relations who, with much show of affection, gushed into the drawing-room with its Japanese plates on the walls. Soon these shabby friends ceased to obtrude themselves and only the best people remained in the Golovins' set.

Young men made up to Lisa, and Petrishchev, an examining magistrate and Dmitri Ivanovich Petrishchev's son and sole heir, began to be so attentive to her that Ivan Ilych had already spoken to Praskovya Fëdorovna about it, and considered whether they should not arrange a party for them, or get up some private theatricals.

So they lived, and all went well, without change, and life flowed pleasantly.

4

They were all in good health. It could not be called ill health if Ivan Ilych sometimes said that he had a queer taste in his mouth and felt some discomfort in his left side.

But this discomfort increased and, though not exactly painful, grew into a sense of pressure in his side accompanied by ill humour. And his irritability became worse and worse and began to mar the agreeable, easy, and correct life that had established itself in the Golovin family. Quarrels between husband and wife became more and more frequent, and soon the ease and amenity disappeared and even the decorum was barely maintained. Scenes again became frequent, and very few of those islets remained on which husband and wife could meet without an explosion. Praskovya Fëdorovna now had good reason to say that her husband's temper was trying. With characteristic exaggeration she said he had always had a dreadful temper, and that it had needed all her good nature to put up with it for twenty years. It was true that now the quarrels were started by him. His bursts of temper always came just before dinner, often just as he began to eat his soup. Sometimes he noticed that a plate or dish was chipped, or the food was not right, or his son put his elbow on the table, or his daughter's hair was not done as he liked it, and for all this he blamed Praskovya Fëdorovna. At first she retorted and said disagreeable things to him, but once or twice he fell into such a rage at the beginning of dinner that she realized it was due to some physical derangement brought on by taking food, and so she restrained herself and did not answer, but only hurried to get the dinner over. She regarded this self-restraint as highly praiseworthy. Having come to the conclusion that her husband had a dreadful temper and made her life miserable, she began to feel sorry for herself, and the more she pitied herself the more she hated her husband. She began to wish he would die; yet she did not want him to die because then his salary would cease. And this irritated her against him still more. She considered herself dreadfully unhappy just because not even his death could save her, and though she concealed her exasperation, that hidden exasperation of hers increased his irritation also.

After one scene in which Ivan Ilych had been particularly unfair and after which he had said in explanation that he certainly was irritable but that it was due to his not being well, she said that if he was ill it should be attended to, and insisted on his going to see a celebrated doctor.

He went. Everything took place as he had expected and as it always does. There was the usual waiting and the important air assumed by the doctor, with which he was so familiar (resembling that which he himself assumed in court), and the sounding and listening, and the questions which called for answers that were foregone conclusions and were evidently unnecessary, and the look of importance which implied that "if only you put yourself in our hands we will arrange everything—we know indubitably how it has to be done, always in the same way for everybody alike." It was all just as it was in the law courts. The doctor put on just the same air towards him as he himself put on towards an accused person.

The doctor said that so-and-so indicated that there was so-and-so inside the patient, but if the investigation of so-and-so did not confirm this, then he must assume that and that. If he assumed that and that, then . . . and so on. To Ivan Ilych only one question was important: was his case serious or not? But the doctor ignored that inappropriate question. From his point of view it was not the one under consideration, the real question was to decide between a floating kidney, chronic catarrh, or appendicitis. It was not a question of Ivan Ilych's life or death, but one between a floating kidney and appendicitis. And that quesiton the doctor solved brilliantly, as it seemed to Ivan Ilych, in favour of the appendix, with the reservation that should an examination of the urine give fresh indications the matter would be reconsidered. All this was just what Ivan Ilych had himself brilliantly accomplished a thousand times in dealing with men on trial. The doctor summed up just as brilliantly, looking over his spectacles triumphantly and even gaily at the accused. From the doctor's summing up Ivan Ilych concluded that things were bad, but that for the doctor, and perhaps for everybody else, it was a matter of indifference, though for him it was bad. And this conclusion struck him painfully, arousing in him a great feeling of pity for himself and of bitterness towards the doctor's indifference to a matter of such importance.

He said nothing of this, but rose, placed the doctor's fee on the table, and remarked with a sigh: "We sick people probably often put inappropriate questions. But tell me, in general, is this complaint dangerous, or not? . . ."

The doctor looked at him sternly over his spectacles with one eye, as if to say: "Prisoner, if you will not keep to the questions put to you, I shall be obliged to have you removed from the court."

"I have already told you what I consider necessary and proper. The analysis may show something more." And the doctor bowed.

Ivan Ilych went out slowly, seated himself disconsolately in his sledge, and drove home. All the way home he was going over what the doctor had said, trying to translate those complicated, obscure, scientific phrases into plain language and find in them an answer to the question: "Is my condition bad? Is it very bad? Or is there as yet nothing much wrong?" And it seemed to him that the meaning of what the doctor had said was that it was very bad. Everything in the streets seemed depressing. The cabmen, the houses, the passers-by, and the shops, were dismal. His ache, this dull gnawing ache that never ceased for a moment, seemed to have acquired a new and more serious significance from the doctor's dubious remarks. Ivan Ilych now watched it with a new and oppressive feeling.

He reached home and began to tell his wife about it. She listened, but in the middle of his account his daughter came in with her hat on, ready to go out with her mother. She sat down reluctantly to listen to this tedious story, but could not stand it long, and her mother too did not hear him to the end.

"Well, I am very glad," she said. "Mind now to take your medicine regularly. Give me the prescription and I'll send Gerasim to the chemist's." And she went to get ready to go out.

While she was in the room Ivan Ilych had hardly taken time to breathe, but he sighed deeply when she left it.

"Well," he thought, "perhaps it isn't so bad after all."

He began taking his medicine and following the doctor's directions, which had been altered after the examination of the urine. But then it happened that there was a contradiction between the indications drawn from the examination of the urine and the symptoms that showed themselves. It turned out that what was happening differed from what the doctor had told him, and that he had either forgotten, or blundered or hidden something from him. He could not, however, be blamed for that, and Ivan Ilych still obeyed his orders implicitly and at first derived some comfort from doing so.

From the time of his visit to the doctor, Ivan Ilych's chief occupation was the exact fulfilment of the doctor's instructions regarding hygiene and the taking of medicine, and the observation of his pain and his excretions. His chief interests came to be people's ailments and people's health. When sickness, deaths, or recoveries were mentioned in his presence, especially when the illness resembled his own, he listened with agitation which he tried to hide, asked questions, and applied what he heard to his own case.

The pain did not grow less, but Ivan Ilych made efforts to force himself to think that he was better. And he could do this so long as nothing agitated him. But as soon as he had any unpleasantness with his wife, or a lack of success in his official work, or held bad cards at bridge, he was at once acutely sensible of his disease. He had formerly borne such mischances, hoping soon to adjust what was wrong, to master it and attain success, or make a grand slam. But now every mischance upset him and plunged him into despair. He would say to himself: "There now, just as I was beginning to get better and the medicine had begun to take effect, comes this accursed misfortune, or unpleasantness . . ." And he was furious with the mishap, or with the people who were causing the unpleasantness and killing him, for he felt that this fury was killing him but could not restrain it. One would have thought that it should have been clear to him that this exasperation with circumstances and people aggravated his illness, and that he ought therefore to ignore unpleasant occurrences. But he drew the very opposite conclusion: he said that he needed peace, and he watched for everything that might disturb it and became irritable at the slightest infringement of it. His condition was rendered worse by the fact that he read medical books and consulted doctors. The progress of his disease was so gradual that he could deceive himself when comparing one day with another—the difference was so slight. But when he consulted the doctors it seemed to him that he was getting worse, and even very rapidly. Yet despite this he was continually consulting them.

That month he went to see another celebrity, who told him almost the same as the first had done but put his questions rather differently, and the interview with this celebrity only increased Ivan Ilych's doubts and fears. A friend of a friend of his, a very good doctor, diagnosed his illness again quite differently from the others, and though he predicted recovery, his questions and suppositions bewildered Ivan Ilych still more and increased his doubts. A homoeopathist diagnosed the disease in yet another way, and prescribed medicine which Ivan Ilych took secretly for a week. But after a week, not feeling any improvement and having lost confidence both in the former doctor's treatment and in this one's, he became still more despondent. One day a lady acquaintance mentioned a cure effected by a wonder-working icon. Ivan Ilych caught himself listening attentively and beginning to believe that it had occurred. This incident alarmed him. "Has my mind really weakened to such an extent?" he asked himself. "Nonsense! It's all rubbish. I mustn't give way to nervous fears but having chosen a doctor must keep strictly to his treatment. That is what I will do. Now it's all settled. I won't think about it, but will follow the treatment seriously till summer, and then we shall see. From now there must be no more of this wavering!" This was easy to say but impossible to carry out. The pain in his side oppressed him and seemed to grow worse and more incessant, while the taste in his mouth grew stranger and stranger. It seemed to him that his breath had a disgusting smell, and he was conscious of a loss of appetite and strength. There was no deceiving himself: something terrible, new, and more important than anything before in his life, was taking place within him of which he alone was aware. Those about him did not understand or would not understand it, but thought everything in the world was going on as usual. That tormented Ivan Ilych more than anything. He saw that his household, especially his wife and daughter, who were in a perfect whirl of visiting, did not understand anything of it and were annoyed that he was so depressed and so exacting, as if he were to blame for it. Though they tried to disguise it he saw that he was an obstacle in their path, and that his wife had adopted a definite line in regard to his illness and kept to it regardless of anything he said or did. Her attitude was this: "You know," she would say to her friends, "Ivan Ilych can't do as other people do, and keep to the treatment prescribed for him. One day he'll take his drops and keep strictly to his diet and go to bed in good time, but the next day unless I watch him he'll suddenly forget his medicine, eat sturgeon—which is forbidden—and sit up playing cards till one o'clock in the morning."

"Oh, come, when was that?" Ivan Ilych would ask in vexation. "Only once at Peter Ivanovich's."

"And yesterday with Shebek."

"Well, even if I hadn't stayed up, this pain would have kept me awake."

"Be that as it may you'll never get well like that, but will always make us wretched."

Praskovya Fëdorovna's attitude to Ivan Ilych's illness, as she expressed it both to others and to him, was that it was his own fault and was another of the annoyances he caused her. Ivan Ilych felt that this opinion escaped her involuntarily—but that did not make it easier for him.

At the law courts too, Ivan Ilych noticed, or thought he noticed, a strange attitude towards himself. It sometimes seemed to him that people were watching him inquisitively as a man whose place might soon be vacant. Then again, his friends would suddenly begin to chaff him in a friendly way about his low spirits, as if the awful, horrible, and unheard-of thing that was going on within him, incessantly gnawing at him and irresistibly drawing him away, was a very agreeable subject for jests. Schwartz in particular irritated him by his jocularity, vivacity, and *savoir-faire,* which reminded him of what he himself had been ten years ago.

Friends came to make up a set and they sat down to cards. They dealt, bending the new cards to soften them, and he sorted the diamonds in his hand and found he had seven. His partner said "No trumps" and supported him with two diamonds. What more could be wished for? It ought to be jolly and lively. They would make a grand slam. But suddenly Ivan Ilych was conscious of that gnawing pain, that taste in his mouth, and it seemed ridiculous that in such circumstances he should be pleased to make a grand slam.

He looked at his partner, Mikhail Mikhailovich, who rapped the table with his strong hand and instead of snatching up the tricks pushed the cards courteously and indulgently towards Ivan Ilych that he might have the pleasure of gathering them up without the trouble of stretching out his hand for them. "Does he think I am too weak to stretch out my arm?" thought Ivan Ilych, and forgetting what he was doing he over-trumped his partner, missing the grand slam by three tricks. And what was most awful of all was that he saw how upset Mikhail Mikhailovich was about it but did not himself care. And it was dreadful to realize why he did not care.

They all saw that he was suffering, and said: "We can stop if you are tired. Take a rest." Lie down? No, he was not at all tired, and he finished the rubber. All were gloomy and silent. Ivan Ilych felt that he had diffused this gloom over them and could not dispel it. They had supper and went away, and Ivan Ilych was left alone with the consciousness that his life was poisoned and was poisoning the lives of others, and that this poison did not weaken but penetrated more and more deeply into his whole being.

With this consciousness, and with physical pain besides that terror, he must go to bed, often to lie awake the greater part of the night. Next morning he had to get up again, dress, go to the law courts, speak, and write; or if he did not go out, spend at home those twenty-four hours a day each of which was a torture. And he had to live thus all alone on the brink of an abyss, with no one who understood or pitied him.

5

So one month passed and then another. Just before the New Year his brother-in-law came to town and stayed at their house. Ivan Ilych was at the law courts and Praskovya Fëdorovna had gone shopping. When Ivan Ilych came home and entered his study he found his brother-in-law there—a healthy, florid man—unpacking his portmanteau himself. He raised his head on hearing Ivan Ilych's footsteps and looked up at him for a moment without a word. That stare told Ivan Ilych everything. His brother-in-law opened his mouth to utter an exclamation of surprise but checked himself, and that action confirmed it all.

"I have changed, eh?"

"Yes, there is a change."

And after that, try as he would to get his brother-in-law to return to the subject of his looks, the latter would say nothing about it. Praskovya Fëdorovna came home and her brother went out to her. Ivan Ilych locked the door and began to examine himself in the glass, first full face, then in profile. He took up a portrait of himself taken with his wife, and compared it with what he saw in the glass. The change in him was immense. Then he bared his arms to the elbow, looked at them, drew the sleeves down again, sat down on an ottoman, and grew blacker than night.

"No, no, this won't do!" he said to himself, and jumped up, went to the table, took up some law papers and began to read them, but could not continue. He unlocked the door and went into the reception-room. The door leading to the drawing-room was shut. He approached it on tiptoe and listened.

"No, you are exaggerating!" Praskovya Fëdorovna was saying.

"Exaggerating! Don't you see it? Why, he's a dead man! Look at his eyes—there's no light in them. But what is it that is wrong with him?"

"No one knows. Nikolaevich [that was another doctor] said something, but I don't know what. And Leshchetitsky [this was the celebrated specialist] said quite the contrary . . . "

Ivan Ilych walked away, went to his own room, lay down, and began musing: "The kidney, a floating kidney." He recalled all the doctors had told him of how it detached itself and swayed about. And by an effort of imagination he tried to catch that kidney and arrest it and support it. So little was needed for this, it seemed to him. "No, I'll go to see Peter Ivanovich again." [That was the friend whose friend was a doctor.] He rang, ordered the carriage, and got ready to go.

"Where are you going, Jean?" asked his wife, with a specially sad and exceptionally kind look.

This exceptionally kind look irritated him. He looked morosely at her.

"I must go to see Peter Ivanovich."

He went to see Peter Ivanovich, and together they went to see his friend, the doctor. He was in, and Ivan Ilych had a long talk with him.

Reviewing the anatomical and physiological details of what in the doctor's opinion was going on inside him, he understood it all.

There was something, a small thing, in the vermiform appendix. It might all come right. Only stimulate the energy of one organ and check the activity of another, then absorption would take place and everything would come right. He got home rather late for dinner, ate his dinner, conversed cheerfully, but could not for a long time bring himself to go back to work in his room. At last, however, he went to his study and did what was necessary, but the consciousness that he had put something aside—an important, intimate matter which he would revert to when his work was done—never left him. When he had finished his work he remembered that this intimate matter was the thought of his vermiform appendix. But he did not give himself up to it, and went to the drawing-room for tea. There were callers there, including the examining magistrate who was a desirable match for his daughter, and they were conversing, playing the piano, and singing. Ivan Ilych, as Praskoyva Fëdorovna remarked, spent that evening more cheerfully than usual, but he never for a moment forgot that he had postponed the important matter of the appendix. At eleven o'clock he said good-night and went to his bedroom. Since his illness he had slept alone in a small room next to his study. He undressed and took up a novel by Zola, but instead of reading it fell into thought, and in his imagination that desired improvement in the vermiform appendix occurred. There was the absorption and evacuation and the re-establishment of normal activity. "Yes, that's it!" he said to himself. "One need only assist nature, that's all." He remembered his medicine, rose, took it, and lay down on his back watching for the beneficent action of the medicine and for it to lessen the pain. "I need only take it regularly and avoid all injurious influences. I am already feeling better, much better." He began touching his side: it was not painful to the touch. "There, I really don't feel it. It's much better already." He put out the light and turned on his side . . . "The appendix is getting better, absorption is occurring." Suddenly he felt the old, familiar, dull, gnawing pain, stubborn and serious. There was the same familiar loathsome taste in his mouth. His heart sank and he felt dazed. "My God! My God!" he muttered. "Again, again! and it will never cease." And suddenly the matter presented itself in a quite different aspect. "Vermiform appendix! Kidney!" he said to himself. "It's not a question of appendix or kidney, but of life and . . . death. Yes, life was there and now it is going, going and I cannot stop it. Yes. Why deceive myself? Isn't it obvious to everyone but me that I'm dying, and that it's only a question of weeks, days . . . it may happen this moment. There was light and now there is darkness. I was here and now I'm going there! Where?" A chill came over him, his breathing ceased, and he felt only the throbbing of his heart.

"When I am not, what will there be? There will be nothing. Then where shall I be when I am no more? Can this be dying? No, I don't want to!" He jumped up and tried to light the candle, felt for it with trembling hands, dropped candle and candlestick on the floor, and fell back on his pillow.

"What's the use? It makes no difference," he said to himself, staring with wide-open eyes into the darkness. "Death. Yes, death. And none of them know or wish to know it, and they have no pity for me. Now they are playing." (He heard through the door the distant sound of a song and its accompaniment.) "It's all the same to them, but they will die too! Fools! I first, and they later, but it will be the same for them. And now they are merry . . . the beasts!"

Anger choked him and he was agonizingly, unbearably, miserable. "It is impossible that all men have been doomed to suffer this awful horror!" He raised himself.

"Something must be wrong. I must calm myself—must think it all over from the beginning." And he again began thinking. "Yes, the beginning of my illness: I knocked my side, but I was quite well that day and the next. It hurt a little, then rather more. I saw the doctor, then followed despondency and anguish, more doctors, and I drew nearer to the abyss. My strength grew less and I kept coming nearer and nearer, and now I have wasted away and there is no light in my eyes. I think of the appendix—but this is death! I think of mending the appendix, and all the while here is death! Can it really be death?" Again terror seized him and he gasped for breath. He leant down and began feeling for the matches, pressing with his elbow on the stand beside the bed. It was in the way and hurt him, he grew furious with it, pressed on it still harder, and upset it. Breathless and in despair he fell on his back, expecting death to come immediately.

Meanwhile the visitors were leaving. Praskovya Fëdorovna was seeing them off. She heard something fall and came in.

"What has happened?"

"Nothing. I knocked it over accidentally."

She went out and returned with a candle. He lay there panting heavily, like a man who has run a thousand yards, and stared upwards at her with a fixed look.

"What is it, Jean?"

"No . . . o . . . thing. I upset it." ("Why speak of it? She won't understand," he thought.)

And in truth she did not understand. She picked up the stand, lit his candle, and hurried away to see another visitor off. When she came back he still lay on his back, looking upwards.

"What is it? Do you feel worse?"

"Yes."

She shook her head and sat down.

"Do you know, Jean, I think we must ask Leshchetitsky to come and see you here."

This meant calling in the famous specialist, regardless of expense. He smiled malignantly and said "No." She remained a little longer and then went up to him and kissed his forehead.

While she was kissing him he hated her from the bottom of his soul and with difficulty refrained from pushing her away.

"Good-night. Please God you'll sleep."

"Yes."

6

Ivan Ilych saw that he was dying, and he was in continual despair.

In the depth of his heart he knew he was dying, but not only was he not accustomed to the thought, he simply did not and could not grasp it.

The syllogism he had learnt from Kiezewetter's Logic: "Caius is a man, men are mortal, therefore Caius is mortal," had always seemed to him correct as applied to Caius, but certainly not as applied to himself. That Caius—man in the abstract—was mortal, was perfectly correct, but he was no Caius, not an abstract man, but a creature quite, quite separate from all others. He had been little Vanya, with a mamma and a papa, with Mitya and Volodya, with the toys, a coachman and a nurse, afterwards with Katenka and with all the joys, griefs, and delights of childhood, boyhood, and youth. What did Caius know of the smell of that striped leather ball Vanya had been so fond of? Had Caius kissed his mother's hand like that, and did the silk of her dress rustle so for Caius? Had he rioted like that at school when the pastry was bad? Had Caius been in love like that? Could Caius preside at a session as he did? "Caius really was mortal, and it was right for him to die; but for me, little Vanya, Ivan Ilych, with all my thoughts and emotions, it's altogether a different matter. It cannot be that I ought to die. That would be too terrible."

Such was his feeling.

"If I had to die like Caius, I should have known it was so. An inner voice would have told me so, but there was nothing of the sort in me and I and all my friends felt that our case was quite different from that of Caius. And now here it is!" he said to himself. "It can't be. It's impossible! But here it is. How is this? How is one to understand it?"

He could not understand it, and tried to drive this false, incorrect, morbid thought away and to replace it by other proper and healthy thoughts. But that thought, and not the thought only but the reality itself, seemed to come and confront him.

And to replace that thought he called up a succession of others, hoping to find in them some support. He tried to get back into the former current of thoughts that had once screened the thought of death for him. But strange to say, all that had formerly shut off, hidden, and destroyed his consciousness of death no longer had that effect. Ivan Ilych now spent most of his time in attempting to re-establish that old current. He would say to himself: "I will take up my duties again—after all I used to live by them." And banishing all doubts he would go to the law courts, enter into conversation with his colleagues, and sit carelessly as was his wont, scanning the crowd with a thoughtful look and leaning both his emaciated arms on the arms of his oak chair; bending over as usual to a colleague and drawing his papers nearer he would interchange whispers with him, and then suddenly raising his eyes and sitting erect would pronounce certain words and open the proceedings. But suddenly in the midst of those proceedings the pain in his side, regardless of the stage the proceedings had reached, would begin its own gnawing work. Ivan Ilych would turn his attention to it and try to drive the thoughts of it away, but without success. *It* would come and stand before him and look at him, and he would be petrified and the light would die out of his eyes, and he would again begin asking himself whether *It* alone was true. And his colleagues and subordinates would see with surprise and distress that he, the brilliant and subtle judge, was becoming confused and making mistakes. He would shake himself, try to pull himself together, manage somehow to bring the sitting to a close, and return home with the sorrowful consciousness that his judicial labours could not as formerly hide from him what he wanted them to hide, and could not deliver him from *It.* And what was worst of all was that *It* drew his attention to itself not in order to take some action but only that he should look at *It,* look it straight in the face: look at it without doing anything, suffer inexpressibly.

And to save himself from this condition Ivan Ilych looked for consolations—new screens—and new screens were found and for a while seemed to save him, but then they immediately fell to pieces or rather became transparent, as if *It* penetrated them and nothing could veil *It.*

In these latter days he would go into the drawing-room he had arranged—that drawing-room where he had fallen and for the sake of which (how bitterly ridiculous it seemed) he had sacrificed his life—for he knew that this illness originated with that knock. He would enter and see that something had scratched the polished table. He would look for the cause of this and find that it was the bronze ornamentation of an album, that had got bent. He would take up the expensive album which he had lovingly arranged, and feel vexed with his daughter and her friends for their untidiness—for the album was torn here and there and some of the photographs turned upside down. He would put it carefully in order and bend the ornamentation back into position. Then it would occur to him to place all those things in another corner of the room, near the plants. He would call the footman, but his daughter or wife would come to help him. They would not agree, and his wife would contradict him, and he would dispute and grow angry. But that was all right, for then he did not think about *It. It* was invisible.

But then, when he was moving something himself, his wife would say: "Let the servants do it. You will hurt yourself again." And suddenly *It* would flash through the screen and he would see it. It was just a flash, and he hoped it would disappear, but he would involuntarily pay attention to his side. "It sits there as before, gnawing just the same!" And he could no longer forget *It,* but could distinctly see it looking at him from behind the flowers. "What is it all for?"

"It really is so! I lost my life over the curtain as I might have done when storming a fort. Is that possible? How terrible and how stupid. It can't be true! It can't, but it is."

He would go to his study, lie down, and again be alone with *It:* face to face with *It.* And nothing could be done with *It* except to look at it and shudder.

7

How it happened it is impossible to say because it came about step by step, unnoticed, but in the third month of Ivan Ilych's illness, his wife, his daughter, his son, his acquaintances, the doctors, the servants, and above all he himself, were aware that the whole interest he had for other people was whether he would soon vacate his place, and at last release the living from the discomfort caused by his presence and be himself released from his sufferings.

He slept less and less. He was given opium and hypodermic injections of morphine, but this did not relieve him. The dull depression he experienced in a somnolent condition at first gave him a little relief, but only as something new, afterwards it became as distressing as the pain itself or even more so.

Special foods were prepared for him by the doctors' orders, but all those foods became increasingly distasteful and disgusting to him.

For his excretions also special arrangements had to be made, and this was a torment to him every time—a torment from the uncleanliness, the unseemliness, and the smell, and from knowing that another person had to take part in it.

But just through this most unpleasant matter, Ivan Ilych obtained comfort. Gerasim, the butler's young assistant, always came in to carry the things out. Gerasim was a clean, fresh peasant lad, grown stout on town food and always cheerful and bright. At first the sight of him, in his clean Russian peasant costume, engaged in that disgusting task embarrassed Ivan Ilych.

Once when he got up from the commode too weak to draw up his trousers, he dropped into a soft armchair and looked with horror at his bare, enfeebled thighs with the muscles so sharply marked on them.

Gerasim with a firm light tread, his heavy boots emitting a pleasant smell of tar and fresh winter air, came in wearing a clean Hessian apron, the sleeves of his print shirt tucked up over his strong bare young arms; and refraining from looking at his sick master out of consideration for his feelings, and restraining the joy of life that beamed from his face, he went up to the commode.

"Gerasim!" said Ivan Ilych in a weak voice.

Gerasim started, evidently afraid he might have committed some blunder, and with a rapid movement turned his fresh, kind, simple young face which just showed the first downy signs of a beard.

"Yes, sir?"

"That must be very unpleasant for you. You must forgive me. I am helpless."

"Oh, why, sir," and Gerasim's eyes beamed and he showed his glistening white teeth, "what's a little trouble? It's a case of illness with you, sir."

And his deft strong hands did their accustomed task, and he went out of the room stepping lightly. Five minutes later he as lightly returned.

Ivan Ilych was still sitting in the same position in the armchair.

"Gerasim," he said when the latter had replaced the freshly-washed utensil. "Please come here and help me." Gerasim went up to him. "Lift me up. It is hard for me to get up, and I have sent Dmitri away."

Gerasim went up to him, grasped his master with his strong arms deftly but gently, in the same way that he stepped—lifted him, supported him with one hand, and with the other drew up his trousers and would have set him down again, but Ivan Ilych asked to be led to the sofa. Gerasim, without an effort and without apparent pressure, led him, almost lifting him, to the sofa and placed him on it.

"Thank you. How easily and well you do it all!"

Gerasim smiled again and turned to leave the room. But Ivan Ilych felt his presence such a comfort that he did not want to let him go.

"One thing more, please move up that chair. No, the other one—under my feet. It is easier for me when my feet are raised."

Gerasim brought the chair, set it down gently in place, and raised Ivan Ilych's legs on to it. It seemed to Ivan Ilych that he felt better while Gerasim was holding up his legs.

"It's better when my legs are higher," he said. "Place that cushion under them."

Gerasim did so. He again lifted the legs and placed them, and again Ivan Ilych felt better while Gerasim held his legs. When he set them down Ivan Ilych fancied he felt worse.

"Gerasim," he said. "Are you busy now?"

"Not at all, sir," said Gerasim, who had learnt from the townfolk how to speak gentlefolk.

"What have you still to do?"

"What have I to do? I've done everything except chopping the logs for tomorrow."

"Then hold my legs up a bit higher, can you?"

"Of course I can. Why not?" And Gerasim raised his master's legs higher and Ivan Ilych thought that in that position he did not feel any pain at all.

"And how about the logs?"

"Don't trouble about that, sir. There's plenty of time."

Ivan Ilych told Gerasim to sit down and hold his legs, and began to talk to him. And strange to say it seemed to him that he felt better while Gerasim held his legs up.

After that Ivan Ilych would sometimes call Gerasim and get him to hold his legs on his shoulders, and he liked talking to him. Gerasim did it all easily, willingly, simply, and with a good nature that touched Ivan Ilych. Health, strength, and vitality in other people were offensive to him, but Gerasim's strength and vitality did not mortify but soothed him.

What tormented Ivan Ilych most was the deception, the lie, which for some reason they all accepted, that he was not dying but was simply ill, and that he only need keep quiet and undergo a treatment and then something very good would result. He however knew that do what they would nothing would come of it, only still more agonizing suffering and death. This deception tortured him—their not wishing to admit what they all knew and what he knew, but wanting to lie to him concerning his terrible condition, and wishing and forcing him to participate in that lie. Those lies—lies enacted over him on the eve of his death and destined to degrade this awful, solemn act to the level of their visitings, their curtains, their sturgeon for dinner—were a terrible agony for Ivan Ilych. And strangely enough, many times when they were going through their antics over him he had been within a hairbreadth of calling out to them: "Stop lying! You know and I know that I am dying. Then at least stop lying about it!" But he had never had the spirit to do it. The awful, terrible act of his dying was, he could see, reduced by those about him to the level of a casual, unpleasant, and almost indecorous incident (as if someone entered a drawing-room diffusing an unpleasant odour) and this was done by that very decorum which he had served all his life long. He saw that no one felt for him, because no one even wished to grasp his position. Only Gerasim recognized it and pitied him. And so Ivan Ilych felt at ease only with him. He felt comforted when Gerasim supported his legs (sometimes all night long) and refused to go to bed, saying: "Don't you worry, Ivan Ilych. I'll get sleep enough later on," or when he suddenly became familiar and exclaimed: "If you weren't sick it would be another matter, but as it is, why should I grudge a little trouble?" Gerasim alone did not lie; everything showed that he alone understood the facts of the case and did not consider it necessary to disguise them, but simply felt sorry for his emaciated and enfeebled master. Once when Ivan Ilych was sending him away he even said straight out: "We shall all of us die, so why should I grudge a little trouble?"—expressing the fact that he did not think his work burdensome, because he was doing it for a dying man and hoped someone would do the same for him when his time came.

Apart from this lying, or because of it, what most tormented Ivan Ilych was that no one pitied him as he wished to be pitied. At certain moments after prolonged suffering he wished most of all (though he would have been ashamed to confess it) for someone to pity him as a sick child is pitied. He longed to be petted and comforted. He knew he was an important functionary, that he had a beard turning grey, and that therefore what he longed for was impossible, but still he longed for it. And in Gerasim's attitude towards him there was something akin to what he wished for, and so that attitude comforted him. Ivan Ilych wanted to weep, wanted to be petted and cried over, and then his colleague Shebek would come, and instead of weeping and being petted, Ivan Ilych would assume a serious, severe, and profound air, and by force of habit would express his opinion on a decision of the Court of Cassation and would stubbornly insist on that view. This falsity around him and within him did more than anything else to poison his last days.

8

It was morning. He knew it was morning because Gerasim had gone, and Peter the footman had come and put out the candles, drawn back one of the curtains, and begun quietly to tidy up. Whether it was morning or evening, Friday or Sunday, made no difference, it was all just the same: the gnawing, unmitigated, agonizing pain, never ceasing for an instant, the consciousness of life inexorably waning but not yet extinguished, the approach of that ever dreaded and hateful Death which was the only reality, and always the same falsity. What were days, weeks, hours, in such a case?

"Will you have some tea, sir?"

"He wants things to be regular, and wishes the gentlefolk to drink tea in the morning," thought Ivan Ilych, and only said "No."

"Wouldn't you like to move onto the sofa, sir?"

"He wants to tidy up the room, and I'm in the way. I am uncleanliness and disorder," he thought, and said only:

"No, leave me alone."

The man went on bustling about. Ivan Ilych stretched out his hand. Peter came up, ready to help.

"What is it, sir?"

"My watch."

Peter took the watch which was close at hand and gave it to his master.

"Half-past eight. Are they up?"

"No, sir, except Vladimir Ivanich" (the son) "who has gone to school. Praskovya Fëdorovna ordered me to wake her if you asked for her. Shall I do so?"

"No, there's no need to." "Perhaps I'd better have some tea," he thought, and added aloud: "Yes, bring me some tea."

Peter went to the door, but Ivan Ilych dreaded being left alone. "How can I keep him here? Oh yes, my medicine." "Peter, give me my medicine." "Why not? Perhaps it may do me some good." He took a spoonful and swallowed it. "No, it won't help. It's all tomfoolery, all deception," he decided as soon as he became aware of the familiar, sickly, hopeless taste. "No, I can't believe in it any longer. But the pain, why this pain? If it would only cease just for a moment!" And he moaned. Peter turned towards him. "It's all right. Go and fetch me some tea."

Peter went out. Left alone Ivan Ilych groaned not so much with pain, terrible though that was, as from mental anguish. Always and for ever the same, always these endless days and nights. If only it would come quicker! If only *what* would come quicker? Death, darkness? . . . No, no! Anything rather than death!

When Peter returned with the tea on a tray, Ivan Ilych stared at him for a time in perplexity, not realizing who and what he was. Peter was disconcerted by that look and his embarrassment brought Ivan Ilych to himself.

"Oh, tea! All right, put it down. Only help me to wash and put on a clean shirt."

And Ivan Ilych began to wash. With pauses for rest, he washed his hands and then his face, cleaned his teeth, brushed his hair, and looked in the glass. He was terrified by what he saw, especially by the limp way in which his hair clung to his pallid forehead.

While his shirt was being changed he knew that he would be still more frightened at the sight of his body, so he avoided looking at it. Finally he was ready. He drew on a dressing-gown, wrapped himself in a plaid, and sat down in the armchair to take his tea. For a moment he felt refreshed, but as soon as he began to drink the tea he was again aware of the same taste, and the pain also returned. He finished it with an effort, and then lay down stretching out his legs, and dismissed Peter.

Always the same. Now a spark of hope flashes up, then a sea of despair rages, and always pain; always pain, always despair, and always the same. When alone he had a dreadful and distressing desire to call someone, but he knew beforehand that with others present it would be still worse. "Another dose of morphine—to lose consciousness. I will tell him, the doctor, that he must think of something else. It's impossible, impossible, to go on like this."

An hour and another pass like that. But now there is a ring at the door bell. Perhaps it's the doctor? It is. He comes in fresh, hearty, plump, and cheerful, with that look on his face that seems to say: "There now, you're in a panic about something, but we'll arrange it all for you directly!" The doctor knows this expression is out of place here, but he has put it on once for all and can't take it off—like a man who has put on a frock-coat in the morning to pay a round of calls.

The doctor rubs his hands vigorously and reassuringly.

"Brr! How cold it is! There's such a sharp frost; just let me warm myself!" he says, as if it were only a matter of waiting till he was warm, and then he would put everything right.

"Well now, how are you?"

Ivan Ilych feels that the doctor would like to say: "Well, how are your affairs?" but that even he feels that this would not do, and says instead: "What sort of a night have you had?"

Ivan Ilych looks at him as much as to say: "Are you really never ashamed of lying?" But the doctor does not wish to understand this question, and Ivan Ilych says: "Just as terrible as ever. The pain never leaves me and never subsides. If only something . . ."

"Yes, you sick people are always like that . . . There, now I think I am warm enough. Even Praskovya Fëdorovna, who is so particular, could find no fault with my temperature. Well, now I can say good-morning," and the doctor presses his patient's hand.

Then, dropping his former playfulness, he begins with a most serious face to examine the patient, feeling his pulse and taking his temperature, and then begins the sounding and auscultation.

Ivan Ilych knows quite well and definitely that all this is nonsense and pure deception, but when the doctor, getting down on his knee, leans over him, putting the ear first higher then lower, and performs various gymnastic movements over him with a significant expression on his face, Ivan Ilych submits to it all as he used to submit to the speeches of the lawyers, though he knew very well they were all lying and why they were lying.

The doctor, kneeling on the sofa, is still sounding him when Praskovya Fëdorovna's silk dress rustles at the door and she is heard scolding Peter for not having let her know of the doctor's arrival.

She comes in, kisses her husband, and at once proceeds to prove that she has been up a long time already, and only owing to a misunderstanding failed to be there when the doctor arrived.

Ivan Ilych looks at her, scans her all over, sets against her the whiteness and plumpness and cleanness of her hands and neck, the gloss of her hair, and the sparkle of her vivacious eyes. He hates her with his whole soul. And the thrill of hatred he feels for her makes him suffer from her touch.

Her attitude towards him and his disease is still the same. Just as the doctor had adopted a certain relation to his patient which he could not abandon, so had she formed one towards him—that he was not doing something he ought to do and was himself to blame, and that she reproached him lovingly for this—and she could not now change that attitude.

"You see he doesn't listen to me and doesn't take his medicine at the proper time. And above all he lies in a position that is no doubt bad for him—with his legs up."

She described how he made Gerasim hold his legs up.

The doctor smiled with a contemptuous affability that said: "What's to be done? These sick people do have foolish fancies of that kind, but we must forgive them."

When the examination was over the doctor looked at his watch, and then Praskovya Fëdorovna announced to Ivan Ilych that it was of course as he pleased, but she had sent today for a celebrated specialist who would examine him and have a consultation with Michael Danilovich (their regular doctor).

"Please don't raise any objections. I am doing this for my own sake," she said ironically, letting it be felt that she was doing this all for his sake and only said this to leave him no right to refuse. He remained silent, knitting his brows. He felt that he was so surrounded and involved in a mesh of falsity that it was hard to unravel anything.

Everything she did for him was entirely for her own sake, and she told him she was doing for herself what she actually was doing for herself, as if that was so incredible that he must understand the opposite.

At half-past eleven the celebrated specialist arrived. Again the sounding began and the significant conversations in his presence and in another room about the kidneys and the appendix, and the questions and answers, with such an air of importance that again, instead of the real question of life and death which now alone confronted him, the question arose of the kidney and appendix which were not behaving as they ought to and would now be attacked by Michael Danilovich and the specialist and forced to mend their ways.

The celebrated specialist took leave of him with a serious though not hopeless look, and in reply to the timid question Ivan Ilych, with eyes glistening with fear and hope, put to him as to whether there was a chance of recovery, said that he could not vouch for it but there was a possibility. The look of hope with which Ivan Ilych watched the doctor out was so pathetic that Praskovya Fëdorovna, seeing it, even wept as she left the room to hand the doctor his fee.

The gleam of hope kindled by the doctor's encouragement did not last long. The same room, the same pictures, curtains, wall-paper, medicine bottles, were all there, and the same aching suffering body, and Ivan Ilych began to moan. They gave him a subcutaneous injection and he sank into oblivion.

It was twilight when he came to. They brought him his dinner and he swallowed some beef tea with difficulty, and then everything was the same again and night was coming on.

After dinner, at seven o'clock, Praskovya Fëdorovna came into the room in evening dress, her full bosom pushed up by her corset, and with traces of powder on her face. She had reminded him in the morning that they were going to the theatre. Sarah Bernhardt was visiting the town and they had a box, which he had insisted on their taking. Now he had forgotten about it and her toilet offended him, but he concealed his vexation when he remembered that he had himself insisted on their securing a box and going because it would be an instructive and aesthetic pleasure for the children.

Praskovya Fëdorovna came in, self-satisfied but yet with a rather guilty air. She sat down and asked how he was, but, as he saw, only for the sake of asking and not in order to learn about it, knowing that there was nothing to learn—and then went on to what she really wanted to say: that she would not on any account have gone but that the box had been taken and Helen and their daughter were going, as well as Petrishchev (the examining magistrate, their daughter's fiancé) and that it was out of the question to let them go alone; but that she would have much preferred to sit with him for a while; and he must be sure to follow the doctor's orders while she was away.

"Oh, and Fëdor Petrovich" (the fiancé) "would like to come in. May he? And Lisa?"

"All right."

Their daughter came in in full evening dress, her fresh young flesh exposed (making a show of that very flesh which in his own case caused so much suffering), strong, healthy, evidently in love, and impatient with illness, suffering, and death, because they interfered with her happiness.

Fëdor Petrovich came in too, in evening dress, his hair curled *à la Capoul,* a tight stiff collar round his long sinewy neck, an enormous white shirt-front and narrow black trousers tightly stretched over his strong thighs. He had one white glove tightly drawn on, and was holding his opera hat in his hand.

Following him the schoolboy crept in unnoticed, in a new uniform, poor little fellow, and wearing gloves. Terribly dark shadows showed under his eyes, the meaning of which Ivan Ilych knew well.

His son had always seemed pathetic to him, and now it was dreadful to see the boy's frightened look of pity. It seemed to Ivan Ilych that Vasya was the only one besides Gerasim who understood and pitied him.

They all sat down and again asked how he was. A silence followed. Lisa asked her mother about the opera-glasses, and there was an altercation between mother and daughter as to who had taken them and where they had been put. This occasioned some unpleasantness.

Fëdor Petrovich inquired of Ivan Ilych whether he had ever seen Sarah Bernhardt. Ivan Ilych did not at first catch the question, but then replied: "No, have you seen her before?"

"Yes, in *Adrienne Lecouvreur.*"

Praskovya Fëdorovna mentioned some rôles in which Sarah Bernhardt was particularly good. Her daughter disagreed. Conversation sprang up as to the elegance and realism of her acting—the sort of conversation that is always repeated and is always the same.

In the midst of the conversation Fëdor Petrovich glanced at Ivan Ilych and became silent. Ivan Ilych was staring with glittering eyes straight before him, evidently indignant with them. This had to be rectified, but it was impossible to do so. The silence had to be broken, but for a time no one dared to break it and they all became afraid that the conventional deception would suddenly become obvious and the truth become plain to all. Lisa was the first to pluck up courage and break the silence, but by trying to hide what everybody was feeling, she betrayed it.

"Well, if we are going it's time to start," she said, looked at her watch, a present from her father, and with a faint and significant smile at Fëdor Petrovich relating to something known only to them. She got up with a rustle of her dress.

They all rose, said good-night, and went away.

When they had gone it seemed to Ivan Ilych that he felt better; the falsity had gone with them. But the pain remained—that same pain and that same fear that made everything monotonously alike, nothing harder and nothing easier. Everything was worse.

Again minute followed minute and hour followed hour. Everything remained the same and there was no cessation. And the inevitable end of it all became more and more terrible.

"Yes, send Gerasim here," he replied to a question Peter asked.

9

His wife returned late at night. She came in on tiptoe, but he heard her, opened his eyes, and made haste to close them again. She wished to send Gerasim away and to sit with him herself, but he opened his eyes and said: "No, go away."

"Are you in great pain?"

"Always the same."

"Take some opium."

He agreed and took some. She went away.

Till about three in the morning he was in a state of stupefied misery. It seemed to him that he and his pain were being thrust into a narrow, deep black sack, but though they were pushed further and further in they could not be pushed to the bottom. And this, terrible enough in itself, was accompanied by suffering. He struggled but yet coooperated. And suddenly he broke through, fell, and regained consciousness. Gerasim was sitting at the foot of the bed dozing quietly, while he himself lay with his emaciated stockinged legs resting on Gerasim's shoulders; the same shaded candle was there and the same unceasing pain.

"Go away, Gerasim," he whispered.

"It's all right, sir. I'll stay a while."

"No. Go away."

He removed his legs from Gerasim's shoulders, turned sideways onto his arm, and felt sorry for himself. He only waited till Gerasim had gone into the next room and then restrained himself no longer but wept like a child. He wept on account of his helplessness, his terrible loneliness, the cruelty of man, the cruelty of God, and the absence of God.

"Why hast Thou done all this? Why hast Thou brought me here? Why, why dost Thou torment me so terribly?"

He did not expect an answer and yet wept because there was no answer and could be none. The pain grew more acute, but he did not stir and did not call. He said to himself: "Go on! Strike me! But what is it for? What have I done to Thee? What is it for?"

Then he grew quiet and not only ceased weeping but even held his breath and became all attention. It was as though he were listening not to an audible voice but to the voice of his soul, to the current of thoughts arising within him.

"What is it you want?" was the first clear conception of expression in words that he heard.

"What do you want? What do you want?" he repeated to himself.

"What do I want? To live and not to suffer," he answered.

And again he listened with such concentrated attention that even his pain did not distract him.

"To live? How?" asked his inner voice.

"Why, to live as I used to—well and pleasantly."

"As you lived before, well and pleasantly?" the voice repeated.

And in imagination he began to recall the best moments of his pleasant life. But strange to say none of those best moments of his pleasant life now seemed at all what they had then seemed—none of them except the first recollections of childhood. There, in childhood, there had been something really pleasant with which it would be possible to live if it could return. But the child who had experienced that happiness existed no longer, it was like a reminiscence of somebody else.

As soon as the period began which had produced the present Ivan Ilych, all that had then seemed joys now melted before his sight and turned into something trivial and often nasty.

And the further he departed from childhood and the nearer he came to the present the more worthless and doubtful were the joys. This began with the School of Law. A little that was really good was still found there—there was light-heartedness, friendship, and hope. But in the upper classes there had already been fewer of such good moments. Then during the first years of his official career, when he was in the service of the Governor, some pleasant moments again occurred: they were the memories of love for a woman. Then all became confused and there was still less of what was good; later on again there was still less that was good, and the further he went the less there was. His marriage, a mere accident, then the disenchantment that followed it, his wife's bad breath and the sensuality and hypocrisy: then that deadly official life and those preoccupations about money, a year of it, and two, and ten, and twenty, and always the same thing. And the longer it lasted the more deadly it became. "It is as if I had been going downhill while I imagined I was going up. And that is really what it was. I was going up in public opinion, but to the same extent life was ebbing away from me. And now it is all done and there is only death."

"Then what does it mean? Why? It can't be that life is so senseless and horrible. But if it really has been so horrible and senseless, why must I die and die in agony? There is something wrong!"

"Maybe I did not live as I ought to have done," it suddenly occurred to him. "But how could that be, when I did everything properly?" he replied, and immediately dismissed from his mind this, the sole solution of all the riddles of life and death, as something quite impossible.

"Then what do you want now? To live? Live how? Live as you lived in the law courts when the usher proclaimed 'The judge is coming!' The judge is coming, the judge!" he repeated to himself. "Here he is, the judge. But I am not guilty!" he exclaimed angrily. "What is it for?" And he ceased crying, but turning his face to the wall continued to ponder on the same question: Why, and for what purpose, is there all this horror? But however much he pondered he found no answer. And whenever the thought occurred to him, as it often did, that it all resulted from his not having lived as he ought to have done, he at once recalled the correctness of his whole life and dismissed so strange an idea.

10

Another fortnight passed. Ivan Ilych now no longer left his sofa. He would not lie in bed but lay on the sofa, facing the wall nearly all the time. He suffered ever the same unceasing agonies and in his loneliness pondered always on the same insoluble question: "What is this? Can it be that it is Death?" And the inner voice answered: "Yes, it is Death."

"Why these sufferings?" And the voice answered, "For no reason—they just are so." Beyond and besides this there was nothing.

From the very beginning of his illness, ever since he had first been to see the doctor, Ivan Ilych's life had been divided between two contrary and alternating moods: now it was despair and the expectation of this uncomprehended and terrible death, and now hope and an intently interested observation of the functioning of his organs. Now before his eyes there was only a kidney or an intestine that temporarily evaded its duty, and now only that incomprehensible and dreadful death from which it was impossible to escape.

These two states of mind had alternated from the very beginning of his illness, but the further it progressed the more doubtful and fantastic became the conception of the kidney, and the more real the sense of impending death.

He had but to call to mind what he had been three months before and what he was now, to call to mind with what regularity he had been going downhill, for every possibility of hope to be shattered.

Latterly during that loneliness in which he found himself as he lay facing the back of the sofa, a loneliness in the midst of a populous town and surrounded by numerous acquaintances and relations but that yet could not have been more complete anywhere—either at the bottom of the sea or under the earth—during that terrible loneliness Ivan Ilych had lived only in memories of the past. Pictures of his past rose before him one after another. They always began with what was nearest in time and then went back to what was the most remote—to his childhood—and rested there. If he thought of the stewed prunes that had been offered him that day, his mind went back to the raw shrivelled French plums of his childhood, their peculiar flavour and the flow of saliva when he sucked their stones, and along with the memory of that taste came a whole series of memories of those days: his nurse, his brother, and their toys. "No, I mustn't think of that . . . It is too painful," Ivan Ilych said to himself, and brought himself back to the present—to the button on the back of the sofa and the creases in its morocco. "Morocco is expensive, but it does not wear well: there had been a quarrel about it. It was a different kind of quarrel and a different kind of morocco that time when we tore father's portfolio and were punished, and Mamma brought us some tarts . . ." And again his thoughts dwelt on his childhood, and again it was painful and he tried to banish them and fix his mind on something else.

Then again together with that chain of memories another series passed through his mind—of how his illness had progressed and grown worse. There also the further back he looked the more life there had been. There had been more of what was good in life and more of life itself. The two merged together. "Just as the pain went on getting worse and worse, so my life grew worse and worse," he thought. "There is one bright spot there at the back, at the beginning of life, and afterwards all becomes blacker and blacker and proceeds more and more rapidly—in inverse ratio to the square of the distance from death," thought Ivan Ilych. And the example of a stone falling downwards with increasing velocity entered his mind. Life, a series of increasing sufferings, flies further and further towards its end—the most terrible suffering. "I am flying . . ." He shuddered, shifted himself, and tried to resist, but was already aware that resistance was impossible, and again with eyes weary of gazing but unable to cease seeing what was before them, he stared at the back of the sofa and waited—awaiting that dreadful fall and shock and destruction.

"Resistance is impossible!" he said to himself. "If I could only understand what it is all for! But that too is impossible. An explanation would be possible if it could be said that I have not lived as I ought to. But it is impossible to say that," and he remembered all the legality, correctitude, and propriety of his life. "That at any rate can certainly not be admitted," he thought, and his lips smiled ironically as if someone could see that smile and be taken in by it. "There is no explanation! Agony, death . . . What for?"

11

Another two weeks went by in this way and during that fortnight an event occurred that Ivan Ilych and his wife had desired. Petrishchev formally proposed. It happened in the evening. The next day Praskovya Fëdorovna came into her husband's room considering how best to inform him of it, but that very night there had been a fresh change for the worse in his condition. She found him lying on the sofa but in a different position. He lay on his back, groaning and staring fixedly in front of him.

She began to remind him of his medicines, but he turned his eyes towards her with such a look that she did not finish what she was saying; so great an animosity, to her in particular, did that look express.

"For Christ's sake let me die in peace!" he said.

She would have gone away, but just then their daughter came in and went up to say good morning. He looked at her as he had done at his wife, and in reply to her inquiry about his health said dryly that he would soon free them all of himself. They were both silent and after sitting with him for a while went away.

"Is it our fault?" Lisa said to her mother. "It's as if we were to blame! I am sorry for papa, but why should we be tortured?"

The doctor came at his usual time. Ivan Ilych answered "Yes" and "No," never taking his angry eyes from him, and at last said: "You know you can do nothing for me, so leave me alone."

"We can ease your sufferings."

"You can't even do that. Let me be."

The doctor went into the drawing-room and told Praskovya Fëdorovna that the case was very serious and that the only resource left was opium to allay her husband's sufferings, which must be terrible.

It was true, as the doctor said, that Ivan Ilych's physical sufferings were terrible, but worse than the physical sufferings were his mental sufferings, which were his chief torture.

His mental sufferings were due to the fact that that night, as he looked at Gerasim's sleepy, good-natured face with its prominent cheek-bones, the question suddenly occurred to him: "What if my whole life has really been wrong?"

It occurred to him that what had appeared perfectly impossible before, namely that he had not spent his life as he should have done, might after all be true. It occurred to him that his scarcely perceptible attempts to struggle against what was considered good by the most highly placed people, those scarcely noticeable impulses which he had immediately suppressed, might have been the real thing, and all the rest false. And his professional duties and the whole arrangement of his life and of his family, and all his social and official interests, might all have been false. He tried to defend all those things to himself and suddenly felt the weakness of what he was defending. There was nothing to defend.

"But if that is so," he said to himself, "and I am leaving this life with the consciousness that I have lost all that was given me and it is impossible to rectify it—what then?"

He lay on his back and began to pass his life in review in quite a new way. In the morning when he saw first his footman, then his wife, then his daughter, and then the doctor, their every word and movement confirmed to him the awful truth that had been revealed to him during the night. In them he saw himself—all that for which he had lived—and saw clearly that it was not real at all, but a terrible and huge deception which had hidden both life and death. This consciousness intensified his physical suffering tenfold. He groaned and tossed about, and pulled at his clothing which choked and stifled him. And he hated them on that account.

He was given a large dose of opium and became unconscious, but at noon his sufferings began again. He drove everybody away and tossed from side to side.

His wife came to him and said:

"Jean, my dear, do this for me. It can't do any harm and often helps. Healthy people often do it."

He opened his eyes wide.

"What? Take communion? Why? It's unnecessary! However . . ."

She began to cry.

"Yes, do, my dear. I'll send for our priest. He is such a nice man."

"All right. Very well," he muttered.

When the priest came and heard his confession, Ivan Ilych was softened and seemed to feel a relief from his doubts and consequently from his sufferings, and for a moment there came a ray of hope. He again began to think of the vermiform appendix and the possibility of correcting it. He received the sacrament with tears in his eyes.

When they laid him down again afterwards he felt a moment's ease, and the hope that he might live awoke in him again. He began to think of the operation that had been suggested to him. "To live! I want to live!" he said to himself.

His wife came to congratulate him after his communion, and when uttering the usual conventional words she added:

"You feel better, don't you?"

Without looking at her he said "Yes."

Her dress, her figure, the expression of her face, the tone of her voice, all revealed the same thing. "This is wrong, it is not as it should be. All you have lived for and still live for is falsehood and deception, hiding life and death from you." And as soon as he admitted that thought, his hatred and his agonizing physical suffering again sprang up, and with that suffering a consciousness of the unavoidable, approaching end. And to this was added a new sensation of grinding shooting pain and a feeling of suffocation.

The expression of his face when he uttered that "yes" was dreadful. Having uttered it, he looked her straight in the eyes, turned on his face with a rapidity extraordinary in his weak state and shouted:

"Go away! Go away and leave me alone!"

12

From that moment the screaming began that continued for three days, and was so terrible that one could not hear it through two closed doors without horror. At the moment he answered his wife he realized that he was lost, that there was no return, that the end had come, the very end, and his doubts were still unsolved and remained doubts.

"Oh! Oh! Oh!" he cried in various intonations. He had begun by screaming "I won't!" and continued screaming on the letter *O.*

For three whole days, during which time did not exist for him, he struggled in that black sack into which he was being thrust by an invisible, resistless force. He struggled as a man condemned to death struggles in the hands of the executioner, knowing that he cannot save himself. And every moment he felt that despite all his efforts he was drawing nearer and nearer to what terrified him. He felt that his agony was due to his being thrust into that black hole and still more to his not being able to get right into it. He was hindered from getting into it by his conviction that his life had been a good one. That very justification of his life held him fast and prevented his moving forward, and it caused him most torment of all.

Suddenly some force struck him in the chest and side, making it still harder to breathe, and he fell through the hole and there at the bottom was a light. What had happened to him was like the sensation one sometimes experiences in a railway carriage when one thinks one is going backwards while one is really going forwards and suddenly becomes aware of the real direction.

"Yes, it was all not the right thing," he said to himself, "but that's no matter. It can be done. But what *is* the right thing?" he asked himself, and suddenly grew quiet.

This occurred at the end of the third day, two hours before his death. Just then his schoolboy son had crept softly in and gone up to the bedside. The dying man was still screaming and waving his arms. His hand fell on the boy's head, and the boy caught it, pressed it to his lips, and began to cry.

At that very moment Ivan Ilych fell through and caught sight of the light, and it was revealed to him that though his life had not been what it should have been, this could still be rectified. He asked himself, "What *is* the right thing?" and grew still, listening. Then he felt that someone was kissing his hand. He opened his eyes, looked at his son, and felt sorry for him. His wife came up to him and he glanced at her. She was gazing at him openmouthed, with undried tears on her nose and cheek and a despairing look on her face. He felt sorry for her too.

"Yes, I am making them wretched," he thought. "They are sorry, but it will be better for them when I die." He wished to say this but had not the strength to utter it. "Besides, why speak? I must act," he thought. With a look at his wife he indicated his son and said: "Take him away . . . sorry for him . . . sorry for you too . . ." He tried to add, "forgive me," but said "forgo" and waved his hand, knowing that He whose understanding mattered would understand.

And suddenly it grew clear to him that what had been oppressing him and would not leave him was dropping away at once from two sides, from ten sides, and from all sides. He was sorry for them, he must act so as not to hurt them and free himself from these sufferings. "How good and how simple!" he thought. "And the pain?" he asked himself. "What has become of it? Where are you, pain?"

He turned his attention to it.

"Yes, here it is. Well, what of it? Let the pain be."

"And death . . . where is it?"

He sought his former accustomed fear of death and did not find it. "Where is it? What death?" There was no fear because there was no death.

In place of death there was light.

"So that's what it is!" he suddenly exclaimed aloud. "What joy!"

To him all this happened in a single instant, and the meaning of that instant did not change. For those present his agony continued for another two hours. Something rattled in his throat, his emaciated body twitched, then the gasping and rattle became less and less frequent.

"It is finished!" said someone near him.

He heard these words and repeated them in his soul.

"Death is finished," he said to himself. "It is no more!"

He drew in a breath, stopped in the midst of a sigh, stretched out, and died.

1886

The Celebrated Jumping Frog of Calaveras County

SAMUEL CLEMENS (MARK TWAIN)

[1835–1910]

In compliance with the request of a friend of mine, who wrote me from the East, I called on good-natured, garrulous old Simon Wheeler, and inquired about my friend's friend, Leonidas W. Smiley, as requested to do, and I hereunto append the result. I have a lurking suspicion that *Leonidas* W. Smiley is a myth; that my friend never knew such a personage; and that he only conjectured that if I asked old Wheeler about him, it would remind him of his infamous *Jim* Smiley, and he would go to work and bore me to death with some exasperating reminiscence of him as long and as tedious as it should be useless to me. If that was the design, it succeeded.

I found Simon Wheeler dozing comfortably by the barroom stove of the dilapidated tavern in the decayed mining camp of Angel's, and I noticed that he was fat and bald-headed, and had an expression of winning gentleness and simplicity upon his tranquil countenance. He roused up, and gave me good day. I told him that a friend of mine had commissioned me to make some inquiries about a cherished companion of his boyhood named *Leonidas* W. Smiley—*Rev. Leonidas* W. Smiley, a young minister of the Gospel, who he had heard was at one time a resident of Angel's Camp. I added that if Mr. Wheeler could tell me anything about this Rev. Leonidas W. Smiley, I would feel under many obligations to him.

Simon Wheeler backed me into a corner and blockaded me there with his chair, and then sat down and reeled off the monotonous narrative which follows this paragraph. He never smiled, he never frowned, he never changed his voice from the gentle-flowing key to which he tuned his initial sentence, he never betrayed the slightest suspicion of enthusiasm; but all through the interminable narrative there ran a vein of impressive earnestness and sincerity, which showed me plainly that, so far from his imagining that there was anything ridiculous or funny about his story, he regarded it as a really important matter, and admired its two heroes as men of transcendent genius in *finesse.* I let him go on his own way, and never interrupted him once.

"Rev. Leonidas W. H'm, Reverend Le—well, there was a feller here once by the name of *Jim* Smiley, in the winter of '49—or maybe it was the spring of '50—I don't recollect exactly, somehow, though what makes me think it was one or the other is because I remember the big flume warn't finished when he first came to the camp; but anyway, he was the curiousest man about always betting on anything that turned up you ever see, if he could get anybody to bet on the other side; and if he couldn't he'd change sides. Any way that suited the other man would suit *him*—any way just so's he got a bet, *he* was satisfied. But still he was lucky, uncommon lucky; he most always come out winner. He was always ready and laying for a chance; there couldn't be no solit'ry thing mentioned but that feller'd offer to bet on it, and take ary side you please, as I was just telling you. If there was a horse-race, you'd find him flush or you'd find him busted at the end of it; if there was a dog-fight, he'd bet on it; if there was a cat-fight, he'd bet on it; if there was a chicken-fight, he'd bet on it; why, if there was two birds setting on a fence, he would bet you which one would fly first; or if there was a camp-meeting, he would be there reg'lar to bet on Parson Walker, which he judged to be the best exhorter about here, and so he was too, and a good man. If he even see a straddle-bug start to go anywheres, he would bet you how long it would take him to get to—to wherever he was going to, and if you took him up, he would foller that straddle-bug to Mexico but what he would find out where he was bound for and how long he was on the road. Lots of the boys here has seen that Smiley, and can tell you about him. Why, it never made no difference to *him*—he'd bet on *any* thing—the dangdest feller. Parson Walker's wife laid very sick once, for a good while, and it seemed as if they warn't going to save her; but one morning he come in, and Smiley up and asked him how she was, and he said she was considerable better—thank the Lord for his inf'nite mercy—and coming on so smart that with the blessing of Prov'dence she'd get well yet; and Smiley, before he thought, says, 'Well, I'll resk two-and-a-half she don't anyway.'

"This-yer Smiley had a mare—the boys called her the fifteen-minute nag, but that was only in fun, you know, because of course she was faster than that—and he used to win money on that horse, for all she was slow and always had the asthma, or the distemper, or the consumption, or something of that kind. They used to give her two or three hundred yards' start, and then pass her under way; but always at the fag end of the race she'd get excited and desperate like, and come cavoting and straddling up, and scattering her legs around limber, sometimes in the air, and sometimes out to one side among the fences, and kicking up m-o-r-e dust and raising m-o-r-e racket with her coughing and sneezing and blowing her nose—and *always* fetch up at the stand just about a neck ahead, as near as you could cipher it down.

"And he had a little small bull-pup, that to look at him you'd think he warn't worth a cent but to set around and look ornery and lay for a chance to steal something. But as soon as money was up on him he was a different dog; his under-jaw'd begin to stick out like the fo'castle of a steamboat, and his teeth would uncover and shine like the furnaces. And a dog might tackle him and bully-rag him, and bite him, and throw him over his shoulder two or three times, and Andrew Jackson—which was the name of the pup—Andrew Jackson would never let on but what *he* was satisfied, and hadn't expected nothing else—and the bets being doubled and doubled on the other side all the time, till the money was all up; and then all of a sudden he would grab that other dog jest by the j'int of his hind leg and freeze to it—not chaw, you understand, but only just grip and hang on till they throwed up the sponge, if it was a year. Smiley always come out winner on that pup, till he harnessed a dog once that didn't have no hind legs, because they'd been sawed off in a circular saw, and when the thing had gone along far enough, and the money was all up, and he come to make a snatch for his pet holt, he see in a minute how he'd been imposed on, and how the other dog had him in the door, so to speak, and he 'peared surprised, and then he looked sorter discouraged-like, and didn't try no more to win the fight, and so he got shucked out bad. He give Smiley a look, as much as to say his heart was broke, and it was *his* fault, for putting up a dog that hadn't no hind legs for him to take holt of, which was his main dependence in a fight, and then he limped off a piece and laid down and died. It was a good pup, was that Andrew Jackson, and would have made a name for hisself if he'd lived, for the stuff was in him and he had genius—I know it, because he hadn't no opportunities to speak of, and it don't stand to reason that a dog could make such a fight as he could under them circumstances if he hadn't no talent. It always makes me feel sorry when I think of that last fight of his'n, and the way it turned out.

"Well, thish-yer Smiley had rat-tarriers, and chicken cocks, and tom-cats and all them kind of things, till you couldn't rest, and you couldn't fetch nothing for him to bet on but he'd match you. He ketched a frog one day, and took him home, and said he cal'lated to educate him; and so he never done nothing for three months but set in his back yard and learn that frog to jump. And you bet you he *did* learn him, too. He'd give him a little punch behind, and the next minute you'd see that frog whirling in the air like a dough-nut—see him turn one summerset, or maybe a couple, if he got a good start, and come down flat-footed and all right, like a cat. He got him up so in the matter of ketching flies, and kep' him in practice so constant, that he'd nail a fly every time as fur as he could see him. Smiley said all a frog wanted was education, and he could do 'most anything—and I believe him. Why, I've seen him set Dan'l Webster down here on this floor—Dan'l Webster was the name of the frog—and sing out, 'Flies, Dan'l, flies!' and quicker'n you could wink he'd spring straight up and snake a fly off'n the counter there, and flop down on the floor ag'in as solid as a gob of mud, and fall to scratching the side of his head with his hind foot as indifferent as if he hadn't no idea he'd been doin' any more'n any frog might do. You never see a frog so modest and straightfor'ard as he was, for all he was so gifted. And when it come to fair and square jumping on a dead level, he could get over more ground at one straddle than any animal of his breed you ever see. Jumping on a dead level was his strong suit, you understand; and when it come to that, Smiley would ante up money on him as long as he had a red. Smiley was monstrous proud of his frog, and well he might be, for fellers that had traveled and been everywheres, all said he laid over any frog that ever *they* see.

"Well, Smiley kep' the beast in a little lattice box, and he used to fetch him downtown sometimes and lay for a bet. One day a feller—a stranger in the camp, he was—come acrost him with his box, and says:

" 'What might it be that you've got in the box?'

"And Smiley says, sorter indifferent-like, 'It might be a parrot, or it might be a canary, maybe, but it ain't—it's only just a frog.'

"And the feller took it, and looked at it careful, and turned it round this way and that, and says, 'H'm—so 'tis. Well, what's *he* good for?'

" 'Well,' Smiley says, easy and careless, 'he's good enough for *one* thing, I should judge—he can outjump any frog in Calaveras County.'

"The feller took the box again, and took another long, particular look, and give it back to Smiley, and says, very deliberate, 'Well,' he says, 'I don't see no p'ints about that frog that's any better'n any other frog.'

" 'Maybe you don't,' Smiley says. 'Maybe you understand frogs and maybe you don't understand 'em; maybe you've had experience, and maybe you ain't only a amature, as it were. Anyways, I've got *my* opinion, and I'll resk forty dollars that he can outjump any frog in Calaveras County.'

"And the feller studied a minute, and then says, kinder sadlike, 'Well, I'm only a stranger here, and I ain't got no frog; but if I had a frog, I'd bet you.'

"And then Smiley says, 'That's all right—that's all right—if you'll hold my box a minute, I'll go and get you a frog.' And so the feller took the box, and put up his forty dollars along with Smiley's, and set down to wait.

"So he set there a good while thinking and thinking to himself, and then he got the frog out and prized his mouth open and took a teaspoon and filled him full of quail-shot—filled him pretty near up to his chin—and set him on the floor. Smiley he went to the swamp and slopped around in the mud for a long time, and finally he ketched a frog, and fetched him in, and give him to this feller, and says:

" 'Now, if you're ready, set him alongside of Dan'l, with his fore paws just even with Dan'l's, and I'll give the word.' Then he says, 'One—two—three—*git!*' and him and the feller touched up the frogs from behind, and the new frog hopped off lively, but Dan'l give a heave, and hysted up his shoulders—so—like a Frenchman, but it warn't no use—he couldn't budge; he was planted as solid as a church, and he couldn't no more stir than if he was anchored out. Smiley was a good deal surprised, and he was disgusted too, but he didn't have no idea what the matter was, of course.

"The feller took the money and started away; and when he was going out at the door, he sorter jerked his thumb over his shoulder—so—at Dan'l, and says again, very deliberate, 'Well,' he says, 'I don't see no p'ints about that frog that's any better'n any other frog.'

"Smiley he stood scratching his head and looking down at Dan'l a long time, and at last he says, 'I do wonder what in the nation that frog throw'd off for—I wonder if there ain't something the matter with him—he 'pears to look mighty baggy, somehow.' And he ketched Dan'l by the nape of the neck, and hefted him, and says, 'Why blame my cats if he don't weigh five pound!' " and turned him upside down and he belched out a double handful of shot. And then he see how it was, and he was the maddest man—he set the frog down and took out after that feller, but he never ketched him. And—"

[Here Simon Wheeler heard his name called from the front yard, and got up to see what was wanted.] And turning to me as he moved away, he said: "Just set where you are, stranger, and rest easy—I ain't going to be gone a second."

But, by your leave, I did not think that a continuation of the history of the enterprising vagabond *Jim* Smiley would be likely to afford me much information concerning the Rev. *Leonidas* W. Smiley, and so I started away.

At the door I met the sociable Wheeler returning, and he buttonholed me and recommended:

"Well, thish-yer Smiley had a yaller one-eyed cow that didn't have no tail, only just a short stump like a bannanner, and—"

However, lacking both time and inclination, I did not wait to hear about the afflicted cow, but took my leave.

1867

An Occurrence at Owl Creek Bridge

AMBROSE BIERCE

[1842–1914?]

I

A man stood upon a railroad bridge in northern Alabama, looking down into the swift water twenty feet below. The man's hands were behind his back, the wrists bound with a cord. A rope closely encircled his neck. It was attached to a stout cross-timber above his head and the slack fell to the level of his knees. Some loose boards laid upon the sleepers supporting the metals of the railway supplied a footing for him and his executioners—two private soldiers of the Federal army, directed by a sergeant who in civil life may have been a deputy sheriff. At a short remove upon the same temporary platform was an officer in the uniform of his rank, armed. He was a captain. A sentinel at each end of the bridge stood with his rifle in the position known as "support," that is to say, vertical in front of the left shoulder, the hammer resting on the forearm thrown straight across the chest—a formal and unnatural position, enforcing an erect carriage of the body. It did not appear to be the duty of these two men to know what was occurring at the center of the bridge; they merely blockaded the two ends of the foot planking that traversed it.

Beyond one of the sentinels nobody was in sight; the railroad ran straight away into a forest for a hundred yards, then, curving, was lost to view. Doubtless there was an outpost farther along. The other bank of the stream was open ground—a gentle acclivity topped with a stockade of vertical tree trunks, loopholed for rifles, with a single embrasure through which protruded the muzzle of a brass cannon commanding the bridge. Midway of the slope between bridge and fort were the spectators—a single company of infantry in line, at "parade rest," the butts of the rifles on the ground, the barrels inclining slightly backward against the right shoulder, the hands crossed upon the stock. A lieutenant stood at the right of the line, the point of his sword upon the ground, his left hand resting upon his right. Excepting the group of four at the center of the bridge, not a man moved. The company faced the bridge, staring stonily, motionless. The sentinels, facing the banks of the stream, might have been statues to adorn the bridge. The captain stood with folded arms, silent, observing the work of his subordinates, but making no sign. Death is a dignitary who when he comes announced is to be received with formal manifestations of respect, even by those most familiar with him. In the code of military etiquette silence and fixity are forms of deference.

The man who was engaged in being hanged was apparently about thirty-five years of age. He was a civilian, if one might judge from his habit, which was that of a planter. His features were good—a straight nose, firm mouth, broad forehead, from which his long, dark hair was combed straight back, falling behind his ears to the collar of his well-fitting frock coat. He wore a mustache and pointed beard, but no whiskers; his eyes were large and dark gray, and had a kindly expression which one would hardly have expected in one whose neck was in the hemp. Evidently this was no vulgar assassin. The liberal military code makes provision for hanging many kinds of persons, and gentlemen are not excluded.

The preparations being complete, the two private soldiers stepped aside and each drew away the plank upon which he had been standing. The sergeant turned to the captain, saluted and placed himself immediately behind that officer, who in turn moved apart one pace. These movements left the condemned man and the sergeant standing on the two ends of the same plank, which spanned three of the crossties of the bridge. The end upon which the civilian stood almost, but not quite, reached a fourth. This plank had been held in place by the weight of the captain; it was now held by that of the sergeant. At a signal from the former the latter would step aside, the plank would tilt and the condemned man go down between two ties. The arrangement commended itself to his judgment as simple and effective. His face had not been covered nor his eyes bandaged. He looked a moment at his "unsteadfast footing," then let his gaze wander to the swirling water of the stream racing madly beneath his feet. A piece of dancing driftwood caught his attention and his eyes followed it down the current. How slowly it appeared to move! What a sluggish stream!

He closed his eyes in order to fix his last thoughts upon his wife and children. The water, touched to gold by the early sun, the brooding mists under the banks at some distance down the stream, the fort, the soldiers, the piece of drift—all had distracted him. And now he became conscious of a new disturbance. Striking through the thought of his dear ones was a sound which he could neither ignore nor understand, a sharp, distinct, metallic percussion like the stroke of a blacksmith's hammer upon the anvil; it had the same ringing quality. He wondered what it was, and whether immeasurably distant or near by—it seemed both. Its recurrence was regular, but as slow as the tolling of a death knell. He awaited each stroke with impatience and—he knew not why—apprehension. The intervals of silence grew progressively longer; the delays became maddening. With their greater infrequency the sounds increased in strength and sharpness. They hurt his ear like the thrust of a knife; he feared he would shriek. What he heard was the ticking of his watch.

He unclosed his eyes and saw again the water below him. "If I could free my hands," he thought, "I might throw off the noose and spring into the stream. By diving I could evade the bullets and, swimming vigorously, reach the bank, take to the woods and get away home. My home, thank God, is as yet outside their lines; my wife and little ones are still beyond the invader's farthest advance."

As these thoughts, which have here to be set down in words, were flashed into the doomed man's brain rather than evolved from it the captain nodded to the sergeant. The sergeant stepped aside.

II

Peyton Farquhar was a well-to-do planter, of an old and highly respected Alabama family. Being a slave owner and like other slave owners a politician he was naturally an original secessionist and ardently devoted to the Southern cause. Circumstances of an imperious nature, which it is unnecessary to relate here, had prevented him from taking service with the gallant army that had fought the disastrous campaigns ending with the fall of Corinth, and he chafed under the inglorious restraint, longing for the release of his energies, the larger life of the soldier, the opportunity for distinction. That opportunity, he felt, would come, as it comes to all in war time. Meanwhile he did what he could. No service was too humble for him to perform in aid of the South, no adventure too perilous for him to undertake if consistent with the character of a civilian who was at heart a soldier, and who in good faith and without too much qualification assented to at least a part of the frankly villainous dictum that all is fair in love and war.

One evening while Farquhar and his wife were sitting on a rustic bench near the entrance to his grounds, a gray-clad soldier rode up to the gate and asked for a drink of water. Mrs. Farquhar was only too happy to serve him with her own white hands. While she was fetching the water her husband approached the dusty horseman and inquired eagerly for news from the front.

"The Yanks are repairing the railroads," said the man, "and are getting ready for another advance. They have reached the Owl Creek bridge, put it in order and built a stockade on the north bank. The commandant has issued an order, which is posted everywhere, declaring that any civilian caught interfering with the railroad, its bridges, tunnels or trains will be summarily hanged. I saw the order."

"How far is it to the Owl Creek bridge?" Farquhar asked.

"About thirty miles."

"Is there no force on this side the creek?"

"Only a picket post half a mile out, on the railroad, and a single sentinel at this end of the bridge."

"Suppose a man—a civilian and student of hanging—should elude the picket post and perhaps get the better of the sentinel," said Farquhar, smiling, "what could he accomplish?"

The soldier reflected. "I was there a month ago," he replied. "I observed that the flood of last winter had lodged a great quantity of driftwood against the wooden pier at this end of the bridge. It is now dry and would burn like tow."

The lady had now brought the water, which the soldier drank. He thanked her ceremoniously, bowed to her husband and rode away. An hour later, after nightfall, he repassed the plantation, going northward in the direction from which he had come. He was a Federal scout.

III

As Peyton Farquhar fell straight downward through the bridge he lost consciousness and was as one already dead. From this state he was awakened—ages later, it seemed to him—by the pain of a sharp pressure upon his throat, followed by a sense of suffocation. Keen, poignant agonies seemed to shoot from his neck downward through every fiber of his body and limbs. These pains appeared to flash along well-defined lines of ramification and to beat with an inconceivably rapid periodicity. They seemed like streams of pulsating fire heating him to an intolerable temperature. As to his head, he was conscious of nothing but a feeling of fulness—of congestion. These sensations were unaccompanied by thought. The intellectual part of his nature was already effaced; he had power only to feel, and feeling was torment. He was conscious of motion. Encompassed in a luminous cloud, of which he was now merely the fiery heart, without material substance, he swung through unthinkable arcs of oscillation, like a vast pendulum. Then all at once, with terrible suddenness, the light about him shot upward with the noise of a loud plash; a frightful roaring was in his ears, and all was cold and dark. The power of thought was restored; he knew that the rope had broken and he had fallen into the stream. There was no additional strangulation; the noose about his neck was already suffocating him and kept the water from his lungs. To die of hanging at the bottom of a river!—the idea seemed to him ludicrous. He opened his eyes in the darkness and saw above him a gleam of light, but how distant, how inaccessible! He was still sinking, for the light became fainter and fainter until it was a mere glimmer. Then it began to grow and brighten, and he knew that he was rising toward the surface—knew it with reluctance, for he was now very comfortable. "To be hanged and drowned," he thought, "that is not so bad; but I do not wish to be shot. No; I will not be shot; that is not fair."

He was not conscious of an effort, but a sharp pain in his wrist appraised him that he was trying to free his hands. He gave the struggle his attention, as an idler might observe the feat of a juggler, without interest in the outcome. What splendid effort!—what magnificent, what superhuman strength! Ah, that was a fine endeavor! Bravo! The cord fell away; his arms parted and floated upward, the hands dimly seen on each side in the growing light. He watched them with a new interest as first one and then the other pounced upon the noose at his neck. They tore it away and thrust it fiercely aside, its undulations resembling those of a water snake. "Put it back, put it back!" He thought he shouted these words to his hands, for the undoing of the noose had been succeeded by the direct pang that he had yet experienced. His neck ached horribly; his brain was on fire; his heart, which had been fluttering faintly, gave a great leap, trying to force itself out at his mouth. His whole body was racked and wrenched with an insupportable anguish! But his disobedient hands gave no heed to the command. They beat the water vigorously with quick, downward strokes, forcing him to the surface. He felt his head emerge; his eyes were blinded by the sunlight; his chest expanded convulsively, and with a supreme and crowning agony his lungs engulfed a great draught of air, which instantly he expelled in a shriek!

He was now in full possession of his physical senses. They were, indeed, preternaturally keen and alert. Something in the awful disturbance of his organic system had so exalted and refined them that they made record of things never before perceived. He felt the ripples upon his face and heard their separate sounds as they struck. He looked at the forest on the bank of the stream, saw the individual trees, the leaves and the veining of each leaf—saw the very insects upon them: the locusts, the brilliant-bodied flies, the gray spiders stretching their webs from twig to twig. He noted the prismatic colors in all the dewdrops upon a million blades of grass. The humming of the gnats that danced above the eddies of the stream, the beating of the dragonflies' wings, the strokes of the waterspiders' legs, like oars which had lifted their boat—all these made audible music. A fish slid along beneath his eyes and he heard the rush of its body parting the water.

He had come to the surface facing down the stream; in a moment the visible world seemed to wheel slowly round, himself the pivotal point, and he saw the bridge, the fort, the soldiers upon the bridge, the captain, the sergeant, the two privates, his executioners. They were in silhouette against the blue sky. They shouted and gesticulated, pointing at him. The captain had drawn his pistol, but did not fire; the others were unarmed. Their movements were grotesque and horrible, their forms gigantic.

Suddenly he heard a sharp report and something struck the water smartly within a few inches of his head, spattering his face with spray. He heard a second report, and saw one of the sentinels with his rifle at his shoulder, a light cloud of blue smoke rising from the muzzle. The man in the water saw the eye of the man on the bridge gazing into his own through the sights of the rifle. He observed that it was a gray eye and remembered having read that gray eyes were keenest, and that all famous marksmen had them. Nevertheless, this one had missed.

A counter-swirl had caught Farquhar and turned him half round; he was again looking into the forest on the bank opposite the fort. The sound of a clear, high voice in a monotonous singsong now rang out behind him and came across the water with a distinctness that pierced and subdued all other sounds, even the beating of the ripples in his ears. Although no soldier, he had frequented camps enough to know the dread significance of that deliberate, drawling, aspirated chant; the lieutenant on shore was taking a part in the morning's work. How coldly and pitilessly—with what an even, calm intonation, presaging, and enforcing tranquility in the men—with what accurately measured intervals fell those cruel words:

"Attention, company! . . . Shoulder arms! . . . Ready! . . . Aim! . . . Fire!"

Farquhar dived—dived as deeply as he could. The water roared in his ears like the voice of Niagara, yet he heard the dulled thunder of the volley and, rising again toward the surface, met shining bits of metal, singularly flattened, oscillating slowly downward. Some of them touched him on the face and hands, then fell away, continuing their descent. One lodged between his collar and neck; it was uncomfortably warm and he snatched it out.

As he rose to the surface, gasping for breath, he saw that he had been a long time under water; he was perceptibly farther downstream—nearer to safety. The soldiers had almost finished reloading; the metal ramrods flashed all at once in the sunshine as they were drawn from the barrels, turned in the air, and thrust into their sockets. The two sentinels fired again, independently and ineffectually.

The hunted man saw all this over his shoulder; he was now swimming vigorously with the current. His brain was as energetic as his arms and legs; he thought with the rapidity of lightning.

"The officer," he reasoned, "will not make that martinet's error a second time. It is as easy to dodge a volley as a single shot. He has probably already given the command to fire at will. God help me, I cannot dodge them all!"

An appalling plash within two yards of him was followed by a loud, rushing sound, diminuendo, which seemed to travel back through the air to the fort and died in an explosion which stirred the very river to its deeps! A rising sheet of water curved over him, fell down upon him, blinded him, strangled him! The cannon had taken a hand in the game. As he shook his head free from the commotion of the smitten water he heard the deflected shot humming through the air ahead, and in an instant it was cracking and smashing the branches in the forest beyond.

"They will not do that again," he thought; "the next time they will use a charge of grape. I must keep my eye upon the gun; the smoke will apprise me—the report arrives too late; it lags behind the missile. That is a good gun."

Suddenly he felt himself whirled round and round—spinning like a top. The water, the banks, the forests, the now distant bridge, fort and men—all were commingled and blurred. Objects were represented by their colors only; circular horizontal streaks of color—that was all he saw. He had been caught in a vortex and was being whirled on with a velocity of advance and gyration that made him giddy and sick. In a few moments he was flung upon the travel at the foot of the left bank of the stream—the southern bank—and behind a projecting point which concealed him from his enemies. The sudden arrest of his motion, the abrasion of one of his hands on the gravel, restored him, and he wept with delight. He dug his fingers into the sand, threw it over himself in handfuls and audibly blessed it. It looked like diamonds, rubies, emeralds; he could think of nothing beautiful which it did not resemble. The trees upon the bank were giant garden plants; he noted a definite order in their arrangement, inhaled the fragrance of their blooms. A strange, roseate light shone through the spaces among their trunks and the wind made in their branches the music of aeolian harps. He had no wish to perfect his escape—was content to remain in that enchanting spot until retaken.

A whiz and rattle of grapeshot among the branches high above his head roused him from his dream. The baffled cannoneer had fired him a random farewell. He sprang to his feet, rushed up the sloping bank, and plunged into the forest.

All that day he traveled, laying his course by the rounding sun. The forest seemed interminable; nowhere did he discover a break in it, not even a woodman's road. He had not known that he lived in so wild a region. There was something uncanny in the revelation.

By nightfall he was fatigued, footsore, famishing. The thought of his wife and children urged him on. At last he found a road which led him in what he knew to be the right direction. It was as wide and straight as a city street, yet it seemed untraveled. No fields bordered it, no dwelling anywhere. Not so much as the barking of a dog suggested human habitation. The black bodies of the trees formed a straight wall on both sides, terminating on the horizon in a point, like a diagram in a lesson in perspective. Overhead, as he looked up through this rift in the wood, shone great golden stars looking unfamiliar and grouped in strange constellations. He was sure they were arranged in some order which had a secret and malign significance. The wood on either side was full of singular noises, among which—once, twice, and again—he distinctly heard whispers in an unknown tongue.

His neck was in pain and lifting his hand to it he found it horribly swollen. He knew that it had a circle of black where the rope had bruised it. His eyes felt congested; he could no longer close them. His tongue was swollen with thirst; he relieved its fever by thrusting it forward from between his teeth into the cold air. How softly the turf had carpeted the untraveled avenue—he could no longer feel the roadway beneath his feet!

Doubtless, despite his suffering, he had fallen asleep while walking, for now he sees another scene—perhaps he has merely recovered from a delirium. He stands at the gate of his own home. All is as he left it, and all bright and beautiful in the morning sunshine. He must have traveled the entire night. As he pushes upon the gate and passes up the wide white walk, he sees a flutter of female garments; his wife, looking fresh and cool and sweet, steps down from the veranda to meet him. At the bottom of the steps she stands waiting, with a smile of ineffable joy, an attitude of matchless grace and dignity. Ah, how beautiful she is! He springs forward with extended arms. As he is about to clasp her he feels a stunning blow upon the back of the neck; a blinding white light blazes all about him with a sound like the shock of a cannon—then all is darkness and silence!

Peyton Farquhar was dead; his body, with a broken neck, swung gently from side to side beneath the timbers of the Owl Creek bridge.

1891

The Beast in the Jungle

HENRY JAMES

[1843–1916]

What determined the speech that startled him in the course of their encounter scarcely matters, being probably but some words spoken by himself quite without intention—spoken as they lingered and slowly moved together after their renewal of acquaintance. He had been conveyed by friends an hour or two before to the house at which she was staying; the party of visitors at the other house, of whom he was one, and thanks to whom it was his theory, as always, that he was lost in the crowd, had been invited over to luncheon. There had been after luncheon much dispersal, all in the interest of the original move, a view of Weatherend itself and the fine things, intrinsic features, pictures, heirlooms, treasures of all the arts, that made the place almost famous; and the great rooms were so numerous that guests could wander at their will, hang back from the principal group and in cases where they took such matters with the least seriousness give themselves up to mysterious appreciations and measurements. There were persons to be observed, singly or in couples, bending toward objects in out-of-the-way corners with their hands on their knees and their heads nodding quite as with the emphasis of an excited sense of smell. When they were two they either mingled their sounds of ecstasy or melted into silences of even deeper import, so that there were aspects of the occasion that gave it for Marcher much the air of the "look round," previous to a sale highly advertised, that excites or quenches, as may be, the dream of acquisition. The dream of acquisition at Weatherend would have had to be wild indeed, and John Marcher found himself, among such suggestions, disconcerted almost equally by the presence of those who knew too much and by that of those who knew nothing. The great rooms caused so much poetry and history to press upon him that he needed some straying apart to feel in a proper relation with them, though this impulse was not, as happened, like the gloating of some of his companions, to be compared to the movements of a dog sniffing a cupboard. It had an issue promptly enough in a direction that was not to have been calculated.

It led, briefly, in the course of the October afternoon, to his closer meeting with May Bartram, whose face, a reminder, yet not quite a remembrance, as they sat much separated at a very long table, had begun merely by troubling him rather pleasantly. It affected him as the sequel of something of which he had lost the beginning. He knew it, and for the time quite welcomed it, as a continuation, but didn't know what it continued, which was an interest or an amusement the greater as he was also somehow aware—yet without a direct sign from her—that the young woman herself hadn't lost the thread. She hadn't lost it, but she wouldn't give it back to him, he saw, without some putting forth of his hand for it; and he not only saw that, but saw several things more, things odd enough in the light of the fact that at the moment some accident of grouping brought them face to face he was still merely fumbling with the idea that any contact between them in the past would have had no importance. If it had had no importance he scarcely knew why his actual impression of her should so seem to have so much; the answer to which, however, was that in such a life as they all appeared to be leading for the moment one could but take things as they came. He was satisfied, without in the least being able to say why, that this young lady might roughly have ranked in the house as a poor relation; satisfied also that she was not there on a brief visit, but was more or less a part of the establishment—almost a working, a remunerated part. Didn't she enjoy at periods a protection that she paid for by helping, among other services, to show the place and explain it, deal with the tiresome people, answer questions about the dates of the building, the styles of the furniture, the authorship of the pictures, the favourite haunts of the ghost? It wasn't that she looked as if you could have given her shillings—it was impossible to look less so. Yet when she finally drifted toward him, distinctly handsome, though ever so much older—older than when he had seen her before—it might have been as an effect of her guessing that he had, within the couple of hours, devoted more imagination to her than to all the others put together, and had thereby penetrated to a kind of truth that the others were too stupid for. She *was* there on harder terms than any one; she was there as a consequence of things suffered, one way and another, in the interval of years; and she remembered him very much as she was remembered—only a good deal better.

By the time they at last thus came to speech they were alone in one of the rooms—remarkable for a fine portrait over the chimney-place—out of which their friends had passed, and the charm of it was that even before they had spoken they had practically arranged with each other to stay behind to talk. The charm, happily, was in other things too—partly in there being scarce a spot at Weatherend without something to stay behind for. It was in the way the autumn day looked into the high windows as it waned; the way the red light, breaking at the close from under a low sombre sky, reached out in a long shaft and played over old wainscots, old tapestry, old gold, old colour. It was most of all perhaps in the way she came to him as if, since she had been turned on to deal with the simpler sort, he might, should he choose to keep the whole thing down, just take her mild attention for a part of her general business. As soon as he heard her voice, however, the gap was filled up and the missing link supplied; the slight irony he divined in her attitude lost its advantage. He almost jumped at it to get there before her. "I met you years and years ago in Rome. I remember all about it." She confessed to disappointment—she had been so sure he didn't; and to prove how well he did he began to pour forth the particular recollections that popped up as he called for them. Her face and her voice, all at his service now, worked the miracle—the impression operating like the torch of a lamplighter who touches into flame, one by one, a long row of gas-jets. Marcher flattered himself the illumination was brilliant, yet he was really still more pleased on her showing him, with amusement, that in his haste to make everything right he had got most things rather wrong. It hadn't been at Rome—it had been at Naples; and it hadn't been eight years before—it had been more nearly ten. She hadn't been, either, with her uncle and aunt, but with her mother and her brother; in addition to which it was not with the Pembles *he* had been, but with the Boyers, coming down in their company from Rome—a point on which she insisted, a little to his confusion, and as to which she had her evidence in hand. The Boyers she had known, but didn't know the Pembles, though she had heard of them, and it was the people he was with who had made them acquainted. The incident of the thunderstorm that had raged round them with such violence as to drive them for refuge into an excavation—this incident had not occurred at the Palace of the Cæsars, but at Pompeii, on an occasion when they had been present there at an important find.

He accepted her amendments, he enjoyed her corrections, though the moral of them was, she pointed out, that he *really* didn't remember the least thing about her; and he only felt it as a drawback that when all was made strictly historic there didn't appear much of anything left. They lingered together still, she neglecting her office—for from the moment he was so clever she had no proper right to him—and both neglecting the house, just waiting as to see if a memory or two more wouldn't again breathe on them. It hadn't taken them many minutes, after all, to put down on the table, like the cards of a pack, those that constituted their respective hands; only what came out was that the pack was unfortunately not perfect—that the past, invoked, invited, encouraged, could give them, naturally, no more than it had. It had made them anciently meet—her at twenty, him at twenty-five; but nothing was so strange, they seemed to say to each other, as that, while so occupied, it hadn't done a little more for them. They looked at each other as with the feeling of an occasion missed; the present would have been so much better if the other, in the far distance, in the foreign land, hadn't been so stupidly meagre. There weren't apparently, all counted, more than a dozen little old things that had succeeded in coming to pass between them; trivialities of youth, simplicities of freshness, stupidities of ignorance, small possible germs, but too deeply buried—too deeply (didn't it seem?) to sprout after so many years. Marcher could only feel he ought to have rendered her some service—saved her from a capsized boat in the Bay or at least recovered her dressing-bag, filched from her cab in the streets of Naples by a lazzarone with a stiletto. Or it would have been nice if he could have been taken with fever all alone at his hotel, and she could have come to look after him, to write to his people, to drive him out in convalescence. *Then* they would be in possession of the something or other that their actual show seemed to lack. It yet somehow presented itself, this show, as too good to be spoiled; so that they were reduced for a few minutes more to wondering a little helplessly why—since they seemed to know a certain number of the same people—their reunion had been so long averted. They didn't use that name for it, but their delay from minute to minute to join the others was a kind of confession that they didn't quite want it to be a failure. Their attempted supposition of reasons for their not having met but showed how little they knew of each other. There came in fact a moment when Marcher felt a positive pang. It was vain to pretend she was an old friend, for all the communities were wanting, in spite of which it was as an old friend that he saw she would have suited him. He had new ones enough—was surrounded with them for instance on the stage of the other house; as a new one he probably wouldn't have so much as noticed her. He would have liked to invent something, get her to make-believe with him that some passage of a romantic or critical kind *had* originally occurred. He was really almost reaching out in imagination—as against time—for something that would do, and saying to himself that if it didn't come this sketch of a fresh start would show for quite awkwardly bungled. They would separate, and now for no second or no third chance. They would have tried and not succeeded. Then it was, just at the turn, as he afterwards made it out to himself, that, everything else failing, she herself decided to take up the case and, as it were, save the situation. He felt as soon as she spoke that she had been consciously keeping back what she said and hoping to get on without it; a scruple in her that immensely touched him when, by the end of three or four minutes more, he was able to measure it. What she brought out, at any rate, quite cleared the air and supplied the link—the link it was so odd he should frivolously have managed to lose.

"You know you told me something I've never forgotten and that again and again has made me think of you since; it was that tremendously hot day when we went to Sorrento, across the bay, for the breeze. What I allude to was what you said to me, on the way back, as we sat under the awning of the boat enjoying the cool. Have you forgotten?"

He had forgotten and was even more surprised than ashamed. But the great thing was that he saw in this no vulgar reminder of any "sweet" speech. The vanity of women had long memories, but she was making no claim on him of a compliment or a mistake. With another woman, a totally different one, he might have feared the recall possibly even some imbecile "offer." So, in having to say that he had indeed forgotten, he was conscious rather of a loss than of a gain; he already saw an interest in the matter of her mention. "I try to think—but I give it up. Yet I remember the Sorrento day."

"I'm not very sure you do," May Bartram after a moment said; "and I'm not very sure I ought to want you to. It's dreadful to bring a person back at any time to what he was ten years before. If you've lived away from it," she smiled, "so much the better."

"And if *you* haven't why should I?" he asked.

"Lived away, you mean, from what I myself was?"

"From what *I* was. I was of course an ass," Marcher went on; "but I would rather know from you just the sort of ass I was than—from the moment you have something in your mind—not know anything."

Still, however, she hesitated. "But if you've completely ceased to be that sort—?"

"Why I can then all the more bear to know. Besides, perhaps I haven't."

"Perhaps. Yet if you haven't," she added, "I should suppose you'd remember. Not indeed that *I* in the least connect with my impression the invidious name you use. If I had only thought you foolish," she explained, "the thing I speak of wouldn't so have remained with me. It was about yourself." She waited as if it might come to him; but as, only meeting her eyes in wonder, he gave no sign, she burnt her ships. "Has it ever happened?"

Then it was that, while he continued to stare, a light broke for him and the blood slowly came to his face, which began to burn with recognition. "Do you mean I told you—?" But he faltered, lest what came to him shouldn't be right, lest he should only give himself away.

"It was something about yourself that it was natural one shouldn't forget—that is if one remembered you at all. That's why I ask you," she smiled, "if the thing you then spoke of has ever come to pass?"

Oh then he saw, but he was lost in wonder and found himself embarrassed. This, he also saw, made her sorry for him, as if her allusion had been a mistake. It took him but a moment, however, to feel it hadn't been, much as it had been a surprise. After the first little shock of it her knowledge on the contrary began, even if rather strangely, to taste sweet to him. She was the only other person in the world then who would have it, and she had had it all these years, while the fact of his having so breathed his secret had unaccountably faded from him. No wonder they couldn't have met as if nothing had happened. "I judge," he finally said, "that I know what you mean. Only I had strangely enough lost any sense of having taken you so far into my confidence."

"Is it because you've taken so many others as well?"

"I've taken nobody. Not a creature since then."

"So that I'm the only person who knows?"

"The only person in the world."

"Well," she quickly replied, "I myself have never spoken. I've never, never repeated of you what you told me." She looked at him so that he perfectly believed her. Their eyes met over it in such a way that he was without a doubt. "And I never will."

She spoke with an earnestness that, as if almost excessive, put him at ease about her possible derision. Somehow the whole question was a new luxury to him—that is from the moment she was in possession. If she didn't take the sarcastic view she clearly took the sympathetic, and that was what he had had, in all the long time, from no one whomsoever. What he felt was that he couldn't at present have begun to tell her, and yet could profit perhaps exquisitely by the accident of having done so of old. "Please don't then. We're just right as it is."

"Oh I am," she laughed, "if you are!" To which she added: "Then you do still feel in the same way?"

It was impossible he shouldn't take to himself that she was really interested, though it all kept coming as perfect surprise. He had thought of himself so long as abominably alone, and lo he wasn't alone a bit. He hadn't been, it appeared, for an hour—since those moments on the Sorrento boat. It was *she* who had been, he seemed to see as he looked at her—she who had been made so by the graceless fact of his lapse of fidelity. To tell her what he had told her—what had it been but to ask something of her? something that she had given, in her charity, without his having, by a remembrance, by a return of the spirit, failing another encounter, so much as thanked her. What he had asked of her had been simply at first not to laugh at him. She had beautifully not done so for ten years, and she was not doing so now. So he had endless gratitude to make up. Only for that he must see just how he had figured to her. "What, exactly, was the account I gave—?"

"Of the way you did feel? Well, it was very simple. You said you had had from your earliest time, as the deepest thing within you, the sense of being kept for something rare and strange, possibly prodigious and terrible, that was sooner or later to happen to you, that you had in your bones the foreboding and the conviction of, and that would perhaps overwhelm you."

"Do you call that very simple?" John Marcher asked.

She thought a moment. "It was perhaps because I seemed, as you spoke, to understand it."

"You do understand it?" he eagerly asked.

Again she kept her kind eyes on him. "You still have the belief?"

"Oh!" he exclaimed helplessly. There was too much to say.

"Whatever it's to be," she clearly made out, "it hasn't yet come."

He shook his head in complete surrender now. "It hasn't yet come. Only, you know, it isn't anything I'm to *do,* to achieve in the world, to be distinguished or admired for. I'm not such an ass as *that.* It would be much better, no doubt, if I were."

"It's to be something you're merely to suffer?"

"Well, say to wait for—to have to meet, to face, to see suddenly break out in my life; possibly destroying all further consciousness, possibly annihilating me; possibly, on the other hand, only altering everything, striking at the root of all my world and leaving me to the consequences, however they shape themselves."

She took this in, but the light in her eyes continued for him not to be that of mockery. "Isn't what you describe perhaps but the expectation—or at any rate the sense of danger, familiar to so many people—of falling in love?"

John Marcher wondered. "Did you ask me that before?"

"No—I wasn't so free-and-easy then. But it's what strikes me now."

"Of course," he said after a moment, "it strikes you. Of course it strikes *me.* Of course what's in store for me may be no more than that. The only thing is," he went on, "that I think if it had been that I should by this time know."

"Do you mean because you've *been* in love?" And then as he but looked at her in silence: "You've been in love, and it hasn't meant such a cataclysm, hasn't proved the great affair?"

"Here I am, you see. It hasn't been overwhelming."

"Then it hasn't been love," said May Bartram.

"Well, I at least thought it was. I took it for that—I've taken it till now. It was agreeable, it was delightful, it was miserable," he explained. "But it wasn't strange. It wasn't what *my* affair's to be."

"You want something all to yourself—something that nobody else knows or *has* known?"

"It isn't a question of what I 'want'—God knows I don't want anything. It's only a question of the apprehension that haunts me—that I live with day by day."

He said this so lucidly and consistently that he could see it further impose itself. If she hadn't been interested before she'd have been interested now. "Is it a sense of coming violence?"

Evidently now too again he liked to talk of it. "I don't think of it as—when it does come—necessarily violent. I only think of it as natural and as of course above all unmistakable. I think of it simply as *the* thing. *The* thing will of itself appear natural."

"Then how will it appear strange?"

Marcher bethought himself. "It won't—to *me.*"

"To whom then?"

"Well," he replied, smiling at last, "say to you."

"Oh then I'm to be present?"

"Why you *are* present—since you know."

"I see." She turned it over. "But I mean at the catastrophe."

At this, for a minute, their lightness gave way to their gravity; it was as if the long look they exchanged held them together. "It will only depend on yourself—if you'll watch with me."

"Are you afraid?" she asked.

"Don't leave me *now,*" he went on.

"Are you afraid?" she repeated.

"Do you think me simply out of my mind?" he pursued instead of answering. "Do I merely strike you as a harmless lunatic?"

"No," said May Bartram. "I understand you. I believe you."

"You mean you feel how my obsession—poor old thing!—may correspond to some possible reality?"

"To some possible reality."

"Then you *will* watch with me?"

She hesitated, then for the third time put her question. "Are you afraid?"

"Did I tell you I was—at Naples?"

"No, you said nothing about it."

"Then I don't know. And I should *like* to know," said John Marcher. "You'll tell me yourself whether you think so. If you'll watch with me you'll see."

"Very good then." They had been moving by this time across the room, and at the door, before passing out, they paused as for the full wind-up of their understanding. "I'll watch with you," said May Bartram.

2

The fact that she "knew"—knew and yet neither chaffed him nor betrayed him—had in a short time begun to constitute between them a goodly bond, which became more marked when, within the year that followed their afternoon at Weatherend, the opportunities for meeting multiplied. The event that thus promoted these occasions was the death of the ancient lady her great-aunt, under whose wing, since losing her mother, she had to such an extent found shelter, and who, though but the widowed mother of the new successor to the property, had succeeded—thanks to a high tone and a high temper—in not forfeiting the supreme position at the great house. The deposition of this personage arrived but with her death, which, followed by many changes, made in particular a difference for the young woman in whom Marcher's expert attention had recognised from the first a dependent with a pride that might ache though it didn't bristle. Nothing for a long time had made him easier than the thought that the aching must have been much soothed by Miss Bartram's now finding herself able to set up a small home in London. She had acquired property, to an amount that made that luxury just possible, under her aunt's extremely complicated will, and when the whole matter began to be straightened out, which indeed took time, she let him know that the happy issue was at last in view. He had seen her again before that day, both because she had more than once accompanied the ancient lady to town and because he had paid another visit to the friends who so conveniently made of Weatherend one of the charms of their own hospitality. These friends had taken him back there; he had achieved there again with Miss Bartram some quiet detachment; and he had in London succeeded in persuading her to more than one brief absence from her aunt. They went together, on these latter occasions, to the National Gallery and the South Kensington Museum, where, among vivid reminders, they talked of Italy at large—not now attempting to recover, as at first, the taste of their youth and their ignorance. That recovery, the first day at Weatherend, had served its purpose well, had given them quite enough; so that they were, to Marcher's sense, no longer hovering about the headwaters of their stream, but had felt their boat pushed sharply off and down the current.

They were literally afloat together; for our gentleman this was marked, quite as marked as that the fortunate cause of it was just the buried treasure of her knowledge. He had with his own hands dug up this little hoard, brought to light—that is to within reach of the dim day constituted by their discretions and privacies—the object of value the hiding-place of which he had, after putting it into the ground himself, so strangely, so long forgotten. The rare luck of his having again just stumbled on the spot made him indifferent to any other question; he would doubtless have devoted more time to the odd accident of his lapse of memory if he hadn't been moved to devote so much to the sweetness, the comfort, as he felt, for the future, that this accident itself had helped to keep fresh. It had never entered into his plan that any one should "know," and mainly for the reason that it wasn't in him to tell any one. That would have been impossible, for nothing but the amusement of a cold world would have waited on it. Since, however, a mysterious fate had opened his mouth betimes, in spite of him, he would count that a compensation and profit by it to the utmost. That the right person *should* know tempered the asperity of his secret more even than his shyness had permitted him to imagine; and May Bartram was clearly right, because—well, because there she was. Her knowledge simply settled it; he would have been sure enough by this time had she been wrong. There was that in his situation, no doubt, that disposed him too much to see her as a mere confidant, taking all her light for him from the fact—the fact only—of her interest in his predicament; from her mercy, sympathy, seriousness, her consent not to regard him as the funniest of the funny. Aware, in fine, that her price for him was just in her giving him this constant sense of his being admirably spared, he was careful to remember that she had also a life of her own, with things that might happen to *her,* things that in friendship one should likewise take account of. Something fairly remarkable came to pass with him, for that matter, in this connexion—something represented by a certain passage of his consciousness, in the suddenest way, from one extreme to the other.

He had thought himself, so long as nobody knew, the most disinterested person in the world, carrying his concentrated burden, his perpetual suspense, ever so quietly, holding his tongue about it, giving others no glimpse of it nor of its effect upon his life, asking of them no allowance and only making on his side all those that were asked. He hadn't disturbed people with the queerness of their having to know a haunted man, though he had had moments of rather special temptation on hearing them say they were forsooth "unsettled." If they were as unsettled as he was—he who had never been settled for an hour in his life—they would know what it meant. Yet it wasn't, all the same, for him to make them, and he listened to them civilly enough. This was why he had such good—though possibly such rather colourless—manners; this was why, above all, he could regard himself, in a greedy world, as decently—as in fact perhaps even a little sublimely—unselfish. Our point is accordingly that he valued this character quite sufficiently to measure his present danger of letting it lapse, against which he promised himself to be much on his guard. He was quite ready, none the less, to be selfish just a little, since surely no more charming occasion for it had come to him. "Just a little," in a word, was just as much as Miss Bartram, taking one day with another, would let him. He never would be in the least coercive, and would keep well before him the lines on which consideration for her—the very highest—ought to proceed. He would thoroughly establish the heads under which her affairs, her requirements, her peculiarities—he went so far as to give them the latitude of that name—would come into their intercourse. All this naturally was a sign of how much he took the intercourse itself for granted. There was nothing more to be done about *that.* It simply existed; had sprung into being with her first penetrating question to him in the autumn light there at Weatherend. The real form it should have taken on the basis that stood out large was the form of their marrying. But the devil in this was that the very basis itself put marrying out of the question. His conviction, his apprehension, his obsession, in short, wasn't a privilege he could invite a woman to share; and that consequence of it was precisely what was the matter with him. Something or other lay in wait for him, amid the twists and the turns of the months and the years, like a crouching beast in the jungle. It signified little whether the crouching beast were destined to slay him or to be slain. The definite point was the inevitable spring of the creature; and the definite lesson from that was that a man of feeling didn't cause himself to be accompanied by a lady on a tiger-hunt. Such was the image under which he had ended by figuring his life.

They had at first, none the less, in the scattered hours spent together, made no allusion to that view of it; which was a sign he was handsomely alert to give that he didn't expect, that he in fact didn't care, always to be talking about it. Such a feature in one's outlook was really like a hump on one's back. The differences it made every minute of the day existed quite independently of discussion. One discussed of course *like* a hunchback, for there was always, if nothing else, the hunchback face. That remained, and she was watching him; but people watched best, as a general thing, in silence, so that such would be predominantly the manner of their vigil. Yet he didn't want, at the same time, to be tense and solemn; tense and solemn was what he imagined he too much showed for with other people. The thing to be, with the one person who knew, was easy and natural—to make the reference rather than be seeming to avoid it, to avoid it rather than be seeming to make it, and to keep it, in any case, familiar, facetious even, rather than pedantic and portentous. Some such consideration as the latter was doubtless in his mind for instance when he wrote pleasantly to Miss Bartram that perhaps the great thing he had so long felt as in the lap of the gods was no more than this circumstance, which touched him so nearly, of her acquiring a house in London. It was the first allusion they had yet again made, needing any other hitherto so little; but when she replied, after having given him the news, that she was by no means satisfied with such a trifle as the climax to so special a suspense, she almost set him wondering if she hadn't even a larger conception of singularity for him than he had for himself. He was at all events destined to become aware little by little, as time went by, that she was all the while looking at his life, judging it, measuring it, in the light of the thing she knew, which grew to be at last, with the consecration of the years, never mentioned between them save as "the real truth" about him. That had always been his own form of reference to it, but she adopted the form so quietly that, looking back at the end of a period, he knew there was no moment at which it was traceable that she had, as he might say, got inside his idea, or exchanged the attitude of beautifully indulging for that of still more beautifully believing him.

It was always open to him to accuse her of seeing him but as the most harmless of maniacs, and this, in the long run—since it covered so much ground—was his easiest description of their friendship. He had a screw loose for her, but she liked him in spite of it and was practically, against the rest of the world, his kind wise keeper, unremunerated but fairly amused and, in the absence of other near ties, not disreputably occupied. The rest of the world of course thought him queer, but she, she only, knew how, and above all why, queer; which was precisely what enabled her to dispose the concealing veil in the right folds. She took his gaiety from him—since it had to pass with them for gaiety—as she took everything else; but she certainly so far justified by her unerring touch his finer sense of the degree to which he had ended by convincing her. *She* at least never spoke of the secret of his life except as "the real truth about you," and she had in fact a wonderful way of making it seem, as such, the secret of her own life too. That was in fine how he so constantly felt her as allowing for him; he couldn't on the whole call it anything else. He allowed for himself, but she, exactly, allowed still more; partly because, better placed for a sight of the matter, she traced his unhappy perversion through reaches of its course into which he could scarce follow it. He knew how he felt, but, besides knowing that, she knew how he *looked* as well; he knew each of the things of importance he was insidiously kept from doing, but she could add up the amount they made, understand how much, with a lighter weight on his spirit, he might have done, and thereby establish how, clever as he was, he fell short. Above all she was in the secret of the difference between the forms he went through—those of his little office under Government, those of caring for his modest patrimony, for his library, for his garden in the country, for the people in London whose invitations he accepted and repaid—and the detachment that reigned beneath them and that made of all behaviour, all that could in the least be called behaviour, a long act of dissimulation. What it had come to was that he wore a mask painted with the social simper, out of the eye-holes of which there looked eyes of an expression not in the least matching the other features. This the stupid world, even after years, had never more than half-discovered. It was only May Bartram who had, and she achieved, by an art indescribable, the feat of at once—or perhaps it was only alternately—meeting the eyes from in front and mingling her own vision, as from over his shoulder, with their peep through the apertures.

So while they grew older together she did watch with him, and so she let this association give shape and colour to her own existence. Beneath *her* forms as well detachment had learned to sit, and behaviour had become for her, in the social sense, a false account of herself. There was but one account of her that would have been true all the while and that she could give straight to nobody, least of all to John Marcher. Her whole attitude was a virtual statement, but the perception of that only seemed called to take its place for him as one of the many things necessarily crowded out of his consciousness. If she had moreover, like himself, to make sacrifices to their real truth, it was to be granted that her compensation might have affected her as more prompt and more natural. They had long periods, in this London time, during which, when they were together, a stranger might have listened to them without in the least pricking up his ears; on the other hand the real truth was equally liable at any moment to rise to the surface, and the auditor would then have wondered indeed what they were talking about. They had from an early hour made up their mind that society was, luckily, unintelligent, and the margin allowed them by this had fairly become one of their commonplaces. Yet there were still moments when the situation turned almost fresh—usually under the effect of some expression drawn from herself. Her expressions doubtless repeated themselves, but her intervals were generous. "What saves us, you know, is that we answer so completely to so usual an appearance: that of the man and woman whose friendship has become such a daily habit—or almost—as to be at last indispensable." That for instance was a remark she had frequently enough had occasion to make, though she had given it at different times different developments. What we are especially concerned with is the turn it happened to take from her one afternoon when he had come to see her in honour of her birthday. This anniversary had fallen on a Sunday, at a season of thick fog and general outward gloom; but he had brought her his customary offering, having known her now long enough to have established a hundred small traditions. It was one of his proofs to himself, the present he made her on her birthday, that he hadn't sunk into real selfishness. It was mostly nothing more than a small trinket, but it was always fine of its kind, and he was regularly careful to pay for it more than he thought he could afford. "Our habit saves you at least, don't you see? because it makes you, after all, for the vulgar, indistinguishable from other men. What's the most inveterate mark of men in general? Why the capacity to spend endless time with dull women—to spend it I won't say without being bored, but without minding that they are, without being driven off at a tangent by it; which comes to the same thing. I'm your dull woman, a part of the daily bread for which you pray at church. That covers your tracks more than anything."

"And what covers yours?" asked Marcher, whom his dull woman could mostly to this extent amuse. "I see of course what you mean by your saving me, in this way and that, so far as other people are concerned—I've seen it all along. Only what is it that saves *you?* I often think, you know, of that."

She looked as if she sometimes thought of that too, but rather in a different way. "Where other people, you mean, are concerned?"

"Well, you're really so in with me, you know—as a sort of result of my being so in with yourself. I mean of my having such an immense regard for you, being so tremendously mindful of all you've done for me. I sometimes ask myself if it's quite fair. Fair I mean to have so involved and—since one may say it—interested you. I almost feel as if you hadn't really had time to do anything else."

"Anything else but be interested?" she asked. "Ah what else does one ever want to be? If I've been 'watching' with you, as we long ago agreed I was to do, watching's always in itself an absorption."

"Oh certainly," John Marcher said, "if you hadn't had your curiosity—! Only doesn't it sometimes come to you as time goes on that your curiosity isn't being particularly repaid?"

May Bartram had a pause. "Do you ask that, by any chance, because you feel at all that yours isn't? I mean because you have to wait so long."

Oh he understood what she meant! "For the thing to happen that never does happen? For the beast to jump out? No, I'm just where I was about it. It isn't a matter as to which I can *choose,* I can decide for a change. It isn't one as to which there *can* be a change. It's in the lap of the gods. One's in the hands of one's law—there one is. As to the form the law will take, the way it will operate, that's its own affair."

"Yes," Miss Bartram replied; "of course one's fate's coming, of course it *has* come in its own form and its own way, all the while. Only, you know, the form and the way in your case were to have been—well, something so exceptional and, as one may say, so particularly *your* own."

Something in this made him look at her with suspicion. "You say 'were to *have* been,' as if in your heart you had begun to doubt."

"Oh!" she vaguely protested.

"As if you believed," he went on, "that nothing will now take place."

She shook her head slowly but rather inscrutably. "You're far from my thought."

He continued to look at her. "What then is the matter with you?"

"Well," she said after another wait, "the matter with me is simply that I'm more sure than ever my curiosity, as you call it, will be but too well repaid."

They were frankly grave now; he had got up from his seat, had turned once more about the little drawing-room to which, year after year, he brought his inevitable topic; in which he had, as he might have said, tasted their intimate community with every sauce, where every object was as familiar to him as the things of his own house and the very carpets were worn with his fitful walk very much as the desks in old counting-houses are worn by the elbows of generations of clerks. The generations of his nervous moods had been at work there, and the place was the written history of his whole middle life. Under the impression of what his friend had just said he knew himself, for some reason, more aware of these things; which made him, after a moment, stop again before her. "Is it possibly that you've grown afraid?"

"Afraid?" He thought, as she repeated the word, that his question had made her, a little, change colour; so that, lest he should have touched on a truth, he explained very kindly: "You remember that that was what you asked *me* long ago—that first day at Weatherend."

"Oh yes, and you told me you didn't know—that I was to see for myself. We've said little about it since, even in so long a time."

"Precisely," Marcher interposed—"quite as if it were too delicate a matter for us to make free with. Quite as if we might find, on pressure, that I *am* afraid. For then," he said, "we shouldn't, should we? quite know what to do."

She had for the time no answer to this question. "There have been days when I thought you were. Only, of course," she added, "there have been days when we have thought almost anything."

"Everything. Oh!" Marcher softly groaned as with a gasp, half-spent, at the face, more uncovered just then than it had been for a long while, of the imagination always with them. It had always had its incalculable moments of glaring out, quite as with the very eyes of the very Beast, and, used as he was to them, they could still draw from him the tribute of a sigh that rose from the depths of his being. All they had thought, first and last, rolled over him; the past seemed to have been reduced to mere barren speculation. This in fact was what the place had just struck him as so full of—the simplification of everything but the state of suspense. That remained only by seeming to hang in the void surrounding it. Even his original fear, if fear it had been, had lost itself in the desert. "I judge, however," he continued, "that you see I'm not afraid now."

"What I see, as I make it out, is that you've achieved something almost unprecedented in the way of getting used to danger. Living with it so long and so closely you've lost your sense of it; you know it's there, but you're indifferent, and you cease even, as of old, to have to whistle in the dark. Considering what the danger is," May Bartram wound up, "I'm bound to say I don't think your attitude could well be surpassed."

John Marcher faintly smiled. "It's heroic?"

"Certainly—call it that."

It was what he would have liked indeed to call it. "I *am* then a man of courage?"

"That's what you were to show me."

He still, however, wondered. "But doesn't the man of courage know what he's afraid of—or *not* afraid of? I don't know *that,* you see. I don't focus it. I can't name it. I only know I'm exposed."

"Yes, but exposed—how shall I say?—so directly. So intimately. That's surely enough."

"Enough to make you feel then—as what we may call the end and the upshot of our watch—that I'm not afraid?"

"You're not afraid. But it isn't," she said, "the end of our watch. That is it isn't the end of yours. You've everything still to see."

"Then why haven't *you?*" he asked. He had had, all along, to-day, the sense of her keeping something back, and he still had it. As this was his first impression of that it quite made a date. The case was the more marked as she didn't at first answer; which in turn made him go on. "You know something I don't." Then his voice, for that of a man of courage, trembled a little. "You know what's to happen." Her silence, with the face she showed, was almost a confession—it made him sure. "You know, and you're afraid to tell me. It's so bad that you're afraid I'll find out."

All this might be true, for she did look as if, unexpectedly to her, he had crossed some mystic line that she had secretly drawn round her. Yet she might, after all, not have worried; and the real climax was that he himself, at all events, needn't. "You'll never find out."

3

It was all to have made, none the less, as I have said, a date; which came out in the fact that again and again, even after long intervals, other things that passed between them wore in relation to this hour but the character of recalls and results. Its immediate effect had been indeed rather to lighten insistence—almost to provoke a reaction; as if their topic had dropped by its own weight and as if moreover, for that matter, Marcher had been visited by one of his occasional warnings against egotism. He had kept up, he felt, and very decently on the whole, his consciousness of the importance of not being selfish, and it was true that he had never sinned in that direction without promptly enough trying to press the scales the other way. He often repaired his fault, the season permitting, by inviting his friend to accompany him to the opera; and it not infrequently thus happened that, to show he didn't wish her to have but one sort of food for her mind, he was the cause of her appearing there with him a dozen nights in the month. It even happened that, seeing her home at such times, he occasionally went in with her to finish, as he called it, the evening, and, the better to make his point, sat down to the frugal but always careful little supper that awaited his pleasure. His point was made, he thought, by his not eternally insisting with her on himself; made for instance, at such hours, when it befell that, her piano at hand and each of them familiar with it, they went over passages of the opera together. It chanced to be on one of these occasions, however, that he reminded her of her not having answered a certain question he had put to her during the talk that had taken place between them on her last birthday. "What is it that saves *you?*"—saved her, he meant, from that appearance of variation from the usual human type. If he had practically escaped remark, as she pretended, by doing, in the most important particular, what most men do—find the answer to life in patching up an alliance of a sort with a woman no better than himself—how had she escaped it, and how could the alliance, such as it was, since they must suppose it had been more or less noticed, have failed to make her rather positively talked about?

"I never said," May Bartram replied, "that it hadn't made me a good deal talked about."

"Ah well then you're not 'saved.' "

"It hasn't been a question for me. If you've had your woman I've had," she said, "my man."

"And you mean that makes you all right?"

Oh it was always as if there were so much to say! "I don't know why it shouldn't make me—humanly, which is what we're speaking of—as right as it makes you."

"I see," Marcher returned. " 'Humanly,' no doubt, as showing that you're living for something. Not, that is, just for me and my secret."

May Bartram smiled. "I don't pretend it exactly shows that I'm not living for you. It's my intimacy with you that's in question."

He laughed as he saw what she meant. "Yes, but since, as you say, I'm only, so far as people make out, ordinary, you're—aren't you? —no more than ordinary either. You help me to pass for a man like another. So if I *am,* as I understand you, you're not compromised. Is that it?"

She had another of her waits, but she spoke clearly enough. "That's it. It's all that concerns me—to help you to pass for a man like another."

He was careful to acknowledge the remark handsomely. "How kind, how beautiful, you are to me! How shall I ever repay you?"

She had her last grave pause, as if there might be a choice of ways. But she chose. "By going on as you are."

It was into this going on as he was that they relapsed, and really for so long a time that the day inevitably came for a further sounding of their depths. These depths, constantly bridged over by a structure firm enough in spite of its lightness and of its occasional oscillation in the somewhat vertiginous air, invited on occasion, in the interest of their nerves, a dropping of the plummet and a measurement of the abyss. A difference had been made moreover, once for all, by the fact that she had all the while not appeared to feel the need of rebutting his charge of an idea within her that she didn't dare to express—a charge uttered just before one of the fullest of their later discussions ended. It had come up for him then that she "knew" something and that what she knew was bad—too bad to tell him. When he had spoken of it as visibly so bad that she was afraid he might find it out, her reply had left the matter too equivocal to be let alone and yet, for Marcher's special sensibility, almost too formidable again to touch. He circled about it at a distance that alternately narrowed and widened and that still wasn't much affected by the consciousness in him that there was nothing she could "know," after all, any better than he did. She had no source of knowledge he hadn't equally—except of course that she might have finer nerves. That was what women had where they were interested; they made out things, where people were concerned, that the people often couldn't have made out for themselves. Their nerves, their sensibility, their imagination, were conductors and revealers, and the beauty of May Bartram was in particular that she had given herself so to his case. He felt in these days what, oddly enough, he had never felt before, the growth of a dread of losing her by some catastrophe—some catastrophe that yet wouldn't at all be *the* catastrophe: partly because she had almost of a sudden begun to strike him as more useful to him than ever yet, and partly by reason of an appearance of uncertainty in her health, coincident and equally new. It was characteristic of the inner detachment he had hitherto so successfully cultivated and to which our whole account of him is a reference, it was characteristic that his complications, such as they were, had never yet seemed so as at this crisis to thicken about him, even to the point of making him ask himself if he were, by any chance, of a truth, within sight or sound, within touch or reach, within the immediate jurisdiction, of the thing that waited.

When the day came, as come it had to, that his friend confessed to him her fear of a deep disorder in her blood, he felt somehow the shadow of a change and the chill of a shock. He immediately began to imagine aggravations and disasters, and above all to think of her peril as the direct menace for himself of personal privation. This indeed gave him one of those partial recoveries of equanimity that were agreeable to him—it showed him that what was still first in his mind was the loss she herself might suffer. "What if she should have to die before knowing, before seeing—?" It would have been brutal, in the early stages of her trouble, to put that question to her; but it had immediately sounded for him to his own concern, and the possibility was what most made him sorry for her. If she did "know," moreover, in the sense of her having had some—what should he think?—mystical irresistible light, this would make the matter not better, but worse, inasmuch as her original adoption of his own curiosity had quite become the basis of her life. She had been living to see what would *be* to be seen, and it would quite lacerate her to have to give up before the accomplishment of the vision. These reflexions, as I say, quickened his generosity; yet, make them as he might, he saw himself, with the lapse of the period, more and more disconcerted. It lapsed for him with a strange steady sweep, and the oddest oddity was that it gave him, independently of the threat of much inconvenience, almost the only positive surprise his career, if career it could be called, had yet offered him. She kept to the house as she had never done; he had to go to her to see her—she could meet him nowhere now, though there was scarce a corner of their loved old London in which she hadn't in the past, at one time or another, done so; and he found her always seated by her fire in the deep old-fashioned chair she was less and less able to leave. He had been struck one day, after an absence exceeding his usual measure, with her suddenly looking much older to him than he had ever thought of her being; then he recognized that the suddenness was all on his side—he had just simply and suddenly noticed. She looked older because inevitably, after so many years, she *was* old, or almost; which was of course true in still greater measure of her companion. If she was old, or almost, John Marcher assuredly was, and yet it was her showing of the lesson, not his own, that brought the truth home to him. His surprises began here; when once they had begun they multiplied; they came rather with a rush: it was as if, in the oddest way in the world, they had all been kept back, sown in a thick cluster, for the late afternoon of life, the time at which for people in general the unexpected has died out.

One of them was that he should have caught himself—for he *had* so done—*really* wondering if the great accident would take form now as nothing more than his being condemned to see this charming woman, this admirable friend, pass away from him. He had never so unreservedly qualified her as while confronted in thought with such a possibility; in spite of which there was small doubt for him that as an answer to his long riddle the mere effacement of even so fine a feature of his situation would be an abject anticlimax. It would represent, as connected with his past attitude, a drop of dignity under the shadow of which his existence could only become the most grotesque of failures. He had been far from holding it a failure—long as he had waited for the appearance that was to make it a success. He had waited for quite another thing, not for such a thing as that. The breath of his good faith came short, however, as he recognised how long he had waited, or how long at least his companion had. That she, at all events, might be recorded as having waited in vain—this affected him sharply, and all the more because of his at first having done little more than amuse himself with the idea. It grew more grave as the gravity of her condition grew, and the state of mind it produced in him, which he himself ended by watching as if it had been some definite disfigurement of his outer person, may pass for another of his surprises. This conjoined itself still with another, the really stupefying consciousness of a question that he would have allowed to shape itself had he dared. What did everything mean—what, that is, did *she* mean, she and her vain waiting and her probable death and the soundless admonition of it all—unless that, at this time of day, it was simply, it was overwhelmingly too late? He had never at any stage of his queer consciousness admitted the whisper of such a correction; he had never till within these last few months been so false to his conviction as not to hold that what was to come to him had time, whether *he* struck himself as having it or not. That at last, at last, he certainly hadn't it, to speak of, or had it but in the scantiest measure—such, soon enough, as things went with him, became the inference with which his old obsession had to reckon: and this it was not helped to do by the more and more confirmed appearance that the great vagueness casting the long shadow in which he had lived had, to attest itself, almost no margin left. Since it was in Time that he was to have met his fate, so it was in Time that his fate was to have acted; and as he waked up to the sense of no longer being young, which was exactly the sense of being stale, just as that, in turn, was the sense of being weak, he waked up to another matter beside. It all hung together; they were subject, he and the great vagueness, to an equal and indivisible law. When the possibilities themselves had accordingly turned stale, when the secret of the gods had grown faint, had perhaps even quite evaporated, that, and that only, was failure. It wouldn't have been failure to be bankrupt, dishonoured, pilloried, hanged; it was failure not to be anything. And so, in the dark valley into which his path had taken its unlooked-for twist, he wondered not a little as he groped. He didn't care what awful crash might overtake him, with what ignominy or what monstrosity he might yet be associated—since he wasn't after all too utterly old to suffer—if it would only be decently proportionate to the posture he had kept, all his life, in the threatened presence of it. He had but one desire left—that he shouldn't have been "sold."

4

Then it was that, one afternoon, while the spring of the year was young and new she met all in her own way his frankest betrayal of these alarms. He had gone in late to see her, but evening hadn't settled and she was presented to him in that long fresh light of waning April days which affects us often with a sadness sharper than the greyest hours of autumn. The week had been warm, the spring was supposed to have begun early, and May Bartram sat, for the first time in the year, without a fire; a fact that, to Marcher's sense, gave the scene of which she formed part a smooth and ultimate look, an air of knowing, in its immaculate order and cold meaningless cheer, that it would never see a fire again. Her own aspect—he could scarce have said why—intensified this note. Almost as white as wax, with the marks and signs in her face as numerous and as fine as if they had been etched by a needle, with soft white draperies relieved by a faded green scarf on the delicate tone of which the years had further refined, she was the picture of a serene and exquisite but impenetrable sphinx, whose head, or indeed all whose person, might have been powdered with silver. She was a sphinx, yet with her white petals and green fronds she might have been a lily too—only an artificial lily, wonderfully imitated and constantly kept, without dust or stain, though not exempt from a slight droop and a complexity of faint creases, under some clear glass bell. The perfection of household care, of high polish and finish, always reigned in her rooms, but they now looked most as if everything had been wound up, tucked in, put away, so that she might sit with folded hands and with nothing more to do. She was "out of it," to Marcher's vision; her work was over; she communicated with him as across some gulf or from some island of rest that she had already reached, and it made him feel strangely abandoned. Was it—or rather wasn't it—that if for so long she had been watching with him the answer to their question must have swum into her ken and taken on its name, so that her occupation was verily gone? He had as much as charged her with this in saying to her, many months before, that she even then knew something she was keeping from him. It was a point he had never since ventured to press, vaguely fearing as he did that it might become a difference, perhaps a disagreement, between them. He had in this later time turned nervous, which was what he in all the other years had never been; and the oddity was that his nervousness should have waited till he had begun to doubt, should have held off so long as he was sure. There was something, it seemed to him, that the wrong word would bring down on his head, something that would so at least ease off his tension. But he wanted not to speak the wrong word; that would make everything ugly. He wanted the knowledge he lacked to drop on him, if drop it could, by its own august weight. If she was to forsake him it was surely for her to take leave. This was why he didn't directly ask her again what she knew; but it was also why, approaching the matter from another side, he said to her in the course of his visit: "What do you regard as the very worst that at this time of day *can* happen to me?"

He had asked her that in the past often enough; they had, with the odd irregular rhythm of their intensities and avoidances, exchanged ideas about it and then had seen the ideas washed away by cool intervals, washed like figures traced in sea-sand. It had ever been the mark of their talk that the oldest allusions in it required but a little dismissal and reaction to come out again, sounding for the hour as new. She could thus at present meet his enquiry quite freshly and patiently. "Oh yes, I've repeatedly thought, only it always seemed to me of old that I couldn't quite make up my mind. I thought of dreadful things, between which it was difficult to choose; and so must you have done."

"Rather! I feel now as if I had scarce done anything else. I appear to myself to have spent my life in thinking of nothing *but* dreadful things. A great many of them I've at different times named to you, but there were others I couldn't name."

"They were too, too dreadful?"

"Too, too dreadful—some of them."

She looked at him a minute, and there came to him as he met it an inconsequent sense that her eyes, when one got their full clearness, were still as beautiful as they had been in youth, only beautiful with a strange cold light—a light that somehow was a part of the effect, if it wasn't rather a part of the cause, of the pale hard sweetness of the season and the hour. "And yet," she said at last, "there are horrors we've mentioned."

It deepened the strangeness to see her, as such a figure in such a picture, talk of "horrors," but she was to do in a few minutes something stranger yet—though even of this he was to take the full measure but afterwards—and the note of it already trembled. It was, for the matter of that, one of the signs that her eyes were having again the high flicker of their prime. He had to admit, however, what she said. "Oh yes, there were times when we did go far." He caught himself in the act of speaking as if it all were over. Well, he wished it were; and the consummation depended for him clearly more and more on his friend.

But she had now a soft smile. "Oh far—!"

It was oddly ironic. "Do you mean you're prepared to go further?"

She was frail and ancient and charming as she continued to look at him, yet it was rather as if she had lost the thread. "Do you consider that we went far?"

"Why I thought it the point you were just making—that we *had* looked most things in the face."

"Including each other?" She still smiled. "But you're quite right.

We've had together great imaginations, often great fears; but some of them have been unspoken."

"Then the worst—we haven't faced that. I *could* face it, I believe, if I knew what you think it. I feel," he explained, "as if I had lost my power to conceive such things." And he wondered if he looked as blank as he sounded. "It's spent."

"Then why do you assume," she asked, "that mine isn't?"

"Because you've given me signs to the contrary. It isn't a question for you of conceiving, imagining, comparing. It isn't a question now of choosing." At last he came out with it. "You know something I don't. You've shown me that before."

These last words had affected her, he made out in a moment, exceedingly, and she spoke with firmness. "I've shown you, my dear, nothing."

He shook his head. "You can't hide it."

"Oh, oh!" May Bartram sounded over what she couldn't hide. It was almost a smothered groan.

"You admitted it months ago, when I spoke of it to you as of something you were afraid I should find out. Your answer was that I couldn't, that I wouldn't, and I don't pretend I have. But you had something therefore in mind, and I now see how it must have been, how it still is, the possibility that, of all possibilities, has settled itself for you as the worst. This," he went on, "is why I appeal to you. I'm only afraid of ignorance to-day—I'm not afraid of knowledge." And then as for a while she said nothing: "What makes me sure is that I see in your face and feel here, in this air and amid these appearances, that you're out of it. You've done. You've had your experience. You leave me to my fate."

Well, she listened, motionless and white in her chair, as on a decision to be made, so that her manner was fairly an avowal, though still, with a small fine inner stiffness, an imperfect surrender. "It *would* be the worst," she finally let herself say. "I mean the thing I've never said."

It hushed him a moment. "More monstrous than all the monstrosities we've named?"

"More monstrous. Isn't that what you sufficiently express," she asked, "in calling it the worst?"

Marcher thought. "Assuredly—if you mean, as I do, something

that includes all the loss and all the shame that are thinkable."

"It would if it *should* happen," said May Bartram. "What we're speaking of, remember, is only my idea."

"It's your belief," Marcher returned. "That's enough for me. I feel your beliefs are right. Therefore if, having this one, you give me no more light on it, you abandon me."

"No, no!" she repeated. "I'm with you—don't you see?—still." And as to make it more vivid to him she rose from her chair—a movement she seldom risked in these days—and showed herself, all draped and all soft, in her fairness and slimness. "I haven't forsaken you."

It was really, in its effort against weakness, a generous assurance, and had the success of the impulse not, happily, been great, it would have touched him to pain more than to pleasure. But the cold charm in her eyes had spread, as she hovered before him, to all the rest of her person, so that it was for the minute almost a recovery of youth. He couldn't pity her for that; he could only take her as she showed—as capable even yet of helping him. It was as if, at the same time, her light might at any instant go out; wherefore he must make the most of it. There passed before him with intensity the three or four things he wanted most to know; but the question that came of itself to his lips really covered the others. "Then tell me if I shall consciously suffer."

She promptly shook her head. "Never!"

It confirmed the authority he imputed to her, and it produced on him an extraordinary effect. "Well, what's better than that? Do you call that the worst?"

"You think nothing is better?" she asked.

She seemed to mean something so special that he again sharply wondered, though still with the dawn of a prospect of relief. "Why not, if one doesn't *know?*" After which, as their eyes, over his question, met in a silence, the dawn deepened and something to his purpose came prodigiously out of her very face. His own, as he took it in, suddenly flushed to the forehead, and he gasped with the force of a perception to which, on the instant, everything fitted. The sound of his gasp filled the air; then he became articulate. "I see—if I don't suffer!"

In her own look, however, was doubt. "You see what?"

"Why what you mean—what you've always meant."

She again shook her head. "What I mean isn't what I've always meant. It's different."

"It's something new?"

She hung back from it a little. "Something new. It's not what you think. I see what you think."

His divination drew breath then; only her correction might be wrong. "It isn't that I *am* a blockhead?" he asked between faintness and grimness. "It isn't that it's all a mistake?"

"A mistake?" she pityingly echoed. *That* possibility, for her, he saw, would be monstrous; and if she guaranteed him the immunity from pain it would accordingly not be what she had in mind. "Oh no," she declared; "it's nothing of that sort. You've been right."

Yet he couldn't help asking himself if she weren't, thus pressed, speaking but to save him. It seemed to him he should be most in a hole if his history should prove all a platitude. "Are you telling me the truth, so that I shan't have been a bigger idiot than I can bear to know? I *haven't* lived with a vain imagination, in the most besotted illusion? I haven't waited but to see the door shut in my face?"

She shook her head again. "However the case stands *that* isn't the truth. Whatever the reality, it *is* a reality. The door isn't shut. The door's open," said May Bartram.

"Then something's to come?"

She waited once again, always with her cold sweet eyes on him. "It's never too late." She had, with her gliding step, diminished the distance between them, and she stood nearer to him, close to him, a minute, as if still charged with the unspoken. Her movement might have been for some finer emphasis on what she was at once hesitating and deciding to say. He had been standing by the chimney-piece, fireless and sparely adorned, a small perfect old French clock and two morsels of rosy Dresden constituting all its furniture; and her hand grasped the shelf while she kept him waiting, grasped it a little as for support and encouragement. She only kept him waiting, however; that is he only waited. It had become suddenly, from her movement and attitude, beautiful and vivid to him that she had something more to give him; her wasted face delicately shone with it—it glittered almost as with the white lustre of silver in her expression. She was right, incontestably, for what he saw in her face was the truth, and strangely, without consequence, while their talk of it as dreadful was still in the air, she appeared to present it as inordinately soft. This, prompting bewilderment, made him but gape the more gratefully for her revelation, so that they continued for some minutes silent, her face shining at him, her contact imponderably pressing, and his stare all kind but all expectant. The end, none the less, was that what he had expected failed to come to him. Something else took place instead, which seemed to consist at first in the mere closing of her eyes. She gave way at the same instant to a slow fine shudder, and though he remained staring—though he stared in fact but the harder—turned off and regained her chair. It was the end of what she had been intending, but it left him thinking only of that.

"Well, you don't say—?"

She had touched in her passage a bell near the chimney and had sunk back strangely pale. "I'm afraid I'm too ill."

"Too ill to tell me?" It sprang up sharp to him, and almost to his lips, the fear she might die without giving him light. He checked himself in time from so expressing his question, but she answered as if she had heard the words.

"Don't you know—now?"

" 'Now'—?" She had spoken as if some difference had been made within the moment. But her maid, quickly obedient to her bell, was already with them. "I know nothing." And he was afterwards to say to himself that he must have spoken with odious impatience, such an impatience as to show that, supremely disconcerted, he washed his hands of the whole question.

"Oh!" said May Bartram.

"Are you in pain?" he asked as the woman went to her.

"No," said May Bartram.

Her maid, who had put an arm round her as if to take her to her room, fixed on him eyes that appealingly contradicted her; in spite of which, however, he showed once more his mystification. "What then has happened?"

She was once more, with her companion's help, on her feet, and, feeling withdrawal imposed on him, he had blankly found his hat and gloves and had reached the door. Yet he waited for her answer. "What *was* to," she said.

5

He came back the next day, but she was then unable to see him, and as it was literally the first time this had occurred in the long stretch of their acquaintance he turned away, defeated and sore, almost angry—or feeling at least that such a break in their custom was really the beginning of the end—and wandered alone with his thoughts, especially with the one he was least able to keep down. She was dying and he would lose her; she was dying and his life would end. He stopped in the Park, into which he had passed, and stared before him at his recurrent doubt. Away from her the doubt pressed again; in her presence he had believed her, but as he felt his forlornness he threw himself into the explanation that, nearest at hand, had most of a miserable warmth for him and least of a cold torment. She had deceived him to save him—to put him off with something in which he should be able to rest. What could the thing that was to happen to him be, after all, but just this thing that had begun to happen? Her dying, her death, his consequent solitude—*that* was what he had figured as the Beast in the Jungle, that was what had been in the lap of the gods. He had had her word for it as he left her—what else on earth could she have meant? It wasn't a thing of a monstrous order; not a fate rare and distinguished; not a stroke of fortune that overwhelmed and immortalised; it had only the stamp of the common doom. But poor Marcher at this hour judged the common doom sufficient. It would serve his turn, and even as the consummation of infinite waiting he would bend his pride to accept it. He sat down on a bench in the twilight. He hadn't been a fool. Something had *been,* as she had said, to come. Before he rose indeed it had quite struck him that the final fact really matched with the long avenue through which he had had to reach it. As sharing his suspense and as giving herself all, giving her life, to bring it to an end, she had come with him every step of the way. He had lived by her aid, and to leave her behind would be cruelly, damnably to miss her. What could be more overwhelming than that?

Well, he was to know within the week, for though she kept him a while at bay, left him restless and wretched during a series of days on each of which he asked about her only again to have to turn away, she ended his trial by receiving him where she had always received him. Yet she had been brought out at some hazard into the presence of so many of the things that were, consciously, vainly, half their past, and there was scant service left in the gentleness of her mere desire, all too visible, to check his obsession and wind up his long trouble. That was clearly what she wanted, the one thing more for her own peace while she could still put out her hand. He was so affected by her state that, once seated by her chair, he was moved to let everything go; it was she herself therefore who brought him back, took up again, before she dismissed him, her last word of the other time. She showed how she wished to leave their business in order. "I'm not sure you understood. You've nothing to wait for more. It *has* come."

Oh how he looked at her! "Really?"

"Really."

"The thing that, as you said, *was* to?"

"The thing that we began in our youth to watch for."

Face to face with her once more he believed her; it was a claim to which he had so abjectly little to oppose. "You mean that it has come as a positive definite occurrence, with a name and a date?"

"Positive. Definite. I don't know about the 'name,' but oh with a date!"

He found himself again too helplessly at sea. "But come in the night—come and passed me by?"

May Bartram had her strange faint smile. "Oh no, it hasn't passed you by!"

"But if I haven't been aware of it and it hasn't touched me—?"

"Ah your not being aware of it"—and she seemed to hesitate an instant to deal with this—"your not being aware of it is the strangeness *in* the strangeness. It's the wonder *of* the wonder." She spoke as with the softness almost of a sick child, yet now at last, at the end of all, with the perfect straightness of a sibyl. She visibly knew that she knew, and the effect on him was of something co-ordinate, in its high character, with the law that had ruled him. It was the true voice of the law; so on her lips would the law itself have sounded. "It *has* touched you," she went on. "It has done its office. It has made you all its own."

"So utterly without my knowing it?"

"So utterly without your knowing it." His hand, as he leaned to her, was on the arm of her chair, and, dimly smiling always now, she placed her own on it. "It's enough if *I* know it."

"Oh!" he confusedly breathed, as she herself of late so often had done.

"What I long ago said is true. You'll never know now, and I think you ought to be content. You've *had* it," said May Bartram.

"But had what?"

"Why what was to have marked you out. The proof of your law. It has acted. I'm too glad," she then bravely added, "to have been able to see what it's *not.*"

He continued to attach his eyes to her, and with the sense that it was all beyond him, and that *she* was too, he would still have sharply challenged her hadn't he so felt it an abuse of her weakness to do more than take devoutly what she gave him, take it hushed as to a revelation. If he did speak, it was out of the foreknowledge of his loneliness to come. "If you're glad of what it's 'not' it might then have been worse?"

She turned her eyes away, she looked straight before her; with which after a moment: "Well, you know our fears."

He wondered. "It's something then we never feared?"

On this slowly she turned to him. "Did we ever dream, with all our dreams, that we should sit and talk of it thus?"

He tried for a little to make out that they had; but it was as if their dreams, numberless enough, were in solution in some thick cold mist through which thought lost itself. "It might have been that we couldn't talk?"

"Well"—she did her best for him—"not from this side. This, you see," she said, "is the *other* side."

"I think," poor Marcher returned, "that all sides are the same to me." Then, however, as she gently shook her head in correction: "We mightn't, as it were, have got across—?"

"To where we are—no. We're *here*"—she made her weak emphasis.

"And much good does it do us!" was her friend's frank comment.

"It does us the good it can. It does us the good that *it* isn't here. It's past, it's behind," said May Bartram. "Before—" but her voice dropped.

He had got up, not to tire her, but it was hard to combat his yearning. She after all told him nothing but that his light had failed —which he knew well enough without her. "Before—?" he blankly echoed.

"Before, you see, it was always to *come.* That kept it present."

"Oh I don't care what comes now! Besides," Marcher added, "it seems to me I liked it better present, as you say, than I can like it absent with *your* absence."

"Oh mine!"—and her pale hands made light of it.

"With the absence of everything." He had a dreadful sense of standing there before her for—so far as anything but this proved, this bottomless drop was concerned—the last time of their life. It rested on him with a weight he felt he could scarce bear, and this weight it apparently was that still pressed out what remained in him of speakable protest. "I believe you; but I can't begin to pretend I understand. *Nothing,* for me, is past; nothing *will* pass till I pass myself, which I pray my stars may be as soon as possible. Say, however," he added, "that I've eaten my cake, as you contend, to the last crumb—how can the thing I've never felt at all be the thing I was marked out to feel?"

She met him perhaps less directly, but she met him unperturbed. "You take your 'feelings' for granted. You were to suffer your fate. That was not necessarily to know it."

"How in the world—when what is such knowledge but suffering?"

She looked up at him a while in silence. "No—you don't understand."

"I suffer," said John Marcher.

"Don't, don't!"

"How can I help at least *that?"*

"Don't!" May Bartram repeated.

She spoke it in a tone so special, in spite of her weakness, that he stared an instant—stared as if some light, hitherto hidden, had shimmered across his vision. Darkness again closed over it, but the gleam had already become for him an idea. "Because I haven't the right—?"

"Don't *know*—when you needn't," she mercifully urged. "You needn't—for we shouldn't."

"Shouldn't?" If he could but know what she meant!

"No—it's too much."

"Too much?" he still asked but, with a mystification that was the next moment of a sudden to give way. Her words, if they meant something, affected him in this light—the light also of her wasted face—as meaning *all,* and the sense of what knowledge had been for herself came over him with a rush which broke through into a question. "Is it of that then you're dying?"

She but watched him, gravely at first, as to see, with this, where he was, and she might have seen something or feared something that moved her sympathy. "I would live for you still—if I could." Her eyes closed for a little, as if, withdrawn into herself, she were for a last time trying. "But I can't!" she said as she raised them again to take leave of him.

She couldn't indeed, as but too promptly and sharply appeared, and he had no vision of her after this that was anything but darkness and doom. They had parted for ever in that strange talk; access to her chamber of pain, rigidly guarded, was almost wholly forbidden him; he was feeling now moreover, in the face of doctors, nurses, the two or three relatives attracted doubtless by the presumption of what she had to "leave," how few were the rights, as they were called in such cases, that he had to put forward, and how odd it might even seem that their intimacy shouldn't have given him more of them. The stupidest fourth cousin had more, even though she had been nothing in such a person's life. She had been a feature of features in *his,* for what else was it to have been so indispensable? Strange beyond saying were the ways of existence, baffling for him the anomaly of his lack, as he felt it to be, of producible claim. A woman might have been, as it were, everything to him, and it might yet present him in no connexion that any one seemed held to recognise. If this was the case in these closing weeks it was the case more sharply on the occasion of the last offices rendered, in the great grey London cemetery, to what had been mortal, to what had been precious, in his friend. The concourse at her grave was not numerous, but he saw himself treated as scarce more nearly concerned with it than if there had been a thousand others. He was in short from this moment face to face with the fact that he was to profit extraordinarily little by the interest May Bartram had taken in him. He couldn't quite have said what he expected, but he hadn't surely expected this approach to a double privation. Not only had her interest failed him, but he seemed to feel himself unattended—and for a reason he couldn't seize—by the distinction, the dignity, the propriety, if nothing else, of the man markedly bereaved. It was as if in the view of society he had not *been* markedly bereaved, as if there still failed some sign or proof of it, and as if none the less his character could never be affirmed nor the deficiency ever made up. There were moments as the weeks went by when he would have liked, by some almost aggressive act, to take his stand on the intimacy of his loss, in order that it *might* be questioned and his retort, to the relief of his spirit, so recorded; but the moments of an irritation more helpless followed fast on these, the moments during which, turning things over with a good conscience but with a bare horizon, he found himself wondering if he oughtn't to have begun, so to speak, further back.

He found himself wondering indeed at many things, and this last speculation had others to keep it company. What could he have done, after all, in her lifetime, without giving them both, as it were, away? He couldn't have made known she was watching him, for that would have published the superstition of the Beast. This was what closed his mouth now—now that the Jungle had been threshed to vacancy and that the Beast had stolen away. It sounded too foolish and too flat; the difference for him in this particular, the extinction in his life of the element of suspense, was such as in fact to surprise him. He could scarce have said what the effect resembled; the abrupt cessation, the positive prohibition, of music perhaps, more than anything else, in some place all adjusted and all accustomed to sonority and to attention. If he could at any rate have conceived lifting the veil from his image at some moment of the past (what had he done, after all, if not lift it to *her?*) so to do this to-day, to talk to people at large of the Jungle cleared and confide to them that he now felt it as safe, would have been not only to see them listen as to a goodwife's tale, but really to hear himself tell one. What it presently came to in truth was that poor Marcher waded through his beaten grass, where no life stirred, where no breath sounded, where no evil eye seemed to gleam from a possible lair, very much as if vaguely looking for the Beast, and still more as if acutely missing it. He walked about in an existence that had grown strangely more spacious, and, stopping fitfully in places where the undergrowth of life struck him as closer, asked himself yearningly, wondered secretly and sorely, if it would have lurked here or there.

It would have at all events *sprung;* what was at least complete was his belief in the truth itself of the assurance given him. The change from his old sense to his new was absolute and final: what was to happen *had* so absolutely and finally happened that he was as little able to know a fear for his future as to know a hope; so absent in short was any question of anything still to come. He was to live entirely with the other question, that of his unidentified past, that of his having to see his fortune impenetrably muffled and masked.

The torment of this vision became then his occupation; he couldn't perhaps have consented to live but for the possibility of guessing. She had told him, his friend, not to guess; she had forbidden him, so far as he might, to know, and she had even in a sort denied the power in him to learn: which were so many things, precisely, to deprive him of rest. It wasn't that he wanted, he argued for fairness, that anything past and done should repeat itself; it was only that he shouldn't, as an anticlimax, have been taken sleeping so sound as not to be able to win back by an effort of thought the lost stuff of consciousness. He declared to himself at moments that he would either win it back or have done with consciousness for ever; he made this idea his one motive in fine, made it so much his passion that none other, to compare with it, seemed ever to have touched him. The lost stuff of consciousness became thus for him as a strayed or stolen child to an unappeasable father; he hunted it up and down very much as if he were knocking at doors and enquiring of the police. This was the spirit in which, inevitably, he set himself to travel; he started on a journey that was to be as long as he could make it; it danced before him that, as the other side of the globe couldn't possibly have less to say to him, it might, by a possibility of suggestion, have more. Before he quitted London, however, he made a pilgrimage to May Bartram's grave, took his way to it through the endless avenues of the grim suburban metropolis, sought it out in the wilderness of tombs, and, though he had come but for the renewal of the act of farewell, found himself, when he had at last stood by it, beguiled into long intensities. He stood for an hour, powerless to turn away and yet powerless to penetrate the darkness of death; fixing with his eyes her inscribed name and date, beating his forehead against the fact of the secret they kept, drawing his breath, while he waited, as if some sense would in pity of him rise from the stones. He kneeled on the stones, however, in vain; they kept what they concealed; and if the face of the tomb did become a face for him it was because her two names became a pair of eyes that didn't know him. He gave them a last long look, but no palest light broke.

6

He stayed away, after this, for a year; he visited the depths of Asia, spending himself on scenes of romantic interest, of superlative sanctity; but what was present to him everywhere was that for a man who had known what *he* had known the world was vulgar and vain. The state of mind in which he had lived for so many years shone out to him, in reflexion, as a light that coloured and refined, a light beside which the glow of the East was garish, cheap and thin. The terrible truth was that he had lost—with everything else—a distinction as well; the things he saw couldn't help being common when he had become common to look at them. He was simply now one of them himself—he was in the dust, without a peg for the sense of difference; and there were hours when, before the temples of gods and the sepulchres of kings, his spirit turned for nobleness of association to the barely discriminated slab in the London suburb. That had become for him, and more intensely with time and distance, his one witness of a past glory. It was all that was left to him for proof or pride, yet the past glories of Pharaohs were nothing to him as he thought of it. Small wonder then that he came back to it on the morrow of his return. He was drawn there this time as irresistibly as the other, yet with a confidence, almost, that was doubtless the effect of the many months that had elapsed. He had lived, in spite of himself, into his change of feeling, and in wandering over the earth had wandered, as might be said, from the circumference to the centre of his desert. He had settled to his safety and accepted perforce his extinction; figuring to himself, with some colour, in the likeness of certain little old men he remembered to have seen, of whom, all meagre and wizened as they might look, it was related that they had in their time fought twenty duels or been loved by ten princesses. They indeed had been wondrous for others while he was but wondrous for himself; which, however, was exactly the cause of his haste to renew the wonder by getting back, as he might put it, into his own presence. That had quickened his steps and checked his delay. If his visit was prompt it was because he had been separated so long from the part of himself that alone he now valued.

It's accordingly not false to say that he reached his goal with a certain elation and stood there again with a certain assurance. The creature beneath the sod *knew* of his rare experience, so that, strangely now, the place had lost for him its mere blankness of expression. It met him in mildness—not, as before, in mockery; it wore for him the air of conscious greeting that we find, after absence, in things that have closely belonged to us and which seem to confess of themselves to the connexion. The plot of ground, the graven tablet, the tended flowers affected him so as belonging to him that he resembled for the hour a contented landlord reviewing a piece of property. Whatever had happened—well, had happened. He had not come back this time with the vanity of that question, his former worrying "What, *what?*" now practically so spent. Yet he would none the less never again so cut himself off from the spot; he would come back to it every month, for if he did nothing else by its aid he at least held up his head. It thus grew for him, in the oddest way, a positive resource; he carried out his idea of periodical returns, which took their place at last among the most inveterate of his habits. What it all amounted to, oddly enough, was that in his finally so simplified world this garden of death gave him the few square feet of earth on which he could still most live. It was as if, being nothing anywhere else for any one, nothing even for himself, he were just everything here, and if not for a crowd of witnesses or indeed for any witness but John Marcher, then by clear right of the register that he could scan like an open page. The open page was the tomb of his friend, and *there* were the facts of the past, there the truth of his life, there the backward reaches in which he could lose himself. He did this from time to time with such effect that he seemed to wander through the old years with his hand in the arm of a companion who was, in the most extraordinary manner, his other, his younger self; and to wander, which was more extraordinary yet, round and round a third presence—not wandering she, but stationary, still, whose eyes, turning with his revolution, never ceased to follow him, and whose seat was his point, so to speak, of orientation. Thus in short he settled to live—feeding all on the sense that he once *had* lived, and dependent on it not alone for a support but for an identity.

It sufficed him in its way for months and the year elapsed; it would doubtless even have carried him further but for an accident, superficially slight, which moved him, quite in another direction, with a force beyond any of his impressions of Egypt or of India. It was a thing of the merest chance—the turn, as he afterwards felt, of a hair, though he was indeed to live to believe that if light hadn't come to him in this particular fashion it would still have come in another. He was to live to believe this, I say, though he was not to live, I may not less definitely mention, to do much else. We allow him at any rate the benefit of the conviction, struggling up for him at the end, that, whatever might have happened or not happened, he would have come round of himself to the light. The incident of an autumn day had put the match to the train laid from of old by his misery. With the light before him he knew that even of late his ache had only been smothered. It was strangely drugged, but it throbbed; at the touch it began to bleed. And the touch, in the event, was the face of a fellow mortal. This face, one grey afternoon when the leaves were thick in the alleys, looked into Marcher's own, at the cemetery, with an expression like the cut of a blade. He felt it, that is, so deep down that he winced at the steady thrust. The person who so mutely assaulted him was a figure he had noticed, on reaching his own goal, absorbed by a grave a short distance away, a grave apparently fresh, so that the emotion of the visitor would probably match it for frankness. This fact alone forbade further attention, though during the time he stayed he remained vaguely conscious of his neighbour, a middle-aged man apparently, in mourning, whose bowed back, among the clustered monuments and mortuary yews, was constantly presented. Marcher's theory that these were elements in contact with which he himself revived, had suffered, on this occasion, it may be granted, a marked, an excessive check. The autumn day was dire for him as none had recently been, and he rested with a heaviness he had not yet known on the low stone table that bore May Bartram's name. He rested without power to move, as if some spring in him, some spell vouchsafed, had suddenly been broken for ever. If he could have done that moment as he wanted he would simply have stretched himself on the slab that was ready to take him, treating it as a place prepared to receive his last sleep. What in all the wide world had he now to keep awake for? He stared before him with the question, and it was then that, as one of the cemetery walks passed near him, he caught the shock of the face.

His neighbour at the other grave had withdrawn, as he himself, with force enough in him, would have done by now, and was advancing along the path on his way to one of the gates. This brought him close, and his pace was slow, so that—and all the more as there was a kind of hunger on his look—the two men were for a minute directly confronted. Marcher knew him at once for one of the deeply stricken—a perception so sharp that nothing else in the picture comparatively lived, neither his dress, his age, nor his presumable character and class; nothing lived but the deep ravage of the features he showed. He *showed* them—that was the point; he was moved, as he passed, by some impulse that was either a signal for sympathy or, more possibly, a challenge to an opposed sorrow. He might already have been aware of our friend, might at some previous hour have noticed in him the smooth habit of the scene, with which the state of his own senses so scantly consorted, and might thereby have been stirred as by an overt discord. What Marcher was at all events conscious of was in the first place that the image of scarred passion presented to him was conscious too—of something that profaned the air; and in the second that, roused, startled, shocked, he was yet the next moment looking after it, as it went, with envy. The most extraordinary thing that had happened to him—though he had given that name to other matters as well—took place, after his immediate vague stare, as a consequence of this impression. The stranger passed, but the raw glare of his grief remained, making our friend wonder in pity what wrong, what wound it expressed, what injury not to be healed. What had the man *had,* to make him by the loss of it so bleed and yet live?

Something—and this reached him with a pang—that *he,* John Marcher, hadn't; the proof of which was precisely John Marcher's arid end. No passion had ever touched him, for this was what passion meant; he had survived and maundered and pined, but where had been *his* deep ravage? The extraordinary thing we speak of was the sudden rush of the result of this question. The sight that had just met his eyes named to him, as in letters of quick flame, something he had utterly, insanely missed, and what he had missed made these things a train of fire, made them mark themselves in an anguish of inward throbs. He had seen *outside* of his life, not learned it within, the way a woman was mourned when she had been loved for herself: such was the force of his conviction of the meaning of the stranger's face, which still flared for him as a smoky torch. It hadn't come to him, the knowledge, on the wings of experience; it had brushed him, jostled him, upset him, with the disrespect of chance, the insolence of accident. Now that the illumination had begun, however, it blazed to the zenith, and what he presently stood there gazing at was the sounded void of his life. He gazed, he drew breath, in pain; he turned in his dismay, and, turning, he had before him in sharper incision than ever the open page of his story. The name on the table smote him as the passage of his neighbour had done, and what it said to him, full in the face, was that *she* was what he had missed. This was the awful thought, the answer to all the past, the vision at the dread clearness of which he grew as cold as the stone beneath him. Everything fell together, confessed, explained, overwhelmed; leaving him most of all stupefied at the blindness he had cherished. The fate he had been marked for he had met with a vengeance—he had emptied the cup to the lees; he had been the man of his time, *the* man, to whom nothing on earth was to have happened. That was the rare stroke—that was his visitation. So he saw it, as we say, in pale horror, while the pieces fitted and fitted. So *she* had seen it while he didn't, and so she served at this hour to drive the truth home. It was the truth, vivid and monstrous, that all the while he had waited the wait was itself his portion. This the companion of his vigil had at a given moment made out, and she had then offered him the chance to baffle his doom. One's doom, however, was never baffled, and on the day she told him his own had come down she had seen him but stupidly stare at the escape she offered him.

The escape would have been to love her; then, *then* he would have lived. *She* had lived—who could say now with what passion?—since she had loved him for himself; whereas he had never thought of her (ah how it hugely glared at him!) but in the chill of his egotism and the light of her use. Her spoken words came back to him—the chain stretched and stretched. The Beast had lurked indeed, and the Beast, at its hour, had sprung; it had sprung in that twilight of the cold April when, pale, ill, wasted, but all beautiful, and perhaps even then recoverable, she had risen from her chair to stand before him and let him imaginably guess. It had sprung as he didn't guess; it had sprung as she hopelessly turned from him, and the mark, by the time he left her, had fallen where it *was* to fall. He had justified his fear and achieved his fate; he had failed, with the last exactitude, of all he was to fail of; and a moan now rose to his lips as he remembered she had prayed he mightn't know. This horror of waking—*this* was knowledge, knowledge under the breath of which the very tears in his eyes seemed to freeze. Through them, none the less, he tried to fix it and hold it; he kept it there before him so that he might feel the pain. That at least, belated and bitter, had something of the taste of life. But the bitterness suddenly sickened him, and it was as if, horribly, he saw, in the truth, in the cruelty of his image, what had been appointed and done. He saw the Jungle of his life and saw the lurking Beast; then, while he looked, perceived it, as by a stir of the air, rise, huge and hideous, for the leap that was to settle him. His eyes darkened—it was close; and, instinctively turning, in his hallucination, to avoid it, he flung himself, face down, on the tomb.

1903

The Necklace

GUY DE MAUPASSANT

[1850–1893]

She was one of those pretty and charming girls who are sometimes, as if by a mistake of destiny, born in a family of clerks. She had no dowry, no expectations, no means of being known, understood, loved, wedded by any rich and distinguished man; and she let herself be married to a little clerk at the Ministry of Public Instruction.

She dressed plainly because she could not dress well, but she was as unhappy as though she had really fallen from her proper station, since with women there is neither caste nor rank: and beauty, grace, and charm act instead of family and birth. Natural fineness, instinct for what is elegant, suppleness of wit, are the sole hierarchy, and make from women of the people the equals of the very greatest ladies.

She suffered ceaselessly, feeling herself born for all the delicacies and all the luxuries. She suffered from the poverty of her dwelling, from the wretched look of the walls, from the worn-out chairs, from the ugliness of the curtains. All those things, of which another woman of her rank would never even have been conscious, tortured her and made her angry. The sight of the little Breton peasant who did her humble housework aroused in her regrets which were despairing, and distracted dreams. She thought of the silent antechambers hung with Oriental tapestry, lit by tall bronze candelabra, and of the two great footmen in knee breeches who sleep in the big armchairs, made drowsy by the heavy warmth of the hot-air stove. She thought of the long *salons* fitted up with ancient silk, of the delicate furniture carrying priceless curiosities, and of the coquettish perfumed boudoirs made for talks at five o'clock with intimate friends, with men famous and sought after, whom all women envy and whose attention they all desire.

When she sat down to dinner, before the round table covered with a tablecloth three days old, opposite her husband, who uncovered the soup tureen and declared with an enchanted air, "Ah, the good *pot-au-feu!* I don't know anything better than that," she thought of dainty dinners, of shining silverware, of tapestry which peopled the walls with ancient personages and with strange birds flying in the midst of a fairy forest; and she thought of delicious dishes served on marvelous plates, and of the whispered gallantries which you listen to with a sphinxlike smile, while you are eating the pink flesh of a trout or the wings of a quail.

She had no dresses, no jewels, nothing. And she loved nothing but that; she felt made for that. She would so have liked to please, to be envied, to be charming, to be sought after.

She had a friend, a former schoolmate at the convent, who was rich, and whom she did not like to go and see any more, because she suffered so much when she came back.

But one evening, her husband returned home with a triumphant air, and holding a large envelope in his hand.

"There," said he. "Here is something for you."

She tore the paper sharply, and drew out a printed card which bore these words:

"The Minister of Public Instruction and Mme. Georges Ramponneau request the honor of M. and Mme. Loisel's company at the palace of the Ministry on Monday evening, January eighteenth."

Instead of being delighted, as her husband hoped, she threw the invitation on the table with disdain, murmuring:

"What do you want me to do with that?"

"But, my dear, I thought you would be glad. You never go out, and this is such a fine opportunity. I had awful trouble to get it. Everyone wants to go; it is very select, and they are not giving many invitations to clerks. The whole official world will be there."

She looked at him with an irritated glance, and said, impatiently:

"And what do you want me to put on my back?"

He had not thought of that; he stammered:

"Why, the dress you go to the theater in. It looks very well, to me."

He stopped, distracted, seeing his wife was crying. Two great tears descended slowly from the corners of her eyes toward the corners of her mouth. He stuttered:

"What's the matter? What's the matter?"

But, by violent effort, she had conquered her grief, and she replied, with a calm voice, while she wiped her wet cheeks:

"Nothing. Only I have no dress and therefore I can't go to this ball. Give your card to some colleague whose wife is better equipped than I."

He was in despair. He resumed:

"Come, let us see, Mathilde. How much would it cost, a suitable dress, which you could use on other occasions, something very simple?"

She reflected several seconds, making her calculations and wondering also what sum she could ask without drawing on herself an immediate refusal and a frightened exclamation from the economical clerk.

Finally, she replied, hesitatingly:

"I don't know exactly, but I think I could manage it with four hundred francs."

He had grown a little pale, because he was laying aside just that amount to buy a gun and treat himself to a little shooting next summer on the plain of Nanterre, with several friends who went to shoot larks down there, of a Sunday.

But he said:

"All right. I will give you four hundred francs. And try to have a pretty dress."

The day of the ball drew near, and Mme. Loisel seemed sad, uneasy, anxious. Her dress was ready, however. Her husband said to her one evening:

"What is the matter? Come, you've been so queer these last three days."

And she answered:

"It annoys me not to have a single jewel, not a single stone, nothing to put on. I shall look like distress. I should almost rather not go at all."

He resumed:

"You might wear natural flowers. It's very stylish at this time of the year. For ten francs you can get two or three magnificent roses."

She was not convinced.

"No; there's nothing more humiliating than to look poor among other women who are rich."

But her husband cried:

"How stupid you are! Go look up your friend Mme. Forestier, and ask her to lend you some jewels. You're quite thick enough with her to do that."

She uttered a cry of joy:

"It's true. I never thought of it."

The next day she went to her friend and told of her distress.

Mme. Forestier went to a wardrobe with a glass door, took out a large jewel-box, brought it back, opened it, and said to Mme. Loisel:

"Choose, my dear."

She saw first of all some bracelets, then a pearl necklace, then a Venetian cross, gold and precious stones of admirable workmanship. She tried on the ornaments before the glass, hesitated, could not make up her mind to part with them, to give them back. She kept asking:

"Haven't you any more?"

"Why, yes. Look. I don't know what you like."

All of a sudden she discovered, in a black satin box, a superb necklace of diamonds, and her heart began to beat with an immoderate desire. Her hands trembled as she took it. She fastened it around her throat, outside her high-necked dress, and remained lost in ecstasy at the sight of herself.

Then she asked, hesitating, filled with anguish:

"Can you lend me that, only that?"

"Why, yes, certainly."

She sprang upon the neck of her friend, kissed her passionately, then fled with her treasure.

The day of the ball arrived. Mme. Loisel made a great success. She was prettier than them all, elegant, gracious, smiling, and crazy with joy. All the men looked at her, asked her name, endeavored to be introduced. All the attachés of the Cabinet wanted to waltz with her. She was remarked by the minister himself.

She danced with intoxication, with passion, made drunk by pleasure, forgetting all, in the triumph of her beauty, in the glory of her success, in a sort of cloud of happiness composed of all this homage, of all this admiration, of all these awakened desires, and of that sense of complete victory which is so sweet to a woman's heart.

She went away about four o'clock in the morning. Her husband had been sleeping since midnight, in a little deserted anteroom, with three other gentlemen whose wives were having a very good time. He threw over her shoulders the wraps which he had brought, modest wraps of common life, whose poverty contrasted with the elegance of the ball dress. She felt this, and wanted to escape so as not to be remarked by the other women, who were enveloping themselves in costly furs.

Loisel held her back.

"Wait a bit. You will catch cold outside. I will go and call a cab."

But she did not listen to him, and rapidly descended the stairs. When they were in the street they did not find a carriage; and they began to look for one, shouting after the cabmen whom they saw passing by at a distance.

They went down toward the Seine, in despair, shivering with cold. At last they found on the quay one of those ancient noctambulant coupés which, exactly as if they were ashamed to show their misery during the day, are never seen round Paris until after nightfall.

It took them to their door in the Rue des Martyrs, and once more, sadly, they climbed up homeward. All was ended, for her. And as to him, he reflected that he must be at the Ministry at ten o'clock.

She removed the wraps which covered her shoulders, before the glass, so as once more to see herself in all her glory. But suddenly she uttered a cry. She no longer had the necklace around her neck!

Her husband, already half undressed, demanded:

"What is the matter with you?"

She turned madly towards him:

"I have—I have—I've lost Mme. Forestier's necklace."

He stood up, distracted.

"What!—how?—impossible!"

And they looked in the folds of her dress, in the folds of her cloak, in her pockets, everywhere. They did not find it.

He asked:

"You're sure you had it on when you left the ball?"

"Yes, I felt it in the vestibule of the palace."

"But if you had lost it in the street we should have heard it fall.

It must be in the cab."

"Yes. Probably. Did you take his number?"

"No. And you, didn't you notice it?"

"No."

They looked, thunderstruck, at one another. At last Loisel put on his clothes.

"I shall go back on foot," said he, "over the whole route which we have taken to see if I can find it."

And he went out. She sat waiting on a chair in her ball dress, without strength to go to bed, overwhelmed, without fire, without a thought.

Her husband came back about seven o'clock. He had found nothing.

He went to Police Headquarters, to the newspaper offices, to offer a reward; he went to the cab companies—everywhere, in fact, whither he was urged by the least suspicion of hope.

She waited all day, in the same condition of mad fear before this terrible calamity.

Loisel returned at night with a hollow, pale face; he had discovered nothing.

"You must write to your friend," said he, "that you have broken the clasp of her necklace and that you are having it mended. That will give us time to turn round."

She wrote at his dictation.

At the end of a week they had lost all hope.

And Loisel, who had aged five years, declared:

"We must consider how to replace that ornament."

The next day they took the box which had contained it, and they went to the jeweler whose name was found within. He consulted his books.

"It was not I, madame, who sold that necklace; I must simply have furnished the case."

Then they went from jeweler to jeweler, searching for a necklace like the other, consulting their memories, sick both of them with chagrin and anguish.

They found, in a shop at the Palais Royal, a string of diamonds which seemed to them exactly like the one they looked for. It was worth forty thousand francs. They could have it for thirty-six.

So they begged the jeweler not to sell it for three days yet. And they made a bargain that he should buy it back for thirty-four thousand francs, in case they found the other one before the end of February.

Loisel possessed eighteen thousand francs which his father had left him. He would borrow the rest.

He did borrow, asking a thousand francs of one, five hundred of another, five louis here, three louis there. He gave notes, took up ruinous obligations, dealt with usurers and all the race of lenders. He compromised all the rest of his life, risked his signature without even knowing if he could meet it; and, frightened by the pains yet to come, by the black misery which was about to fall upon him, by the prospect of all the physical privation and of all the moral tortures which he was to suffer, he went to get the new necklace, putting down upon the merchant's counter thirty-six thousand francs.

When Mme. Loisel took back the necklace, Mme. Forestier said to her, with a chilly manner:

"You should have returned it sooner; I might have needed it."

She did not open the case, as her friend had so much feared. If she had detected the substitution, what would she have thought, what would she have said? Would she not have taken Mme. Loisel for a thief?

Mme. Loisel now knew the horrible existence of the needy. She took her part, moreover, all of a sudden, with heroism. That dreadful debt must be paid. She would pay it. They dismissed their servant; they changed their lodgings; they rented a garret under the roof.

She came to know what heavy housework meant and the odious cares of the kitchen. She washed the dishes, using her rosy nails on the greasy pots and pans. She washed the dirty linen, the shirts, and the dishcloths, which she dried upon a line; she carried the slops down to the street every morning, and carried up the water, stopping for breath at every landing. And, dressed like a woman of the people, she went to the fruiterer, the grocer, the butcher, her basket on her arm, bargaining, insulted, defending her miserable money sou by sou.

Each month they had to meet some notes, renew others, obtain more time.

Her husband worked in the evening making a fair copy of some tradesman's accounts, and late at night he often copied manuscript for five sous a page.

And this life lasted for ten years.

At the end of ten years, they had paid everything, everything, with the rates of usury, and the accumulations of the compound interest.

Mme. Loisel looked old now. She had become the woman of impoverished households—strong and hard and rough. With frowsy hair, skirts askew, and red hands, she talked loud while washing the floor with great swishes of water. But sometimes, when her husband was at the office, she sat down near the window, and she thought of that gay evening of long ago, of that ball where she had been so beautiful and so fêted.

What would have happened if she had not lost that necklace? Who knows? Who knows? How life is strange and changeful! How little a thing is needed for us to be lost or to be saved!

But, one Sunday, having gone to take a walk in the Champs Elysées to refresh herself from the labor of the week, she suddenly perceived a woman who was leading a child. It was Mme. Forestier, still young, still beautiful, still charming.

Mme. Loisel felt moved. Was she going to speak to her? Yes, certainly. And now that she had paid, she was going to tell her all about it. Why not?

She went up.

"Good-day, Jeanne."

The other, astonished to be familiarly addressed by this plain goodwife, did not recognize her at all, and stammered:

"But—madam!—I do not know—You must be mistaken."

"No. I am Mathilde Loisel."

Her friend uttered a cry.

"Oh, my poor Mathilde! How you are changed!"

"Yes, I have had days hard enough, since I have seen you, days wretched enough—and that because of you!"

"Of me! How so?"

"Do you remember that diamond necklace which you lent me to wear at the ministerial ball?"

"Yes. Well?"

"Well, I lost it."

"What do you mean? You brought it back."

"I brought you back another just like it. And for this we have been ten years paying. You can understand that it was not easy for us, us who had nothing. At last it is ended, and I am very glad."

Mme. Forestier had stopped.

"You say that you bought a necklace of diamonds to replace mine?"

"Yes. You never noticed it, then! They were very like."

And she smiled with a joy which was proud and naïve at once.

Mme. Forestier, strongly moved, took her two hands.

"Oh, my poor Mathilde! Why, my necklace was paste. It was worth at most five hundred francs!"

1884

The Secret Sharer

JOSEPH CONRAD

[1857–1924]

I

On my right hand there were lines of fishing stakes resembling a mysterious system of half-submerged bamboo fences, incomprehensible in its division of the domain of tropical fishes, and crazy of aspect as if abandoned forever by some nomad tribe of fishermen now gone to the other end of the ocean; for there was no sign of human habitation as far as the eye could reach. To the left a group of barren islets, suggesting ruins of stone walls, towers, and blockhouses, had its foundations set in a blue sea that itself looked solid, so still and stable did it lie below my feet; even the track of light from the westering sun shone smoothly, without that animated glitter which tells of an imperceptible ripple. And when I turned my head to take a parting glance at the tug which had just left us anchored outside the bar, I saw the straight line of the flat shore joined to the stable sea, edge to edge, with a perfect and unmarked closeness, in one leveled floor half brown, half blue under the enormous dome of the sky. Corresponding in their insignificance to the islets of the sea, two small clumps of trees, one on each side of the only fault in the impeccable joint, marked the mouth of the river Meinam we had just left on the first preparatory stage of our homeward journey; and, far back on the inland level, a larger and loftier mass, the grove surrounding the great Paknam pagoda, was the only thing on which the eye could rest from the vain task of exploring the monotonous sweep of the horizon. Here and there gleams as of a few scattered pieces of silver marked the windings of the great river; and on the nearest of them, just within the bar, the tug steaming right into the land became lost to my sight, hull and funnel and masts, as though the impassive earth had swallowed her up without an effort, without a tremor. My eye followed the light cloud of her smoke, now here, now there, above the plain, according to the devious curves of the stream, but always fainter and farther away, till I lost it at last behind the miter-shaped hill of the great pagoda. And then I was left alone with my ship, anchored at the head of the Gulf of Siam.

She floated at the starting point of a long journey, very still in an immense stillness, the shadows of her spars flung far to the eastward by the setting sun. At that moment I was alone on her decks. There was not a sound in her—and around us nothing moved, nothing lived, not a canoe on the water, not a bird in the air, not a cloud in the sky. In this breathless pause at the threshold of a long passage we seemed to be measuring our fitness for a long and arduous enterprise, the appointed task of both our existences to be carried out, far from all human eyes, with only sky and sea for spectators and for judges.

There must have been some glare in the air to interfere with one's sight, because it was only just before the sun left us that my roaming eyes made out beyond the highest ridge of the principal islet of the group something which did away with the solemnity of perfect solitude. The tide of darkness flowed on swiftly; and with tropical suddenness a swarm of stars came out above the shadowy earth, while I lingered yet, my hand resting lightly on my ship's rail as if on the shoulder of a trusted friend. But, with all that multitude of celestial bodies staring down at one, the comfort of quiet communion with her was gone for good. And there were also disturbing sounds by this time—voices, footsteps forward; the steward flitted along the main deck, a busily ministering spirit; a hand bell tinkled urgently under the poop deck. . . .

I found my two officers waiting for me near the supper table, in the lighted cuddy. We sat down at once, and as I helped the chief mate, I said:

"Are you aware that there is a ship anchored inside the islands? I saw her mastheads above the ridge as the sun went down."

He raised sharply his simple face, overcharged by a terrible growth of whisker, and emitted his usual ejaculations: "Bless my soul, sir! You don't say so!"

My second mate was a sound-cheeked, silent young man, grave beyond his years, I thought; but as our eyes happened to meet I detected a slight quiver on his lips. I looked down at once. It was not my part to encourage sneering on board my ship. It must be said, too, that I knew very little of my officers. In consequence of certain events of no particular significance, except to myself, I had been appointed to the command only a fortnight before. Neither did I know much of the hands forward. All these people had been together for eighteen months or so, and my position was that of the only stranger on board. I mention this because it has some bearing on what is to follow. But what I felt most was my being a stranger to the ship; and if truth must be told, I was somewhat of a stranger to myself. The youngest man on board (barring the second mate), and untried as yet by a position of the fullest responsibility, I was willing to take the adequacy of the others for granted. They had simply to be equal to their tasks: but I wondered how far I should turn out faithful to that ideal conception of one's own personality every man sets up for himself secretly.

Meantime the chief mate, with an almost visible effect of collaboration on the part of his round eyes and frightful whiskers, was trying to evolve a theory of the anchored ship. His dominant trait was to take all things into earnest consideration. He was of a painstaking turn of mind. As he used to say, he "liked to account to himself" for practically everything that came in his way, down to a miserable scorpion he had found in his cabin a week before. The why and the wherefore of that scorpion—how it got on board and came to select his room rather than the pantry (which was a dark place and more what a scorpion would be partial to), and how on earth it managed to drown itself in the inkwell of his writing desk—had exercised him infinitely. The ship within the islands was much more easily accounted for; and just as we were about to rise from the table he made his pronouncement. She was, he doubted not, a ship from home lately arrived. Probably she drew too much water to cross the bar except at the top of spring tides. Therefore she went into that natural harbor to wait for a few days in preference to remaining in an open roadstead.

"That's so," confirmed the second mate, suddenly, in his slightly hoarse voice. "She draws over twenty feet. She's the Liverpool ship

Sephora with a cargo of coal. Hundred and twenty-three days from Cardiff."

We looked at him in surprise.

"The tugboat skipper told me when he came on board for your letters, sir," explained the young man. "He expects to take her up the river the day after tomorrow."

After thus overwhelming us with the extent of his information he slipped out of the cabin. The mate observed regretfully that he "could not account for that young fellow's whims." What prevented him telling us all about it at once, he wanted to know.

I detained him as he was making a move. For the last two days the crew had had plenty of hard work, and the night before they had very little sleep. I felt painfully that I—a stranger—was doing something unusual when I directed him to let all hands turn in without setting an anchor watch. I proposed to keep on deck myself till one o'clock or thereabouts. I would get the second mate to relieve me at that hour.

"He will turn out the cook and the steward at four," I concluded, "and then give you a call. Of course at the lightest sign of any sort of wind we'll have the hands up and make a start at once."

He concealed his astonishment. "Very well, sir." Outside the cuddy he put his head in the second mate's door to inform him of my unheard-of caprice to take a five hours' anchor watch on myself. I heard the other raise his voice incredulously: "What? The captain himself?" Then a few more murmurs, a door closed, then another. A few moments later I went on deck.

My strangeness, which had made me sleepless, had prompted that unconventional arrangement, as if I had expected in those solitary hours of the night to get on terms with the ship of which I knew nothing, manned by men of whom I knew very little more. Fast alongside a wharf, littered like any ship in port with a tangle of unrelated things, invaded by unrelated shore people, I had hardly seen her yet properly. Now, as she lay cleared for sea, the stretch of her main deck seemed to me very fine under the stars. Very fine, very roomy for her size, and very inviting. I descended the poop and paced the waist, my mind picturing to myself the coming passage through the Malay Archipelago, down the Indian Ocean, and up the Atlantic. All its phases were familiar enough to me, every characteristic, all the alternatives which were likely to face me on the high seas—everything! . . . except the novel responsibility of command. But I took heart from the reasonable thought that the ship was like other ships, the men like other men, and that the sea was not likely to keep any special surprises expressly for my discomfiture.

Arrived at that comforting conclusion, I bethought myself of a cigar and went below to get it. All was still down there. Everybody at the after end of the ship was sleeping profoundly. I came out again on the quarter-deck, agreeably at ease in my sleeping suit on that warm breathless night, barefooted, a glowing cigar in my teeth, and, going forward, I was met by the profound silence of the fore end of the ship. Only as I passed the door of the forecastle I heard a deep, quiet, trustful sigh of some sleeper inside. And suddenly I rejoiced in the great security of the sea as compared with the unrest of the land, in my choice of that untempted life presenting no disquieting problems, invested with an elementary moral beauty by the absolute straightforwardness of its appeal and by the singleness of its purpose.

The riding light in the fore-rigging burned with a clear, untroubled, as if symbolic, flame, confident and bright in the mysterious shades of the night. Passing on my way aft along the other side of the ship, I observed that the rope side ladder, put over, no doubt, for the master of the tug when he came to fetch away our letters, had not been hauled in as it should have been. I became annoyed at this, for exactitude in small matters is the very soul of discipline. Then I reflected that I had myself peremptorily dismissed my officers from duty, and by my own act had prevented the anchor watch being formally set and things properly attended to. I asked myself whether it was wise ever to interfere with the established routine of duties even from the kindest of motives. My action might have made me appear eccentric. Goodness only knew how that absurdly whiskered mate would "account" for my conduct, and what the whole ship thought of that informality of their new captain. I was vexed with myself.

Not from compunction certainly, but, as it were mechanically, I proceeded to get the ladder in myself. Now a side ladder of that sort is a light affair and comes in easily, yet my vigorous tug, which should have brought it flying on board, merely recoiled upon my body in a totally unexpected jerk. What the devil! . . . I was so astounded by the immovableness of that ladder that I remained stock-still, trying to account for it to myself like that imbecile mate of mine. In the end, of course, I put my head over the rail.

The side of the ship made an opaque belt of shadow on the darkling glassy shimmer of the sea. But I saw at once something elongated and pale floating very close to the ladder. Before I could form a guess a faint flash of phosphorescent light, which seemed to issue suddenly from the naked body of a man, flickered in the sleeping water with the elusive, silent play of summer lightning in a night sky. With a gasp I saw revealed to my stare a pair of feet, the long legs, a broad livid back immersed right up to the neck in a greenish cadaverous glow. One hand, awash, clutched the bottom rung of the ladder. He was complete but for the head. A headless corpse! The cigar dropped out of my gaping mouth with a tiny plop and a short hiss quite audible in the absolute stillness of all things under heaven. At that I suppose he raised up his face, a dimly pale oval in the shadow of the ship's side. But even then I could only barely make out down there the shape of his black-haired head. However, it was enough for the horrid, frost-bound sensation which had gripped me about the chest to pass off. The moment of vain exclamations was past, too. I only climbed on the spare spar and leaned over the rail as far as I could, to bring my eyes nearer to that mystery floating alongside.

As he hung by the ladder, like a resting swimmer, the sea lightning played about his limbs at every stir; and he appeared in it ghastly, silvery, fishlike. He remained as mute as a fish, too. He made no motion to get out of the water, either. It was inconceivable that he should not attempt to come on board, and strangely troubling to suspect that perhaps he did not want to. And my first words were prompted by just that troubled incertitude.

"What's the matter?" I asked in my ordinary tone, speaking down to the face upturned exactly under mine.

"Cramp," it answered, no louder. Then slightly anxious, "I say, no need to call anyone."

"I was not going to," I said.

"Are you alone on deck?"

"Yes."

I had somehow the impression that he was on the point of letting go the ladder to swim away beyond my ken—mysterious as he came. But, for the moment, this being appearing as if he had risen from the bottom of the sea (it was certainly the nearest land to the ship) wanted only to know the time. I told him. And he, down there, tentatively:

"I suppose your captain's turned in?"

"I am sure he isn't," I said.

He seemed to struggle with himself, for I heard something like the low, bitter murmur of doubt. "What's the good?" His next words came out with a hesitating effort.

"Look here, my man. Could you call him out quietly?"

I thought the time had come to declare myself.

"*I* am the captain."

I heard a "By Jove!" whispered at the level of the water. The phosphorescence flashed in the swirl of the water all about his limbs, his other hand seized the ladder.

"My name's Leggatt."

The voice was calm and resolute. A good voice. The self-possession of that man had somehow induced a corresponding state in myself. It was very quietly that I remarked:

"You must be a good swimmer."

"Yes. I've been in the water practically since nine o'clock. The question for me now is whether I am to let go this ladder and go on swimming till I sink from exhaustion, or—to come on board here."

I felt this was no mere formula of desperate speech, but a real alternative in the view of a strong soul. I should have gathered from this that he was young; indeed, it is only the young who are ever confronted by such clear issues. But at this time it was pure intuition on my part. A mysterious communication was established already between us two—in the face of that silent darkened tropical sea. I was young, too; young enough to make no comment. The man in the water began suddenly to climb up the ladder, and I hastened away from the rail to fetch some clothes.

Before entering the cabin I stood still, listening in the lobby at the foot of the stairs. A faint snore came through the closed door of the chief mate's room. The second mate's door was on the hook, but the darkness in there was absolutely soundless. He, too, was young and could sleep like a stone. Remained the steward, but he was not likely to wake up before he was called. I got a sleeping suit out of my room and, coming back on deck, saw the naked man from the sea sitting on the main hatch, glimmering white in the darkness, his elbows on his knees and his head in his hands. In a moment he had concealed his damp body in a sleeping suit of the same gray-stripe pattern as the one I was wearing and followed me like my double on the poop. Together we moved right aft, barefooted, silent.

"What is it?" I asked in a deadened voice, taking the lighted lamp out of the binnacle, and raising it to his face.

"An ugly business."

He had rather regular features; a good mouth; light eyes under somewhat heavy, dark eyebrows; a smooth, square forehead; no growth on his cheeks; a small, brown mustache, and a well-shaped, round chin. His expression was concentrated, meditative, under the inspecting light of the lamp I held up to his face; such as a man thinking hard in solitude might wear. My sleeping suit was just right for his size. A well-knit young fellow of twenty-five at most. He caught his lower lip with the edge of white, even teeth.

"Yes," I said, replacing the lamp in the binnacle. The warm, heavy tropical night closed upon his head again.

"There's a ship over there," he murmured.

"Yes, I know. The *Sephora.* Did you know of us?"

"Hadn't the slightest idea. I am the mate of her—" He paused and corrected himself. "I should say I was."

"Aha! Something wrong?"

"Yes. Very wrong indeed. I've killed a man."

"What do you mean? Just now?"

"No, on the passage. Weeks ago. Thirty-nine south. When I say a man—"

"Fit of temper," I suggested, confidently.

The shadowy, dark head, like mine, seemed to nod imperceptibly above the ghostly gray of my sleeping suit. It was, in the night, as though I had been faced by my own reflection in the depths of a somber and immense mirror.

"A pretty thing to have to own up to for a Conway boy," murmured my double, distinctly.

"You're a Conway boy?"

"I am," he said, as if startled. Then, slowly . . . "Perhaps you too —"

It was so; but being a couple of years older I had left before he joined. After a quick interchange of dates a silence fell; and I thought suddenly of my absurd mate with his terrific whiskers and the "Bless my soul—you don't say so" type of intellect. My double gave me an inkling of his thoughts by saying:

"My father's a parson in Norfolk. Do you see me before a judge and jury on that charge? For myself I can't see the necessity. There are fellows that an angel from heaven—And I am not that. He was one of those creatures that are just simmering all the time with a silly sort of wickedness. Miserable devils that have no business to live at all. He wouldn't do his duty and wouldn't let anybody else do theirs. But what's the good of talking! You know well enough the sort of ill-conditioned snarling cur—"

He appealed to me as if our experiences had been as identical as our clothes. And I knew well enough the pestiferous danger of such a character where there are no means of legal repression. And I knew well enough also that my double there was no homicidal ruffian. I did not think of asking him for details, and he told me the story roughly in brusque, disconnected sentences. I needed no more. I saw it all going on as though I were myself inside that other sleeping suit.

"It happened while we were setting a reefed foresail, at dusk. Reefed foresail! You understand the sort of weather. The only sail we had left to keep the ship running; so you may guess what it had been like for days. Anxious sort of job, that. He gave me some of his cursed insolence at the sheet. I tell you I was overdone with this terrific weather that seemed to have no end to it. Terrific, I tell you—and a deep ship. I believe the fellow himself was half crazed with funk. It was no time for gentlemanly reproof, so I turned round and felled him like an ox. He up and at me. We closed just as an awful sea made for the ship. All hands saw it coming and took to the rigging, but I had him by the throat, and went on shaking him like a rat, the men above us yelling, 'Look out! look out!' Then a crash as if the sky had fallen on my head. They say that for over ten minutes hardly anything was to be seen of the ship—just the three masts and a bit of the forecastle head and of the poop all awash driving along in a smother of foam. It was a miracle that they found us, jammed together behind the forebits. It's clear that I meant business, because I was holding him by the throat still when they picked us up. He was black in the face. It was too much for them. It seems they rushed us aft together, gripped as we were, screaming

'Murder!' like a lot of lunatics, and broke into the cuddy. And the ship running for her life, touch and go all the time, any minute her last in a sea fit to turn your hair gray only a-looking at it. I understand that the skipper, too, started raving like the rest of them. The man had been deprived of sleep for more than a week, and to have this sprung on him at the height of a furious gale nearly drove him out of his mind. I wonder they didn't fling me overboard after getting the carcass of their precious shipmate out of my fingers. They had rather a job to separate us, I've been told. A sufficiently fierce story to make an old judge and a respectable jury sit up a bit. The first thing I heard when I came to myself was the maddening howling of that endless gale, and on that the voice of the old man. He was hanging on to my bunk, staring into my face out of his sou'wester.

" 'Mr. Leggatt, you have killed a man. You can act no longer as chief mate of this ship.' "

His care to subdue his voice made it sound monotonous. He rested a hand on the end of the skylight to steady himself with, and all that time did not stir a limb, so far as I could see. "Nice little tale for a quiet tea party," he concluded in the same tone.

One of my hands, too, rested on the end of the skylight; neither did I stir a limb, so far as I knew. We stood less than a foot from each other. It occurred to me that if old "Bless my soul—you don't say so" were to put his head up the companion and catch sight of us, he would think he was seeing double, or imagine himself come upon a scene of weird witchcraft; the strange captain having a quiet confabulation by the wheel with his own gray ghost. I became very much concerned to prevent anything of the sort. I heard the other's soothing undertone.

"My father's a parson in Norfolk," it said. Evidently he had forgotten he had told me this important fact before. Truly a nice little tale.

"You had better slip down into my stateroom now," I said, moving off stealthily. My double followed my movements; our bare feet made no sound; I let him in, closed the door with care, and, after giving a call to the second mate, returned on deck for my relief.

"Not much sign of any wind yet," I remarked when he approached.

"No, sir. Not much," he assented, sleepily, in his hoarse voice, with just enough deference, no more, and barely suppressing a yawn.

"Well, that's all you have to look out for. You have got your orders."

"Yes, sir."

I paced a turn or two on the poop and saw him take up his position face forward with his elbow in the rat-lines of the mizzen-rigging before I went below. The mate's faint snoring was still going on peacefully. The cuddy lamp was burning over the table on which stood a vase with flowers, a polite attention from the ships' provision merchant—the last flowers we should see for the next three months at the very least. Two bunches of bananas hung from the beam symmetrically, one on each side of the rudder casing. Everything was as before in the ship—except that two of her captain's sleeping suits were simultaneously in use, one motionless in the cuddy, the other keeping very still in the captain's stateroom.

It must be explained here that my cabin had the form of the capital letter L, the door being within the angle and opening into the short part of the letter. A couch was to the left, the bed-place to the right; my writing desk and the chronometers' table faced the door. But anyone opening it, unless he stepped right inside, had no view of what I call the long (or vertical) part of the letter. It contained some lockers surmounted by a bookcase; and a few clothes, a thick jacket or two, caps, oilskin coat, and such like, hung on hooks. There was at the bottom of that part a door opening into my bathroom, which could be entered also directly from the saloon. But that way was never used.

The mysterious arrival had discovered the advantage of this particular shape. Entering my room, lighted strongly by a big bulkhead lamp swung on gimbals above my writing desk, I did not see him anywhere till he stepped out quietly from behind the coats hung in the recessed part.

"I heard somebody moving about, and went in there at once," he whispered.

I, too, spoke under my breath.

"Nobody is likely to come in here without knocking and getting permission."

He nodded. His face was thin and the sunburn faded, as though he had been ill. And no wonder. He had been, I heard presently, kept under arrest in his cabin for nearly seven weeks. But there was nothing sickly in his eyes or in his expression. He was not a bit like me, really; yet, as we stood leaning over my bed-place, whispering side by side, with our dark heads together and our backs to the door, anybody bold enough to open it stealthily would have been treated to the uncanny sight of a double captain busy talking in whispers with his other self.

"But all this doesn't tell me how you came to hang on to our side ladder," I inquired, in the hardly audible murmurs we used, after he had told me something more of the proceedings on board the *Sephora* once the bad weather was over.

"When we sighted Java Head I had had time to think all those matters out several times over. I had six weeks of doing nothing else, and with only an hour or so every evening for a tramp on the quarter-deck."

He whispered, his arms folded on the side of my bed-place, staring through the open port. And I could imagine perfectly the manner of this thinking out—a stubborn if not a steadfast operation; something of which I should have been perfectly incapable.

"I reckoned it would be dark before we closed with the land," he continued, so low that I had to strain my hearing, near as we were to each other, shoulder touching shoulder almost. "So I asked to speak to the old man. He always seemed very sick when he came to see me—as if he could not look me in the face. You know, that foresail saved the ship. She was too deep to have run long under bare poles. And it was I that managed to set it for him. Anyway, he came. When I had him in my cabin—he stood by the door looking at me as if I had the halter around my neck already—I asked him right away to leave my cabin door unlocked at night while the ship was going through Sunda Straits. There would be the Java coast within two or three miles, off Angier Point. I wanted nothing more. I've had a prize for swimming my second year in the Conway."

"I can believe it," I breathed out.

"God only knows why they locked me in every night. To see some of their faces you'd have thought they were afraid I'd go about at night strangling people. Am I a murdering brute? Do I look it? By Jove! if I had been he wouldn't have trusted himself like that into my room. You'll say I might have chucked him aside and bolted out, there and then—it was dark already. Well, no. And for the same reason I wouldn't think of trying to smash the door. There would have been a rush to stop me at the noise, and I did not mean to get into a confounded scrimmage. Somebody else might have got killed —for I would not have broken out only to get chucked back, and I did not want any more of that work. He refused, looking more sick than ever. He was afraid of the men, and also of that old second mate of his who had been sailing with him for years—a gray-headed old humbug; and his steward, too, had been with him devil knows how long—seventeen years or more—a dogmatic sort of loafer who hated me like poison, just because I was the chief mate. No chief mate ever made more than one voyage in the *Sephora,* you know. Those two old chaps ran the ship. Devil only knows what the skipper wasn't afraid of (all his nerve went to pieces altogether in that hellish spell of bad weather we had)—of what the law would do to him—of his wife, perhaps. Oh, yes! she's on board. Though I don't think she would have meddled. She would have been only too glad to have me out of the ship in any way. The 'brand of Cain' business, don't you see. That's all right. I was ready enough to go off wandering on the face of the earth—and that was price enough to pay for an Abel of that sort. Anyhow, he wouldn't listen to me. 'This thing must take its course. I represent the law here.' He was shaking life a leaf. 'So you won't?' 'No!' 'Then I hope you will be able to sleep on that,' I said, and turned my back on him. 'I wonder that you can,' cries he, and locks the door.

"Well, after that, I couldn't. Not very well. That was three weeks ago. We have had a slow passage through the Java Sea; drifted about Carimata for ten days. When we anchored here they thought, I suppose, it was all right. The nearest land (and that's five miles) is the ship's destination; the consul would soon set about catching me; and there would have been no object in bolting to these islets there. I don't suppose there's a drop of water on them. I don't know how it was, but tonight that steward, after bringing me my supper, went out to let me eat it, and left the door unlocked. And I ate it—all there was, too. After I had finished I strolled out on the quarter-deck. I don't know that I meant to do anything. A breath of fresh air was all I wanted, I believe. Then a sudden temptation came over me. I kicked off my slippers and was in the water before I had made up my mind fairly. Somebody heard the splash and they raised an awful hullabaloo. 'He's gone! Lower the boats! He's committed suicide! No, he's swimming.' Certainly I was swimming. It's not so easy for a swimmer like me to commit suicide by drowning. I landed on the nearest islet before the boat left the ship's side. I heard them pulling about in the dark, hailing, and so on, but after a bit they gave up. Everything quieted down and the anchorage became as still as death. I sat down on a stone and began to think. I felt certain they would start searching for me at daylight. There was no place to hide on those stony things—and if there had been, what would have been the good? But now I was clear of that ship, I was not going back. So after a while I took off all my clothes, tied them up in a bundle with a stone inside, and dropped them in the deep water on the outer side of the islet. That was suicide enough for me. Let them think what they liked, but I didn't mean to drown myself. I meant to swim till I sank—but that's not the same thing. I struck out for another of these little islands, and it was from that one that I first saw your riding light. Something to swim for. I went on easily, and on the way I came upon a flat rock a foot or two above water. In the daytime, I dare say, you might make it out with a glass from your poop. I scrambled up on it and rested myself for a bit. Then I made another start. That last spell must have been over a mile."

His whisper was getting fainter and fainter, and all the time he stared straight out through the porthole, in which there was not even a star to be seen. I had not interrupted him. There was something that made comment impossible in his narrative, or perhaps in himself; a sort of feeling, a quality, which I can't find a name for. And when he ceased, all I found was a futile whisper: "So you swam for our light?"

"Yes—straight for it. It was something to swim for. I couldn't see any stars low down because the coast was in the way, and I couldn't see the land, either. The water was like glass. One might have been swimming in a confounded thousand-feet deep cistern with no place for scrambling out anywhere; but what I didn't like was the notion of swimming round and round like a crazed bullock before I gave out; and as I didn't mean to go back . . . No. Do you see me being hauled back, stark naked, off one of these little islands by the scruff of the neck and fighting like a wild beast? Somebody would have got killed for certain, and I did not want any of that. So I went on. Then your ladder—"

"Why didn't you hail the ship?" I asked, a little louder.

He touched my shoulder lightly. Lazy footsteps came right over our heads and stopped. The second mate had crossed from the other side of the poop and might have been hanging over the rail, for all we knew.

"He couldn't hear us talking—could he?" My double breathed into my very ear, anxiously.

His anxiety was an answer, a sufficient answer, to the question I had put to him. An answer containing all the difficulty of that situation. I closed the porthole quietly, to make sure. A louder word might have been overheard.

"Who's that?" he whispered then.

"My second mate. But I don't know much more of the fellow than you do."

And I told him a little about myself. I had been appointed to take charge while I least expected anything of the sort, not quite a fortnight ago. I didn't know either the ship or the people. Hadn't had the time in port to look about me or size anybody up. And as to the crew, all they knew was that I was appointed to take the ship home. For the rest, I was almost as much of a stranger on board as himself, I said. And at the moment I felt it most acutely. I felt that it would take very little to make me a suspect person in the eyes of the ship's company.

He had turned about meantime; and we, the two strangers in the ship, faced each other in identical attitudes.

"Your ladder—" he murmured, after a silence. "Who'd have thought of finding a ladder hanging over at night in a ship anchored out here! I felt just then a very unpleasant faintness. After the life I've been leading for nine weeks, anybody would have got out of condition. I wasn't capable of swimming round as far as your rudder chains. And, lo and behold! there was a ladder to get hold of. After I gripped it I said to myself, 'What's the good?' When I saw a man's head looking over I thought I would swim away presently and leave him shouting—in whatever language it was. I didn't mind being looked at. I—I liked it. And then you speaking to me so quietly—as if you had expected me—made me hold on a little longer. It had been a confounded lonely time—I don't mean while swimming. I was glad to talk a little to somebody that didn't belong to the *Sephora.* As to asking for the captain, that was a mere impulse. It could have been no use, with all the ship knowing about me and the other people pretty certain to be round here in the morning. I don't know —I wanted to be seen, to talk with somebody, before I went on. I don't know what I would have said. . . . 'Fine night, isn't it?' or something of the sort."

"Do you think they will be round here presently?" I asked with some incredulity.

"Quite likely," he said, faintly.

He looked extremely haggard all of a sudden. His head rolled on his shoulders.

"H'm. We shall see then. Meantime get into that bed," I whispered. "Want help? There."

It was a rather high bed-place with a set of drawers underneath. This amazing swimmer really needed the lift I gave him by seizing his leg. He tumbled in, rolled over on his back, and flung one arm across his eyes. And then, with his face nearly hidden, he must have looked exactly as I used to look in that bed. I gazed upon my other self for a while before drawing across carefully the two green serge curtains which ran on a brass rod. I thought for a moment of pinning them together for greater safety, but I sat down on the couch, and once there I felt unwilling to rise and hunt for a pin. I would do it in a moment. I was extremely tired, in a peculiarly intimate way, by the strain of stealthiness, by the effort of whispering and the general secrecy of this excitement. It was three o'clock by now and I had been on my feet since nine, but I was not sleepy; I could not have gone to sleep. I sat there, fagged out, looking at the curtains, trying to clear my mind of the confused sensation of being in two places at once, and greatly bothered by an exasperating knocking in my head. It was a relief to discover suddenly that it was not in my head at all, but on the outside of the door. Before I could collect myself the words "Come in" were out of my mouth, and the steward entered with a tray, bringing in my morning coffee. I had slept, after all, and I was so frightened that I shouted, "This way! I am here, steward," as though he had been miles away. He put down the tray on the table next the couch and only then said, very quietly, "I can see you are here, sir." I felt him give me a keen look, but I dared not meet his eyes just then. He must have wondered why I had drawn the curtains of my bed before going to sleep on the couch. He went out, hooking the door open as usual.

I heard the crew washing decks above me. I knew I would have been told at once if there had been any wind. Calm, I thought, and I was doubly vexed. Indeed, I felt dual more than ever. The steward reappeared suddenly in the doorway. I jumped up from the couch so quickly that he gave a start.

"What do you want here?"

"Close your port, sir—they are washing decks."

"It is closed," I said, reddening.

"Very well, sir." But he did not move from the doorway and returned my stare in an extraordinary, equivocal manner for a time. Then his eyes wavered, all his expression changed, and in a voice unusually gentle, almost coaxingly:

"May I come in to take the empty cup away, sir?"

"Of course!" I turned my back on him while he popped in and out. Then I unhooked and closed the door and even pushed the bolt. This sort of thing could not go on very long. The cabin was as hot as an oven, too. I took a peep at my double, and discovered that he had not moved, his arm was still over his eyes; but his chest heaved; his hair was wet; his chin glistened with perspiration. I reached over him and opened the port.

"I must show myself on deck," I reflected.

Of course, theoretically, I could do what I liked, with no one to say nay to me within the whole circle of the horizon; but to lock my cabin door and take the key away I did not dare. Directly I put my head out of the companion I saw the group of my two officers, the second mate barefooted, the chief mate in long india-rubber boots, near the break of the poop, and the steward halfway down the poop ladder talking to them eagerly. He happened to catch sight of me and dived, the second ran down on the main deck shouting some order or other, and the chief mate came to meet me, touching his cap.

There was a sort of curiosity in his eye that I did not like. I don't know whether the steward had told them that I was "queer" only, or downright drunk, but I know the man meant to have a good look at me. I watched him coming with a smile which, as he got into point-blank range, took effect and froze his very whiskers. I did not give him time to open his lips.

"Square the yards by lifts and braces before the hands go to breakfast."

It was the first particular order I had given on board that ship; and

I stayed on deck to see it executed, too. I had felt the need of asserting myself without loss of time. That sneering young cub got taken down a peg or two on that occasion, and I also seized the opportunity of having a good look at the face of every foremast man as they filed past me to go to the after braces. At breakfast time, eating nothing myself, I presided with such frigid dignity that the two mates were only too glad to escape from the cabin as soon as decency permitted; and all the time the dual working of my mind distracted me almost to the point of insanity. I was constantly watching myself, my secret self, as dependent on my actions as my own personality, sleeping in that bed, behind that door which faced me as I sat at the head of the table. It was very much like being mad, only it was worse because one was aware of it.

I had to shake him for a solid minute, but when at last he opened his eyes it was in the full possession of his senses, with an inquiring look.

"All's well so far," I whispered. "Now you must vanish into the bathroom."

He did so, as noiseless as a ghost, and I then rang for the steward, and facing him boldly, directed him to tidy up my stateroom while I was having my bath—"and be quick about it." As my tone admitted of no excuses, he said, "Yes, sir," and ran off to fetch his dustpan and brushes. I took a bath and did most of my dressing, splashing, and whistling softly for the steward's edification, while the secret sharer of my life stood drawn up bolt upright in that little space, his face looking very sunken in daylight, his eyelids lowered under the stern, dark line of his eyebrows drawn together by a slight frown.

When I left him there to go back to my room the steward was finished dusting. I sent for the mate and engaged him in some insignificant conversation. It was, as it were, trifling with the terrific character of whiskers; but my object was to give him an opportunity for a good look at my cabin. And then I could at last shut, with a clear conscience, the door of my stateroom and get my double back into the recessed part. There was nothing else for it. He had to sit still on a small folding stool, half smothered by the heavy coats hanging there. We listened to the steward going into the bathroom out of the saloon, filling the water bottles there, scrubbing the bath, setting things to rights, whisk, bang, clatter—out again into the saloon—turn the key—click. Such was my scheme for keeping my second self invisible. Nothing better could be contrived under the circumstances. And there we sat; I at my writing desk ready to appear busy with some papers, he behind me, out of sight of the door. It would not have been prudent to talk in daytime; and I could not have stood the excitement of that queer sense of whispering to myself. Now and then, glancing over my shoulder, I saw him far back there, sitting rigidly on the low stool, his bare feet close together, his arms folded, his head hanging on his breast—and perfectly still. Anybody would have taken him for me.

I was fascinated by it myself. Every moment I had to glance over my shoulder. I was looking at him when a voice outside the door said:

"Beg pardon, sir."

"Well!" . . . I kept my eyes on him, and so, when the voice outside the door announced, "There's a ship's boat coming our way, sir," I saw him give a start—the first movement he had made for hours. But he did not raise his bowed head.

"All right. Get the ladder over."

I hesitated. Should I whisper something to him? But what? His immobility seemed to have been never disturbed. What could I tell him he did not know already? . . . Finally I went on deck.

II

The skipper of the *Sephora* had a thin red whisker all round his face, and the sort of complexion that goes with hair of that color; also the particular, rather smeary shade of blue in the eyes. He was not exactly a showy figure; his shoulders were high, his stature but middling—one leg slightly more bandy than the other. He shook hands, looking vaguely around. A spiritless tenacity was his main characteristic, I judged. I behaved with a politeness which seemed to disconcert him. Perhaps he was shy. He mumbled to me as if he were ashamed of what he was saying; gave his name (it was something like Archbold—but at this distance of years I hardly am sure), his ship's name, and a few other particulars of that sort, in the manner of a criminal making a reluctant and doleful confession. He had had terrible weather on the passage out—terrible—terrible—wife aboard, too.

By this time we were seated in the cabin and the steward brought in a tray with a bottle and glasses. "Thanks! No." Never took liquor. Would have some water, though. He drank two tumblerfuls. Terrible thirsty work. Ever since daylight had been exploring the islands round his ship.

"What was that for—fun?" I asked, with an appearance of polite interest.

"No!" He sighed. "Painful duty."

As he persisted in his mumbling and I wanted my double to hear every word, I hit upon the notion of informing him that I regretted to say I was hard of hearing.

"Such a young man, too!" he nodded, keeping his smeary blue, unintelligent eyes fastened upon me. What was the cause of it—some disease? he inquired, without the least sympathy and as if he thought that, if so, I'd got no more than I deserved.

"Yes; disease," I admitted in a cheerful tone which seemed to shock him. But my point was gained, because he had to raise his voice to give me his tale. It is not worth while to record that version. It was just over two months since all this had happened, and he had thought so much about it that he seemed completely muddled as to its bearings, but still immensely impressed.

"What would you think of such a thing happening on board your own ship? I've had the *Sephora* for these fifteen years. I am a well-known shipmaster."

He was densely distressed—and perhaps I should have sympathized with him if I had been able to detach my mental vision from the unsuspected sharer of my cabin as though he were my second self. There he was on the other side of the bulkhead, four or five feet from us, no more, as we sat in the saloon. I looked politely at Captain Archbold (if that was his name), but it was the other I saw, in a gray sleeping suit, seated on a low stool, his bare feet close together, his arms folded, and every word said between us falling into the ears of his dark head bowed on his chest.

"I have been at sea now, man and boy, for seven-and-thirty years, and I've never heard of such a thing happening in an English ship. And that it should be my ship. Wife on board, too."

I was hardly listening to him.

"Don't you think," I said, "that the heavy sea which, you told me, came aboard just then might have killed the man? I have seen the sheer weight of a sea kill a man very neatly, by simply breaking his neck."

"Good God!" he uttered, impressively, fixing his smeary blue eyes on me. "The sea! No man killed by the sea ever looked like that." He seemed positively scandalized at my suggestion. And as I gazed at him, certainly not prepared for anything original on his part, he advanced his head close to mine and thrust his tongue out at me so suddenly that I couldn't help starting back.

After scoring over my calmness in this graphic way he nodded wisely. If I had seen the sight, he assured me, I would never forget it as long as I lived. The weather was too bad to give the corpse a proper sea burial. So next day at dawn they took it up on the poop, covering its face with a bit of bunting; he read a short prayer, and then, just as it was, in its oilskins and long boots, they launched it amongst those mountainous seas that seemed ready every moment to swallow up the ship herself and the terrified lives on board of her.

"That reefed foresail saved you," I threw in.

"Under God—it did," he exclaimed fervently. "It was by a special mercy, I firmly believe, that it stood some of those hurricane squalls."

"It was the setting of that sail which—" I began.

"God's own hand in it," he interrupted me. "Nothing less could have done it. I don't mind telling you that I hardly dared give the order. It seemed impossible that we could touch anything without losing it, and then our last hope would have been gone."

The terror of that gale was on him yet. I let him go on for a bit, then said, casually—as if returning to a minor subject:

"You were very anxious to give up your mate to the shore people, I believe?"

He was. To the law. His obscure tenacity on that point had in it something incomprehensible and a little awful; something, as it were, mystical, quite apart from his anxiety that he should not be suspected of "countenancing any doings of that sort." Seven-and-thirty virtuous years at sea, of which over twenty of immaculate command, and the last fifteen in the *Sephora,* seemed to have laid him under some pitiless obligation.

"And you know," he went on, groping shamefacedly amongst his feelings, "I did not engage that young fellow. His people had some interest with my owners. I was in a way forced to take him on. He looked very smart, very gentlemanly, and all that. But do you know —I never liked him, somehow. I am a plain man. You see, he wasn't exactly the sort for the chief mate of a ship like the *Sephora.*"

I had become so connected in thoughts and impressions with the secret sharer of my cabin that I felt as if I, personally, were being given to understand that I, too, was not the sort that would have done for the chief mate of a ship like the *Sephora.* I had no doubt of it in my mind.

"Not at all the style of man. You understand," he insisted, superfluously, looking hard at me.

I smiled urbanely. He seemed at a loss for a while.

"I suppose I must report a suicide."

"Beg pardon?"

"Sui-cide! That's what I'll have to write to my owners directly I get in."

"Unless you manage to recover him before tomorrow," I assented, dispassionately. . . . "I mean, alive."

He mumbled something which I really did not catch, and I turned my ear to him in a puzzled manner. He fairly bawled:

"The land—I say, the mainland is at least seven miles off my anchorage."

"About that."

My lack of excitement, of curiosity, of surprise, of any sort of pronounced interest, began to arouse his distrust. But except for the felicitous pretense of deafness I had not tried to pretend anything. I had felt utterly incapable of playing the part of ignorance properly, and therefore was afraid to try. It is also certain that he had brought some ready-made suspicions with him, and that he viewed my politeness as a strange and unnatural phenomenon. And yet how else could I have received him? Not heartily! That was impossible for psychological reasons, which I need not state here. My only object was to keep off his inquiries. Surlily? Yes, but surliness might have provoked a point-blank question. From its novelty to him and from its nature, punctilious courtesy was the manner best calculated to restrain the man. But there was the danger of his breaking through my defense bluntly. I could not, I think, have met him by a direct lie, also for psychological (not moral) reasons. If he had only known how afraid I was of his putting my feeling of identity with the other to the test! But, strangely enough—(I thought of it only afterward)—I believe that he was not a little disconcerted by the reverse side of that weird situation, by something in me that reminded him of the man he was seeking—suggested a mysterious similitude to the young fellow he had distrusted and disliked from the first.

However that might have been, the silence was not very prolonged. He took another oblique step.

"I reckon I had no more than a two-mile pull to your ship. Not a bit more."

"And quite enough, too, in this awful heat," I said.

Another pause full of mistrust followed. Necessity, they say, is mother of invention, but fear, too, is not barren of ingenious suggestions. And I was afraid he would ask me point-blank for news of my other self.

"Nice little saloon, isn't it?" I remarked, as if noticing for the first time the way his eyes roamed from one closed door to the other. "And very well fitted out, too. Here, for instance," I continued reaching over the back of my seat negligently and flinging the door open, "is my bathroom."

He made an eager movement, but hardly gave it a glance. I got up, shut the door of the bathroom, and invited him to have a look round, as if I were very proud of my accommodation. He had to rise and be shown round, but he went through the business without any raptures whatever.

"And now we'll have a look at my stateroom," I declared, in a voice as loud as I dared to make it, crossing the cabin to the starboard side with purposely heavy steps.

He followed me in and gazed around. My intelligent double had vanished. I played my part.

"Very convenient—isn't it?"

"Very nice. Very comf . . ." He didn't finish, and went out brusquely as if to escape from some unrighteous wiles of mine. But it was not to be. I had been too frightened not to feel vengeful; I felt I had him on the run, and I meant to keep him on the run. My polite insistence must have had something menacing in it, because he gave in suddenly. And I did not let him off a single item; mate's room, pantry, storerooms, the very sail locker which was also under the poop—he had to look into them all. When at last I showed him out on the quarter-deck he drew a long, spiritless sigh, and mumbled dismally that he must really be going back to his ship now. I desired my mate, who had joined us, to see to the captain's boat.

The man of whiskers gave a blast on the whistle which he used to wear hanging round his neck, and yelled, "*Sephora* away!" My double down there in my cabin must have heard, and certainly could not feel more relieved than I. Four fellows came running out from somewhere forward and went over the side, while my own men, appearing on deck too, lined the rail. I escorted my visitor to the gangway ceremoniously, and nearly overdid it. He was a tenacious beast. On the very ladder he lingered, and in that unique, guiltily conscientious manner of sticking to the point:

"I say . . . you . . . you don't think that—"

I covered his voice loudly:

"Certainly not. . . . I am delighted. Good-by."

I had an idea of what he meant to say, and just saved myself by the privilege of defective hearing. He was too shaken generally to insist, but my mate, close witness of that parting, looked mystified and his face took on a thoughtful cast. As I did not want to appear as if I wished to avoid all communication with my officers, he had the opportunity to address me.

"Seems a very nice man. His boat's crew told our chaps a very extraordinary story, if what I am told by the steward is true. I suppose you had it from the captain, sir?"

"Yes. I had a story from the captain."

"A very horrible affair—isn't it, sir?"

"It is."

"Beats all these tales we hear about murders in Yankee ships."

"I don't think it beats them. I don't think it resembles them in the least."

"Bless my soul—you don't say so! But of course I've no acquaintance whatever with American ships, not I, so I couldn't go against your knowledge. It's horrible enough for me. . . . But the queerest part is that these fellows seemed to have some idea the man was hidden aboard here. They had really. Did you ever hear of such a thing?"

"Preposterous—isn't it?"

We were walking to and fro athwart the quarter-deck. No one of the crew forward could be seen (the day was Sunday), and the mate pursued:

"There was some little dispute about it. Our chaps took offense. 'As if we would harbor a thing like that,' they said. 'Wouldn't you like to look for him in our coal hole?' Quite a tiff. But they made it up in the end. I suppose he did drown himself. Don't you, sir?"

"I don't suppose anything."

"You have no doubt in the matter, sir?"

"None whatever."

I left him suddenly. I felt I was producing a bad impression, but with my double down there it was most trying to be on deck. And it was almost as trying to be below. Altogether a nerve-trying situation. But on the whole I felt less torn in two when I was with him. There was no one in the whole ship whom I dared take into my confidence. Since the hands had got to know his story, it would have been impossible to pass him off for anyone else, and an accidental discovery was to be dreaded now more than ever. . . .

The steward being engaged in laying the table for dinner, we could talk only with our eyes when I first went down. Later in the afternoon we had a cautious try at whispering. The Sunday quietness of the ship was against us; the stillness of air and water around her was against us; the elements, the men were against us—everything was against us in our secret partnership; time itself—for this could not go on forever. The very trust in Providence was, I suppose, denied to his guilt. Shall I confess that this thought cast me down very much? And as to the chapter of accidents which counts for so much in the book of success, I could only hope that it was closed. For what favorable accident could be expected?

"Did you hear everything?" were my first words as soon as we took up our position side by side, leaning over my bed-place.

He had. And the proof of it was his earnest whisper, "The man told you he hardly dared to give the order."

I understood the reference to be to that saving foresail.

"Yes. He was afraid of it being lost in the setting."

"I assure you he never gave the order. He may think he did, but he never gave it. He stood there with me on the break of the poop after the maintopsail blew away, and whimpered about our last hope—positively whimpered about it and nothing else—and the night coming on! To hear one's skipper go on like that in such weather was enough to drive any fellow out of his mind. It worked me up into a sort of desperation. I just took it into my hands and went away from him, boiling, and—But what's the use telling you? *You* know! . . . Do you think that if I had not been pretty fierce with them I should have got the men to do anything? Not it! The bosun perhaps? Perhaps! It wasn't a heavy sea—it was a sea gone mad! I suppose the end of the world will be something like that; and a man may have the heart to see it coming once and be done with it—but to have to face it day after day—I don't blame anybody. I was precious little better than the rest. Only—I was an officer of that old coal-wagon, anyhow—"

"I quite understand," I conveyed that sincere assurance into his ear. He was out of breath with whispering; I could hear him pant slightly. It was all very simple. The same strung-up force which had given twenty-four men a chance, at least, for their lives, had, in a sort of recoil, crushed an unworthy mutinous existence.

But I had no leisure to weigh the merits of the matter—footsteps in the saloon, a heavy knock. "There's enough wind to get under way with, sir." Here was the call of a new claim upon my thoughts and even upon my feelings.

"Turn the hands up," I cried through the door. "I'll be on deck directly."

I was going out to make the acquaintance of my ship. Before I left the cabin our eyes met—the eyes of the only two strangers on board. I pointed to the recessed part where the little campstool awaited him and laid my finger on my lips. He made a gesture—somewhat vague—a little mysterious, accompanied by a faint smile, as if of regret.

This is not the place to enlarge upon the sensations of a man who feels for the first time a ship move under his feet to his own independent word. In my case they were not unalloyed. I was not wholly alone with my command; for there was that stranger in my cabin. Or rather, I was not completely and wholly with her. Part of me was absent. That mental feeling of being in two places at once affected me physically as if the mood of secrecy had penetrated my very soul. Before an hour had elapsed since the ship had begun to move, having occasion to ask the mate (he stood by my side) to take a compass bearing of the Pagoda, I caught myself reaching up to his ear in whispers. I say I caught myself, but enough had escaped to startle the man. I can't describe it otherwise than by saying that he shied. A grave, preoccupied manner, as though he were in possession of some perplexing intelligence, did not leave him henceforth. A little later I moved away from the rail to look at the compass with such a stealthy gait that the helmsman noticed it—and I could not help noticing the unusual roundness of his eyes. These are trifling instances, though it's to no commander's advantage to be suspected of ludicrous eccentricities. But I was also more seriously affected. There are to a seaman certain words, gestures, that should in given conditions come as naturally, as instinctively as the winking of a menaced eye. A certain order should spring on to his lips without thinking; a certain sign should get itself made, so to speak, without reflection. But all unconscious alertness had abandoned me. I had to make an effort of will to recall myself back (from the cabin) to the conditions of the moment. I felt that I was appearing an irresolute commander to those people who were watching me more or less critically.

And, besides, there were the scares. On the second day out, for instance, coming off the deck in the afternoon (I had straw slippers on my bare feet) I stopped at the open pantry door and spoke to the steward. He was doing something there with his back to me. At the sound of my voice he nearly jumped out of his skin, as the saying is, and incidentally broke a cup.

"What on earth's the matter with you?" I asked, astonished.

He was extremely confused. "Beg your pardon, sir. I made sure you were in your cabin."

"You see I wasn't."

"No, sir. I could have sworn I had heard you moving in there not a moment ago. It's most extraordinary . . . very sorry, sir."

I passed on with an inward shudder. I was so identified with my secret double that I did not even mention the fact in those scanty, fearful whispers we exchanged. I suppose he had made some slight noise of some kind or other. It would have been miraculous if he hadn't at one time or another. And yet, haggard as he appeared, he looked always perfectly self-controlled, more than calm—almost invulnerable. On my suggestion he remained almost entirely in the bathroom, which, upon the whole, was the safest place. There could be really no shadow of an excuse for anyone ever wanting to go in there, once the steward had done with it. It was a very tiny place. Sometimes he reclined on the floor, his legs bent, his head sustained on one elbow. At others I would find him on the campstool, sitting in his gray sleeping suit and with his cropped dark hair like a patient, unmoved convict. At night I would smuggle him into my bed-place, and we would whisper together, with the regular foot-falls of the officer of the watch passing and repassing over our heads. It was an infinitely miserable time. It was lucky that some tins of fine preserves were stowed in a locker in my stateroom; hard bread I could always get hold of; and so he lived on stewed chicken, paté de foie gras, asparagus, cooked oysters, sardines—on all sorts of abominable sham delicacies out of tins. My early morning coffee he always drank; and it was all I dared do for him in that respect.

Every day there was the horrible maneuvering to go through so that my room and then the bathroom should be done in the usual way. I came to hate the sight of the steward, to abhor the voice of that harmless man. I felt that it was he who would bring on the disaster of discovery. It hung like a sword over our heads.

The fourth day out, I think (we were working down the east side of the Gulf of Siam, tack for tack, in light winds and smooth water) —the fourth day, I say, of this miserable juggling with the unavoidable, as we sat at our evening meal, that man, whose slightest movement I dreaded, after putting down the dishes ran up on deck busily. This could not be dangerous. Presently he came down again; and then it appeared that he had remembered a coat of mine which I had thrown over a rail to dry after having been wetted in a shower which had passed over the ship in the afternoon. Sitting stolidly at the head of the table I became terrified at the sight of the garment on his arm. Of course he made for my door. There was no time to lose.

"Steward," I thundered. My nerves were so shaken that I could not govern my voice and conceal my agitation. This was the sort of thing that made my terrifically whiskered mate tap his forehead with his forefinger. I had detected him using that gesture while talking on deck with a confidential air to the carpenter. It was too far to hear a word, but I had no doubt that this pantomime could only refer to the strange new captain.

"Yes, sir," the pale-faced steward turned resignedly to me. It was this maddening course of being shouted at, checked without rhyme or reason, arbitrarily chased out of my cabin, suddenly called into it, sent flying out of his pantry on incomprehensible errands, that accounted for the growing wretchedness of his expression.

"Where are you going with that coat?"

"To your room, sir."

"Is there another shower coming?"

"I'm sure I don't know, sir. Shall I go up again and see, sir?"

"No! never mind."

My object was attained, as of course my other self in there would have heard everything that passed. During this interlude my two officers never raised their eyes off their respective plates; but the lip of that confounded cub, the second mate, quivered visibly.

I expected the steward to hook my coat on and come out at once. He was very slow about it; but I dominated my nervousness sufficiently not to shout after him. Suddenly I became aware (it could be heard plainly enough) that the fellow for some reason or other was opening the door of the bathroom. It was the end. The place was literally not big enough to swing a cat in. My voice died in my throat and I went stony all over. I expected to hear a yell of surprise and terror, and made a movement, but had not the strength to get on my legs. Everything remained still. Had my second self taken the poor wretch by the throat? I don't know what I would have done next moment if I had not seen the steward come out of my room, close the door, and then stand quietly by the sideboard.

Saved, I thought. But, no! Lost! Gone! He was gone!

I laid my knife and fork down and leaned back in my chair. My head swam. After a while, when sufficiently recovered to speak in a steady voice, I instructed my mate to put the ship round at eight o'clock himself.

"I won't come on deck," I went on. "I think I'll turn in, and unless the wind shifts I don't want to be disturbed before midnight. I feel a bit seedy."

"You did look middling bad a little while ago," the chief mate remarked without showing any great concern.

They both went out, and I stared at the steward clearing the table. There was nothing to be read on that wretched man's face. But why did he avoid my eyes I asked myself. Then I thought I should like to hear the sound of his voice.

"Steward!"

"Sir!" Startled as usual.

"Where did you hang up that coat?"

"In the bathroom, sir." The usual anxious tone. "It's not quite dry yet, sir."

For some time longer I sat in the cuddy. Had my double vanished as he had come? But of his coming there was an explanation, whereas his disappearance would be inexplicable. . . . I went slowly into my dark room, shut the door, lighted the lamp, and for a time dared not turn round. When at last I did I saw him standing bolt upright in the narrow recessed part. It would not be true to say I had a shock, but an irresistible doubt of his bodily existence flitted through my mind. Can it be, I asked myself, that he is not visible to other eyes than mine? It was like being haunted. Motionless, with a grave face, he raised his hands slightly at me in a gesture which meant clearly, "Heavens! what a narrow escape!" Narrow indeed. I think I had come creeping quietly as near insanity as any man who has not actually gone over the border. That gesture restrained me, so to speak.

The mate with the terrific whiskers was now putting the ship on the other tack. In the moment of profound silence which follows upon the hands going to their stations I heard on the poop his raised voice: "Hard alee!" and the distant shout of the order repeated on the maindeck. The sails, in that light breeze, made but a faint fluttering noise. It ceased. The ship was coming round slowly; I held my breath in the renewed stillness of expectation; one wouldn't have thought that there was a single living soul on her decks. A sudden brisk shout, "Mainsail haul!" broke the spell, and in the noisy cries and rush overhead of the men running away with the main brace we two, down in my cabin, came together in our usual position by the bed-place.

He did not wait for my question. "I heard him fumbling here and just managed to squat myself down in the bath," he whispered to me. "The fellow only opened the door and put his arm in to hang the coat up. All the same—"

"I never thought of that," I whispered back, even more appalled than before at the closeness of the shave, and marveling at that something unyielding in his character which was carrying him through so finely. There was no agitation in his whisper. Whoever was being driven distracted, it was not he. He was sane. And the proof of his sanity was continued when he took up the whispering again.

"It would never do for me to come to life again."

It was something that a ghost might have said. But what he was alluding to was his old captain's reluctant admission of the theory of suicide. It would obviously serve his turn—if I had understood at all the view which seemed to govern the unalterable purpose of his action.

"You must maroon me as soon as ever you can get amongst these islands off the Cambodje shore," he went on.

"Maroon you! We are not living in a boy's adventure tale," I protested. His scornful whispering took me up.

"We aren't indeed! There's nothing of a boy's tale in this. But there's nothing else for it. I want no more. You don't suppose I am afraid of what can be done to me? Prison or gallows or whatever they may please. But you don't see me coming back to explain such things to an old fellow in a wig and twelve respectable tradesmen, do you? What can they know whether I am guilty or not—or of *what* I am guilty, either? That's my affair. What does the Bible say? 'Driven off the face of the earth.' Very well. I am off the face of the earth now. As I came at night so I shall go."

"Impossible!" I murmured. "You can't."

"Can't? . . . Not naked like a soul on the Day of Judgment. I shall freeze on to this sleeping suit. The Last Day is not yet—and . . . you have understood thoroughly. Didn't you?"

I felt suddenly ashamed of myself. I may say truly that I understood—and my hesitation in letting that man swim away from my ship's side had been a mere sham sentiment, a sort of cowardice.

"It can't be done now till next night," I breathed out. "The ship is on the offshore tack and the wind may fail us."

"As long as I know that you understand," he whispered. "But of course you do. It's a great satisfaction to have got somebody to understand. You seem to have been there on purpose." And in the same whisper, as if we two whenever we talked had to say things to each other which were not fit for the world to hear, he added, "It's very wonderful."

We remained side by side talking in our secret way—but sometimes silent or just exchanging a whispered word or two at long intervals. And as usual he stared through the port. A breath of wind came now and again into our faces. The ship might have been moored in dock, so gently and on an even keel she slipped through the water, that did not murmur even at our passage, shadowy and silent like a phantom sea.

At midnight I went on deck, and to my mate's great surprise put the ship round on the other tack. His terrible whiskers flitted round me in silent criticism. I certainly should not have done it if it had been only a question of getting out of that sleepy gulf as quickly as possible. I believe he told the second mate, who relieved him, that it was a great want of judgment. The other only yawned. That intolerable cub shuffled about so sleepily and lolled against the rails in such a slack, improper fashion that I came down on him sharply.

"Aren't you properly awake yet?"

"Yes, sir! I am awake."

"Well, then, be good enough to hold yourself as if you were. And keep a lookout. If there's any current we'll be closing with some islands before daylight."

The east side of the gulf is fringed with islands, some solitary, others in groups. On the blue background of the high coast they seem to float on silvery patches of calm water, arid and gray, or dark green and rounded like clumps of evergreen bushes, with the larger ones, a mile or two long, showing the outlines of ridges, ribs of gray rock under the dark mantle of matted leafage. Unknown to trade, to travel, almost to geography, the manner of life they harbor is an unsolved secret. There must be villages—settlements of fishermen at least—on the largest of them, and some communication with the world is probably kept up by native craft. But all forenoon, as we headed for them, fanned along by the faintest of breezes, I saw no sign of man or canoe in the field of the telescope I kept on pointing at the scattered group.

At noon I gave no orders for a change of course, and the mate's whiskers became much concerned and seemed to be offering themselves unduly to my notice. At last I said:

"I am going to stand right in. Quite in—as far as I can take her."

The stare of extreme surprise imparted an air of ferocity also to his eyes, and he looked truly terrific for a moment.

"We're not doing well in the middle of the gulf," I continued, casually. "I am going to look for the land breezes tonight."

"Bless my soul! Do you mean, sir, in the dark amongst the lot of all them islands and reefs and shoals?"

"Well—if there are any regular land breezes at all on this coast one must get close inshore to find them, mustn't one?"

"Bless my soul!" he exclaimed again under his breath. All that afternoon he wore a dreamy, contemplative appearance which in him was a mark of perplexity. After dinner I went into my stateroom as if I meant to take some rest. There we two bent our dark heads over a half-unrolled chart lying on my bed.

"There," I said. "It's got to be Koh-ring. I've been looking at it ever since sunrise. It has got two hills and a low point. It must be inhabited. And on the coast opposite there is what looks like the mouth of a biggish river—with some town, no doubt, not far up. It's the best chance for you that I can see.

"Anything. Koh-ring let it be."

He looked thoughtfully at the chart as if surveying chances and distances from a lofty height—and following with his eyes his own figure wandering on the blank land of Cochin China, and then passing off that piece of paper clean out of sight into uncharted regions. And it was as if the ship had two captains to plan her course for her. I had been so worried and restless running up and down that I had not had the patience to dress that day. I had remained in my sleeping suit, with straw slippers and a soft floppy hat. The closeness of the heat in the gulf had been most oppressive, and the crew were used to see me wandering in that airy attire.

"She will clear the south point as she heads now," I whispered into his ear. "Goodness only knows when, though, but certainly after dark. I'll edge her in to half a mile, as far as I may be able to judge in the dark—"

"Be careful," he murmured, warningly—and I realized suddenly that all my future, the only future for which I was fit, would perhaps go irretrievably to pieces in any mishap to my first command.

I could not stop a moment longer in the room. I motioned him to get out of sight and made my way on the poop. That unplayful cub had the watch. I walked up and down for a while thinking things out, then beckoned him over.

"Send a couple of hands to open the two quarter-deck ports," I said, mildly.

He actually had the impudence, or else so forgot himself in his wonder at such an incomprehensible order, as to repeat:

"Open the quarter-deck ports! What for, sir?"

"The only reason you need concern yourself about is because I tell you to do so. Have them open wide and fastened properly."

He reddened and went off, but I believe made some jeering remark to the carpenter as to the sensible practice of ventilating a ship's quarter-deck. I know he popped into the mate's cabin to impart the fact to him because the whiskers came on deck, as it were by chance, and stole glances at me from below—for signs of lunacy or drunkenness, I suppose.

A little before supper, feeling more restless than ever, I rejoined, for a moment, my second self. And to find him sitting so quietly was surprising, like something against nature, inhuman.

I developed my plan in a hurried whisper.

"I shall stand in as close as I dare and then put her round. I shall presently find means to smuggle you out of here into the sail locker, which communicates with the lobby. But there is an opening, a sort of square for hauling the sails out, which gives straight on the quarter-deck and which is never closed in fine weather, so as to give air to the sails. When the ship's way is deadened in stays and all the hands are aft at the main braces you shall have a clear road to slip out and get overboard through the open quarter-deck port. I've had them both fastened up. Use a rope's end to lower yourself into the water so as to avoid a splash—you know. It could be heard and cause some beastly complication."

He kept silent for a while, then whispered, "I understand."

"I won't be there to see you go," I began with an effort. "The rest . . . I only hope I have understood, too."

"You have. From first to last," and for the first time there seemed to be a faltering, something strained in his whisper. He caught hold of my arm, but the ringing of the supper bell made me start. He didn't, though; he only released his grip.

After supper I didn't come below again till well past eight o'clock. The faint, steady breeze was loaded with dew; and the wet, darkened sails held all there was of propelling power in it. The night, clear and starry, sparkled darkly, and the opaque, lightless patches shifting slowly against the low stars were the drifting islets. On the port bow there was a big one more distant and shadowily imposing by the great space of sky it eclipsed.

On opening the door I had a back view of my very own self looking at a chart. He had come out of the recess and was standing near the table.

"Quite dark enough," I whispered.

He stepped back and leaned against my bed with a level, quiet glance. I sat on the couch. We had nothing to say to each other. Over our heads the officer of the watch moved here and there. Then I heard him move quickly. I knew what that meant. He was making for the companion; and presently his voice was outside my door.

"We are drawing in pretty fast, sir. Land looks rather close."

"Very well," I answered. "I am coming on deck directly."

I waited till he was gone out of the cuddy, then rose. My double moved too. The time had come to exchange our last whispers, for neither of us was ever to hear each other's natural voice.

"Look here!" I opened a drawer and took out three sovereigns. "Take this, anyhow. I've got six and I'd give you the lot, only I must keep a little money to buy some fruit and vegetables for the crew from native boats as we go through Sunda Straits."

He shook his head.

"Take it," I urged him, whispering desperately. "No one can tell what—"

He smiled and slapped meaningly the only pocket of the sleeping jacket. It was not safe, certainly. But I produced a large old silk handkerchief of mine, and tying the three pieces of gold in a corner, pressed it on him. He was touched, I suppose, because he took it at last and tied it quickly round his waist under the jacket, on his bare skin.

Our eyes met; several seconds elapsed, till, our glances still mingled, I extended my hand and turned the lamp out. Then I passed through the cuddy, leaving the door of my room wide open. . . . "Steward!"

He was still lingering in the pantry in the greatness of his zeal, giving a rub-up to a plated cruet stand the last thing before going to bed. Being careful not to wake up the mate, whose room was opposite, I spoke in an undertone.

He looked round anxiously. "Sir!"

"Can you get me a little hot water from the galley?"

"I am afraid, sir, the galley fire's been out for some time now."

"Go and see."

He fled up the stairs.

"Now," I whispered, loudly, into the saloon—too loudly, perhaps, but I was afraid I couldn't make a sound. He was by my side in an instant—the double captain slipped past the stairs—through the tiny dark passage . . . a sliding door. We were in the sail locker, scrambling on our knees over the sails. A sudden thought struck me. I saw myself wandering barefooted, bareheaded, the sun beating on my dark poll. I snatched off my floppy hat and tried hurriedly in the dark to ram it on my other self. He dodged and fended off silently. I wonder what he thought had come to me before he understood and suddenly desisted. Our hands met gropingly, lingered united in a steady, motionless clasp for a second. . . . No word was breathed by either of us when they separated.

I was standing quietly by the pantry door when the steward returned.

"Sorry, sir. Kettle barely warm. Shall I light the spirit lamp?"

"Never mind."

I came out on deck slowly. It was now a matter of conscience to shave the land as close as possible—for now he must go overboard whenever the ship was put in stays. Must! There could be no going back for him. After a moment I walked over to leeward and my heart flew into my mouth at the nearness of the land on the bow. Under any other circumstances I would not have held on a minute longer. The second mate had followed me anxiously.

I looked on till I felt I could command my voice.

"She will weather," I said then in a quiet tone.

"Are you going to try that, sir?" he stammered out incredulously.

I took no notice of him and raised my tone just enough to be heard by the helmsman.

"Keep her good full."

"Good full, sir."

The wind fanned my cheek, the sails slept, the world was silent. The strain of watching the dark loom of the land grow bigger and denser was too much for me. I had shut my eyes—because the ship must go closer. She must! The stillness was intolerable. Were we standing still?

When I opened my eyes the second view started my heart with a thump. The black southern hill of Koh-ring seemed to hang right over the ship like a towering fragment of the everlasting night. On that enormous mass of blackness there was not a gleam to be seen, not a sound to be heard. It was gliding irresistibly toward us and yet seemed already within reach of the hand. I saw the vague figures of the watch grouped in the waist, gazing in awed silence.

"Are you going on, sir?" inquired an unsteady voice at my elbow.

I ignored it. I had to go on.

"Keep her full. Don't check her way. That won't do now," I said warningly.

"I can't see the sails very well," the helmsman answered me, in strange, quavering tones.

Was she close enough? Already she was, I won't say in the shadow of the land, but in the very blackness of it, already swallowed up as it were, gone too close to be recalled, gone from me altogether.

"Give the mate a call," I said to the young man who stood at my elbow still as death. "And turn all hands up."

My tone had a borrowed loudness reverberated from the height of the land. Several voices cried out together: "We are all on deck, sir."

Then stillness again, with the great shadow gliding closer, towering higher, without a light, without a sound. Such a hush had fallen on the ship that she might have been a bark of the dead floating in slowly under the very gate of Erebus.

"My God! Where are we?"

It was the mate moaning at my elbow. He was thunderstruck, and as it were deprived of the moral support of his whiskers. He clapped his hands and absolutely cried out, "Lost!"

"Be quiet," I said sternly.

He lowered his tone, but I saw the shadowy gesture of his despair. "What are we doing here?"

"Looking for the land wind."

He made as if to tear his hair, and addressed me recklessly.

"She will never get out. You have done it, sir. I knew it'd end in something like this. She will never weather, and you are too close now to stay. She'll drift ashore before she's round. O my God!"

I caught his arm as he was raising it to batter his poor devoted head, and shook it violently.

"She's ashore already," he wailed, trying to tear himself away.

"Is she? . . . Keep good full there!"

"Good full, sir," cried the helmsman in a frightened, thin, child-like voice.

I hadn't let go the mate's arm and went on shaking it. "Ready about, do you hear? You go forward"—shake—"and stop there"—

shake—"and hold your noise"—shake—"and see these head sheets properly overhauled"—shake, shake—shake.

And all the time I dared not look toward the land lest my heart should fail me. I released my grip at last and he ran forward as if fleeing for dear life.

I wondered what my double there in the sail locker thought of this commotion. He was able to hear everything—and perhaps he was able to understand why, on my conscience, it had to be thus close—no less. My first order "Hard alee!" re-echoed ominously under the towering shadow of Koh-ring as if I had shouted in a mountain gorge. And then I watched the land intently. In that smooth water and light wind it was impossible to feel the ship coming-to. No! I could not feel her. And my second self was making now ready to slip out and lower himself overboard. Perhaps he was gone already . . . ?

The great black mass brooding over our very mastheads began to pivot away from the ship's side silently. And now I forgot the secret stranger ready to depart, and remembered only that I was a total stranger to the ship. I did not know her. Would she do it? How was she to be handled?

I swung the mainyard and waited helplessly. She was perhaps stopped, and her very fate hung in the balance, with the black mass of Koh-ring like the gate of the everlasting night towering over her taffrail. What would she do now? Had she way on her yet? I stepped to the side swiftly, and on the shadowy water I could see nothing except a faint phosphorescent flash revealing the glassy smoothness of the sleeping surface. It was impossible to tell—and I had not learned yet the feel of my ship. Was she moving? What I needed was something easily seen, a piece of paper, which I could throw overboard and watch. I had nothing on me. To run down for it I didn't dare. There was no time. All at once my strained, yearning stare distinguished a white object floating within a yard of the ship's side. White on the black water. A phosphorescent flash passed under it. What was that thing? . . . I recognized my own floppy hat. It must have fallen off his head . . . and he didn't bother. Now I had what I wanted—the saving mark for my eyes. But I hardly thought of my other self, now gone from the ship, to be hidden forever from all friendly faces, to be a fugitive and a vagabond on the earth, with no brand of the curse on his sane forehead to stay a slaying hand . . . too proud to explain.

And I watched the hat—the expression of my sudden pity for his mere flesh. It had been meant to save his homeless head from the dangers of the sun. And now—behold—it was saving the ship, by serving me for a mark to help out the ignorance of my strangeness. Ha! It was drifting forward, warning me just in time that the ship had gathered sternway.

"Shift the helm," I said in a low voice to the seaman standing still like a statue.

The man's eyes glistened wildly in the binnacle light as he jumped round to the other side and spun round the wheel.

I walked to the break of the poop. On the overshadowed deck all hands stood by the forebraces waiting for my order. The stars ahead seemed to be gliding from right to left. And all was so still in the world that I heard the quiet remark "She's round," passed in a tone of intense relief between two seamen.

"Let go and haul."

The foreyards ran round with a great noise, amidst cheery cries. And now the frightful whiskers made themselves heard giving various orders. Already the ship was drawing ahead. And I was alone with her. Nothing! no one in the world should stand now between us, throwing a shadow on the way of silent knowledge and mute affection, the perfect communion of a seaman with his first command.

Walking to the taffrail, I was in time to make out, on the very edge of a darkness thrown by a towering black mass like the very gateway of Erebus—yes, I was in time to catch an evanescent glimpse of my white hat left behind to mark the spot where the secret sharer of my cabin and of my thoughts, as though he were my second self, had lowered himself into the water to take his punishment: a free man, a proud swimmer striking out for a new destiny.

1910

The Lady With the Dog

ANTON CHEKHOV

[1860–1904]

I

People were telling one another that a newcomer had been seen on the promenade—a lady with a dog. Dmitri Dmitrich Gurov had been a fortnight in Yalta, and was accustomed to its ways, and he, too, had begun to take an interest in fresh arrivals. From his seat in Vernet's outdoor café, he caught sight of a young woman in a toque, passing along the promenade; she was fair and not very tall; after her trotted a white pomeranian.

Later he encountered her in the municipal park, and in the square, several times a day. She was always alone, wearing the same toque, and the pomeranian always trotted at her side. Nobody knew who she was, and people referred to her simply as "the lady with the dog."

"If she's here without her husband, and without any friends," thought Gurov, "it wouldn't be a bad idea to make her acquaintance."

He was not yet forty, but had a twelve-year-old daughter and two schoolboy sons. He had been talked into marrying in his second year at college, and his wife now looked nearly twice as old as he was. She was a tall, black-browed woman, erect, dignified, imposing, and, as she said of herself, a "thinker." She was a great reader, omitted the "hard sign"* at the end of words in her letters, and called her husband "Dimitri" instead of Dmitri; and though he

*Certain progressive intellectuals omitted the hard sign after consonants in writing, thus anticipating the reform in the Russian alphabet introduced later on.—*Tr.*

secretly considered her shallow, narrowminded, and dowdy, he stood in awe of her, and disliked being at home. It was long since he had first begun deceiving her and he was now constantly unfaithful to her, and this was no doubt why he spoke slightingly of women, to whom he referred as *the lower race.*

He considered that the ample lessons he had received from bitter experience entitled him to call them whatever he liked, but without this "lower race" he could not have existed a single day. He was bored and ill-at-ease in the company of men, with whom he was always cold and reserved, but felt quite at home among women, and knew exactly what to say to them, and how to behave; he could even be silent in their company without feeling the slightest awkwardness. There was an elusive charm in his appearance and disposition which attracted women and caught their sympathies. He knew this and was himself attracted to them by some invisible force.

Repeated and bitter experience had taught him that every fresh intimacy, while at first introducing such pleasant variety into everyday life, and offering itself as a charming, light adventure, inevitably developed, among decent people (especially in Moscow, where they are so irresolute and slow to move), into a problem of excessive complication leading to an intolerably irksome situation. But every time he encountered an attractive woman he forgot all about this experience, the desire for life surged up in him, and everything suddenly seemed simple and amusing.

One evening, then, while he was dining at the restaurant in the park, the lady in the toque came strolling up and took a seat at a neighbouring table. Her expression, gait, dress, coiffure, all told him that she was from the upper classes, that she was married, that she was in Yalta for the first time, alone and bored. . . . The accounts of the laxity of morals among visitors to Yalta are greatly exaggerated, and he paid no heed to them, knowing that for the most part they were invented by people who would gladly have transgressed themselves, had they known how to set about it. But when the lady sat down at a neighbouring table a few yards away from him, these stories of easy conquests, of excursions to the mountains, came back to him, and the seductive idea of a brisk transitory liaison, an affair with a woman whose very name he did not know, suddenly took possession of his mind.

He snapped his fingers at the pomeranian, and when it trotted up to him, shook his forefinger at it. The pomeranian growled. Gurov shook his finger again.

The lady glanced at him and instantly lowered her eyes.

"He doesn't bite," she said, and blushed.

"May I give him a bone?" he asked, and on her nod of consent added in friendly tones: "Have you been long in Yalta?"

"About five days."

"And I am dragging out my second week here."

Neither spoke for a few minutes.

"The days pass quickly, and yet one is so bored here," she said, not looking at him.

"It's the thing to say it's boring here. People never complain of boredom in God-forsaken holes like Belyev or Zhizdra, but when they get here it's: 'Oh, the dullness! Oh, the dust!' You'd think they'd come from Grenada to say the least of it."

She laughed. Then they both went on eating in silence, like complete strangers. But after dinner they left the restaurant together, and embarked upon the light, jesting talk of people free and contented, for whom it is all the same where they go, or what they talk about. They strolled along, remarking on the strange light over the sea. The water was a warm, tender purple, the moonlight lay on its surface in a golden strip. They said how close it was, after the hot day. Gurov told her he was from Moscow, that he was really a philologist, but worked in a bank; that he had at one time trained himself to sing in a private opera company, but had given up the idea; that he owned two houses in Moscow. . . . And from her he learned that she had grown up in Petersburg, but had got married in the town of S., where she had been living two years, that she would stay another month in Yalta, and that perhaps her husband, who also needed a rest, would join her. She was quite unable to explain whether her husband was a member of the gubernia council, or on the board of the Zemstvo, and was greatly amused at herself for this. Further, Gurov learned that her name was Anna Sergeyevna.

Back in his own room he thought about her, and felt sure he would meet her the next day. It was inevitable. As he went to bed he reminded himself that only a very short time ago she had been a schoolgirl, like his own daughter, learning her lessons, he remembered how much there was of shyness and constraint in her laughter, in her way of conversing with a stranger—it was probably the first time in her life that she found herself alone, and in a situation in which men could follow her and watch her, and speak to her, all the time with a secret aim she could not fail to divine. He recalled her slender, delicate neck, her fine grey eyes.

"And yet there's something pathetic about her," he thought to himself as he fell asleep.

II

A week had passed since the beginning of their acquaintance. It was a holiday. Indoors it was stuffy, but the dust rose in clouds out of doors, and people's hats blew off. It was a thirsty day and Gurov kept going to the outdoor café for fruit-drinks and ices to offer Anna Sergeyevna. The heat was overpowering.

In the evening, when the wind had dropped, they walked to the pier to see the steamer in. There were a great many people strolling about the landing-place; some, bunches of flowers in their hands, were meeting friends. Two peculiarities of the smart Yalta crowd stood out distinctly—the elderly ladies all tried to dress very young, and there seemed to be an inordinate number of generals about.

Owing to the roughness of the sea the steamer arrived late, after the sun had gone down, and it had to manoeuvre for some time before it could get alongside the pier. Anna Sergeyevna scanned the steamer and passengers through her lorgnette, as if looking for someone she knew, and when she turned to Gurov her eyes were glistening. She talked a great deal, firing off abrupt questions and forgetting immediately what it was she had wanted to know. Then she lost her lorgnette in the crush.

The smart crowd began dispersing, features could no longer be made out, the wind had quite dropped, and Gurov and Anna Sergeyevna stood there as if waiting for someone else to come off the steamer. Anna Sergeyevna had fallen silent, every now and then smelling her flowers, but not looking at Gurov.

"It's turning out a fine evening," he said. "What shall we do? We might go for a drive."

She made no reply.

He looked steadily at her and suddenly took her in his arms and kissed her lips, and the fragrance and dampness of the flowers closed round him, but the next moment he looked behind him in alarm—had anyone seen them?

"Let's go to your room," he murmured.

And they walked off together, very quickly.

Her room was stuffy and smelt of some scent she had bought in the Japanese shop. Gurov looked at her, thinking to himself: "How full of strange encounters life is!" He could remember carefree, good-natured women who were exhilarated by love-making and grateful to him for the happiness he gave them, however short-lived; and there had been others—his wife among them—whose caresses were insincere, affected, hysterical, mixed up with a great deal of quite unnecessary talk, and whose expression seemed to say that all this was not just love-making or passion, but something much more significant; then there had been two or three beautiful, cold women, over whose features flitted a predatory expression, betraying a determination to wring from life more than it could give, women no longer in their first youth, capricious, irrational, despotic, brainless, and when Gurov had cooled to these, their beauty aroused in him nothing but repulsion, and the lace trimming on their underclothes reminded him of fish-scales.

But here the timidity and awkwardness of youth and inexperience were still apparent; and there was a feeling of embarrassment in the atmosphere, as if someone had just knocked at the door. Anna Sergeyevna, "the lady with the dog," seemed to regard the affair as something very special, very serious, as if she had become a fallen woman, an attitude he found odd and disconcerting. Her features lengthened and drooped, and her long hair hung mournfully on either side of her face. She assumed a pose of dismal meditation, like a repentant sinner in some classical painting.

"It isn't right," she said. "You will never respect me any more."

On the table was a water-melon. Gurov cut himself a slice from it and began slowly eating it. At least half an hour passed in silence.

Anna Sergeyevna was very touching, revealing the purity of a decent, naive woman who had seen very little of life. The solitary candle burning on the table scarcely lit up her face, but it was obvious that her heart was heavy.

"Why should I stop respecting you?" asked Gurov. "You don't know what you're saying."

"May God forgive me!" she exclaimed, and her eyes filled with tears. "It's terrible."

"No need to seek to justify yourself."

"How can I justify myself? I'm a wicked, fallen woman, I despise myself and have not the least thought of self-justification. It isn't my husband I have deceived, it's myself. And not only now, I have been deceiving myself for ever so long. My husband is no doubt an honest, worthy man, but he's a flunkey. I don't know what it is he does at his office, but I know he's a flunkey. I was only twenty when I married him, and I was devoured by curiosity, I wanted something higher. I told myself that there must be a different kind of life. I wanted to live, to live. . . . I was burning with curiosity . . . you'll never understand that, but I swear to God I could no longer control myself, nothing could hold me back, I told my husband I was ill, and I came here. . . . And I started going about like one possessed, like a madwoman . . . and now I have become an ordinary, worthless woman, and everyone has the right to despise me."

Gurov listened to her, bored to death. The naive accents, the remorse, all was so unexpected, so out of place. But for the tears in her eyes, she might have been jesting or play-acting.

"I don't understand," he said gently. "What is it you want?"

She hid her face against his breast and pressed closer to him.

"Do believe me, I implore you to believe me," she said. "I love all that is honest and pure in life, vice is revolting to me. I don't know what I'm doing. The common people say they are snared by the devil. And now I can say that I have been snared by the devil, too."

"Come, come," he murmured.

He gazed into her fixed, terrified eyes, kissed her, and soothed her with gentle affectionate words, and gradually she calmed down and regained her cheerfulness. Soon they were laughing together again.

When, a little later, they went out, there was not a soul on the promenade, the town and its cypresses looked dead, but the sea was still roaring as it dashed against the beach. A solitary fishing-boat tossed on the waves, its lamp blinking sleepily.

They found a droshky and drove to Oreanda.

"I discovered your name in the hall, just now," said Gurov, "written up on the board. Von Diederitz. Is your husband a German?"

"No. His grandfather was, I think, but he belongs to the Orthodox church himself."

When they got out of the droshky at Oreanda they sat down on a bench not far from the church, and looked down at the sea, without talking. Yalta could be dimly discerned through the morning mist, and white clouds rested motionless on the summits of the mountains. Not a leaf stirred, the grasshoppers chirruped, and the monotonous hollow roar of the sea came up to them, speaking of peace, of the eternal sleep lying in wait for us all. The sea had roared like this long before there was any Yalta or Oreanda, it was roaring now, and it would go on roaring, just as indifferently and hollowly, when we had passed away. And it may be that in this continuity, this utter indifference to life and death, lies the secret of our ultimate salvation, of the stream of life on our planet, and of its never-ceasing movement towards perfection.

Side by side with a young woman, who looked so exquisite in the early light, soothed and enchanted by the sight of all this magical beauty—sea, mountains, clouds and the vast expanse of the sky—Gurov told himself that, when you came to think of it, everything in the world is beautiful really, everything but our own thoughts and actions, when we lose sight of the higher aims of life, and of our dignity as human beings.

Someone approached them—a watchman, probably—looked at them and went away. And there was something mysterious and beautiful even in this. The steamer from Feodosia could be seen coming towards the pier, lit up by the dawn, its lamps out.

"There's dew on the grass," said Anna Sergeyevna, breaking the silence.

"Yes. Time to go home."

They went back to the town.

After this they met every day at noon on the promenade, lunching and dining together, going for walks, and admiring the sea. She complained of sleeplessness, of palpitations, asked the same questions over and over again, alternately surrendering to jealousy and the fear that he did not really respect her. And often, when there was nobody in sight in the square or the park, he would draw her to him and kiss her passionately. The utter idleness, these kisses in broad daylight, accompanied by furtive glances and the fear of discovery, the heat, the smell of the sea, and the idle, smart, well-fed people continually crossing their field of vision, seemed to have given him a new lease on life. He told Anna Sergeyevna she was beautiful and seductive, made love to her with impetuous passion, and never left her side, while she was always pensive, always trying to force from him the admission that he did not respect her, that he did not love her a bit, and considered her just an ordinary woman. Almost every night they drove out of town, to Oreanda, the waterfall, or some other beauty-spot. And these excursions were invariably a success, each contributing fresh impressions of majestic beauty.

All this time they kept expecting her husband to arrive. But a letter came in which he told his wife that he was having trouble with his eyes, and implored her to come home as soon as possible. Anna Sergeyevna made hasty preparations for leaving.

"It's a good thing I'm going," she said to Gurov. "It's the intervention of fate."

She left Yalta in a carriage, and he went with her as far as the railway station. The drive took nearly a whole day. When she got into the express train, after the second bell had been rung, she said:

"Let me have one more look at you. . . . One last look. That's right."

She did not weep, but was mournful, and seemed ill, the muscles of her cheeks twitching.

"I shall think of you . . . I shall think of you all the time," she said. "God bless you! Think kindly of me. We are parting for ever, it must be so, because we ought never to have met. Good-bye—God bless you."

The train steamed rapidly out of the station, its lights soon disappearing, and a minute later even the sound it made was silenced, as if everything were conspiring to bring this sweet oblivion, this madness, to an end as quickly as possible. And Gurov, standing alone on the platform and gazing into the dark distance, listened to the shrilling of the grasshoppers and the humming of the telegraph wires, with a feeling that he had only just waked up. And he told himself that this had been just one more of the many adventures in his life, and that it, too, was over, leaving nothing but a memory. . . . He was moved and sad, and felt a slight remorse. After all, this young woman whom he would never again see had not been really happy with him. He had been friendly and affectionate with her, but in his whole behaviour, in the tones of his voice, in his very caresses, there had been a shade of irony, the insulting indulgence of the fortunate male, who was, moreover, almost twice her age. She had insisted in calling him good, remarkable, high-minded. Evidently he had appeared to her different from his real self, in a word he had involuntarily deceived her. . . .

There was an autumnal feeling in the air, and the evening was chilly.

"It's time for me to be going north, too," thought Gurov, as he walked away from the platform. "High time!"

III

When he got back to Moscow it was beginning to look like winter, the stoves were heated every day, and it was still dark when the children got up to go to school and drank their tea, so that the nurse had to light the lamp for a short time. Frost had set in. When the first snow falls, and one goes for one's first sleigh-ride, it is pleasant to see the white ground, the white roofs; one breathes freely and lightly, and remembers the days of one's youth. The ancient lime-trees and birches, white with rime, have a good-natured look, they are closer to the heart than cypresses and palms, and beneath their branches one is no longer haunted by the memory of mountains and the sea.

Gurov had always lived in Moscow, and he returned to Moscow on a fine frosty day, and when he put on his fur-lined overcoat and thick gloves, and sauntered down Petrovka Street, and when, on Saturday evening, he heard the church bells ringing, his recent journey and the places he had visited lost their charm for him. He became gradually immersed in Moscow life, reading with avidity three newspapers a day, while declaring he never read Moscow newspapers on principle. Once more he was caught up in a whirl of restaurants, clubs, banquets, and celebrations, once more glowed with the flattering consciousness that well-known lawyers and actors came to his house, that he played cards in the Medical Club opposite a professor.

He had believed that in a month's time Anna Sergeyevna would be nothing but a wistful memory, and that hereafter, with her wistful smile, she would only occasionally appear to him in dreams, like others before her. But the month was now well over and winter was in full swing, and all was as clear in his memory as if he had only parted with Anna Sergeyevna the day before. And his recollections grew ever more insistent. When the voices of his children at their lessons reached him in his study through the evening stillness, when he heard a song, or the sounds of a musical-box in a restaurant, when the wind howled in the chimney, it all came back to him: early morning on the pier, the misty mountains, the steamer from Feodosia, the kisses. He would pace up and down his room for a long time, smiling at his memories, and then memory turned into dreaming, and what had happened mingled in his imagination with what was going to happen. Anna Sergeyevna did not come to him in his dreams, she accompanied him everywhere, like his shadow, following him everywhere he went. When he closed his eyes, she seemed to stand before him in the flesh, still lovelier, younger, tenderer than she had really been, and looking back, he saw himself, too, as better than he had been in Yalta. In the evenings she looked out at him from the bookshelves, the fire-place, the corner, he could hear her breathing, the sweet rustle of her skirts. In the streets he followed women with his eyes, to see if there were any like her. . . .

He began to feel an overwhelming desire to share his memories with someone. But he could not speak of his love at home, and outside his home who was there for him to confide in? Not the tenants living in his house, and certainly not his colleagues at the bank. And what was there to tell? Was it love that he had felt? Had there been anything exquisite, poetic, anything instructive or even amusing about his relations with Anna Sergeyevna? He had to content himself with uttering vague generalizations about love and women, and nobody guessed what he meant, though his wife's dark eyebrows twitched as she said:

"The role of a coxcomb doesn't suit you a bit, Dimitri."

One evening, leaving the Medical Club with one of his card-partners, a government official, he could not refrain from remarking:

"If you only knew what a charming woman I met in Yalta!"

The official got into his sleigh, and just before driving off turned and called out:

"Dmitri Dmitrich!"

"Yes?"

"You were quite right, you know—the sturgeon was just a *leetle* off."

These words, in themselves so commonplace, for some reason infuriated Gurov, seemed to him humiliating, gross. What savage manners, what people! What wasted evenings, what tedious, empty days! Frantic card-playing, gluttony, drunkenness, perpetual talk always about the same thing. The greater part of one's time and energy went on business that was no use to anyone, and on discussing the same thing over and over again, and there was nothing to show for it all but a stunted, earth-bound existence and a round of trivialities, and there was nowhere to escape to, you might as well be in a mad-house or a convict settlement.

Gurov lay awake all night, raging, and went about the whole of the next day with a headache. He slept badly on the succeeding nights, too, sitting up in bed, thinking, or pacing the floor of his room. He was sick of his children, sick of the bank, felt not the slightest desire to go anywhere or talk about anything.

When the Christmas holidays came, he packed his things, telling his wife he had to go to Petersburg in the interests of a certain young man, and set off for the town of S. To what end? He hardly knew himself. He only knew that he must see Anna Sergeyevna, must speak to her, arrange a meeting, if possible.

He arrived at S. in the morning and engaged the best room in the hotel, which had a carpet of grey military frieze, and a dusty ink-pot on the table, surmounted by a headless rider, holding his hat in his raised hand. The hall porter told him what he wanted to know: von Diederitz had a house of his own in Staro-Goncharnaya Street. It wasn't far from the hotel, he lived on a grand scale, luxuriously, kept carriage-horses, the whole town knew him. The hall porter pronounced the name "Drideritz."

Gurov strolled over to Staro-Goncharnaya Street and discovered the house. In front of it was a long grey fence with inverted nails hammered into the tops of the palings.

"A fence like that is enough to make anyone want to run away," thought Gurov, looking at the windows of the house and the fence.

He reasoned that since it was a holiday, her husband would probably be at home. In any case it would be tactless to embarrass her by calling at the house. And a note might fall into the hands of the husband, and bring about catastrophe. The best thing would be to wait about on the chance of seeing her. And he walked up and down the street, hovering in the vicinity of the fence, watching for his chance. A beggar entered the gate, only to be attacked by dogs, then, an hour later, the faint, vague sounds of a piano reached his ears. That would be Anna Sergeyevna playing. Suddenly the front door opened and an old woman came out, followed by a familiar white pomeranian. Gurov tried to call to it, but his heart beat violently, and in his agitation he could not remember its name.

He walked on, hating the grey fence more and more, and now ready to tell himself irately that Anna Sergeyevna had forgotten him, had already, perhaps, found distraction in another—what could be more natural in a young woman who had to look at this accursed fence from morning to night? He went back to his hotel and sat on the sofa in his room for some time, not knowing what to do, then he ordered dinner, and after dinner, had a long sleep.

"What a foolish, restless business," he thought, waking up and looking towards the dark window-panes. It was evening by now. "Well, I've had my sleep out. And what am I to do in the night?"

He sat up in bed, covered by the cheap grey quilt, which reminded him of a hospital blanket, and in his vexation he fell to taunting himself.

"You and your lady with a dog . . . there's adventure for you! See what you get for your pains."

On his arrival at the station that morning he had noticed a poster announcing in enormous letters the first performance at the local theatre of *The Geisha.* Remembering this, he got up and made for the theatre.

"It's highly probable that she goes to first-nights," he told himself.

The theatre was full. It was a typical provincial theatre, with a mist collecting over the chandeliers, and the crowd in the gallery fidgeting noisily. In the first row of the stalls the local dandies stood waiting for the curtain to go up, their hands clasped behind them. There, in the front seat of the Governor's box, sat the Governor's daughter, wearing a boa, the Governor himself hiding modestly behind the drapes, so that only his hands were visible. The curtain stirred, the orchestra took a long time tuning up their instruments. Gurov's eyes roamed eagerly over the audience as they filed in and occupied their seats.

Anna Sergeyevna came in, too. She seated herself in the third row of the stalls, and when Gurov's glance fell on her, his heart seemed to stop, and he knew in a flash that the whole world contained no one nearer or dearer to him, no one more important to his happiness. This little woman, lost in the provincial crowd, in no way remarkable, holding a silly lorgnette in her hand, now filled his whole life, was his grief, his joy, all that he desired. Lulled by the sounds coming from the wretched orchestra, with its feeble, amateurish violinists, he thought how beautiful she was . . . thought and dreamed. . . .

Anna Sergeyevna was accompanied by a tall, round-shouldered young man with small whiskers, who nodded at every step before taking the seat beside her and seemed to be continually bowing to someone. This must be her husband, whom, in a fit of bitterness, at Yalta, she had called a "flunkey." And there really was something of the lackey's servility in his lanky figure, his side-whiskers, and the little bald spot on the top of his head. And he smiled sweetly, and the badge of some scientific society gleaming in his buttonhole was like the number on a footman's livery.

The husband went out to smoke in the first interval, and she was left alone in her seat. Gurov, who had taken a seat in the stalls, went up to her and said in a trembling voice, with a forced smile: "How d'you do?"

She glanced up at him and turned pale, then looked at him again in alarm, unable to believe her eyes, squeezing her fan and lorgnette in one hand, evidently struggling to overcome a feeling of faintness. Neither of them said a word. She sat there, and he stood beside her, disconcerted by her embarrassment, and not daring to sit down. The violins and flutes sang out as they were tuned, and there was a tense sensation in the atmosphere, as if they were being watched from all the boxes. At last she got up and moved rapidly towards one of the exits. He followed her and they wandered aimlessly along corridors, up and down stairs; figures flashed by in the uniforms of legal officials, high-school teachers and civil servants, all wearing badges; ladies, coats hanging from pegs flashed by; there was a sharp draught, bringing with it an odour of cigarette-stubs. And Gurov, whose heart was beating violently, thought:

"What on earth are all these people, this orchestra for? . . ."

The next minute he suddenly remembered how, after seeing

Anna Sergeyevna off that evening at the station, he had told himself that all was over, and they would never meet again. And how far away the end seemed to be now!

She stopped on a dark narrow staircase over which was a notice bearing the inscription "To the upper circle."

"How you frightened me!" she said, breathing heavily, still pale and half-stunned. "Oh, how you frightened me! I'm almost dead! Why did you come? Oh, why?"

"But, Anna," he said, in low, hasty tones. "But, Anna. . . . Try to understand . . . do try. . . ."

She cast him a glance of fear, entreaty, love, and then gazed at him steadily, as if to fix his features firmly in her memory.

"I've been so unhappy," she continued, taking no notice of his words. "I could think of nothing but you the whole time, I lived on the thoughts of you. I tried to forget—why, oh, why did you come?"

On the landing above them were two schoolboys, smoking and looking down, but Gurov did not care, and, drawing Anna Sergeyevna towards him, began kissing her face, her lips, her hands.

"What are you doing, oh, what are you doing?" she said in horror, drawing back. "We have both gone mad. Go away this very night, this moment. . . . By all that is sacred, I implore you. . . . Somebody is coming."

Someone was ascending the stairs.

"You must go away," went on Anna Sergeyevna in a whisper. "D'you hear me, Dmitri Dmitrich? I'll come to you in Moscow. I have never been happy, I am unhappy now, and I shall never be happy—never! Do not make me suffer still more! I will come to you in Moscow, I swear it! And now we must part! My dear one, my kind one, my darling, we must part."

She pressed his hand and hurried down the stairs, looking back at him continually, and her eyes showed that she was in truth unhappy. Gurov stood where he was for a short time, listening, and when all was quiet went to look for his coat, and left the theatre.

IV

And Anna Sergeyevna began going to Moscow to see him. Every two or three months she left the town of S., telling her husband that she was going to consult a specialist on female diseases, and her husband believed her and did not believe her. In Moscow she always stayed at the "Slavyanski Bazaar," sending a man in a red cap to Gurov the moment she arrived. Gurov went to her, and no one in Moscow knew anything about it.

One winter morning he went to see her as usual (the messenger had been to him the evening before, but had not found him at home). His daughter was with him for her school was on the way, and he thought he might as well see her to it.

"It is three degrees above zero," said Gurov to his daughter, "and yet it is snowing. You see it is only above zero close to the ground, the temperature in the upper layers of the atmosphere is quite different."

"Why doesn't it ever thunder in winter, Papa?"

He explained this, too. As he was speaking, he kept reminding himself that he was going to a rendezvous and that not a living soul knew about it, or, probably, ever would. He led a double life—one in public, in the sight of all whom it concerned, full of conventional truth and conventional deception, exactly like the lives of his friends and acquaintances, and another which flowed in secret. And, owing to some strange, possibly quite accidental chain of circumstances, everything that was important, interesting, essential, everything about which he was sincere and never deceived himself, everything that composed the kernel of his life, went on in secret, while everything that was false in him, everything that composed the husk in which he hid himself and the truth which was in him —his work at the bank, discussions at the club, his "lower race," his attendance at anniversary celebrations with his wife—was on the surface. He began to judge others by himself, no longer believing what he saw, and always assuming that the real, the only interesting life of every individual goes on as under cover of night, secretly. Every individual existence revolves around mystery, and perhaps that is the chief reason that all cultivated individuals insisted so strongly on the respect due to personal secrets.

After leaving his daughter at the door of her school Gurov set off for the "Slavyanski Bazaar." Taking off his overcoat in the lobby, he went upstairs and knocked softly on the door. Anna Sergeyevna, wearing the grey dress he liked most, exhausted by her journey and by suspense, had been expecting him since the evening before. She was pale and looked at him without smiling, but was in his arms almost before he was fairly in the room. Their kiss was lingering, prolonged, as if they had not met for years.

"Well, how are you?" he asked. "Anything new?"

"Wait, I'll tell you in a minute. . . . I can't. . . ."

She could not speak, because she was crying. Turning away, she held her handkerchief to her eyes.

"I'll wait till she's had her cry out," he thought, and sank into a chair.

He rang for tea, and a little later, while he was drinking it, she was still standing there, her face to the window. She wept from emotion, from her bitter consciousness of the sadness of their life; they could only see one another in secret, hiding from people, as if they were thieves. Was not their life a broken one?

"Don't cry," he said.

It was quite obvious to him that this love of theirs would not soon come to an end, and that no one could say when this end would be. Anna Sergeyevna loved him ever more fondly, worshipped him, and there would have been no point in telling her that one day it must end. Indeed, she would not have believed him.

He moved over and took her by the shoulders, intending to fondle her with light words, but suddenly he caught sight of himself in the looking-glass.

His hair was already beginning to turn grey. It struck him as strange that he should have aged so much in the last few years. The shoulders on which his hands lay were warm and quivering. He felt a pity for this life, still so warm and exquisite, but probably soon to fade and droop like his own. Why did she love him so? Women had always believed him different from what he really was, had loved in him not himself but the man their imagination pictured him, a man they had sought for eagerly all their lives. And afterwards when they discovered their mistake, they went on loving him just the same. And not one of them had ever been happy with him. Time had passed, he had met one woman after another, become intimate with each, parted with each, but had never loved. There had been all sorts of things between them, but never love.

And only now, when he was grey-haired, had he fallen in love properly, thoroughly, for the first time in his life.

He and Anna Sergeyevna loved one another as people who are very close and intimate, as husband and wife, as dear friends love one another. It seemed to them that fate had intended them for one another, and they could not understand why she should have a husband, and he a wife. They were like two migrating birds, the male and the female, who had been caught and put into separate cages. They forgave one another all that they were ashamed of in the past, in their present, and felt that this love of theirs had changed them both.

Formerly, in moments of melancholy, he had consoled himself by the first argument that came into his head, but now arguments were nothing to him, he felt profound pity, desired to be sincere, tender.

"Stop crying, my dearest," he said. "You've had your cry, now stop. . . . Now let us have a talk, let us try and think what we are to do."

Then they discussed their situation for a long time, trying to think how they could get rid of the necessity for hiding, deception, living in different towns, being so long without meeting. How were they to shake off these intolerable fetters?

"How? How?" he repeated, clutching his head. "How?"

And it seemed to them that they were within an inch of arriving at a decision, and that then a new, beautiful life would begin. And they both realized that the end was still far, far away, and that the hardest, the most complicated part was only just beginning.

1899

The Bride Comes to Yellow Sky

STEPHEN CRANE

[1871–1900]

I

The great Pullman was whirling onward with such dignity of motion that a glance from the window seemed simply to prove that the plains of Texas were pouring eastward. Vast flats of green grass, dull-hued spaces of mesquit and cactus, little groups of frame houses, woods of light and tender trees, all were sweeping into the east, sweeping over the horizon, a precipice.

A newly married pair had boarded this coach at San Antonio. The man's face was reddened from many days in the wind and sun, and a direct result of his new black clothes was that his brick-coloured hands were constantly performing in a most conscious fashion. From time to time he looked down respectfully at his attire. He sat with a hand on each knee, like a man waiting in a barber's shop. The glances he devoted to other passengers were furtive and shy.

The bride was not pretty, nor was she very young. She wore a dress of blue cashmere, with small reservations of velvet here and there, and with steel buttons abounding. She continually twisted her head to regard her puff sleeves, very stiff, straight, and high. They embarrassed her. It was quite apparent that she had cooked, and that she expected to cook, dutifully. The blushes caused by the careless scrutiny of some passengers as she had entered the car were strange to see upon this plain, under-class countenance, which was drawn in placid, almost emotionless lines.

They were evidently very happy. "Ever been in a parlour-car before?" he asked, smiling with delight.

"No," she answered; "I never was. It's fine, ain't it?"

"Great! And then after a while we'll go forward to the diner, and get a big lay-out. Finest meal in the world. Charge a dollar."

"Oh, do they?" cried the bride. "Charge a dollar? Why, that's too much—for us—ain't it, Jack?"

"Not this trip, anyhow," he answered bravely. "We're going to go the whole thing."

Later he explained to her about the trains. "You see, it's a thousand miles from one end of Texas to the other; and this train runs right across it, and never stops but four times." He had the pride of an owner. He pointed out to her the dazzling fittings of the coach; and in truth her eyes opened wider as she contemplated the sea-green figured velvet, the shining brass, silver, and glass, the wood that gleamed as darkly brilliant as the surface of a pool of oil. At one end a bronze figure sturdily held a support for a separated chamber, and at convenient places on the ceiling were frescos in olive and silver.

To the minds of the pair, their surroundings reflected the glory of their marriage that morning in San Antonio; this was the environment of their new estate; and the man's face in particular beamed with an elation that made him appear ridiculous to the negro porter. This individual at times surveyed them from afar with an amused and superior grin. On other occasions he bullied them with skill in ways that did not make it exactly plain to them that they were being bullied. He subtly used all the manners of the most unconquerable kind of snobbery. He oppressed them; but of this oppression they had small knowledge, and they speedily forgot that infrequently a number of travellers covered them with stares of derisive enjoyment. Historically there was supposed to be something infinitely humorous in their situation.

"We are due in Yellow Sky at 3:42," he said, looking tenderly into her eyes.

"Oh, are we?" she said, as if she had not been aware of it. To evince surprise at her husband's statement was part of her wifely amiability. She took from a pocket a little silver watch; and as she held it before her, and stared at it with a frown of attention, the new husband's face shone.

"I bought it in San Anton' from a friend of mine," he told her gleefully.

"It's seventeen minutes past twelve," she said, looking up at him with a kind of shy and clumsy coquetry. A passenger, noting this play, grew excessively sardonic, and winked at himself in one of the numerous mirrors.

At last they went to the dining-car. Two rows of negro waiters, in glowing white suits, surveyed their entrance with the interest, and also the equanimity, of men who had been forewarned. The pair fell to the lot of a waiter who happened to feel pleasure in steering them through their meal. He viewed them with the manner of a fatherly pilot, his countenance radiant with benevolence. The patronage, entwined with the ordinary deference, was not plain to them. And yet, as they returned to their coach, they showed in their faces a sense of escape.

To the left, miles down a long purple slope, was a little ribbon of mist where moved the keening Rio Grande. The train was approaching it at an angle, and the apex was Yellow Sky. Presently it was apparent that, as the distance from Yellow Sky grew shorter, the husband became commensurately restless. His brick-red hands were more insistent in their prominence. Occasionally he was even rather absent-minded and far-away when the bride leaned forward and addressed him.

As a matter of truth, Jack Potter was beginning to find the shadow of a deed weigh upon him like a leaden slab. He, the town marshal of Yellow Sky, a man known, liked, and feared in his corner, a prominent person, had gone to San Antonio to meet a girl he believed he loved, and there, after the usual prayers, had actually induced her to marry him, without consulting Yellow Sky for any part of the transaction. He was now bringing his bride before an innocent and unsuspecting community.

Of course people in Yellow Sky married as it pleased them, in accordance with a general custom; but such was Potter's thought of his duty to his friends, or of their idea of his duty, or of an unspoken form which does not control men in these matters, that he felt he was heinous. He had committed an extraordinary crime. Face to face with this girl in San Antonio, and spurred by his sharp impulse, he had gone headlong over all the social hedges. At San Antonio he was like a man hidden in the dark. A knife to sever any friendly duty, any form, was easy to his hand in that remote city. But the hour of Yellow Sky—the hour of daylight—was approaching.

He knew full well that his marriage was an important thing to his town. It could only be exceeded by the burning of the new hotel. His friends could not forgive him. Frequently he had reflected on the advisability of telling them by telegraph, but a new cowardice had been upon him. He feared to do it. And now the train was hurrying him toward a scene of amazement, glee, and reproach. He glanced out of the window at the line of haze swinging slowly in toward the train.

Yellow Sky had a kind of brass band, which played painfully, to the delight of the populace. He laughed without heart as he thought of it. If the citizens could dream of his prospective arrival with his bride, they would parade the band at the station and escort them, amid cheers and laughing congratulations, to his adobe home.

He resolved that he would use all the devices of speed and plains-craft in making the journey from the station to his house. Once within that safe citadel, he could issue some sort of vocal bulletin, and then not go among the citizens until they had time to wear off a little of their enthusiasm.

The bride looked anxiously at him. "What's worrying you, Jack?"

He laughed again. "I'm not worrying, girl; I'm only thinking of Yellow Sky."

She flushed in comprehension.

A sense of mutual guilt invaded their minds and developed a finer tenderness. They looked at each other with eyes softly aglow. But Potter often laughed the same nervous laugh; the flush upon the bride's face seemed quite permanent.

The traitor to the feelings of Yellow Sky narrowly watched the speeding landscape. "We're nearly there," he said.

Presently the porter came and announced the proximity of Potter's home. He held a brush in his hand, and, with all his airy superiority gone, he brushed Potter's new clothes as the latter slowly turned this way and that way. Potter fumbled out a coin and gave it to the porter, as he had seen others do. It was a heavy and muscle-bound business, as that of a man shoeing his first horse.

The porter took their bag, and as the train began to slow they moved forward to the hooded platform of the car. Presently the two engines and their string of coaches rushed into the station of Yellow Sky.

"They have to take water here," said Potter, from a constricted throat and in mournful cadence, as one announcing death. Before the train stopped his eye had swept the length of the platform, and he was glad and astonished to see there was none upon it but the station-agent, who, with a slightly hurried and anxious air, was walking toward the water-tanks. When the train had halted, the porter alighted first, and placed in position a little temporary step.

"Come on, girl," said Potter, hoarsely. As he helped her down they each laughed on a false note. He took the bag from the negro, and bade his wife cling to his arm. As they slunk rapidly away, his hang-dog glance perceived that they were unloading the two trunks, and also that the station-agent, far ahead near the baggage-car, had turned and was running toward him, making gestures. He laughed, and groaned as he laughed, when he noted the first effect of his marital bliss upon Yellow Sky. He gripped his wife's arm firmly to his side, and they fled. Behind them the porter stood, chuckling fatuously.

II

The California express on the Southern Railway was due at Yellow Sky in twenty-one minutes. There were six men at the bar of the Weary Gentleman saloon. One was a drummer who talked a great deal and rapidly; three were Texans who did not care to talk at that time; and two were Mexican sheepherders, who did not talk as a general practice in the Weary Gentleman saloon. The barkeeper's dog lay on the board walk that crossed in front of the door. His head was on his paws, and he glanced drowsily here and there with the constant vigilance of a dog that is kicked on occasion. Across the sandy street were some vivid green grass-plots, so wonderful in appearance, amid the sands that burned near them in a blazing sun, that they caused a doubt in the mind. They exactly resembled the grass mats used to represent lawns on the stage. At the cooler end of the railway station, a man without a coat sat in a tilted chair and smoked his pipe. The fresh-cut bank of the Rio Grande circled near the town, and there could be seen beyond it a great plum-coloured plain of mesquit.

Save for the busy drummer and his companions in the saloon, Yellow Sky was dozing. The new-comer leaned gracefully upon the bar, and recited many tales with the confidence of a bard who has come upon a new field.

"—and at the moment that the old man fell downstairs with the bureau in his arms, the old woman was coming up with two scuttles of coal, and of course—"

The drummer's tale was interrupted by a young man who suddenly appeared in the open door. He cried: "Scratchy Wilson's drunk, and has turned loose with both hands." The two Mexicans at once set down their glasses and faded out of the rear entrance of the saloon.

The drummer, innocent and jocular, answered: "All right, old man. S'pose he has? Come in and have a drink, anyhow."

But the information had made such an obvious cleft in every skull in the room that the drummer was obliged to see its importance. All had become instantly solemn. "Say," said he, mystified, "what is this?" His three companions made the introductory gesture of eloquent speech; but the young man at the door forestalled them.

"It means, my friend," he answered, as he came into the saloon, "that for the next two hours this town won't be a health resort."

The barkeeper went to the door, and locked and barred it; reaching out of the window, he pulled in heavy wooden shutters, and barred them. Immediately a solemn, chapel-like gloom was upon the place. The drummer was looking from one to another.

"But say," he cried, "what is this, anyhow? You don't mean there is going to be a gun-fight?"

"Don't know whether there'll be a fight or not," answered one man, grimly; "but there'll be some shootin'—some good shootin'."

The young man who had warned them waved his hand. "Oh, there'll be a fight fast enough, if any one wants it. Anybody can get a fight out there in the street. There's a fight just waiting."

The drummer seemed to be swayed between the interest of a foreigner and a perception of personal danger.

"What did you say his name was?" he asked.

"Scratchy Wilson," they answered in chorus.

"And will he kill anybody? What are you going to do? Does this happen often? Does he rampage around like this once a week or so? Can he break in that door?"

"No; he can't break down that door," replied the barkeeper. "He's tried it three times. But when he comes you'd better lay down on the floor, stranger. He's dead sure to shoot at it, and a bullet may come through."

Thereafter the drummer kept a strict eye upon the door. The time had not yet been called for him to hug the floor, but, as a minor precaution, he sidled near to the wall. "Will he kill anybody?" he said again.

The men laughed low and scornfully at the question.

"He's out to shoot, and he's out for trouble. Don't see any good in experimentin' with him."

"But what do you do in a case like this? What do you do?"

A man responded: "Why, he and Jack Potter—"

"But," in chorus the other men interrupted, "Jack Potter's in San Anton'."

"Well, who is he? What's he got to do with it?"

"Oh, he's the town marshal. He goes out and fights Scratchy when he gets on one of these tears."

"Wow!" said the drummer, mopping his brow. "Nice job he's got."

The voices had toned away to mere whisperings. The drummer wished to ask further questions, which were born of an increasing anxiety and bewilderment; but when he attempted them, the men merely looked at him in irritation and motioned him to remain silent. A tense waiting hush was upon them. In the deep shadows of the room their eyes shone as they listened for sounds from the street. One man made three gestures at the barkeeper; and the latter, moving like a ghost, handed him a glass and a bottle. The man poured a full glass of whisky, and set down the bottle noiselessly. He gulped the whisky in a swallow, and turned again toward the door in immovable silence. The drummer saw that the barkeeper, without a sound, had taken a Winchester from beneath the bar. Later he saw this individual beckoning to him, so he tiptoed across the room.

"You better come with me back of the bar."

"No, thanks," said the drummer, perspiring; "I'd rather be where I can make a break for the back door."

Whereupon the man of bottles made a kindly but peremptory gesture. The drummer obeyed it, and, finding himself seated on a box with his head below the level of the bar, balm was laid upon his soul at sight of various zinc and copper fittings that bore a resemblance to armour-plate. The barkeeper took a seat comfortably upon an adjacent box.

"You see," he whispered, "this here Scratchy Wilson is a wonder with a gun—a perfect wonder; and when he goes on the war-trail, we hunt our holes—naturally. He's about the last one of the old gang that used to hang out along the river here. He's a terror when he's drunk. When he's sober he's all right—kind of simple—wouldn't hurt a fly—nicest fellow in town. But when he's drunk—whoo!"

There were periods of stillness. "I wish Jack Potter was back from San Anton'," said the barkeeper. "He shot Wilson up once—in the leg—and he would sail in and pull out the kinks in this thing."

Presently they heard from a distance the sound of a shot, followed by three wild yowls. It instantly removed a bond from the men in the darkened saloon. There was a shuffling of feet. They looked at each other. "Here he comes," they said.

III

A man in a maroon-coloured flannel shirt, which had been purchased for purposes of decoration, and made principally by some Jewish women on the East Side of New York, rounded a corner and walked into the middle of the main street of Yellow Sky. In either hand the man held a long, heavy, blue-black revolver. Often he yelled, and these cries rang through a semblance of a deserted village, shrilly flying over the roofs in a volume that seemed to have no relation to the ordinary vocal strength of a man. It was as if the surrounding stillness formed the arch of a tomb over him. These cries of ferocious challenge rang against walls of silence. And his boots had red tops with gilded imprints, of the kind beloved in winter by little sledding boys on the hillsides of New England.

The man's face flamed in a rage begot of whisky. His eyes, rolling, and yet keen for ambush, hunted the still doorways and windows. He walked with the creeping movement of the midnight cat. As it occurred to him, he roared menacing information. The long revolvers in his hands were as easy as straws; they were moved with an electric swiftness. The little fingers of each hand played sometimes in a musician's way. Plain from the low collar of the shirt, the cords of his neck straightened and sank, straightened and sank, as passion moved him. The only sounds were his terrible invitations. The calm adobes preserved their demeanour at the passing of this small thing in the middle of the street.

There was no offer of fight—no offer of fight. The man called to the sky. There were no attractions. He bellowed and fumed and swayed his revolvers here and everywhere.

The dog of the barkeeper of the Weary Gentleman saloon had not appreciated the advance of events. He yet lay dozing in front of his master's door. At sight of the dog, the man paused and raised his revolver humorously. At sight of the man, the dog sprang up and walked diagonally away, with a sullen head, and growling. The man yelled, and the dog broke into a gallop. As it was about to enter an alley, there was a loud noise, a whistling, and something spat the ground directly before it. The dog screamed, and, wheeling in terror, galloped headlong in a new direction. Again there was a noise, a whistling, and sand was kicked viciously before it. Fear-stricken, the dog turned and flurried like an animal in a pen. The man stood laughing, his weapons at his hips.

Ultimately the man was attracted by the closed door of the Weary Gentleman saloon. He went to it and, hammering with a revolver, demanded drink.

The door remaining imperturbable, he picked a bit of paper from the walk, and nailed it to the framework with a knife. He then turned his back contemptuously upon this popular resort and, walking to the opposite side of the street and spinning there on his heel quickly and lithely, fired at the bit of paper. He missed it by a half-inch. He swore at himself, and went away. Later he comfortably fusilladed the windows of his most intimate friend. The man was playing with this town; it was a toy for him.

But still there was no offer of fight. The name of Jack Potter, his ancient antagonist, entered his mind, and he concluded that it would be a glad thing if he should go to Potter's house, and by bombardment induce him to come out and fight. He moved in the direction of his desire, chanting Apache scalp-music.

When he arrived at it, Potter's house presented the same still front as had the other adobes. Taking up a strategic position, the man howled a challenge. But this house regarded him as might a great stone god. It gave no sign. After a decent wait, the man howled further challenges, mingling with them wonderful epithets.

Paul's Case

WILLA CATHER

[1873–1947]

It was Paul's afternoon to appear before the faculty of the Pittsburgh High School to account for his various misdemeanors. He had been suspended a week ago, and his father had called at the Principal's office and confessed his perplexity about his son. Paul entered the faculty room suave and smiling. His clothes were a trifle outgrown, and the tan velvet on the collar of his open overcoat was frayed and worn; but for all that there was something of the dandy about him, and he wore an opal pin in his neatly knotted black four-in-hand, and a red carnation in his buttonhole. This latter adornment the faculty somehow felt was not properly significant of the contrite spirit befitting a boy under the ban of suspension.

Paul was tall for his age and very thin, with high, cramped shoulders and a narrow chest. His eyes were remarkable for a certain hysterical brilliancy, and he continually used them in a conscious, theatrical sort of way, peculiarly offensive in a boy. The pupils were abnormally large, as though he were addicted to belladonna, but there was a glassy glitter about them which that drug does not produce.

When questioned by the Principal as to why he was there, Paul stated, politely enough, that he wanted to come back to school. This was a lie, but Paul was quite accustomed to lying; found it, indeed, indispensable for overcoming friction. His teachers were asked to state their respective charges against him, which they did with such a rancour and aggrievedness as evinced that this was not a usual case. Disorder and impertinence were among the offences named, yet each of his instructors felt that it was scarcely possible to put into words the real cause of the trouble, which lay in a sort of hysterically defiant manner of the boy's; in the contempt which they all knew he felt for them, and which he seemingly made not the least effort to conceal. Once, when he had been making a synopsis of a paragraph at the blackboard, his English teacher had stepped to his side and attempted to guide his hand. Paul had started back with a shudder and thrust his hands violently behind him. The astonished woman could scarcely have been more hurt and embarrassed had he struck at her. The insult was so involuntary and definitely personal as to be unforgettable. In one way and another, he had made all his teachers, men and women alike, conscious of the same feeling of physical aversion. In one class he habitually sat with his hand shading his eyes; in another he always looked out of the window during the recitation; in another he made a running commentary on the lecture, with humorous intent.

His teachers felt this afternoon that his whole attitude was symbolized by his shrug and his flippantly red carnation flower, and they fell upon him without mercy, his English teacher leading the pack. He stood through it smiling, his pale lips parted over his white teeth. (His lips were continually twitching, and he had a habit of raising his eyebrows that was contemptuous and irritating to the last degree.) Older boys than Paul had broken down and shed tears under that ordeal, but his set smile did not once desert him, and his only sign of discomfort was the nervous trembling of the fingers that toyed with the buttons of his overcoat, and an occasional jerking of the other hand which held his hat. Paul was always smiling, always glancing about him, seeming to feel that people might be watching him and trying to detect something. This conscious expression, since it was as far as possible from boyish mirthfulness, was usually attributed to insolence or "smartness."

As the inquisition proceeded, one of his instructors repeated an impertinent remark of the boy's, and the Principal asked him whether he thought that a courteous speech to make to a woman. Paul shrugged his shoulders slightly and his eyebrows twitched.

"I don't know," he replied. "I didn't mean to be polite or impolite, either. I guess it's a sort of way I have, of saying things regardless."

The Principal asked him whether he didn't think that a way it would be well to get rid of. Paul grinned and said he guessed so. When he was told that he could go, he bowed gracefully and went out. His bow was like a repetition of the scandalous red carnation.

His teachers were in despair, and his drawing-master voiced the feeling of them all when he declared there was something about the boy which none of them understood. He added: "I don't really believe that smile of his comes altogether from insolence; there's something sort of haunted about it. The boy is not strong, for one thing. There is something wrong about the fellow."

The drawing-master had come to realize that, in looking at Paul, one saw only his white teeth and the forced animation of his eyes. One warm afternoon the boy had gone to sleep at his drawing-board, and his master had noted with amazement what a white, blue-veined face it was; drawn and wrinkled like an old man's about the eyes, the lips twitching even in his sleep.

His teachers left the building dissatisfied and unhappy; humiliated to have felt so vindictive toward a mere boy, to have uttered this feeling in cutting terms, and to have set each other on, as it were, in the gruesome game of intemperate reproach. One of them remembered having seen a miserable street cat set at bay by a ring of tormentors.

As for Paul, he ran down the hill whistling the Soldiers' Chorus from "Faust," looking behind him now and then to see whether some of his teachers were not there to witness his light-heartedness. As it was now late in the afternoon and Paul was on duty that evening as usher at Carnegie Hall, he decided that he would not go home to supper.

When he reached the concert hall, the doors were not yet open. It was chilly outside, and he decided to go up into the picture gallery—always deserted at this hour—where there were some of Raffelli's gay studies of Paris streets and an airy blue Venetian scene or two that always exhilarated him. He was delighted to find no one in the gallery but the old guard, who sat in the corner, a newspaper on his knee, a black patch over one eye and the other closed. Paul possessed himself of the place and walked confidently up and down, whistling under his breath. After a while he sat down before a blue Rico and lost himself. When he bethought him to look at his watch, it was after seven o'clock, and he rose with a start and ran downstairs, making a face at Augustus Caesar, peering out from the cast-room, and an evil gesture at the Venus of Milo as he passed her on the stairway.

When Paul reached the ushers' dressing-room, half a dozen boys were there already, and he began excitedly to tumble into his uniform. It was one of the few that at all approached fitting, and Paul thought it very becoming—though he knew the tight, straight coat accentuated his narrow chest, about which he was exceedingly sensitive. He was always excited while he dressed, twanging all over to the tuning of the strings and the preliminary flourishes of the horns in the music-room; but tonight he seemed quite beside himself, and he teased and plagued the boys until, telling him that he was crazy, they put him down on the floor and sat on him.

Somewhat calmed by his suppression, Paul dashed out to the front of the house to seat the early comers. He was a model usher. Gracious and smiling he ran up and down the aisles. Nothing was too much trouble for him; he carried messages and brought programmes as though it were his greatest pleasure in life, and all the people in his section thought him a charming boy, feeling that he remembered and admired them. As the house filled, he grew more and more vivacious and animated, and the colour came to his cheeks and lips. It was very much as though this were a great reception and Paul were the host. Just as the musicians came out to take their places, his English teacher arrived with cheques for the seats which a prominent manufacturer had taken for the season. She betrayed some embarrassment when she handed Paul the tickets, and a hauteur which subsequently made her feel very foolish. Paul was startled for a moment, and had the feeling of wanting to put her out; what business had she here among all these fine people and gay colours? He looked her over and decided that she was not appropriately dressed and must be a fool to sit downstairs in such togs. The tickets had probably been sent her out of kindness, he reflected, as he put down a seat for her, and she had about as much right to sit there as he had.

When the symphony began, Paul sank into one of the rear seats with a long sigh of relief, and lost himself as he had done before the Rico. It was not that symphonies, as such, meant anything in particular to Paul, but the first sight of the instruments seemed to free some hilarious spirit within him; something that struggled there like the Genius in the bottle found by the Arab fisherman. He felt a sudden zest of life; the lights danced before his eyes and the concert hall blazed into unimaginable splendour. When the soprano soloist came on, Paul forgot even the nastiness of his teacher's being there, and gave himself up to the peculiar intoxication such personages always had for him. The soloist chanced to be a German woman, by no means in her first youth, and the mother of many children; but she wore a satin gown and a tiara, and she had that indefinable air of achievement, that world-shine upon her, which always blinded Paul to any possible defects.

After a concert was over, Paul was often irritable and wretched until he got to sleep—and to-night he was even more than usually restless. He had the feeling of not being able to let down; of its being impossible to give up his delicious excitement which was the only thing that could be called living at all. During the last number he withdrew and, after hastily changing his clothes in the dressing-room, slipped out to the side door where the singer's carriage stood. Here he began pacing rapidly up and down the walk, waiting to see her come out.

Over yonder the Schenley, in its vacant stretch, loomed big and square through the fine rain, the windows of its twelve stories glowing like those of a lighted cardboard house under a Christmas tree. All the actors and singers of any importance stayed there when they were in Pittsburgh, and a number of the big manufacturers of the place lived there in the winter. Paul had often hung about the hotel, watching the people go in and out, longing to enter and leave schoolmasters and dull care behind him forever.

At last the singer came out, accompanied by the conductor, who helped her into her carriage and closed the door with a cordial *auf wiedersehen*—which set Paul to wondering whether she were not an old sweetheart of his. Paul followed the carriage over to the hotel, walking so rapidly as not to be far from the entrance when the singer alighted and disappeared behind the swinging glass doors which were opened by a Negro in a tall hat and a long coat. In the moment that the door was ajar, it seemed to Paul that he, too, entered. He seemed to feel himself go after her up the steps, into the warm, lighted building, into an exotic, a tropical world of shiny, glistening surfaces and basking ease. He reflected upon the mysterious dishes that were brought into the dining-room, the green bottles in buckets of ice, as he had seen them in the supper-party pictures of the Sunday supplement. A quick gust of wind brought the rain down with sudden vehemence, and Paul was startled to find that he was still outside in the slush of the gravel driveway; that his boots were letting in the water and his scanty overcoat was clinging wet about him; that the lights in front of the concert hall were out, and that the rain was driving in sheets between him and the orange glow of the windows above him. There it was, what he wanted—tangibly before him, like the fairy world of a Christmas pantomime; as the rain beat in his face, Paul wondered whether he were destined always to shiver in the black night outside, looking up at it.

He turned and walked reluctantly toward the car tracks. The end had to come sometime; his father in his night-clothes at the top of the stairs, explanations that did not explain, hastily improvised fictions that were forever tripping him up, his upstairs room and its horrible yellow wallpaper, the creaking bureau with the greasy plush collar-box, and over his painted wooden bed the pictures of George Washington and John Calvin, and the framed motto, 'Feed my Lambs,' which had been worked in red worsted by his mother, whom Paul could not remember.

Half an hour later, Paul alighted from the Negley Avenue car and went slowly down one of the side streets off the main thoroughfare. It was a highly respectable street, where all the houses were exactly alike, and where business men of moderate means begot and reared large families of children, all of whom went to Sabbath School and learned the shorter catechism, and were interested in arithmetic; all of whom were as exactly alike as their homes, and of a piece with the monotony in which they lived. Paul never went up Cordelia Street without a shudder of loathing. His home was next the house of the Cumberland minister. He approached it to-night with the nerveless sense of defeat, the hopeless feeling of sinking back forever into ugliness and commonness that he had always had when he came home. The moment he turned into Cordelia Street he felt the waters close above his head. After each of these orgies of living, he experienced all the physical depression which follows a debauch; the loathing of respectable beds, of common food, of a house permeated by kitchen odours; a shuddering repulsion for the flavourless, colourless mass of every-day existence; a morbid desire for cool things and soft lights and fresh flowers.

The nearer he approached the house, the more absolutely unequal Paul felt to the sight of it all: his ugly sleeping chamber; the old bathroom with the grimy zinc tub, the cracked mirror, the dripping spigots; his father, at the top of the stairs, his hairy legs sticking out from his nightshirt, his feet thrust into carpet slippers. He was so much later than usual that there would certainly be enquiries and reproaches. Paul stopped short before the door. He felt that he could not be accosted by his father to-night; that he could not toss again on that miserable bed. He would not go in. He would tell his father that he had no car-fare, and it was raining so hard he had gone home with one of the boys and stayed all night.

Meanwhile, he was wet and cold. He went around to the back of the house and tried one of the basement windows, found it open, and raised it cautiously, and scrambled down the cellar wall to the floor. There he stood, holding his breath, terrified by the noise he had made; but the floor above him was silent, and there was no creak on the stairs. He found a soap-box, and carried it over to the soft ring of light that streamed from the furnace door, and sat down. He was horribly afraid of rats, so he did not try to sleep, but sat looking distrustfully at the dark, still terrified lest he might have awakened his father.

In such reactions, after one of the experiences which made days and nights out of the dreary blanks of the calendar, when his senses were deadened, Paul's head was always singularly clear. Suppose his father had heard him getting in at the window and had come down and shot him for a burglar? Then again, suppose his father had come down, pistol in hand, and he had cried out in time to save himself, and his father had been horrified to think how nearly he had killed him? Then again, suppose a day should come when his father would remember that night, and wish there had been no warning cry to stay his hand? With this last supposition Paul entertained himself until daybreak.

The following Sunday was fine; the sodden November chill was broken by the last flash of autumnal summer. In the morning Paul had to go to church and Sabbath School, as always. On seasonable Sunday afternoons the burghers of Cordelia Street usually sat out on their front "stoops," and talked to their neighbours on the next stoop, or called to those across the street in neighbourly fashion. The men sat placidly on gay cushions placed upon the steps that led down to the sidewalk, while the women, in their Sunday "waists," sat in rockers on the cramped porches, pretending to be greatly at their ease. The children played in the streets; there were so many of them that the place resembled the recreation grounds of a kindergarten. The men on the steps, all in their shirt-sleeves, their vests unbuttoned, sat with their legs well apart, their stomachs comfortably protruding, and talked of the prices of things, or told anecdotes of the sagacity of their various chiefs and overlords. They occasionally looked over the multitude of squabbling children, listened affectionately to their high-pitched, nasal voices, smiling to see their own proclivities reproduced in their offspring, and interspersed their legends of the iron kings with remarks about their sons' progress at school, their grades in arithmetic, and the amounts they had saved in their toy banks.

On this last Sunday of November, Paul sat all afternoon on the lowest step of his "stoop," staring into the street, while his sisters, in their rockers, were talking to the minister's daughters next door about how many shirtwaists they had made in the last week, and how many waffles someone had eaten at the last church supper. When the weather was warm, and his father was in a particularly jovial frame of mind, the girls made lemonade, which was always brought out in a red-glass pitcher, ornamented with forget-me-nots in blue enamel. This the girls thought very fine, and the neighbours joked about the suspicious colour of the pitcher.

To-day Paul's father, on the top step, was talking to a young man who shifted a restless baby from knee to knee. He happened to be the young man who was daily held up to Paul as a model, and after whom it was his father's dearest hope that he would pattern. This young man was of a ruddy complexion, with a compressed, red mouth, and faded, nearsighted eyes, over which he wore thick spectacles, with gold bows that curved about his ears. He was clerk to one of the magnates of a great steel corporation, and was looked upon in Cordelia Street as a young man with a future. There was a story that, some five years ago—he was now barely twenty-six—he had been a trifle "dissipated," but in order to curb his appetites and save the loss of time and strength that a sowing of wild oats might have entailed, he had taken his chief's advice, oft reiterated to his employees, and at twenty-one had married the first woman whom he could persuade to share his fortunes. She happened to be an angular schoolmistress, much older than he, who also wore thick glasses, and who had now borne him four children, all nearsighted like herself.

The young man was relating how his chief, now cruising in the Mediterranean, kept in touch with all the details of the business, arranging his office hours on his yacht just as though he were at home, and "knocking off work enough to keep two stenographers busy." His father told, in turn, the plan his corporation was considering, of putting in an electric railway plant at Cairo. Paul snapped his teeth; he had an awful apprehension that they might spoil it all before he got there. Yet he rather liked to hear these legends of the iron kings, that were told and retold on Sundays and holidays; these stories of palaces in Venice, yachts on the Mediterranean, and high play at Monte Carlo appealed to his fancy, and he was interested in the triumphs of cash-boys who had become famous, though he had no mind for the cash-boy stage.

After supper was over, and he had helped to dry the dishes, Paul nervously asked his father whether he could go to George's to get some help in his geometry, and still more nervously asked for car-fare. This latter request he had to repeat, as his father, on principle, did not like to hear requests for money, whether much or little. He asked Paul whether he could not go to some boy who lived nearer, and told him that he ought not to leave his school work until Sunday; but he gave him the dime. He was not a poor man, but he had a worthy ambition to come up in the world. His only reason for allowing Paul to usher was that he thought a boy ought to be earning a little.

Paul bounded upstairs, scrubbed the greasy odour of the dishwater from his hands with the ill-smelling soap he hated, and then shook over his fingers a few drops of violet water from the bottle he kept hidden in his drawer. He left the house with his geometry conspicuously under his arm, and the moment he got out of Cordelia Street and boarded a downtown car, he shook off the lethargy of two deadening days, and began to live again.

The leading juvenile of the permanent stock company which played at one of the downtown theatres was an acquaintance of Paul's, and the boy had been invited to drop in at the Sunday-night rehearsals whenever he could. For more than a year Paul had spent every available moment loitering about Charley Edwards's dressing-room. He had won a place among Edwards's following not only because the young actor, who could not afford to employ a dresser, often found him useful, but because he recognized in Paul something akin to what churchmen term "vocation."

It was at the theatre and at Carnegie Hall that Paul really lived; the rest was but a sleep and a forgetting. This was Paul's fairy tale, and it had for him all the allurement of a secret love. The moment he inhaled the gassy, painty, dusty odour behind the scenes, he breathed like a prisoner set free, and felt within him the possibility of doing or saying splendid, brilliant things. The moment the cracked orchestra beat out the overture from "Martha," or jerked at the serenade from "Rigoletto," all stupid and ugly things slid from him, and his senses were deliciously, yet delicately fired.

Perhaps it was because, in Paul's world, the natural nearly always wore the guise of ugliness, that a certain element of artificiality seemed to him necessary in beauty. Perhaps it was because his experience of life elsewhere was so full of Sabbath-School picnics, petty economies, wholesome advice as to how to succeed in life, and the unescapable odours of cooking, that he found this existence so alluring, these smartly clad men and women so attractive, that he was so moved by these starry apple orchards that bloomed perennially under the limelight. It would be difficult to put it strongly enough how convincingly the stage entrance of the theatre was for Paul the actual portal of Romance. Certainly none of the company ever suspected it, least of all Charley Edwards. It was very like the old stories that used to float about London of fabulously rich Jews, who had subterranean halls, with palms, and fountains, and soft lamps and richly apparelled women who never saw the disenchanting light of London day. So, in the midst of that smoke-palled city, enamoured of figures and grimy toil, Paul had his secret temple, his wishing-carpet, his bit of blue-and-white Mediterranean shore bathed in perpetual sunshine.

Several of Paul's teachers had a theory that his imagination had been perverted by garish fiction; but the truth was he scarcely ever read at all. The books at home were not such as would either tempt or corrupt a youthful mind, and as for reading the novels that some of his friends urged upon him—well, he got what he wanted much more quickly from music; any sort of music, from an orchestra to a barrel-organ. He needed only the spark, the indescribable thrill that made his imagination master of his senses, and he could make plots and pictures enough of his own. It was equally true that he was not stage-struck—not, at any rate, in the usual acceptation of that expression. He had no desire to become an actor, any more than he had to become a musician. He felt no necessity to do any of these things; what he wanted was to see, to be in the atmosphere, float on the wave of it, to be carried out, blue league after league, away from everything.

After a night behind the scenes, Paul found the schoolroom more than ever repulsive; the bare floors and naked walls; the prosy men who never wore frock coats, or violets in their buttonholes; the women with their dull gowns, shrill voices, and pitiful seriousness about prepositions that govern the dative. He could not bear to have the other pupils think, for a moment, that he took these people seriously; he must convey to them that he considered it all trivial, and was there only by way of a joke, anyway. He had autographed pictures of all the members of the stock company which he showed his classmates, telling them the most incredible stories of his familiarity with these people, of his acquaintance with the soloists who came to Carnegie Hall, his suppers with them and the flowers he sent them. When these stories lost their effect, and his audience grew listless, he would bid all the boys goodbye, announcing that he was going to travel for a while; going to Naples, to California, to Egypt. Then, next Monday, he would slip back, conscious and nervously smiling; his sister was ill, and he would have to defer his voyage until spring.

Matters went steadily worse with Paul at school. In the itch to let his instructors know how heartily he despised them, and how thoroughly he was appreciated elsewhere, he mentioned once or twice that he had no time to fool with theorems; adding—with a twitch of the eyebrows and a touch of that nervous bravado which so perplexed them—that he was helping the people down at the stock company; they were old friends of his.

The upshot of the matter was that the Principal went to Paul's father, and Paul was taken out of school and put to work. The manager at Carnegie Hall was told to get another usher in his stead; the doorkeeper at the theatre was warned not to admit him to the house; and Charley Edwards remorsefully promised the boy's father not to see him again.

The members of the stock company were vastly amused when some of Paul's stories reached them—especially the women. They were hard-working women, most of them supporting indolent husbands or brothers, and they laughed rather bitterly at having stirred the boy to such fervid and florid inventions. They agreed with the faculty and with his father, that Paul's was a bad case.

The east-bound train was ploughing through a January snowstorm; the dull dawn was beginning to show grey when the engine whistled a mile out of Newark. Paul started up from the seat where he had lain curled in uneasy slumber, rubbed the breath-misted window-glass with his hand, and peered out. The snow was whirling in curling eddies above the white bottom lands, and the drifts lay already deep in the fields and along the fences, while here and there the tall dead grass and dried weed stalks protruded black above it. Lights shone from the scattered houses, and a gang of labourers who stood beside the track waved their lanterns.

Paul had slept very little, and he felt grimy and uncomfortable. He had made the all-night journey in a day coach because he was afraid if he took a Pullman he might be seen by some Pittsburgh business man who had noticed him in Denny and Carson's office. When the whistle woke him, he clutched quickly at his breast pocket, glancing about him with an uncertain smile. But the little, clay-bespattered Italians were still sleeping, the slatternly women across the aisle were in open-mouthed oblivion, and even the crumby, crying babies were for the time stilled. Paul settled back to struggle with his impatience as best he could.

When he arrived at the Jersey City station, he hurried through his breakfast, manifestly ill at ease and keeping a sharp eye about him. After he reached the Twenty-Third Street station, he consulted a cabman, and had himself driven to a men's furnishing establishment which was just opening for the day. He spent upward of two hours there, buying with endless reconsidering and great care. His new street suit he put on in the fitting-room; the frock coat and dress clothes he had bundled into the cab with his new shirts. Then he drove to a hatter's and a shoe house. His next errand was at Tiffany's, where he selected silver-mounted brushes and a scarf-pin. He would not wait to have his silver marked, he said. Lastly, he stopped at a trunk shop on Broadway, and had his purchases packed into various travelling-bags.

It was a little after one o'clock when he drove up to the Waldorf, and, after settling with the cabman, went into the office. He registered from Washington; said his mother and father had been abroad, and that he had come down to await the arrival of their steamer. He told his story plausibly and had no trouble, since he offered to pay for them in advance, in engaging his rooms; a sleeping-room, sitting-room, and bath.

Not once, but a hundred times Paul had planned this entry into New York. He had gone over every detail of it with Charley Edwards, and in his scrapbook at home there were pages of description about New York hotels, cut from the Sunday papers.

When he was shown to his sitting-room on the eighth floor, he saw at a glance that everything was as it should be; there was but one detail in his mental picture that the place did not realize, so he rang for the bell-boy and sent him down for flowers. He moved about nervously until the boy returned, putting away his new linen and fingering it delightedly as he did so. When the flowers came, he put them hastily into water, and then tumbled into a hot bath. Presently he came out of his white bathroom, resplendent in his new silk underwear, and playing with the tassels of his red robe. The snow was whirling so fiercely outside his windows that he could scarcely see across the street; but within, the air was deliciously soft and fragrant. He put the violets and jonquils on the tabouret beside the couch, and threw himself down with a long sigh, covering himself with a Roman blanket. He was thoroughly tired; he had been in such haste, he had stood up to such a strain, covered so much ground in the last twenty-four hours, that he wanted to think how it had all come about. Lulled by the sound of the wind, the warm air, and the cool fragrance of the flowers, he sank into deep, drowsy retrospection.

It had been wonderfully simple; when they had shut him out of the theatre and concert hall, when they had taken away his bone, the whole thing was virtually determined. The rest was a mere matter of opportunity. The only thing that at all surprised him was his own courage—for he realized well enough that he had always been tormented by fear, a sort of apprehensive dread which, of late years, as the meshes of the lies he had told closed about him, had been pulling the muscles of his body tighter and tighter. Until now, he could not remember a time when he had not been dreading something. Even when he was a little boy, it was always there—behind him, or before, or on either side. There had always been the shadowed corner, the dark place into which he dared not look, but from which something seemed always to be watching him—and Paul had done things that were not pretty to watch, he knew.

But now he had a curious sense of relief, as though he had at last thrown down the gauntlet to the thing in the corner.

Yet it was but a day since he had been sulking in the traces; but yesterday afternoon that he had been sent to the bank with Denny and Carson's deposit, as usual—but this time he was instructed to leave the book to be balanced. There was above two thousand dollars in cheques, and nearly a thousand in the banknotes which he had taken from the book and quietly transferred to his pocket. At the bank he had made out a new deposit slip. His nerves had been steady enough to permit of his returning to the office, where he had finished his work and asked for a full day's holiday to-morrow, Saturday, giving a perfectly reasonable pretext. The bank book, he knew, would not be returned before Monday or Tuesday, and his father would be out of town for the next week. From the time he slipped the banknotes into his pocket until he boarded the night train for New York, he had not known a moment's hesitation.

How astonishingly easy it had all been; here he was, the thing done; and this time there would be no awakening, no figure at the top of the stairs. He watched the snowflakes whirling by his window until he fell asleep.

When he awoke, it was four o'clock in the afternoon. He bounded up with a start; one of his precious days gone already! He spent nearly an hour in dressing, watching every stage of his toilet carefully in the mirror. Everything was quite perfect; he was exactly the kind of boy he had always wanted to be.

When he went downstairs, Paul took a carriage and drove up Fifth Avenue toward the Park. The snow had somewhat abated; carriages and tradesmen's wagons were hurrying soundlessly to and fro in the winter twilight; boys in woollen mufflers were shovelling off the doorsteps; the Avenue stages made fine spots of colour against the white street. Here and there on the corners whole flower gardens blooming behind glass windows, against which the snowflakes stuck and melted; violets, roses, carnations, lilies-of-the-valley—somehow vastly more lovely and alluring that they blossomed thus unnaturally in the snow. The Park itself was a wonderful stage winter-piece.

When he returned, the pause of the twilight had ceased, and the tune of the streets had changed. The snow was falling faster, lights streamed from the hotels that reared their many stories fearlessly up into the storm, defying the raging Atlantic winds. A long, black stream of carriages poured down the Avenue, intersected here and there by other streams, tending horizontally. There were a score of cabs about the entrance of his hotel, and his driver had to wait. Boys in livery were running in and out of the awning stretched across the sidewalk, up and down the red velvet carpet laid from the door to the street. Above, about, within it all, was the rumble and roar, the hurry and toss of thousands of human beings as hot for pleasure as himself, and on every side of him towered the glaring affirmation of the omnipotence of wealth.

The boy set his teeth and drew his shoulders together in a spasm of realization; the plot of all dramas, the text of all romances, the nerve-stuff of all sensations was whirling about him like the snow-flakes. He burnt like a fagot in a tempest.

When Paul came down to dinner, the music of the orchestra floated up the elevator shaft to greet him. As he stepped into the thronged corridor, he sank back into one of the chairs against the wall to get his breath. The lights, the chatter, the perfumes, the bewildering medley of colour—he had, for a moment, the feeling of not being able to stand it. But only for a moment; these were his own people, he told himself. He went slowly about the corridors, through the writing-rooms, smoking-rooms, reception-rooms, as though he were exploring the chambers of an enchanted palace, built and peopled for him alone.

When he reached the dining-room he sat down at a table near a window. The flowers, the white linen, the many-coloured wine-glasses, the gay toilettes of the women, the low popping of corks, the undulating repetitions of the "Blue Danube" from the orchestra, all flooded Paul's dream with bewildering radiance. When the roseate tinge of his champagne was added—that cold, precious, bubbling stuff that creamed and foamed in his glass—Paul wondered that there were honest men in the world at all. This was what all the world was fighting for, he reflected; this was what all the struggle was about. He doubted the reality of his past. Had he ever known a place called Cordelia Street, a place where fagged-looking business men boarded the early car? Mere rivets in a machine they seemed to Paul—sickening men, with combings of children's hair always hanging to their coats, and the smell of cooking in their clothes. Cordelia Street—Ah, that belonged to another time and country! Had he not always been thus, had he not sat here night after night, from as far back as he could remember, looking pensively over just such shimmering textures, and slowly twirling the stem of a glass like this one between his thumb and middle finger? He rather thought he had.

He was not in the least abashed or lonely. He had no especial desire to meet or to know any of these people; all he demanded was the right to look on and conjecture, to watch the pageant. The mere stage properties were all he contended for. Nor was he lonely later in the evening, in his loge at the Opera. He was entirely rid of his nervous misgivings, of his forced aggressiveness, of the imperative desire to show himself different from his surroundings. He felt now that his surroundings explained him. Nobody questioned the purple; he had only to wear it passively. He had only to glance down at his dress coat to reassure himself that here it would be impossible for anyone to humiliate him.

He found it hard to leave his beautiful sitting-room to go to bed that night, and sat long watching the raging storm from his turret window. When he went to sleep, it was with the lights turned on in his bedroom; partly because of his old timidity, and partly so that, if he should wake in the night, there would be no wretched moment of doubt, no horrible suspicion of yellow wallpaper, or of Washington and Calvin above his bed.

On Sunday morning the city was practically snowbound. Paul breakfasted late, and in the afternoon he fell in with a wild San Francisco boy, a freshman at Yale, who said he had run down for a "little flyer" over Sunday. The young man offered to show Paul the night side of the town, and the two boys went off together after dinner, not returning to the hotel until seven o'clock the next morning. They had started out in the confiding warmth of a champagne friendship, but their parting in the elevator was singularly cool. The freshman pulled himself together to make his train, and Paul went to bed. He awoke at two o'clock in the afternoon, very thirsty and dizzy, and rang for ice-water, coffee, and the Pittsburgh papers.

On the part of the hotel management, Paul excited no suspicion. There was this to be said for him, that he wore his spoils with dignity and in no way made himself conspicuous. His chief greediness lay in his ears and eyes, and his excesses were not offensive ones. His dearest pleasures were the grey winter twilights in his sitting-room; his quiet enjoyment of his flowers, his clothes, his wide divan, his cigarette, and his sense of power. He could not remember a time when he had felt so at peace with himself. The mere release from the necessity of petty lying, lying every day and every day, restored his self-respect. He had never lied for pleasure, even at school; but to make himself noticed and admired, to assert his difference from other Cordelia Street boys; and he felt a good deal more manly, more honest, even, now that he had no need for boastful pretensions, now that he could, as his actor friends used to say, "dress the part." It was characteristic that remorse did not occur to him. His golden days went by without a shadow, and he made each as perfect as he could.

On the eighth day after his arrival in New York, he found the whole affair exploited in the Pittsburgh papers, exploited with a wealth of detail which indicated that local news of a sensational nature was at a low ebb. The firm of Denny and Carson announced that the boy's father had refunded the full amount of his theft, and that they had no intention of prosecuting. The Cumberland minister had been interviewed, and expressed his hope of yet reclaiming the motherless lad, and Paul's Sabbath-School teacher declared that she would spare no effort to that end. The rumour had reached Pittsburgh that the boy had been seen in a New York hotel, and his father had gone East to find him and bring him home.

Paul had just come in to dress for dinner; he sank into the chair, weak in the knees, and clasped his head in his hands. It was to be worse than jail, even; the tepid waters of Cordelia Street were to close over him finally and forever. The grey monotony stretched before him in hopeless, unrelieved years;—Sabbath-School, Young People's Meeting, the yellow-papered room, the damp dish-towels; it all rushed back upon him with sickening vividness. He had the old feeling that the orchestra had suddenly stopped, the sinking sensation that the play was over. The sweat broke out on his face, and he sprang to his feet, looked about him with his white, conscious smile, and winked at himself in the mirror. With something of the childish belief in miracles with which he had so often gone to class, all his lessons unlearned, Paul dressed and dashed whistling down the corridor to the elevator.

He had no sooner entered the dining-room and caught the measure of the music than his remembrance was lightened by his old elastic power of claiming the moment, mounting with it, and finding it all-sufficient. The glare and glitter about him, the mere scenic accessories had again, and for the last time, their old potency. He would show himself that he was game, he would finish the thing splendidly. He doubted, more than ever, the existence of Cordelia Street, and for the first time he drank his wine recklessly. Was he not, after all, one of these fortunate beings? Was he not still himself, and in his own place? He drummed a nervous accompaniment to the music and looked about him, telling himself over and over that it had paid.

He reflected drowsily, to the swell of the violin and the chill sweetness of his wine, that he might have done it more wisely. He might have caught an outbound steamer and been well out of their clutches before now. But the other side of the world had seemed too far away and too uncertain then; he could not have waited for it; his need had been too sharp. If he had to choose over again, he would do the same thing to-morrow. He looked affectionately about the dining-room, now gilded with a soft mist. Ah, it had paid indeed!

Paul was awakened next morning by a painful throbbing in his head and feet. He had thrown himself across the bed without undressing, and had slept with his shoes on. His limbs and hands were lead-heavy, and his tongue and throat were parched. There came upon him one of those fateful attacks of clear-headedness that never occurred except when he was physically exhausted and his nerves hung loose. He lay still and closed his eyes and let the tide of realities wash over him.

His father was in New York; "stopping at some joint or other," he told himself. The memory of successive summers on the front stoop fell upon him like a weight of black water. He had not a hundred dollars left; and he knew now, more than ever, that money was everything, the wall that stood between all he loathed and all he wanted. The thing was winding itself up; he had thought of that on his first glorious day in New York, and had even provided a way to snap the thread. It lay on his dressing-table now; he had got it out last night when he came blindly up from dinner—but the shiny metal hurt his eyes, and he disliked the look of it, anyway.

He rose and moved about with a painful effort, succumbing now and again to attacks of nausea. It was the old depression exaggerated; all the world had become Cordelia Street. Yet somehow he was not afraid of anything, was absolutely calm; perhaps because he had looked into the dark corner at last, and knew. It was bad enough, what he saw there; but somehow not so bad as his long fear of it had been. He saw everything clearly now. He had a feeling that he had made the best of it, that he had lived the sort of life he was meant to live, and for half an hour he sat staring at the revolver. But he told himself that was not the way, so he went downstairs and took a cab to the ferry.

When Paul arrived at Newark, he got off the train and took another cab, directing the driver to follow the Pennsylvania tracks out of the town. The snow lay heavy on the roadways and had drifted deep in the open fields. Only here and there the dead grass or dried weed stalks projected, singularly black, above it.

Once well into the country, Paul dismissed the carriage and walked, floundering along the tracks, his mind a medley of irrelevant things. He seemed to hold in his brain an actual picture of everything he had seen that morning. He remembered every feature of both his drivers, the toothless old woman from whom he had bought the red flowers in his coat, the agent from whom he had got his ticket, and all of his fellow-passengers on the ferry. His mind, unable to cope with vital matters near at hand, worked feverishly and deftly at sorting and grouping these images. They made for him a part of the ugliness of the world, of the ache in his head, and the bitter burning on his tongue. He stooped and put a handful of snow into his mouth as he walked, but that, too, seemed hot. When he reached a little hillside, where the tracks ran through a cut some twenty feet below him, he stopped and sat down.

The carnations in his coat were drooping with the cold, he noticed; their red glory over. It occurred to him that all the flowers he had seen in the show windows that first night must have gone the same way, long before this. It was only one splendid breath they had, in spite of their brave mockery at the winter outside the glass. It was a losing game in the end, it seemed, this revolt against the homilies by which the world is run. Paul took one of the blossoms carefully from his coat and scooped a little hole in the snow, where he covered it up. Then he dozed awhile, from his weak condition, seeming insensible to the cold.

The sound of an approaching train woke him and he started to his feet, remembering only his resolution, and afraid lest he should be too late. He stood watching the approaching locomotive, his teeth chattering, his lips drawn away from them in a frightened smile; once or twice he glanced nervously sidewise, as though he were being watched. When the right moment came, he jumped. As he fell, the folly of his haste occurred to him with merciless clearness, the vastness of what he had left undone. There flashed through his brain, clearer than ever before, the blue of Adriatic water, the yellow of Algerian sands.

He felt something strike his chest—his body was being thrown swiftly through the air, on and on, immeasurably far and fast, while his limbs gently relaxed. Then, because the picture-making mechanism was crushed, the disturbing visions flashed into black, and Paul dropped back into the immense design of things.

1905

Disorder and Early Sorrow

THOMAS MANN

[1875–1955]

The principal dish at dinner had been croquettes made of turnip greens. So there follows a trifle, concocted out of one of those dessert powders we use nowadays, that taste like almond soap. Xaver, the youthful manservant, in his outgrown striped jacket, white woollen gloves, and yellow sandals, hands it round, and the "big folk" take this opportunity to remind their father, tactfully, that company is coming today.

The "big folk" are two, Ingrid and Bert. Ingrid is brown-eyed, eighteen, and perfectly delightful. She is on the eve of her exams, and will probably pass them, if only because she knows how to wind masters, and even headmasters, round her finger. She does not, however, mean to use her certificate once she gets it; having leanings towards the stage, on the ground of her ingratiating smile, her equally ingratiating voice, and a marked and irresistible talent for burlesque. Bert is blond and seventeen. He intends to get done with school somehow, anyhow, and fling himself into the arms of life. He will be a dancer, or a cabaret actor, possibly even a waiter—but not a waiter anywhere else save at the Cairo, the night-club, whither he has once already taken flight, at five in the morning, and been brought back crestfallen. Bert bears a strong resemblance to the youthful manservant Xaver Kleinsgutl, of about the same age as himself; not because he looks common—in features he is strikingly like his father, Professor Cornelius—but by reason of an approximation of types, due in its turn to far-reaching compromises in matters of dress and bearing generally. Both lads wear their heavy hair very long on top, with a cursory parting in the middle, and give their heads the same characteristic toss to throw it off the forehead. When one of them leaves the house, by the garden gate, bareheaded in all weathers, in a blouse rakishly girt with a leather strap, and sheers off bent well over with his head on one side; or else mounts his push-bike—Xaver makes free with his employers', of both sexes, or even, in acutely irresponsible mood, with the Professor's own—Dr. Cornelius from his bedroom window cannot, for the life of him, tell whether he is looking at his son or his servant. Both, he thinks, look like young moujiks. And both are impassioned cigarette-smokers, though Bert has not the means to compete with Xaver, who smokes as many as thirty a day, of a brand named after a popular cinema star. The big folk call their father and mother the "old folk"—not behind their backs, but as a form of address and in all affection: "Hullo, old folk," they will say; though Cornelius is only forty-seven years old and his wife eight years younger. And the Professor's parents, who lead in his household the humble and hesitant life of the really old, are on the big folk's lips the "ancients." As for the "little folk," Ellie and Snapper, who take their meals upstairs with blue-faced Ann—so-called because of her prevailing facial hue—Ellie and Snapper follow their mother's example and address their father by his first name, Abel. Unutterably comic it sounds, in its pert, confiding familiarity; particularly on the lips, in the sweet accents, of five-year-old Eleanor, who is the image of Frau Cornelius's baby pictures and whom the Professor loves above everything else in the world.

"Darling old thing," says Ingrid affably, laying her large but shapely hand on his, as he presides in proper middle-class style over the family table, with her on his left and the mother opposite: "Parent mine, may I ever so gently jog your memory, for you have probably forgotten: this is the afternoon we were to have our little jollification, our turkey-trot with eats to match. You haven't a thing to do but just bear up and not funk it; everything will be over by nine o'clock."

"Oh—ah!" says Cornelius, his face falling. "Good!" he goes on, and nods his head to show himself in harmony with the inevitable. "I only meant—is this really the day? Thursday, yes. How time flies! Well, what time are they coming?"

"Half past four they'll be dropping in, I should say," answers Ingrid, to whom her brother leaves the major rôle in all dealings with the father. Upstairs, while he is resting, he will hear scarcely anything, and from seven to eight he takes his walk. He can slip out by the terrace if he likes.

"Tut!" says Cornelius deprecatingly, as who should say: "You exaggerate." But Bert puts in: "It's the one evening in the week Wanja doesn't have to play. Any other night he'd have to leave by half past six, which would be painful for all concerned."

Wanja is Ivan Herzl, the celebrated young leading man at the Stadttheater. Bert and Ingrid are on intimate terms with him, they often visit him in his dressing-room and have tea. He is an artist of the modern school, who stands on the stage in strange and, to the Professor's mind, utterly affected dancing attitudes, and shrieks lamentably. To a professor of history, all highly repugnant; but Bert has entirely succumbed to Herzl's influence, blackens the lower rim of his eyelids—despite painful but fruitless scenes with the father—and with youthful carelessness of the ancestral anguish declares that not only will he take Herzl for his model if he becomes a dancer, in case he turns out to be a waiter at the Cairo he means to walk precisely thus.

Cornelius slightly raises his brows and makes his son a little bow—indicative of the unassumingness and self-abnegation that befits his age. You could not call it a mocking bow or suggestive in any special sense. Bert may refer it to himself or equally to his so talented friend.

"Who else is coming?" next inquires the master of the house. They mention various people, names all more or less familiar, from the city, from the suburban colony, from Ingrid's school. They still have some telephoning to do, they say. They have to phone Max. This is Max Hergesell, an engineering student; Ingrid utters his name in the nasal drawl which according to her is the traditional intonation of all the Hergesells. She goes on to parody it in the most abandonedly funny and lifelike way, and the parents laugh until they nearly choke over the wretched trifle. For even in these times when something funny happens people have to laugh.

From time to time the telephone bell rings in the Professor's study, and the big folk run across, knowing it is their affair. Many people had to give up their telephones the last time the price rose, but so far the Corneliuses have been able to keep theirs, just as they have kept their villa, which was built before the war, by dint of the salary Cornelius draws as professor of history—a million marks, and more or less adequate to the chances and changes of post-war life. The house is comfortable, even elegant, though sadly in need of repairs that cannot be made for lack of materials, and at present disfigured by iron stoves with long pipes. Even so, it is still the proper setting of the upper middle class, though they themselves look odd enough in it, with their worn and turned clothing and altered way of life. The children, of course, know nothing else; to them it is normal and regular, they belong by birth to the "villa proletariat." The problem of clothing troubles them not at all. They and their like have evolved a costume to fit the time, by poverty out of taste for innovation: in summer it consists of scarcely more than a belted linen smock and sandals. The middle-class parents find things rather more difficult.

The big folk's table-napkins hang over their chair-backs, they talk with their friends over the telephone. These friends are the invited guests who have rung up to accept or decline or arrange; and the conversation is carried on in the jargon of the clan, full of slang and high spirits, of which the old folk understand hardly a word. These consult together meantime about the hospitality to be offered to the impending guests. The Professor displays a middle-class ambitiousness: he wants to serve a sweet—or something that looks like a sweet—after the Italian salad and brown-bread sandwiches. But Frau Cornelius says that would be going too far. The guests would not expect it, she is sure—and the big folk, returning once more to their trifle, agree with her.

The mother of the family is of the same general type as Ingrid, though not so tall. She is languid; the fantastic difficulties of the housekeeping have broken and worn her. She really ought to go and take a cure, but feels incapable; the floor is always swaying under her feet, and everything seems upside down. She speaks of what is uppermost in her mind: the eggs, they simply must be bought today. Six thousand marks apiece they are, and just so many are to be had on this one day of the week at one single shop fifteen minutes' journey away. Whatever else they do, the big folk must go and fetch them immediately after luncheon, with Danny, their neighbour's son, who will soon be calling for them; and Xaver Kleinsgutl will don civilian garb and attend his young master and mistress. For no single household is allowed more than five eggs a week; therefore the young people will enter the shop singly, one after another, under assumed names, and thus wring twenty eggs from the shopkeeper for the Cornelius family. This enterprise is the sporting event of the week for all participants, not excepting the moujik Kleinsgutl, and most of all for Ingrid and Bert, who delight in misleading and mystifying their fellowmen and would revel in the performance even if it did not achieve one single egg. They adore impersonating fictitious characters; they love to sit in a bus and carry on long lifelike conversations in a dialect which they otherwise never speak, the most commonplace dialogue about politics and people and the price of food, while the whole bus listens open-mouthed to this incredibly ordinary prattle, though with a dark suspicion all the while that something is wrong somewhere. The conversation waxes ever more shameless, it enters into revolting detail about these people who do not exist. Ingrid can make her voice sound ever so common and twittering and shrill as she impersonates a shop-girl with an illegitimate child, said child being a son with sadistic tendencies, who lately out in the country treated a cow with such unnatural cruelty that no Christian could have borne to see it. Bert nearly explodes at her twittering, but restrains himself and displays a grisly sympathy; he and the unhappy shop-girl entering into a long, stupid, depraved, and shuddery conversation over the particular morbid cruelty involved; until an old gentleman opposite, sitting with his ticket folded between his index finger and his seal ring, can bear it no more and makes public protest against the nature of the themes these young folk are discussing with such particularity. He uses the Greek plural: "themata." Whereat Ingrid pretends to be dissolving in tears, and Bert behaves as though his wrath against the old gentleman was with difficulty being held in check and would probably burst out before long. He clenches his fists, he gnashes his teeth, he shakes from head to foot; and the unhappy old gentleman, whose intentions had been of the best, hastily leaves the bus at the next stop.

Such are the diversions of the big folk. The telephone plays a prominent part in them: they ring up any and everybody—members of government, opera singers, dignitaries of the Church—in the character of shop assistants, or perhaps as Lord or Lady Doolittle. They are only with difficulty persuaded that they have the wrong number. Once they emptied their parents' card-tray and distributed its contents among the neighbours' letter-boxes, wantonly, yet not without enough impish sense of the fitness of things to make it highly upsetting, God only knowing why certain people should have called where they did.

Xaver comes in to clear away, tossing the hair out of his eyes. Now that he has taken off his gloves you can see the yellow chain-ring on his left hand. And as the Professor finishes his watery eight-thousand-mark beer and lights a cigarette, the little folk can be heard scrambling down the stair, coming, by established custom, for their after-dinner call on Father and Mother. They storm the dining-room, after a struggle with the latch, clutched by both pairs of little hands at once; their clumsy small feet twinkle over the carpet, in red felt slippers with the socks falling down on them. With prattle and shoutings each makes for his own place: Snapper to Mother, to climb on her lap, boast of all he has eaten, and thump his fat little tum; Ellie to her Abel, so much hers because she is so very much his; because she consciously luxuriates in the deep tenderness—like all deep feeling, concealing a melancholy strain—with which he holds her small form embraced; in the love in his eyes as he kisses her little fairy hand or the sweet brow with its delicate tracery of tiny blue veins.

The little folk look like each other, with the strong undefined likeness of brother and sister. In clothing and hair-cut they are twins. Yet they are sharply distinguished after all, and quite on sex lines. It is a little Adam and a little Eve. Not only is Snapper the sturdier and more compact, he appears consciously to emphasize his four-year-old masculinity in speech, manner, and carriage, lifting his shoulders and letting the little arms hang down quite like a young American athlete, drawing down his mouth when he talks and seeking to give his voice a gruff and forthright ring. But all this masculinity is the result of effort rather than natively his. Born and brought up in these desolate, distracted times, he has been endowed by them with an unstable and hypersensitive nervous system and suffers greatly under life's disharmonies. He is prone to sudden anger and outbursts of bitter tears, stamping his feet at every trifle; for this reason he is his mother's special nursling and care. His round, round eyes are chestnut brown and already inclined to squint, so that he will need glasses in the near future. His little nose is long, the mouth small—the father's nose and mouth they are, more plainly than ever since the Professor shaved his pointed beard and goes smooth-faced. The pointed beard had become impossible— even professors must make some concession to the changing times.

But the little daughter sits on her father's knee, his Eleonorchen, his little Eve, so much more gracious a little being, so much sweeter-faced than her brother—and he holds his cigarette away from her while she fingers his glasses with her dainty wee hands. The lenses are divided for reading and distance, and each day they tease her curiosity afresh.

At bottom he suspects that his wife's partiality may have a firmer basis than his own: that Snapper's refractory masculinity perhaps is solider stuff than his own little girl's more explicit charm and grace. But the heart will not be commanded, that he knows; and once and for all his heart belongs to the little one, as it has since the day she came, since the first time he saw her. Almost always when he holds her in his arms he remembers that first time: remembers the sunny room in the Women's Hospital, where Ellie first saw the light, twelve years after Bert was born. He remembers how he drew near, the mother smiling the while, and cautiously put aside the canopy of the diminutive bed that stood beside the large one. There lay the little miracle among the pillows: so well formed, so encompassed, as it were, with the harmony of sweet proportions, with little hands that even then, though so much tinier, were beautiful as now; with wide-open eyes blue as the sky and brighter than the sunshine—and almost in that very second he felt himself captured and held fast. This was love at first sight, love everlasting: a feeling unknown, unhoped for, unexpected—in so far as it could be a matter of conscious awareness; it took entire possession of him, and he understood, with joyous amazement, that this was for life.

But he understood more. He knows, does Dr. Cornelius, that there is something not quite right about his feeling, so unaware, so undreamed of, so involuntary. He has a shrewd suspicion that it is not by accident it has so utterly mastered him and bound itself up with his existence; that he had—even subconsciously—been preparing for it, or, more precisely, been prepared for it. There is, in short, something in him which at a given moment was ready to issue in such a feeling; and this something, highly extraordinary to relate, is his essence and quality as a professor of history. Dr. Cornelius, however, does not actually say this, even to himself; he merely realizes it, at odd times, and smiles a private smile. He knows that history professors do not love history because it is something that comes to pass, but only because it is something that *has* come to pass; that they hate a revolution like the present one because they feel it is lawless, incoherent, irrelevant—in a word, unhistoric; that their hearts belong to the coherent, disciplined, historic past. For the temper of timelessness, the temper of eternity—thus the scholar communes with himself when he takes his walk by the river before supper—that temper broods over the past; and it is a temper much better suited to the nervous system of a history professor than are the excesses of the present. The past is immortalized; that is to say, it is dead; and death is the root of all godliness and all abiding significance. Dr. Cornelius, walking alone in the dark, has a profound insight into this truth. It is this conservative instinct of his, his sense of the eternal, that has found in his love for his little daughter a way to save itself from the wounding inflicted by the times. For father love, and a little child on its mother's breast—are not these timeless, and thus very, very holy and beautiful? Yet Cornelius, pondering there in the dark, descries something not perfectly right and good in his love. Theoretically, in the interests of science, he admits it to himself. There is something ulterior about it, in the nature of it; that something is hostility, hostility against the history of today, which is still in the making and thus not history at all, in behalf of the genuine history that has already happened—that is to say, death. Yes, passing strange though all this is, yet it is true; true in a sense, that is. His devotion to this priceless little morsel of life and new growth has something to do with death, it clings to death as against life; and that is neither right nor beautiful—in a sense. Though only the most fanatical asceticism could be capable, on no other ground than such casual scientific perception, of tearing this purest and most precious of feelings out of his heart.

He holds his darling on his lap and her slim rosy legs hang down. He raises his brows as he talks to her, tenderly, with a half-teasing note of respect, and listens enchanted to her high, sweet little voice calling him Abel. He exchanges a look with the mother, who is caressing her Snapper and reading him a gentle lecture. He must be more reasonable, he must learn self-control; today again, under the manifold exasperations of life, he has given way to rage and behaved like a howling dervish. Cornelius casts a mistrustful glance at the big folk now and then, too; he thinks it not unlikely they are not unaware of those scientific preoccupations of his evening walks. If such be the case they do not show it. They stand there leaning their arms on their chair-backs and with a benevolence not untinctured with irony look on at the parental happiness.

The children's frocks are of a heavy, brick-red stuff, embroidered in modern "arty" style. They once belonged to Ingrid and Bert and are precisely alike, save that little knickers come out beneath Snapper's smock. And both have their hair bobbed. Snapper's is a streaky blond, inclined to turn dark. It is bristly and sticky and looks for all the world like a droll, badly fitting wig. But Ellie's is chestnut brown, glossy and fine as silk, as pleasing as her whole little personality. It covers her ears—and these ears are not a pair, one of them being the right size, the other distinctly too large. Her father will sometimes uncover this little abnormality and exclaim over it as though he had never noticed it before, which both makes Ellie giggle and covers her with shame. Her eyes are now golden brown, set far apart and with sweet gleams in them—such a clear and lovely look! The brows above are blond; the nose still unformed, with thick nostrils and almost circular holes; the mouth large and expressive, with a beautifully arching and mobile upper lip. When she laughs, dimples come in her cheeks and she shows her teeth like loosely strung pearls. So far she has lost but one tooth, which her father gently twisted out with his handkerchief after it had grown very wobbling. During this small operation she had paled and trembled very much. Her cheeks have the softness proper to her years, but they are not chubby; indeed, they are rather concave, due to her facial structure, with its somewhat prominent jaw. On one, close to the soft fall of her hair, is a downy freckle.

Ellie is not too well pleased with her looks—a sign that already she troubles about such things. Sadly she thinks it is best to admit it once for all, her face is "homely"; though the rest of her, "on the other hand," is not bad at all. She loves expressions like "on the other hand"; they sound choice and grown-up to her, and she likes to string them together, one after the other: "very likely," "probably," "after all." Snapper is self-critical too, though more in the moral sphere: he suffers from remorse for his attacks of rage and considers himself a tremendous sinner. He is quite certain that heaven is not for such as he; he is sure to go to "the bad place" when he dies, and no persuasions will convince him to the contrary—as that God sees the heart and gladly makes allowances. Obstinately he shakes his head, with a comic, crooked little peruke, and vows there is no place for him in heaven. When he has a cold he is immediately quite choked with mucus; rattles and rumbles from top to toe if you even look at him; his temperature flies up at once and he simply puffs. Nursy is pessimistic on the score of his constitution: such fat-blooded children as he might get a stroke any minute. Once she even thought she saw the moment at hand: Snapper had been in one of his berserker rages, and in the ensuing fit of penitence stood himself in the corner with his back to the room. Suddenly Nursy noticed that his face had gone all blue, far bluer, even, than her own. She raised the alarm, crying out that the child's all too rich blood had at length brought him to his final hour; and Snapper, to his vast astonishment, found himself, so far from being rebuked for evil-doing, encompassed in tenderness and anxiety—until it turned out that his colour was not caused by apoplexy but by the distempering on the nursery wall, which had come off on his tear-wet face.

Nursy has come downstairs too, and stands by the door, sleek-haired, owl-eyed, with her hands folded over her white apron, and a severely dignified manner born of her limited intelligence. She is very proud of the care and training she gives her nurslings and declares that they are "enveloping wonderfully." She has had seventeen suppurated teeth lately removed from her jaws and been measured for a set of symmetrical yellow ones in dark rubber gums; these now embellish her peasant face. She is obsessed with the strange conviction that these teeth of hers are the subject of general conversation, that, as it were, the sparrows on the house-tops chatter of them. "Everybody knows I've had a false set put in," she will say; "there has been a great deal of foolish talk about them." She is much given to dark hints and veiled innuendo: speaks, for instance, of a certain Dr. Bleifuss, whom every child knows, and "there are even some in the house who pretend to be him." All one can do with talk like this is charitably to pass it over in silence. But she teaches the children nursery rhymes: gems like:

Puff, puff, here comes the train!
Puff, puff, toot, toot,
Away it goes again.

Or that gastronomical jingle, so suited, in its sparseness, to the times, and yet seemingly with a blitheness of its own:

Monday we begin the week,
Tuesday there's a bone to pick.
Wednesday we're half way through,
Thursday what a great to-do!
Friday we eat what fish we're able,
Saturday we dance round the table.
Sunday brings us pork and greens—
Here's a feast for kings and queens!

Also a certain four-line stanza with a romantic appeal, unutterable and unuttered:

Open the gate, open the gate
And let the carriage drive in.
Who is it in the carriage sits:
A lordly sir with golden hair.

Or, finally that ballad about golden-haired Marianne who sat on a, sat on a, sat on a stone, and combed out her, combed out her, combed out her hair; and about bloodthirsty Rudolph, who pulled out a, pulled out a, pulled out a knife—and his ensuing direful end. Ellie enunciates all these ballads charmingly, with her mobile little lips, and sings them in her sweet little voice—much better than Snapper. She does everything better than he does, and he pays her honest admiration and homage and obeys her in all things except when visited by one of his attacks. Sometimes she teaches him, instructs him upon the birds in the picture-book and tells him their proper names: "This is a chaffinch, Buddy, this is a bullfinch, this is a cowfinch." He has to repeat them after her. She gives him medical instruction too, teaches him the names of diseases, such as infammation of the lungs, infammation of the blood, infammation of the air. If he does not pay attention and cannot say the words after her, she stands him in the corner. Once she even boxed his ears, but was so ashamed that she stood herself in the corner for a long time. Yes, they are fast friends, two souls with but a single thought, and have all their adventures in common. They come home from a walk and relate as with one voice that they have seen two moollies and a teenty-weenty baby calf. They are on familiar terms with the kitchen, which consists of Xaver and the ladies Hinterhofer, two sisters once of the lower middle class who, in these evil days, are reduced to living *"au pair"* as the phrase goes and officiating as cook and housemaid for their board and keep. The little ones have a feeling that Xaver and the Hinterhofers are on much the same footing with their father and mother as they are themselves. At least sometimes, when they have been scolded, they go downstairs and announce that the master and mistress are cross. But playing with the servants lacks charm compared with the joys of playing upstairs. The kitchen could never rise to the height of the games their father can invent. For instance, there is "four gentlemen taking a walk." When they play it Abel will crook his knees until he is the same height with themselves and go walking with them, hand in hand. They never get enough of this sport; they could walk round and round the dining-room a whole day on end, five gentlemen in all, counting the diminished Abel.

Then there is the thrilling cushion game. One of the children, usually Ellie, seats herself, unbeknownst to Abel, in his seat at table. Still as a mouse she awaits his coming. He draws near with his head in the air, descanting in loud, clear tones upon the surpassing comfort of his chair; and sits down on top of Ellie. "What's this, what's this?" says he. And bounces about, deaf to the smothered giggles exploding behind him. "Why have they put a cushion in my chair? And what a queer, hard, awkward-shaped cushion it is!" he goes on. "Frightfully uncomfortable to sit on!" And keeps pushing and bouncing about more and more on the astonishing cushion and clutching behind him into the rapturous giggling and squeaking, until at last he turns round, and the game ends with a magnificent climax of discovery and recognition. They might go through all this a hundred times without diminishing by an iota its power to thrill.

Today is no time for such joys. The imminent festivity disturbs the atmosphere, and besides there is work to be done, and, above all, the eggs to be got. Ellie has just time to recite "Puff, puff," and Cornelius to discover that her ears are not mates, when they are interrupted by the arrival of Danny, come to fetch Bert and Ingrid. Xaver, meantime, has exchanged his striped livery for an ordinary coat, in which he looks rather rough-and-ready, though as brisk and attractive as ever. So then Nursy and the children ascend to the upper regions, the Professor withdraws to his study to read, as always after dinner, and his wife bends her energies upon the sandwiches and salad that must be prepared. And she has another errand as well. Before the young people arrive she has to take her shopping-basket and dash into town on her bicycle, to turn into provisions a sum of money she has in hand, which she dares not keep lest it lose all value.

Cornelius reads, leaning back in his chair, with his cigar between his middle and index fingers. First he reads Macaulay on the origin of the English public debt at the end of the seventeenth century; then an article in a French periodical on the rapid increase in the Spanish debt towards the end of the sixteenth. Both these for his lecture on the morrow. He intends to compare the astonishing prosperity which accompanied the phenomenon in England with its fatal effects a hundred years earlier in Spain, and to analyse the ethical and psychological grounds of the difference in results. For that will give him a chance to refer back from the England of William III, which is the actual subject in hand, to the time of Philip II and the Counter-Reformation, which is his own special field. He has already written a valuable work on this period; it is much cited and got him his professorship. While his cigar burns down and gets strong, he excogitates a few pensive sentences in a key of gentle melancholy, to be delivered before his class next day: about the practically hopeless struggle carried on by the belated Philip against the whole trend of history: against the new, the kingdom- disrupting power of the Germanic ideal of freedom and individual liberty. And about the persistent, futile struggle of the aristocracy, condemned by God and rejected of man, against the forces of progress and change. He savours his sentences; keeps on polishing them while he puts back the books he has been using; then goes upstairs for the usual pause in his day's work, the hour with drawn blinds and closed eyes, which he so imperatively needs. But today, he recalls, he will rest under disturbed conditions, amid the bustle of preparations for the feast. He smiles to find his heart giving a mild flutter at the thought. Disjointed phrases on the theme of black-clad Philip and his times mingle with a confused consciousness that they will soon be dancing down below. For five minutes or so he falls asleep.

As he lies and rests he can hear the sound of the garden gate and the repeated ringing at the bell. Each time a little pang goes through him, of excitement and suspense, at the thought that the young people have begun to fill the floor below. And each time he smiles at himself again—though even his smile is slightly nervous, is tinged with the pleasurable anticipations people always feel before a party. At half past four—it is already dark—he gets up and washes at the wash-stand. The basin has been out of repair for two years. It is supposed to tip, but has broken away from its socket on one side and cannot be mended because there is nobody to mend it; neither replaced because no shop can supply another. So it has to be hung up above the vent and emptied by lifting in both hands and pouring out the water. Cornelius shakes his head over this basin, as he does several times a day—whenever, in fact, he has occasion to use it. He finishes his toilet with care, standing under the ceiling light to polish his glasses till they shine. Then he goes downstairs.

On his way to the dining-room he hears the gramophone already going, and the sound of voices. He puts on a polite, society air; at his tongue's end is the phrase he means to utter: "Pray don't let me disturb you," as he passes directly into the dining-room for his tea. "Pray don't let me disturb you"—it seems to him precisely the *mot juste,* towards the guests cordial and considerate, for himself a very bulwark.

The lower floor is lighted up, all the bulbs in the chandelier are burning save one that has burned out. Cornelius pauses on a lower step and surveys the entrance hall. It looks pleasant and cosy in the bright light, with its copy of Marée over the brick chimney-piece, its wainscoted walls—wainscoted in soft wood—and red-carpeted floor, where the guests stand in groups, chatting, each with his tea-cup and slice of bread-and-butter spread with anchovy paste. There is a festal haze, faint scents of hair and clothing and human breath come to him across the room, it is all characteristic and familiar and highly evocative. The door into the dressing-room is open, guests are still arriving.

A large group of people is rather bewildering at first sight. The Professor takes in only the general scene. He does not see Ingrid, who is standing just at the foot of the steps, in a dark silk frock with a pleated collar falling softly over the shoulders, and bare arms. She smiles up at him, nodding and showing her lovely teeth.

"Rested?" she asks, for his private ear. With a quite unwarranted start he recognizes her, and she presents some of her friends.

"May I introduce Herr Zuber?" she says. "And this is Fräulein Plaichinger."

Herr Zuber is insignificant. But Fräulein Plaichinger is a perfect Germania, blond and voluptuous, arrayed in floating draperies. She has a snub nose, and answers the Professor's salutation in the high, shrill pipe so many stout women have.

"Delighted to meet you," he says. "How nice of you to come! A classmate of Ingrid's, I suppose?"

And Herr Zuber is a golfing partner of Ingrid's. He is in business; he works in his uncle's brewery. Cornelius makes a few jokes about the thinness of the beer and professes to believe that Herr Zuber could easily do something about the quality if he would. "But pray don't let me disturb you," he goes on, and turns towards the dining-room.

"There comes Max," says Ingrid. "Max, you sweep, what do you mean by rolling up at this time of day?" For such is the way they talk to each other, offensively to an older ear; of social forms, of hospitable warmth, there is no faintest trace. They all call each other by their first names.

A young man comes up to them out of the dressing-room and makes his bow; he has an expanse of white shirt-front and a little black string tie. He is as pretty as a picture, dark, with rosy cheeks, clean-shaven of course, but with just a sketch of side-whisker. Not a ridiculous or flashy beauty, not like a gypsy fiddler, but just charming to look at, in a winning, well-bred way, with kind dark eyes. He even wears his dinner-jacket a little awkwardly.

"Please don't scold me, Cornelia," he says; "it's the idiotic lectures." And Ingrid presents him to her father as Herr Hergesell.

Well, and so this is Herr Hergesell. He knows his manners, does Herr Hergesell, and thanks the master of the house quite ingratiatingly for his invitation as they shake hands. "I certainly seem to have missed the bus," says he jocosely. "Of course I have lectures today up to four o'clock; I would have; and after that I had to go home to change." Then he talks about his pumps, with which he has just been struggling in the dressing-room.

"I brought them with me in a bag," he goes on. "Mustn't tramp all over the carpet in our brogues—it's not done. Well, I was ass enough not to fetch along a shoe-horn, and I find I simply can't get in! What a sell! They are the tightest I've ever had, the numbers don't tell you a thing, and all the leather today is just cast iron. It's not leather at all. My poor finger"—he confidingly displays a reddened digit and once more characterizes the whole thing as a "sell," and a putrid sell into the bargain. He really does talk just as Ingrid said he did, with a peculiar nasal drawl, not affectedly in the least, but merely because that is the way of all the Hergesells.

Dr. Cornelius says it is very careless of them not to keep a shoehorn in the cloak-room and displays proper sympathy with the mangled finger. "But now you *really* must not let me disturb you any longer," he goes on. *"Auf wiedersehen!"* And he crosses the hall into the dining-room.

There are guests there too, drinking tea; the family table is pulled out. But the Professor goes at once to his own little upholstered corner with the electric light bulb above it—the nook where he usually drinks his tea. His wife is sitting there talking with Bert and two other young men, one of them Herzl, whom Cornelius knows and greets; the other a typical "Wandervogel" named Möller, a youth who obviously neither owns nor cares to own the correct evening dress of the middle classes (in fact, there is no such thing any more), nor to ape the manners of a gentleman (and, in fact, there is no such thing any more either). He has a wilderness of hair, horned spectacles, and a long neck, and wears golf stockings and a belted blouse. His regular occupation, the Professor learns, is banking, but he is by way of being an amateur folk-lorist and collects folk-songs from all localities and in all languages. He sings them, too, and at Ingrid's command has brought his guitar; it is hanging in the dressing-room in an oilcloth case. Herzl, the actor, is small and slight, but he has a strong growth of black beard, as you can tell by the thick coat of powder on his cheeks. His eyes are larger than life, with a deep and melancholy glow. He has put on rouge besides the powder—those dull carmine high-lights on the cheeks can be nothing but a cosmetic. "Queer," thinks the Professor. "You would think a man would be one thing or the other—not melancholic and use face paint at the same time. It's a psychological contradiction. How can a melancholy man rouge? But here we have a perfect illustration of the abnormality of the artist soul-form. It can make possible a contradiction like this—perhaps it even consists in the contradiction. All very interesting—and no reason whatever for not being polite to him. Politeness is a primitive convention—and legitimate. . . . Do take some lemon, Herr Hofschauspieler!"

Court actors and court theatres—there are no such things any more, really. But Herzl relishes the sound of the title, notwithstanding he is a revolutionary artist. This must be another contradiction inherent in his soul-form; so, at least, the Professor assumes, and he is probably right. The flattery he is guilty of is a sort of atonement for his previous hard thoughts about the rouge.

"Thank you so much—it's really too good of you, sir," says Herzl, quite embarrassed. He is so overcome that he almost stammers; only his perfect enunciation saves him. His whole bearing towards his hostess and the master of the house is exaggeratedly polite. It is almost as though he had a bad conscience in respect of his rouge; as though an inward compulsion had driven him to put it on, but now, seeing it through the Professor's eyes, he disapproves of it himself, and thinks, by an air of humility toward the whole of unrouged society, to mitigate its effect.

They drink their tea and chat: about Möller's folk-songs, about Basque folk-songs and Spanish folk-songs; from which they pass to the new production of *Don Carlos* at the Stadttheater, in which Herzl plays the title-rôle. He talks about his own rendering of the part and says he hopes his conception of the character has unity. They go on to criticize the rest of the cast, the setting, and the production as a whole; and Cornelius is struck, rather painfully, to find the conversation trending towards his own special province, back to Spain and the Counter-Reformation. He has done nothing at all to give it this turn, he is perfectly innocent, and hopes it does not look as though he has sought an occasion to play the professor. He wonders, and falls silent, feeling relieved when the little folk come up to the table. Ellie and Snapper have on their blue velvet Sunday frocks; they are permitted to partake in the festivities up to bedtime. They look shy and large-eyed as they say how-do-you-do to the strangers and, under pressure, repeat their names and ages. Herr Möller does nothing but gaze at them solemnly, but Herzl is simply ravished. He rolls his eyes up to heaven and puts his hands over his mouth; he positively blesses them. It all, no doubt, comes from his heart, but he is so addicted to theatrical methods of making an impression and getting an effect that both words and behaviour ring frightfully false. And even his enthusiasm for the little folk looks too much like part of his general craving to make up for the rouge on his cheeks.

The tea-table has meanwhile emptied of guests, and dancing is going on in the hall. The children run off, the Professor prepares to retire. "Go and enjoy yourselves," he says to Möller and Herzl, who have sprung from their chairs as he rises from his. They shake hands and he withdraws into his study, his peaceful kingdom, where he lets down the blinds, turns on the desk lamp, and sits down to his work.

It is work which can be done, if necessary, under disturbed conditions: nothing but a few letters and a few notes. Of course, Cornelius's mind wanders. Vague impressions float through it: Herr Hergesell's refractory pumps, the high pipe in that plump body of the Plaichinger female. As he writes, or leans back in his chair and stares into space, his thoughts go back to Herr Möller's collection of Basque folk-songs, to Herzl's posings and humility, to "his" Carlos and the court of Philip II. There is something strange, he thinks, about conversations. They are so ductile, they will flow of their own accord in the direction of one's dominating interest. Often and often he has seen this happen. And while he is thinking, he is listening to the sounds next door—rather subdued, he finds them. He hears only voices, no sound of footsteps. The dancers do not glide or circle round the room; they merely walk about over the carpet, which does not hamper their movements in the least. Their way of holding each other is quite different and strange, and they move to the strains of the gramophone, to the weird music of the new world. He concentrates on the music and makes out that it is a jazz-band record, with various percussion instruments and the clack and clatter of castanets, which, however, are not even faintly suggestive of Spain, but merely jazz like the rest. No, not Spain. . . . His thoughts are back at their old round.

Half an hour goes by. It occurs to him it would be no more than friendly to go and contribute a box of cigarettes to the festivities next door. Too bad to ask the young people to smoke their own—though they have probably never thought of it. He goes into the empty dining-room and takes a box from his supply in the cupboard: not the best ones, nor yet the brand he himself prefers, but a certain long, thin kind he is not averse to getting rid of—after all, they are nothing but youngsters. He takes the box into the hall, holds it up with a smile, and deposits it on the mantel-shelf. After which he gives a look round and returns to his own room.

There comes a lull in dance and music. The guests stand about the room in groups or round the table at the window or are seated in a circle by the fireplace. Even the built-in stairs, with their worn velvet carpet, are crowded with young folk as in an amphitheatre: Max Hergesell is there, leaning back with one elbow on the step above and gesticulating with his free hand as he talks to the shrill, voluptuous Plaichinger. The floor of the hall is nearly empty, save just in the centre: there, directly beneath the chandelier, the two little ones in their blue velvet frocks clutch each other in an awkward embrace and twirl silently round and round, oblivious of all else. Cornelius, as he passes, strokes their hair, with a friendly word; it does not distract them from their small solemn preoccupation. But at his own door he turns to glance round and sees young Hergesell push himself off the stair by his elbow—probably because he noticed the Professor. He comes down into the arena, takes Ellie out of her brother's arms, and dances with her himself. It looks very comic, without the music, and he crouches down just as Cornelius does when he goes walking with the four gentlemen, holding the fluttered Ellie as though she were grown up and taking little "shimmying" steps. Everybody watches with huge enjoyment, the gramophone is put on again, dancing becomes general. The Professor stands and looks, with his hand on the door-knob. He nods and laughs; when he finally shuts himself into his study the mechanical smile still lingers on his lips.

Again he turns over pages by his desk lamp, takes notes, attends to a few simple matters. After a while he notices that the guests have forsaken the entrance hall for his wife's drawing-room, into which there is a door from his own study as well. He hears their voices and the sounds of a guitar being tuned. Herr Möller, it seems, is to sing—and does so. He twangs the strings of his instrument and sings in a powerful bass a ballad in a strange tongue, possibly Swedish. The Professor does not succeed in identifying it, though he listens attentively to the end, after which there is great applause. The sound is deadened by the portière that hangs over the dividing door. The young bank-clerk begins another song. Cornelius goes softly in.

It is half-dark in the drawing-room; the only light is from the shaded standard lamp, beneath which Möller sits, on the divan, with his legs crossed, picking his strings. His audience is grouped easily about; as there are not enough seats, some stand, and more, among them many young ladies, are simply sitting on the floor with their hands clasped round their knees or even with their legs stretched out before them. Hergesell sits thus, in his dinner jacket, next the piano, with Fräulein Plaichinger beside him. Frau Cornelius is holding both children on her lap as she sits in her easy-chair opposite the singer. Snapper, the Boeotian, begins to talk loud and clear in the middle of the song and has to be intimidated with hushings and finger-shakings. Never, never would Ellie allow herself to be guilty of such conduct. She sits there daintily erect and still on her mother's knee. The Professor tries to catch her eye and exchange a private signal with his little girl; but she does not see him. Neither does she seem to be looking at the singer. Her gaze is directed lower down.

Möller sings the "joli tambour":

Sire, mon roi, donnez-moi votre fille—

They are all enchanted. "How good!" Hergesell is heard to say, in the odd, nasally condescending Hergesell tone. The next one is a beggar ballad, to a tune composed by young Möller himself; it elicits a storm of applause:

Gypsy lassie a-goin' to the fair,
Huzza!
Gypsy laddie a-goin' to be there—
Huzza, diddlety umpty dido!

Laughter and high spirits, sheer reckless hilarity, reigns after this jovial ballad. "Frightfully good!" Hergesell comments again, as before. Follows another popular song, this time a Hungarian one; Möller sings it in its own outlandish tongue, and most effectively. The Professor applauds with ostentation. It warms his heart and does him good, this outcropping of artistic, historic, and cultural elements all amongst the shimmying. He goes up to young Möller and congratulates him, talks about the songs and their sources, and Möller promises to lend him a certain annotated book of folk songs. Cornelius is the more cordial because all the time, as fathers do, he has been comparing the parts and achievements of this young stranger with those of his own son, and being gnawed by envy and chagrin. This young Möller, he is thinking, is a capable bank-clerk (though about Möller's capacity he knows nothing whatever) and has this special gift besides, which must have taken talent and energy to cultivate. "And here is my poor Bert, who knows nothing and can do nothing and thinks of nothing except playing the clown, without even talent for that!" He tries to be just; he tells himself that, after all, Bert has innate refinement; that probably there is a good deal more to him than there is to the successful Möller; that perhaps he has even something of the poet in him, and his dancing and table-waiting are due to mere boyish folly and the distraught times. But paternal envy and pessimism win the upper hand; when Möller begins another song, Dr. Cornelius goes back to his room.

He works as before, with divided attention, at this and that, while it gets on for seven o'clock. Then he remembers a letter he may just as well write, a short letter and not very important, but letter- writing is wonderful for the way it takes up the time, and it is almost half past when he has finished. At half past eight the Italian salad will be served; so now is the prescribed moment for the Professor to go out into the wintry darkness to post his letters and take his daily quantum of fresh air and exercise. They are dancing again, and he will have to pass through the hall to get his hat and coat; but they are used to him now, he need not stop and beg them not to be disturbed. He lays away his papers, takes up the letters he has written, and goes out. But he sees his wife sitting near the door of his room and pauses a little by her easy-chair.

She is watching the dancing. Now and then the big folk or some of their guests stop to speak to her; the party is at its height, and there are more onlookers than these two: blue-faced Ann is standing at the bottom of the stairs, in all the dignity of her limitations. She is waiting for the children, who simply cannot get their fill of these unwonted festivities, and watching over Snapper, lest his all too rich blood be churned to the danger-point by too much twirling round. And not only the nursery but the kitchen takes an interest: Xaver and the two ladies Hinterhofer are standing by the pantry door looking on with relish. Fräulein Walburga, the elder of the two sunken sisters (the culinary section—she objects to being called a cook), is a whimsical, good-natured sort, brown-eyed, wearing glasses with thick circular lenses; the nose-piece is wound with a bit of rag to keep it from pressing on her nose. Fräulein Cecilia is younger, though not so precisely young either. Her bearing is as self-assertive as usual, this being her way of sustaining her dignity as a former member of the middle class. For Fräulein Cecilia feels acutely her descent into the ranks of domestic service. She positively declines to wear a cap or other badge of servitude, and her hardest trial is on the Wednesday evening when she has to serve the dinner while Xaver has his afternoon out. She hands the dishes with averted face and elevated nose—a fallen queen; and so distressing is it to behold her degradation that one evening when the little folk happened to be at table and saw her they both with one accord burst into tears. Such anguish is unknown to young Xaver. He enjoys serving and does it with an ease born of practice as well as talent, for he was once a "piccolo." But otherwise he is a thorough-paced good-for-nothing and windbag—with quite distinct traits of character of his own, as his long-suffering employers are always ready to concede, but perfectly impossible and a bag of wind for all that. One must just take him as he is, they think, and not expect figs from thistles. He is the child and product of the disrupted times, a perfect specimen of his generation, follower of the revolution, Bolshevist sympathizer. The Professor's name for him is the "minute-man," because he is always to be counted on in any sudden crisis, if only to address his sense of humour or love of novelty, and will display therein amazing readiness and resources. But he utterly lacks a sense of duty and can as little be trained to the performance of the daily round and common task as some kinds of dog can be taught to jump over a stick. It goes so plainly against the grain that criticism is disarmed. One becomes resigned. On grounds that appealed to him as unusual and amusing he would be ready to turn out of his bed at any hour of the night. But he simply cannot get up before eight in the morning, he cannot do it, he will not jump over the stick. Yet all day long the evidence of this free and untrammelled existence, the sound of his mouth-organ, his joyous whistle, or his raucous but expressive voice lifted in song, rises to the hearing of the world above-stairs; and the smoke of his cigarettes fills the pantry. While the Hinterhofer ladies work he stands and looks on. Of a morning while the Professor is breakfasting, he tears the leaf off the study calendar—but does not lift a finger to dust the room. Dr. Cornelius has often told him to leave the calendar alone, for he tends to tear off two leaves at a time and thus to add to the general confusion. But young Xaver appears to find joy in this activity, and will not be deprived of it.

Again, he is fond of children, a winning trait. He will throw himself into games with the little folk in the garden, make and mend their toys with great ingenuity, even read aloud from their books—and very droll it sounds in his thick-lipped pronunciation. With his whole soul he loves the cinema; after an evening spent there he inclines to melancholy and yearning and talking to himself. Vague hopes stir in him that some day he may make his fortune in that gay world and belong to it by rights—hopes based on his shock of hair and his physical agility and daring. He likes to climb the ash tree in the front garden, mounting branch by branch to the very top and frightening everybody to death who sees him. Once there he lights a cigarette and smokes it as he sways to and fro, keeping a look-out for a cinema director who might chance to come along and engage him.

If he changed his striped jacket for mufti, he might easily dance with the others and no one would notice the difference. For the big folk's friends are rather anomalous in their clothing: evening dress is worn by a few, but it is by no means the rule. There is quite a sprinkling of guests, both male and female, in the same general style as Möller the ballad-singer. The Professor is familiar with the circumstances of most of this young generation he is watching as he stands beside his wife's chair; he has heard them spoken of by name. They are students at the high school or at the School of Applied Art; they lead, at least the masculine portion, that precarious and scrambling existence which is purely the product of the time. There is a tall, pale, spindling youth, the son of a dentist, who lives by speculation. From all the Professor hears, he is a perfect Aladdin. He keeps a car, treats his friends to champagne suppers, and showers presents upon them on every occasion, costly little trifles in mother-of-pearl and gold. So today he has brought gifts to the young givers of the feast: for Bert a gold lead-pencil, and for Ingrid a pair of ear-rings of barbaric size, great gold circlets that fortunately do not have to go through the little earlobe, but are fastened over it by means of a clip. The big folk come laughing to their parents to display these trophies; and the parents shake their heads even while they admire—Aladdin bowing over and over from afar.

The young people appear to be absorbed in their dancing—if the performance they are carrying out with so much still concentration can be called dancing. They stride across the carpet, slowly, according to some unfathomable prescript, strangely embraced; in the newest attitude, tummy advanced and shoulders high, waggling the hips. They do not get tired, because nobody could. There is no such thing as heightened colour or heaving bosoms. Two girls may dance together or two young men—it is all the same. They move to the exotic strains of the gramophone, played with the loudest needles to procure the maximum of sound: shimmies, foxtrots, one-steps, double foxes, African shimmies, Java dances, and Creole polkas, the wild musky melodies follow one another, now furious, now languishing, a monotonous Negro programme in unfamiliar rhythm, to a clacking, clashing, and strumming orchestral accompaniment.

"What is that record?" Cornelius inquires of Ingrid, as she passes him by in the arms of the pale young speculator, with reference to the piece then playing, whose alternate languors and furies he finds comparatively pleasing and showing a certain resourcefulness in detail.

"*Prince of Pappenheim:* 'Console thee, dearest child,' " she answers, and smiles pleasantly back at him with her white teeth.

The cigarette smoke wreathes beneath the chandelier. The air is blue with a festal haze compact of sweet and thrilling ingredients that stir the blood with memories of green-sick pains and are particularly poignant to those whose youth—like the Professor's own—has been over-sensitive. . . . The little folk are still on the floor. They are allowed to stop up until eight, so great is their delight in the party. The guests have got used to their presence; in their own way, they have their place in the doings of the evening. They have separated, anyhow: Snapper revolves all alone in the middle of the carpet, in his little blue velvet smock, while Ellie is running after one of the dancing couples, trying to hold the man fast by his coat. It is Max Hergesell and Fräulein Plaichinger. They dance well, it is a pleasure to watch them. One has to admit that these mad modern dances, when the right people dance them, are not so bad after all—they have something quite taking. Young Hergesell is a capital leader, dances according to rule, yet with individuality. So it looks. With what aplomb can he walk backwards—when space permits! And he knows how to be graceful standing still in a crowd. And his partner supports him well, being unsuspectedly lithe and buoyant, as fat people often are. They look at each other, they are talking, paying no heed to Ellie, though others are smiling to see the child's persistence. Dr. Cornelius tries to catch up his little sweetheart as she passes and draw her to him. But Ellie eludes him, almost peevishly; her dear Abel is nothing to her now. She braces her little arms against his chest and turns her face away with a persecuted look. Then escapes to follow her fancy once more.

The Professor feels an involuntary twinge. Uppermost in his heart is hatred for this party, with its power to intoxicate and estrange his darling child. His love for her—that not quite disinterested, not quite unexceptionable love of his—is easily wounded. He wears a mechanical smile, but his eyes have clouded, and he stares fixedly at a point in the carpet, between the dancers' feet.

"The children ought to go to bed," he tells his wife. But she pleads for another quarter of an hour; she has promised already, and they do love it so! He smiles again and shakes his head, stands so a moment and then goes across to the cloak-room, which is full of coats and hats and scarves and overshoes. He has trouble in rummaging out his own coat, and Max Hergesell comes out of the hall, wiping his brow.

"Going out, sir?" he asks, in Hergesellian accents, dutifully helping the older man on with his coat. "Silly business this, with my pumps," he says. "They pinch like hell. The brutes are simply too tight for me, quite apart from the bad leather. They press just here on the ball of my great toe"—he stands on one foot and holds the other in his hand—"it's simply unbearable. There's nothing for it but to take them off; my brogues will have to do the business. . . . Oh, let me help you, sir."

"Thanks," says Cornelius. "Don't trouble. Get rid of your own tormentors. . . . Oh, thanks very much!" For Hergesell has gone on one knee to snap the fasteners of his snow-boots.

Once more the Professor expresses his gratitude; he is pleased and touched by so much sincere respect and youthful readiness to serve. "Go and enjoy yourself," he counsels. "Change your shoes and make up for what you have been suffering. Nobody can dance in shoes that pinch. Good-bye, I must be off to get a breath of fresh air."

"I'm going to dance with Ellie now," calls Hergesell after him. "She'll be a first-rate dancer when she grows up, and that I'll swear to."

"Think so?" Cornelius answers, already half out. "Well, you are a connoisseur, I'm sure. Don't get curvature of the spine with stooping."

He nods again and goes. "Fine lad," he thinks as he shuts the door. "Student of engineering. Knows what he's bound for, got a good clear head, and so well set up and pleasant too." And again paternal envy rises as he compares his poor Bert's status with this young man's, which he puts in the rosiest light that his son's may look the darker. Thus he sets out on his evening walk.

He goes up the avenue, crosses the bridge, and walks along the bank on the other side as far as the next bridge but one. The air is wet and cold, with a little snow now and then. He turns up his coat-collar and slips the crook of his cane over the arm behind his back. Now and then he ventilates his lungs with a long deep breath of the night air. As usual when he walks, his mind reverts to his professional preoccupations, he thinks about his lectures and the things he means to say tomorrow about Philip's struggle against the Germanic revolution, things steeped in melancholy and penetratingly just. Above all just, he thinks. For in one's dealings with the young it behooves one to display the scientific spirit, to exhibit the principles of enlightenment—not only for purposes of mental discipline, but on the human and individual side, in order not to wound them or indirectly offend their political sensibilities; particularly in these days, when there is so much tinder in the air, opinions are so frightfully split up and chaotic, and you may so easily incur attacks from one party or the other, or even give rise to scandal, by taking sides on a point of history. "And taking sides is unhistoric anyhow," so he muses. "Only justice, only impartiality is historic." And could not, properly considered, be otherwise. . . . For justice can have nothing of youthful fire and blithe, fresh, loyal conviction. It is by nature melancholy. And, being so, has secret affinity with the lost cause and the forlorn hope rather than with the fresh and blithe and loyal—perhaps this affinity is its very essence and without it it would not exist at all! . . . "And is there then no such thing as justice?" the Professor asks himself, and ponders the question so deeply that he absently posts his letters in the next box and turns round to go home. This thought of his is unsettling and disturbing to the scientific mind—but is it not after all itself scientific, psychological, conscientious, and therefore to be accepted without prejudice, no matter how upsetting? In the midst of which musings Dr. Cornelius finds himself back at his own door.

On the outer threshold stands Xaver, and seems to be looking for him.

"Herr Professor," says Xaver, tossing back his hair, "go upstairs to Ellie straight off. She's in a bad way."

"What's the matter?" asks Cornelius in alarm. "Is she ill?"

"No-o, not to say ill," answers Xaver. "She's just in a bad way and crying fit to bust her little heart. It's along o' that chap with the shirt-front that danced with her—Herr Hergesell. She couldn't be got to go upstairs peaceably, not at no price at all, and she's b'en crying bucketfuls."

"Nonsense," says the Professor, who has entered and is tossing off his things in the cloak-room. He says no more; opens the glass door and without a glance at the guests turns swiftly to the stairs. Takes them two at a time, crosses the upper hall and the small room leading into the nursery. Xaver follows at his heels, but stops at the nursery door.

A bright light still burns within, showing the gay frieze that runs all round the room, the large row of shelves heaped with a confusion of toys, the rocking-horse on his swaying platform, with red-varnished nostrils and raised hoofs. On the linoleum lie other toys—building blocks, railway trains, a little trumpet. The two white cribs stand not far apart, Ellie's in the window corner, Snapper's out in the room.

Snapper is asleep. He has said his prayers in loud, ringing tones, prompted by Nurse, and gone off at once into vehement, profound, and rosy slumber—from which a cannon-ball fired at close range could not rouse him. He lies with both fists flung back on the pillows on either side of the tousled head with its funny crooked little slumber-tossed wig.

A circle of females surrounds Ellie's bed: not only blue-faced Ann is there, but the Hinterhofer ladies too, talking to each other and to her. They make way as the Professor comes up and reveal the child sitting all pale among her pillows, sobbing and weeping more bitterly than he has ever seen her sob and weep in her life. Her lovely little hands lie on the coverlet in front of her, the nightgown with its narrow lace border has slipped down from her shoulder—such a thin, birdlike little shoulder—and the sweet head Cornelius loves so well, set on the neck like a flower on its stalk, her head is on one side, with the eyes rolled up to the corner between wall and ceiling above her head. For there she seems to envisage the anguish of her heart and even to nod to it—either on purpose or because her head wobbles as her body is shaken with the violence of her sobs. Her eyes rain down tears. The bow-shaped lips are parted, like a little *mater dolorosa's,* and from them issue long, low wails that in nothing resemble the unnecessary and exasperating shrieks of a naughty child, but rise from the deep extremity of her heart and wake in the Professor's own a sympathy that is well-nigh intolerable. He has never seen his darling so before. His feelings find immediate vent in an attack on the ladies Hinterhofer.

"What about the supper?" he asks sharply. "There must be a great deal to do. Is my wife being left to do it alone?"

For the acute sensibilities of the former middle class this is quite enough. The ladies withdraw in righteous indignation, and Xaver Kleingutl jeers at them as they pass out. Having been born to low life instead of achieving it, he never loses a chance to mock at their fallen state.

"Childie, childie," murmurs Cornelius, and sitting down by the crib enfolds the anguished Ellie in his arms. "What is the trouble with my darling?"

She bedews his face with her tears.

"Abel . . . Abel . . ." she stammers between sobs. "Why—isn't Max—my brother? Max ought to be—my brother!"

Alas, alas! What mischance is this? Is this what the party has wrought, with its fatal atmosphere? Cornelius glances helplessly up at blue-faced Ann standing there in all the dignity of her limitations with her hands before her on her apron. She purses up her mouth and makes a long face. "It's pretty young," she says, "for the female instincts to be showing up."

"Hold your tongue," snaps Cornelius, in his agony. He has this much to be thankful for, that Ellie does not turn from him now; she does not push him away as she did downstairs, but clings to him in her need, while she reiterates her absurd, bewildered prayer that Max might be her brother, or with a fresh burst of desire demands to be taken downstairs so that he can dance with her again. But Max, of course, is dancing with Fräulein Plaichinger, that behemoth who is his rightful partner and has every claim upon him; whereas Ellie—never, thinks the Professor, his heart torn with the violence of his pity, never has she looked so tiny and birdlike as now, when she nestles to him shaken with sobs and all unaware of what is happening in her little soul. No, she does not know. She does not comprehend that her suffering is on account of Fräulein Plaichinger, fat, overgrown, and utterly within her rights in dancing with Max Hergesell, whereas Ellie may only do it once, by way of a joke, although she is incomparably the more charming of the two. Yet it would be quite mad to reproach young Hergesell with the state of affairs or to make fantastic demands upon him. No, Ellie's suffering is without help or healing and must be covered up. Yet just as it is without understanding, so it is also without restraint—and that is what makes it so horribly painful. Xaver and blue-faced Ann do not feel this pain, it does not affect them—either because of native callousness or because they accept it as the way of nature. But the Professor's fatherly heart is quite torn by it, and by a distressful horror of this passion, so hopeless and so absurd.

Of no avail to hold forth to poor Ellie on the subject of the perfectly good little brother she already has. She only casts a distraught and scornful glance over at the other crib, where Snapper lies vehemently slumbering, and with fresh tears calls again for Max. Of no avail either the promise of a long, long walk tomorrow, all five gentlemen, round and round the dining-room table; or a dramatic description of the thrilling cushion games they will play. No, she will listen to none of all this, nor to lying down and going to sleep. She will not sleep, she will sit bolt upright and suffer. . . . But on a sudden they stop and listen, Abel and Ellie; listen to something miraculous that is coming to pass, that is approaching by strides, two strides, to the nursery door, that now overwhelmingly appears. . . .

It is Xaver's work, not a doubt of that. He has not remained by the door where he stood to gloat over the ejection of the Hinterhofers. No, he has bestirred himself, taken a notion; likewise steps to carry it out. Downstairs he has gone, twitched Herr Hergesell's sleeve, and made a thick-lipped request. So here they both are. Xaver, having done his part, remains by the door; but Max Hergesell comes up to Ellie's crib; in his dinner-jacket, with his sketchy side-whisker and charming black eyes; obviously quite pleased with his rôle of swan knight and fairy prince, as one who should say: "See, here am I, now all losses are restored and sorrows end."

Cornelius is almost as much overcome as Ellie herself.

"Just look," he says feebly, "look who's here. This is uncommonly good of you, Herr Hergesell."

"Not a bit of it," says Hergesell. "Why shouldn't I come to say good-night to my fair partner?"

And he approaches the bars of the crib, behind which Ellie sits struck mute. She smiles blissfully through her tears. A funny, high little note that is half a sigh of relief comes from her lips, then she looks dumbly up at her swan knight with her golden-brown eyes—tear-swollen though they are, so much more beautiful than the fat Plaichinger's. She does not put up her arms. Her joy, like her grief, is without understanding; but she does not do that. The lovely little hands lie quiet on the coverlet, and Max Hergesell stands with his arms leaning over the rail as on a balcony.

"And now," he says smartly, "she need not 'sit the livelong night and weep upon her bed'!" He looks at the Professor to make sure he is receiving due credit for the quotation. "Ha ha!" he laughs, "she's beginning young. 'Console thee, dearest child!' Never mind, you're all right! Just as you are you'll be wonderful! You've only got to grow up. . . . And you'll lie down and go to sleep like a good girl, now I've come to say good-night? And not cry any more, little Lorelei?"

Ellie looks up at him, transfigured. One birdlike shoulder is bare; the Professor draws the lace-trimmed nighty over it. There comes into his mind a sentimental story he once read about a dying child who longs to see a clown he had once, with unforgettable ecstasy, beheld in a circus. And they bring the clown to the bedside marvelously arrayed, embroidered before and behind with silver butterflies; and the child dies happy. Max Hergesell is not embroidered, and Ellie, thank God, is not going to die, she has only "been in a bad way." But, after all, the effect is the same. Young Hergesell leans over the bars of the crib and rattles on, more for the father's ear than the child's, but Ellie does not know that—and the father's feelings towards him are a most singular mixture of thankfulness, embarrassment, and hatred.

"Good night, little Lorelei," says Hergesell, and gives her his hand through the bars. Her pretty, soft, white little hand is swallowed up in the grasp of his big, strong, red one. "Sleep well," he says, "and sweet dreams! But don't dream about me—God forbid! Not at your age—ha ha!" And then the fairy clown's visit is at an end. Cornelius accompanies him to the door. "No, no positively, no thanks called for, don't mention it," he large-heartedly protests; and Xaver goes downstairs with him, to help serve the Italian salad.

But Dr. Cornelius returns to Ellie, who is now lying down, with her cheek pressed into her flat little pillow.

"Well, wasn't that lovely?" he says as he smooths the covers. She nods, with one last little sob. For a quarter of an hour he sits beside her and watches while she falls asleep in her turn, beside the little brother who found the right way so much earlier than she. Her silky brown hair takes the enchanting fall it always does when she sleeps; deep, deep lie the lashes over the eyes that late so abundantly poured forth their sorrow; the angelic mouth with its bowed upper lip is peacefully relaxed and a little open. Only now and then comes a belated catch in her slow breathing.

And her small hands, like pink and white flowers, lie so quietly, one on the coverlet, the other on the pillow by her face—Dr. Cornelius, gazing, feels his heart melt with tenderness as with strong wine.

"How good," he thinks, "that she breathes in oblivion with every breath she draws! That in childhood each night is a deep, wide gulf between one day and the next. Tomorrow, beyond all doubt, young Hergesell will be a pale shadow, powerless to darken her little heart. Tomorrow, forgetful of all but present joy, she will walk with Abel and Snapper, all five gentlemen, round and round the table, will play the ever-thrilling cushion game."

Heaven be praised for that!

1925

The Egg

SHERWOOD ANDERSON

[1876–1941]

My father was, I am sure, intended by nature to be a cheerful, kindly man. Until he was thirty-four years old he worked as a farm-hand for a man named Thomas Butterworth whose place lay near the town of Bidwell, Ohio. He had then a horse of his own and on Saturday evenings drove into town to spend a few hours in social intercourse with other farm-hands. In town he drank several glasses of beer and stood about in Ben Head's saloon—crowded on Saturday evenings with visiting farm-hands. Songs were sung and glasses thumped on the bar. At ten o'clock father drove home along a lonely country road, made his horse comfortable for the night and himself went to bed, quite happy in his position in life. He had at that time no notion of trying to rise in the world.

It was in the spring of his thirty-fifth year that father married my mother, then a country school-teacher, and in the following spring I came wriggling and crying into the world. Something happened to the two people. They became ambitious. The American passion for getting up in the world took possession of them.

It may have been that mother was responsible. Being a school-teacher she had no doubt read books and magazines. She had, I presume, read of how Garfield, Lincoln, and other Americans rose from poverty to fame and greatness and as I lay beside her—in the days of her lying-in—she may have dreamed that I would some day rule men and cities. At any rate she induced father to give up his place as a farm-hand, sell his horse and embark on an independent enterprise of his own. She was a tall silent woman with a long nose and troubled grey eyes. For herself she wanted nothing. For father and myself she was incurably ambitious.

The first venture into which the two people went turned out badly. They rented ten acres of poor stony land on Grigg's Road, eight miles from Bidwell, and launched into chicken raising. I grew into boyhood on the place and got my first impressions of life there. From the beginning they were impressions of disaster and if, in my turn, I am a gloomy man inclined to see the darker side of life, I attribute it to the fact that what should have been for me the happy joyous days of childhood were spent on a chicken farm.

One unversed in such matters can have no notion of the many and tragic things that can happen to a chicken. It is born out of an egg, lives for a few weeks as a tiny fluffy thing such as you will see pictured on Easter cards, then becomes hideously naked, eats quantities of corn and meal bought by the sweat of your father's brow, gets diseases called pip, cholera, and other names, stands looking with stupid eyes at the sun, becomes sick and dies. A few hens and now and then a rooster, intended to serve God's mysterious ends, struggle through to maturity. The hens lay eggs out of which come other chickens and the dreadful cycle is thus made complete. It is all unbelievably complex. Most philosophers must have been raised on chicken farms. One hopes for so much from a chicken and is so dreadfully disillusioned. Small chickens, just setting out on the journey of life, look so bright and alert and they are in fact so dreadfully stupid. They are so much like people they mix one up in one's judgments of life. If disease does not kill them they wait until your expectations are thoroughly aroused and then walk under the wheels of a wagon—to go squashed and dead back to their maker. Vermin infest their youth, and fortunes must be spent for curative powders. In later life I have seen how a literature has been built up on the subject of fortunes to be made out of the raising of chickens. It is intended to be read by the gods who have just eaten of the tree of the knowledge of good and evil. It is a hopeful literature and declares that much may be done by simple ambitious people who own a few hens. Do not be led astray by it. It was not written for you. Go hunt for gold on the frozen hills of Alaska, put your faith in the honesty of a politician, believe if you will that the world is daily growing better and that good will triumph over evil, but do not read and believe the literature that is written concerning the hen. It was not written for you.

I, however, digress. My tale does not primarily concern itself with the hen. If correctly told it will centre on the egg. For ten years my father and mother struggled to make our chicken farm pay and then they gave up that struggle and began another. They moved into the town of Bidwell, Ohio and embarked in the restaurant business. After ten years of worry with incubators that did not hatch, and with tiny—and in their own way lovely—balls of fluff that passed on into semi-naked pullethood and from that into dead henhood, we threw all aside and packing our belongings on a wagon drove down Grigg's Road toward Bidwell, a tiny caravan of hope looking for a new place from which to start on our upward journey through life.

We must have been a sad looking lot, not, I fancy, unlike refugees fleeing from a battlefield. Mother and I walked in the road. The wagon that contained our goods had been borrowed for the day from Mr. Albert Griggs, a neighbor. Out of its sides stuck the legs of cheap chairs and at the back of the pile of beds, tables, and boxes filled with kitchen utensils was a crate of live chickens, and on top of that the baby carriage in which I had been wheeled about in my infancy. Why we stuck to the baby carriage I don't know. It was unlikely other children would be born and the wheels were broken. People who have few possessions cling tightly to those they have. That is one of the facts that make life so discouraging.

Father rode on top of the wagon. He was then a bald-headed man of forty-five, a little fat and from long association with mother and the chickens he had become habitually silent and discouraged. All during our ten years on the chicken farm he had worked as a laborer on neighboring farms and most of the money he had earned had been spent for remedies to cure chicken diseases, on Wilmer's White Wonder Cholera Cure or Professor Bidlow's Egg Producer or some other preparations that mother found advertised in the poultry papers. There were two little patches of hair on father's head just above his ears. I remember that as a child I used to sit looking at him when he had gone to sleep in a chair before the stove on Sunday afternoons in the winter. I had at that time already begun to read books and have notions of my own and the bald path that led over the top of his head was, I fancied, something like a broad road, such a road as Caesar might have made on which to lead his legions out of Rome and into the wonders of an unknown world. The tufts of hair that grew above father's ears were, I thought, like forests. I fell into a half-sleeping, half-waking state and dreamed I was a tiny thing going along the road into a far beautiful place where there were no chicken farms and where life was a happy eggless affair.

One might write a book concerning our flight from the chicken farm into town. Mother and I walked the entire eight miles—she to be sure that nothing fell from the wagon and I to see the wonder of the world. On the seat of the wagon beside father was his greatest treasure. I will tell you of that.

On a chicken farm where hundreds and even thousands of chickens come out of eggs surprising things sometimes happen. Grotesques are born out of eggs as out of people. The accident does not often occur—perhaps once in a thousand births. A chicken is, you see, born that has four legs, two pairs of wings, two heads or what not. The things do not live. They go quickly back to the hand of their maker that has for a moment trembled. The fact that the poor little things could not live was one of the tragedies of life to father. He had some sort of notion that if he could but bring into henhood or roosterhood a five-legged hen or a two-headed rooster his fortune would be made. He dreamed of taking the wonder about to county fairs and of growing rich by exhibiting it to other farmhands.

At any rate he saved all the little monstrous things that had been born on our chicken farm. They were preserved in alcohol and put each in its own glass bottle. These he had carefully put into a box and on our journey into town it was carried on the wagon seat beside him. He drove the horses with one hand and with the other clung to the box. When we got to our destination the box was taken down at once and the bottles removed. All during our days as keepers of a restaurant in the town of Bidwell, Ohio, the grotesques in their little glass bottles sat on a shelf back of the counter. Mother sometimes protested but father was a rock on the subject of his treasure. The grotesques were, he declared, valuable. People, he said, liked to look at strange and wonderful things.

Did I say that we embarked in the restaurant business in the town of Bidwell, Ohio? I exaggerated a little. The town itself lay at the foot of a low hill and on the shore of a small river. The railroad did not run through the town and the station was a mile away to the north at a place called Pickleville. There had been a cider mill and pickle factory at the station, but before the time of our coming they had both gone out of business. In the morning and in the evening busses came down to the station along a road called Turner's Pike from the hotel on the main street of Bidwell. Our going to the out of the way place to embark in the restaurant business was mother's idea. She talked of it for a year and then one day went off and rented an empty store building opposite the railroad station. It was her idea that the restaurant would be profitable. Travelling men, she said, would be always waiting around to take trains out of town and town people would come to the station to await incoming trains. They would come to the restaurant to buy pieces of pie and drink coffee. Now that I am older I know that she had another motive in going. She was ambitious for me. She wanted me to rise in the world, to get into a town school and become a man of the towns.

At Pickleville father and mother worked hard as they always had done. At first there was the necessity of putting our place into shape to be a restaurant. That took a month. Father built a shelf on which he put tins of vegetables. He painted a sign on which he put his name in large red letters. Below his name was the sharp command —"EAT HERE"—that was so seldom obeyed. A show case was bought and filled with cigars and tobacco. Mother scrubbed the floor and the walls of the room. I went to school in the town and was glad to be away from the farm and from the presence of the discouraged, sad-looking chickens. Still I was not very joyous. In the evening I walked home from school along Turner's Pike and remembered the children I had seen playing in the town school yard. A troop of little girls had gone hopping about and singing. I tried that. Down along the frozen road I went hopping solemnly on one leg. "Hippity Hop To The Barber Shop," I sang shrilly. Then I stopped and looked doubtfully about. I was afraid of being seen in my gay mood. It must have seemed to me that I was doing a thing that should not be done by one who, like myself, had been raised on a chicken farm where death was a daily visitor.

Mother decided that our restaurant should remain open at night. At ten in the evening a passenger train went north past our door followed by a local freight. The freight crew had switching to do in Pickleville and when the work was done they came to our restaurant for hot coffee and food. Sometimes one of them ordered a fried egg. In the morning at four they returned north-bound and again visited us. A little trade began to grow up. Mother slept at night and during the day tended the restaurant and fed our boarders while father slept. He slept in the same bed mother had occupied during the night and I went off to the town of Bidwell and to school. During the long nights, while mother and I slept, father cooked meats that were to go into sandwiches for the lunch baskets of our boarders. Then an idea in regard to getting up in the world came into his head. The American spirit took hold of him. He also became ambitious.

In the long nights when there was little to do father had time to think. That was his undoing. He decided that he had in the past been an unsuccessful man because he had not been cheerful enough and that in the future he would adopt a cheerful outlook on life. In the early morning he came upstairs and got into bed with mother. She woke and the two talked. From my bed in the corner I listened.

It was father's idea that both he and mother should try to entertain the people who came to eat at our restaurant. I cannot now remember his words, but he gave the impression of one about to become in some obscure way a kind of public entertainer. When people, particularly young people from the town of Bidwell, came into our place, as on very rare occasions they did, bright entertaining conversation was to be made. From father's words I gathered that something of the jolly inn-keeper effect was to be sought. Mother must have been doubtful from the first, but she said nothing discouraging. It was father's notion that a passion for the company of himself and mother would spring up in the breasts of the younger people of the town of Bidwell. In the evening bright happy groups would come singing down Turner's Pike. They would troop shouting with joy and laughter into our place. There would be song and festivity. I do not mean to give the impression that father spoke so elaborately of the matter. He was as I have said an uncommunicative man. "They want some place to go. I tell you they want some place to go," he said over and over. That was as far as he got. My own imagination has filled in the blanks.

For two or three weeks this notion of father's invaded our house. We did not talk much, but in our daily lives tried earnestly to make smiles take the place of glum looks. Mother smiled at the boarders and I, catching the infection, smiled at our cat. Father became a little feverish in his anxiety to please. There was no doubt, lurking somewhere in him, a touch of the spirit of the showman. He did not waste much of his ammunition on the railroad men he served at night but seemed to be waiting for a young man or woman from Bidwell to come in to show what he could do. On the counter in the restaurant there was a wire basket kept always filled with eggs, and it must have been before his eyes when the idea of being entertaining was born in his brain. There was something pre-natal about the way eggs kept themselves connected with the development of his idea. At any rate an egg ruined his new impulse in life. Late one night I was awakened by a roar of anger coming from father's throat. Both mother and I sat upright in our beds. With trembling hands she lighted a lamp that stood on a table by her head. Downstairs the front door of our restaurant went shut with a bang and in a few minutes father tramped up the stairs. He held an egg in his hand and his hand trembled as though he were having a chill. There was a half insane light in his eyes. As he stood glaring at us I was sure he intended throwing the egg at either mother or me. Then he laid it gently on the table beside the lamp and dropped on his knees beside mother's bed. He began to cry like a boy and I, carried away by his grief, cried with him. The two of us filled the little upstairs room with our wailing voices. It is ridiculous, but of the picture we made I can remember only the fact that mother's hand continually stroked the bald patch that ran across the top of his head. I have forgotten what mother said to him and how she induced him to tell her of what had happened downstairs. His explanation also has gone out of my mind. I remember only my own grief and fright and the shiny path over father's head glowing in the lamp light as he knelt by the bed.

As to what happened downstairs. For some unexplainable reason I know the story as well as though I had been a witness to my father's discomfiture. One in time gets to know many unexplainable things. On that evening young Joe Kane, son of a merchant of Bidwell, came to Pickleville to meet his father, who was expected on the ten o'clock evening train from the South. The train was three hours late and Joe came into our place to loaf about and to wait for its arrival. The local freight train came in and the freight crew were fed. Joe was left alone in the restaurant with father.

From the moment he came into our place the Bidwell young man must have been puzzled by my father's actions. It was his notion that father was angry at him for hanging around. He noticed that the restaurant keeper was apparently disturbed by his presence and he thought of going out. However, it began to rain and he did not fancy the long walk to town and back. He bought a five-cent cigar and ordered a cup of coffee. He had a newspaper in his pocket and took it out and began to read. "I'm waiting for the evening train. It's late," he said apologetically.

For a long time father, whom Joe Kane had never seen before, remained silently gazing at his visitor. He was no doubt suffering an attack of stage fright. As so often happens in life he had thought so much and so often of the situation that now confronted him that he was somewhat nervous in its presence.

For one thing, he did not know what to do with his hands. He thrust one of them nervously over the counter and shook hands with Joe Kane. "How-de-do," he said. Joe Kane put his newspaper down and stared at him. Father's eyes lighted on the basket of eggs that sat on the counter and he began to talk. "Well," he began hesitatingly, "well, you have heard of Christopher Columbus, eh?" He seemed to be angry. "That Christopher Columbus was a cheat," he declared emphatically. "He talked of making an egg stand on its end. He talked, he did and then he went and broke the end of the egg."

My father seemed to his visitor to be beside himself at the duplicity of Christopher Columbus. He muttered and swore. He declared it was wrong to teach children that Christopher Columbus was a great man when, after all, he cheated at the critical moment. He had declared he would make an egg stand on end and then when his bluff had been called he had done a trick. Still grumbling at Columbus, father took an egg from the basket on the counter and began to walk up and down. He rolled the egg between the palms of his hands. He smiled genially. He began to mumble words regarding the effect to be produced on an egg by the electricity that comes out of the human body. He declared that without breaking its shell and by virtue of rolling it back and forth in his hands he could stand the egg on its end. He explained that the warmth of his hands and the gentle rolling movement he gave the egg created a new centre of gravity, and Joe Kane was mildly interested. "I have handled thousands of eggs," father said. "No one knows more about eggs than I do."

He stood the egg on the counter and it fell on its side. He tried the trick again and again, each time rolling the egg between the palms of his hands and saying the words regarding the wonders of electricity and the laws of gravity. When after a half hour's effort he did succeed in making the egg stand for a moment he looked up to find that his visitor was no longer watching. By the time he had succeeded in calling Joe Kane's attention to the success of his effort the egg had again rolled over and lay on its side.

Afire with the showman's passion and at the same time a good deal disconcerted by the failure of his first effort, father now took the bottles containing the poultry monstrosities down from their place on the shelf and began to show them to his visitor. "How would you like to have seven legs and two heads like this fellow?" he asked, exhibiting the most remarkable of his treasures. A cheerful smile played over his face. He reached over the counter and tried to slap Joe Kane on the shoulder as he had seen men do in Ben Head's saloon when he was a young farmhand and drove to town on Saturday evenings. His visitor was made a little ill by the sight of the body of the terribly deformed bird floating in the alcohol in the bottle and got up to go. Coming from behind the counter father took hold of the young man's arm and led him back to his seat. He grew a little angry and for a moment had to turn his face away and force himself to smile. Then he put the bottles back on the shelf. In an outburst of generosity he fairly compelled Joe Kane to have a fresh cup of coffee and another cigar at his expense. Then he took a pan and filling it with vinegar, taken from a jug that sat beneath the counter, he declared himself about to do a new trick. "I will heat this egg in this pan of vinegar," he said. "Then I will put it through the neck of a bottle without breaking the shell. When the egg is inside the bottle it will resume its normal shape and the shell will become hard again. Then I will give the bottle with the egg in it to you. You can take it about with you wherever you go. People will want to know how you got the egg in the bottle. Don't tell them. Keep them guessing. This is the way to have fun with this trick."

Father grinned and winked at his visitor. Joe Kane decided that the man who confronted him was mildly insane but harmless. He drank the cup of coffee that had been given him and began to read his paper again. When the egg had been heated in vinegar father carried it on a spoon to the counter and going into a back room got an empty bottle. He was angry because his visitor did not watch him as he began to do his trick, but nevertheless went cheerfully to work. For a long time he struggled, trying to get the egg to go through the neck of the bottle. He put the pan of vinegar back on the stove, intending to reheat the egg, then picked it up and burned his fingers. After a second bath in the hot vinegar the shell of the egg had been softened a little but not enough for his purpose. He worked and worked and a spirit of desperate determination took possession of him. When he thought that at last the trick was about to be consummated the delayed train came in at the station and Joe Kane started to go nonchalantly out at the door. Father made a last desperate effort to conquer the egg and make it do the things that would establish his reputation as one who knew how to entertain guests who came into his restaurant. He worried the egg. He attempted to be somewhat rough with it. He swore and the sweat stood out on his forehead. The egg broke under his hand. When the contents spurted over his clothes, Joe Kane, who had stopped at the door, turned and laughed.

A roar of anger rose from my father's throat. He danced and shouted a string of inarticulate words. Grabbing another egg from the basket on the counter, he threw it, just missing the head of the young man as he dodged through the door and escaped.

Father came upstairs to mother and me with an egg in his hand. I do not know what he intended to do. I imagine he had some idea of destroying it, of destroying all eggs, and that he intended to let mother and me see him begin. When, however, he got into the presence of mother something happened to him. He laid the egg gently on the table and dropped on his knees by the bed as I have already explained. He later decided to close the restaurant for the night and to come upstairs and get into bed. When he did so he blew out the light and after much muttered conversation both he and mother went to sleep. I suppose I went to sleep also, but my sleep was troubled. I awoke at dawn and for a long time looked at the egg that lay on the table. I wondered why eggs had to be and why from the egg came the hen who again laid the egg. The question got into my blood. It has stayed there, I imagine, because I am the son of my father. At any rate, the problem remains unsolved in my mind. And that, I conclude, is but another evidence of the complete and final triumph of the egg—at least as far as my family is concerned.

1920

Araby

JAMES JOYCE

[1882–1941]

North Richmond Street, being blind, was a quiet street except at the hour when the Christian Brothers' School set the boys free. An uninhabited house of two storeys stood at the blind end, detached from its neighbours in a square ground. The other houses of the street, conscious of decent lives within them, gazed at one another with brown imperturbable faces.

The former tenant of our house, a priest, had died in the back drawing-room. Air, musty from having been long enclosed, hung in all the rooms, and the waste room behind the kitchen was littered with old useless papers. Among these I found a few paper-covered books, the pages of which were curled and damp: *The Abbot,* by Walter Scott, *The Devout Communicant* and *The Memoirs of Vidocq.* I liked the last best because its leaves were yellow. The wild garden behind the house contained a central apple-tree and a few straggling bushes under one of which I found the late tenant's rusty bicycle-pump. He had been a very charitable priest; in his will he had left all his money to institutions and the furniture of his house to his sister.

When the short days of winter came dusk fell before we had well eaten our dinners. When we met in the street the houses had grown sombre. The space of sky above us was the colour of ever-changing violet and towards it the lamps of the street lifted their feeble lanterns. The cold air stung us and we played till our bodies glowed. Our shouts echoed in the silent street. The career of our play brought us through the dark muddy lanes behind the houses where we ran the gauntlet of the rough tribes from the cottages, to the back doors of the dark dripping gardens where odours arose from the ashpits, to the dark odorous stables where a coachman smoothed and combed the horse or shook music from the buckled harness. When we returned to the street light from the kitchen windows had filled the areas. If my uncle was seen turning the corner we hid in the shadow until we had seen him safely housed. Or if Mangan's sister came out on the doorstep to call her brother in to his tea we watched her from our shadow peer up and down the street. We waited to see whether she would remain or go in and, if she remained, we left our shadow and walked up to Mangan's steps resignedly. She was waiting for us, her figure defined by the light from the half-opened door. Her brother always teased her before he obeyed and I stood by the railings looking at her. Her dress swung as she moved her body and the soft rope of her hair tossed from side to side.

Every morning I lay on the floor in the front parlour watching her door. The blind was pulled down to within an inch of the sash so that I could not be seen. When she came out on the doorstep my heart leaped. I ran to the hall, seized my books and followed her. I kept her brown figure always in my eye and, when we came near the point at which our ways diverged, I quickened my pace and passed her. This happened morning after morning. I had never spoken to her, except for a few casual words, and yet her name was like a summons to all my foolish blood.

Her image accompanied me even in places the most hostile to romance. On Saturday evenings when my aunt went marketing I had to go to carry some of the parcels. We walked through the flaring streets, jostled by drunken men and bargaining women, amid the curses of labourers, the shrill litanies of shop-boys who stood on guard by the barrels of pigs' cheeks, the nasal chanting of street-singers, who sang a *come-all-you* about O'Donovan Rossa, or a ballad about the troubles in our native land. These noises converged in a single sensation of life for me: I imagined that I bore my chalice safely through a throng of foes. Her name sprang to my lips at moments in strange prayers and praises which I myself did not understand. My eyes were often full of tears (I could not tell why) and at times a flood from my heart seemed to pour itself out into my bosom. I thought little of the future. I did not know whether I would ever speak to her or not or, if I spoke to her, how I could tell her of my confused adoration. But my body was like a harp and her words and gestures were like fingers running upon the wires.

One evening I went into the back drawing-room in which the priest had died. It was a dark rainy evening and there was no sound in the house. Through one of the broken panes I heard the rain impinge upon the earth, the fine incessant needles of water playing in the sodden beds. Some distant lamp or lighted window gleamed below me. I was thankful that I could see so little. All my senses seemed to desire to veil themselves and, feeling that I was about to slip from them, I pressed the palms of my hands together until they trembled, murmuring: *"O love! O love!"* many times.

At last she spoke to me. When she addressed the first words to me I was so confused that I did not know what to answer. She asked me was I going to *Araby.* I forgot whether I answered yes or no. It would be a splendid bazaar, she said she would love to go.

"And why can't you?" I asked.

While she spoke she turned a silver bracelet round and round her wrist. She could not go, she said, because there would be a retreat that week in her convent. Her brother and two other boys were fighting for their caps and I was alone at the railings. She held one of the spikes, bowing her head towards me. The light from the lamp opposite our door caught the white curve of her neck, lit up her hair that rested there and, falling, lit up the hand upon the railing. It fell over one side of her dress and caught the white border of a petticoat, just visible as she stood at ease.

"It's well for you," she said.

"If I go," I said, "I will bring you something."

What innumerable follies laid waste my waking and sleeping thoughts after that evening! I wished to annihilate the tedious intervening days. I chafed against the work of school. At night in my bedroom and by day in the classroom her image came between me and the page I strove to read. The syllables of the word *Araby* were called to me through the silence in which my soul luxuriated and cast an Eastern enchantment over me. I asked for leave to go to the bazaar on Saturday night. My aunt was surprised and hoped it was not some Freemason affair. I answered few questions in class. I watched my master's face pass from amiability to sternness; he hoped I was not beginning to idle. I could not call my wandering thoughts together. I had hardly any patience with the serious work of life which, now that it stood between me and my desire, seemed to me child's play, ugly monotonous child's play.

On Saturday morning I reminded my uncle that I wished to go

to the bazaar in the evening. He was fussing at the hallstand, looking for the hatbrush, and answered me curtly:

"Yes, boy, I know."

As he was in the hall I could not go into the front parlour and lie at the window. I left the house in bad humour and walked slowly towards the school. The air was pitilessly raw and already my heart misgave me.

When I came home to dinner my uncle had not yet been home. Still it was early. I sat staring at the clock for some time and, when its ticking began to irritate me, I left the room. I mounted the staircase and gained the upper part of the house. The high cold empty gloomy rooms liberated me and I went from room to room singing. From the front window I saw my companions playing below in the street. Their cries reached me weakened and indistinct and, leaning my forehead against the cool glass, I looked over at the dark house where she lived. I may have stood there for an hour, seeing nothing but the brown-clad figure cast by my imagination, touched discreetly by the lamplight at the curved neck, at the hand upon the railings and at the border below the dress.

When I came downstairs again I found Mrs. Mercer sitting at the fire. She was an old garrulous woman, a pawnbroker's widow, who collected used stamps for some pious purpose. I had to endure the gossip of the tea-table. The meal was prolonged beyond an hour and still my uncle did not come. Mrs. Mercer stood up to go: she was sorry she couldn't wait any longer, but it was after eight o'clock and she did not like to be out late, as the night air was bad for her. When she had gone I began to walk up and down the room, clenching my fists. My aunt said:

"I'm afraid you may put off your bazaar for this night of Our Lord."

At nine o'clock I heard my uncle's latchkey in the halldoor. I heard him talking to himself and heard the hallstand rocking when it had received the weight of his overcoat. I could interpret these signs. When he was midway through his dinner I asked him to give me the money to go to the bazaar. He had forgotten.

"The people are in bed and after their first sleep now," he said.

I did not smile. My aunt said to him energetically:

"Can't you give him the money and let him go? You've kept him late enough as it is."

My uncle said he was very sorry he had forgotten. He said he believed in the old saying: "All work and no play makes Jack a dull boy." He asked me where I was going and, when I had told him a second time he asked me did I know *The Arab's Farewell to his Steed.* When I left the kitchen he was about to recite the opening lines of the piece to my aunt.

I held a florin tightly in my hand as I strode down Buckingham Street towards the station. The sight of the streets thronged with buyers and glaring with gas recalled to me the purpose of my journey. I took my seat in a third-class carriage of a deserted train. After an intolerable delay the train moved out of the station slowly. It crept onward among ruinous houses and over the twinkling river. At Westland Row Station a crowd of people pressed to the carriage doors; but the porters moved them back, saying that it was a special train for the bazaar. I remained alone in the bare carriage. In a few minutes the train drew up beside an improvised wooden platform. I passed out on to the road and saw by the lighted dial of a clock that it was ten minutes to ten. In front of me was a large building which displayed the magical name.

I could not find any sixpenny entrance and, fearing that the bazaar would be closed, I passed in quickly through a turnstile, handing a shilling to a weary-looking man. I found myself in a big hall girdled at half its height by a gallery. Nearly all the stalls were closed and the greater part of the hall was in darkness. I recognised a silence like that which pervades a church after a service. I walked into the centre of the bazaar timidly. A few people were gathered about the stalls which were still open. Before a curtain, over which the words *Café Chantant* were written in coloured lamps, two men were counting money on a salver. I listened to the fall of the coins.

Remembering with difficulty why I had come I went over to one of the stalls and examined porcelain vases and flowered tea-sets. At the door of the stall a young lady was talking and laughing with two young gentlemen. I remarked their English accents and listened vaguely to their conversation.

"O, I never said such a thing!"

"O, but you did!"

"O, but I didn't!"

"Didn't she say that?"

"Yes. I heard her."

"O, there's a . . . fib!"

Observing me the young lady came over and asked me did I wish to buy anything. The tone of her voice was not encouraging; she seemed to have spoken to me out of a sense of duty. I looked humbly at the great jars that stood like eastern guards at either side of the dark entrance to the stall and murmured:

"No, thank you."

The young lady changed the position of one of the vases and went back to the two young men. They began to talk of the same subject. Once or twice the young lady glanced at me over her shoulder.

I lingered before her stall, though I knew my stay was useless, to make my interest in her wares seem the more real. Then I turned away slowly and walked down the middle of the bazaar. I allowed the two pennies to fall against the sixpence in my pocket. I heard a voice call from one end of the gallery that the light was out. The upper part of the hall was now completely dark.

Gazing up into the darkness I saw myself as a creature driven and derided by vanity; and my eyes burned with anguish and anger.

1914

Kew Gardens

VIRGINIA WOOLF

[1882–1941]

From the oval-shaped flower-bed there rose perhaps a hundred stalks spreading into heart-shaped or tongue-shaped leaves half-way up and unfurling at the tip red or blue or yellow petals marked with spots of colour raised upon the surface; and from the red, blue or yellow gloom of the throat emerged a straight bar, rough with gold dust and slightly clubbed at the end. The petals were voluminous enough to be stirred by the summer breeze, and when they moved, the red, blue and yellow lights passed one over the other, staining an inch of the brown earth beneath with a spot of the most intricate colour. The light fell either upon the smooth, grey back of a pebble, or, the shell of a snail with its brown, circular veins, or falling into a raindrop, it expanded with such intensity of red, blue and yellow the thin walls of water that one expected them to burst and disappear. Instead, the drop was left in a second silver grey once more, and the light now settled upon the flesh of a leaf, revealing the branching thread of fibre beneath the surface, and again it moved on and spread its illumination in the vast green spaces beneath the dome of the heart-shaped and tongue-shaped leaves. Then the breeze stirred rather more briskly overhead and the colour was flashed into the air above, into the eyes of the men and women who walk in Kew Gardens in July.

The figures of these men and women straggled past the flower-bed with a curiously irregular movement not unlike that of the white and blue butterflies who crossed the turf in zig-zag flights from bed to bed. The man was about six inches in front of the woman, strolling carelessly, while she bore on with greater purpose, only turning her head now and then to see that the children were not too far behind. The man kept this distance in front of the woman purposely, though perhaps unconsciously, for he wished to go on with his thoughts.

"Fifteen years ago I came here with Lily," he thought. "We sat somewhere over there by a lake and I begged her to marry me all through the hot afternoon. How the dragonfly kept circling round us: how clearly I see the dragonfly and her shoe with the square silver buckle at the toe. All the time I spoke I saw her shoe and when it moved impatiently I knew without looking up what she was going to say: the whole of her seemed to be in her shoe. And my love, my desire, were in the dragonfly; for some reason I thought that if it settled there, on that leaf, the broad one with the red flower in the middle of it, if the dragonfly settled on the leaf she would say 'Yes' at once. But the dragonfly went round and round: it never settled anywhere—of course not, happily not, or I shouldn't be walking here with Eleanor and the children. Tell me, Eleanor. D'you ever think of the past?"

"Why do you ask, Simon?"

"Because I've been thinking of the past. I've been thinking of Lily, the woman I might have married. . . . Well, why are you silent? Do you mind my thinking of the past?"

"Why should I mind, Simon? Doesn't one always think of the past, in a garden with men and women lying under the trees. Aren't they one's past, all that remains of it, those men and women, those ghosts lying under the trees, . . . one's happiness, one's reality?"

"For me, a square silver shoe buckle and a dragonfly—"

"For me, a kiss. Imagine six little girls sitting before their easels twenty years ago, down by the side of a lake, painting the water-lilies, the first red water-lilies I'd ever seen. And suddenly a kiss, there on the back of my neck. And my hand shook all the afternoon so that I couldn't paint. I took out my watch and marked the hour when I would allow myself to think of the kiss for five minutes only—it was so precious—the kiss of an old grey-haired woman with a wart on her nose, the mother of all my kisses all my life. Come, Caroline, come, Hubert."

They walked on past the flower-bed, now walking four abreast, and soon diminished in size among the trees and looked half transparent as the sunlight and shade swam over their backs in large trembling irregular patches.

In the oval flower-bed the snail, whose shell had been stained red, blue and yellow for the space of two minutes or so, now appeared to be moving very slightly in its shell, and next began to labour over the crumbs of loose earth which broke away and rolled down as it passed over them. It appeared to have a definite goal in front of it, differing in this respect from the singular high stepping angular green insect who attempted to cross in front of it, and waited for a second with its antennae trembling as if in deliberation, and then stepped off as rapidly and strangely in the opposite direction. Brown cliffs with deep green lakes in the hollows, flat, blade-like trees that waved from root to tip, round boulders of grey stone, vast crumpled surfaces of a thin crackling texture—all these objects lay across the snail's progress between one stalk and another to his goal. Before he had decided whether to circumvent the arched tent of a dead leaf or to breast it there came past the bed the feet of other human beings.

This time they were both men. The younger of the two wore an expression of perhaps unnatural calm; he raised his eyes and fixed them very steadily in front of him while his companion spoke, and directly his companion had done speaking he looked on the ground again and sometimes opened his lips only after a long pause and sometimes did not open them at all. The elder man had a curiously uneven and shaky method of walking, jerking his hand forward and throwing up his head abruptly, rather in the manner of an impatient carriage horse tired of waiting outside a house; but in the man these gestures were irresolute and pointless. He talked almost incessantly; he smiled to himself and again began to talk, as if the smile had been an answer. He was talking about spirits—the spirits of the dead, who, according to him, were even now telling him all sorts of odd things about their experiences in Heaven.

"Heaven was known to the ancients as Thessaly, William, and now, with this war, the spirit matter is rolling between the hills like thunder." He paused, seemed to listen, smiled, jerked his head and continued:

"You have a small electric battery and a piece of rubber to insulate the wire—isolate?—insulate?—well, we'll skip the details, no good going into details that wouldn't be understood—and in short the little machine stands in any convenient position by the head of the bed, we will say, on a neat mahogany stand. All arrangements being properly fixed by workmen under my direction, the widow applies her ear and summons the spirit by sign as agreed. Women! Widows! Women in black—"

Here he seemed to have caught sight of a woman's dress in the distance, which in the shade looked a purple black. He took off his hat, placed his hand upon his heart, and hurried towards her muttering and gesticulating feverishly. But William caught him by the sleeve and touched a flower with the tip of his walking-stick in order to divert the old man's attention. After looking at it for a moment in some confusion the old man bent his ear to it and seemed to answer a voice speaking from it, for he began talking about the forests of Uruguay which he had visited hundreds of years ago in company with the most beautiful young woman in Europe. He could be heard murmuring about forests of Uruguay blanketed with the wax petals of tropical roses, nightingales, sea beaches, mermaids, and women drowned at sea, as he suffered himself to be moved on by William, upon whose face the look of stoical patience grew slowly deeper and deeper.

Following his steps so closely as to be slightly puzzled by his gestures came two elderly women of the lower middle class, one stout and ponderous, the other rosy cheeked and nimble. Like most people of their station they were frankly fascinated by other signs of eccentricity betokening a disordered brain, especially in the well-to-do; but they were too far off to be certain whether the gestures were merely eccentric or genuinely mad. After they had scrutinized the old man's back in silence for a moment and given each other a queer, sly look, they went on energetically piecing together their very complicated dialogue:

"Nell, Bert, Lot, Cess, Phil, Pa, he says, I says, she says, I says, I says—"

"My Bert, Sis, Bill, Grandad, the old man, sugar,
Sugar, flour, kippers, greens,
Sugar, sugar, sugar."

The ponderous woman looked through the pattern of falling words at the flowers standing cool, firm, and upright in the earth, with a curious expression. She saw them as a sleeper waking from a heavy sleep sees a brass candlestick reflecting the light in an unfamiliar way, and closes his eyes and opens them, and seeing the brass candlestick again, finally starts broad awake and stares at the candlestick with all his powers. So the heavy woman came to a standstill opposite the oval-shaped flower-bed, and ceased even to pretend to listen to what the other woman was saying. She stood there letting the words fall over her, swaying the top part of her body slowly backwards and forwards, looking at the flowers. Then she suggested that they should find a seat and have their tea.

The snail had now considered every possible method of reaching his goal without going round the dead leaf or climbing over it. Let alone the effort needed for climbing, a leaf, he was doubtful whether the thin texture which vibrated with such an alarming crackle when touched even by the tips of his horns would bear his weight; and this determined him finally to creep beneath it, for there was a point where the leaf curved high enough from the ground to admit him. He had just inserted his head in the opening and was taking stock of the high brown roof and was getting used to the cool brown light when two other people came past outside on the turf. This time they were both young, a young man and a young woman. They were both in the prime of youth, the season before the smooth pink folds of the flower have burst their gummy case, when the wings of the butterfly, though fully grown, are motionless in the sun.

"Lucky it isn't Friday," he observed.

"Why? D'you believe in luck?"

"They make you pay sixpence on Friday."

"What's a sixpence anyway? Isn't it worth sixpence?"

"What's 'it'—what do you mean by 'it'?"

"O, anything—I mean—you know what I mean."

Long pauses came between each of these remarks; they were uttered in toneless and monotonous voices. The couple stood still on the edge of the flower-bed, and together pressed the end of her parasol deep down into the soft earth. The action and the fact that his hand rested on the top of hers expressed their feelings in a strange way, as these short insignificant words also expressed something, words with short wings for their heavy body of meaning, inadequate to carry them far and thus alighting awkwardly upon the very common objects that surrounded them, and were to their inexperienced touch so massive; but who knows (so they thought as they pressed the parasol into the earth) what precipices aren't concealed in them, or what slopes of ice don't shine in the sun on the other side? Who knows? Who has ever seen this before? Even when she wondered what sort of tea they gave you at Kew, he felt that something loomed up behind her words, and stood vast and solid behind them; and the mist very slowly rose and uncovered—O, Heavens, what were those shapes?—little white tables, and waitresses who looked first at her and then at him; and there was a bill that he would pay with a real two-shilling piece, and it was real, all real, he assured himself, fingering the coin in his pocket, real to everyone except to him and to her; even to him it began to seem real; and then—but it was too exciting to stand and think any longer, and he pulled the parasol out of the earth with a jerk and was impatient to find the place where one had tea with other people, like other people.

"Come along, Trissie; it's time we had our tea."

"Wherever *does* one have one's tea?" she asked with the oddest thrill of excitement in her voice, looking vaguely round and letting herself be drawn on down the grass path, trailing her parasol; turning her head this way and that way forgetting her tea, wishing to go down there and then down there, remembering orchids and cranes among wild flowers, a Chinese pagoda and a crimson crested bird; but he bore her on.

Thus one couple after another with much the same irregular and aimless movement passed the flower-bed and were enveloped in layer after layer of green-blue vapour, in which at first their bodies had substance and a dash of colour, but later both substance and colour dissolved in the green-blue atmosphere. How hot it was! So hot that even the thrush chose to hop, like a mechanical bird, in the shadow of the flowers, with long pauses between one movement and the next; instead of rambling vaguely the white butterflies danced one above another, making with their white shifting flakes the outline of a shattered marble column above the tallest flowers; the glass roofs of the palm house shone as if a whole market full of shiny green umbrellas had opened in the sun; and in the drone of the aeroplane the voice of the summer sky murmured its fierce soul. Yellow and black, pink and snow white, shapes of all these colours, men, women, and children were spotted for a second upon the horizon, and then, seeing the breadth of yellow that lay upon the grass, they wavered and sought shade beneath the trees, dissolving like drops of water in the yellow and green atmosphere, staining it faintly with red and blue. It seemed as if all gross and heavy bodies had sunk down in the heat motionless and lay huddled upon the ground, but their voices went wavering from them as if they were flames lolling from the thick waxen bodies of candles. Voices. Yes, voices. Wordless voices, breaking the silence suddenly with such depth of contentment, such passion of desire, or, in the voices of children, such freshness of surprise; breaking the silence? But there was no silence; all the time the motor omnibuses were turning their wheels and changing their gear; like a vast nest of Chinese boxes all of wrought steel turning ceaselessly one within another the city murmured; on the top of which the voices cried aloud and the petals of myriads of flowers flashed their colours into the air.

1919

A Hunger Artist*

FRANZ KAFKA

[1883–1924]

During these last decades the interest in professional fasting has markedly diminished. It used to pay very well to stage such great performances under one's own management, but today that is quite impossible. We live in a different world now. At one time the whole town took a lively interest in the hunger artist; from day to day of his fast the excitement mounted; everybody wanted to see him at least once a day; there were people who bought season tickets for the last few days and sat from morning till night in front of his small barred cage; even in the nighttime there were visiting hours, when the whole effect was heightened by torch flares; on fine days the cage was set out in the open air, and then it was the children's special treat to see the hunger artist; for their elders he was often just a joke that happened to be in fashion, but the children stood open-mouthed, holding each other's hands for greater security, marveling at him as he sat there pallid in black tights, with his ribs sticking out so prominently, not even on a seat but down among straw on the ground, sometimes giving a courteous nod, answering questions with a constrained smile, or perhaps stretching an arm through the bars so that one might feel how thin it was, and then again withdrawing deep into himself, paying no attention to anyone or anything, not even to the all-important striking of the clock that was the only piece of furniture in his cage, but merely staring into vacancy with half-shut eyes, now and then taking a sip from a tiny glass of water to moisten his lips.

*Translated by Edwin and Willa Muir.

Besides casual onlookers there were also relays of permanent watchers selected by the public, usually butchers, strangely enough, and it was their task to watch the hunger artist day and night, three of them at a time, in case he should have some secret recourse to nourishment. This was nothing but a formality, instituted to reassure the masses, for the initiates knew well enough that during his fast the artist would never in any circumstances, not even under forcible compulsion, swallow the smallest morsel of food; the honor of his profession forbade it. Not every watcher, of course, was capable of understanding this; there were often groups of night watchers who were very lax in carrying out their duties and deliberately huddled together in a retired corner to play cards with great absorption, obviously intending to give the hunger artist the chance of a little refreshment, which they supposed he could draw from some private hoard. Nothing annoyed the artist more than such watchers; they made him miserable; they made his fast seem unendurable; sometimes he mastered his feebleness sufficiently to sing during their watch for as long as he could keep going, to show them how unjust their suspicions were. But that was of little use; they only wondered at his cleverness in being able to fill his mouth even while singing. Much more to his taste were the watchers who sat close up to the bars, who were not content with the dim night lighting of the hall but focused him in the full glare of the electric pocket torch given them by the impresario. The harsh light did not trouble him at all, in any case he could never sleep properly, and he could always drowse a little, whatever the light, at any hour, even when the hall was thronged with noisy onlookers. He was quite happy at the prospect of spending a sleepless night with such watchers; he was ready to exchange jokes with them, to tell them stories out of his nomadic life, anything at all to keep them awake and demonstrate to them again that he had no eatables in his cage and that he was fasting as not one of them could fast. But his happiest moment was when the morning came and an enormous breakfast was brought them, at his expense, on which they flung themselves with the keen appetite of healthy men after a weary night of wakefulness. Of course there were people who argued that this breakfast was an unfair attempt to bribe the watchers, but that was going rather too far, and when they were invited to take on a night's vigil without a breakfast, merely for the sake of the cause, they made themselves scarce, although they stuck stubbornly to their suspicions.

Such suspicions, anyhow, were a necessary accompaniment to the profession of fasting. No one could possibly watch the hunger artist continuously, day and night, and so no one could produce first-hand evidence that the fast had really been rigorous and continuous; only the artist himself could know that, he was therefore bound to be the sole completely satisfied spectator of his own fast. Yet for other reasons he was never satisfied; it was not perhaps mere fasting that had brought him to such skeleton thinness that many people had regretfully to keep away from his exhibitions, because the sight of him was too much for them, perhaps it was dissatisfaction with himself that had worn him down. For he alone knew, what no other initiate knew, how easy it was to fast. It was the easiest thing in the world. He made no secret of this, yet people did not believe him, at the best they set him down as modest, most of them, however, thought he was out for publicity or else was some kind of cheat who found it easy to fast because he had discovered a way of making it easy, and then had the impudence to admit the fact, more or less. He had to put up with all that, and in the course of time had got used to it, but his inner dissatisfaction always rankled, and never yet, after any term of fasting—this must be granted to his credit—had he left the cage of his own free will. The longest period of fasting was fixed by his impresario at forty days, beyond that term he was not allowed to go, not even in great cities, and there was good reason for it, too. Experience had proved that for about forty days the interest of the public could be stimulated by a steadily increasing pressure of advertisement, but after that the town began to lose interest, sympathetic support began notably to fall off; there were of course local variations as between one town and another or one country and another, but as a general rule forty days marked the limit. So on the fortieth day the flower bedecked cage was opened, enthusiastic spectators filled the hall, a military band played, two doctors entered the cage to measure the results of the fast, which were announced through a megaphone, and finally two young ladies appeared, blissful at having been selected for the honor, to help the hunger artist down the few steps leading to a small table on which was spread a carefully chosen invalid repast. And at this very moment the artist always turned stubborn. True, he would entrust his bony arms to the outstretched helping hands of the ladies bending over him, but stand up he would not. Why stop fasting at this particular moment, after forty days of it? He had held out for a long time, an illimitably long time; why stop now, when he was in his best fasting form, or rather, not yet quite in his best fasting form? Why should he be cheated of the fame he would get for fasting longer, for being not only the record hunger artist of all time, which presumably he was already, but for beating his own record by a performance beyond human imagination, since he felt that there were no limits to his capacity for fasting? His public pretended to admire him so much, why should it have so little patience with him; if he could endure fasting longer, why shouldn't the public endure it? Besides, he was tired, he was comfortable sitting in the straw, and now he was supposed to lift himself to his full height and go down to a meal the very thought of which gave him a nausea that only the presence of the ladies kept him from betraying, and even that with an effort. And he looked up into the eyes of the ladies who were apparently so friendly and in reality so cruel, and shook his head, which felt too heavy on its strengthless neck. But then there happened yet again what always happened. The impresario came forward, without a word—for the band made speech impossible—lifted his arms in the air above the artist, as if inviting Heaven to look down upon its creature here in the straw, this suffering martyr, which indeed he was, although in quite another sense; grasped him round the emaciated waist, with exaggerated caution, so that the frail condition he was in might be appreciated; and committed him to the care of the blenching ladies, not without secretly giving him a shaking so that his legs and body tottered and swayed. The artist now submitted completely; his head lolled on his breast as if it had landed there by chance; his body was hollowed out; his legs in a spasm of self-preservation clung close to each other at the knees, yet scraped on the ground as if it were not really solid ground, as if they were only trying to find solid ground; and the whole weight of his body, a feather-weight after all, relapsed onto one of the ladies, who, looking round for help and panting a little—this post of honor was not at all what she had expected it to be—first stretched her neck as far as she could to keep her face at least free from contact with the artist, when finding this impossible, and her more fortunate companion not coming to her aid but merely holding extended on her own trembling hand the little bunch of knucklebones that was the artist's, to the great delight of the spectators burst into tears and had to be replaced by an attendant who had long been stationed in readiness. Then came the food, a little of which the impresario managed to get between the artist's lips, while he sat in a kind of half-fainting trance, to the accompaniment of cheerful patter designed to distract the public's attention from the artist's condition; after that, a toast was drunk to the public, supposedly prompted by a whisper from the artist in the impresario's ear; the band confirmed it with a mighty flourish, the spectators melted away, and no one had any cause to be dissatisfied with the proceedings, no one except the hunger artist himself, he only, as always.

So he lived for many years, with small regular intervals of recuperation, in visible glory, honored by the world, yet in spite of that troubled in spirit, and all the more troubled because no one would take his trouble seriously. What comfort could he possibly need? What more could he possibly wish for? And if some good-natured person, feeling sorry for him, tried to console him by pointing out that his melancholy was probably caused by fasting, it could happen, especially when he had been fasting for some time, that he reacted with an outburst of fury and to the general alarm began to shake the bars of his cage like a wild animal. Yet the impresario had a way of punishing these outbreaks which he rather enjoyed putting into operation. He would apologize publicly for the artist's behavior, which was only to be excused, he admitted, because of the irritability caused by fasting; a condition hardly to be understood by well-fed people; then by natural transition he went on to mention the artist's equally incomprehensible boast that he could fast for much longer than he was doing; he praised the high ambition, the good will, the great self-denial undoubtedly implicit in such a statement; and then quite simply countered it by bringing out photographs, which were also on sale to the public, showing the artist on the fortieth day of a fast lying in bed almost dead from exhaustion. This perversion of the truth, familiar to the artist though it was, always unnerved him afresh and proved too much for him. What was a consequence of the premature ending of his fast was here presented as the cause of it! To fight against this lack of understanding, against a whole world of non-understanding, was impossible. Time and again in good faith he stood by the bars listening to the impresario, but as soon as the photographs appeared he always let go and sank with a groan back on to his straw, and the reassured public could once more come close and gaze at him.

A few years later when the witnesses of such scenes called them to mind, they often failed to understand themselves at all. For meanwhile the aforementioned change in public interest had set in; it seemed to happen almost overnight; there may have been profound causes for it, but who was going to bother about that; at any rate the pampered hunger artist suddenly found himself deserted one fine day by the amusement seekers, who went streaming past him to other more favored attractions. For the last time the impresario hurried him over half Europe to discover whether the old interest might still survive here and there; all in vain; everywhere, as if by secret agreement, a positive revulsion from professional fasting was in evidence. Of course it could not really have sprung up so suddenly as all that, and many premonitory symptoms which had not been sufficiently remarked or suppressed during the rush and glitter of success now came retrospectively to mind, but it was now too late to take any countermeasures. Fasting would surely come into fashion again at some future date, yet that was no comfort for those living in the present. What, then, was the hunger artist to do? He had been applauded by thousands in his time and could hardly come down to showing himself in a street booth at village fairs, and as for adopting another profession, he was not only too old for that but too fanatically devoted to fasting. So he took leave of the impresario, his partner in an unparalleled career, and hired himself to a large circus; in order to spare his own feelings he avoided reading the conditions of his contract.

A large circus with its enormous traffic in replacing and recruiting men, animals and apparatus can always find a use for people at any time, even for a hunger artist, provided of course that he does not ask too much, and in this particular case anyhow it was not only the artist who was taken on but his famous and long-known name as well, indeed considering the peculiar nature of his performance, which was not impaired by advancing age, it could not be objected that here was an artist past his prime, no longer at the height of his professional skill, seeking a refuge in some quiet corner of a circus; on the contrary, the hunger artist averred that he could fast as well as ever, which was entirely credible, he even alleged that if he were allowed to fast as he liked, and this was at once promised him without more ado, he could astound the world by establishing a record never yet achieved, a statement which certainly provoked a smile among the other professionals, since it left out of account the change in public opinion, which the hunger artist in his zeal conveniently forgot.

He had not, however, actually lost his sense of the real situation and took it as a matter of course that he and his cage should be stationed, not in the middle of the ring as a main attraction, but outside, near the animal cages, on a site that was after all easily accessible. Large and gaily painted placards made a frame for the cage and announced what was to be seen inside it. When the public came thronging out in the intervals to see the animals, they could hardly avoid passing the hunger artist's cage and stopping there for a moment, perhaps they might even have stayed longer had not those pressing behind them in the narrow gangway, who did not understand why they should be held up on their way toward the excitements of the menagerie, made it impossible for anyone to stand gazing quietly for any length of time. And that was the reason why the hunger artist, who had of course been looking forward to these visiting hours as the main achievement of his life, began instead to shrink from them. At first he could hardly wait for the intervals; it was exhilarating to watch the crowds come streaming his way, until only too soon—not even the most obstinate self-deception, clung to almost consciously, could hold out against the fact—the conviction was borne in upon him that these people, most of them, to judge from their actions, again and again, without exception, were all on their way to the menagerie. And the first sight of them from the distance remained the best. For when they reached his cage he was at once deafened by the storm of shouting and abuse that arose from the two contending factions, which renewed themselves continuously, of those who wanted to stop and stare at him

—he soon began to dislike them more than the others—not out of real interest but only out of obstinate self-assertiveness, and those who wanted to go straight on to the animals. When the first great rush was past, the stragglers came along, and these, whom nothing could have prevented from stopping to look at him as long as they had breath, raced past with long strides, hardly even glancing at him, in their haste to get to the menagerie in time. And all too rarely did it happen that he had a stroke of luck, when some father of a family fetched up before him with his children, pointed a finger at the hunger artist and explained at length what the phenomenon meant, telling stories of earlier years when he himself had watched similar but much more thrilling performances, and the children, still rather uncomprehending, since neither inside nor outside school had they been sufficiently prepared for this lesson—what did they care about fasting?—yet showed by the brightness of their intent eyes that new and better times might be coming. Perhaps, said the hunger artist to himself many a time, things would be a little better if his cage were set not quite so near the menagerie. That made it too easy for people to make their choice, to say nothing of what he suffered from the stench of the menagerie, the animals' restlessness by night, the carrying past of raw lumps of flesh for the beasts of prey, the roaring at feeding times, which depressed him continually. But he did not dare to lodge a complaint with the management; after all, he had the animals to thank for the troops of people who passed his cage, among whom there might always be one here and there to take an interest in him, and who could tell where they might seclude him if he called attention to his existence and thereby to the fact that, strictly speaking, he was only an impediment on the way to the menagerie.

A small impediment, to be sure, one that grew steadily less. People grew familiar with the strange idea that they could be expected, in times like these, to take an interest in a hunger artist, and with this familiarity the verdict went out against him. He might fast as much as he could, and he did so; but nothing could save him now, people passed him by. Just try to explain to anyone the art of fasting! Anyone who has no feeling for it cannot be made to understand it. The fine placards grew dirty and illegible, they were torn down; the little notice board telling the number of fast days achieved, which at first was changed carefully every day, had long stayed at the same figure, for after the first few weeks even this small task seemed pointless to the staff; and so the artist simply fasted on and on, as he had once dreamed of doing, and it was no trouble to him, just as he had always foretold, but no one counted the days, no one, not even the artist himself, knew what records he was already breaking, and his heart grew heavy. And when once in a time some leisurely passer-by stopped, made merry over the old figure on the board and spoke of swindling, that was in its way the stupidest lie ever invented by indifference and inborn malice, since it was not the hunger artist who was cheating; he was working honestly, but the world was cheating him of his reward.

Many more days went by, however, and that too came to an end. An overseer's eye fell on the cage one day and asked the attendants why this perfectly good cage should be left standing there unused with dirty straw inside it; nobody knew, until one man, helped out by the notice board, remembered about the hunger artist. They poked into the straw with sticks and found him in it. "Are you still fasting?" asked the overseer. "When on earth do you mean to stop?" "Forgive me, everybody," whispered the hunger artist; only the overseer, who had his ear to the bars, understood him. "Of course," said the overseer, and tapped his forehead with a finger to let the attendants know what state the man was in, "we forgive you." "I always wanted you to admire my fasting," said the hunger artist. "We do admire it," said the overseer, affably. "But you shouldn't admire it," said the hunger artist. "Well, then we don't admire it," said the overseer, "but why shouldn't we admire it?" "Because I have to fast, I can't help it," said the hunger artist. "What a fellow you are," said the overseer, "and why can't you help it?" "Because," said the hunger artist, lifting his head a little and speaking, with his lips pursed, as if for a kiss, right into the overseer's ear, so that no syllable might be lost, "because I couldn't find the food I liked. If I had found it, believe me, I should have made no fuss and stuffed myself like you or anyone else." These were his last words, but in his dimming eyes remained the firm though no longer proud persuasion that he was still continuing to fast.

"Well, clear this out now!" said the overseer, and they buried the hunger artist, straw and all. Into the cage they put a young panther. Even the most insensitive felt it refreshing to see this wild creature

The narrator switches his sympathies.

leaping around the cage that had so long been dreary. The panther was all right. The food he liked was brought him without hesitation by the attendants; he seemed not even to miss his freedom; his noble body, furnished almost to the bursting point with all that it needed, seemed to carry freedom around with it too; somewhere in his jaws it seemed to lurk; and the joy of life streamed with such ardent passion from his throat that for the onlookers it was not easy to stand the shock of it. But they braced themselves, crowded round the cage, and did not want ever to move away.

1922

The Use of Force

WILLIAM CARLOS WILLIAMS

[1883–1963]

They were new patients to me, all I had was the name, Olson. Please come down as soon as you can, my daughter is very sick.

When I arrived I was met by the mother, a big startled-looking woman, very clean and apologetic who merely said, Is this the doctor? and let me in. In the back, she added? You must excuse us, doctor, we have her in the kitchen where it is warm. It is very damp here sometimes.

The child was fully dressed and sitting on her father's lap near the kitchen table. He tried to get up, but I motioned for him not to bother, took off my overcoat and started to look things over. I could see that they were all very nervous, eyeing me up and down distrustfully. As often, in such cases, they weren't telling me more than they had to, it was up to me to tell them; that's why they were spending three dollars on me.

The child was fairly eating me up with her cold, steady eyes, and no expression to her face whatever. She did not move and seemed, inwardly, quiet; an unusually attractive little thing, and as strong as a heifer in appearance. But her face was flushed, she was breathing rapidly, and I realized that she had a high fever. She had magnificent blond hair, in profusion. One of those picture children often reproduced in advertising leaflets and the photogravure sections of the Sunday papers.

She's had a fever for three days, began the father and we don't know what it comes from. My wife has given her things, you know, like people do, but it don't do no good. And there's been a lot of sickness around. So we tho't you'd better look her over and tell us what is the matter.

As doctors often do I took a trial shot at it as a point of departure. Has she had a sore throat?

Both parents answered me together, No . . . No, she says her throat don't hurt her.

Does your throat hurt you? added the mother to the child. But the little girl's expression didn't change nor did she move her eyes from my face.

Have you looked?

I tried to, said the mother, but I couldn't see.

As it happens we had been having a number of cases of diphtheria in the school to which this child went during that month and we were all, quite apparently, thinking of that, though no one had as yet spoken of the thing.

Well, I said, suppose we take a look at the throat first. I smiled in my best professional manner and asking for the child's first name I said, come on, Mathilda, open your mouth and let's take a look at your throat.

Nothing doing.

Aw, come on, I coaxed, just open your mouth wide and let me take a look. Look, I said opening both hands wide, I haven't anything in my hands. Just open up and let me see.

Such a nice man, put in the mother. Look how kind he is to you. Come on, do what he tells you to. He won't hurt you.

At that I ground my teeth in disgust. If only they wouldn't use the word "hurt" I might be able to get somewhere. But I did not allow myself to be hurried or disturbed but speaking quietly and slowly I approached the child again.

As I moved my chair a little nearer suddenly with one cat-like movement both her hands clawed instinctively for my eyes and she almost reached them too. In fact she knocked my glasses flying and they fell, though unbroken, several feet away from me on the kitchen floor.

Both the mother and father almost turned themselves inside out in embarrassment and apology. You bad girl, said the mother, taking her and shaking her by one arm. Look what you've done. The nice man . . .

For heaven's sake, I broke in. Don't call me a nice man to her. I'm here to look at her throat on the chance that she might have diphtheria and possibly die of it. But that's nothing to her. Look here, I said to the child, we're going to look at your throat. You're old enough to understand what I'm saying. Will you open it now by yourself or shall we have to open it for you?

Not a move. Even her expression hadn't changed. Her breaths however were coming faster and faster. Then the battle began. I had to do it. I had to have a throat culture for her own protection. But first I told the parents that it was entirely up to them. I explained the danger but said that I would not insist on a throat examination so long as they would take the responsibility.

If you don't do what the doctor says you'll have to go to the hospital, the mother admonished her severely.

Oh yeah? I had to smile to myself. After all, I had already fallen in love with the savage brat, the parents were contemptible to me. In the ensuing struggle they grew more and more abject, crushed, exhausted while she surely rose to magnificent heights of insane fury of effort bred of her terror of me.

The father tried his best, and he was a big man but the fact that she was his daughter, his shame at her behavior and his dread of hurting her made him release her just at the critical moment several times when I had almost achieved success, till I wanted to kill him. But his dread also that she might have diphtheria made him tell me to go on, go on though he himself was almost fainting, while the mother moved back and forth behind us raising and lowering her hands in an agony of apprehension.

Put her in front of you on your lap, I ordered, and hold both her wrists.

But as soon as he did the child let out a scream. Don't, you're hurting me. Let go of my hands. Let them go I tell you. Then she shrieked terrifyingly, hysterically. Stop it! Stop it! You're killing me!

Do you think she can stand it, doctor! said the mother.

You get out, said the husband to his wife. Do you want her to die of diphtheria?

Come on now, hold her, I said.

Then I grasped the child's head with my left hand and tried to get the wooden tongue depressor between her teeth. She fought, with clenched teeth, desperately! But now I also had grown furious—at a child. I tried to hold myself down but I couldn't. I know how to expose a throat for inspection. And I did my best. When finally I got the wooden spatula behind the last teeth and just the point of it into the mouth cavity, she opened up for an instant but before I could see anything she came down again and gripping the wooden blade between her molars she reduced it to splinters before I could get it out again.

Aren't you ashamed, the mother yelled at her. Aren't you ashamed to act like that in front of the doctor?

Get me a smooth-handled spoon of some sort, I told the mother. We're going through with this. The child's mouth was already bleeding. Her tongue was cut and she was screaming in wild hysterical shrieks. Perhaps I should have desisted and come back in an hour or more. No doubt it would have been better. But I have seen at least two children lying dead in bed of neglect in such cases, and feeling that I must get a diagnosis, now or never I went at it again. But the worst of it was that I too had got beyond reason. I could have torn the child apart in my own fury and enjoyed it. It was a pleasure to attack her. My face was burning with it.

The damned little brat must be protected against her own idiocy, one says to one's self at such times. Others must be protected against her. It is social necessity. And all these things are true. But a blind fury, a feeling of adult shame, bred of a longing for muscular release are the operatives. One goes on to the end.

In a final unreasoning assault I overpowered the child's neck and jaws. I forced the heavy silver spoon back of her teeth and down her throat till she gagged. And there it was—both tonsils covered with membrane. She had fought valiantly to keep me from knowing her secret. She had been hiding that sore throat for three days at least and lying to her parents in order to escape just such an outcome as this.

Now truly she *was* furious. She had been on the defensive before but now she attacked. Tried to get off her father's lap and fly at me while tears of defeat blinded her eyes.

1938

Haircut

RING LARDNER

[1885–1933]

I got another barber that comes over from Carterville and helps me out Saturdays, but the rest of the time I can get along all right alone. You can see for yourself that this ain't no New York City and besides that, the most of the boys works all day and don't have no leisure to drop in here and get themselves prettied up.

You're a newcomer, ain't you? I thought I hadn't seen you round before. I hope you like it good enough to stay. As I say, we ain't no New York City or Chicago, but we have pretty good times. Not as good, though, since Jim Kendall got killed. When he was alive, him and Hod Meyers used to keep this town in an uproar. I bet they was more laughin' done here than any town its size in America.

Jim was comical, and Hod was pretty near a match for him. Since Jim's gone, Hod tries to hold his end up just the same as ever, but it's tough goin' when you ain't got nobody to kind of work with.

They used to be plenty fun in here Saturdays. This place is jam-packed Saturdays, from four o'clock on. Jim and Hod would show up right after their supper, round six o'clock. Jim would set himself down in that big chair, nearest the blue spittoon. Whoever had been settin' in that chair, why they'd get up when Jim come in and give it to him.

You'd of thought it was a reserved seat like they have sometimes in a theayter. Hod would generally always stand or walk up and down, or some Saturdays, of course, he'd be settin' in this chair part of the time, gettin' a haircut.

Well, Jim would set there a w'ile without openin' his mouth only to spit, and then finally he'd say to me, "Whitey,"—my right name, that is, my right first name, is Dick, but everybody round here calls me Whitey—Jim would say, "Whitey, your nose looks like a rosebud tonight. You must of been drinkin' some of your aw de cologne."

So I'd say, "No, Jim, but you look like you'd been drinking somethin' of that kind or somethin' worse."

Jim would have to laugh at that, but then he'd speak up and say, "No, I ain't had nothin' to drink, but that ain't sayin' I wouldn't like somethin'. I wouldn't even mind if it was wood alcohol."

Then Hod Meyers would say, "Neither would your wife." That would set everybody to laughin' because Jim and his wife wasn't on very good terms. She'd of divorced him only they wasn't no chance to get alimony and she didn't have no way to take care of herself and the kids. She couldn't never understand Jim. He *was* kind of rough, but a good fella at heart.

Him and Hod had all kinds of sport with Milt Sheppard. I don't suppose you've seen Milt. Well, he's got an Adam's apple that looks more like a mushmelon. So I'd be shavin' Milt and when I'd start to shave down here on his neck, Hod would holler, "Hey, Whitey, wait a minute! Before you cut into it, let's make up a pool and see who can guess closest to the number of seeds."

And Jim would say, "If Milt hadn't of been so hoggish, he'd of ordered a half a canteloupe instead of a whole one and it might not of stuck in his throat."

All the boys would roar at this and Milt himself would force a smile, though the joke was on him. Jim certainly was a card!

There's his shavin' mug, settin' on the shelf, right next to Charley Vail's. "Charles M. Vail." That's the druggist. He comes in regular for his shave, three times a week. And Jim's is the cup next to Charley's. "James H. Kendall." Jim won't need no shavin' mug no more, but I'll leave it there just the same for old time's sake. Jim certainly was a character!

Years ago, Jim used to travel for a canned goods concern over in Carterville. They sold canned goods. Jim had the whole northern half of the State and was on the road five days out of every week. He'd drop in here Saturdays and tell his experiences for that week. It was rich.

I guess he paid more attention to playin' jokes than makin' sales. Finally the concern let him out and he come right home here and told everybody he'd been fired instead of sayin' he'd resigned like most fellas would of.

It was a Saturday and the shop was full and Jim got up out of that chair and says, "Gentlemen, I got an important announcement to make. I been fired from my job."

Well, they asked him if he was in earnest and he said he was and nobody could think of nothin' to say till Jim finally broke the ice himself. He says, "I been sellin' canned goods and now I'm canned goods myself."

You see, the concern he'd been workin' for was a factory that made canned goods. Over in Carterville. And now Jim said he was canned himself. He was certainly a card!

Jim had a great trick that he used to play w'ile he was travelin'. For instance, he'd be ridin' on a train and they'd come to some little town like—well, like—we'll say, like Benton. Jim would look out the train window and read the signs on the stores.

For instance, they'd be a sign, "Henry Smith, Dry Goods." Well, Jim would write down the name and the name of the town and when he got to wherever he was goin' he'd mail back a postal card to Henry Smith at Benton and not sign no name to it, but he'd write on the card, well, somethin' like "Ask your wife about that book agent that spent the afternoon last week," or "Ask your Missus who kept her from gettin' lonesome the last time you was in Carterville." And he'd sign the card, "A Friend."

Of course, he never knew what really come of none of these jokes, but he could picture what *probably* happened and that was enough.

Jim didn't work very steady after he lost his position with the Carterville people. What he did earn, doin' odd jobs round town, why he spent pretty near all of it on gin and his family might of starved if the stores hadn't of carried them along. Jim's wife tried her hand at dressmakin', but they ain't nobody goin' to get rich makin' dresses in this town.

As I say, she'd of divorced Jim, only she seen that she couldn't support herself and the kids and she was always hopin' that some day Jim would cut his habits and give her more than two or three dollars a week.

They was a time when she would go to whoever he was workin' for and ask them to give her his wages, but after she done this once or twice, he beat her to it by borrowin' most of his pay in advance. He told it all round town, how he had outfoxed his Missus. He certainly was a caution!

But he wasn't satisfied with just outwittin' her. He was sore the way she had acted, tryin' to grab off his pay. And he made up his mind he'd get even. Well, he waited till Evans's Circus was advertised to come to town. Then he told his wife and kiddies that he was goin' to take them to the circus. The day of the circus, he told them he would get the tickets and meet them outside the entrance to the tent.

Well, he didn't have no intentions of bein' there or buyin' tickets or nothin'. He got full of gin and laid round Wright's poolroom all day. His wife and the kids waited and waited and of course he didn't show up. His wife didn't have a dime with her, or nowhere else, I guess. So she finally had to tell the kids it was all off and they cried like they wasn't never goin' to stop.

Well, it seems, w'ile they was cryin', Doc Stair came along and he asked what was the matter, but Mrs. Kendall was stubborn and wouldn't tell him, but the kids told him and he insisted on takin' them and their mother in the show. Jim found this out afterwards and it was one reason why he had it in for Doc Stair.

Doc Stair come here about a year and a half ago. He's a mighty handsome young fella and his clothes always look like he has them made to order. He goes to Detroit two or three times a year and w'ile he's there he must have a tailor take his measure and then make him a suit to order. They cost pretty near twice as much, but they fit a whole lot better than if you just bought them in a store.

For a w'ile everybody was wonderin' why a young doctor like Doc Stair should come to a town like this where we already got old Doc Gamble and Doc Foote that's both been here for years and all the practice in town was always divided between the two of them.

Then they was a story got round that Doc Stair's gal had throwed him over, a gal up in the Northern Peninsula somewheres, and the reason he come here was to hide himself away and forget it. He said himself that he thought they wasn't nothin' like general practice in a place like ours to fit a man to be a good all round doctor. And that's why he'd came.

Anyways, it wasn't long before he was makin' enough to live on, though they tell me that he never dunned nobody for what they owed him, and the folks here certainly has got the owin' habit, even in my business. If I had all that was comin' to me for just shaves alone, I could go to Carterville and put up at the Mercer for a week and see a different picture every night. For instance, they's old George Purdy—but I guess I should't ought to be gossipin'.

Well, last year, our coroner died, died of the flu. Ken Beatty, that was his name. He was the coroner. So they had to choose another man to be coroner in his place and they picked Doc Stair. He laughed at first and said he didn't want it, but they made him take it. It ain't no job anybody would fight for and what a man makes out of it in a year would just about buy seeds for their garden. Doc's the kind, though, that can't say no to nothin' if you keep at him long enough.

But I was goin' to tell you about a poor boy we got here in town—Paul Dickson. He fell out of a tree when he was about ten years old. Lit on his head and it done somethin' to him and he ain't never been right. No harm in him, but just silly. Jim Kendall used to call him cuckoo; that's a name Jim had for anybody that was off their head, only he called people's head their bean. That was another of his gags, callin' head bean and callin' crazy people cuckoo. Only poor Paul ain't crazy, but just silly.

You can imagine that Jim used to have all kinds of fun with Paul. He'd send him to the White Front Garage for a left-handed monkey wrench. Of course they ain't no such a thing as a left-handed monkey wrench.

And once we had a kind of a fair here and they was a baseball game between the fats and the leans and before the game started Jim called Paul over and sent him way down to Schrader's hardware store to get a key for the pitcher's box.

They wasn't nothin' in the way of gags that Jim couldn't think up, when he put his mind to it.

Poor Paul was always kind of suspicious of people, maybe on account of how Jim had kept foolin' him. Paul wouldn't have much to do with anybody only his own mother and Doc Stair and a girl here in town named Julie Gregg. That is, she ain't a girl no more, but pretty near thirty or over.

When Doc first come to town, Paul seemed to feel like here was a real friend and he hung round Doc's office most of the w'ile; the only time he wasn't there was when he'd go home to eat or sleep or when he seen Julie Gregg doin' her shoppin'.

When he looked out Doc's window and seen her, he'd run downstairs and join her and tag along with her to the different stores. The poor boy was crazy about Julie and she always treated him mighty nice and made him feel like he was welcome, though of course it wasn't nothin' but pity on her side.

Doc done all he could to improve Paul's mind and he told me once that he really thought the boy was gettin' better, that they was times when he was as bright and sensible as anybody else.

But I was goin' to tell you about Julie Gregg. Old Man Gregg was in the lumber business, but got to drinkin' and lost most of his money and when he died, he didn't leave nothin' but the house and just enough insurance for the girl to skimp along on.

Her mother was a kind of half invalid and didn't hardly ever leave the house. Julie wanted to sell the place and move somewheres else after the old man died, but the mother said she was born here and would die here. It was tough on Julie, as the young people round this town—well, she's too good for them.

She's been away to school and Chicago and New York and different places and they ain't no subject she can't talk on, where you take the rest of the young folks here and you mention anything to them outside of Gloria Swanson or Tommy Meighan and they think you're delirious. Did you see Gloria in *Wages of Virtue*? You missed somethin'!

Well, Doc Stair hadn't been here more than a week when he come in one day to get shaved and I recognized who he was as he had been pointed out to me, so I told him about my old lady. She's been ailin' for a couple years and either Doc Gamble or Doc Foote, neither one, seemed to be helpin' her. So he said he would come out and see her, but if she was able to get out herself, it would be better to bring her to his office where he could make a completer examination.

So I took her to his office and w'ile I was waiting for her in the reception room, in come Julie Gregg. When somebody comes in Doc Stair's office, they's a bell that rings in his inside office so he can tell they's somebody to see him.

So he left my old lady inside and come out to the front office and that's the first time him and Julie met and I guess it was what they call love at first sight. But it wasn't fifty-fifty. This young fella was the slickest lookin' fella she'd ever seen in this town and she went wild over him. To him she was just a young lady that wanted to see the doctor.

She'd came on about the same business I had. Her mother had been doctorin' for years with Doc Gamble and Doc Foote and without no results. So she'd heard they was a new doc in town and decided to give him a try. He promised to call and see her mother that same day.

I said a minute ago that it was love at first sight on her part. I'm not only judgin' by how she acted afterwards but how she looked at him that first day in his office. I ain't no mind reader, but it was wrote all over her face that she was gone.

Now Jim Kendall, besides bein' a jokesmith and a pretty good drinker, well, Jim was quite a lady-killer. I guess he run pretty wild durin' the time he was on the road for them Carterville people, and besides that, he'd had a couple little affairs of the heart right here in town. As I say, his wife could of divorced him, only she couldn't.

But Jim was like the majority of men, and women, too, I guess. He wanted what he couldn't get. He wanted Julie Gregg and worked his head off tryin' to land her. Only he'd of said bean instead of head.

Well, Jim's habits and his jokes didn't appeal to Julie and of course he was a married man, so he didn't have no more chance than, well, than a rabbit. That's an expression of Jim's himself. When somebody didn't have no chance to get elected or somethin', Jim would always say they didn't have no more chance than a rabbit.

He didn't make no bones about how he felt. Right in here, more than once, in front of the whole crowd, he said he was stuck on Julie and anybody that could get her for him was welcome to his house and his wife and kids included. But she wouldn't have nothin' to do with him; wouldn't even speak to him on the street. He finally seen he wasn't gettin' nowheres with his usual line so he decided to try the rough stuff. He went right up to her house one evenin' and when she opened the door he forced his way in and grabbed her. But she broke loose and before he could stop her, she run in the next room and locked the door and phoned to Joe

Barnes. Joe's the marshal. Jim could hear who she was phonin' to and he beat it before Joe got there.

Joe was an old friend of Julie's pa. Joe went to Jim the next day and told him what would happen if he ever done it again.

I don't know how the news of this little affair leaked out. Chances is that Joe Barnes told his wife and she told somebody else's wife and they told their husband. Anyways, it did leak out and Hod Meyers had the nerve to kid Jim about it, right here in this shop. Jim didn't deny nothin' and kind of laughed it off and said for us all to wait; that lots of people had tried to make a monkey out of him, but he always got even.

Meanw'ile everybody in town was wise to Julie's bein' wild mad over the Doc. I don't suppose she had any idear how her face changed when him and her was together; of course she couldn't of, or she'd of kept away from him. And she didn't know that we was all noticin' how many times she made excuses to go up to his office or pass it on the other side of the street and look up in his window to see if he was there. I felt sorry for her and so did most other people.

Hod Meyers kept rubbin' it into Jim about how the Doc had cut him out. Jim didn't pay no attention to the kiddin' and you could see he was plannin' one of his jokes.

One trick Jim had was the knack of changin' his voice. He could make you think he was a girl talkin' and he could mimic any man's voice. To show you how good he was along this line, I'll tell you the joke he played on me once.

You know, in most towns of any size, when a man is dead and needs a shave, why the barber that shaves him soaks him five dollars for the job; that is, he don't soak *him,* but whoever ordered the shave. I just charge three dollars because personally I don't mind much shavin' a dead person. They lay a whole lot stiller than live customers. The only thing is that you don't feel like talkin' to them and you get kind of lonesome.

Well, about the coldest day we ever had here, two years ago last winter, the phone rung at the house w'ile I was home to dinner and I answered the phone and it was a woman's voice and she said she was Mrs. John Scott and her husband was dead and would I come out and shave him.

Old John had always been a good customer of mine. But they

live seven miles out in the country, on the Streeter road. Still I didn't see how I could say no.

So I said I would be there, but would have to come in a jitney and it might cost three or four dollars besides the price of the shave. So she, or the voice, said that was all right, so I got Frank Abbott to drive me out to the place and when I got there, who should open the door but old John himself! He wasn't no more dead than, well, than a rabbit.

It didn't take no private detective to figure out who had played me this little joke. Nobody could of thought it up but Jim Kendall. He certainly was a card!

I tell you this incident just to show you how he could disguise his voice and make you believe it was somebody else talkin'. I'd of swore it was Mrs. Scott had called me. Anyways, some woman.

Well, Jim waited till he had Doc Stair's voice down pat; then he went after revenge.

He called Julie up on a night when he knew Doc was over in Carterville. She never questioned but what it was Doc's voice. Jim said he must see her that night; he couldn't wait no longer to tell her somethin'. She was all excited and told him to come to the house. But he said he was expectin' an important long distance call and wouldn't she please forget her manners for once and come to his office. He said they couldn't nothin' hurt her and nobody would see her and he just *must* talk to her a little w'ile. Well, poor Julie fell for it.

Doc always keeps a night light in his office, so it looked to Julie like they was somebody there.

Meanw'ile Jim Kendall had went to Wright's poolroom, where they was a whole gang amusin' themselves. The most of them had drank plenty of gin, and they was a rough bunch even when sober. They was always strong for Jim's jokes and when he told them to come with him and see some fun they give up their card games and pool games and followed along.

Doc's office is on the second floor. Right outside his door they's a flight of stairs leadin' to the floor above. Jim and his gang hid in the dark behind these stairs.

Well, Julie come up to Doc's door and rung the bell and they was nothin' doin'. She rung it again and she rung it seven or eight times. Then she tried the door and found it locked. Then Jim made some kind of a noise and she heard it and waited a minute, and then she says, "Is that you, Ralph?" Ralph is Doc's first name.

They was no answer and it must of came to her all of a sudden that she'd been bunked. She pretty near fell downstairs and the whole gang after her. They chased her all the way home, hollerin', "Is that you, Ralph?" and "Oh, Ralphie, dear, is that you?" Jim says he couldn't holler it himself, as he was laughin' too hard.

Poor Julie! She didn't show up here on Main Street for a long, long time afterward.

And of course Jim and his gang told everybody in town, everybody but Doc Stair. They was scared to tell him, and he might of never knowed only for Paul Dickson. The poor cuckoo, as Jim called him, he was here in the shop one night when Jim was still gloatin' yet over what he'd done to Julie. And Paul took in as much of it as he could understand and he run to Doc with the story.

It's a cinch Doc went up in the air and swore he'd make Jim suffer. But it was a kind of a delicate thing, because if it got out that he had beat Jim up, Julie was bound to hear of it and then she'd know that Doc knew and of course knowin' that he knew would make it worse for her than ever. He was goin' to do somethin', but it took a lot of figurin'.

Well, it was a couple days later when Jim was here in the shop again, and so was the cuckoo. Jim was goin' duck-shootin' the next day and had come in lookin' for Hod Meyers to go with him. I happened to know that Hod went over to Carterville and wouldn't be home till the end of the week. So Jim said he hated to go alone and he guessed he would call it off. Then poor Paul spoke up and said if Jim would take him he would go along. Jim thought a w'ile and then he said, well, he guessed a half-wit was better than nothin'.

I suppose he was plottin' to get Paul out in the boat and play some joke on him, like pushin' him in the water. Anyways, he said Paul could go. He asked him had he ever shot a duck and Paul said no, he'd never even had a gun in his hands. So Jim said he could set in the boat and watch him if he behaved himself, he might lend him his gun for a couple of shots. They made a date to meet in the mornin' and that's the last I seen of Jim alive.

Next mornin', I hadn't been open more than ten minutes when Doc Stair come in. He looked kind of nervous. He asked me had I seen Paul Dickson. I said no, but I knew where he was, out duck-shootin' with Jim Kendall. So Doc says that's what he had heard, and he couldn't understand it because Paul had told him he wouldn't never have no more to do with Jim as long as he lived.

He said Paul had told him about the joke Jim had played on Julie. He said Paul had asked him what he thought of the joke and the Doc had told him anybody that would do a thing like that ought not to be let live.

I said it had been a kind of a raw thing, but Jim just couldn't resist no kind of a joke, no matter how raw. I said I thought he was all right at heart, but just bubblin' over with mischief. Doc turned and walked out.

At noon he got a phone call from old John Scott. The lake where Jim and Paul had went shootin' is on John's place. Paul had came runnin' up to the house a few minutes before and said they'd been an accident. Jim had shot a few ducks and then give the gun to Paul and told him to try his luck. Paul hadn't never handled a gun and he was nervous. He was shakin' so hard that he couldn't control the gun. He let fire and Jim sunk back in the boat, dead.

Doc Stair, bein' the coroner, jumped in Frank Abbott's flivver and rushed out to Scott's farm. Paul and old John was down on the shore of the lake. Paul had rowed the boat to shore, but they'd left the body in it, waitin' for Doc to come.

Doc examined the body and said they might as well fetch it back to town. They was no use leavin' it there or callin' a jury, as it was a plain case of accidental shootin'.

Personally I wouldn't never leave a person shoot a gun in the same boat I was in unless I was sure they knew somethin' about guns. Jim was a sucker to leave a new beginner have his gun, let alone a half-wit. It probably served Jim right, what he got. But still we miss him round here. He certainly was a card!

Comb it wet or dry?

1925

The Rocking-Horse Winner

D. H. LAWRENCE

[1885–1930]

There was a woman who was beautiful, who started with all the advantages, yet she had no luck. She married for love, and the love turned to dust. She had bonny children, yet she felt they had been thrust upon her, and she could not love them. They looked at her coldly, as if they were finding fault with her. And hurriedly she felt she must cover up some fault in herself. Yet what it was that she must cover up she never knew. Nevertheless, when her children were present, she always felt the centre of her heart go hard. This troubled her, and in her manner she was all the more gentle and anxious for her children, as if she loved them very much. Only she herself knew that at the centre of her heart was a hard little place that could not feel love, no, not for anybody. Everybody else said of her: "She is such a good mother. She adores her children." Only she herself, and her children themselves, knew it was not so. They read it in each other's eyes.

There were a boy and two little girls. They lived in a pleasant house, with a garden, and they had discreet servants, and felt themselves superior to anyone in the neighbourhood.

Although they lived in style, they felt always an anxiety in the house. There was never enough money. The mother had a small income, and the father had a small income, but not nearly enough for the social position which they had to keep up. The father went into town to some office. But though he had good prospects, these prospects never materialized. There was always the grinding sense of the shortage of money, though the style was always kept up.

At last the mother said: "I will see if I can't make something." But she did not know where to begin. She racked her brains, and tried this thing and the other, but could not find anything successful. The failure made deep lines come into her face. Her children were growing up, they would have to go to school. There must be more money, there must be more money. The father, who was always very handsome and expensive in his tastes, seemed as if he never would be able to do anything worth doing. And the mother, who had a great belief in herself, did not succeed any better, and her tastes were just as expensive.

And so the house came to be haunted by the unspoken phrase: There must be more money! There must be more money! The children could hear it all the time, though nobody said it aloud. They heard it at Christmas, when the expensive and splendid toys filled the nursery. Behind the shining modern rocking horse, behind the smart doll's-house, a voice would start whispering: "There must be more money! There must be more money!" And the children would stop playing, to listen for a moment. They would look into each other's eyes, to see if they had all heard. And each one saw in the eyes of the other two that they too had heard. "There must be more money! There must be more money!"

It came whispering from the springs of the still-swaying rocking horse, and even the horse, bending his wooden, champing head, heard it. The big doll, sitting so pink and smirking in her new pram, could hear it quite plainly, and seemed to be smirking all the more self-consciously because of it. The foolish puppy, too, that took the place of the Teddy bear, he was looking so extraordinarily foolish for no other reason but that he heard the secret whisper all over the house: "There must be more money!"

Yet nobody ever said it aloud. The whisper was everywhere, and therefore no one spoke it. Just as no one ever says: "We are breathing!" in spite of the fact that breath is coming and going all the time.

"Mother," said the boy Paul one day, "why don't we keep a car of our own? Why do we always use uncle's, or else a taxi?"

"Because we're the poor members of the family," said the mother.

"But why are we, mother?"

"Well—I suppose," she said slowly and bitterly, "it's because your father has no luck."

The boy was silent for some time.

"Is luck money, mother?" he asked, rather timidly.

"No, Paul. Not quite. It's what causes you to have money."

"Oh!" said Paul vaguely. "I thought when Uncle Oscar said filthy lucker, it meant money."

"Filthy lucre does mean money," said the mother. "But it's lucre, not luck."

"Oh!" said the boy. "Then what is luck, mother?"

"It's what causes you to have money. If you're lucky you have money. That's why it's better to be born lucky than rich. If you're rich, you may lose your money. But if you're lucky, you will always get more money."

"Oh! Will you? And is father not lucky?"

"Very unlucky, I should say," she said bitterly.

The boy watched her with unsure eyes.

"Why?" he asked.

"I don't know. Nobody ever knows why one person is lucky and another unlucky."

"Don't they? Nobody at all? Does nobody know?"

"Perhaps God. But He never tells."

"He ought to, then. And aren't you lucky either, mother?"

"I can't be, if I married an unlucky husband."

"But by yourself, aren't you?"

"I used to think I was, before I married. Now I think I am very unlucky indeed."

"Why?"

"Well—never mind! Perhaps I'm not really," she said.

The child looked at her, to see if she meant it. But he saw, by the lines of her mouth, that she was only trying to hide something from him.

"Well, anyhow," he said stoutly, "I'm a lucky person."

"Why?" said his mother, with a sudden laugh.

He stared at her. He didn't even know why he had said it.

"God told me," he asserted, brazening it out.

"I hope He did, dear!" she said, again with a laugh, but rather bitter.

"He did, mother!"

"Excellent!" said the mother, using one of her husband's exclamations.

The boy saw she did not believe him; or, rather, that she paid no attention to his assertion. This angered him somewhat, and made him want to compel her attention.

He went off by himself, vaguely, in a childish way, seeking for the clue to "luck." Absorbed, taking no heed of other people, he went about with a sort of stealth, seeking inwardly for luck. He wanted luck, he wanted it, he wanted it. When the two girls were playing dolls in the nursery, he would sit on his big rocking horse, charging madly into space, with a frenzy that made the little girls peer at him uneasily. Wildly the horse careered, the waving dark hair of the boy tossed, his eyes had a strange glare in them. The little girls dared not speak to him.

When he had ridden to the end of his mad little journey, he climbed down and stood in front of his rocking horse, staring fixedly into its lowered face. Its red mouth was slightly open, its big eye was wide and glassy-bright.

"Now!" he would silently command the snorting steed. "Now, take me to where there is luck! Now take me!"

And he would slash the horse on the neck with the little whip he had asked Uncle Oscar for. He knew the horse could take him to where there was luck, if only he forced it. So he would mount again, and start on his furious ride, hoping at last to get there. He knew he could get there.

"You'll break your horse, Paul!" said the nurse.

"He's always riding like that! I wish he'd leave off!" said his elder sister Joan.

But he only glared down on them in silence. Nurse gave him up. She could make nothing of him. Anyhow he was growing beyond her.

One day his mother and his Uncle Oscar came in when he was on one of his furious rides. He did not speak to them.

"Hallo, you young jockey! Riding a winner?" said his uncle.

"Aren't you growing too big for a rocking horse? You're not a very little boy any longer, you know," said his mother.

But Paul only gave a blue glare from his big, rather close-set eyes. He would speak to nobody when he was in full tilt. His mother watched him with an anxious expression on her face.

At last he suddenly stopped forcing his horse into the mechanical gallop, and slid down.

"Well, I got there!" he announced fiercely, his blue eyes still flaring, and his sturdy long legs straddling apart.

"Where did you get to?" asked his mother.

"Where I wanted to go," he flared back at her.

"That's right, son!" said Uncle Oscar. "Don't you stop till you get there. What's the horse's name?"

"He doesn't have a name," said the boy.

"Gets on without all right?" asked the uncle.

"Well, he has different names. He was called Sansovino last week."

"Sansovino, eh? Won the Ascot. How did you know his name?"

"He always talks about horse races with Bassett," said Joan.

The uncle was delighted to find that his small nephew was posted with all the racing news. Bassett, the young gardener, who had been wounded in the left foot in the war and had got his present job through Oscar Cresswell, whose batman he had been, was a perfect blade of the "turf." He lived in the racing events, and the small boy lived with him.

Oscar Cresswell got it all from Bassett.

"Master Paul comes and asks me, so I can't do more than tell him, sir," said Bassett, his face terribly serious, as if he were speaking of religious matters.

"And does he ever put anything on a horse he fancies?"

"Well—I don't want to give him away—he's a young sport, a fine sport, sir. Would you mind asking him yourself? He sort of takes a pleasure in it, and perhaps he'd feel I was giving him away, sir, if you don't mind."

Bassett was serious as a church.

The uncle went back to his nephew, and took him off for a ride in the car.

"Say, Paul, old man, do you ever put anything on a horse?" the uncle asked.

The boy watched the handsome man closely.

"Why, do you think I oughtn't to?" he parried.

"Not a bit of it! I thought perhaps you might give me a tip for the Lincoln."

The car sped on into the country, going down to Uncle Oscar's place in Hampshire.

"Honour bright?" said the nephew.

"Honour bright, son!" said the uncle.

"Well, then, Daffodil."

"Daffodil! I doubt it, sonny. What about Mirza?"

"I only know the winner," said the boy. "That's Daffodil."

"Daffodil, eh?"

There was a pause. Daffodil was an obscure horse comparatively.

"Uncle!"

"Yes, son?"

"You won't let it go any further, will you? I promised Bassett."

"Bassett be damned, old man! What's he got to do with it?"

"We're partners. We've been partners from the first. Uncle, he lent me my first five shillings, which I lost. I promised him, honour bright, it was only between me and him; only you gave me that ten-shilling note I started winning with, so I thought you were lucky. You won't let it go any further, will you?"

The boy gazed at his uncle from those big, hot, blue eyes, set rather close together. The uncle stirred and laughed uneasily.

"Right you are, son! I'll keep your tip private. Daffodil, eh? How much are you putting on him?"

"All except twenty pounds," said the boy. "I keep that in reserve."

The uncle thought it a good joke.

"You keep twenty pounds in reserve, do you, you young romancer? What are you betting, then?"

"I'm betting three hundred," said the boy gravely. "But it's between you and me, Uncle Oscar! Honour bright?"

The uncle burst into a roar of laughter.

"It's between you and me all right, you young Nat Gould," he said, laughing. "But where's your three hundred?"

"Bassett keeps it for me. We're partners."

"You are, are you! And what is Bassett putting on Daffodil?"

"He won't go quite as high as I do, I expect. Perhaps he'll go a hundred and fifty."

"What, pennies?" laughed the uncle.

"Pounds," said the child, with a surprised look at his uncle. "Bassett keeps a bigger reserve than I do."

Between wonder and amusement Uncle Oscar was silent. He pursued the matter no further, but he determined to take his nephew with him to the Lincoln races.

"Now, son," he said, "I'm putting twenty on Mirza, and I'll put five for you on any horse you fancy. What's your pick?"

"Daffodil, uncle."

"No, not the fiver on Daffodil!"

"I should if it was my own fiver," said the child.

"Good! Good! Right you are! A fiver for me and a fiver for you on Daffodil."

The child had never been to a race meeting before, and his eyes were blue fire. He pursed his mouth tight, and watched. A Frenchman just in front had put his money on Lancelot. Wild with excitement, he flayed his arms up and down, yelling "Lancelot! Lancelot!" in his French accent.

Daffodil came in first, Lancelot second, Mirza third. The child, flushed and with eyes blazing, was curiously serene. His uncle brought him four five-pound notes, four to one.

"What am I to do with these?" he cried, waving them before the boy's eyes.

"I suppose we'll talk to Bassett," said the boy. "I expect I have fifteen hundred now; and twenty in reserve; and this twenty."

His uncle studied him for some moments.

"Look here, son!" he said. "You're not serious about Bassett and that fifteen hundred, are you?"

"Yes, I am. But it's between you and me, uncle. Honour bright!"

"Honour bright all right, son! But I must talk to Bassett."

"If you'd like to be a partner, uncle, with Bassett and me, we could all be partners. Only, you'd have to promise, honour bright, uncle, not to let it go beyond us three. Bassett and I are lucky, and you must be lucky, because it was your ten shillings I started winning with . . ."

Uncle Oscar took both Bassett and Paul into Richmond Park for an afternoon, and there they talked.

"It's like this, you see, sir," Bassett said. "Master Paul would get me talking about racing events, spinning yarns, you know, sir. And he was always keen on knowing if I'd made or if I'd lost. It's about a year since, now, that I put five shillings on Blush of Dawn for him—and we lost. Then the luck turned, with that ten shillings he had from you, that we put on Singhalese. And since that time, it's been pretty steady, all things considering. What do you say, Master Paul?"

"We're all right when we're sure," said Paul. "It's when we're not quite sure that we go down."

"Oh, but we're careful then," said Bassett.

"But when are you sure?" smiled Uncle Oscar.

"It's Master Paul, sir," said Bassett, in a secret, religious voice. "It's as if he had it from heaven. Like Daffodil, now, for the Lincoln. That was as sure as eggs."

"Did you put anything on Daffodil?" asked Oscar Cresswell.

"Yes, sir, I made my bit."

"And my nephew?"

Bassett was obstinately silent, looking at Paul.

"I made twelve hundred, didn't I, Bassett? I told uncle I was putting three hundred on Daffodil."

"That's right," said Bassett, nodding.

"But where's the money?" asked the uncle.

"I keep it safe locked up, sir. Master Paul he can have it any minute he likes to ask for it."

"What, fifteen hundred pounds?"

"And twenty! and forty, that is, with the twenty he made on the course."

"It's amazing!" said the uncle.

"If Master Paul offers you to be partners, sir, I would, if I were you; if you'll excuse me," said Bassett.

Oscar Cresswell thought about it.

"I'll see the money," he said.

They drove home again, and sure enough, Bassett came round to the garden-house with fifteen hundred pounds in notes. The twenty pounds reserve was left with Joe Glee, in the Turf Commission deposit.

"You see, it's all right, uncle, when I'm sure! Then we go strong, for all we're worth. Don't we, Bassett?"

"We do that, Master Paul."

"And when are you sure?" said the uncle, laughing.

"Oh, well, sometimes I'm absolutely sure, like about Daffodil," said the boy; "and sometimes I have an idea; and sometimes I haven't even an idea, have I, Bassett? Then we're careful, because we mostly go down."

"You do, do you! And when you're sure, like about Daffodil, what makes you sure, sonny?"

"Oh, well, I don't know," said the boy uneasily. "I'm sure, you know, uncle; that's all."

"It's as if he had it from heaven, sir," Bassett reiterated.

"I should say so!" said the uncle.

But he became a partner. And when the Leger was coming on, Paul was "sure" about Lively Spark, which was a quite inconsiderable horse. The boy insisted on putting a thousand on the horse, Bassett went for five hundred, and Oscar Cresswell two hundred. Lively Spark came in first, and the betting had been ten to one against him. Paul had made ten thousand.

"You see," he said, "I was absolutely sure of him."

Even Oscar Cresswell had cleared two thousand.

"Look here, son," he said, "this sort of thing makes me nervous."

"It needn't, uncle! Perhaps I shan't be sure again for a long time."

"But what are you going to do with your money?" asked the uncle.

"Of course," said the boy, "I started it for mother. She said she had no luck, because father is unlucky, so I thought if I was lucky, it might stop whispering."

"What might stop whispering?"

"Our house. I hate our house for whispering."

"What does it whisper?"

"Why—why"—the boy fidgeted—"why, I don't know. But it's always short of money, you know, uncle."

"I know it, son, I know it."

"You know people send mother writs, don't you, uncle?"

"I'm afraid I do," said the uncle.

"And then the house whispers, like people laughing at you behind your back. It's awful, that is! I thought if I was lucky . . ."

"You might stop it," added the uncle.

The boy watched him with big blue eyes that had an uncanny cold fire in them, and he said never a word.

"Well, then!" said the uncle. "What are we doing?"

"I shouldn't like mother to know I was lucky," said the boy.

"Why not, son?"

"She'd stop me."

"I don't think she would."

"Oh!"—and the boy writhed in an odd way—"I don't want her to know, uncle."

"All right, son! We'll manage it without her knowing."

They managed it very easily. Paul, at the other's suggestion, handed over five thousand pounds to his uncle, who deposited it with the family lawyer, who was then to inform Paul's mother that a relative had put five thousand pounds into his hands, which sum was to be paid out a thousand pounds at a time, on the mother's birthday, for the next five years.

"So she'll have a birthday present of a thousand pounds for five successive years," said Uncle Oscar. "I hope it won't make it all the harder for her later."

Paul's mother had her birthday in November. The house had been "whispering" worse than ever lately, and, even in spite of his luck, Paul could not bear up against it. He was very anxious to see the effect of the birthday letter, telling his mother about the thousand pounds.

When there were no visitors, Paul now took his meals with his parents, as he was beyond the nursery control. His mother went into town nearly every day. She had discovered that she had an odd knack of sketching furs and dress materials, so she worked secretly in the studio of a friend who was the chief "artist" for the leading drapers. She drew the figures of ladies in furs and ladies in silk and sequins for the newspaper advertisements. This young woman artist earned several thousand pounds a year, but Paul's mother only made several hundreds, and she was again dissatisfied. She so wanted to be first in something, and she did not succeed, even in making sketches for drapery advertisements.

She was down to breakfast on the morning of her birthday. Paul watched her face as she read her letters. He knew the lawyer's letter. As his mother read it, her face hardened and became more expressionless. Then a cold, determined look came on her mouth. She hid the letter under the pile of others, and said not a word about it.

"Didn't you have anything nice in the post for your birthday, mother?" said Paul.

"Quite moderately nice," she said, her voice cold and absent.

She went away to town without saying more.

But in the afternoon Uncle Oscar appeared. He said Paul's mother had had a long interview with the lawyer, asking if the whole five thousand could be advanced at once, as she was in debt.

"What do you think, uncle?" said the boy.

"I leave it to you, son."

"Oh, let her have it, then! We can get some more with the other," said the boy.

"A bird in the hand is worth two in the bush, laddie!" said Uncle Oscar.

"But I'm sure to know for the Grand National; or the Lincolnshire; or else the Derby. I'm sure to know for one of them," said Paul.

So Uncle Oscar signed the agreement, and Paul's mother touched the whole five thousand. Then something very curious happened. The voices in the house suddenly went mad, like a chorus of frogs on a spring evening. There were certain new furnishings, and Paul had a tutor. He was really going to Eton, his father's school, in the following autumn. There were flowers in the winter, and a blossoming of the luxury Paul's mother had been used to. And yet the voices in the house, behind the sprays of mimosa and almond blossom, and from under the piles of iridescent cushions, simply trilled and screamed in a sort of ecstasy: "There must be more money! Oh-h-h, there must be more money. Oh, now, now-w! Now-w-w—there must be more money—more than ever! More than ever!"

It frightened Paul terribly. He studied away at his Latin and Greek with his tutors. But his intense hours were spent with Bassett. The Grand National had gone by: he had not "known," and had lost a hundred pounds. Summer was at hand. He was in agony for the Lincoln. But even for the Lincoln he didn't "know" and he lost fifty pounds. He became wild-eyed and strange, as if something were going to explode in him.

"Let it alone, son! Don't you bother about it!" urged Uncle Oscar. But it was as if the boy couldn't really hear what his uncle was saying.

"I've got to know for the Derby! I've got to know for the Derby!" the child reiterated, his big blue eyes blazing with a sort of madness.

His mother noticed how overwrought he was.

"You'd better go to the seaside. Wouldn't you like to go now to the seaside, instead of waiting? I think you'd better," she said, looking down at him anxiously, her heart curiously heavy because of him.

But the child lifted his uncanny blue eyes.

"I couldn't possibly go before the Derby, mother!" he said. "I couldn't possibly!"

"Why not?" she said, her voice becoming heavy when she was opposed. "Why not? You can still go from the seaside to see the Derby with your Uncle Oscar, if that's what you wish. No need for you to wait here. Besides, I think you care too much about these races. It's a bad sign. My family has been a gambling family, and you won't know till you grow up how much damage it has done. But it has done damage. I shall have to send Bassett away, and ask Uncle Oscar not to talk racing to you, unless you promise to be reasonable about it; go away to the seaside and forget it. You're all nerves!"

"I'll do what you like, mother, so long as you don't send me away till after the Derby," the boy said.

"Send you away from where? Just from this house?"

"Yes," he said, gazing at her.

"Why, you curious child, what makes you care about this house so much, suddenly? I never knew you loved it."

He gazed at her without speaking. He had a secret within a secret, something he had not divulged, even to Bassett or to his Uncle Oscar.

But his mother, after standing undecided and a little bit sullen for some moments, said:

"Very well, then! Don't go to the seaside till after the Derby, if you don't wish it. But promise me you won't let your nerves go to pieces. Promise you won't think so much about horse racing and events, as you call them!"

"Oh, no," said the boy casually. "I won't think much about them, mother. You needn't worry. I wouldn't worry, mother, if I were you."

"If you were me and I were you," said his mother, "I wonder what we should do!"

"But you know you needn't worry, mother, don't you?" the boy repeated.

"I should be awfully glad to know it," she said wearily.

"Oh, well, you can, you know. I mean, you ought to know you needn't worry," he insisted.

"Ought I? Then I'll see about it," she said.

Paul's secret of secrets was his wooden horse, that which had no name. Since he was emancipated from a nurse and a nursery-governess, he had had his rocking horse removed to his own bedroom at the top of the house.

"Surely, you're too big for a rocking horse!" his mother had remonstrated.

"Well, you see, mother, till I can have a real horse, I like to have some sort of animal about," had been his quaint answer.

"Do you feel he keeps you company?" she laughed.

"Oh, yes! He's very good, he always keeps me company, when I'm there," said Paul.

So the horse, rather shabby, stood in an arrested prance in the boy's bedroom.

The Derby was drawing near, and the boy grew more and more tense. He hardly heard what was spoken to him, he was very frail, and his eyes were really uncanny. His mother had sudden seizures of uneasiness about him. Sometimes, for half-an-hour, she would feel a sudden anxiety about him that was almost anguish. She wanted to rush to him at once, and know he was safe.

Two nights before the Derby, she was at a big party in town, when one of her rushes of anxiety about her boy, her first-born, gripped her heart till she could hardly speak. She fought with the feeling, might and main, for she believed in common sense. But it was too strong. She had to leave the dance and go downstairs to telephone to the country. The children's nursery-governess was terribly surprised and startled at being rung up in the night.

"Are the children all right, Miss Wilmot?"

"Oh, yes, they are quite all right."

"Master Paul? Is he all right?"

"He went to bed as right as a trivet. Shall I run up and look at him?"

"No," said Paul's mother reluctantly. "No! Don't trouble. It's all right. Don't sit up. We shall be home fairly soon." She did not want her son's privacy intruded upon.

"Very good," said the governess.

It was about one o'clock when Paul's mother and father drove up to their house. All was still. Paul's mother went to her room and slipped off her white fur coat. She had told her maid not to wait up for her. She heard her husband downstairs, mixing a whisky-and-soda.

And then, because of the strange anxiety at her heart, she stole upstairs to her son's room. Noiselessly she went along the upper corridor. Was there a faint noise? What was it?

She stood, with arrested muscles, outside his door, listening. There was a strange, heavy, and yet not loud noise. Her heart stood still. It was a soundless noise, yet rushing and powerful. Something huge, in violent, hushed motion. What was it? What in God's name was it? She ought to know. She felt that she knew the noise. She knew what it was.

Yet she could not place it. She couldn't say what it was. And on and on it went, like a madness.

Softly, frozen with anxiety and fear, she turned the door handle.

The room was dark. Yet in the space near the window, she heard and saw something plunging to and fro. She gazed in fear and amazement.

Then suddenly she switched on the light, and saw her son, in his green pyjamas, madly surging on the rocking horse. The blaze of light suddenly lit him up, as he urged the wooden horse, and lit her up, as she stood, blonde, in her dress of pale green and crystal, in the doorway.

"Paul!" she cried. "Whatever are you doing?"

"It's Malabar!" he screamed, in a powerful, strange voice. "It's Malabar."

His eyes blazed at her for one strange and senseless second, as he ceased urging his wooden horse. Then he fell with a crash to the ground, and she, all her tormented motherhood flooding upon her, rushed to gather him up.

But he was unconscious, and unconscious he remained, with some brain-fever. He talked and tossed, and his mother sat stonily by his side.

"Malabar! It's Malabar! Bassett, Bassett, I know it! It's Malabar!"

So the child cried, trying to get up and urge the rocking horse that gave him his inspiration.

"What does he mean by Malabar?" asked the heart-frozen mother.

"I don't know," said the father stonily.

"What does he mean by Malabar?" she asked her brother Oscar.

"It's one of the horses running for the Derby," was the answer.

And, in spite of himself, Oscar Cresswell spoke to Bassett, and himself put a thousand on Malabar: at fourteen to one.

The third day of the illness was critical: they were waiting for a change. The boy, with his rather long, curly hair, was tossing ceaselessly on the pillow. He neither slept nor regained consciousness, and his eyes were like blue stones. His mother sat, feeling her heart had gone, turned actually into a stone.

In the evening, Oscar Cresswell did not come, but Bassett sent a message, saying could he come up for one moment, just one moment? Paul's mother was very angry at the intrusion, but on second thought she agreed. The boy was the same. Perhaps Bassett might bring him to consciousness.

The gardener, a shortish fellow with a little brown moustache, and sharp little brown eyes, tiptoed into the room, touched his imaginary cap to Paul's mother, and stole to the bedside, staring with glittering, smallish eyes, at the tossing, dying child.

"Master Paul!" he whispered. "Master Paul! Malabar come in first all right, a clean win. I did as you told me. You've made over seventy thousand pounds, you have; you've got over eighty thousand. Malabar came in all right, Master Paul."

"Malabar! Malabar! Did I say Malabar, mother? Did I say Malabar? Do you think I'm lucky, mother? I knew Malabar, didn't I? Over eighty thousand pounds! I call that lucky, don't you, mother? Over eighty thousand pounds! I knew, didn't I know I knew? Malabar came in all right. If I ride my horse till I'm sure, then I tell you, Bassett, you can go as high as you like. Did you go for all you were worth, Bassett?"

"I went a thousand on it, Master Paul."

"I never told you, mother, that if I can ride my horse, and get there, then I'm absolutely sure—oh, absolutely! Mother, did I ever tell you? I'm lucky."

"No, you never did," said the mother.

But the boy died in the night.

And even as he lay dead, his mother heard her brother's voice saying to her: "My God, Hester, you're eighty-odd thousand to the good and a poor devil of a son to the bad. But, poor devil, poor devil, he's best gone out of a life where he rides his rocking horse to find a winner."

1932

A Dill Pickle

KATHERINE MANSFIELD

[1888–1923]

And then, after six years, she saw him again. He was seated at one of those little bamboo tables decorated with a Japanese vase of paper daffodils. There was a tall plate of fruit in front of him, and very carefully, in a way she recognized immediately as his "special" way, he was peeling an orange.

He must have felt that shock of recognition in her for he looked up and met her eyes. Incredible! He didn't know her! She smiled; he frowned. She came towards him. He closed his eyes an instant, but opening them his face lit up as though he had struck a match in a dark room. He laid down the orange and pushed back his chair, and she took her little warm hand out of her muff and gave it to him.

"Vera!" he exclaimed. "How strange. Really, for a moment I didn't know you. Won't you sit down? You've had lunch? Won't you have some coffee?"

She hesitated, but of course she meant to.

"Yes, I'd like some coffee." And she sat down opposite him.

"You've changed. You've changed very much," he said, staring at her with that eager, lighted look. "You look so well. I've never seen you look so well before."

"Really?" She raised her veil and unbuttoned her high fur collar. "I don't feel very well. I can't bear this weather, you know."

"Ah, no. You hate the cold. . . ."

"Loathe it." She shuddered. "And the worst of it is that the older one grows . . ."

He interrupted her. "Excuse me," and tapped on the table for the waitress. "Please bring some coffee and cream." To her: "You are sure you won't eat anything? Some fruit, perhaps. The fruit here is very good."

"No, thanks. Nothing."

"Then that's settled." And smiling just a hint too broadly he took up the orange again. "You were saying—the older one grows—"

"The colder," she laughed. But she was thinking how well she remembered that trick of his—the trick of interrupting her—and of how it used to exasperate her six years ago. She used to feel then as though he, quite suddenly, in the middle of what she was saying, put his hand over her lips, turned from her, attended to something different, and then took his hand away, and with just the same slightly too broad smile, gave her his attention again. . . . Now we are ready. That is settled.

"The colder!" He echoed her words, laughing too. "Ah, ah. You still say the same things. And there is another thing about you that is not changed at all—your beautiful voice—your beautiful way of speaking." Now he was very grave; he leaned towards her, and she smelled the warm, stinging scent of the orange peel. "You have only to say one word and I would know your voice among all other voices. I don't know what it is—I've often wondered—that makes your voice such a—haunting memory. . . . Do you remember that first afternoon we spent together at Kew Gardens? You were so surprised because I did not know the names of any flowers. I am still just as ignorant for all your telling me. But whenever it is very fine and warm, and I see some bright colours—it's awfully strange—I hear your voice saying: 'Geranium, marigold and verbena.' And I feel those three words are all I recall of some forgotten, heavenly language. . . . You remember that afternoon?"

"Oh, yes, very well." She drew a long, soft breath, as though the paper daffodils between them were almost too sweet to bear. Yet, what had remained in her mind of that particular afternoon was an absurd scene over the tea table. A great many people taking tea in a Chinese pagoda, and he behaving like a maniac about the wasps—waving them away, flapping at them with his straw hat, serious and infuriated out of all proportion to the occasion. How delighted the sniggering tea drinkers had been. And how she had suffered.

But now, as he spoke, that memory faded. His was the truer. Yes, it had been a wonderful afternoon, full of geranium and marigold and verbena, and—warm sunshine. Her thoughts lingered over the last two words as though she sang them.

In the warmth, as it were, another memory unfolded. She saw herself sitting on a lawn. He lay beside her, and suddenly, after a long silence, he rolled over and put his head in her lap.

"I wish," he said, in a low, troubled voice, "I wish that I had taken poison and were about to die—here now!"

At that moment a little girl in a white dress, holding a long, dripping water lily, dodged from behind a bush, stared at them, and dodged back again. But he did not see. She leaned over him.

"Ah, why do you say that? I could not say that."

But he gave a kind of soft moan, and taking her hand he held it to his cheek.

"Because I know I am going to love you too much—far too much. And I shall suffer so terribly, Vera, because you never, never will love me."

He was certainly far better looking now than he had been then. He had lost all that dreamy vagueness and indecision. Now he had the air of a man who has found his place in life, and fills it with a confidence and an assurance which was, to say the least, impressive. He must have made money, too. His clothes were admirable, and at that moment he pulled a Russian cigarette case out of his pocket.

"Won't you smoke?"

"Yes, I will." She hovered over them. "They look very good."

"I think they are. I get them made for me by a little man in St. James's Street. I don't smoke very much. I'm not like you—but when I do, they must be delicious, very fresh cigarettes. Smoking isn't a habit with me; it's a luxury—like perfume. Are you still so fond of perfumes? Ah, when I was in Russia . . ."

She broke in: "You've really been to Russia?"

"Oh, yes. I was there for over a year. Have you forgotten how we used to talk of going there?"

"No, I've not forgotten."

He gave a strange half laugh and leaned back in his chair. "Isn't it curious. I have really carried out all those journeys that we planned. Yes, I have been to all those places that we talked of, and stayed in them long enough to—as you used to say, 'air oneself' in them. In fact, I have spent the last three years of my life travelling all the time. Spain, Corsica, Siberia, Russia, Egypt. The only country left is China, and I mean to go there, too, when the war is over."

As he spoke, so lightly, tapping the end of his cigarette against the ash-tray, she felt the strange beast that had slumbered so long within her bosom stir, stretch itself, yawn, prick up its ears, and suddenly bound to its feet, and fix its longing, hungry stare upon those far away places. But all she said was, smiling gently: "How I envy you."

He accepted that. "It has been," he said, "very wonderful—especially Russia. Russia was all that we had imagined, and far, far more. I even spent some days on a river boat on the Volga. Do you remember that boatman's song that you used to play?"

"Yes." It began to play in her mind as she spoke.

"Do you ever play it now?"

"No, I've no piano."

He was amazed at that. "But what has become of your beautiful piano?"

She made a little grimace. "Sold. Ages ago."

"But you were so fond of music," he wondered.

"I've no time for it now," said she.

He let it go at that. "That river life," he went on, "is something quite special. After a day or two you cannot realize that you have ever known another. And it is not necessary to know the language—the life of the boat creates a bond between you and the people that's more than sufficient. You eat with them, pass the day with them, and in the evening there is that endless singing."

She shivered, hearing the boatman's song break out again loud and tragic, and seeing the boat floating on the darkening river with melancholy trees on either side. . . . "Yes, I should like that," said she, stroking her muff.

"You'd like almost everything about Russian life," he said warmly. "It's so informal, so impulsive, so free without question. And then the peasants are so splendid. They are such human beings—yes, that is it. Even the man who drives your carriage has—has some real part in what is happening. I remember the evening a party of us, two friends of mine and the wife of one of them, went for a picnic by the Black Sea. We took supper and champagne and ate and drank on the grass. And while we were eating the coachman came up. 'Have a dill pickle,' he said. He wanted to share with us. That seemed to me so right, so—you know what I mean?"

And she seemed at that moment to be sitting on the grass beside the mysteriously Black Sea, black as velvet, and rippling against the banks in silent, velvet waves. She saw the carraige drawn up to one side of the road, and the little group on the grass, their faces and hands white in the moonlight. She saw the pale dress of the woman outspread and her folded parasol, lying on the grass like a huge pearl crochet hook. Apart from them, with his supper in a cloth on his knees, sat the coachman. "Have a dill pickle," said he, and although she was not certain what a dill pickle was, she saw the greenish glass jar with a red chili like a parrot's beak glimmering through. She sucked in her cheeks; the dill pickle was terribly sour. . . .

"Yes, I know perfectly what you mean," she said.

In the pause that followed they looked at each other. In the past when they had looked at each other like that they had felt such a boundless understanding between them that their souls had, as it were, put their arms round each other and dropped into the same sea, content to be drowned, like mournful lovers. But now, the surprising thing was that it was he who held back. He who said:

"What a marvellous listener you are. When you look at me with those wild eyes I feel that I could tell you things that I would never breathe to another human being."

Was there just a hint of mockery in his voice or was it her fancy? She could not be sure.

"Before I met you," he said, "I had never spoken of myself to anybody. How well I remember one night, the night that I brought you the little Christmas tree, telling you all about my childhood. And of how I was so miserable that I ran away and lived under a cart in our yard for two days without being discovered. And you listened, and your eyes shone, and I felt that you had even made the little Christmas tree listen too, as in a fairy story."

But of that evening she had remembered a little pot of caviare. It had cost seven and sixpence. He could not get over it. Think of it—a tiny jar like that costing seven and sixpence. While she ate it he watched her, delighted and shocked.

"No, really, that is eating money. You could not get seven shillings into a little pot that size. Only think of the profit they must make. . . ." And he had begun some immensely complicated calculations. . . . But now good-bye to the caviare. The Christmas tree was on the table, and the little boy lay under the cart with his head pillowed on the yard dog.

"The dog was called Bosun," she cried delightedly.

But he did not follow. "Which dog? Had you a dog? I don't remember a dog at all."

"No, no. I mean the yard dog when you were a little boy." He laughed and snapped the cigarette case to.

"Was he? Do you know I had forgotten that. It seems such ages ago. I cannot believe that it is only six years. After I had recognized you to-day—I had to take such a leap—I had to take a leap over my whole life to get back to that time. I was such a kid then." He drummed on the table. "I've often thought how I must have bored you. And now I understand so perfectly why you wrote to me as you did—although at the time that letter nearly finished my life. I found it again the other day, and I couldn't help laughing as I read it. It was so clever—such a true picture of me." He glanced up. "You're not going?"

She had buttoned her collar again and drawn down her veil.

"Yes, I am afraid I must," she said, and managed a smile. Now she knew that he had been mocking.

"Ah, no, please," he pleaded. "Don't go just for a moment," and he caught up one of her gloves from the table and clutched at it as if that would hold her. "I see so few people to talk to nowadays, that I have turned into a sort of barbarian," he said. "Have I said something to hurt you?"

"Not a bit," she lied. But as she watched him draw her glove through his fingers, gently, gently, her anger really did die down, and besides, at the moment he looked more like himself of six years ago. . . .

"What I really wanted then," he said softly, "was to be a sort of carpet—to make myself into a sort of carpet for you to walk on so that you need not be hurt by the sharp stones and the mud that you hated so. It was nothing more positive than that—nothing more selfish. Only I did desire, eventually, to turn into a magic carpet and carry you away to all those lands you longed to see."

As he spoke she lifted her head as though she drank something; the strange beast in her bosom began to purr. . . .

"I felt that you were more lonely than anybody else in the world," he went on, "and yet, perhaps, that you were the only person in the world who was really, truly alive. Born out of your time," he murmured, stroking the glove, "fated."

Ah, God! What had she done! How had she dared to throw away her happiness like this. This was the only man who had ever understood her. Was it too late? Could it be too late? *She* was that glove that he held in his fingers. . . .

"And then the fact that you had no friends and never had made friends with people. How I understood that, for neither had I. Is it just the same now?"

"Yes," she breathed. "Just the same. I am as alone as ever."

"So am I," he laughed gently, "just the same."

Suddenly with a quick gesture he handed her back the glove and scraped his chair on the floor. "But what seemed to me so mysterious then is perfectly plain to me now. And to you, too, of course. . . . It simply was that we were such egoists, so self-engrossed, so wrapped up in ourselves that we hadn't a corner in our hearts for anybody else. Do you know," he cried, naïve and hearty, and dreadfully like another side of that old self again, "I began studying a Mind System when I was in Russia, and I found that we were not peculiar at all. It's quite a well known form of . . ."

She had gone. He sat there, thunder-struck, astounded beyond words. . . . And then he asked the waitress for his bill.

"But the cream has not been touched," he said. "Please do not charge me for it."

1917

The Grave

KATHERINE ANNE PORTER

[1890–1980]

The grandfather, dead for more than thirty years, had been twice disturbed in his long repose by the constancy and possessiveness of his widow. She removed his bones first to Louisiana and then to Texas as if she had set out to find her own burial place, knowing well she would never return to the places she had left. In Texas she set up a small cemetery in a corner of her first farm, and as the family connection grew, and oddments of relations came over from Kentucky to settle, it contained at last about twenty graves. After the grandmother's death, part of her land was to be sold for the benefit of certain of her children, and the cemetery happened to lie in the part set aside for sale. It was necessary to take up the bodies and bury them again in the family plot in the big new public cemetery, where the grandmother had been buried. At last her husband was to lie beside her for eternity, as she had planned.

The family cemetery had been a pleasant small neglected garden of tangled rose bushes and ragged cedar trees and cypress, the simple flat stones rising out of uncropped sweet-smelling wild grass. The graves were lying open and empty one burning day when Miranda and her brother Paul, who often went together to hunt rabbits and doves, propped their twenty-two Winchester rifles carefully against the rail fence, climbed over and explored among the graves. She was nine years old and he was twelve.

They peered into the pits all shaped alike with such purposeful accuracy, and looking at each other with pleased adventurous eyes, they said in solemn tones: "These were graves!" trying by words to shape a special, suitable emotion in their minds, but they felt nothing except an agreeable thrill of wonder: they were seeing a new sight, doing something they had not done before. In them both there was also a small disappointment at the entire commonplaceness of the actual spectacle. Even if it had once contained a coffin for years upon years, when the coffin was gone a grave was just a hole in the ground. Miranda leaped into the pit that had held her grandfather's bones. Scratching around aimlessly and pleasurably as any young animal, she scooped up a lump of earth and weighted it in her palm. It had a pleasantly sweet, corrupt smell, being mixed with cedar needles and small leaves, and as the crumbs fell apart, she saw a silver dove no larger than a hazel nut, with spread wings and a neat fan-shaped tail. The breast had a deep round hollow in it. Turning it up to the fierce sunlight, she saw that the inside of the hollow was cut in little whorls. She scrambled out, over the pile of loose earth that had fallen back into one end of the grave, calling to Paul that she had found something, he must guess what . . . His head appeared smiling over the rim of another grave. He waved a closed hand at her. "I've got something too!" They ran to compare treasures, making a game of it, so many guesses each, all wrong, and a final showdown with opened palms. Paul had found a thin wide gold ring carved with intricate flowers and leaves. Miranda was smitten at sight of the ring and wished to have it. Paul seemed more impressed by the dove. They made a trade, with some little bickering. After he had got the dove in his hand, Paul said, "Don't you know what this is? This is a screw head for a *coffin!* . . . I'll bet nobody else in the world has one like this!"

Miranda glanced at it without covetousness. She had the gold ring on her thumb; it fitted perfectly. "Maybe we ought to go now," she said, "maybe one of the niggers 'll see us and tell somebody." They knew the land had been sold, the cemetery was no longer theirs, and they felt like trespassers. They climbed back over the fence, slung their rifles loosely under their arms—they had been shooting at targets with various kinds of firearms since they were seven years old—and set out to look for the rabbits and doves or whatever small game might happen along. On these expeditions Miranda always followed at Paul's heels along the path, obeying instructions about handling her gun when going through fences; learning how to stand it up properly so it would not slip and fire unexpectedly; how to wait her time for a shot and not just bang away in the air without looking, spoiling shots for Paul, who really could hit things if given a chance. Now and then, in her excitement at seeing birds whizz up suddenly before her face, or a rabbit leap across her very toes, she lost her head, and almost without sighting she flung her rifle up and pulled the trigger. She hardly ever hit any sort of mark. She had no proper sense of hunting at all. Her brother would be often completely disgusted with her. "You don't care whether you get your bird or not," he said. "That's no way to hunt." Miranda could not understand his indignation. She had seen him smash his hat and yell with fury when he had missed his aim. "What I like about shooting," said Miranda, with exasperating inconsequence, "is pulling the trigger and hearing the noise."

"Then, by golly," said Paul, "whyn't you go back to the range and shoot at bullseyes?"

"I'd just as soon," said Miranda, "only like this, we walk around more."

"Well, you just stay behind and stop spoiling my shots," said Paul, who, when he made a kill, wanted to be certain he had made it. Miranda, who alone brought down a bird once in twenty rounds, always claimed as her own any game they got when they fired at the same moment. It was tiresome and unfair and her brother was sick of it.

"Now, the first dove we see, or the first rabbit, is mine," he told her. "And the next will be yours. Remember that and don't get smarty."

"What about snakes?" asked Miranda idly. "Can I have the first snake?"

Waving her thumb gently and watching her gold ring glitter, Miranda lost interest in shooting. She was wearing her summer roughing outfit: dark blue overalls, a light blue shirt, a hired-man's straw hat, and thick brown sandals. Her brother had the same outfit except his was a sober hickory-nut color. Ordinarily Miranda preferred her overalls to any other dress, though it was making rather a scandal in the countryside, for the year was 1903, and in the back country the law of female decorum had teeth in it. Her father had been criticized for letting his girls dress like boys and go careering around astride barebacked horses. Big sister Maria, the really independent and fearless one, in spite of her rather affected ways, rode at a dead run with only a rope knotted around her horse's nose. It was said the motherless family was running down, with the Grandmother no longer there to hold it together. It was known that she had discriminated against her son Harry in her will, and that he was in straits about money. Some of his old neighbors reflected with vicious satisfaction that now he would probably not be so stiff-necked, nor have any more high-stepping horses either. Miranda knew this, though she could not say how. She had met along the road old women of the kind who smoked corn-cob pipes, who had treated her grandmother with most sincere respect. They slanted their gummy old eyes side-ways at the granddaughter and said, "Ain't you ashamed of yoself, Missy? It's aginst the Scriptures to dress like that. Whut yo Pappy thinkin about?" Miranda, with her powerful social sense, which was like a fine set of antennae radiating from every pore of her skin, would feel ashamed because she knew well it was rude and ill-bred to shock anybody, even bad-tempered old crones, though she had faith in her father's judgment and was perfectly comfortable in the clothes. Her father had said, "They're just what you need, and they'll save your dresses for school . . ." This sounded quite simple and natural to her. She had been brought up in rigorous economy. Wastefulness was vulgar. It was also a sin. These were truths; she had heard them repeated many times and never once disputed.

Now the ring, shining with the serene purity of fine gold on her rather grubby thumb, turned her feelings against her overalls and sockless feet, toes sticking through the thick brown leather straps. She wanted to go back to the farmhouse, take a good cold bath, dust herself with plenty of Maria's violet talcum powder—provided Maria was not present to object, of course—put on the thinnest, most becoming dress she owned, with a big sash, and sit in a wicker chair under the trees . . . These things were not all she wanted, of course; she had vague stirrings of desire for luxury and a grand way of living which could not take precise form in her imagination but were founded on family legend of past wealth and leisure. These immediate comforts were what she could have, and she wanted them at once. She lagged rather far behind Paul, and once she thought of just turning back without a word and going home. She stopped, thinking that Paul would never do that to her, and so she would have to tell him. When a rabbit leaped, she let Paul have it without dispute. He killed it with one shot.

When she came up with him, he was already kneeling, examining the wound, the rabbit trailing from his hands. "Right through the head," he said complacently, as if he had aimed for it. He took out his sharp, competent bowie knife and started to skin the body. He did it very cleanly and quickly. Uncle Jimbilly knew how to prepare the skins so that Miranda always had fur coats for her dolls, for though she never cared much for her dolls she liked seeing them in fur coats. The children knelt facing each other over the dead animal. Miranda watched admiringly while her brother stripped the skin away as if he were taking off a glove. The flayed flesh emerged dark scarlet, sleek, firm; Miranda with thumb and finger felt the long fine muscles with the silvery flat strips binding them to the joints. Brother lifted the oddly bloated belly. "Look," he said, in a low amazed voice. "It was going to have young ones."

Very carefully he slit the thin flesh from the center ribs to the flanks, and a scarlet bag appeared. He slit again and pulled the bag open, and there lay a bundle of tiny rabbits, each wrapped in a thin scarlet veil. The brother pulled these off and there they were, dark gray, their sleek wet down lying in minute even ripples, like a baby's head just washed, their unbelievably small delicate ears folded close, their little blind faces almost featureless.

Miranda said, "Oh, I want to *see,*" under her breath. She looked and looked—excited but not frightened, for she was accustomed to the sight of animals killed in hunting—filled with pity and astonishment and a kind of shocked delight in the wonderful little creatures for their own sakes, they were so pretty. She touched one of them ever so carefully, "Ah, there's blood running over them," she said and began to tremble without knowing why. Yet she wanted most deeply to see and to know. Having seen, she felt at once as if she had known all along. The very memory of her former ignorance faded, she had always known just this. No one had ever told her anything outright, she had been rather unobservant of the animal life around her because she was so accustomed to animals. They seemed simply disorderly and unaccountably rude in their habits, but altogether natural and not very interesting. Her brother had spoken as if he had known about everything all along. He may have seen all this before. He had never said a word to her, but she knew now a part at least of what he knew. She understood a little of the secret, formless intuitions in her own mind and body, which had been clearing up, taking form, so gradually and so steadily she had not realized that she was learning what she had to know. Paul said cautiously, as if he were talking about something forbidden: "They were just about ready to be born." His voice dropped on the last word. "I know," said Miranda, "like kittens. I know, like babies." She was quietly and terribly agitated, standing again with her rifle under her arm, looking down at the bloody heap. "I don't want the skin," she said, "I won't have it." Paul buried the young rabbits again in their mother's body, wrapped the skin around her, carried her to a clump of sage bushes, and hid her away. He came out again at once and said to Miranda, with an eager friendliness, a confidential tone quite unusual in him, as if he were taking her into an important secret on equal terms: "Listen now. Now you listen to me, and don't ever forget. Don't you ever tell a living soul that you saw this. Don't tell a soul. Don't tell Dad because I'll get into trouble. He'll say I'm leading you into things you ought not to do. He's always saying that. So now don't you go and forget and blab out sometime the way you're always doing . . . Now, that's a secret. Don't you tell."

Miranda never told, she did not even wish to tell anybody. She thought about the whole worrisome affair with confused unhappiness for a few days. Then it sank quietly into her mind and was heaped over by accumulated thousands of impressions, for nearly twenty years. One day she was picking her path among the puddles and crushed refuse of a market street in a strange city of a strange country, when without warning, plain and clear in its true colors as if she looked through a frame upon a scene that had not stirred nor changed since the moment it happened, the episode of that far-off day leaped from its burial place before her mind's eye. She was so reasonlessly horrified she halted suddenly staring, the scene before her eyes dimmed by the vision back of them. An Indian vendor had held up before her a tray of dyed sugar sweets, in the shapes of all kinds of small creatures: birds, baby chicks, baby rabbits, lambs, baby pigs. They were in gay colors and smelled of vanilla, maybe. . . . It was a very hot day and the smell in the market, with its piles of raw flesh and wilting flowers, was like the mingled sweetness and corruption she had smelled that other day in the empty cemetery at home: the day she had remembered always until now vaguely as the time she and her brother had found treasure in the opened graves. Instantly upon this thought the dreadful vision faded, and she saw clearly her brother, whose childhood face she had forgotten, standing again in the blazing sunshine, again twelve years old, a pleased sober smile in his eyes, turning the silver dove over and over in his hands.

1944

My First Goose

ISAAC BABEL

[1894–1941?]

Savitsky, Commander of the VI Division, rose when he saw me, and I wondered at the beauty of his giant's body. He rose, the purple of his riding breeches and the crimson of his little tilted cap and the decorations stuck on his chest cleaving the hut as a standard cleaves the sky. A smell of scent and the sickly sweet freshness of soap emanated from him. His long legs were like girls sheathed to the neck in shining riding boots.

He smiled at me, struck his riding whip on the table, and drew toward him an order that the Chief of Staff had just finished dictating. It was an order for Ivan Chesnokov to advance on Chugunov-Dobryvodka with the regiment entrusted to him, to make contact with the enemy and destroy the same.

"For which destruction," the Commander began to write, smearing the whole sheet, "I make this same Chesnokov entirely responsible, up to and including the supreme penalty, and will if necessary strike him down on the spot; which you, Chesnokov, who have been working with me at the front for some months now, cannot doubt."

The Commander signed the order with a flourish, tossed it to his orderlies and turned upon me gray eyes that danced with merriment.

I handed him a paper with my appointment to the Staff of the Division.

"Put it down in the Order of the Day," said the Commander. "Put him down for every satisfaction save the front one. Can you read and write?"

"Yes, I can read and write," I replied, envying the flower and iron of that youthfulness. "I graduated in law from St Petersburg University."

"Oh, are you one of those grinds?" he laughed. "Specs on your nose, too! What a nasty little object! They've sent you along without making any enquiries; and this is a hot place for specs. Think you'll get on with us?"

"I'll get on all right," I answered, and went off to the village with the quartermaster to find a billet for the night.

The quartermaster carried my trunk on his shoulder. Before us stretched the village street. The dying sun, round and yellow as a pumpkin, was giving up its roseate ghost to the skies.

We went up to a hut painted over with garlands. The quartermaster stopped, and said suddenly, with a guilty smile:

"Nuisance with specs. Can't do anything to stop it, either. Not a life for the brainy type here. But you go and mess up a lady, and a good lady too, and you'll have the boys patting you on the back."

He hesitated, my little trunk on his shoulder; then he came quite close to me, only to dart away again despairingly and run to the nearest yard. Cossacks were sitting there, shaving one another.

"Here, you soldiers," said the quartermaster, setting my little trunk down on the ground. "Comrade Savitsky's orders are that you're to take this chap in your billets, so no nonsense about it, because the chap's been through a lot in the learning line."

The quartermaster, purple in the face, left us without looking back. I raised my hand to my cap and saluted the Cossacks. A lad with long straight flaxen hair and the handsome face of the Ryazan Cossacks went over to my little trunk and tossed it out at the gate. Then he turned his back on me and with remarkable skill emitted a series of shameful noises.

"To your guns—number double-zero!" an older Cossack shouted at him, and burst out laughing. "Running fire!"

His guileless art exhausted, the lad made off. Then, crawling over the ground, I began to gather together the manuscript and tattered garments that had fallen out of the trunk. I gathered them up and carried them to the other end of the yard. Near the hut, on a brick stove, stood a cauldron in which pork was cooking. The steam that rose from it was like the far-off smoke of home in the village, and it mingled hunger with desperate loneliness in my head. Then I covered my little broken trunk with hay, turning it into a pillow, and lay down on the ground to read in *Pravda* Lenin's speech at the Second Congress of the Comintern. The sun fell upon me from behind the toothed hillocks, the Cossacks trod on my feet, the lad made fun of me untiringly, the beloved lines came toward me along a thorny path and could not reach me. Then I put aside the paper and went out to the landlady, who was spinning on the porch.

"Landlady," I said, "I've got to eat."

The old woman raised to me the diffused whites of her purblind eyes and lowered them again.

"Comrade," she said, after a pause, "what with all this going on, I want to go and hang myself."

"Christ!" I muttered, and pushed the old woman in the chest with my fist. "You don't suppose I'm going to go into explanations with you, do you?"

And turning around I saw somebody's sword lying within reach. A severe-looking goose was waddling about the yard, inoffensively preening its feathers. I overtook it and pressed it to the ground. Its head cracked beneath my boot, cracked and emptied itself. The white neck lay stretched out in the dung, the wings twitched.

"Christ!" I said, digging into the goose with my sword. "Go and cook it for me, landlady."

Her blind eyes and glasses glistening, the old woman picked up the slaughtered bird, wrapped it in her apron, and started to bear it off toward the kitchen.

"Comrade," she said to me, after a while, "I want to go and hang myself." And she closed the door behind her.

The Cossacks in the yard were already sitting around their cauldron. They sat motionless, stiff as heathen priests at a sacrifice, and had not looked at the goose.

"The lad's all right," one of them said, winking and scooping up the cabbage soup with his spoon.

The Cossacks commenced their supper with all the elegance and restraint of peasants who respect one another. And I wiped the sword with sand, went out at the gate, and came in again, depressed. Already the moon hung above the yard like a cheap earring.

"Hey, you," suddenly said Surovkov, an older Cossack. "Sit down and feed with us till your goose is done."

He produced a spare spoon from his boot and handed it to me.

We supped up the cabbage soup they had made and ate the pork.

"What's in the newspaper?" asked the flaxen-haired lad, making room for me.

"Lenin writes in the paper," I said, pulling out *Pravda.* "Lenin writes that there's a shortage of everything."

And loudly, like a triumphant man hard of hearing, I read Lenin's speech out to the Cossacks.

Evening wrapped about me the quickening moisture of its twilight sheets; evening laid a mother's hand upon my burning forehead. I read on and rejoiced, spying out exultingly the secret curve of Lenin's straight line.

"Truth tickles everyone's nostrils," said Surovkov, when I had come to the end. "The question is, how's it to be pulled from the heap. But he goes and strikes at it straight off like a hen pecking at a grain!"

This remark about Lenin was made by Surokov, platoon commander of the Staff Squadron; after which we lay down to sleep in the hayloft. We slept, all six of us, beneath a wooden roof that let in the stars, warming one another, our legs intermingled. I dreamed: and in my dreams saw women. But my heart, stained with bloodshed, grated and brimmed over.

1924

The Secret Life of Walter Mitty

JAMES THURBER

[1894–1961]

"We're going through!" The Commander's voice was like thin ice breaking. He wore his full-dress uniform, with the heavily braided white cap pulled down rakishly over one cold gray eye. "We can't make it, sir. It's spoiling for a hurricane, if you ask me." "I'm not asking you, Lieutenant Berg," said the Commander. "Throw on the power lights! Rev her up to 8,500! We're going through!" The pounding of the cylinders increased: ta-pocketa-pocketa-pocketa *-pocketa-pocketa.* The Commander stared at the ice forming on the pilot window. He walked over and twisted a row of complicated dials. "Switch on No. 8 auxiliary!" he shouted. "Switch on No. 8 auxiliary!" repeated Lieutenant Berg. "Full strength in No. 3 turret!" shouted the Commander. "Full strength in No. 3 turret!" The crew, bending to their various tasks in the huge, hurtling eight-engined Navy hydroplane, looked at each other and grinned. "The Old Man'll get us through," they said to one another. "The Old Man ain't afraid of Hell!" . . .

"Not so fast! You're driving too fast!" said Mrs. Mitty. "What are you driving so fast for?"

"Hmm?" said Walter Mitty. He looked at his wife, in the seat beside him, with shocked astonishment. She seemed grossly unfamiliar, like a strange woman who had yelled at him in a crowd. "You were up to fifty-five," she said. "You know I don't like to go more than forty. You were up to fifty-five." Walter Mitty drove on toward Waterbury in silence, the roaring of the SN202 through the worst storm in twenty years of Navy flying fading in the remote, intimate airways of his mind. "You're tensed up again," said Mrs. Mitty. "It's one of your days. I wish you'd let Dr. Renshaw look you over."

Walter Mitty stopped the car in front of the building where his wife went to have her hair done. "Remember to get those overshoes while I'm having my hair done," she said. "I don't need overshoes," said Mitty. She put her mirror back into her bag. "We've been all through that," she said, getting out of the car. "You're not a young man any longer." He raced the engine a little. "Why don't you wear your gloves? Have you lost your gloves?" Walter Mitty reached in a pocket and brought out the gloves. He put them on, but after she had turned and gone into the building and he had driven on to a red light, he took them off again. "Pick it up, brother!" snapped a cop as the light changed, and Mitty hastily pulled on his gloves and lurched ahead. He drove around the streets aimlessly for a time, and then he drove past the hospital on his way to the parking lot.

. . . "It's the millionaire banker, Wellington McMillan," said the pretty nurse. "Yes?" said Walter Mitty, removing his gloves slowly. "Who has the case?" "Dr. Renshaw and Dr. Benbow, but there are two specialists here, Dr. Remington from New York and Mr. Pritchard-Mitford from London. He flew over." A door opened down a long, cool corridor and Dr. Renshaw came out. He looked distraught and haggard. "Hello, Mitty," he said. "We're having the devil's own time with McMillan, the millionaire banker and close personal friend of Roosevelt. Obstreosis of the ductal tract. Tertiary. Wish you'd take a look at him." "Glad to," said Mitty.

In the operating room there were whispered introductions: "Dr. Remington, Dr. Mitty. Mr. Pritchard-Mitford, Dr. Mitty." "I've read your book on streptothricosis," said Pritchard-Mitford, shaking hands. "A brilliant performance, sir." "Thank you," said Walter Mitty. "Didn't know you were in the States, Mitty," grumbled Remington. "Coals to Newcastle, bringing Mitford and me here for a tertiary." "You are very kind," said Mitty. A huge, complicated machine, connected to the operating table, with many tubes and wires, began at this moment to go pocketa-pocketa-pocketa. "The new anesthetizer is giving way!" shouted an interne. "There is no one in the East who knows how to fix it!" "Quiet, man!" said Mitty, in a low, cool voice. He sprang to the machine, which was now going pocketa-pocketa-queep-pocketa-queep. He began fingering delicately a row of glistening dials. "Give me a fountain pen!" he snapped. Someone handed him a fountain pen. He pulled a faulty piston out of the machine and inserted the pen in its place. "That will hold for ten minutes," he said. "Get on with the operation." A nurse hurried over and whispered to Renshaw, and Mitty saw the man turn pale. "Coreopsis has set in," said Renshaw nervously. "If you would take over, Mitty?" Mitty looked at him and at the craven figure of Benbow, who drank, and at the grave, uncertain faces of the two great specialists. "If you wish," he said. They slipped a white gown on him; he adjusted a mask and drew on thin gloves; nurses handed him shining. . . .

"Back it up, Mac! Look out for that Buick!" Walter Mitty jammed on the brakes. "Wrong lane, Mac," said the parking-lot attendant, looking at Mitty closely. "Gee. Yeh," muttered Mitty. He began cautiously to back out of the lane marked "Exit Only." "Leave her sit there," said the attendant. "I'll put her away." Mitty got out of the car. "Hey, better leave the key." "Oh," said Mitty, handing the man the ignition key. The attendant vaulted into the car, backed it up with insolent skill, and put it where it belonged.

They're so damn cocky, thought Walter Mitty, walking along Main Street; they think they know everything. Once he had tried to take his chains off, outside New Milford, and he had got them wound around the axles. A man had had to come out in a wrecking car and unwind them, a young, grinning garageman. Since then Mrs. Mitty always made him drive to a garage to have the chains taken off. The next time, he thought, I'll wear my right arm in a sling; they won't grin at me then. I'll have my right arm in a sling and they'll see I couldn't possibly take the chains off myself. He kicked at the slush on the sidewalk. "Overshoes," he said to himself, and he began looking for a shoe store.

When he came out into the street again, with the overshoes in a box under his arm, Walter Mitty began to wonder what the other thing was his wife had told him to get. She had told him twice, before they set out from their house for Waterbury. In a way he hated these weekly trips to town—he was always getting something wrong. Kleenex, he thought, Squibb's, razor blades? No. Toothpaste, toothbrush, bicarbonate, carborundum, initiative and referendum? He gave it up. But she would remember it. "Where's the what's-its-name?" she would ask. "Don't tell me you forgot the what's-its-name?" A newsboy went by shouting something about the Waterbury trial.

. . . "Perhaps this will refresh your memory." The District Attorney suddenly thrust a heavy automatic at the quiet figure on the witness stand. "Have you ever seen this before?" Walter Mitty took the gun and examined it expertly. "This is my Webley-Vickers 50.80," he said calmly. An excited buzz ran around the courtroom. The judge rapped for order. "You are a crack shot with any sort of firearms, I believe?" said the District Attorney, insinuatingly. "Objection!" shouted Mitty's attorney. "We have shown that the defendant could not have fired the shot. We have shown that he wore his right arm in a sling on the night of the fourteenth of July." Walter Mitty raised his hand briefly and the bickering attorneys were stilled. "With any known make of gun," he said evenly, "I could have killed Gregory Fitzhurst at three hundred feet *with my left hand.*" Pandemonium broke loose in the courtroom. A woman's scream rose above the bedlam and suddenly a lovely, dark-haired girl was in Walter Mitty's arms. The District Attorney struck at her savagely. Without rising from his chair, Mitty let the man have it on the point of the chin. "You miserable cur!" . . .

"Puppy biscuit," said Walter Mitty. He stopped walking and the buildings of Waterbury rose up out of the misty courtroom and surrounded him again. A woman who was passing laughed. "He said 'Puppy biscuit,' " she said to her companion. "That man said 'Puppy biscuit' to himself." Walter Mitty hurried on. He went into an A & P, not the first one he came to but a smaller one farther up the street. "I want some biscuit for small, young dogs," he said to the clerk. "Any special brand, sir?" The greatest pistol shot in the world thought a moment. "It says 'Puppies Bark for It' on the box," said Walter Mitty.

His wife would be through at the hairdresser's in fifteen minutes, Mitty saw in looking at his watch, unless they had trouble drying it; sometimes they had trouble drying it. She didn't like to get to the hotel first; she would want him to be there waiting for her as usual. He found a big leather chair in the lobby, facing a window, and he put the overshoes and the puppy biscuit on the floor beside it. He picked up an old copy of *Liberty* and sank down into the chair. "Can Germany Conquer the World Through the Air?" Walter Mitty looked at the pictures of bombing planes and of ruined streets.

. . . "The cannonading has got the wind up in young Raleigh, sir," said the sergeant. Captain Mitty looked up at him through tousled hair. "Get him to bed," he said wearily. "With the others. I'll fly alone." "But you can't, sir," said the sergeant anxiously. "It takes two men to handle that bomber and the Archies are pounding hell out of the air. Von Richtman's circus is between here and Saulier." "Somebody's got to get that ammunition dump," said Mitty. "I'm going over. Spot of brandy?" He poured a drink for the sergeant and one for himself. War thundered and whined around the dugout and battered at the door. There was a rending of wood and splinters flew through the room. "A bit of a near thing," said Captain Mitty carelessly. "The box barrage is closing in," said the sergeant. "We only live once, Sergeant," said Mitty, with his faint, fleeting smile. "Or do we?" He poured another brandy and tossed it off. "I never see a man could hold his brandy like you, sir," said the sergeant. "Begging your pardon, sir." Captain Mitty stood up and strapped on his huge Webley-Vickers automatic. "It's forty kilometers through hell, sir," said the sergeant. Mitty finished one last brandy. "After all," he said softly, "what isn't?" The pounding of the cannon increased; there was the rat-tat-tatting of machine guns, and from somewhere came the menacing pocketa-pocketa-pocketa of the new flame-throwers. Walter Mitty walked to the door of the dugout humming "Auprès de Ma Blonde." He turned and waved to the sergeant. "Cheerio!" he said. . . .

Something struck his shoulder. "I've been looking all over this hotel for you," said Mrs. Mitty. "Why do you have to hide in this old chair? How did you expect me to find you?" "Things close in," said Walter Mitty vaguely. "What?" Mrs. Mitty said. "Did you get the what's-its-name? The puppy biscuit? What's in the box?" "Overshoes," said Mitty. "Couldn't you have put them on in the store?" "I was thinking," said Walter Mitty. "Does it ever occur to you that I am sometimes thinking?" She looked at him. "I'm going to take your temperature when I get you home," she said.

They went out through the revolving doors that made a faintly derisive whistling sound when you pushed them. It was two blocks to the parking lot. At the drugstore on the corner she said, "Wait here for me. I forgot something. I won't be a minute." She was more than a minute. Walter Mitty lighted a cigarette. It began to rain, rain with sleet in it. He stood up against the wall of the drugstore, smoking. . . . He put his shoulders back and his heels together. "To hell with the handkerchief," said Walter Mitty scornfully. He took one last drag on his cigarette and snapped it away. Then, with that faint, fleeting smile playing about his lips, he faced the firing squad; erect and motionless, proud and disdainful, Walter Mitty the Undefeated, inscrutable to the last.

1942

Babylon Revisited

F. SCOTT FITZGERALD

[1896–1940]

I

"And where's Mr. Campbell?" Charlie asked.

"Gone to Switzerland. Mr. Campbell's a pretty sick man, Mr. Wales."

"I'm sorry to hear that. And George Hardt?" Charlie inquired.

"Back in America, gone to work."

"And where is the Snow Bird?"

"He was in here last week. Anyway, his friend, Mr. Schaeffer, is in Paris."

Two familiar names from the long list of a year and a half ago. Charlie scribbled an address in his notebook and tore out the page.

"If you see Mr. Schaeffer, give him this," he said. "It's my brother-in-law's address. I haven't settled on a hotel yet."

He was not really disappointed to find Paris was so empty. But the stillness in the Ritz bar was strange and portentous. It was not an American bar any more—he felt polite in it, and not as if he owned it. It had gone back into France. He felt tne stillness from the moment he got out of the taxi and saw the doorman, usually in a frenzy of activity at this hour, gossiping with a *chasseur* by the servants' entrance.

Passing through the corridor, he heard only a single, bored voice in the once-glamorous women's room. When he turned into the bar he travelled the twenty feet of green carpet with his eyes fixed straight ahead by old habit; and then, with his foot firmly on the rail, he turned and surveyed the room, encountering only a single pair of eyes that fluttered up from a newspaper in the corner. Charlie asked for the head barman, Paul, who in the latter days of the bull market had come to work in his own custom-built car—disembarking, however, with due nicety at the nearest corner. But Paul was at his country house today and Alix giving him information.

"No, no more," Charlie said, "I'm going slow these days."

Alix congratulated him: "You were going pretty strong a couple of years ago."

"I'll stick to it all right," Charlie assured him. "I've stuck to it for over a year and a half now."

"How do you find conditions in America?"

"I haven't been to America for months. I'm in business in Prague, representing a couple of concerns there. They don't know about me down there."

Alix smiled.

"Remember the night of George Hardt's bachelor dinner here?" said Charlie. "By the way, what's become of Claude Fessenden?"

Alix lowered his voice confidentially: "He's in Paris, but he doesn't come here any more. Paul doesn't allow it. He ran up a bill of thirty thousand francs, charging all his drinks and his lunches, and usually his dinner, for more than a year. And when Paul finally told him he had to pay, he gave him a bad check."

Alix shook his head sadly.

"I don't understand it, such a dandy fellow. Now he's all bloated up—" He made a plump apple of his hands.

Charlie watched a group of strident queens installing themselves in a corner.

"Nothing affects them," he thought. "Stocks rise and fall, people loaf or work, but they go on forever." The place oppressed him. He called for the dice and shook with Alix for the drink.

"Here for long, Mr. Wales?"

"I'm here for four or five days to see my little girl."

"Oh-h! You have a little girl?"

Outside, the fire-red, gas-blue, ghost-green signs shone smokily through the tranquil rain. It was late afternoon and the streets were in movement; the *bistros* gleamed. At the corner of the Boulevard des Capucines he took a taxi. The Place de la Concorde moved by in pink majesty; they crossed the logical Seine, and Charlie felt the sudden provincial quality of the Left Bank.

Charlie directed his taxi to the Avenue de l'Opéra, which was out of his way. But he wanted to see the blue hour spread over the magnificent façade, and imagine that the cab horns, playing endlessly the first few bars of *Le Plus que Lent,* were the trumpets of the Second Empire. They were closing the iron grill in front of Brentano's Book-store, and people were already at dinner behind the trim little bourgeois hedge of Duval's. He had never eaten at a really cheap restaurant in Paris. Five-course dinner, four francs fifty, eighteen cents, wine included. For some odd reason he wished that he had.

As they rolled on to the Left Bank and he felt its sudden provincialism, he thought, "I spoiled this city for myself. I didn't realize it, but the days came along one after another, and then two years were gone, and everything was gone, and I was gone."

He was thirty-five, and good to look at. The Irish mobility of his face was sobered by a deep wrinkle between his eyes. As he rang his brother-in-law's bell in the Rue Palatine, the wrinkle deepened till it pulled down his brows; he felt a cramping sensation in his belly. From behind the maid who opened the door darted a lovely little girl of nine who shrieked "Daddy!" and flew up, struggling like a fish, into his arms. She pulled his head around by one ear and set her cheek against his.

"My old pie," he said.

"Oh, daddy, daddy, daddy, daddy, dads, dads, dads!"

She drew him into the salon, where the family waited, a boy and girl his daughter's age, his sister-in-law and her husband. He greeted Marion with his voice pitched carefully to avoid either feigned enthusiasm or dislike, but her response was more frankly tepid, though she minimized her expression of unalterable distrust by directing her regard toward his child. The two men clasped hands in a friendly way and Lincoln Peters rested his for a moment on Charlie's shoulder.

The room was warm and comfortably American. The three children moved intimately about, playing through the yellow oblongs that led to other rooms; the cheer of six o'clock spoke in the eager smacks of the fire and the sounds of French activity in the kitchen. But Charlie did not relax; his heart sat up rigidly in his body and he drew confidence from his daughter, who from time to time came close to him, holding in her arms the doll he had brought.

"Really extremely well," he declared in answer to Lincoln's question. "There's a lot of business there that isn't moving at all, but we're doing even better than ever. In fact, damn well. I'm bringing my sister over from America next month to keep house for me. My income last year was bigger than it was when I had money. You see, the Czechs—"

His boasting was for a specific purpose; but after a moment, seeing a faint restiveness in Lincoln's eye, he changed the subject:

"Those are fine children of yours, well brought up, good manners."

"We think Honoria's a great little girl too."

Marion Peters came back from the kitchen. She was a tall woman with worried eyes, who had once possessed a fresh American loveliness. Charlie had never been sensitive to it and was always surprised when people spoke of how pretty she had been. From the first there had been an instinctive antipathy between them.

"Well, how do you find Honoria?" she asked.

"Wonderful. I was astonished how much she's grown in ten months. All the children are looking well."

"We haven't had a doctor for a year. How do you like being back in Paris?"

"It seems very funny to see so few Americans around."

"I'm delighted," Marion said vehemently. "Now at least you can go into a store without their assuming you're a millionaire. We've suffered like everybody, but on the whole it's a good deal pleasanter."

"But it was nice while it lasted," Charlie said. "We were a sort of royalty, almost infallible, with a sort of magic around us. In the bar this afternoon"—he stumbled, seeing his mistake—"there wasn't a man I knew."

She looked at him keenly. "I should think you'd have had enough of bars."

"I only stayed a minute. I take one drink every afternoon, and no more."

"Don't you want a cocktail before dinner?" Lincoln asked.

"I take only one drink every afternoon, and I've had that."

"I hope you keep to it," said Marion.

Her dislike was evident in the coldness with which she spoke, but Charlie only smiled; he had larger plans. Her very aggressiveness gave him an advantage, and he knew enough to wait. He wanted them to initiate the discussion of what they knew had brought him to Paris.

At dinner he couldn't decide whether Honoria was most like him or her mother. Fortunate if she didn't combine the traits of both that had brought them to disaster. A great wave of protectiveness went over him. He thought he knew what to do for her. He believed in character; he wanted to jump back a whole generation and trust in character again as the eternally valuable element. Everything else wore out.

He left soon after dinner, but not to go home. He was curious to see Paris by night with clearer and more judicious eyes than those of other days. He bought a *strapontin* for the Casino and watched Josephine Baker go through her chocolate arabesques.

After an hour he left and strolled toward Montmartre, up the Rue Pigalle into the Place Blanche. The rain had stopped and there were a few people in evening clothes disembarking from taxis in front of cabarets, and *cocottes* prowling singly or in pairs, and many Negroes. He passed a lighted door from which issued music, and stopped with the sense of familiarity; it was Bricktop's, where he had parted with so many hours and so much money. A few doors farther on he found another ancient rendezvous and incautiously put his head inside. Immediately an eager orchestra burst into sound, a pair of professional dancers leaped to their feet and a maître d'hôtel swooped toward him, crying, "Crowd just arriving, sir!" But he withdrew quickly.

"You have to be damn drunk," he thought.

Zelli's was closed, the bleak and sinister cheap hotels surrounding it were dark; up in the Rue Blanche there was more light and a local, colloquial French crowd. The Poet's Cave had disappeared, but the two great mouths of the Café of Heaven and the Café of Hell still yawned—even devoured, as he watched, the meagre contents of a tourist bus—a German, a Japanese, and an American couple who glanced at him with frightened eyes.

So much for the effort and ingenuity of Montmartre. All the catering to vice and waste was on an utterly childish scale, and he suddenly realized the meaning of the word "dissipate"—to dissipate into thin air; to make nothing out of something. In the little hours of the night every move from place to place was an enormous human jump, an increase of paying for the privilege of slower and slower motion.

He remembered thousand-franc notes given to an orchestra for playing a single number, hundred-franc notes tossed to a doorman for calling a cab.

But it hadn't been given for nothing.

It had been given, even the most wildly squandered sum, as an offering to destiny that he might not remember the things most worth remembering, the things that now he would always remember—his child taken from his control, his wife escaped to a grave in Vermont.

In the glare of a *brasserie* a woman spoke to him. He bought her some eggs and coffee, and then, eluding her encouraging stare, gave her a twenty-franc note and took a taxi to his hotel.

II

He woke upon a fine fall day—football weather. The depression of yesterday was gone and he liked the people on the streets. At noon he sat opposite Honoria at Le Grand Vatel, the only restaurant he could think of not reminiscent of champagne dinners and long luncheons that began at two and ended in a blurred and vague twilight.

"Now, how about vegetables? Oughtn't you to have some vegetables?"

"Well, yes."

"Here's *épinards* and *chou-fleur* and carrots and *haricots.*"

"I'd like *chou-fleur.*"

"Wouldn't you like to have two vegetables?"

"I usually only have one at lunch."

The waiter was pretending to be inordinately fond of children. *"Qu'elle est mignonne, la petite! Elle parle exactement comme une française."*

"How about dessert? Shall we wait and see?"

The waiter disappeared. Honoria looked at her father expectantly.

"What are we going to do?"

"First, we're going to that toy store in the Rue Saint-Honoré and buy you anything you like. And then we're going to the vaudeville at the Empire."

She hesitated. "I like it about the vaudeville, but not the toy store."

"Why not?"

"Well, you brought me this doll." She had it with her. "And I've got lots of things. And we're not rich any more, are we?"

"We never were. But today you are to have anything you want."

"All right," she agreed resignedly.

When there had been her mother and a French nurse he had been inclined to be strict; now he extended himself, reached out for a new tolerance; he must be both parents to her and not shut any of her out of communication.

"I want to get to know you," he said gravely. "First let me introduce myself. My name is Charles J. Wales, of Prague."

"Oh, daddy!" her voice cracked with laughter.

"And who are you, please?" he persisted, and she accepted a rôle immediately: "Honoria Wales, Rue Palatine, Paris."

"Married or single?"

"No, not married. Single."

He indicated the doll. "But I see you have a child, madame."

Unwilling to disinherit it, she took it to her heart and thought quickly: "Yes, I've been married, but I'm not married now. My husband is dead."

He went on quickly, "And the child's name?"

"Simone. That's after my best friend at school."

"I'm very pleased that you're doing so well at school."

"I'm third this month," she boasted. "Elsie"—that was her cousin—"is only about eighteenth, and Richard is about at the bottom."

"You like Richard and Elsie, don't you?"

"Oh, yes, I like Richard quite well and I like her all right."

Cautiously and casually he asked: "And Aunt Marion and Uncle Lincoln—which do you like best?"

"Oh, Uncle Lincoln, I guess."

He was increasingly aware of her presence. As they came in, a murmur of ". . . adorable" followed them, and now the people at the next table bent all their silences upon her, staring as if she were something no more conscious than a flower.

"Why don't I live with you?" she asked suddenly. "Because mamma's dead?"

"You must stay here and learn more French. It would have been hard for daddy to take care of you so well."

"I don't really need much taking care of any more. I do everything for myself."

Going out of the restaurant, a man and a woman unexpectedly hailed him.

"Well, the old Wales!"

"Hello there, Lorraine. . . . Dunc."

Sudden ghosts out of the past: Duncan Schaeffer, a friend from college. Lorraine Quarrles, a lovely, pale blonde of thirty; one of a crowd who had helped them make months into days in the lavish times of three years ago.

"My husband couldn't come this year," she said, in answer to his question. "We're poor as hell. So he gave me two hundred a month and told me I could do my worst on that. . . . This your little girl?"

"What about coming back and sitting down?" Duncan asked.

"Can't do it." He was glad for an excuse. As always, he felt Lorraine's passionate, provocative attraction, but his own rhythm was different now.

"Well, how about dinner?" she asked.

"I'm not free. Give me your address and let me call you."

"Charlie, I believe you're sober," she said judicially. "I honestly believe he's sober, Dunc. Pinch him and see if he's sober."

Charlie indicated Honoria with his head. They both laughed.

"What's your address?" said Duncan sceptically.

He hesitated, unwilling to give the name of his hotel.

"I'm not settled yet. I'd better call you. We're going to see the vaudeville at the Empire."

"There! That's what I want to do," Lorraine said. "I want to see some clowns and acrobats and jugglers. That's just what we'll do, Dunc."

"We've got to do an errand first," said Charlie. "Perhaps we'll see you there."

"All right, you snob. . . . Good-by, beautiful little girl."

"Good-by."

Honoria bobbed politely.

Somehow, an unwelcome encounter. They liked him because he

was functioning, because he was serious; they wanted to see him, because he was stronger than they were now, because they wanted to draw a certain sustenance from his strength.

At the Empire, Honoria proudly refused to sit upon her father's folded coat. She was already an individual with a code of her own, and Charlie was more and more absorbed by the desire of putting a little of himself into her before she crystallized utterly. It was hopeless to try to know her in so short a time.

Between the acts they came upon Duncan and Lorraine in the lobby where the band was playing.

"Have a drink?"

"All right, but not up at the bar. We'll take a table."

"The perfect father."

Listening abstractedly to Lorraine, Charlie watched Honoria's eyes leave their table, and he followed them wistfully about the room, wondering what they saw. He met her glance and she smiled.

"I liked that lemonade," she said.

What had she said? What had he expected? Going home in a taxi afterward, he pulled her over until her head rested against his chest.

"Darling, do you ever think about your mother?"

"Yes, sometimes," she answered vaguely.

"I don't want you to forget her. Have you got a picture of her?"

"Yes, I think so. Anyhow, Aunt Marion has. Why don't you want me to forget her?"

"She loved you very much."

"I loved her too."

They were silent for a moment.

"Daddy, I want to come and live with you," she said suddenly.

His heart leaped; he had wanted it to come like this.

"Aren't you perfectly happy?"

"Yes, but I love you better than anybody. And you love me better than anybody, don't you, now that mummy's dead?"

"Of course I do. But you won't always like me best, honey. You'll grow up and meet somebody your own age and go marry him and forget you ever had a daddy."

"Yes, that's true," she agreed tranquilly.

He didn't go in. He was coming back at nine o'clock and he wanted to keep himself fresh and new for the thing he must say then.

"When you're safe inside, just show yourself in that window."

"All right. Good-by, dads, dads, dads, dads."

He waited in the dark street until she appeared, all warm and glowing, in the window above and kissed her fingers out into the night.

III

They were waiting. Marion sat behind the coffee service in a dignified black dinner dress that just faintly suggested mourning. Lincoln was walking up and down with the animation of one who had already been talking. They were as anxious as he was to get into the question. He opened it almost immediately:

"I suppose you know what I want to see you about—why I really came to Paris."

Marion played with the black stars on her necklace and frowned.

"I'm awfully anxious to have a home," he continued. "And I'm awfully anxious to have Honoria in it. I appreciate your taking in Honoria for her mother's sake, but things have changed now"—he hesitated and then continued more forcibly—"changed radically with me, and I want to ask you to reconsider the matter. It would be silly for me to deny that about three years ago I was acting badly —"

Marion looked up at him with hard eyes.

"—but all that's over. As I told you, I haven't had more than a drink a day for over a year, and I take that drink deliberately, so that the idea of alcohol won't get too big in my imagination. You see the idea?"

"No," said Marion succinctly.

"It's a sort of stint I set myself. It keeps the matter in proportion."

"I get you," said Lincoln. "You don't want to admit it's got any attraction for you."

"Something like that. Sometimes I forget and don't take it. But I try to take it. Anyhow, I couldn't afford to drink in my position. The people I represent are more than satisfied with what I've done, and I'm bringing my sister over from Burlington to keep house for me, and I want awfully to have Honoria too. You know that even when her mother and I weren't getting along well we never let anything that happened touch Honoria. I know she's fond of me and I know I'm able to take care of her and—well, there you are. How do you feel about it?"

He knew that now he would have to take a beating. It would last an hour or two hours, and it would be difficult, but if he modulated his inevitable resentment to the chastened attitude of the reformed sinner, he might win his point in the end.

Keep your temper, he told himself. You don't want to be justified. You want Honoria.

Lincoln spoke first: "We've been talking it over ever since we got your letter last month. We're happy to have Honoria here. She's a dear little thing, and we're glad to be able to help her, but of course that isn't the question—"

Marion interrupted suddenly. "How long are you going to stay sober, Charlie?" she asked.

"Permanently, I hope."

"How can anybody count on that?"

"You know I never did drink heavily until I gave up business and came over here with nothing to do. Then Helen and I began to run around with—"

"Please leave Helen out of it. I can't bear to hear you talk about her like that."

He stared at her grimly, he had never been certain how fond of each other the sisters were in life.

"My drinking only lasted about a year and a half—from the time we came over until I—collapsed."

"It was time enough."

"It was time enough," he agreed.

"My duty is entirely to Helen," she said. "I try to think what she would have wanted me to do. Frankly, from the night you did that terrible thing you haven't really existed for me. I can't help that. She was my sister."

"Yes."

"When she was dying she asked me to look out for Honoria. If you hadn't been in a sanitarium then, it might have helped matters."

He had no answer.

"I'll never in my life be able to forget the morning when Helen knocked at my door, soaked to the skin and shivering, and said you'd locked her out."

Charlie gripped the sides of the chair. This was more difficult than he expected; he wanted to launch out into a long expostulation and explanation, but he only said: "The night I locked her out—" and she interrupted, "I don't feel up to going over that again."

After a moment's silence Lincoln said: "We're getting off the subject. You want Marion to set aside her legal guardianship and give you Honoria. I think the main point for her is whether she has confidence in you or not."

"I don't blame Marion," Charlie said slowly, "but I think she can have entire confidence in me. I had a good record up to three years ago. Of course, it's within human possibilities I might go wrong any time. But if we wait much longer I'll lose Honoria's childhood and my chance for a home." He shook his head, "I'll simply lose her, don't you see?"

"Yes, I see," said Lincoln.

"Why didn't you think of all this before?" Marion asked.

"I suppose I did, from time to time, but Helen and I were getting along badly. When I consented to the guardianship, I was flat on my back in a sanitarium and the market had cleaned me out. I knew I'd acted badly, and I thought if it would bring any peace to Helen, I'd agree to anything. But now it's different. I'm functioning, I'm behaving damn well, so far as—"

"Please don't swear at me," Marion said.

He looked at her, startled. With each remark the force of her dislike became more and more apparent. She had built up all her fear of life into one wall and faced it toward him. This trivial reproof was possibly the result of some trouble with the cook several hours before. Charlie became increasingly alarmed at leaving Honoria in this atmosphere of hostility against himself; sooner or later it would come out, in a word here, a shake of the head there, and some of that distrust would be irrevocably implanted in Honoria. But he pulled his temper down out of his face and shut it up inside him; he had won a point, for Lincoln realized the absurdity of Marion's remark and asked her lightly since when she had objected to the word "damn."

"Another thing," Charlie said: "I'm able to give her certain advantages now. I'm going to take a French governess to Prague with me. I've got a lease on a new apartment—"

He stopped, realizing that he was blundering. They couldn't be expected to accept with equanimity the fact that his income was again twice as large as their own.

"I suppose you can give her more luxuries than we can," said Marion. "When you were throwing away money we were living along watching every ten francs. . . . I suppose you'll start doing it again."

"Oh, no," he said. "I've learned. I worked hard for ten years, you know—until I got lucky in the market, like so many people. Terribly lucky. It didn't seem any use working any more, so I quit. It won't happen again."

There was a long silence. All of them felt their nerves straining, and for the first time in a year Charlie wanted a drink. He was sure now that Lincoln Peters wanted him to have his child.

Marion shuddered suddenly; part of her saw that Charlie's feet were planted on the earth now, and her own maternal feeling recognized the naturalness of his desire; but she had lived for a long time with a prejudice—a prejudice founded on a curious disbelief in her sister's happiness, and which, in the shock of one terrible night, had turned to hatred for him. It had all happened at a point in her life where the discouragement of ill health and adverse circumstances made it necessary for her to believe in tangible villainy and a tangible villain.

"I can't help what I think!" she cried out suddenly. "How much you were responsible for Helen's death, I don't know. It's something you'll have to square with your own conscience."

An electric current of agony surged through him; for a moment he was almost on his feet, an unuttered sound echoing in his throat. He hung on to himself for a moment, another moment.

"Hold on there," said Lincoln uncomfortably. "I never thought you were responsible for that."

"Helen died of heart trouble," Charlie said dully.

"Yes, heart trouble." Marion spoke as if the phrase had another meaning for her.

Then, in the flatness that followed her outburst, she saw him plainly and she knew he had somehow arrived at control over the situation. Glancing at her husband, she found no help from him, and as abruptly as if it were a matter of no importance, she threw up the sponge.

"Do what you like!" she cried, springing up from her chair.

"She's your child. I'm not the person to stand in your way. I think if it were my child I'd rather see her—" She managed to check herself. "You two decide it. I can't stand this. I'm sick. I'm going to bed."

She hurried from the room; after a moment Lincoln said:

"This has been a hard day for her. You know how strongly she feels—" His voice was almost apologetic: "When a woman gets an idea in her head."

"Of course."

"It's going to be all right. I think she sees now that you—can provide for the child, and so we can't very well stand in your way or Honoria's way."

"Thank you, Lincoln."

"I'd better go along and see how she is."

"I'm going."

He was still trembling when he reached the street, but a walk down the Rue Bonaparte to the quais set him up, and as he crossed the Seine, fresh and new by the quai lamps, he felt exultant. But back in his room he couldn't sleep. The image of Helen haunted him. Helen whom he had loved so until they had senselessly begun to abuse each other's love, tear it into shreds. On that terrible February night that Marion remembered so vividly, a slow quarrel had gone on for hours. There was a scene at the Florida, and then he attempted to take her home, and then she kissed young Webb at a table; after that there was what she had hysterically said. When he arrived home alone he turned the key in the lock in wild anger. How could he know she would arrive an hour later alone, that there would be a snowstorm in which she wandered about in slippers, too confused to find a taxi? Then the aftermath, her escaping pneumonia by a miracle, and all the attendant horror. They were "reconciled," but that was the beginning of the end, and Marion, who had seen with her own eyes and who imagined it to be one of many scenes from her sister's martyrdom, never forgot.

Going over it again brought Helen nearer, and in the white, soft light that steals upon half sleep near morning he found himself talking to her again. She said that he was perfectly right about Honoria and that she wanted Honoria to be with him. She said she was glad he was being good and doing better. She said a lot of other things—very friendly things—but she was in a swing in a white dress, and swinging faster and faster all the time, so that at the end he could not hear clearly all that she said.

IV

He woke up feeling happy. The door of the world was open again. He made plans, visits, futures for Honoria and himself, but suddenly he grew sad, remembering all the plans he and Helen had made. She had not planned to die. The present was the thing—work to do and someone to love. But not to love too much, for he knew the injury that a father can do to a daughter or a mother to a son by attaching them too closely: afterward, out in the world, the child would seek in the marriage partner the same blind tenderness and, failing probably to find it, turn against love and life.

It was another bright, crisp day. He called Lincoln Peters at the bank where he worked and asked if he could count on taking Honoria when he left for Prague. Lincoln agreed that there was no reason for delay. One thing—the legal guardianship. Marion wanted to retain that a while longer. She was upset by the whole matter, and it would oil things if she felt that the situation was still in her control for another year. Charlie agreed, wanting only the tangible, visible child.

Then the question of a governess. Charlie sat in a gloomy agency and talked to a cross Béarnaise and to a buxom Breton peasant, neither of whom he could have endured. There were others whom he would see tomorrow.

He lunched with Lincoln Peters at Griffons, trying to keep down his exultation.

"There's nothing quite like your own child," Lincoln said. "But you understand how Marion feels too."

"She's forgotten how hard I worked for seven years there," Charlie said. "She just remembers one night."

"There's another thing." Lincoln hesitated. "While you and Helen were tearing around Europe throwing money away, we were just getting along. I didn't touch any of the prosperity because I never got ahead enough to carry anything but my insurance. I think Marion felt there was some kind of injustice in it—you not even working toward the end, and getting richer and richer."

"It went just as quick as it came," said Charlie.

"Yes, a lot of it stayed in the hands of *chasseurs* and saxophone players and maîtres d'hôtel—well, the big party's over now. I just said that to explain Marion's feeling about those crazy years. If you drop in about six o'clock tonight before Marion's too tired, we'll settle the details on the spot."

Back at his hotel, Charlie found a *pneumatique* that had been redirected from the Ritz bar where Charlie had left his address for the purpose of finding a certain man.

> DEAR CHARLIE: You were so strange when we saw you the other day that I wondered if I did something to offend you. If so, I'm not conscious of it. In fact, I have thought about you too much for the last year, and it's always been in the back of my mind that I might see you if I came over here. We *did* have such good times that crazy spring, like the night you and I stole the butcher's tricycle, and the time we tried to call on the president and you had the old derby rim and the wire cane. Everybody seems so old lately, but I don't feel old a bit. Couldn't we get together some time today for old time's sake? I've got a vile hangover for the moment, but will be feeling better this afternoon and will look for you about five in the sweat-shop at the Ritz.
>
> Always devotedly,
>
> LORRAINE.

His first feeling was one of awe that he had actually, in his mature years, stolen a tricycle and pedalled Lorraine all over the Étoile between the small hours and dawn. In retrospect it was a nightmare. Locking out Helen didn't fit in with any other act of his life, but the tricycle incident did—it was one of many. How many weeks or months of dissipation to arrive at that condition of utter irresponsibility?

He tried to picture how Lorraine had appeared to him then—very attractive; Helen was unhappy about it, though she said nothing. Yesterday, in the restaurant, Lorraine had seemed trite, blurred, worn away. He emphatically did not want to see her, and he was glad Alix had not given away his hotel address. It was a relief to think, instead, of Honoria, to think of Sundays spent with her and of saying good morning to her and of knowing she was there in his house at night, drawing her breath in the darkness.

At five he took a taxi and bought presents for all the Peters—a piquant cloth doll, a box of Roman soldiers, flowers for Marion, big linen handkerchiefs for Lincoln.

He saw, when he arrived in the apartment, that Marion had accepted the inevitable. She greeted him now as though he were a recalcitrant member of the family, rather than a menacing outsider. Honoria had been told she was going; Charlie was glad to see that her tact made her conceal her excessive happiness. Only on his lap did she whisper her delight and the question "When?" before she slipped away with the other children.

He and Marion were alone for a minute in the room, and on an impulse he spoke out boldly:

"Family quarrels are bitter things. They don't go according to any rules. They're not like aches or wounds; they're more like splits in the skin that won't heal because there's not enough material. I wish you and I could be on better terms."

"Some things are hard to forget," she answered. "It's a question of confidence." There was no answer to this and presently she asked, "When do you propose to take her?"

"As soon as I can get a governess. I hoped the day after tomorrow."

"That's impossible. I've got to get her things in shape. Not before Saturday."

He yielded. Coming back into the room, Lincoln offered him a drink.

"I'll take my daily whisky," he said.

It was warm here, it was a home, people together by a fire. The children felt very safe and important; the mother and father were serious, watchful. They had things to do for the children more important than his visit here. A spoonful of medicine was, after all, more important than the strained relations between Marion and himself. They were not dull people, but they were very much in the grip of life and circumstances. He wondered if he couldn't do something to get Lincoln out of his rut at the bank.

A long peal at the door-bell; the *bonne de toute faire* passed through and down the corridor, closely followed by the voices, which developed under the light into Duncan Shaeffer and Lorraine Quarrles.

They were gay, they were hilarious, they were roaring with laughter. For a moment Charlie was astounded; unable to understand how they ferreted out the Peters' address.

"Ah-h-h!" Duncan wagged his finger roguishly at Charlie. "Ah-h-h!"

They both slid down another cascade of laughter. Anxious and at a loss, Charlie shook hands with them quickly and presented them to Lincoln and Marion. Marion nodded, scarcely speaking. She had drawn back a step toward the fire; her little girl stood beside her, and Marion put an arm about her shoulder.

With growing annoyance at the intrusion, Charlie waited for them to explain themselves. After some concentration Duncan said:

"We came to invite you out to dinner. Lorraine and I insist that all this shishi, cagey business 'bout your address got to stop."

Charlie came closer to them, as if to force them backward down the corridor.

"Sorry, but I can't. Tell me where you'll be and I'll phone you in half an hour."

This made no impression. Lorraine sat down suddenly on the side of a chair, and focusing her eyes on Richard, cried, "Oh, what a nice little boy! Come here, little boy." Richard glanced at his mother, but did not move. With a perceptible shrug of her shoulders, Lorraine turned back to Charlie:

"Come and dine. Sure your cousins won' mine. See you so sel'om. Or solemn."

"I can't," said Charlie sharply. "You two have dinner and I'll phone you."

Her voice became suddenly unpleasant. "All right, we'll go. But I remember once when you hammered on my door at four A.M. I was enough of a good sport to give you a drink. Come on, Dunc."

Still in slow motion, with blurred, angry faces, with uncertain feet, they retired along the corridor.

"Good night," Charlie said.

"Good night!" responded Lorraine emphatically.

When he went back into the salon Marion had not moved, only now her son was standing in the circle of her other arm. Lincoln was still swinging Honoria back and forth like a pendulum from side to side.

"What an outrage!" Charlie broke out. "What an absolute outrage!"

Neither of them answered. Charlie dropped into an armchair, picked up his drink, set it down again and said:

"People I haven't seen for two years having the colossal nerve—"

He broke off. Marion had made the sound "Oh!" in one swift, furious breath, turned her body from him with a jerk and left the room.

Lincoln set down Honoria carefully.

"You children go in and start your soup," he said, and when they obeyed, he said to Charlie:

"Marion's not well and she can't stand shocks. That kind of people make her really physically sick."

"I didn't tell them to come here. They wormed your name out of somebody. They deliberately—"

"Well, it's too bad. It doesn't help matters. Excuse me a minute."

Left alone, Charlie sat tense in his chair. In the next room he could hear the children eating, talking in monosyllables, already oblivious to the scene between their elders. He heard a murmur of conversation from a farther room and then the ticking bell of a telephone receiver picked up, and in a panic he moved to the other side of the room and out of earshot.

In a minute Lincoln came back. "Look here, Charlie. I think we'd better call off dinner for tonight. Marion's in bad shape."

"Is she angry with me?"

"Sort of," he said, almost roughly. "She's not strong and—"

"You mean she's changed her mind about Honoria?"

"She's pretty bitter right now. I don't know. You phone me at the bank tomorrow."

"I wish you'd explain to her I never dreamed these people would come here. I'm just as sore as you are."

"I couldn't explain anything to her now."

Charlie got up. He took his coat and hat and started down the corridor. Then he opened the door of the dining room and said in a strange voice, "Good night, children."

Honoria rose and ran around the table to hug him.

"Good night, sweetheart," he said vaguely, and then trying to make his voice more tender, trying to conciliate something, "Good night, dear children."

V

Charlie went directly to the Ritz bar with the furious idea of finding Lorraine and Duncan, but they were not there, and he realized that in any case there was nothing he could do. He had not touched his drink at the Peters', and now he ordered a whisky-and-soda. Paul came over to say hello.

"It's a great change," he said sadly. "We do about half the business we did. So many fellows I hear about back in the States lost everything, maybe not in the first crash, but then in the second. Your friend George Hardt lost every cent, I hear. Are you back in the States?"

"No, I'm in business in Prague."

"I heard that you lost a lot in the crash."

"I did," and he added grimly, "but I lost everything I wanted in the boom."

"Selling short?"

"Something like that."

Again the memory of those days swept over him like a nightmare —the people they had met travelling; the people who couldn't add a row of figures or speak a coherent sentence. The little man Helen had consented to dance with at the ship's party, who had insulted her ten feet from the table; the women and girls carried screaming with drinks or drugs out of public places—

—The men who locked their wives out in the snow, because the snow of twenty-nine wasn't real snow. If you didn't want it to be snow, you just paid some money.

He went to the phone and called the Peters' apartment; Lincoln answered.

"I called up because this thing is on my mind. Has Marion said anything definite?"

"Marion's sick," Lincoln answered shortly. "I know this thing isn't altogether your fault, but I can't have her go to pieces about it. I'm afraid we'll have to let it slide for six months; I can't take the chance of working her up to this state again."

"I see."

"I'm sorry, Charlie."

He went back to his table. His whisky glass was empty, but he shook his head when Alix looked at it questioningly. There wasn't much he could do now except send Honoria some things; he would send her a lot of things tomorrow. He thought rather angrily that this was just money—he had given so many people money. . . .

"No, no more," he said to another waiter. "What do I owe you?"

He would come back some day; they couldn't make him pay forever. But he wanted his child, and nothing was much good now, beside that fact. He wasn't young any more, with a lot of nice thoughts and dreams to have by himself. He was absolutely sure Helen wouldn't have wanted him to be so alone.

1931

Barn Burning

WILLIAM FAULKNER

[1897–1962]

The store in which the Justice of the Peace's court was sitting smelled of cheese. The boy, crouched on his nail keg at the back of the crowded room, knew he smelled cheese, and more: from where he sat he could see the ranked shelves close-packed with the solid, squat, dynamic shapes of tin cans whose labels his stomach read, not from the lettering which meant nothing to his mind but from the scarlet devils and the silver curve of fish—this, the cheese which he knew he smelled and the hermetic meat which his intestines believed he smelled coming in intermittent gusts momentary and brief between the other constant one, the smell and sense just a little of fear because mostly of despair and grief, the old fierce pull of blood. He could not see the table where the Justice sat and before which his father and his father's enemy *(our enemy* he thought in that despair; *ourn! mine and hisn both! He's my father!)* stood, but he could hear them, the two of them that is, because his father had said no word yet:

"But what proof have you, Mr. Harris?"

"I told you. The hog got into my corn. I caught it up and sent it back to him. He had no fence that would hold it. I told him so, warned him. The next time I put the hog in my pen. When he came to get it I gave him enough wire to patch up his pen. The next time I put the hog up and kept it. I rode down to his house and saw the wire I gave him still rolled on to the spool in his yard. I told him he could have the hog when he paid me a dollar pound fee. That evening a nigger came with the dollar and got the hog. He was a strange nigger. He said, 'He say to tell you wood and hay kin burn.' I said, 'What?' 'That whut he say to tell you,' the nigger said. 'Wood and hay kin burn.' That night my barn burned. I got the stock out but I lost the barn."

"Where is the nigger? Have you got him?"

"He was a strange nigger, I tell you. I don't know what became of him."

"But that's not proof. Don't you see that's not proof?"

"Get that boy up here. He knows." For a moment the boy thought too that the man meant his older brother until Harris said, "Not him. The little one. The boy," and, crouching, small for his age, small and wiry like his father, in patched and faded jeans even too small for him, with straight, uncombed, brown hair and eyes gray and wild as storm scud, he saw the men between himself and the table part and become a lane of grim faces, at the end of which he saw the Justice, a shabby, collarless, graying man in spectacles, beckoning him. He felt no floor under his bare feet; he seemed to walk beneath the palpable weight of the grim turning faces. His father, stiff in his black Sunday coat donned not for the trial but for the moving, did not even look at him. *He aims for me to lie,* he thought, again with that frantic grief and despair. *And I will have to do hit.*

"What's your name, boy?" the Justice said.

"Colonel Sartoris Snopes," the boy whispered.

"Hey?" the Justice said. "Talk louder. Colonel Sartoris? I reckon anybody named for Colonel Sartoris in this country can't help but tell the truth, can they?" The boy said nothing. *Enemy! Enemy!* he thought; for a moment he could not even see, could not see that the Justice's face was kindly nor discern that his voice was troubled when he spoke to the man named Harris: "Do you want me to question this boy?" But he could hear, and during those subsequent long seconds while there was absolutely no sound in the crowded little room save that of quiet and intent breathing it was as if he had swung outward at the end of a grape vine, over a ravine, and at the top of the swing had been caught in a prolonged instant of mesmerized gravity, weightless in time.

"No!" Harris said violently, explosively. "Damnation! Send him out of here!" Now time, the fluid world, rushed beneath him again, the voices coming to him again through the smell of cheese and sealed meat, the fear and despair and the old grief of blood:

"This case is closed. I can't find against you, Snopes, but I can give you advice. Leave this country and don't come back to it."

His father spoke for the first time, his voice cold and harsh, level, without emphasis: "I aim to. I don't figure to stay in a country among people who . . ." he said something unprintable and vile, addressed to no one.

"That'll do," the Justice said. "Take your wagon and get out of this country before dark. Case dismissed."

His father turned, and he followed the stiff black coat, the wiry figure walking a little stiffly from where a Confederate provost's man's musket ball had taken him in the heel on a stolen horse thirty years ago, followed the two backs now, since his older brother had appeared from somewhere in the crowd, no taller than the father but thicker, chewing tobacco steadily, between the two lines of grim-faced men and out of the store and across the worn gallery and down the sagging steps and among the dogs and half-grown boys in the mild May dust, where as he passed a voice hissed:

"Barn burner!"

Again he could not see, whirling; there was a face in a red haze, moonlike, bigger than the full moon, the owner of it half again his size, he leaping in the red haze toward the face, feeling no blow, feeling no shock when his head struck the earth, scrabbling up and leaping again, feeling no blow this time either and tasting no blood, scrabbling up to see the other boy in full flight and himself already leaping into pursuit as his father's hand jerked him back, the harsh, cold voice speaking above him: "Go get in the wagon."

It stood in a grove of locusts and mulberries across the road. His two hulking sisters in their Sunday dresses and his mother and her sister in calico and sunbonnets were already in it, sitting on and among the sorry residue of the dozen and more movings which even the boy could remember—the battered stove, the broken beds and chairs, the clock inlaid with mother-of-pearl, which would not run, stopped at some fourteen minutes past two o'clock of a dead and forgotten day and time, which had been his mother's dowry. She was crying, though when she saw him she drew her sleeve across her face and began to descend from the wagon. "Get back," the father said.

"He's hurt. I got to get some water and wash his . . ."

"Get back in the wagon," his father said. He got in too, over the tail-gate. His father mounted to the seat where the older brother already sat and struck the gaunt mules two savage blows with the peeled willow, but without heat. It was not even sadistic; it was exactly that same quality which in later years would cause his descendants to over-run the engine before putting a motor car into motion, striking and reining back in the same movement. The wagon went on, the store with its quiet crowd of grimly watching men dropped behind; a curve in the road hid it. *Forever* he thought. *Maybe he's done satisfied now, now that he has . . .* stopping himself, not to say it aloud even to himself. His mother's hand touched his shoulder.

"Does hit hurt?" she said.

"Naw," he said. "Hit don't hurt. Lemme be."

"Can't you wipe some of the blood off before hit dries?"

"I'll wash to-night," he said. "Lemme be, I tell you."

The wagon went on. He did not know where they were going. None of them ever did or ever asked, because it was always somewhere, always a house of sorts waiting for them a day or two days or even three days away. Likely his father had already arranged to make a crop on another farm before he . . . Again he had to stop himself. He (the father) always did. There was something about his wolflike independence and even courage when the advantage was at least neutral which impressed strangers, as if they got from his latent ravening ferocity not so much a sense of dependability as a feeling that his ferocious conviction in the rightness of his own actions would be of advantage to all whose interest lay with his.

That night they camped, in a grove of oaks and beeches where a spring ran. The nights were still cool and they had a fire against it, of a rail lifted from a nearby fence and cut into lengths—a small fire, neat, niggard almost, a shrewd fire; such fires were his father's habit and custom always, even in freezing weather. Older, the boy might have remarked this and wondered why not a big one; why should not a man who had not only seen the waste and extravagance of war, but who had in his blood an inherent voracious prodigality with material not his own, have burned everything in sight? Then he might have gone a step farther and thought that that was the reason: that niggard blaze was the living fruit of nights passed during those four years in the woods hiding from all men, blue or gray, with his strings of horses (captured horses, he called them). And older still, he might have divined the true reason: that the element of fire spoke to some deep mainspring of his father's being, as the element of steel or of powder spoke to other men, as the one weapon for the preservation of integrity, else breath were not worth the breathing, and hence to be regarded with respect and used with discretion.

But he did not think this now and he had seen those same niggard blazes all his life. He merely ate his supper beside it and was already half asleep over his iron plate when his father called him, and once more he followed the stiff back, the stiff and ruthless limp, up the slope and on to the starlit road where, turning, he could see his father against the stars but without face or depth—a shape black, flat, and bloodless as though cut from tin in the iron folds of the frockcoat which had not been made for him, the voice harsh like tin and without heat like tin:

"You were fixing to tell them. You would have told him." He didn't answer. His father struck him with the flat of his hand on the side of the head, hard but without heat, exactly as he had struck the two mules at the store, exactly as he would strike either of them with any stick in order to kill a horse fly, his voice still without heat or anger: "You're getting to be a man. You got to learn. You got to learn to stick to your own blood or you ain't going to have any blood to stick to you. Do you think either of them, any man there this morning, would? Don't you know all they wanted was a chance to get at me because they knew I had them beat? Eh?" Later, twenty years later, he was to tell himself, "If I had said they wanted only truth, justice, he would have hit me again." But now he said nothing. He was not crying. He just stood there. "Answer me," his father said.

"Yes," he whispered. His father turned.

"Get on to bed. We'll be there to-morrow."

To-morrow they were there. In the early afternoon the wagon stopped before a paintless two-room house identical almost with the dozen others it had stopped before even in the boy's ten years, and again, as on the other dozen occasions, his mother and aunt got down and began to unload the wagon, although his two sisters and his father and brother had not moved.

"Likely hit ain't fitten for hawgs," one of the sisters said.

"Nevertheless, fit it will and you'll hog it and like it," his father said. "Get out of them chairs and help your Ma unload."

The two sisters got down, big, bovine, in a flutter of cheap ribbons; one of them drew from the jumbled wagon bed a battered lantern, the other a worn broom. His father handed the reins to the older son and began to climb stiffly over the wheel. "When they get unloaded, take the team to the barn and feed them." Then he said, and at first the boy thought he was still speaking to his brother: "Come with me."

"Me?" he said.

"Yes," his father said. "You."

"Abner," his mother said. His father paused and looked back—the harsh level stare beneath the shaggy, graying, irascible brows.

"I reckon I'll have a word with the man that aims to begin tomorrow owning me body and soul for the next eight months."

They went back up the road. A week ago—or before last night, that is—he would have asked where they were going, but not now. His father had struck him before last night but never before had he paused afterward to explain why; it was as if the blow and the following calm, outrageous voice still rang, repercussed, divulging nothing to him save the terrible handicap of being young, the light weight of his few years, just heavy enough to prevent his soaring free of the world as it seemed to be ordered but not heavy enough to keep him footed solid in it, to resist it and try to change the course of its events.

Presently he could see the grove of oaks and cedars and the other flowering trees and shrubs where the house would be, though not the house yet. They walked beside a fence massed with honeysuckle and Cherokee roses and came to a gate swinging open between two brick pillars, and now, beyond a sweep of drive, he saw the house for the first time and at that instant he forgot his father and the terror and despair both, and even when he remembered his father again (who had not stopped) the terror and despair did not return. Because, for all the twelve movings, they had sojourned until now in a poor country, a land of small farms and fields and houses, and he had never seen a house like this before. *Hit's big as a courthouse* he thought quietly, with a surge of peace and joy whose reason he could not have thought into words, being too young for that: *They are safe from him. People whose lives are a part of this peace and dignity are beyond his touch, he no more to them than a buzzing wasp: capable of stinging for a little moment but that's all; the spell of this peace and dignity rendering even the barns and stable and cribs which belong to it impervious to the puny flames he might contrive . . .* this, the peace and joy, ebbing for an instant as he looked again at the stiff black back, the stiff and implacable limp of the figure which was not dwarfed by the house, for the reason that it had never looked big anywhere and which now, against the serene columned backdrop, had more than ever that impervious quality of something cut ruthlessly from tin, depthless, as though, sidewise to the sun, it would cast no shadow. Watching him, the boy remarked the absolutely undeviating course which his father held and saw the stiff foot come squarely down in a pile of fresh droppings where a horse had stood in the drive and which his father could have avoided by a simple change of stride. But it ebbed only for a moment, though he could not have thought this into words either, walking on in the spell of the house, which he could even want but without envy, without sorrow, certainly never with that ravening and jealous rage which unknown to him walked in the ironlike black coat before him: *Maybe he will feel it too. Maybe it will even change him now from what maybe he couldn't help but be.*

They crossed the portico. Now he could hear his father's stiff foot as it came down on the boards with clocklike finality, a sound out of all proportion to the displacement of the body it bore and which was not dwarfed either by the white door before it, as though it had attained to a sort of vicious and ravening minimum not to be dwarfed by anything—the flat, wide, black hat, the formal coat of broadcloth which had once been black but which had now that friction-glazed greenish cast of the bodies of old house flies, the lifted sleeve which was too large, the lifted hand like a curled claw. The door opened so promptly that the boy knew the Negro must have been watching them all the time, an old man with neat grizzled hair, in a linen jacket, who stood barring the door with his body, saying, "Wipe yo foots, white man, fo you come in here. Major ain't home nohow."

"Get out of my way, nigger," his father said, without heat too, flinging the door back and the Negro also and entering, his hat still on his head. And now the boy saw the prints of the stiff foot on the doorjamb and saw them appear on the pale rug behind the machinelike deliberation of the foot which seemed to bear (or transmit) twice the weight which the body compassed. The Negro was shouting "Miss Lula! Miss Lula!" somewhere behind them, then the boy, deluged as though by a warm wave by a suave turn of carpeted stair and a pendant glitter of chandeliers and a mute gleam of gold frames, heard the swift feet and saw her too, a lady—perhaps he had never seen her like before either—in a gray, smooth gown with lace at the throat and an apron tied at the waist and the sleeves turned back, wiping cake or biscuit dough from her hands with a towel as she came up the hall, looking not at his father at all but at the tracks on the blond rug with an expression of incredulous amazement.

"I tried," the Negro cried. "I tole him to . . ."

"Will you please go away?" she said in a shaking voice. "Major de Spain is not at home. Will you please go away?"

His father had not spoken again. He did not speak again. He did not even look at her. He just stood stiff in the center of the rug, in his hat, the shaggy iron-gray brows twitching slightly above the pebble-colored eyes as he appeared to examine the house with brief deliberation. Then with the same deliberation he turned; the boy watched him pivot on the good leg and saw the stiff foot drag round the arc of the turning, leaving a final long and fading smear. His father never looked at it, he never once looked down at the rug. The Negro held the door. It closed behind them, upon the hysteric and indistinguishable woman-wail. His father stopped at the top of the steps and scraped his boot clean on the edge of it. At the gate he stopped again. He stood for a moment, planted stiffly on the stiff foot, looking back at the house. "Pretty and white, ain't it?" he said. "That's sweat. Nigger sweat. Maybe it ain't white enough yet to suit him. Maybe he wants to mix some white sweat with it."

Two hours later the boy was chopping wood behind the house within which his mother and aunt and the two sisters (the mother and aunt, not the two girls, he knew that; even at this distance and muffled by walls the flat loud voices of the two girls emanated an incorrigible idle inertia) were setting up the stove to prepare a meal, when he heard the hooves and saw the linen-clad man on a fine sorrel mare, whom he recognized even before he saw the rolled rug in front of the Negro youth following on a fat bay carriage horse—a suffused, angry face vanishing, still at full gallop, beyond the corner of the house where his father and brother were sitting in the two tilted chairs; and a moment later, almost before he could have put the axe down, he heard the hooves again and watched the sorrel mare go back out of the yard, already galloping again. Then his father began to shout one of the sisters' names, who presently emerged backward from the kitchen door dragging the rolled rug along the ground by one end while the other sister walked behind it.

"If you ain't going to tote, go on and set up the wash pot," the first said.

"You, Sarty!" the second shouted. "Set up the wash pot!" His father appeared at the door, framed against that shabbiness, as he had been against that other bland perfection, impervious to either, the mother's anxious face at his shoulder.

"Go on," the father said. "Pick it up." The two sisters stooped, broad, lethargic; stooping, they presented an incredible expanse of pale cloth and a flutter of tawdry ribbons.

"If I thought enough of a rug to have to git hit all the way from France I wouldn't keep hit where folks coming in would have to tromp on hit," the first said. They raised the rug.

"Abner," the mother said. "Let me do it."

"You go back and git dinner," his father said. "I'll tend to this."

From the woodpile through the rest of the afternoon the boy watched them, the rug spread flat in the dust beside the bubbling wash-pot, the two sisters stooping over it with that profound and lethargic reluctance, while the father stood over them in turn, implacable and grim, driving them though never raising his voice again. He could smell the harsh homemade lye they were using; he saw his mother come to the door once and look toward them with an expression not anxious now but very like despair; he saw his father turn, and he fell to with the axe and saw from the corner of his eye his father raise from the ground a flattish fragment of field stone and examine it and return to the pot, and this time his mother actually spoke: "Abner. Abner. Please don't. Please, Abner."

Then he was done too. It was dusk; the whippoorwills had already begun. He could smell coffee from the room where they would presently eat the cold food remaining from the mid-afternoon meal, though when he entered the house he realized they were having coffee again probably because there was a fire on the hearth, before which the rug now lay spread over the backs of the two chairs. The tracks of his father's foot were gone. Where they had been were now long, water-cloudy scoriations resembling the sporadic course of a lilliputian mowing machine.

It still hung there while they ate the cold food and then went to bed, scattered without order or claim up and down the two rooms, his mother in one bed, where his father would later lie, the older brother in the other, himself, the aunt, and the two sisters on pallets on the floor. But his father was not in bed yet. The last thing the boy remembered was the depthless, harsh silhouette of the hat and coat bending over the rug and it seemed to him that he had not even closed his eyes when the silhouette was standing over him, the fire almost dead behind it, the stiff foot prodding him awake. "Catch up the mule," his father said.

When he returned with the mule his father was standing in the black door, the rolled rug over his shoulder. "Ain't you going to ride?" he said.

"No. Give me your foot."

He bent his knee into his father's hand, the wiry, surprising power flowed smoothly, rising, he rising with it, on to the mule's bare back (they had owned a saddle once; the boy could remember it though not when or where) and with the same effortlessness his father swung the rug up in front of him. Now in the starlight they retraced the afternoon's path, up the dusty road rife with honeysuckle, through the gate and up the black tunnel of the drive to the lightless house, where he sat on the mule and felt the rough warp of the rug drag across his thighs and vanish.

"Don't you want me to help?" he whispered. His father did not answer and now he heard again that stiff foot striking the hollow portico with that wooden and clocklike deliberation, that outrageous overstatement of the weight it carried. The rug, hunched, not flung (the boy could tell that even in the darkness) from his father's shoulder struck the angle of wall and floor with a sound unbelievably loud, thunderous, then the foot again, unhurried and enormous; a light came on in the house and the boy sat, tense, breathing steadily and quietly and just a little fast, though the foot itself did not increase its beat at all, descending the steps now; now the boy could see him.

"Don't you want to ride now?" he whispered. "We kin both ride now," the light within the house altering now, flaring up and sinking. *He's coming down the stairs now,* he thought. He had already ridden the mule up beside the horse block; presently his father was up behind him and he doubled the reins over and slashed the mule across the neck, but before the animal could begin to trot the hard, thin arm came round him, the hard, knotted hand jerking the mule back to a walk.

In the first red rays of the sun they were in the lot, putting plow gear on the mules. This time the sorrel mare was in the lot before he heard it at all, the rider collarless and even bareheaded, trembling, speaking in a shaking voice as the woman in the house had done. His father merely looking up once before stooping again to the hame he was buckling, so that the man on the mare spoke to his stooping back:

"You must realize you have ruined that rug. Wasn't there anybody here, any of your women . . ." he ceased, shaking, the boy watching him, the older brother leaning now in the stable door, chewing, blinking slowly and steadily at nothing apparently. "It cost a hundred dollars. But you never had a hundred dollars. You never will. So I'm going to charge you twenty bushels of corn against your crop. I'll add it in your contract and when you come to the commissary you can sign it. That won't keep Mrs. de Spain quiet but maybe it will teach you to wipe your feet off before you enter her house again."

Then he was gone. The boy looked at his father, who still had not spoken or even looked up again, who was now adjusting the logger-head in the hame.

"Pap," he said. His father looked at him—the inscrutable face, the shaggy brows beneath which the gray eyes glinted coldly. Suddenly the boy went toward him, fast, stopping as suddenly. "You done the best you could!" he cried. "If he wanted hit done different why didn't he wait and tell you how? He won't git no twenty bushels! He won't git none! We'll gether hit and hide hit! I kin watch . . ."

"Did you put the cutter back in that straight stock like I told you?"

"No, sir," he said.

"Then go do it."

That was Wednesday. During the rest of that week he worked steadily, at what was within his scope and some which was beyond it, with an industry that did not need to be driven nor even commanded twice; he had this from his mother, with the difference that some at least of what he did he liked to do, such as splitting wood with the half-size axe which his mother and aunt had earned, or saved money somehow, to present him with at Christmas. In company with the two older women (and on one afternoon, even one of the sisters), he built pens for the shoat and the cow which were a part of his father's contract with the landlord, and one afternoon, his father being absent, gone somewhere on one of the mules, he went to the field.

They were running a middle buster now, his brother holding the plow straight while he handled the reins, and walking beside the straining mule, the rich black soil shearing cool and damp against his bare ankles, he thought *Maybe this is the end of it. Maybe even that twenty bushels that seems hard to have to pay for just a rug will be a cheap price for him to stop forever and always from being what he used to be;* thinking, dreaming now, so that his brother had to speak sharply to him to mind the mule: *Maybe he even won't collect the twenty bushels. Maybe it will all add up and balance and vanish—corn, rug, fire; the terror and grief, the being pulled two ways like between two teams of horses—gone, done with for ever and ever.*

Then it was Saturday; he looked up from beneath the mule he was harnessing and saw his father in the black coat and hat. "Not that," his father said. "The wagon gear." And then, two hours later, sitting in the wagon bed behind his father and brother on the seat, the wagon accomplished a final curve, and he saw the weathered paintless store with its tattered tobacco- and patent-medicine posters and the tethered wagons and saddle animals below the gallery. He mounted the gnawed steps behind his father and brother, and there again was the lane of quiet, watching faces for the three of them to walk through. He saw the man in spectacles sitting at the plank table and he did not need to be told this was a Justice of the Peace; he sent one glare of fierce, exultant, partisan defiance at the man in collar and cravat now, whom he had seen but twice before in his life, and that on a galloping horse, who now wore on his face an expression not of rage but of amazed unbelief which the boy could not have known was at the incredible circumstance of being sued by one of his own tenants, and came and stood against his father and cried at the Justice: "He ain't done it! He ain't burnt . . ."

"Go back to the wagon," his father said.

"Burnt?" the Justice said. "Do I understand this rug was burned too?"

"Does anybody here claim it was?" his father said. "Go back to the wagon." But he did not, he merely retreated to the rear of the room, crowded as that other had been, but not to sit down this time, instead, to stand pressing among the motionless bodies, listening to the voices:

"And you claim twenty bushels of corn is too high for the damage you did to the rug?"

"He brought the rug to me and said he wanted the tracks washed out of it. I washed the tracks out and took the rug back to him."

"But you didn't carry the rug back to him in the same condition it was in before you made the tracks on it."

His father did not answer, and now for perhaps half a minute there was no sound at all save that of breathing, the faint, steady suspiration of complete and intent listening.

"You decline to answer that, Mr. Snopes?" Again his father did not answer. "I'm going to find against you, Mr. Snopes. I'm going to find that you were responsible for the injury to Major de Spain's rug and hold you liable for it. But twenty bushels of corn seems a little high for a man in your circumstances to have to pay. Major de Spain claims it cost a hundred dollars. October corn will be worth about fifty cents. I figure that if Major de Spain can stand a ninety-five dollar loss on something he paid cash for, you can stand a five-dollar loss you haven't earned yet. I hold you in damages to Major de Spain to the amount of ten bushels of corn over and above your contract with him, to be paid to him out of your crop at gathering time. Court adjourned."

It had taken no time hardly, the morning was but half begun. He thought they would return home and perhaps back to the field, since they were late, far behind all other farmers. But instead his father passed on behind the wagon, merely indicating with his hand for the older brother to follow with it, and crossed the road toward the blacksmith shop opposite, pressing on after his father, overtaking him, speaking, whispering up at the harsh, calm face beneath the weathered hat: "He won't git no ten bushels neither. He won't git one. We'll . . ." until his father glanced for an instant down at him, the face absolutely calm, the grizzled eyebrows tangled above the cold eyes, the voice almost pleasant, almost gentle:

"You think so? Well, we'll wait till October anyway."

The matter of the wagon—the setting of a spoke or two and the tightening of the tires—did not take long either, the business of the tires accomplished by driving the wagon into the spring branch behind the shop and letting it stand there, the mules nuzzling into the water from time to time, and the boy on the seat with the idle reins, looking up the slope and through the sooty tunnel of the shed where the slow hammer rang and where his father sat on an upended cypress bolt, easily, either talking or listening, still sitting there when the boy brought the dripping wagon up out of the branch and halted it before the door.

"Take them on to the shade and hitch," his father said. He did so and returned. His father and the smith and a third man squatting on his heels inside the door were talking, about crops and animals; the boy, squatting too in the ammoniac dust and hoof-parings and scales of rust, heard his father tell a long and unhurried story out of the time before the birth of the older brother even when he had been a professional horsetrader. And then his father came up beside him where he stood before a tattered last year's circus poster on the other side of the store, gazing rapt and quiet at the scarlet horses, the incredible poisings and convolutions of tulle and tights and the painted leers of comedians, and said, "It's time to eat."

But not at home. Squatting beside his brother against the front wall, he watched his father emerge from the store and produce from a paper sack a segment of cheese and divide it carefully and deliberately into three with his pocket knife and produce crackers from the same sack. They all three squatted on the gallery and ate, slowly, without talking; then in the store again, they drank from a tin dipper tepid water smelling of the cedar bucket and of living beech trees. And still they did not go home. It was a horse lot this time, a tall rail fence upon and along which men stood and sat and out of which one by one horses were led, to be walked and trotted and then cantered back and forth along the road while the slow swapping and buying went on and the sun began to slant westward, they—the three of them—watching and listening, the older brother with his muddy eyes and his steady, inevitable tobacco, the father commenting now and then on certain of the animals, to no one in particular.

It was after sundown when they reached home. They ate supper by lamplight, then, sitting on the doorstep, the boy watched the night fully accomplish, listening to the whippoorwills and the frogs, when he heard his mother's voice: "Abner! No! No! Oh, God. Oh, God. Abner!" and he rose, whirled, and saw the altered light through the door where a candle stub now burned in a bottle neck on the table and his father, still in the hat and coat, at once formal and burlesque as though dressed carefully for some shabby and ceremonial violence, emptying the reservoir of the lamp back into the five-gallon kerosene can from which it had been filled, while the mother tugged at his arm until he shifted the lamp to the other hand and flung her back, not savagely or viciously, just hard, into the wall, her hands flung out against the wall for balance, her mouth open and in her face the same quality of hopeless despair as had been in her voice. Then his father saw him standing in the door.

"Go to the barn and get that can of oil we were oiling the wagon with," he said. The boy did not move. Then he could speak.

"What . . ." he cried. "What are you . . ."

"Go get that oil," his father said. "Go."

Then he was moving, running, outside the house, toward the stable: this the old habit, the old blood which he had not been permitted to choose for himself, which had been bequeathed him willy nilly and which had run for so long (and who knew where, battening on what of outrage and savagery and lust) before it came to him. *I could keep on,* he thought. *I could run on and on and never look back, never need to see his face again. Only I can't. I can't,* the rusted can in his hand now, the liquid sploshing in it as he ran back to the house and into it, into the sound of his mother's weeping in the next room, and handed the can to his father.

"Ain't you going to even send a nigger?" he cried. "At least you sent a nigger before!"

This time his father didn't strike him. The hand came even faster than the blow had, the same hand which had set the can on the table with almost excruciating care flashing from the can toward him too quick for him to follow it, gripping him by the back of his shirt and on to tiptoe before he had seen it quit the can, the face stooping at him in breathless and frozen ferocity, the cold, dead voice speaking over him to the older brother who leaned against the table, chewing with that steady, curious, sidewise motion of cows:

"Empty the can into the big one and go on. I'll catch up with you."

"Better tie him up to the bedpost," the brother said.

"Do like I told you," the father said. Then the boy was moving, his bunched shirt and the hard, bony hand between his shoulder-blades, his toes just touching the floor, across the room and into the other one, past the sisters sitting with spread heavy thighs in the two chairs over the cold hearth, and to where his mother and aunt sat side by side on the bed, the aunt's arms about his mother's shoulders.

"Hold him," the father said. The aunt made a startled movement. "Not you," the father said. "Lennie. Take hold of him. I want to see you do it." His mother took him by the wrist. "You'll hold him better than that. If he gets loose don't you know what he is going to do? He will go up yonder." He jerked his head toward the road. "Maybe I'd better tie him."

"I'll hold him," his mother whispered.

"See you do then." Then his father was gone, the stiff foot heavy and measured upon the boards, ceasing at last.

Then he began to struggle. His mother caught him in both arms, he jerking and wrenching at them. He would be stronger in the end, he knew that. But he had no time to wait for it. "Lemme go!" he cried. "I don't want to have to hit you!"

"Let him go!" the aunt said. "If he don't go, before God, I am going up there myself!"

"Don't you see I can't?" his mother cried. "Sarty! Sarty! No! No! Help me, Lizzie!"

Then he was free. His aunt grasped at him but it was too late. He whirled, running, his mother stumbled forward on to her knees behind him, crying to the nearer sister: "Catch him, Net! Catch him!" But that was too late too, the sister (the sisters were twins, born at the same time, yet either of them now gave the impression of being, encompassing as much living meat and volume and weight as any other two of the family) not yet having begun to rise from the chair, her head, face, alone merely turned, presenting to him in the flying instant an astonishing expanse of young female features untroubled by any surprise even, wearing only an expression of bovine interest. Then he was out of the room, out of the house, in the mild dust of the starlit road and the heavy rifeness of honeysuckle, the pale ribbon unspooling with terrific slowness under his running feet, reaching the gate at last and turning in, running, his heart and lungs drumming, on up the drive toward the lighted house, the lighted door. He did not knock, he burst in, sobbing for breath, incapable for the moment of speech; he saw the astonished face of the Negro in the linen jacket without knowing when the Negro had appeared.

"De Spain!" he cried, panted. "Where's . . ." then he saw the white man too emerging from a white door down the hall. "Barn!" he cried. "Barn!"

"What?" the white man said. "Barn?"

"Yes!" the boy cried. "Barn!"

"Catch him!" the white man shouted.

But it was too late this time too. The Negro grasped his shirt, but the entire sleeve, rotten with washing, carried away, and he was out that door too and in the drive again, and had actually never ceased to run even while he was screaming into the white man's face.

Behind him the white man was shouting, "My horse! Fetch my horse!" and he thought for an instant of cutting across the park and climbing the fence into the road, but he did not know the park nor how high the vine-massed fence might be and he dared not risk it. So he ran on down the drive, blood and breath roaring; presently he was in the road again though he could not see it. He could not hear either: the galloping mare was almost upon him before he heard her, and even then he held his course, as if the very urgency of his wild grief and need must in a moment more find him wings, waiting until the ultimate instant to hurl himself aside and into the weed-choked roadside ditch as the horse thundered past and on, for an instant in furious silhouette against the stars, the tranquil early summer night sky which, even before the shape of the horse and rider vanished, stained abruptly and violently upward: a long, swirling roar incredible and soundless, blotting the stars, and he springing up and into the road again, running again, knowing it was too late yet still running even after he heard the shot and, an instant later, two shots, pausing now without knowing he had ceased to run, crying "Pap! Pap!", running again before he knew he had begun to run, stumbling, tripping over something and scrabbling up again without ceasing to run, looking backward over his shoulder at the glare as he got up, running on among the invisible trees, panting, sobbing, "Father! Father!"

At midnight he was sitting on the crest of a hill. He did not know it was midnight and he did not know how far he had come. But there was no glare behind him now and he sat now, his back toward what he had called home for four days anyhow, his face toward the dark woods which he would enter when breath was strong again, small, shaking steadily in the chill darkness, hugging himself into the remainder of his thin, rotten shirt, the grief and despair now no longer terror and fear but just grief and despair. *Father. My father,* he thought. "He was brave!" He cried suddenly, aloud but not loud, no more than a whisper: "He was! He was in the war! He was in Colonel Sartoris' cav'ry!" not knowing that his father had gone to that war a private in the fine old European sense, wearing no uniform, admitting the authority of and giving fidelity to no man or army or flag, going to war as Malbrouck himself did: for booty—it meant nothing and less than nothing to him if it were enemy booty or his own.

The slow constellations wheeled on. It would be dawn and then sun-up after a while and he would be hungry. But that would be to-morrow and now he was only cold, and walking would cure that. His breathing was easier now and he decided to get up and go on, and then he found that he had been asleep because he knew it was almost dawn, the night almost over. He could tell that from the whippoorwills. They were everywhere now among the dark trees below him, constant and inflectioned and ceaseless, so that, as the instant for giving over to the day birds drew nearer and nearer, there was no interval at all between them. He got up. He was a little stiff, but walking would cure that too as it would the cold, and soon there would be the sun. He went on down the hill, toward the dark woods within which the liquid silver voices of the birds called unceasing—the rapid and urgent beating of the urgent and quiring heart of the late spring night. He did not look back.

1939

The Secret Miracle

JORGE LUIS BORGES

[b. 1899]

> *And God had him die for a hundred years and then revived him and said:*
> *"How long have you been here?"*
> *"A day or a part of a day," he answered.*
>
> KORAN, II, 261

The night of March 14, 1943, in an apartment in the Zeltnergasse of Prague, Jaromir Hladik, the author of the unfinished drama entitled *The Enemies,* of *Vindication of Eternity,* and of a study of the indirect Jewish sources of Jakob Böhme, had a dream of a long game of chess. The players were not two persons, but two illustrious families; the game had been going on for centuries. Nobody could remember what the stakes were, but it was rumored that they were enormous, perhaps infinite; the chessmen and the board were in a secret tower. Jaromir (in his dream) was the first-born of one of the contending families. The clock struck the hour for the game, which could not be postponed. The dreamer raced over the sands of a rainy desert, and was unable to recall either the pieces or the rules of chess. At that moment he awoke. The clangor of the rain and of the terrible clocks ceased. A rhythmic, unanimous noise, punctuated by shouts of command, arose from the Zeltnergasse. It was dawn, and the armored vanguard of the Third Reich was entering Prague.

On the nineteenth the authorities received a denunciation; that same nineteenth, toward evening, Jaromir Hladik was arrested. He was taken to an aseptic, white barracks on the opposite bank of the

Moldau. He was unable to refute a single one of the Gestapo's charges; his mother's family name was Jaroslavski, he was of Jewish blood, his study on Böhme had a marked Jewish emphasis, his signature had been one more on the protest against the *Anschluss.* In 1928 he had translated the *Sepher Yezirah* for the publishing house of Hermann Barsdorf. The fulsome catalogue of the firm had exaggerated, for publicity purposes, the translator's reputation, and the catalogue had been examined by Julius Rothe, one of the officials who held Hladik's fate in his hands. There is not a person who, except in the field of his own specialization, is not credulous; two or three adjectives in Gothic type were enough to persuade Julius Rothe of Hladik's importance, and he ordered him sentenced to death *pour encourager les autres.* The execution was set for March 29th, at 9:00 A.M. This delay (whose importance the reader will grasp later) was owing to the desire on the authorities' part to proceed impersonally and slowly, after the manner of vegetables and plants.

Hladik's first reaction was mere terror. He felt he would not have shrunk from the gallows, the block, or the knife, but that death by a firing squad was unbearable. In vain he tried to convince himself that the plain, unvarnished fact of dying was the fearsome thing, not the attendant circumstances. He never wearied of conjuring up these circumstances, senselessly trying to exhaust all their possible variations. He infinitely anticipated the process of his dying, from the sleepless dawn to the mysterious volley. Before the day set by Julius Rothe he died hundreds of deaths in courtyards whose forms and angles strained geometrical probabilities, machine-gunned by variable soldiers in changing numbers, who at times killed him from a distance, at others from close by. He faced these imaginary executions with real terror (perhaps with real bravery); each simulacrum lasted a few seconds. When the circle was closed, Jaromir returned once more and interminably to the tremulous vespers of his death. Then he reflected that reality does not usually coincide with our anticipation of it; with a logic of his own he inferred that to foresee a circumstantial detail is to prevent its happening. Trusting in this weak magic, he invented, *so that they would not happen,* the most gruesome details. Finally, as was natural, he came to fear that they were prophetic. Miserable in the night, he endeavored to find some way to hold fast to the fleeting substance of time. He knew that it was rushing headlong toward the dawn of the twenty-ninth. He reasoned aloud: "I am now in the night of the twenty-second; while this night lasts (and for six nights more), I am invulnerable, immortal." The nights of sleep seemed to him deep, dark pools in which he could submerge himself. There were moments when he longed impatiently for the final burst of fire that would free him, for better or for worse, from the vain compulsion of his imaginings. On the twenty-eighth, as the last sunset was reverberating from the high barred windows, the thought of his drama, *The Enemies,* deflected him from these abject considerations.

Hladik had rounded forty. Aside from a few friendships and many habits, the problematic exercise of literature constituted his life. Like all writers, he measured the achievements of others by what they had accomplished, asking of them that they measure him by what he envisaged or planned. All the books he had published had left him with a complex feeling of repentance. His studies of the work of Böhme, of Ibn Ezra, and of Fludd had been characterized essentially by mere application; his translation of the *Sepher Yezirah,* by carelessness, fatigue, and conjecture. *Vindication of Eternity* perhaps had fewer shortcomings. The first volume gave a history of man's various concepts of eternity, from the immutable Being of Parmenides to the modifiable Past of Hinton. The second denied (with Francis Bradley) that all the events of the universe make up a temporal series, arguing that the number of man's possible experiences is not infinite, and that a single "repetition" suffices to prove that time is a fallacy . . . Unfortunately, the arguments that demonstrate this fallacy are equally fallacious. Hladik was in the habit of going over them with a kind of contemptuous perplexity. He had also composed a series of Expressionist poems; to the poet's chagrin they had been included in an anthology published in 1924, and no subsequent anthology but inherited them. From all this equivocal, uninspired past Hladik had hoped to redeem himself with his drama in verse, *The Enemies.* (Hladik felt the verse form to be essential because it makes it impossible for the spectators to lose sight of irreality, one of art's requisites.)

The drama observed the unities of time, place, and action. The scene was laid in Hradcany, in the library of Baron von Roemerstadt, on one of the last afternoons of the nineteenth century. In the first scene of the first act a strange man visits Roemerstadt. (A clock was striking seven, the vehemence of the setting sun's rays glorified the windows, a passionate, familiar Hungarian music floated in the air.) This visit is followed by others; Roemerstadt does not know the people who are importuning him, but he has the uncomfortable feeling that he has seen them somewhere, perhaps in a dream. They all fawn upon him, but it is apparent—first to the audience and then to the Baron—that they are secret enemies, in league to ruin him. Roemerstadt succeeds in checking or evading their involved schemings. In the dialogue mention is made of his sweetheart, Julia von Weidenau, and a certain Jaroslav Kubin, who at one time pressed his attentions on her. Kubin has now lost his mind, and believes himself to be Roemerstadt. The dangers increase; Roemerstadt, at the end of the second act, is forced to kill one of the conspirators. The third and final act opens. The incoherencies gradually increase; actors who had seemed out of the play reappear; the man Roemerstadt killed returns for a moment. Someone points out that evening has not fallen; the clock strikes seven, the high windows reverberate in the western sun, the air carries an impassioned Hungarian melody. The first actor comes on and repeats the lines he had spoken in the first scene of the first act. Roemerstadt speaks to him without surprise; the audience understands that Roemerstadt is the miserable Jaroslav Kubin. The drama has never taken place; it is the circular delirium that Kubin lives and relives endlessly.

Hladik had never asked himself whether this tragicomedy of errors was preposterous or admirable, well thought out or slipshod. He felt that the plot I have just sketched was best contrived to cover up his defects and point up his abilities and held the possibility of allowing him to redeem (symbolically) the meaning of his life. He had finished the first act and one or two scenes of the third; the metrical nature of the work made it possible for him to keep working it over, changing the hexameters, without the manuscript in front of him. He thought how he still had two acts to do, and that he was going to die very soon. He spoke with God in the darkness: "If in some fashion I exist, if I am not one of Your repetitions and mistakes, I exist as the author of *The Enemies.* To finish this drama, which can justify me and justify You, I need another year. Grant me these days, You to whom the centuries and time belong." This was the last night, the most dreadful of all, but ten minutes later sleep flooded over him like a dark water.

Toward dawn he dreamed that he had concealed himself in one of the naves of the Clementine Library. A librarian wearing dark glasses asked him: "What are you looking for?" Hladik answered: "I am looking for God." The librarian said to him: "God is in one of the letters on one of the pages of one of the four hundred thousand volumes of the Clementine. My fathers and the fathers of my fathers have searched for this letter; I have grown blind seeking it." He removed his glasses, and Hladik saw his eyes, which were dead. A reader came in to return an atlas. "This atlas is worthless," he said, and handed it to Hladik, who opened it at random. He saw a map of India as in a daze. Suddenly sure of himself, he touched one of the tiniest letters. A ubiquitous voice said to him: "The time of your labor has been granted." At this point Hladik awoke.

He remembered that men's dreams belong to God, and that Maimonides had written that the words heard in a dream are divine when they are distinct and clear and the person uttering them cannot be seen. He dressed: two soldiers came into the cell and ordered him to follow them.

From behind the door, Hladik had envisaged a labyrinth of passageways, stairs, and separate buildings. The reality was less spectacular: they descended to an inner court by a narrow iron stairway. Several soldiers—some with uniform unbuttoned—were examining a motorcycle and discussing it. The sergeant looked at the clock; it was 8:44. They had to wait until it struck nine. Hladik, more insignificant than pitiable, sat down on a pile of wood. He noticed that the soldiers' eyes avoided his. To ease his wait, the sergeant handed him a cigarette. Hladik did not smoke; he accepted it out of politeness or humility. As he lighted it, he noticed that his hands were shaking. The day was clouding over; the soldiers spoke in a low voice as though he were already dead. Vainly he tried to recall the woman of whom Julia von Weidenau was the symbol.

The squad formed and stood at attention. Hladik, standing against the barracks wall, waited for the volley. Someone pointed out that the wall was going to be stained with blood; the victim was ordered to step forward a few paces. Incongruously, this reminded Hladik of the fumbling preparations of photographers. A big drop of rain struck one of Hladik's temples and rolled slowly down his cheek; the sergeant shouted the final order.

The physical universe came to a halt.

The guns converged on Hladik, but the men who were to kill him stood motionless. The sergeant's arm eternized an unfinished gesture. On a paving stone of the courtyard a bee cast an unchanging shadow. The wind had ceased, as in a picture. Hladik attempted a cry, a word, a movement of the hand. He realized that he was paralyzed. Not a sound reached him from the halted world. He thought: "I am in hell, I am dead." He thought: "I am mad." He thought: "Time has stopped." Then he reflected that if that was the case, his mind would have stopped too. He wanted to test this; he repeated (without moving his lips) Vergil's mysterious fourth Eclogue. He imagined that the now remote soldiers must be sharing his anxiety; he longed to be able to communicate with them. It astonished him not to feel the least fatigue, not even the numbness of his protracted immobility. After an indeterminate time he fell asleep. When he awoke the world continued motionless and mute. The drop of water still clung to his cheek, the shadow of the bee to the stone. The smoke from the cigarette he had thrown away had not dispersed. Another "day" went by before Hladik understood.

He had asked God for a whole year to finish his work; His omnipotence had granted it. God had worked a secret miracle for him; German lead would kill him at the set hour, but in his mind a year would go by between the order and its execution. From perplexity he passed to stupor, from stupor to resignation, from resignation to sudden gratitude.

He had no document but his memory; the training he had acquired with each added hexameter gave him a discipline unsuspected by those who set down and forget temporary, incomplete paragraphs. He was not working for posterity or even for God, whose literary tastes were unknown to him. Meticulously, motionlessly, secretly, he wrought in time his lofty, invisible labyrinth. He worked the third act over twice. He eliminated certain symbols as over-obvious, such as the repeated striking of the clock, the music. Nothing hurried him. He omitted, he condensed, he amplified. In certain instances he came back to the original version. He came to feel an affection for the courtyard, the barracks; one of the faces before him modified his conception of Roemerstadt's character. He discovered that the wearying cacophonies that bothered Flaubert so much are mere visual superstitions, weakness and limitation of the written word, not the spoken . . . He concluded his drama. He had only the problem of a single phrase. He found it. The drop of water slid down his cheek. He opened his mouth in a maddened cry, moved his face, dropped under the quadruple blast.

Jaromir Hladik died on March 29, at 9:02 A.M.

1943

The Snows of Kilimanjaro

ERNEST HEMINGWAY

[1899–1961]

Kilimanjaro is a snow covered mountain 19,710 feet high, and is said to be the highest mountain in Africa. Its western summit is called the Masai "Ngàje Ngài," the House of God. Close to the western summit there is the dried and frozen carcass of a leopard. No one has explained what the leopard was seeking at that altitude.

"The marvellous thing is that it's painless," he said. "That's how you know when it starts."

"Is it really?"

"Absolutely. I'm awfully sorry about the odor though. That must bother you."

"Don't! Please don't."

"Look at them," he said. "Now is it sight or is it scent that brings them like that?"

The cot the man lay on was in the wide shade of a mimosa tree and as he looked out past the shade onto the glare of the plain there were three of the big birds squatted obscenely, while in the sky a dozen more sailed, making quick-moving shadows as they passed.

"They've been there since the day the truck broke down," he said. "Today's the first time any have lit on the ground. I watched the way they sailed very carefully at first in case I ever wanted to use them in a story. That's funny now."

"I wish you wouldn't," she said.

"I'm only talking," he said. "It's much easier if I talk. But I don't want to bother you."

"You know it doesn't bother me," she said. "It's that I've gotten so very nervous not being able to do anything. I think we might make it as easy as we can until the plane comes."

"Or until the plane doesn't come."

"Please tell me what I can do. There must be something I can do."

"You can take the leg off and that might stop it, though I doubt it. Or you can shoot me. You're a good shot now. I taught you to shoot didn't I?"

"Please don't talk that way. Couldn't I read to you?"

"Read what?"

"Anything in the book bag that we haven't read."

"I can't listen to it," he said. "Talking is the easiest. We quarrel and that makes the time pass."

"I don't quarrel. I never want to quarrel. Let's not quarrel any more. No matter how nervous we get. Maybe they will be back with another truck today. Maybe the plane will come."

"I don't want to move," the man said. "There is no sense in moving now except to make it easier for you."

"That's cowardly."

"Can't you let a man die as comfortably as he can without calling him names? What's the use of slanging me?"

"You're not going to die."

"Don't be silly. I'm dying now. Ask those bastards." He looked over to where the huge, filthy birds sat, their naked heads sunk in the hunched feathers. A fourth planed down, to run quick-legged and then waddle slowly toward the others.

"They are around every camp. You never notice them. You can't die if you don't give up."

"Where did you read that? You're such a bloody fool."

"You might think about some one else."

"For Christ's sake," he said, "That's been my trade."

He lay then and was quiet for a while and looked across the heat shimmer of the plain to the edge of the bush. There were a few Tommies that showed minute and white against the yellow and, far off, he saw a herd of zebra, white against the green of the bush. This was a pleasant camp under big trees against a hill, with good water, and close by, a nearly dry water hole where sand grouse flighted in the mornings.

"Wouldn't you like me to read?" she asked. She was sitting on a canvas chair beside his cot. "There's a breeze coming up."

"No thanks."

"Maybe the truck will come."

"I don't give a damn about the truck."

"I do."

"You give a damn about so many things that I don't."

"Not so many, Harry."

"What about a drink?"

"It's supposed to be bad for you. It said in Black's to avoid all alcohol. You shouldn't drink."

"Molo!" he shouted.

"Yes Bwana."

"Bring whiskey-soda."

"Yes Bwana."

"You shouldn't," she said. "That's what I mean by giving up. It says it's bad for you. I know it's bad for you."

"No," he said. "It's good for me."

So now it was all over, he thought. So now he would never have a chance to finish it. So this was the way it ended in a bickering over a drink. Since the gangrene started in his right leg he had no pain and with the pain the horror had gone and all he felt now was a great tiredness and anger that this was the end of it. For this, that now was coming, he had very little curiosity. For years it had obsessed him; but now it meant nothing in itself. It was strange how easy being tired enough made it.

Now he would never write the things that he had saved to write until he knew enough to write them well. Well, he would not have to fail at trying to write them either. Maybe you could never write them, and that was why you put them off and delayed the starting. Well he would never know, now.

"I wish we'd never come," the woman said. She was looking at him holding the glass and biting her lip. "You never would have gotten anything like this in Paris. You always said you loved Paris. We could have stayed in Paris or gone anywhere. I'd have gone anywhere. I said I'd go anywhere you wanted. If you wanted to shoot we could have gone shooting in Hungary and been comfortable."

"Your bloody money," he said.

"That's not fair," she said. "It was always yours as much as mine. I left everything and I went wherever you wanted to go and I've done what you wanted to do. But I wish we'd never come here."

"You said you loved it."

"I did when you were all right. But now I hate it. I don't see why that had to happen to your leg. What have we done to have that happen to us?"

"I suppose what I did was to forget to put iodine on it when I first scratched it. Then I didn't pay any attention to it because I never infect. Then, later, when it got bad, it was probably using that weak carbolic solution when the other antiseptics ran out that paralyzed the minute blood vessels and started the gangrene." He looked at her, "What else?"

"I don't mean that."

"If we would have hired a good mechanic instead of a half baked kikuyu driver, he would have checked the oil and never burned out that bearing in the truck."

"I don't mean that."

"If you hadn't left your own people, your goddamned Old Westbury, Saratoga, Palm Beach people to take me on—"

"Why, I loved you. That's not fair. I love you now. I'll always love you. Don't you love me?"

"No," said the man. "I don't think so. I never have."

"Harry, what are you saying? You're out of your head."

"No. I haven't any head to go out of."

"Don't drink that," she said. "Darling, please don't drink that. We have to do everything we can."

"You do it," he said. "I'm tired."

Now in his mind he saw a railway station at Karagatch and he was standing with his pack and that was the headlight of the Simplon-Orient cutting the dark now and he was leaving Thrace then after the retreat. That was one of the things he had saved to write, with, in the morning at breakfast, looking out the window and seeing snow on the mountains in Bulgaria and Nansen's Secretary asking the old man if it were snow and the old man looking at it and saying, No, that's not snow. It's too early for snow. And the Secretary repeating to the other girls, No, you see. It's not snow and them all saying, It's not snow we were mistaken. But it was the snow all right and he sent them on into it when he evolved exchange of populations. And it was snow they tramped along in until they died that winter.

It was snow too that fell all Christmas week that year up in the Gauertal, that year they lived in the woodcutter's house with the big square porcelain stove that filled half the room, and they slept on mattresses filled with beech leaves, the time the deserter came with his feet bloody in the snow. He said the police were right behind him and they gave him woolen socks and held the gendarmes talking until the tracks had drifted over.

In Schrunz, on Christmas day, the snow was so bright it hurt your eyes when you looked out from the weinstube and saw every one coming home from church. That was where they walked up the sleigh-smoothed urine-yellowed road along the river with the steep pine hills, skis heavy on the shoulder, and where they ran that great run down the glacier above the Madlener-haus, the snow as smooth to see as cake frosting and as light as powder and he remembered the noiseless rush the speed made as you dropped down like a bird.

They were snow-bound a week in the Madlener-haus that time in the blizzard playing cards in the smoke by the lantern light and the stakes were higher all the time as Herr Lent lost more. Finally he lost it all. Everything, the skischule money and all the season's profit and then his capital. He could see him with his long nose, picking up the cards and then opening, "Sans Voir." There was always gambling then. When there was no snow you gambled and when there was too much you gambled. He thought of all the time in his life he had spent gambling.

But he had never written a line of that, nor of that cold, bright Christmas day with the mountains showing across the plain that Barker had flown across the lines to bomb the Austrian officers' leave train, machine-gunning them as they scattered and ran. He remembered Barker afterwards coming into the mess and starting to tell about it. And how quiet it got and then somebody saying, "You bloody murderous bastard."

Those were the same Austrians they killed then that he skied with later. No not the same. Hans, that he skied with all that year, had been in the Kaiser-Jägers and when they went hunting hares together up the little valley above the saw-mill they had talked of the fighting on Pasubio and of the attack on Pertica and Asalone and he had never written a word of that. Nor of Monte Corno, nor the Siete Commum, nor of Arsiedo.

How many winters had he lived in the Voralberg and the Arlberg? It was four and then he remembered the man who had the fox to sell when they had walked into Bludenz, that time to buy presents, and the cherry-pit taste of good kirsch, the fast-slipping rush of running powder-snow on crust, singing "Hi! Ho! said Rolly!" as you ran down the last stretch to the steep drop, taking it straight, then running the orchard in three turns and out across the ditch and onto the icy road behind the inn. Knocking your bindings loose, kicking the skis free and leaning them up against the wooden wall of the inn, the lamplight coming from the window, where inside, in the smoky, new-wine smelling warmth, they were playing the accordion.

"Where did we stay in Paris?" he asked the woman who was sitting by him in a canvas chair, now, in Africa.

"At the Crillon. You know that."

"Why do I know that?"

"That's where we always stayed."

"No. Not always."

"There and at the Pavillion Henri-Quatre in St. Germain. You said you loved it there."

"Love is a dunghill," said Harry. "And I'm the cock that gets on it to crow."

"If you have to go away," she said, "is it absolutely necessary to kill off everything you leave behind? I mean do you have to take away everything? Do you have to kill your horse, and your wife and burn your saddle and your armour?"

"Yes," he said. "Your damned money was my armour. My Swift and my Armour."

"Don't."

"All right. I'll stop that. I don't want to hurt you."

"It's a little bit late now."

"All right then. I'll go on hurting you. It's more amusing. The only thing I ever really liked to do with you I can't do now."

"No, that's not true. You liked to do many things and everything you wanted to do I did."

"Oh, for Christ sake stop bragging, will you?"

He looked at her and saw her crying.

"Listen," he said. "Do you think that it is fun to do this? I don't know why I'm doing it. It's trying to kill to keep yourself alive, I imagine. I was all right when we started talking. I didn't mean to start this, and now I'm crazy as a coot and being as cruel to you as I can be. Don't pay any attention, darling, to what I say. I love you, really. You know I love you. I've never loved any one else the way I love you."

He slipped into the familiar lie he made his bread and butter by.

"You're sweet to me."

"You bitch," he said. "You rich bitch. That's poetry. I'm full of poetry now. Rot and poetry. Rotten poetry."

"Stop it. Harry, why do you have to turn into a devil now?"

"I don't like to leave anything," the man said. "I don't like to leave things behind."

It was evening now and he had been asleep. The sun was gone behind the hill and there was a shadow all across the plain and the small animals were feeding close to camp; quick dropping heads and switching tails, he watched them keeping well out away from the bush now. The birds no longer waited on the ground. They were all perched heavily in a tree. There were many more of them. His personal boy was sitting by the bed.

"Memsahib's gone to shoot," the boy said. "Does Bwana want?"

"Nothing."

She had gone to kill a piece of meat and, knowing how he liked to watch the game, she had gone well away so she would not disturb this little pocket of the plain that he could see. She was always thoughtful, he thought. On anything she knew about, or had read, or that she had ever heard.

It was not her fault that when he went to her he was already over. How could a woman know that you meant nothing that you said; that you spoke only from habit and to be comfortable? After he no longer meant what he said, his lies were more successful with women than when he had told them the truth.

It was not so much that he lied as that there was no truth to tell. He had had his life and it was over and then he went on living it again with different people and more money, with the best of the same places, and some new ones.

You kept from thinking and it was all marvellous. You were equipped with good insides so that you did not go to pieces that way, the way most of them had, and you made an attitude that you cared nothing for the work you used to do, now that you could no longer do it. But, in yourself, you said that you would write about these people; about the very rich; that you were really not of them but a spy in their country; that you would leave it and write of it and for once it would be written by some one who knew what he was writing of. But he would never do it, because each day of not writing, of comfort, of being that which he despised, dulled his ability and softened his will to work so that, finally, he did no work at all. The people he knew now were all much more comfortable when he did not work. Africa was where he had been happiest in the good time of his life, so he had come out here to start again. They had made this safari with the minimum of comfort. There was no hardship; but there was no luxury and he had thought that he could get back into training that way. That in some way he could work the fat off his soul the way a fighter went into the mountains to work and train in order to burn it out of his body.

She had liked it. She said she loved it. She loved anything that was exciting, that involved a change of scene, where there were new people and where things were pleasant. And he had felt the illusion of returning strength of will to work. Now if this was how it ended, and he knew it was, he must not turn like some snake biting itself because its back was broken. It wasn't this woman's fault. If it had not been she it would have been another. If he lived by a lie he should try to die by it. He heard a shot beyond the hill.

She shot very well this good, this rich bitch, this kindly caretaker and destroyer of his talent. Nonsense. He had destroyed his talent himself. Why should he blame this woman because she kept him well? He had destroyed his talent by not using it, by betrayals of himself and what he believed in, by drinking so much that he blunted the edge of his perceptions, by laziness, by sloth, and by snobbery, by pride and by prejudice, by hook and by crook. What was this? A catalogue of old books? What was his talent anyway? It was a talent all right but instead of using it, he had traded on it. It was never what he had done, but always what he could do. And he had chosen to make his living with something else instead of a pen or a pencil. It was strange, too, wasn't it, that when he fell in love with another woman, that woman should always have more money than the last one? But when he no longer was in love, when he was only lying, as to this woman, now, who had the most money of all, who had all the money there was, who had had a husband and children, who had taken lovers and been dissatisfied with them, and who loved him dearly as a writer, as a man, as a companion and as a proud possession; it was strange that when he did not love her at all and was lying, that he should be able to give her more for her money than when he had really loved.

We must all be cut out for what we do, he thought. However you make your living is where your talent lies. He had sold vitality, in one form or another, all his life and when your affections are not too involved you give much better value for the money. He had found that out but he would never write that, now, either. No, he would not write that, although it was well worth writing.

Now she came in sight, walking across the open toward the camp.

She was wearing jodphurs and carrying her rifle. The two boys had a Tommie slung and they were coming along behind her. She was still a good-looking woman, he thought, and she had a pleasant body. She had a great talent and appreciation for the bed, she was not pretty, but he liked her face, she read enormously, liked to ride and shoot and, certainly, she drank too much. Her husband had died when she was still a comparatively young woman and for a while she had devoted herself to her two just-grown children, who did not need her and were embarrassed at having her about, to her stable of horses, to books, and to bottles. She liked to read in the evening before dinner and she drank Scotch and soda while she read. By dinner she was fairly drunk and after a bottle of wine at dinner she was usually drunk enough to sleep.

That was before the lovers. After she had the lovers she did not drink so much because she did not have to be drunk to sleep. But the lovers bored her. She had been married to a man who had never bored her and these people bored her very much.

Then one of her two children was killed in a plane crash and after that was over she did not want the lovers, and drink being no anæsthetic she had to make another life. Suddenly, she had been acutely frightened of being alone. But she wanted some one that she respected with her.

It had begun very simply. She liked what he wrote and she had always envied the life he led. She thought he did exactly what he wanted to. The steps by which she had acquired him and the way in which she had finally fallen in love with him were all part of a regular progression in which she had built herself a new life and he had traded away what remained of his old life.

He had traded it for security, for comfort too, there was no denying that, and for what else? He did not know. She would have bought him anything he wanted. He knew that. She was a damned nice woman too. He would as soon be in bed with her as any one; rather with her, because she was richer, because she was very pleasant and appreciative and because she never made scenes. And now this life that she had built again was coming to a term because he had not used iodine two weeks ago when a thorn had scratched his knee as they moved forward trying to photograph a herd of waterbuck standing, their heads up, peering while their nostrils searched the air, their ears spread wide to hear the first noise that would send them rushing into the bush. They had bolted, too, before he got the picture.

Here she came now.

He turned his head on the cot to look toward her. "Hello," he said.

"I shot a Tommy ram," she told him. "He'll make you good broth and I'll have them mash some potatoes with the Klim. How do you feel?"

"Much better."

"Isn't that lovely? You know I thought perhaps you would. You were sleeping when I left."

"I had a good sleep. Did you walk far?"

"No. Just around behind the hill. I made quite a good shot on the Tommy."

"You shoot marvellously, you know."

"I love it. I've loved Africa. Really. If *you're* all right it's the most fun that I've ever had. You don't know the fun it's been to shoot with you. I've loved the country."

"I love it too."

"Darling, you don't know how marvellous it is to see you feeling better. I couldn't stand it when you felt that way. You won't talk to me like that again, will you? Promise me?"

"No," he said. "I don't remember what I said."

"You don't have to destroy me. Do you? I'm only a middle-aged woman who loves you and wants to do what you want to do. I've been destroyed two or three times already. You wouldn't want to destroy me again, would you?"

"I'd like to destroy you a few times in bed," he said.

"Yes. That's the good destruction. That's the way we're made to be destroyed. The plane will be here tomorrow."

"How do you know?"

"I'm sure. It's bound to come. The boys have the wood all ready and the grass to make the smudge. I went down and looked at it again today. There's plenty of room to land and we have the smudges ready at both ends."

"What makes you think it will come tomorrow?"

"I'm sure it will. It's overdue now. Then, in town, they will fix up your leg and then we will have some good destruction. Not that dreadful talking kind."

"Should we have a drink? The sun is down."

"Do you think you should?"

"I'm having one."

"We'll have one together. *Molo, letti dui whiskey-soda!*" she called.

"You'd better put on your mosquito boots," he told her.

"I'll wait till I bathe . . ."

While it grew dark they drank and just before it was dark and there was no longer enough light to shoot, a hyena crossed the open on his way around the hill.

"That bastard crosses there every night," the man said. "Every night for two weeks."

"He's the one makes the noise at night. I don't mind it. They're a filthy animal though."

Drinking together, with no pain now except the discomfort of lying in the one position, the boys lighting a fire, its shadow jumping on the tents, he could feel the return of acquiescence in this life of pleasant surrender. She *was* very good to him. He had been cruel and unjust in the afternoon. She was a fine woman, marvellous really. And just then it occurred to him that he was going to die.

It came with a rush; not as a rush of water nor of wind; but of a sudden evil-smelling emptiness and the odd thing was that the hyena slipped lightly along the edge of it.

"What is it, Harry?" she asked him.

"Nothing," he said. "You had better move over to the other side. To windward."

"Did Molo change the dressing?"

"Yes. I'm just using the boric now."

"How do you feel?"

"A little wobbly."

"I'm going in to bathe," she said. "I'll be right out. I'll eat with you and then we'll put the cot in."

So, he said to himself, we did well to stop the quarrelling. He had never quarrelled much with this woman, while with the women that he loved he had quarrelled so much they had finally, always, with the corrosion of the quarrelling, killed what they had together. He had loved too much, demanded too much, and he wore it all out.

He thought about alone in Constantinople that time, having quarrelled in Paris before he had gone out. He had whored the whole time and then, when that was over, and he had failed to kill his loneliness, but only made it worse, he had written her, the first one, the one who left him, a letter telling her how he had never been able to kill it. . . . How when he thought he saw her outside the Regence *one time it made him go all faint and sick inside, and that he would follow a woman who looked like her in some way, along the Boulevard, afraid to see it was not she, afraid to lose the feeling it gave him. How every one he had slept with had only made him miss her more. How what she had done could never matter since he knew he could not cure himself of loving her. He wrote this letter at the Club, cold sober, and mailed it to New York asking her to write him at the office in Paris. That seemed safe. And that night missing her so much it made him feel hollow sick inside, he wandered up past Taxim's, picked a girl up and took her out to supper. He had gone to a place to dance with her afterward, she danced badly, and left her for a hot Armenian slut, that swung her belly against him so it almost scalded. He took her away from a British gunner subaltern after a row. The gunner asked him outside and they fought in the street on the cobbles in the dark. He'd hit him twice, hard, on the side of the jaw and when he didn't go down he knew he was in for a fight. The gunner hit him in the body, then beside his eye. He swung with his left again and landed and the gunner fell on him and grabbed his coat and tore the sleeve off and he clubbed him twice behind the ear and then smashed him with his right as he pushed him away. When the gunner went down his head hit first and he ran with the girl because they heard the M.P.'s coming. They got into a taxi and drove out to Rimmily Hissa along the Bosphorus, and around, and back in the cool night and went to bed and she felt as over-ripe as she looked but smooth, rose-petal, syrupy, smooth-bellied, big-breasted and needed no pillow under her buttocks, and he left her before she was awake looking blousy enough in the first daylight and turned up at the Pera Palace with a black eye, carrying his coat because one sleeve was missing.*

That same night he left for Anatolia and he remembered, later on that trip, riding all day through fields of the poppies that they raised for opium and how strange it made you feel, finally, and all the distances seemed wrong, to where they had made the attack with the newly arrived Constantine officers, that did not know a god-damned thing, and the artillery had fired into the troops and the British observer had cried like a child.

That was the day he'd first seen dead men wearing white ballet skirts and upturned shoes with pompons on them. The Turks had come steadily and lumpily and he had seen the skirted men running and the officers shooting into them and running themselves and he and the British observer had run too until his lungs ached and his mouth was full of the taste of pennies and they stopped behind some rocks and there were the Turks coming as lumpily as ever. Later he had seen the things that he could never think of and later still he had seen much worse. So when he got back to Paris that time he could not talk about it or stand to have it mentioned. And there in the café as he passed was that American poet with a pile of saucers in front of him and a stupid look on his potato face talking about the Dada movement with a Roumanian who said his name was Tristan Tzara, who always wore a monocle and had a headache, and, back at the apartment with his wife that now he loved again, the quarrel all over, the madness all over, glad to be home, the office sent his mail up to the flat. So then the letter in answer to the one he'd written came in on a platter one morning and when he saw the handwriting he went cold all over and tried to slip the letter underneath another. But his wife said, "Who is that letter from, dear?" and that was the end of the beginning of that.

He remembered the good times with them all, and the quarrels. They always picked the finest places to have the quarrels. And why had they always quarrelled when he was feeling best? He had never written any of that because, at first, he never wanted to hurt any one and then it seemed as though there was enough to write without it. But he had always thought that he would write it finally. There was so much to write. He had seen the world change; not just the events; although he had seen many of them and had watched the people, but he had seen the subtler change and he could remember how the people were at different times. He had been in it and he had watched it and it was his duty to write of it; but now he never would.

"How do you feel?" she said. She had come out from the tent now after her bath.

"All right."

"Could you eat now?" He saw Molo behind her with the folding table and the other boy with the dishes.

"I want to write," he said.

"You ought to take some broth to keep your strength up."

"I'm going to die tonight," he said. "I don't need my strength up."

"Don't be melodramatic, Harry, please," she said.

"Why don't you use your nose? I'm rotted half way up my thigh now. What the hell should I fool with broth for? Molo bring whiskey-soda."

"Please take the broth," she said gently.

"All right."

The broth was too hot. He had to hold it in the cup until it cooled enough to take it and then he just got it down without gagging.

"You're a fine woman," he said. "Don't pay any attention to me."

She looked at him with her well-known, well-loved face from *Spur* and *Town and Country,* only a little the worse for drink, only a little the worse for bed, but *Town and Country* never showed those good breasts and those useful thighs and those lightly small-of-back-caressing hands, and as he looked and saw her well known pleasant smile, he felt death come again. This time there was no rush. It was a puff, as of a wind that makes a candle flicker and the flame go tall.

"They can bring my net out later and hang it from the tree and build the fire up. I'm not going in the tent tonight. It's not worth moving. It's a clear night. There won't be any rain."

So this was how you died, in whispers that you did not hear. Well, there would be no more quarrelling. He could promise that. The one experience that he had never had he was not going to spoil now. He probably would. You spoiled everything. But perhaps he wouldn't.

"You can't take dictation, can you?"

"I never learned," she told him.

"That's all right."

There wasn't time, of course, although it seemed as though it telescoped so that you might put it all into one paragraph if you could get it right.

There was a log house, chinked white with mortar, on a hill above the lake. There was a bell on a pole by the door to call the people in to meals. Behind the house were fields and behind the fields was the timber. A line of lombardy poplars ran from the house to the dock. Other poplars ran along the point. A road went up to the hills along the edge of the timber and along that road he picked blackberries. Then that log house was burned down and all the guns that had been on deer foot racks above the open fire place were burned and afterwards their barrels, with the lead melted in the magazines, and the stocks burned away, lay out on the heap of ashes that were used to make lye for the big iron soap kettles, and you asked Grandfather if you could have them to play with, and he said, no. You see they were his guns still and he never bought any others. Nor did he hunt any more. The house was rebuilt in the same place out of lumber now and painted white and from its porch you saw the poplars and the lake beyond; but there were never any more guns. The barrels of the guns that had hung on the deer feet on the wall of the log house lay out there on the heap of ashes and no one ever touched them.

In the Black Forest, after the war, we rented a trout stream and there were two ways to walk to it. One was down the valley from Triberg and around the valley road in the shade of the trees that bordered the white road, and then up a side road that went up through the hills past many small farms, with the big Schwarzwald houses, until that road crossed the stream. That was where our fishing began.

The other way was to climb steeply up to the edge of the woods and then go across the top of the hills through the pine woods, and then out to the edge of a meadow and down across this meadow to the bridge. There were birches along the stream and it was not big, but narrow, clear and fast, with pools where it had cut under the roots of the birches. At the Hotel in Triberg the proprietor had a fine season. It was very pleasant and we were all great friends. The next year came the inflation and the money he had made the year before was not enough to buy supplies to open the hotel and he hanged himself.

You could dictate that, but you could not dictate the Place Contrescarpe where the flower sellers dyed their flowers in the street and the dye ran over the paving where the autobus started and the old men and the women, always drunk on wine and bad marc; and the children with their noses running in the cold; the smell of dirty sweat and poverty and drunkenness at the Café des Amateurs and the whores at the Bal Musette they lived above. The Concierge who entertained the trooper of the Garde Republicaine in her loge, his horse-hair-plumed helmet on a chair. The locataire across the hall whose husband was a bicycle racer and her joy that morning at the Cremerie when she had opened L'Auto and seen where he placed third in Paris-Tours, his first big race. She had blushed and laughed and then gone upstairs crying with the yellow sporting paper in her hand. The husband of the woman who ran the Bal Musette drove a taxi and when he, Harry, had to take an early plane the husband knocked upon the door to wake him and they each drank a glass of white wine at the zinc of the bar before they started. He knew his neighbors in that quarter then because they all were poor.

Around that Place there were two kinds; the drunkards and the sportifs. The drunkards killed their poverty that way; the sportifs took it out in exercise. They were the descendants of the Communards and it was no struggle for them to know their politics. They knew who had shot their fathers, their relatives, their brothers, and their friends when the Versailles troops came in and took the town after the Commune and executed any one they could catch with calloused hands, or who wore a cap, or carried any other sign he was a working man. And in that poverty, and in that quarter across the street from a Boucherie Chevaline and a wine co-operative he had written the start of all he was to do. There never was another part of Paris that he loved like that, the sprawling trees, the old white plastered houses painted brown below, the long green of the autobus in that round square, the purple flower dye upon the paving, the sudden drop down the hill of the rue Cardinal Lemoine to the River, and the other way the narrow crowded world of the rue Mouffetard. The street that ran up toward the Pantheon and the other that he always took with the bicycle, the only asphalted street in all that quarter, smooth under the tires, with the high narrow houses and the cheap tall hotel where Paul Verlaine had died. There were only two rooms in the apartments where they lived and he had a room on the top floor of that hotel that cost him sixty francs a month where he did his writing, and from it he could see the roofs and chimney pots and all the hills of Paris.

From the apartment you could only see the wood and coal man's place. He sold wine too, bad wine. The golden horse's head outside the Boucherie Chevaline where the carcasses hung yellow gold and red in the open window, and the green painted co-operative where they bought their wine; good wine and cheap. The rest was plaster walls and the windows of the neighbors. The neighbors who, at night, when some one lay drunk in the street, moaning and groaning in that typical French ivresse *that you were propaganded to believe did not exist, would open their windows and then the murmur of talk.*

"Where is the policeman? When you don't want him the bugger is always there. He's sleeping with some concierge. Ge the Agent.*" Till some one threw a bucket of water from a window and the moaning stopped. "What's that? Water. Ah, that's intelligent." And the windows shutting. Marie, his femme de menage, protesting against the eight-hour day saying, "If a husband works until six he gets only a little drunk on the way home and does not waste too much. If he works only until five he is drunk every night and one has no money. It is the wife of the working man who suffers from this shortening of hours."*

"Wouldn't you like some more broth?" the woman asked him now.

"No, thank you very much. It is awfully good."

"Try just a little."

"I would like a whiskey-soda."

"It's not good for you."

"No. It's bad for me. Cole Porter wrote the words and the music. This knowledge that you're going mad for me."

"You know I like you to drink."

"Oh yes. Only it's bad for me."

When she goes, he thought. I'll have all I want. Not all I want but all there is. Ayee he was tired. Too tired. He was going to sleep a little while. He lay still and death was not there. It must have gone around another street. It went in pairs, on bicycles, and moved absolutely silently on the pavements.

No, he had never written about Paris. Not the Paris that he cared about. But what about the rest that he had never written?

What about the ranch and the silvered gray of the sage brush, the quick, clear water in the irrigation ditches, and the heavy green of the alfalfa. The trail went up into the hills and the cattle in the summer were shy as deer. The bawling and the steady noise and slow moving mass raising a dust as you brought them down in the fall. And behind the mountains, the clear sharpness of the peak in the evening light and, riding down along the trail in the moonlight, bright across the valley. Now he remembered coming down through the timber in the dark holding the horse's tail when you could not see and all the stories that he meant to write.

About the half-wit chore boy who was left at the ranch that time and told not to let any one get any hay, and that old bastard from the Forks who had beaten the boy when he had worked for him stopping to get some feed. The boy refusing and the old man saying he would beat him again. The boy got the rifle from the kitchen and shot him when he tried to come into the barn and when they came back to the ranch he'd been dead a week, frozen in the corral, and the dogs had eaten part of him. But what was left you packed on a sled wrapped in a blanket and roped on and you got the boy to help you haul it, and the two of you took it out over the road on skis, and sixty miles down to town to turn the boy over. He having no idea that he would be arrested. Thinking he had done his duty and that you were his friend and he would be rewarded. He'd helped to haul the old man in so everybody could know how bad the old man had been and how he'd tried to steal some feed that didn't belong to him, and when the sheriff put the handcuffs on the boy he couldn't believe it. Then he'd started to cry. That was one story he had saved to write. He knew at least twenty good stories from out there and he had never written one. Why?

"You tell them why," he said.

"Why what, dear?"

"Why nothing."

She didn't drink so much, now, since she had him. But if he lived he would never write about her, he knew that now. Nor about any of them. The rich were dull and they drank too much, or they played too much backgammon. They were dull and they were repetitious. He remembered poor Julian and his romantic awe of them and how he had started a story once that began, "The very rich are different from you and me." And how some one had said to Julian, Yes, they have more money. But that was not humorous to Julian. He thought they were a special glamourous race and when he found they weren't it wrecked him just as much as any other thing that wrecked him.

He had been contemptuous of those who wrecked. You did not have to like it because you understood it. He could beat anything, he thought, because no thing could hurt him if he did not care.

All right. Now he would not care for death. One thing he had always dreaded was the pain. He could stand pain as well as any man, until it went on too long, and wore him out, but here he had something that had hurt frightfully and just when he had felt it breaking him, the pain had stopped.

He remembered long ago when Williamson, the bombing officer, had been hit by a stick bomb some one in a German patrol had thrown as he was coming in through the wire that night and, screaming, had begged every one to kill him. He was a fat man, very brave, and a good officer, although addicted to fantastic shows. But that night he was caught in the wire, with a flare lighting him up and his bowels spilled out into the wire, so when they brought him in, alive, they had to cut him loose. Shoot me, Harry. For Christ sake shoot me. They had had an argument one time about our Lord never sending you anything you could not bear and some one's theory had been that meant that at a certain time the pain passed you out automatically. But he had always remembered Williamson, that night. Nothing passed out Williamson until he gave him all his morphine tablets that he had always saved to use himself and then they did not work right away.

Still this now, that he had, was very easy; and if it was no worse as it went on there was nothing to worry about. Except that he would rather be in better company.

He thought a little about the company that he would like to have.

No, he thought, when everything you do, you do too long, and do too late, you can't expect to find the people still there. The people all are gone. The party's over and you are with your hostess now.

I'm getting as bored with dying as with everything else, he thought.

"It's a bore," he said out loud.

"What is, my dear?"

"Anything you do too bloody long."

He looked at her face between him and the fire. She was leaning back in the chair and the firelight shone on her pleasantly lined face and he could see that she was sleepy. He heard the hyena make a noise just outside the range of the fire.

"I've been writing," he said. "But I got tired."

"Do you think you will be able to sleep?"

"Pretty sure. Why don't you turn in?"

"I like to sit here with you."

"Do you feel anything strange?" he asked her.

"No. Just a little sleepy."

"I do," he said.

He had just felt death come by again.

"You know the only thing I've never lost is curiosity," he said to her.

"You've never lost anything. You're the most complete man I've ever known."

"Christ," he said. "How little a woman knows. What is that? Your intuition?"

Because, just then, death had come and rested its head on the foot of the cot and he could smell its breath.

"Never believe any of that about a scythe and a skull," he told her. "It can be two bicycle policemen as easily, or be a bird. Or it can have a wide snout like a hyena."

It had moved up on him now, but it had no shape any more. It simply occupied space.

"Tell it to go away."

It did not go away but moved a little closer.

"You've got a hell of a breath," he told it. "You stinking bastard."

It moved up closer to him still and now he could not speak to it, and when it saw he could not speak it came a little closer, and now he tried to send it away without speaking, but it moved in on him so its weight was all upon his chest, and while it crouched there and he could not move, or speak, he heard the woman say, "Bwana is asleep now. Take the cot up very gently and carry it into the tent."

He could not speak to tell her to make it go away and it crouched now, heavier, so he could not breathe. And then, while they lifted the cot, suddenly it was all right and the weight went from his chest.

It was morning and had been morning for some time and he heard the plane. It showed very tiny and then made a wide circle and the boys ran out and lit the fires, using kerosene, and piled on grass so there were two big smudges at each end of the level place and the morning breeze blew them toward the camp and the plane circled twice more, low this time, and then glided down and levelled off and landed smoothly and, coming walking toward him, was old Compton in slacks, a tweed jacket and a brown felt hat.

"What's the matter, old cock?" Compton said.

"Bad leg," he told him. "Will you have some breakfast?"

"Thanks. I'll just have some tea. It's the Puss Moth you know. I won't be able to take the Memsahib. There's only room for one. Your lorry is on the way."

Helen had taken Compton aside and was speaking to him. Compton came back more cheery than ever.

"We'll get you right in," he said. "I'll be back for the Mem. Now I'm afraid I'll have to stop at Arusha to refuel. We'd better get going."

"What about the tea?"

"I don't really care about it you know."

The boys had picked up the cot and carried it around the green tents and down along the rock and out onto the plain and along past the smudges that were burning brightly now, the grass all consumed, and the wind fanning the fire, to the little plane. It was difficult getting him in, but once in he lay back in the leather seat, and the leg was stuck straight out to one side of the seat where Compton sat. Compton started the motor and got in. He waved to Helen and to the boys and, as the clatter moved into the old familiar roar, they swung around with Compie watching for wart-hog holes and roared, bumping, along the stretch between the fires and with the last bump rose and he saw them all standing below, waving, and the camp beside the hill, flattening now, and the plain spreading, clumps of trees, and the bush flattening, while the game trails ran now smoothly to the dry waterholes, and there was a new water that he had never known of. The zebra, small rounded backs now, and the wildebeeste, big-headed dots seeming to climb as they moved in long fingers across the plain, now scattering as the shadow came toward them, they were tiny now, and the movement had no gallop, and the plain as far as you could see, gray-yellow now and ahead old Compie's tweed back and the brown felt hat. Then they were over the first hills and the wildebeeste were trailing up them, and then they were over mountains with sudden depths of green-rising forest and the solid bamboo slopes, and then the heavy forest again, sculptured into peaks and hollows until they crossed, and hills sloped down and then another plain, hot now, and purple brown, bumpy with heat and Compie looking back to see how he was riding. Then there were other mountains dark ahead.

And then instead of going on to Arusha they turned left, he evidently figured that they had the gas, and looking down he saw a pink sifting cloud, moving over the ground, and in the air, like the first snow in a blizzard, that comes from nowhere, and he knew the locusts were coming up from the South. Then they began to climb and they were going to the East it seemed, and then it darkened and they were in a storm, the rain so thick it seemed like flying through a waterfall, and then they were out and Compie turned his head and grinned and pointed and there, ahead, all he could see, as wide as all the world, great, high, and unbelievably white in the sun, was the square top of Kilimanjaro. And then he knew that there was where he was going.

Just then the hyena stopped whimpering in the night and started to make a strange, human, almost crying sound. The woman heard it and stirred uneasily. She did not wake. In her dream she was at the house on Long Island and it was the night before her daughter's début. Somehow her father was there and he had been very rude. Then the noise the hyena made was so loud she woke and for a moment she did not know where she was and she was very afraid. Then she took the flashlight and shone it on the other cot that they had carried in after Harry had gone to sleep. She could see his bulk under the mosquito bar but somehow he had gotten his leg out and it hung down alongside the cot. The dressings had all come down and she could not look at it.

"Molo," she called, "Molo! Molo!"

Then she said, "Harry, Harry!" Then her voice rising, "Harry! Please, Oh Harry!"

There was no answer and she could not hear him breathing.

Outside the tent the hyena made the same strange noise that had awakened her. But she did not hear him for the beating of her heart.

1936

The Vane Sisters

VLADIMIR NABOKOV

[1899–1977]

I might never have heard of Cynthia's death, had I not run, that night, into D., whom I had also lost track of for the last four years or so; and I might never have run into D., had I not got involved in a series of trivial investigations.

The day, a compunctious Sunday after a week of blizzards, had been part jewel, part mud. In the midst of my usual afternoon stroll through the small hilly town attached to the girls' college where I taught French literature, I had stopped to watch a family of brilliant icicles drip-dripping from the eaves of a frame house. So clear-cut were their pointed shadows on the white boards behind them that I was sure the shadows of the falling drops should be visible too. But they were not. The roof jutted too far out, perhaps, or the angle of vision was faulty, or, again, I did not chance to be watching the right icicle when the right drop fell. There was a rhythm, an alternation in the dropping that I found as teasing as a coin trick. It led me to inspect the corners of several house blocks, and this brought me to Kelly Road, and right to the house where D. used to live when he was instructor here. And as I looked up at the eaves of the adjacent garage with its full display of transparent stalactites backed by their blue silhouettes, I was rewarded at last, upon choosing one, by the sight of what might be described as the dot of an exclamation mark leaving its ordinary position to glide down very fast—a jot faster than the thaw-drop it raced. This twinned twinkle was delightful but not completely satisfying; or rather it only sharpened my appetite for other tidbits of light and shade, and I walked on in a state of raw awareness that seemed to transform the whole of my being into one big eyeball rolling in the world's socket.

Through peacocked lashes I saw the dazzling diamond reflection of the low sun on the round back of a parked automobile. To all kinds of things a vivid pictorial sense had been restored by the sponge of the thaw. Water in overlapping festoons flowed down one sloping street and turned gracefully into another. With ever so slight a note of meretricious appeal, narrow passages between buildings revealed treasures of brick and purple. I remarked for the first time the humble fluting—last echoes of grooves on the shafts of columns—ornamenting a garbage can, and I also saw the rippling upon its lid—circles diverging from a fantastically ancient center. Erect, dark-headed shapes of dead snow (left by the blades of a bulldozer last Friday) were lined up like rudimentary penguins along the curbs, above the brilliant vibration of live gutters.

I walked up, and I walked down, and I walked straight into a delicately dying sky, and finally the sequence of observed and observant things brought me, at my usual eating time, to a street so distant from my usual eating place that I decided to try a restaurant which stood on the fringe of the town. Night had fallen without sound or ceremony when I came out again. The lean ghost, the elongated umbra cast by a parking meter upon some damp snow, had a strange ruddy tinge; this I made out to be due to the tawny red light of the restaurant sign above the sidewalk; and it was then—as I sauntered there, wondering rather wearily if in the course of my return tramp I might be lucky enough to find the same in neon blue, it was then that a car crunched to a standstill near me and D. got out of it with an exclamation of feigned pleasure.

He was passing, on his way from Albany to Boston, through the town he had dwelt in before, and more than once in my life have I felt that stab of vicarious emotion followed by a rush of personal irritation against travelers who seem to feel nothing at all upon revisiting spots that ought to harass them at every step with wailing and writhing memories. He ushered me back into the bar that I had just left, and after the usual exchange of buoyant platitudes came the inevitable vacuum which he filled with the random words: "Say, I never thought there was anything wrong with Cynthia Vane's heart. My lawyer tells me she died last week."

II

He was still young, still brash, still shifty, still married to the gentle, exquisitely pretty woman who had never learned or suspected anything about his disastrous affair with Cynthia's hysterical young sister, who in her turn had known nothing of the interview I had had with Cynthia when she suddenly summoned me to Boston to make me swear I would talk to D. and get him "kicked out" if he did not stop seeing Sybil at once—or did not divorce his wife (whom incidentally she visualized through the prism of Sybil's wild talk as a termagant and a fright). I had cornered him immediately. He had said there was nothing to worry about—had made up his mind, anyway, to give up his college job and move with his wife to Albany where he would work in his father's firm; and the whole matter, which had threatened to become one of those hopelessly entangled situations that drag on for years, with peripheral sets of well-meaning friends endlessly discussing it in universal secrecy—and even founding, among themselves, new intimacies upon its alien woes—came to an abrupt end.

I remember sitting next day at my raised desk in the large classroom where a mid-year examination in French Lit was being held on the eve of Sybil's suicide. She came in on high heels, with a suitcase, dumped it in a corner where several other bags were stacked, with a single shrug slipped her fur coat off her thin shoulders, folded it on her bag, and with two or three other girls stopped before my desk to ask when would I mail them their grades. It would take me a week, beginning from tomorrow, I said, to read the stuff. I also remember wondering whether D. had already informed her of his decision—and I felt acutely unhappy about my dutiful little student as during one hundred and fifty minutes my gaze kept reverting to her, so childishly slight in close-fitting gray, and kept observing that carefully waved dark hair, that small, small-flowered hat with a little hyaline veil as worn that season and under it her small face broken into a cubist pattern by scars due to a skin disease, pathetically masked by a sun-lamp tan that hardened her features, whose charm was further impaired by her having painted everything that could be painted, so that the pale gums of her teeth between cherry-red chapped lips and the diluted black ink of her eyes under darkened lids were the only visible openings into her beauty.

Next day, having arranged the ugly copybooks alphabetically, I plunged into their chaos of scripts and came prematurely to Valevsky and Vane, whose books I had somehow misplaced. The first was dressed up for the occasion in a semblance of legibility, but Sybil's work displayed her usual combination of several demon hands. She had begun in very pale, very hard pencil which had conspicuously embossed the blank verse, but had produced little of permanent value on the upper-side of the page. Happily the tip soon broke, and Sybil continued in another, darker lead, gradually lapsing into the blurred thickness of what looked almost like charcoal, to which, by sucking the blunt point, she had contributed some traces of lipstick. Her work, although even poorer than I had expected, bore all the signs of a kind of desperate conscientiousness, with underscores, transposes, unnecessary footnotes, as if she were intent upon rounding up things in the most respectable manner possible. Then she had borrowed Mary Valevsky's fountain pen and added: *"Cette examain est finie ainsi que ma vie. Adieu, jeunes filles!* Please, *Monsieur le Professeur,* contact *ma soeur** and tell her that Death was not better than D minus, but definitely better than Life minus D."

I lost no time in ringing up Cynthia who told me it was all over—had been all over since eight in the morning—and asked me to bring her the note, and when I did, beamed through her tears with proud admiration for the whimsical use ("Just like her!") Sybil had made of an examination in French literature. In no time she "fixed" two highballs, while never parting with Sybil's notebook—by now splashed with soda water and tears—and went on studying the death message, whereupon I was impelled to point out to her the grammatical mistakes in it and to explain the way "girl" is translated in American colleges lest students innocently bandy around the French equivalent of "wench," or worse. These rather tasteless trivialities pleased Cynthia hugely as she rose, with gasps, above the heaving surface of her grief. And then, holding that limp notebook as if it were a kind of passport to a casual Elysium (where

*"This examination is finished thus as [is] my life. Adieu, girls! Please, Professor, contact my sister. . . ."

pencil points do not nap and a dreamy young beauty with an impeccable complexion winds a lock of her hair on a dreamy forefinger, as she meditates over some celestial test), Cynthia led me upstairs, to a chilly little bedroom just to show me, as if I were the police or a sympathetic Irish neighbor, two empty pill bottles and the tumbled bed from which a tender, inessential body, that D. must have known down to its last velvet detail, had been already removed.

III

It was four or five months after her sister's death that I began seeing Cynthia fairly often. By the time I had come to New York for some vocational research in the Public Library she had also moved to that city where for some odd reason (in vague connection, I presume, with artistic motives) she had taken what people, immune to gooseflesh, term a "cold water" flat, down in the scale of the city's transverse streets. What attracted me were neither her ways, which I thought repulsively vivacious, nor her looks, which other men thought striking. She had wide-spaced eyes very much like her sister's, of a frank, frightened blue with dark points in a radial arrangement. The interval between her thick black eyebrows was always shiny, and shiny too were the fleshy volutes of her nostrils. The coarse texture of her epiderm looked almost masculine, and, in the stark lamplight of her studio, you could see the pores of her thirty-two-year-old face fairly gaping at you like something in an aquarium. She used cosmetics with as much zest as her little sister had, but with an additional slovenliness that would result in her big front teeth getting some of the rouge. She was handsomely dark, wore a not too tasteless mixture of fairly smart heterogeneous things, and had a so-called good figure; but all of her was curiously frowsy, after a way I obscurely associated with left-wing enthusiasms in politics and "advanced" banalities in art, although, actually, she cared for neither. Her coily hair-do, on a part-and-bun basis, might have looked feral and bizarre had it not been thoroughly domesticated by its own soft unkemptness at the vulnerable nape. Her fingernails were gaudily painted, but badly bitten and not clean. Her lovers were a silent young photographer with a sudden laugh and two older men, brothers, who owned a small printing establishment across the street. I wondered at their tastes whenever I glimpsed, with a secret shudder, the higgledy-piggledy striation of black hairs that showed all along her pale shins through the nylon of her stockings with the scientific distinctness of a preparation flattened under glass; or when I felt, at her every movement, the dullish, stalish, not particularly conspicuous but all-pervading and depressing emanation that her seldom bathed flesh spread from under weary perfumes and creams.

Her father had gambled away the greater part of a comfortable fortune, and her mother's first husband had been of Slav origin, but otherwise Cynthia Vane belonged to a good, respectable family. For aught we know, it may have gone back to kings and soothsayers in the mists of ultimate islands. Transferred to a newer world, to a landscape of doomed, splendid deciduous trees, her ancestry presented, in one of its first phases, a white churchful of farmers against a black thunderhead, and then an imposing array of townsmen engaged in mercantile pursuits, as well as a number of learned men, such as Dr. Jonathan Vane, the gaunt bore (1780–1839), who perished in the conflagration of the steamer "Lexington" to become later an habitué of Cynthia's tilting table. I have always wished to stand genealogy on its head, and here I have an opportunity to do so, for it is the last scion, Cynthia, and Cynthia alone, who will remain of any importance in the Vane dynasty. I am alluding of course to her artistic gift, to her delightful, gay, but not very popular paintings which the friends of her friends bought at long intervals—and I dearly should like to know where they went after her death, those honest and poetical pictures that illumined her living room—the wonderfully detailed images of metallic things, and my favorite "Seen Through a Windshield"—a windshield partly covered with rime, with a brilliant trickle (from an imaginary car roof) across its transparent part and, through it all, the sapphire flame of the sky and a green and white fir tree.

IV

Cynthia had a feeling that her dead sister was not altogether pleased with her—had discovered by now that she and I had conspired to break her romance; and so, in order to disarm her shade, Cynthia reverted to a rather primitive type of sacrificial offering (tinged, however, with something of Sybil's humor), and began to send to

D.'s business address, at deliberately unfixed dates, such trifles as snapshots of Sybil's tomb in a poor light; cuttings of her own hair which was indistinguishable from Sybil's; a New England sectional map with an inked-in cross, midway between two chaste towns, to mark the spot where D. and Sybil had stopped on October the twenty-third, in broad daylight, at a lenient motel, in a pink and brown forest; and, twice, a stuffed skunk.

Being as a conversationalist more voluble than explicit, she never could describe in full the theory of intervenient auras that she had somehow evolved. Fundamentally there was nothing particularly new about her private creed since it presupposed a fairly conventional hereafter, a silent solarium of immortal souls (spliced with mortal antecedents) whose main recreation consisted of periodical hoverings over the dear quick. The interesting point was a curious practical twist that Cynthia gave to her tame metaphysics. She was sure that her existence was influenced by all sorts of dead friends each of whom took turns in directing her fate much as if she were a stray kitten which a schoolgirl in passing gathers up, and presses to her cheek, and carefully puts down again, near some suburban hedge—to be stroked presently by another transient hand or carried off to a world of doors by some hospitable lady.

For a few hours, or for several days in a row, and sometimes recurrently, in an irregular series, for months or years, anything that happened to Cynthia, after a given person had died, would be, she said, in the manner and mood of that person. The event might be extraordinary, changing the course of one's life; or it might be a string of minute incidents just sufficiently clear to stand out in relief against one's usual day and then shading off into still vaguer trivia as the aura gradually faded. The influence might be good or bad; the main thing was that its source could be identified. It was like walking through a person's soul, she said. I tried to argue that she might not always be able to determine the exact source since not everybody has a recognizable soul; that there are anonymous letters and Christmas presents which anybody might send; that, in fact, what Cynthia called "a usual day" might be itself a weak solution of mixed auras or simply the routine shift of a humdrum guardian angel. And what about God? Did or did not people who would resent any omnipotent dictator on earth look forward to one in heaven? And wars? What a dreadful idea—dead soldiers still fighting with living ones, or phantom armies trying to get at each other through the lives of crippled old men.

But Cynthia was above generalities as she was beyond logic. "Ah, that's Paul," she would say when the soup spitefully boiled over, or: "I guess good Betty Brown is dead"—when she won a beautiful and very welcome vacuum cleaner in a charity lottery. And, with Jamesian meanderings that exasperated my French mind, she would go back to a time when Betty and Paul had not yet departed, and tell me of the showers of well-meant, but odd and quite unacceptable bounties—beginning with an old purse that contained a check for three dollars which she picked up in the street and, of course, returned (to the aforesaid Betty Brown—this is where she first comes in—a decrepit colored woman hardly able to walk), and ending with an insulting proposal from an old beau of hers (this is where Paul comes in) to paint "straight" pictures of his house and family for a reasonable remuneration—all of which followed upon the demise of a certain Mrs. Page, a kindly but petty old party who had pestered her with bits of matter-of-fact advice since Cynthia had been a child.

Sybil's personality, she said, had a rainbow edge as if a little out of focus. She said that had I known Sybil better I would have at once understood how Sybil-like was the aura of minor events which, in spells, had suffused her, Cynthia's, existence after Sybil's suicide. Ever since they had lost their mother they had intended to give up their Boston home and move to New York, where Cynthia's paintings, they thought, would have a chance to be more widely admired; but the old home had clung to them with all its plush tentacles. Dead Sybil, however, had proceeded to separate the house from its view—a thing that affects fatally the sense of home. Right across the narrow street a building project had come into loud, ugly scaffolded life. A pair of familiar poplars died that spring, turning to blond skeletons. Workmen came and broke up the warm-colored lovely old sidewalk that had a special violet sheen on wet April days and had echoed so memorably to the morning footsteps of museum-bound Mr. Lever, who upon retiring from business at sixty had devoted a full quarter of a century exclusively to the study of snails.

Speaking of old men, one should add that sometimes these posthumous auspices and interventions were in the nature of parody. Cynthia had been on friendly terms with an eccentric librarian called Porlock who in the last years of his dusty life had been engaged in examining old books for miraculous misprints such as the substitution of "l" for the second "h" in the word "hither." Contrary to Cynthia, he cared nothing for the thrill of obscure predictions; all he sought was the freak itself, the chance that mimics choice, the flaw that looks like a flower; and Cynthia, a much more perverse amateur of misshapen or illicitly connected words, puns, logogriphs, and so on, had helped the poor crank to pursue a quest that in the light of the example she cited struck me as statistically insane. Anyway, she said, on the third day after his death she was reading a magazine and had just come across a quotation from an imperishable poem (that she, with other gullible readers, believed to have been really composed in a dream) when it dawned upon her that "Alph" was a prophetic sequence of the initial letters of Anna Livia Plurabelle (another sacred river running through, or rather around, yet another fake dream), while the additional "h" modestly stood, as a private signpost, for the word that had so hypnotized Mr. Porlock. And I wish I could recollect that novel or short story (by some contemporary writer, I believe) in which, unknown to its author, the first letters of the words in its last paragraph formed, as deciphered by Cynthia, a message from his dead mother.

V

I am sorry to say that not content with these ingenious fancies Cynthia showed a ridiculous fondness for spiritualism. I refused to accompany her to sittings in which paid mediums took part: I knew too much about that from other sources. I did consent, however, to attend little farces rigged up by Cynthia and her two poker-faced gentlemen-friends of the printing shop. They were podgy, polite, and rather eerie old fellows, but I satisfied myself that they possessed considerable wit and culture. We sat down at a light little table, and crackling tremors started almost as soon as we laid our fingertips upon it. I was treated to an assortment of ghosts who rapped out their reports most readily though refusing to elucidate anything that I did not quite catch. Oscar Wilde came in and in rapid garbled French, with the usual anglicisms, obscurely accused Cynthia's dead parents of what appeared in my jottings as *"plagiatisme."* A brisk spirit contributed the unsolicited information that he, John Moore, and his brother Bill had been coal miners in Colorado and had perished in an avalanche at "Crested Beauty" in January 1883. Frederic Myers, an old hand at the game, hammered out a piece of verse (oddly resembling Cynthia's own fugitive productions) which in part reads in my notes:

What is this—a conjurer's rabbit,
Or a flawy but genuine gleam—
Which can check the perilous habit
And dispel the dolorous dream?

Finally, with a great crash and all kinds of shudderings and jig-like movements on the part of the table, Leo Tolstoy visited our little group and, when asked to identify himself by specific traits of terrene habitation, launched upon a complex description of what seemed to be some Russian type of architectural woodwork ("figures on boards—man, horse, cock, man, horse, cock"), all of which was difficult to take down, hard to understand, and impossible to verify.

I attended two or three other sittings which were even sillier but I must confess that I preferred the childish entertainment they afforded and the cider we drank (Podgy and Pudgy were teetotallers) to Cynthia's awful house parties.

She gave them at the Wheelers' nice flat next door—the sort of arrangement dear to her centrifugal nature, but then, of course, her own living room always looked like a dirty old palette. Following a barbaric, unhygienic, and adulterous custom, the guests' coats, still warm on the inside, were carried by quiet, baldish Bob Wheeler into the sanctity of a tidy bedroom and heaped on the conjugal bed. It was also he who poured out the drinks, which were passed around by the young photographer while Cynthia and Mrs. Wheeler took care of the canapés.

A late arrival had the impression of lots of loud people unnecessarily grouped within a smoke-blue space between two mirrors gorged with reflections. Because, I suppose, Cynthia wished to be the youngest in the room, the women she used to invite, married or single, were, at the best, in their precarious forties; some of them would bring from their homes, in dark taxis, intact vestiges of good looks, which, however, they lost as the party progressed. It has always amazed me—the capacity sociable week-end revelers have of finding almost at once, by a purely empiric but very precise method, a common denominator of drunkenness, to which everybody loyally sticks before descending, all together, to the next level. The rich friendliness of the matrons was marked by tomboyish overtones, while the fixed inward look of amiably tight men was like a sacrilegious parody of pregnancy. Although some of the guests were connected in one way or another with the arts, there was no inspired talk, no wreathed, elbow-propped heads, and of course no flute girls. From some vantage point where she had been sitting in a stranded mermaid pose on the pale carpet with one or two younger fellows, Cynthia, her face varnished with a film of beaming sweat, would creep up on her knees, a proffered plate of nuts in one hand, and crisply tap with the other the athletic leg of Cochran or Corcoran, an art dealer, ensconced, on a pearl-gray sofa, between two flushed, happily disintegrating ladies.

At a further stage there would come spurts of more riotous gaiety. Corcoran or Coransky would grab Cynthia or some other wandering woman by the shoulder and lead her into a corner to confront her with a grinning imbroglio of private jokes and rumors, whereupon, with a laugh and a toss of her head, she would break away. And still later there would be flurries of intersexual chumminess, jocular reconciliations, a bare fleshy arm flung around another woman's husband (he standing very upright in the midst of a swaying room), or a sudden rush of flirtatious anger, of clumsy pursuit—and the quiet half smile of Bob Wheeler picking up glasses that grew like mushrooms in the shade of chairs.

After one last party of that sort, I wrote Cynthia a perfectly harmless and, on the whole, well-meant note, in which I poked a little Latin fun at some of her guests. I also apologized for not having touched her whisky, saying that as a Frenchman I preferred the grape to the grain. A few days later I met her on the steps of the Public Library, in the broken sun, under a weak cloudburst, opening her amber umbrella, struggling with a couple of armpitted books (of which I relieved her for a moment), "Footfalls on the Boundary of Another World," by Robert Dale Owen, and something on "Spiritualism and Christianity"; when, suddenly, with no provocation on my part, she blazed out at me with vulgar vehemence, using poisonous words, saying—through pear-shaped drops of sparse rain—that I was a prig and a snob; that I only saw the gestures and disguises of people; that Corcoran had rescued from drowning, in two different oceans, two men—by an irrelevant coincidence both called Corcoran; that romping and screeching Joan Winter had a little girl doomed to grow completely blind in a few months; and that the woman in green with the freckled chest whom I had snubbed in some way or other had written a national best-seller in 1932. Strange Cynthia! I had been told she could be thunderously rude to people whom she liked and respected; one had, however, to draw the line somewhere and since I had by then sufficiently studied her interesting auras and other odds and ids, I decided to stop seeing her altogether.

VI

The night D. informed me of Cynthia's death I returned after eleven to the two-storied house I shared, in horizontal section, with an emeritus professor's widow. Upon reaching the porch I looked with the apprehension of solitude at the two kinds of darkness in the two rows of windows: the darkness of absence and the darkness of sleep.

I could do something about the first but could not duplicate the second. My bed gave me no sense of safety; its springs only made my nerves bounce. I plunged into Shakespeare's sonnets—and found myself idiotically checking the first letters of the lines to see what sacramental words they might form. I got FATE (LXX), ATOM (CXX) and, twice, TAFT (LXXXVIII, CXXXI). Every now and then I would glance around to see how the objects in my room were behaving. It was strange to think that if bombs began to fall I would feel little more than a gambler's excitement (and a great deal of earthy relief) whereas my heart would burst if a certain suspiciously tense-looking little bottle on yonder shelf moved a fraction of an inch to one side. The silence, too, was suspiciously compact as if deliberately forming a black backdrop for the nerve flash caused by any small sound of unknown origin. All traffic was dead. In vain did I pray for the groan of a truck up Perkins Street. The woman above who used to drive me crazy by the booming thuds occasioned by what seemed monstrous feet of stone (actually, in diurnal life, she was a small dumpy creature resembling a mummified guinea pig) would have earned my blessings had she now trudged to her bathroom. I put out my light and cleared my throat several times so as to be responsible for at least *that* sound. I thumbed a mental ride with a very remote automobile but it dropped me before I had a chance to doze off. Presently a crackle (due, I hoped, to a discarded and crushed sheet of paper opening like a mean, stubborn night flower)—started and stopped in the waste-paper basket, and my bed-table responded with a little click. It would have been just like Cynthia to put on right then a cheap poltergeist show.

I decided to fight Cynthia. I reviewed in thought the modern era of raps and apparitions, beginning with the knockings of 1848, at the hamlet of Hydesville, N.Y., and ending with grotesque phenomena at Cambridge, Mass.; I evoked the ankle-bones and other anatomical castanets of the Fox sisters (as described by the sages of the University of Buffalo); the mysteriously uniform type of delicate adolescent in bleak Epworth or Tedworth, radiating the same disturbances as in old Peru; solemn Victorian orgies with roses falling and accordions floating to the strains of sacred music; professional impostors regurgitating moist cheesecloth; Mr. Duncan, a lady medium's dignified husband, who, when asked if he would submit to a search, excused himself on the ground of soiled underwear; old Alfred Russel Wallace, the naïve naturalist, refusing to believe that the white form with bare feet and unperforated earlobes before him, at a private pandemonium in Boston, could be prim Miss Cook whom he had just seen asleep, in her curtained corner, all dressed in black, wearing laced-up boots and earrings; two other investigators, small, puny, but reasonably intelligent and active men, closely clinging with arms and legs about Eusapia, a large, plump elderly female reeking of garlic, who still managed to fool them; and the sceptical and embarrassed magician, instructed by charming Margery's "control" not to get lost in the bathrobe's lining but to follow up the left stocking until he reached the bare thigh—upon the warm skin of which he felt a "teleplastic" mass that appeared to the touch uncommonly like cold, uncooked liver.

VII

I was appealing to flesh, and the corruption of flesh, to refute and defeat the possible persistence of discarnate life. Alas, these conjurations only enhanced my fear of Cynthia's phantom. Atavistic peace came with dawn, and when I slipped into sleep, the sun through the tawny window shades penetrated a dream that somehow was full of Cynthia.

This was disappointing. Secure in the fortress of daylight, I said to myself that I had expected more. She, a painter of glass-bright minutiæ—and now so vague! I lay in bed, thinking my dream over and listening to the sparrows outside: Who knows, if recorded and then run backward, those bird sounds might not become human speech, voiced words, just as the latter become a twitter when reversed? I set myself to re-read my dream—backward, diagonally, up, down—trying hard to unravel something Cynthia-like in it, something strange and suggestive that must be there.

I could isolate, consciously, little. Everything seemed blurred, yellow-clouded, yielding nothing tangible. Her inept acrostics, maudlin evasions, theopathies—every recollection formed ripples of mysterious meaning. Everything seemed yellowly blurred, illusive, lost.

1959

The Chrysanthemums

JOHN STEINBECK

[1902–1968]

The high grey-flannel fog of winter closed off the Salinas Valley from the sky and from all the rest of the world. On every side it sat like a lid on the mountains and made of the great valley a closed pot. On the broad, level land floor the gang plows bit deep and left the black earth shining like metal where the shares had cut. On the foothill ranches across the Salinas River, the yellow stubble fields seemed to be bathed in pale cold sunshine, but there was no sunshine in the valley now in December. The thick willow scrub along the river flamed with sharp and positive yellow leaves.

It was a time of quiet and of waiting. The air was cold and tender. A light wind blew up from the southwest so that the farmers were mildly hopeful of a good rain before long; but fog and rain do not go together.

Across the river, on Henry Allen's foothill ranch there was little work to be done, for the hay was cut and stored and the orchards were plowed up to receive the rain deeply when it should come. The cattle on the higher slopes were becoming shaggy and rough-coated.

Elisa Allen, working in her flower garden, looked down across the yard and saw Henry, her husband, talking to two men in business suits. The three of them stood by the tractor shed, each man with one foot on the side of the little Fordson. They smoked cigarettes and studied the machine as they talked.

Elisa watched them for a moment and then went back to her work. She was thirty-five. Her face was lean and strong and her eyes were as clear as water. Her figure looked blocked and heavy in her gardening costume, a man's black hat pulled low down over her eyes, clod-hopper shoes, a figured print dress almost completely covered by a big corduroy apron with four big pockets to hold the snips, the trowel and scratcher, the seeds and the knife she worked with. She wore heavy leather gloves to protect her hands while she worked.

She was cutting down the old year's chrysanthemum stalks with a pair of short and powerful scissors. She looked down toward the men by the tractor shed now and then. Her face was eager and mature and handsome; even her work with the scissors was over-eager, over-powerful. The chrysanthemum stems seemed too small and easy for her energy.

She brushed a cloud of hair out of her eyes with the back of her glove, and left a smudge of earth on the cheek in doing it. Behind her stood the neat white farm house with red geraniums close-banked around it as high as the windows. It was a hard-swept looking little house, with hard-polished windows, and a clean mud-mat on the front steps.

Elisa cast another glance toward the tractor shed. The strangers were getting into their Ford coupe. She took off a glove and put her strong fingers down into the forest of new green chrysanthemum sprouts that were growing around the old roots. She spread the leaves and looked down among the close-growing stems. No aphids were there, no sowbugs or snails or cutworms. Her terrier fingers destroyed such pests before they could get started.

Elisa started at the sound of her husband's voice. He had come near quietly, and he leaned over the wire fence that protected her flower garden from cattle and dogs and chickens.

"At it again," he said. "You've got a strong new crop coming."

Elisa straightened her back and pulled on the gardening glove again. "Yes. They'll be strong this coming year." In her tone and on her face there was a little smugness.

"You've got a gift with things," Henry observed. "Some of those yellow chrysanthemums you had this year were ten inches across. I wish you'd work out in the orchard and raise some apples that big."

Her eyes sharpened. "Maybe I could do it, too. I've a gift with things, all right. My mother had it. She could stick anything in the ground and make it grow. She said it was having planters' hands that knew how to do it."

"Well, it sure works with flowers," he said.

"Henry, who were those men you were talking to?"

"Why, sure, that's what I came to tell you. They were from the Western Meat Company. I sold those thirty head of three-year-old steers. Got nearly my own price, too."

"Good," she said. "Good for you."

"And I thought," he continued, "I thought how it's Saturday afternoon, and we might go into Salinas for dinner at a restaurant, and then to a picture show—to celebrate, you see."

"Good," she repeated. "Oh, yes. That will be good."

Henry put on his joking tone. "There's fights tonight. How'd you like to go to the fights?"

"Oh, no," she said breathlessly. "No, I wouldn't like fights."

"Just fooling, Elisa. We'll go to a movie. Let's see. It's two now. I'm going to take Scotty and bring down those steers from the hill. It'll take us maybe two hours. We'll go in town about five and have dinner at the Cominos Hotel. Like that?"

"Of course I'll like it. It's good to eat away from home."

"All right, then. I'll go get up a couple of horses."

She said, "I'll have plenty of time to transplant some of these sets, I guess."

She heard her husband calling Scotty down by the barn. And a little later she saw the two men ride up the pale yellow hillside in search of the steers.

There was a little square sandy bed kept for rooting the chrysanthemums. With her trowel she turned the soil over and over, and smoothed it and patted it firm. Then she dug ten parallel trenches to receive the sets. Back at the chrysanthemum bed she pulled out the little crisp shoots, trimmed off the leaves of each one with her scissors and laid it on a small orderly pile.

A squeak of wheels and plod of hoofs came from the road. Elisa looked up. The country road ran along the dense bank of willows and cottonwoods that bordered the river, and up this road came a curious vehicle, curiously drawn. It was an old spring-wagon, with a round canvas top on it like the cover of a prairie schooner. It was drawn by an old bay horse and a little grey-and-white burro. A big stubble-bearded man sat between the cover flaps and drove the crawling team. Underneath the wagon, between the hind wheels, a lean and rangy mongrel dog walked sedately. Words were painted on the canvas in clumsy, crooked letters. "Pots, pans, knives, sisors, lawn mores. Fixed." Two rows of articles and the triumphantly definitive "Fixed" below. The black paint had run down in little sharp points beneath each letter.

Elisa, squatting on the ground, watched to see the crazy, loose-jointed wagon pass by. But it didn't pass. It turned into the farm road in front of her house, crooked old wheels skirling and squeaking. The rangy dog darted from between the wheels and ran ahead. Instantly the two ranch shepherds flew out at him. Then all three stopped, and with stiff and quivering tails, with taut straight legs, with ambassadorial dignity, they slowly circled, sniffing daintily. The caravan pulled up to Elisa's wire fence and stopped. Now the newcomer dog, feeling outnumbered, lowered his tail and retired under the wagon with raised hackles and bared teeth.

The man on the wagon seat called out. "That's a bad dog in a fight when he gets started."

Elisa laughed. "I see he is. How soon does he generally get started?"

The man caught up her laughter and echoed it heartily. "Sometimes not for weeks and weeks," he said. He climbed stiffly down over the wheel. The horse and the donkey drooped like unwatered flowers.

Elisa saw that he was a very big man. Although his hair and beard were greying, he did not look old. His worn black suit was wrinkled and spotted with grease. The laughter had disappeared from his face and eyes the moment his laughing voice ceased. His eyes were dark, and they were full of the brooding that gets in the eyes of teamsters and of sailors. The calloused hands he rested on the wire fence were cracked, and every crack was a black line. He took off his battered hat.

"I'm off my general road, ma'am," he said. "Does this dirt road cut over across the river to the Los Angeles highway?"

Elisa stood up and shoved the thick scissors in her apron pocket. "Well, yes, it does, but it winds around and then fords the river. I don't think your team could pull through the sand."

He replied with some asperity, "It might surprise you what them beasts can pull through."

"When they get started?" she asked.

He smiled for a second. "Yes. When they get started."

"Well," said Elisa, "I think you'll save time if you go back to the Salinas road and pick up the highway there."

He drew a big finger down the chicken wire and made it sing. "I ain't in any hurry, ma'am. I go from Seattle to San Diego and back every year. Takes all my time. About six months each way. I aim to follow nice weather."

Elisa took off her gloves and stuffed them in the apron pocket with the scissors. She touched the under edge of her man's hat, searching for fugitive hairs. "That sounds like a nice kind of a way to live," she said.

He leaned confidentially over the fence. "Maybe you noticed the writing on my wagon. I mend pots and sharpen knives and scissors. You got any of them things to do?"

"Oh, no," she said quickly. "Nothing like that." Her eyes hardened with resistance.

"Scissors is the worst thing," he explained. "Most people just ruin scissors trying to sharpen 'em, but I know how. I got a special tool. It's a little bobbit kind of thing, and patented. But it sure does the trick."

"No. My scissors are all sharp."

"All right, then. Take a pot," he continued earnestly, "a bent pot, or a pot with a hole. I can make it like new so you don't have to buy no new ones. That's a saving for you."

"No," she said shortly. "I tell you I have nothing like that for you to do."

His face fell to an exaggerated sadness. His voice took on a whining undertone. "I ain't had a thing to do today. Maybe I won't have no supper tonight. You see I'm off my regular road. I know folks on the highway clear from Seattle to San Diego. They save their things for me to sharpen up because they know I do it so good and save them money."

"I'm sorry," Elisa said irritably. "I haven't anything for you to do."

His eyes left her face and fell to searching the ground. They roamed about until they came to the chrysanthemum bed where she had been working. "What's them plants, ma'am?"

The irritation and resistance melted from Elisa's face. "Oh, those are chrysanthemums, giant whites and yellows. I raise them every year, bigger than anybody around here."

"Kind of a long-stemmed flower? Looks like a quick puff of colored smoke?" he asked.

"That's it. What a nice way to describe them."

"They smell kind of nasty till you get used to them," he said.

"It's a good bitter smell," she retorted, "not nasty at all."

He changed his tone quickly. "I like the smell myself."

"I had ten-inch blooms this year," she said.

The man leaned farther over the fence. "Look. I know a lady down the road a piece, has got the nicest garden you ever seen. Got nearly every kind of flower but no chrysanthemums. Last time I was mending a copper-bottom washtub for her (that's a hard job but I do it good), she said to me, 'If you ever run acrost some nice chrysanthemums I wish you'd try to get me a few seeds.' That's what she told me."

Elisa's eye grew alert and eager. "She couldn't have known much about chrysanthemums. You can raise them from seed, but it's much easier to root the little sprouts you see there."

"Oh," he said. "I s'pose I can't take none to her, then."

"Why yes you can," Elisa cried. "I can put some in damp sand, and you can carry them right along with you. They'll take root in the pot if you keep them damp. And then she can transplant them."

"She'd sure like to have some, ma'am. You say they're nice ones?"

"Beautiful," she said. "Oh, beautiful." Her eyes shone. She tore off the battered hat and shook out her dark pretty hair. "I'll put them in a flower pot, and you can take them right with you. Come into the yard."

While the man came through the picket gate Elisa ran excitedly along the geranium-bordered path to the back of the house. And she returned carrying a big red flower pot. The gloves were forgotten now. She kneeled on the ground by the starting bed and dug up the sandy soil with her fingers and scooped it into the bright new flower pot. Then she picked up the little pile of shoots she had prepared. With her strong fingers she pressed them into the sand and tamped around them with her knuckles. The man stood over her. "I'll tell you what to do," she said. "You remember so you can tell the lady."

"Yes, I'll try to remember."

"Well, look. These will take root in about a month. Then she must set them out, about a foot apart in good rich earth like this, see?" She lifted a handful of dark soil for him to look at. "They'll grow fast and tall. Now remember this. In July tell her to cut them down, about eight inches from the ground."

"Before they bloom?" he asked.

"Yes, before they bloom." Her face was tight with eagerness. "They'll grow right up again. About the last of September the buds will start."

She stopped and seemed perplexed. "It's the budding that takes the most care," she said hesitantly. "I don't know how to tell you." She looked deep into his eyes, searchingly. Her mouth opened a little, and she seemed to be listening. "I'll try to tell you," she said. "Did you ever hear of planting hands?"

"Can't say I have, ma'am."

"Well, I can only tell you what it feels like. It's when you're picking off the buds you don't want. Everything goes right down into your fingertips. You watch your fingers work. They do it themselves. You can feel how it is. They pick and pick the buds. They never make a mistake. They're with the plant. Do you see? Your fingers and the plant. You can feel that, right up your arm. They know. They never make a mistake. You can feel it. When you're like that you can't do anything wrong. Do you see that? Can you understand that?"

She was kneeling on the ground looking up at him. Her breast swelled passionately.

The man's eyes narrowed. He looked away self-consciously. "Maybe I know," he said. "Sometimes in the night in the wagon there—"

Elisa's voice grew husky. She broke in on him. "I've never lived as you do, but I know what you mean. When the night is dark—why, the stars are sharp-pointed, and there's quiet. Why, you rise up and up! Every pointed star gets driven into your body. It's like that. Hot and sharp and—lovely."

Kneeling there, her hand went out toward his legs in the greasy black trousers. Her hesitant fingers almost touched the cloth. Then her hand dropped to the ground. She crouched low like a fawning dog.

He said, "It's nice, just like you say. Only when you don't have no dinner, it ain't."

She stood up then, very straight, and her face was ashamed. She held the flower pot out to him and placed it gently in his arms. "Here. Put it in your wagon, on the seat, where you can watch it. Maybe I can find something for you to do."

At the back of the house she dug in the can pile and found two old and battered aluminum saucepans. She carried them back and gave them to him. "Here, maybe you can fix these."

His manner changed. He became professional. "Good as new I can fix them." At the back of his wagon he set a little anvil, and out of an oily tool box dug a small machine hammer. Elisa came through the gate to watch him while he pounded out the dents in the kettles. His mouth grew sure and knowing. At a difficult part of the work he sucked his under-lip.

"You sleep right in the wagon?" Elisa asked.

"Right in the wagon, ma'am. Rain or shine I'm dry as a cow in there."

"It must be nice," she said. "It must be very nice. I wish women could do such things."

"It ain't the right kind of a life for a woman."

Her upper lip raised a little, showing her teeth. "How do you know? How can you tell?" she said.

"I don't know, ma'am," he protested. "Of course I don't know. Now here's your kettles, done. You don't have to buy no new ones."

"How much?"

"Oh, fifty cents'll do. I keep my prices down and my work good. That's why I have all them satisfied customers up and down the highway."

Elisa brought him a fifty-cent piece from the house and dropped it in his hand. "You might be surprised to have a rival some time. I can sharpen scissors, too. And I can beat the dents out of little pots. I could show you what a woman might do."

He put his hammer back in the oily box and shoved the little anvil out of sight. "It would be a lonely life for a woman, ma'am, and a scarey life, too, with animals creeping under the wagon all night." He climbed over the single-tree, steadying himself with a hand on the burro's white rump. He settled himself in the seat, picked up the lines. "Thank you kindly, ma'am," he said. "I'll do like you told me; I'll go back and catch the Salinas road."

"Mind," she called, "if you're long in getting there, keep the sand damp."

"Sand, ma'am? . . . Sand? Oh, sure. You mean around the chrysanthemums. Sure I will." He clucked his tongue. The beasts leaned luxuriously into their collars. The mongrel dog took his place between the back wheels. The wagon turned and crawled out the entrance road and back the way it had come, along the river.

Elisa stood in front of her wire fence watching the slow progress of the caravan. Her shoulders were straight, her head thrown back, her eyes half-closed, so that the scene came vaguely into them. Her lips moved silently, forming the words "Good-bye—good-bye." Then she whispered, "That's a bright direction. There's a glowing there." The sound of her whisper startled her. She shook herself free and looked about to see whether anyone had been listening. Only the dogs had heard. They lifted their heads toward her from their sleeping in the dust, and then stretched out their chins and settled asleep again. Elisa turned and ran hurriedly into the house.

In the kitchen she reached behind the stove and felt the water tank. It was full of hot water from the noonday cooking. In the bathroom she tore off her soiled clothes and flung them into the corner. And then she scrubbed herself with a little block of pumice, legs and thighs, loins and chest and arms, until her skin was scratched and red. When she had dried herself she stood in front of a mirror in her bedroom and looked at her body. She tightened her stomach and threw out her chest. She turned and looked over her shoulder at her back.

After a while she began to dress, slowly. She put on her newest underclothing and her nicest stockings and the dress which was the symbol of her prettiness. She worked carefully on her hair, penciled her eyebrows and roughed her lips.

Before she was finished she heard the little thunder of hoofs and the shouts of Henry and his helper as they drove the red steers into the corral. She heard the gate bang shut and set herself for Henry's arrival.

His step sounded on the porch. He entered the house calling, "Elisa, where are you?"

"In my room, dressing. I'm not ready. There's hot water for your bath. Hurry up. It's getting late."

When she heard him splashing in the tub, Elisa laid his dark suit on the bed, and shirt and socks and tie beside it. She stood his polished shoes on the floor beside the bed. Then she went to the porch and sat primly and stiffly down. She looked toward the river road where the willow-line was still yellow with frosted leaves so that under the high grey fog they seemed a thin band of sunshine. This was the only color in the grey afternoon. She sat unmoving for a long time. Her eyes blinked rarely.

Henry came banging out of the door, shoving his tie inside his vest as he came. Elisa stiffened and her face grew tight. Henry stopped short and looked at her. "Why—why, Elisa. You look so nice!"

"Nice? You think I look nice? What do you mean by 'nice'?"

Henry blundered on. "I don't know. I mean you look different, strong and happy."

"I am strong? Yes, strong. What do you mean 'strong'?"

He looked bewildered. "You're playing some kind of game," he said helplessly. "It's a kind of a play. You look strong enough to break a calf over your knee, happy enough to eat it like a watermelon."

For a second she lost her rigidity. "Henry! Don't talk like that. You didn't know what you said." She grew complete again. "I'm strong," she boasted. "I never knew before how strong."

Henry looked down toward the tractor shed, and when he brought his eyes back to her, they were his own again. "I'll get out the car. You can put on your coat while I'm starting."

Elisa went into the house. She heard him drive to the gate and idle down his motor, and then she took a long time to put on her hat. She pulled it here and pressed it there. When Henry turned the motor off she slipped into her coat and went out.

The little roadster bounced along on the dirt road by the river, raising the birds and driving the rabbits into the brush. Two cranes flapped heavily over the willow-line and dropped into the river-bed.

Far ahead on the road Elisa saw a dark speck. She knew.

She tried not to look as they passed it, but her eyes would not obey. She whispered to herself sadly, "He might have thrown them off the road. That wouldn't have been much trouble, not very much. But he kept the pot," she explained. "He had to keep the pot. That's why he couldn't get them off the road."

The roadster turned a bend and she saw the caravan ahead. She swung full around toward her husband so she could not see the little covered wagon and the mismatched team as the car passed them.

In a moment it was over. The thing was done. She did not look back. She said loudly, to be heard above the motor, "It will be good, tonight, a good dinner."

"Now you're changed again," Henry complained. He took one hand from the wheel and patted her knee. "I ought to take you in to dinner oftener. It would be good for both of us. We get so heavy out on the ranch."

"Henry," she asked, "could we have wine at dinner?"

"Sure we could. Say! That will be fine."

She was silent for a while; then she said, "Henry, at those prize fights, do the men hurt each other very much?"

"Sometimes a little, not often. Why?"

"Well, I've read how they break noses, and blood runs down their chests. I've read how the fighting gloves get heavy and soggy with blood."

He looked around at her. "What's the matter, Elisa? I didn't know you read things like that." He brought the car to a stop, then turned to the right over the Salinas River bridge.

"Do any women ever go to the fights?" she asked.

"Oh, sure, some. What's the matter, Elisa? Do you want to go? I don't think you'd like it, but I'll take you if you really want to go."

She relaxed limply in the seat. "Oh, no. No. I don't want to go. I'm sure I don't." Her face was turned away from him. "It will be enough if we can have wine. It will be plenty." She turned up her coat collar so he could not see that she was crying weakly—like an old woman.

1937

First Confession

FRANK O'CONNOR

[1903–1966]

All the trouble began when my grandfather died and my grandmother—my father's mother—came to live with us. Relations in the one house are a strain at the best of times, but, to make matters worse, my grandmother was a real old countrywoman and quite unsuited to the life in town. She had a fat, wrinkled old face, and, to Mother's great indignation, went round the house in bare feet—the boots had her crippled, she said. For dinner she had a jug of porter and a pot of potatoes with—sometimes—a bit of salt fish, and she poured out the potatoes on the table and ate them slowly, with great relish, using her fingers by way of a fork.

Now, girls are supposed to be fastidious, but I was the one who suffered most from this. Nora, my sister, just sucked up to the old woman for the penny she got every Friday out of the old-age pension, a thing I could not do. I was too honest, that was my trouble; and when I was playing with Bill Connell, the sergeant-major's son, and saw my grandmother steering up the path with the jug of porter sticking out from beneath her shawl I was mortified. I made excuses not to let him come into the house, because I could never be sure what she would be up to when we went in.

When Mother was at work and my grandmother made the dinner I wouldn't touch it. Nora once tried to make me, but I hid under the table from her and took the bread-knife with me for protection. Nora let on to be very indignant (she wasn't, of course, but she knew Mother saw through her, so she sided with Gran) and came after me. I lashed out at her with the bread-knife, and after that she left me alone. I stayed there till Mother came in from work and made my dinner, but when Father came in later Nora said in a shocked voice: "Oh, Dadda, do you know what Jackie did at dinnertime?" Then, of course, it all came out; Father gave me a flaking; Mother interfered, and for days after that he didn't speak to me and Mother barely spoke to Nora. And all because of that old woman! God knows, I was heart-scalded.

Then, to crown my misfortunes, I had to make my first confession and communion. It was an old woman called Ryan who prepared us for these. She was about the one age with Gran; she was well-to-do, lived in a big house on Montenotte, wore a black cloak and bonnet, and came every day to school at three o'clock when we should have been going home, and talked to us of hell. She may have mentioned the other place as well, but that could only have been by accident, for hell had the first place in her heart.

She lit a candle, took out a new half-crown, and offered it to the first boy who would hold one finger—only one finger! in the flame for five minutes by the school clock. Being always very ambitious I was tempted to volunteer, but I thought it might look greedy. Then she asked were we afraid of holding one finger—only one finger!—in a little candle flame for five minutes and not afraid of burning all over in roasting hot furnaces for all eternity. "All eternity! Just think of that! A whole lifetime goes by and it's nothing, not even a drop in the ocean of your sufferings." The woman was really interesting about hell, but my attention was all fixed on the half-crown. At the end of the lesson she put it back in her purse. It was a great disappointment; a religious woman like that, you wouldn't think she'd bother about a thing like a half-crown.

Another day she said she knew a priest who woke one night to find a fellow he didn't recognize leaning over the end of his bed. The priest was a bit frightened—naturally enough—but he asked the fellow what he wanted, and the fellow said in a deep, husky voice that he wanted to go to confession. The priest said it was an awkward time and wouldn't it do in the morning, but the fellow said that last time he went to confession, there was one sin he kept back, being ashamed to mention it, and now it was always on his mind. Then the priest knew it was a bad case, because the fellow was after making a bad confession and committing a mortal sin. He got up to dress, and just then the cock crew in the yard outside, and—lo and behold!—when the priest looked round there was no sign of the fellow, only a smell of burning timber, and when the priest looked at his bed didn't he see the print of two hands burned in it? That was because the fellow had made a bad confession. This story made a shocking impression on me.

But the worst of all was when she showed us how to examine our conscience. Did we take the name of the Lord, our God, in vain? Did we honour our father and our mother? (I asked her did this include grandmothers and she said it did.) Did we love our neighbours as ourselves? Did we covet our neighbour's goods? (I thought of the way I felt about the penny that Nora got every Friday.) I decided that, between one thing and another, I must have broken the whole ten commandments, all on account of that old woman, and so far as I could see, so long as she remained in the house I had no hope of ever doing anything else.

I was scared to death of confession. The day the whole class went I let on to have a toothache, hoping my absence wouldn't be noticed; but at three o'clock, just as I was feeling safe, along comes a chap with a message from Mrs. Ryan that I was to go to confession myself on Saturday and be at the chapel for communion with the rest. To make it worse, Mother couldn't come with me and sent Nora instead.

Now, that girl had ways of tormenting me that Mother never knew of. She held my hand as we went down the hill, smiling sadly and saying how sorry she was for me, as if she were bringing me to the hospital for an operation.

"Oh, God help us!" she moaned. "Isn't it a terrible pity you weren't a good boy? Oh, Jackie, my heart bleeds for you! How will you ever think of all your sins? Don't forget you have to tell him about the time you kicked Gran on the shin."

"Lemme go!" I said, trying to drag myself free of her. "I don't want to go to confession at all."

"But sure, you'll have to go to confession, Jackie," she replied in the same regretful tone. "Sure, if you didn't, the parish priest would be up to the house, looking for you. 'Tisn't, God knows, that I'm not sorry for you. Do you remember the time you tried to kill me with the bread-knife under the table? And the language you used to me? I don't know what he'll do with you at all, Jackie. He might have to send you up to the bishop."

I remember thinking bitterly that she didn't know the half of what I had to tell—if I told it. I knew I couldn't tell it, and understood perfectly why the fellow in Mrs. Ryan's story made a bad confession; it seemed to me a great shame that people wouldn't stop criticizing him. I remember that steep hill down to the church, and the sunlit hillsides beyond the valley of the river, which I saw in the gaps between the houses like Adam's last glimpse of Paradise.

Then, when she had manœuvred me down the long flight of steps to the chapel yard, Nora suddenly changed her tone. She became the raging malicious devil she really was.

"There you are!" she said with a yelp of triumph, hurling me through the church door. "And I hope he'll give you the penitential psalms, you dirty little caffler."

I knew then I was lost, given up to eternal justice. The door with the coloured-glass panels swung shut behind me, the sunlight went out and gave place to deep shadow, and the wind whistled outside so that the silence within seemed to crackle like ice under my feet. Nora sat in front of me by the confession box. There were a couple of old women ahead of her, and then a miserable-looking poor devil came and wedged me in at the other side, so that I couldn't escape even if I had the courage. He joined his hands and rolled his eyes in the direction of the roof, muttering aspirations in an anguished tone, and I wondered had he a grandmother too. Only a grandmother could account for a fellow behaving in that heartbroken way, but he was better off than I, for he at least could go and confess his sins; while I would make a bad confession and then die in the night and be continually coming back and burning people's furniture.

Nora's turn came, and I heard the sound of something slamming, and then her voice as if butter wouldn't melt in her mouth, and then another slam, and out she came. God, the hypocrisy of women! Her eyes were lowered, her head was bowed, and her hands were joined very low down on her stomach, and she walked up the aisle to the side altar looking like a saint. You never saw such an exhibition of devotion; and I remembered the devilish malice with which she had tormented me all the way from our door, and wondered were all religious people like that, really. It was my turn now. With the fear of damnation in my soul I went in, and the confessional door closed of itself behind me.

It was pitch-dark and I couldn't see priest or anything else. Then

I really began to be frightened. In the darkness it was a matter between God and me, and He had all the odds. He knew what my intentions were before I even started; I had no chance. All I had ever been told about confession got mixed up in my mind, and I knelt to one wall and said; "Bless me, father, for I have sinned; this is my first confession." I waited for a few minutes, but nothing happened, so I tried it on the other wall. Nothing happened there either. He had me spotted all right.

It must have been then that I noticed the shelf at about one height with my head. It was really a place for grown-up people to rest their elbows, but in my distracted state I thought it was probably the place you were supposed to kneel. Of course, it was on the high side and not very deep, but I was always good at climbing and managed to get up all right. Staying up was the trouble. There was room only for my knees, and nothing you could get a grip on but a sort of wooden moulding a bit above it. I held on to the moulding and repeated the words a little louder, and this time something happened all right. A slide was slammed back; a little light entered the box, and a man's voice said: "Who's there?"

"'Tis me, father," I said for fear he mightn't see me and go away again. I couldn't see him at all. The place the voice came from was under the moulding, about level with my knees, so I took a good grip of the moulding and swung myself down till I saw the astonished face of a young priest looking up at me. He had to put his head on one side to see me, and I had to put mine on one side to see him, so we were more or less talking to one another upside-down. It struck me as a queer way of hearing confessions, but I didn't feel it my place to criticize.

"Bless me, father, for I have sinned; this is my first confession," I rattled off all in one breath, and swung myself down the least shade more to make it easier for him.

"What are you doing up there?" he shouted in an angry voice, and the strain the politeness was putting on my hold of the moulding, and the shock of being addressed in such an uncivil tone, were too much for me. I lost my grip, tumbled, and hit the door an unmerciful wallop before I found myself flat on my back in the middle of the aisle. The people who had been waiting stood up with their mouths open. The priest opened the door of the middle box and came out, pushing his biretta back from his forehead; he looked something terrible. Then Nora came scampering down the aisle.

"Oh, you dirty little caffler!" she said. "I might have known you'd do it. I might have known you'd disgrace me. I can't leave you out of my sight for one minute."

Before I could even get to my feet to defend myself she bent down and gave me a clip across the ear. This reminded me that I was so stunned I had even forgotten to cry, so that people might think I wasn't hurt at all, when in fact I was probably maimed for life. I gave a roar out of me.

"What's this all about?" the priest hissed, getting angrier than ever and pushing Nora off me. "How dare you hit the child like that, you little vixen?"

"But I can't do my penance with him, father," Nora cried, cocking an outraged eye up at him.

"Well, go and do it, or I'll give you some more to do," he said, giving me a hand up. "Was it coming to confession you were, my poor man?" he asked me.

"'Twas, father," said I with a sob.

"Oh," he said respectfully, "a big hefty fellow like you must have terrible sins. Is this your first?"

"'Tis, father," said I.

"Worse and worse," he said gloomily. "The crimes of a lifetime. I don't know will I get rid of you at all today. You'd better wait now till I'm finished with these old ones. You can see by the looks of them they haven't much to tell."

"I will, father," I said with something approaching joy.

The relief of it was really enormous. Nora stuck out her tongue at me from behind his back, but I couldn't even be bothered retorting. I knew from the very moment that man opened his mouth that he was intelligent above the ordinary. When I had time to think, I saw how right I was. It only stood to reason that a fellow confessing after seven years would have more to tell than people that went every week. The crimes of a lifetime, exactly as he said. It was only what he expected, and the rest was the cackle of old women and girls with their talk of hell, the bishop, and the penitential psalms. That was all they knew. I started to make my examination of conscience, and barring the one bad business of my grandmother it didn't seem so bad.

The next time, the priest steered me into the confession box himself and left the shutter back the way I could see him get in and sit down at the further side of the grille from me.

"Well, now," he said, "what do they call you?"

"Jackie, father," said I.

"And what's a-trouble to you, Jackie?"

"Father," I said, feeling I might as well get it over while I had him in good humour, "I had it all arranged to kill my grandmother."

He seemed a bit shaken by that, all right, because he said nothing for quite a while.

"My goodness," he said at last, "that'd be a shocking thing to do. What put that into your head?"

"Father," I said, feeling very sorry for myself, "she's an awful woman."

"Is she?" he asked. "What way is she awful?"

"She takes porter, father," I said, knowing well from the way Mother talked of it that this was a mortal sin, and hoping it would make the priest take a more favourable view of my case.

"Oh, my!" he said, and I could see he was impressed.

"And snuff, father," said I.

"That's a bad case, sure enough, Jackie," he said.

"And she goes round in her bare feet, father," I went on in a rush of self-pity, "and she knows I don't like her, and she gives pennies to Nora and none to me, and my da sides with her and flakes me, and one night I was so heart-scalded I made up my mind I'd have to kill her."

"And what would you do with the body?" he asked with great interest.

"I was thinking I could chop that up and carry it away in a barrow I have," I said.

"Begor, Jackie," he said, "do you know you're a terrible child?"

"I know, father," I said, for I was just thinking the same thing myself. "I tried to kill Nora too with a bread-knife under the table, only I missed her."

"Is that the little girl that was beating you just now?" he asked.

"'Tis, father."

"Someone will go for her with a bread-knife one day, and he won't miss her," he said rather cryptically. "You must have great courage. Between ourselves, there's a lot of people I'd like to do the same to but I'd never have the nerve. Hanging is an awful death."

"Is it, father?" I asked with the deepest interest—I was always very keen on hanging. "Did you ever see a fellow hanged?"

"Dozens of them," he said solemnly. "And they all died roaring."

"Jay!" I said.

"Oh, a horrible death!" he said with great satisfaction. "Lots of the fellows I saw killed their grandmothers too, but they all said 'twas never worth it."

He had me there for a full ten minutes talking, and then walked out the chapel yard with me. I was genuinely sorry to part with him, because he was the most entertaining character I'd ever met in the religious line. Outside, after the shadow of the church, the sunlight was like the roaring of waves on a beach; it dazzled me; and when the frozen silence melted and I heard the screech of trams on the road, my heart soared. I knew now I wouldn't die in the night and come back, leaving marks on my mother's furniture. It would be a great worry to her, and the poor soul had enough.

Nora was sitting on the railing, waiting for me, and she put on a very sour puss when she saw the priest with me. She was mad jealous because a priest had never come out of the church with her.

"Well," she asked coldly, after he left me, "what did he give you?"

"Three Hail Marys," I said.

"Three Hail Marys," she repeated incredulously. "You mustn't have told him anything."

"I told him everything," I said confidently.

"About Gran and all?"

"About Gran and all."

(All she wanted was to be able to go home and say I'd made a bad confession.)

"Did you tell him you went for me with the bread-knife?" she asked with a frown.

"I did to be sure."

"And he only gave you three Hail Marys?"

"That's all."

She slowly got down from the railing with a baffled air. Clearly, this was beyond her. As we mounted the steps back to the main road she looked at me suspiciously.

"What are you sucking?" she asked.

"Bullseyes."

"Was it the priest gave them to you?"

"'Twas."

"Lord God," she wailed bitterly, "some people have all the luck! 'Tis no advantage to anybody trying to be good. I might just as well be a sinner like you."

1952

The Man Who Was Almost a Man

RICHARD WRIGHT

[1908–1960]

Dave struck out across the fields, looking homeward through paling light. Whuts the usa talkin wid em niggers in the field? Anyhow, his mother was putting supper on the table. Them niggers can't understand *nothing.* One of these days he was going to get a gun and practice shooting, then they can't talk to him as though he were a little boy. He slowed, looking at the ground. Shucks, Ah ain scareda them even ef they are biggern me! Aw, Ah know whut Ahma do. . . . Ahm going by ol Joe's sto n git that Sears Roebuck catlog n look at them guns. Mabbe Ma will lemme buy one when she gits mah pay from ol man Hawkins. Ahma beg her t gimme some money. Ahm ol enough to hava gun. Ahm seventeen. Almost a man. He strode, feeling his long, loose-jointed limbs. Shucks, a man oughta hava little gun aftah he done worked hard all day. . . .

He came in sight of Joe's store. A yellow lantern glowed on the front porch. He mounted steps and went through the screen door, hearing it bang behind him. There was a strong smell of coal oil and mackerel fish. He felt very confident until he saw fat Joe walk in through the rear door, then his courage began to ooze.

'Howdy, Dave! Whutcha want?'

'How yuh, Mistah Joe? Aw, Ah don wanna buy nothing. Ah jus wanted t see ef yuhd lemme look at tha ol catlog erwhile.'

'Sure! You wanna see it here?'

'Nawsuh. Ah wans t take it home wid me. Ahll bring it back termorrow when Ah come in from the fiels.'

'You plannin on buyin something?'

'Yessuh.'

'Your ma letting you have your own money now?'

'Shucks. Mistah Joe, Ahm gittin t be a man like anybody else!'

Joe laughed and wiped his greasy white face with a red bandanna.

'Whut you plannin on buyin?'

Dave looked at the floor, scratched his head, scratched his thigh, and smiled. Then he looked up shyly.

'Ahll tell yuh, Mistah Joe, ef yuh promise yuh won't tell.'

'I promise.'

'Waal, Ahma buy a gun.'

'A gun? Whut you want with a gun?'

'Ah wanna keep it.'

'You ain't nothing but a boy. You don't need a gun.'

'Aw, lemme have the catalog, Mistah Joe. Ahll bring it back.'

Joe walked through the rear door. Dave was elated. He looked around at barrels of sugar and flour. He heard Joe coming back. He craned his neck to see if he were bringing the book. Yeah, he's got it! Gawddog, he's got it!

'Here; but be sure you bring it back. It's the only one I got.'

'Sho, Mistah Joe.'

'Say, if you wanna buy a gun, why don't you buy one from me. I gotta gun to sell.'

'Will it shoot?'

'Sure it'll shoot.'

'Whut kind is it?'

'Oh, it's kinda old. . . . A Lefthand Wheeler. A pistol. A big one.'

'Is it got bullets in it?'

'It's loaded.'

'Kin Ah see it?'

'Where's your money?'

'Whut yuh wan fer it?'

'I'll let you have it for two dollars.'

'Just *two* dollahs? Shucks, Ah could buy tha when Ah git mah pay.'

'I'll have it here when you want it.'

'Awright, suh. Ah be in fer it.'

He went through the door, hearing it slam again behind him.

Ahma git some money from Ma n buy me a gun! Only *two* dollahs! He tucked the thick catalogue under his arm and hurried.

'Where yuh been, boy?' His mother held a steaming dish of black-eyed peas.

'Aw, Ma, Ah jus stopped down the road t talk wid th boys.'

'Yuh know bettah than t keep suppah waitin.'

He sat down, resting the catalogue on the edge of the table.

'Yuh git up from there and git to the well n wash yosef! Ah ain feedin no hogs in mah house!'

She grabbed his shoulder and pushed him. He stumbled out of the room, then came back to get the catalogue.

'Whut this?'

'Aw, Ma, it's jusa catlog.'

'Who yuh git it from?'

'From Joe, down at the sto.'

'Waal, thas good. We kin use it around the house.'

'Naw, Ma.' He grabbed for it. 'Gimme mah catlog, Ma.'

She held onto it and glared at him.

'Quit hollerin at me! Whuts wrong wid yuh? Yuh crazy?'

'But Ma, please. It ain mine! It's Joe's! He tol me t bring it back t im termorrow.'

She gave up the book. He stumbled down the back steps, hugging the thick book under his arm. When he had splashed water on his face and hands, he groped back to the kitchen and fumbled in a corner for the towel. He bumped into a chair; it clattered to the floor. The catalogue sprawled at his feet. When he had dried his eyes he snatched up the book and held it again under his arm. His mother stood watching him.

'Now, ef yuh gonna acka fool over that ol book, Ahll take it n burn it up.'

'Naw, Ma, please.'

'Waal, set down n be still!'

He sat and drew the oil lamp close. He thumbed page after page, unaware of the food his mother set on the table. His father came in. Then his small brother.

'Whutcha got there, Dave?' his father asked.

'Jusa catlog,' he answered, not looking up.

'Ywah, here they is!' His eyes glowed at blue and black revolvers.

He glanced up, feeling sudden guilt. His father was watching him. He eased the book under the table and rested it on his knees. After the blessing was asked, he ate. He scooped up peas and swallowed fat meat without chewing. Buttermilk helped to wash it down. He did not want to mention money before his father. He would do much better by cornering his mother when she was alone. He looked at his father uneasily out of the edge of his eye.

'Boy, how come yuh don quit foolin wid tha book n eat yo suppah?'

'Yessuh.'

'How yuh n ol man Hawkins gittin erlong?'

'Suh?'

'Can't yuh hear? Why don yuh lissen? Ah ast yuh how wuz yuh n ol man Hawkins gittin erlong?'

'Oh, swell, Pa. Ah plows mo lan than anybody over there.'

'Waal, yuh oughta keep yo min on whut yuh doin.'

'Yessuh.'

He poured his plate full of molasses and sopped at it slowly with a chunk of cornbread. When all but his mother had left the kitchen, he still sat and looked again at the guns in the catalogue. Lawd, ef Ah only had tha pretty one! He could almost feel the slickness of the weapon with his fingers. If he had a gun like that he would polish it and keep it shining so it would never rust. N Ahd keep it loaded, by Gawd!

'Ma?'

'Hunh?'

'Ol man Hawkins give yuh mah money yit?'

'Yeah, but ain no usa yuh thinkin bout thowin nona it erway. Ahm keepin tha money sos yuh kin have cloes t go to school this winter.'

He rose and went to her side with the open catalogue in his palms. She was washing dishes, her head bent low over a pan. Shyly he raised the open book. When he spoke his voice was husky, faint.

'Ma, Gawd knows Ah wans one of these.'

'One of whut?' she asked, not raising her eyes.

'One of *these,*' he said again, not daring even to point. She glanced up at the page, then at him with wide eyes.

'Nigger is yuh gone plum crazy?'

'Ah, Ma——'

'Git outta here! Don yuh talk t me bout no gun! Yuh a fool!'

'Ma, Ah kin buy one fer *two* dollahs.'

'Not ef Ah knows it yuh ain!'

'But yuh promised me one——'

'Ah don care whut Ah promised! Yuh ain nothing but a boy yit!'

'Ma, ef yuh lemme buy one Ahll *never* ast yuh fer nothing no mo.'

'Ah tol yuh t git outta here! Yuh ain gonna toucha penny of tha money fer no gun! Thas how come Ah has Mistah Hawkins t pay yo wages t me, cause Ah knows yuh ain got no sense.'

'But Ma, we needa gun. Pa ain got no gun. We needa gun in the house. Yuh kin never tell whut might happen.'

'Now don yuh try to maka fool outta me, boy! Ef we did hava gun yuh wouldn't have it!'

He laid the catalogue down and slipped his arm around her waist.

'Aw, Ma, Ah done worked hard alla summer n ain ast yuh fer nothin, is Ah, now?'

'Thas whut yuh spose t do!'

'But Ma, Ah wans a gun. Yuh kin lemme have two dollahs outta mah money. Please, Ma. I kin give it to Pa . . . Please, Ma! Ah loves yuh, Ma.'

When she spoke her voice came soft and low.

'Whut yuh wan wida gun, Dave? Yuh don need no gun. Yuhll git in trouble. N ef yo Pa jus *thought* Ah let yuh have money t buy a gun he'd hava fit.'

'Ahll hide it, Ma, it ain but two dollahs.'

'Lawd, chil, whuts wrong wid yuh?'

'Ain nothing wrong, Ma. Ahm almos a man now. Ah wans a gun.'

'Who gonna sell yuh a gun?'

'Ol Joe at the sto.'

'N it don cos but two dollahs?'

'Thas all, Ma. Just two dollahs. Please, Ma.'

She was stacking the plates away; her hands moved slowly, reflectively. Dave kept an anxious silence. Finally, she turned to him.

'Ahll let yuh git tha gun ef yuh promise me one thing.'

'Whuts tha, Ma?'

'Yuh bring it straight back t *me,* yuh hear? Itll be fer Pa.'

'Yessum! Lemme go now, Ma.'

She stooped, turned slightly to one side, raised the hem of her dress, rolled down the top of her stocking, and came up with a slender wad of bills.

'Here,' she said. 'Lawd knows yuh don need no gun. But yer Pa does. Yuh bring it right back t *me,* yuh hear? Ahma put it up. Now ef yuh don, Ahma have yuh Pa lick yuh so hard yuh won ferget it.'

'Yessum.'

He took the money, ran down the steps, and across the yard.

'Dave! Yuuuuuh Daaaaave!'

He heard, but he was not going to stop now. 'Naw, Lawd!'

The first movement he made the following morning was to reach under his pillow for the gun. In the gray light of dawn he held it loosely, feeling a sense of power. Could killa man wida gun like this. Kill anybody, black er white. And if he were holding his gun in his hand nobody could run over him; they would have to respect him. It was a big gun, with a long barrel and a heavy handle. He raised and lowered it in his hand, marveling at its weight.

He had not come straight home with it as his mother had asked; instead he had stayed out in the fields, holding the weapon in his hand, aiming it now and then at some imaginary foe. But he had not fired it; he had been afraid that his father might hear. Also he was not sure he knew how to fire it.

To avoid surrendering the pistol he had not come into the house until he knew that all were asleep. When his mother had tiptoed to his bedside late that night and demanded the gun, he had first played 'possum; then he had told her that the gun was hidden outdoors, that he would bring it to her in the morning. Now he lay turning it slowly in his hands. He broke it, took out the cartridges, felt them, and then put them back.

He slid out of bed, got a long strip of old flannel from a trunk, wrapped the gun in it, and tied it to his naked thigh while it was still loaded. He did not go in to breakfast. Even though it was not yet daylight, he started for Jim Hawkins' plantation. Just as the sun was rising he reached the barns where the mules and plows were kept.

'Hey! That you, Dave?'

He turned. Jim Hawkins stood eying him suspiciously.

'Whatre yuh doing here so early?'

'Ah didn't know Ah wuz gittin up so early, Mistah Hawkins. Ah wuz fixin t hitch up ol Jenny n take her t the fiels.'

'Good. Since you're here so early, how about plowing that stretch down by the woods?'

'Suits me, Mistah Hawkins.'

'O.K. Go to it!'

He hitched Jenny to a plow and started across the fields. Hot dog! This was just what he wanted. If he could get down by the woods, he could shoot his gun and nobody would hear. He walked behind the plow, hearing the traces creaking, feeling the gun tied tight to his thigh.

When he reached the woods, he plowed two whole rows before he decided to take out the gun. Finally, he stopped, looked in all directions, then untied the gun and held it in his hand. He turned to the mule and smiled.

'Know whut this is, Jenny? Naw, yuh wouldn't know! Yuhs jusa ol mule! Anyhow, this is a gun, n it kin shoot, by Gawd!'

He held the gun at arm's length. Whut t hell, Ahma shoot this thing! He looked at Jenny again.

'Lissen here, Jenny! When Ah pull this ol trigger Ah don wan yuh t run n acka fool now.'

Jenny stood with head down, her short ears pricked straight. Dave walked off about twenty feet, held the gun far out from him, at arm's length, and turned his head. Hell, he told himself, Ah ain afraid. The gun felt loose in his fingers; he waved it wildly for a moment. Then he shut his eyes and tightened his forefinger. *Blooom!* A report half-deafened him and he thought his right hand was torn from his arm. He heard Jenny whinnying and galloping over the field, and he found himself on his knees, squeezing his fingers hard between his legs. His hand was numb; he jammed it into his mouth, trying to warm it, trying to stop the pain. The gun lay at his feet. He did not quite know what had happened. He stood up and stared at the gun as though it were a live thing. He gritted his teeth and kicked the gun. Yuh almos broke mah arm! He turned to look for Jenny; she was far over the fields, tossing her head and kicking wildly.

'Hol on there, ol mule!'

When he caught up with her she stood trembling, walling her big white eyes at him. The plow was far away; the traces had broken. Then Dave stopped short, looking, not believing. Jenny was bleeding. Her left side was red and wet with blood. He went closer. Lawd have mercy! Wondah did Ah shoot this mule? He grabbed for Jenny's mane. She flinched, snorted, whirled, tossing her head.

'Hol on now! Hol on.'

Then he saw the hole in Jenny's side, right between the ribs. It was round, wet, red. A crimson stream streaked down the front leg, flowing fast. Good Gawd! Ah wuznt shootin at tha mule. . . . He felt panic. He knew he had to stop that blood, or Jenny would bleed to death. He had never seen so much blood in all his life. He ran the mule for half a mile, trying to catch her. Finally she stopped, breathing hard, stumpy tail half arched. He caught her mane and led her back to where the plow and gun lay. Then he stopped and grabbed handfuls of damp black earth and tried to plug the bullet hole. Jenny shuddered, whinnied, and broke from him.

'Hol on! Hol on now!'

He tried to plug it again, but blood came anyhow. His fingers were hot and sticky. He rubbed dirt hard into his palms, trying to dry them. Then again he attempted to plug the bullet hole, but Jenny shied away, kicking her heels high. He stood helpless. He had to do something. He ran at Jenny; she dodged him. He watched a red stream of blood flow down Jenny's leg and form a bright pool at her feet.

'Jenny . . . Jenny . . .' he called weakly.

His lips trembled. She's bleeding t death! He looked in the direction of home, wanting to go back, wanting to get help. But he saw the pistol lying in the damp black clay. He had a queer feeling that if he only did something, this would not be; Jenny would not be there bleeding to death.

When he went to her this time, she did not move. She stood with sleepy, dreamy eyes; and when he touched her she gave a low-pitched whinny and knelt to the ground, her front knees slopping in blood.

'Jenny . . . Jenny . . .' he whispered.

For a long time she held her neck erect; then her head sank, slowly. Her ribs swelled with a mighty heave and she went over.

Dave's stomach felt empty, very empty. He picked up the gun

and held it gingerly between his thumb and forefinger. He buried it at the foot of a tree. He took a stick and tried to cover the pool of blood with dirt—but what was the use? There was Jenny lying with her mouth open and her eyes walled and glassy. He could not tell Jim Hawkins he had shot his mule. But he had to tell something. Yeah, Ahll tell em Jenny started gittin wil n fell on the joint of the plow. . . . But that would hardly happen to a mule. He walked across the field slowly, head down.

It was sunset. Two of Jim Hawkins' men were over near the edge of the woods digging a hole in which to bury Jenny. Dave was surrounded by a knot of people; all of them were looking down at the dead mule.

'I don't see how in the world it happened,' said Jim Hawkins for the tenth time.

The crowd parted and Dave's mother, father, and small brother pushed into the center.

'Where Dave?' his mother called.

'There he is,' said Jim Hawkins.

His mother grabbed him.

'Whut happened, Dave? Whut yuh done?'

'Nothing.'

'C'mon, boy, talk,' his father said.

Dave took a deep breath and told the story he knew nobody believed.

'Waal,' he drawled, 'Ah brung ol Jenny down here sos Ah could do mah plowin. Ah plowed bout two rows, just like yuh see.' He stopped and pointed at the long rows of upturned earth. 'Then something musta been wrong wid ol Jenny. She wouldn't ack right atall. She started snortin n kickin her heels. Ah tried to hol her, but she pulled erway, rearin n goin on. Then when the point of the plow was stickin up in the air, she swung erroun n twisted hersef back on it. . . . She stuck hersef n started t bleed. N fo Ah could do anything, she wuz dead.'

'Did you ever hear of anything like that in all your life?' asked Jim Hawkins.

There were white and black standing in the crowd. They murmured. Dave's mother came close to him and looked hard into his face.

'Tell the truth, Dave,' she said.

'Looks like a bullet hole ter me,' said one man.

'Dave, whut yuh do wid tha gun?' his mother asked.

The crowd surged in, looking at him. He jammed his hands into his pockets, shook his head slowly from left to right, and backed away. His eyes were wide and painful.

'Did he hava gun?' asked Jim Hawkins.

'By Gawd, Ah tol yuh tha wuz a *gun* wound,' said a man, slapping his thigh.

His father caught his shoulders and shook him till his teeth rattled.

'Tell whut happened, yuh rascal! Tell whut . . .'

Dave looked at Jenny's stiff legs and began to cry.

'Whut yuh do wid tha gun?' his mother asked.

'Whut wuz he doin wida gun?' his father asked.

'Come on and tell the truth,' said Hawkins. 'Ain't nobody going to hurt you . . .'

His mother crowded close to him.

'Did yuh shoot tha mule, Dave?'

Dave cried, seeing blurred white and black faces.

"Ahh ddinnt gggo tt sshoooot hher. . . . Ah ssswear off Gawd Ahh ddint. . . . Ah wuz a-tryin t sssee ef the ol gggun would sshoot—'

'Where yuh git the gun from?' his father asked.

'Ah got it from Joe, at the sto.'

'Where yuh git the money?'

'Ma give it t me.'

'He kept worryin me, Bob. . . . Ah had t. . . . Ah tol im t bring the gun right back t me. . . . It was fer yuh, the gun.'

'But how yuh happen to shoot that mule?' asked Jim Hawkins.

'Ah wuznt shootin at the mule, Mistah Hawkins. The gun jumped when Ah pulled the trigger . . . N fo Ah knowed anything Jenny wuz there a-bleedin.'

Somebody in the crowd laughed. Jim Hawkins walked close to Dave and looked into his face.

'Well, looks like you have bought you a mule, Dave.'

'Ah swear fo Gawd, Ah didn't go t kill the mule, Mistah Hawkins!'

'But you killed her!'

All the crowd was laughing now. They stood on tiptoe and poked heads over one another's shoulders.

'Well, boy, looks like yuh done bought a dead mule! Hahaha!'

'Ain tha ershame.'

'Hohohohoho.'

Dave stood head down, twisting his feet in the dirt.

'Well, you needn't worry about it, Bob,' said Jim Hawkins to Dave's father. 'Just let the boy keep on working and pay me two dollars a month.'

'Whut yuh wan fer yo mule, Mistah Hawkins?'

Jim Hawkins screwed up his eyes.

'Fifty dollars.'

'Whut yuh do wid tha gun?' Dave's father demanded.

Dave said nothing.

'Yuh wan me t take a tree lim n beat yuh till yuh talk!'

'Nawsuh!'

'Whut yuh do wid it?'

'Ah throwed it erway.'

'Where?'

'Ah . . . Ah throwed it in the creek.'

'Waal, c mon home. N firs thing in the mawnin git to tha creek n fin tha gun.'

'Yessuh.'

'Whut yuh pay fer it?'

'Two dollahs.'

'Take tha gun n git yo money back n carry it t Mistah Hawkins, yuh hear? N don fergit Ahma lam yo black bottom good fer this! Now march yosef on home, suh!'

Dave turned and walked slowly. He heard people laughing. Dave glared, his eyes welling with tears. Hot anger bubbled in him. Then he swallowed and stumbled on.

That night Dave did not sleep. He was glad that he had gotten out of killing the mule so easily, but he was hurt. Something hot seemed to turn over inside him each time he remembered how they had laughed. He tossed on his bed, feeling his hard pillow. N Pa says he's gonna beat me. . . . He remembered other beatings, and his back quivered. Naw, naw, Ah sho don wan im t beat me tha way no mo. . . . Dam em *all!* Nobody ever gave him anything. All he did was work. They treat me lika mule. . . . N then they beat me. . . . He gritted his teeth. N Ma had t tell on me.

Well, if he had to, he would take old man Hawkins that two dollars. But that meant selling the gun. And he wanted to keep that gun. Fifty dollahs fer a dead mule.

He turned over, thinking of how he had fired the gun. He had an itch to fire it again. Ef other men kin shoota gun, by Gawd, Ah kin! He was still listening. Mebbe they all sleepin now. . . . The house was still. He heard the soft breathing of his brother. Yes, now! He would go down and get that gun and see if he could fire it! He eased out of bed and slipped into overalls.

The moon was bright. He ran almost all the way to the edge of the woods. He stumbled over the ground, looking for the spot where he had buried the gun. Yeah, here it is. Like a hungry dog scratching for a bone he pawed it up. He puffed his black cheeks and blew dirt from the trigger and barrel. He broke it and found four cartridges unshot. He looked around; the fields were filled with silence and moonlight. He clutched the gun stiff and hard in his fingers. But as soon as he wanted to pull the trigger, he shut his eyes and turned his head. Naw, Ah can't shoot wid mah eyes closed n mah head turned. With effort he held his eyes open; then he squeezed. *Blooooom!* He was stiff, not breathing. The gun was still in his hands. Dammit, he'd done it! He fired again. *Bloooom!* He smiled. *Bloooom! Bloooom! Click, click.* There! It was empty. If anybody could shoot a gun, he could. He put the gun into his hip pocket and started across the fields.

When he reached the top of a ridge he stood straight and proud in the moonlight, looking at Jim Hawkins' big white house, feeling the gun sagging in his pocket. Lawd, ef Ah had jus one mo bullet Ahd taka shot at tha house. Ahd like t scare ol man Hawkins jusa little. . . . Jussa enough t let im know Dave Sanders is a man.

To his left the road curved, running to the tracks of the Illinois Central. He jerked his head, listening. From far off came a faint *hoooof-hoooof; hoooof-hoooof; hoooof-hoooof . . .* Tha's number eight. He took a swift look at Jim Hawkins' white house; he thought of pa, of ma, of his little brother, and the boys. He thought of the dead mule and heard *hoooof-hoooof; hoooof-hoooof; hoooof-hoooof* . . . He stood rigid. Two dollahs a mont. Les see now. . . . Tha means itll take bout two years. Shucks! Ahll be dam!

He started down the road, toward the tracks. Yeah, here she comes! He stood beside the track and held himself stiffly. Here she comes, erroun the ben. . . . C mon, yuh slow poke! C mon! He had his hand on his gun; something quivered in his stomach. Then the train thundered past, the gray and brown box cars rumbling and clinking. He gripped the gun tightly; then he jerked his hand out of his pocket. Ah betcha Bill wouldn't do it! Ah betcha. . . . The cars slid past, steel grinding upon steel. Ahm riding yuh ternight so hep me Gawd! He was hot all over. He hesitated just a moment; then he grabbed, pulled atop of a car, and lay flat. He felt his pocket; the gun was still there. Ahead the long rails were glinting in the moonlight, stretching away, away to somewhere, somewhere where he could be a man. . . .

1940

A Worn Path

EUDORA WELTY

[b. 1909]

It was December—a bright frozen day in the early morning. Far out in the country there was an old Negro woman with her head tied in a red rag, coming along a path through the pinewoods. Her name was Phoenix Jackson. She was very old and small and she walked slowly in the dark pine shadows, moving a little from side to side in her steps, with the balanced heaviness and lightness of a pendulum in a grandfather clock. She carried a thin, small cane made from an umbrella, and with this she kept tapping the frozen earth in front of her. This made a grave and persistent noise in the still air, that seemed meditative like the chirping of a solitary little bird.

She wore a dark striped dress reaching down to her shoe tops, and an equally long apron of bleached sugar sacks, with a full pocket: all neat and tidy, but every time she took a step she might have fallen over her shoe-laces, which dragged from her unlaced shoes. She looked straight ahead. Her eyes were blue with age. Her skin had a pattern all its own of numberless branching wrinkles and as though a whole little tree stood in the middle of her forehead, but a golden color ran underneath, and the two knobs of her cheeks were illuminated by a yellow burning under the dark. Under the red rag her hair came down on her neck in the frailest of ringlets, still black, and with an odor like copper.

Now and then there was a quivering in the thicket. Old Phoenix said, "Out of my way, all you foxes, owls, beetles, jack rabbits, coons, and wild animals! . . . Keep out from under these feet, little bob-whites. . . . Keep the big wild hogs out of my path. Don't let none of those come running my direction. I got a long way." Under her small black-freckled hand her cane, limber as a buggy whip, would switch at the brush as if to rouse up any hiding things.

On she went. The woods were deep and still. The sun made the pine needles almost too bright to look at, up where the wind rocked. The cones dropped as light as feathers. Down in the hollow was the mourning dove—it was not too late for him.

The path ran up a hill. "Seem like there is chains about my feet, time I get this far," she said, in the voice of argument old people keep to use with themselves. "Something always take a hold of me on this hill—pleads I should stay."

After she got to the top she turned and gave a full, severe look behind her where she had come. "Up through pines," she said at length. "Now down through oaks."

Her eyes opened their widest, and she started down gently. But before she got to the bottom of the hill a bush caught her dress.

Her fingers were busy and intent, but her skirts were full and long, so that before she could pull them free in one place they were caught in another. It was not possible to allow the dress to tear. "I in the thorny bush," she said. "Thorns, you doing your appointed work. Never want to let folks pass—no sir. Old eyes thought you was a pretty little *green* bush."

Finally, trembling all over, she stood free, and after a moment dared to stoop for her cane.

"Sun so high!" she cried, leaning back and looking, while the thick tears went over her eyes. "The time getting all gone here."

At the foot of this hill was a place where a log was laid across the creek.

"Now comes the trial," said Phoenix.

Putting her right foot out, she mounted the log and shut her eyes. Lifting her skirt, levelling her cane fiercely before her, like a festival figure in some parade, she began to march across. Then she opened her eyes and she was safe on the other side.

"I wasn't as old as I thought," she said.

But she sat down to rest. She spread her skirts on the bank around her and folded her hands over her knees. Up above her was a tree in a pearly cloud of mistletoe. She did not dare to close her eyes, and when a little boy brought her a little plate with a slice of marble-cake on it she spoke to him. "That would be acceptable," she said. But when she went to take it there was just her own hand in the air.

So she left that tree, and had to go through a barbed-wire fence. There she had to creep and crawl, spreading her knees and stretching her fingers like a baby trying to climb the steps. But she talked loudly to herself: she could not let her dress be torn now, so late in the day, and she could not pay for having her arm or her leg sawed off if she got caught fast where she was.

At last she was safe through the fence and risen up out in the clearing. Big dead trees, like black men with one arm, were standing in the purple stalks of the withered cotton field. There sat a buzzard.

"Who you watching?"

In the furrow she made her way along.

"Glad this not the season for bulls," she said, looking sideways, "and the good Lord made his snakes to curl up and sleep in the winter. A pleasure I don't see no two-headed snake coming around that tree, where it come once. It took a while to get by him, back in the summer."

She passed through the old cotton and went into a field of dead corn. It whispered and shook and was taller than her head. "Through the maze now," she said, for there was no path.

Then there was something tall, black, and skinny there, moving before her.

At first she took it for a man. It could have been a man dancing in the field. But she stood still and listened, and it did not make a sound. It was as silent as a ghost.

"Ghost," she said sharply, "who be you the ghost of? For I have heard of nary death close by."

But there was no answer—only the ragged dancing in the wind.

She shut her eyes, reached out her hand, and touched a sleeve. She found a coat and inside that an emptiness, cold as ice.

"You scarecrow," she said. Her face lighted. "I ought to be shut up for good," she said with laughter. "My senses is gone. I too old. I the oldest people I ever know. Dance, old scarecrow," she said, "while I dancing with you."

She kicked her foot over the furrow, and with mouth drawn down, shook her head once or twice in a little strutting way. Some husks blew down and whirled in streamers about her skirts.

Then she went on, parting her way from side to side with the cane, through the whispering field. At last she came to the end, to a wagon track where the silver grass blew between the red ruts. The quail were walking around like pullets, seeming all dainty and unseen.

"Walk pretty," she said. "This the easy place. This the easy going."

She followed the track, swaying through the quiet bare fields, through the little strings of trees silver in their dead leaves, past cabins silver from weather, with the doors and windows boarded shut, all like old women under a spell sitting there. "I walking in their sleep," she said, nodding her head vigorously.

In a ravine she went where a spring was silently flowing through a hollow log. Old Phoenix bent and drank. "Sweet-gum makes the water sweet," she said, and drank more. "Nobody know who made this well, for it was here when I was born."

The track crossed a swampy part where the moss hung as white as lace from every limb. "Sleep on, alligators, and blow your bubbles." Then the track went into the road.

Deep, deep the road went down between the high green-colored banks. Overhead the live-oaks met, and it was as dark as a cave.

A black dog with a lolling tongue came up out of the weeds by the ditch. She was meditating, and not ready, and when he came at her she only hit him a little with her cane. Over she went in the ditch, like a little puff of milk-weed.

Down there, her senses drifted away. A dream visited her, and she reached her hand up, but nothing reached down and gave her a pull. So she lay there and presently went to talking. "Old woman," she said to herself, "that black dog come up out of the weeds to stall you off, and now there he sitting on his fine tail, smiling at you."

A white man finally came along and found her—a hunter, a young man, with his dog on a chain.

"Well, Granny!" he laughed. "What are you doing there?"

"Lying on my back like a June-bug waiting to be turned over, mister," she said, reaching up her hand.

He lifted her up, gave her a swing in the air, and set her down, "Anything broken, Granny?"

"No sir, them old dead weeds is springy enough," said Phoenix, when she had got her breath. "I thank you for your trouble."

"Where do you live, Granny?" he asked, while the two dogs were growling at each other.

"Away back yonder, sir, behind the ridge. You can't even see it from here."

"On your way home?"

"No, sir, I going to town."

"Why, that's too far! That's as far as I walk when I come out myself, and I get something for my trouble." He patted the stuffed bag he carried, and there hung down a little closed claw. It was one of the bob-whites, with its beak hooked bitterly to show it was dead. "Now you go on home, Granny!"

"I bound to go to town, mister," said Phoenix. "The time come around."

He gave another laugh, filling the whole landscape. "I know you old colored people! Wouldn't miss going to town to see Santa Claus!"

But something held Old Phoenix very still. The deep lines in her face went into a fierce and different radiation. Without warning, she had seen with her own eyes a flashing nickel fall out of the man's pocket onto the ground.

"How old are you, Granny?" he was saying.

"There is no telling, mister," she said, "no telling."

Then she gave a little cry and clapped her hands and said, "Git on away from here, dog! Look! Look at that dog!" She laughed as if in admiration. "He ain't scared of nobody. He a big black dog." She whispered, "Sic him!"

"Watch me get rid of that cur," said the man. "Sic him, Pete! Sic him!"

Phoenix heard the dogs fighting, and heard the man running and throwing sticks. She even heard a gunshot. But she was slowly bending forward by that time, further and further forward, the lids stretched down over her eyes, as if she were doing this in her sleep. Her chin was lowered almost to her knees. The yellow palm of her hand came out from the fold of her apron. Her fingers slid down and along the ground under the piece of money with the grace and care they would have in lifting an egg from under a sitting hen. Then she slowly straightened up, she stood erect, and the nickel was in her apron pocket. A bird flew by. Her lips moved. "God watching me the whole time. I come to stealing."

The man came back, and his own dog panted about them. "Well, I scared him off that time," he said, and then he laughed and lifted his gun and pointed it at Phoenix.

She stood straight and faced him.

"Doesn't the gun scare you?" he said, still pointing it.

"No, sir, I seen plenty go off closer by, in my day, and for less than what I done," she said, holding utterly still.

He smiled, and shouldered the gun. "Well, Granny," he said, "you must be a hundred years old, and scared of nothing. I'd give you a dime if I had any money with me. But you take my advice and stay home, and nothing will happen to you."

"I bound to go on my way, mister," said Phoenix. She inclined her head in the red rag. Then they went in different directions, but she could hear the gun shooting again and again over the hill.

She walked on. The shadows hung from the oak trees to the road like curtains. Then she smelled wood-smoke, and smelled the river, and she saw a steeple and the cabins on their steep steps. Dozens of little black children whirled around her. There ahead was Natchez shining. Bells were ringing. She walked on.

In the paved city it was Christmas time. There were red and green electric lights strung and crisscrossed everywhere, and all turned on in the daytime. Old Phoenix would have been lost if she had not distrusted her eyesight and depended on her feet to know where to take her.

She paused quietly on the sidewalk where people were passing by. A lady came along in the crowd, carrying an armful of red-, green-, and silver-wrapped presents; she gave off perfume like the red roses in hot summer, and Phoenix stopped her.

"Please, missy, will you lace up my shoe?" She held up her foot.

"What do you want, Grandma?"

"See my shoe," said Phoenix. "Do all right for out in the country, but wouldn't look right to go in a big building."

"Stand still then, Grandma," said the lady. She put her packages down on the sidewalk beside her and laced and tied both shoes tightly.

"Can't lace 'em with a cane," said Phoenix. "Thank you, missy.

I doesn't mind asking a nice lady to tie up my shoe, when I gets out on the street."

Moving slowly and from side to side, she went into the big building and into a tower of steps, where she walked up and around and around until her feet knew to stop.

She entered a door, and there she saw nailed up on the wall the document that had been stamped with the gold seal and framed in the gold frame, which matched the dream that was hung up in her head.

"Here I be," she said. There was a fixed and ceremonial stiffness over her body.

"A charity case, I suppose," said an attendant who sat at the desk before her.

But Phoenix only looked above her head. There was sweat on her face, the wrinkles in her skin shone like a bright net.

"Speak up, Grandma," the woman said. "What's your name? We must have your history, you know. Have you been here before? What seems to be the trouble with you?"

Old Phoenix only gave a twitch to her face as if a fly were bothering her.

"Are you deaf?" cried the attendant.

But then the nurse came in.

"Oh, that's just old Aunt Phoenix," she said. "She doesn't come for herself—she has a little grandson. She makes these trips just as regular as clockwork. She lives away back off the Old Natchez Trace." She bent down. "Well, Aunt Phoenix, why don't you just take a seat? We won't keep you standing after your long trip." She pointed.

The old woman sat down, bolt upright in the chair.

"Now, how is the boy?" asked the nurse.

Old Phoenix did not speak.

"I said, how is the boy?"

But Phoenix only waited and stared straight ahead, her face very solemn and withdrawn into rigidity.

"Is his throat any better?" asked the nurse. "Aunt Phoenix, don't you hear me? Is your grandson's throat any better since the last time you came for the medicine?"

With her hands on her knees, the old woman waited, silent, erect and motionless, just as if she were in armour.

"You mustn't take up our time this way, Aunt Phoenix," the nurse said. "Tell us quickly about your grandson, and get it over. He isn't dead, is he?"

At last there came a flicker and then a flame of comprehension across her face, and she spoke.

"My grandson. It was my memory had left me. There I sat and forgot why I made my long trip."

"Forgot?" The nurse frowned. "After you came so far?"

Then Phoenix was like an old woman begging a dignified forgiveness for waking up frightened in the night. "I never did go to school, I was too old at the Surrender," she said in a soft voice. "I'm an old woman without an education. It was my memory fail me. My little grandson, he is just the same, and I forgot it in the coming."

"Throat never heals, does it?" said the nurse, speaking in a loud, sure voice to Old Phoenix. By now she had a card with something written on it, a little list. "Yes. Swallowed lye. When was it— January—two-three years ago—"

Phoenix spoke unasked now. "No, missy, he not dead, he just the same. Every little while his throat begin to close up again, and he not able to swallow. He not get his breath. He not able to help himself. So the time come around, and I go on another trip for the soothingmedicine."

"All right. The doctor said as long as you came to get it, you could have it," said the nurse. "But it's an obstinate case."

"My little grandson, he sit up there in the house all wrapped up, waiting by himself," Phoenix went on. "We is the only two left in the world. He suffer and it don't seem to put him back at all. He got a sweet look. He going to last. He wear a little patch quilt and peep out holding his mouth open like a little bird. I remembers so plain now. I not going to forget him again, no, the whole enduring time. I could tell him from all the others in creation."

"All right." The nurse was trying to hush her now. She brought her a bottle of medicine. "Charity," she said, making a check mark in a book.

Old Phoenix held the bottle close to her eyes and then carefully put it into her pocket.

"I thank you," she said.

"It's Christmas time, Grandma," said the attendant. "Could I give you a few pennies out of my purse?"

"Five pennies is a nickel," said Phoenix stiffly.

"Here's a nickel," said the attendant.

Phoenix rose carefully and held out her hand. She received the nickel and then fished the other nickel out of her pocket and laid it beside the new one. She stared at her palm closely, with her head on one side.

Then she gave a tap with her cane on the floor.

"This is what come to me to do," she said. "I going to the store and buy my child a little windmill they sells, made out of paper. He going to find it hard to believe there such a thing in the world. I'll march myself back where he waiting, holding it straight up in this hand."

She lifted her free hand, gave a little nod, turned round, and walked out of the doctor's office. Then her slow step began on the stairs, going down.

1941

The Country Husband

JOHN CHEEVER

[1912–1982]

To begin at the beginning, the airplane from Minneapolis in which Francis Weed was traveling East ran into heavy weather. The sky had been a hazy blue, with the clouds below the plane lying so close together that nothing could be seen of the earth. Then mist began to form outside the windows, and they flew into a white cloud of such density that it reflected the exhaust fires. The color of the cloud darkened to gray, and the plane began to rock. Francis had been in heavy weather before, but he had never been shaken up so much. The man in the seat beside him pulled a flask out of his pocket and took a drink. Francis smiled at his neighbor, but the man looked away; he wasn't sharing his painkiller with anyone. The plane had begun to drop and flounder wildly. A child was crying. The air in the cabin was overheated and stale, and Francis' left foot went to sleep. He read a little from a paper book that he had bought at the airport, but the violence of the storm divided his attention. It was black outside the ports. The exhaust fires blazed and shed sparks in the dark, and, inside, the shaded lights, the stuffiness, and the window curtains gave the cabin an atmosphere of intense and misplaced domesticity. Then the lights flickered and went out. "You know what I've always wanted to do?" the man beside Francis said suddenly. "I've always wanted to buy a farm in New Hampshire and raise beef cattle." The stewardess announced that they were going to make an emergency landing. All but the child saw in their minds the spreading wings of the Angel of Death. The pilot could be heard singing faintly, "I've got sixpence, jolly, jolly sixpence. I've got sixpence to last me all my life . . ." There was no other sound.

The loud groaning of the hydraulic valves swallowed up the pilot's song, and there was a shrieking high in the air, like automobile brakes, and the plane hit flat on its belly in a cornfield and shook them so violently that an old man up forward howled, "Me kidneys! Me kidneys!" The stewardess flung open the door, and someone opened an emergency door at the back, letting in the sweet noise of their continuing mortality—the idle splash and smell of a heavy rain. Anxious for their lives, they filed out of the doors and scattered over the cornfield in all directions, praying that the thread would hold. It did. Nothing happened. When it was clear that the plane would not burn or explode, the crew and the stewardess gathered the passengers together and led them to the shelter of a barn. They were not far from Philadelphia, and in a little while a string of taxis took them into the city. "It's just like the Marne," someone said, but there was surprisingly little relaxation of that suspiciousness with which many Americans regard their fellow-travelers.

In Philadelphia, Francis Weed got a train to New York. At the end of that journey, he crossed the city and caught, just as it was about to pull out, the commuting train that he took five nights a week to his home in Shady Hill.

He sat with Trace Bearden. "You know, I was in that plane that just crashed outside Philadelphia," he said. "We came down in a field . . ." He had traveled faster than the newspapers or the train, and the weather in New York was sunny and mild. It was a day in late September, as fragrant and shapely as an apple. Trace listened to the story, but how could he get excited? Francis had no powers that would let him re-create a brush with death— particularly in the atmosphere of a commuting train, journeying through a sunny countryside where already, in the slum gardens, there were signs of harvest. Trace picked up his newspaper, and Francis was left alone with his thoughts. He said good night to Trace on the platform at Shady Hill and drove in his secondhand Volkswagen up to the Blenhollow neighborhood, where he lived.

The Weeds' Dutch Colonial house was larger than it appeared to be from the driveway. The living room was spacious and divided like Gaul into three parts. Around an ell to the left as one entered from the vestibule was the long table, laid for six, with candles and a bowl of fruit in the center. The sounds and smells that came from the open kitchen door were appetizing, for Julia Weed was a good cook. The largest part of the living room centered around a fireplace. On the right were some bookshelves and a piano. The room was polished and tranquil, and from the windows that opened to the west there was some late-summer sunlight, brilliant and as clear as water. Nothing here was neglected; nothing had not been burnished. It was not the kind of household where, after prying open a stuck cigarette box, you would find an old shirt button and a tarnished nickel. The hearth was swept, the roses on the piano were reflected in the polish of the broad top, and there was an album of Schubert waltzes on the rack. Louisa Weed, a pretty girl of nine, was looking out the western windows. Her younger brother Henry was standing beside her. Her still younger brother, Toby, was studying the figures of some tonsured monks drinking beer on the polished brass of the wood box. Francis, taking off his hat and putting down his paper, was not consciously pleased with the scene; he was not that reflective. It was his element, his creation, and he returned to it with that sense of lightness and strength with which any creature returns to its home. "Hi, everybody," he said. "The plane from Minneapolis . . ."

Nine times out of ten, Francis would be greeted with affection, but tonight the children are absorbed in their own antagonisms. Francis has not finished his sentence about the plane crash before Henry plants a kick in Louisa's behind. Louisa swings around, saying, "*Damn* you!" Francis makes the mistake of scolding Louisa for bad language before he punishes Henry. Now Louisa turns on her father and accuses him of favoritism. Henry is always right; she is persecuted and lonely; her lot is hopeless. Francis turns to his son, but the boy has justification for the kick—she hit him first; she hit him on the ear, which is dangerous. Louisa agrees with this passionately. She hit him on the ear, and she *meant* to hit him on the ear, because he messed up her china collection. Henry says that this is a lie. Little Toby turns away from the wood box to throw in some evidence for Louisa. Henry claps his hand over little Toby's mouth. Francis separates the two boys but accidentally pushes Toby into the wood box. Toby begins to cry. Louisa is already crying. Just then, Julia Weed comes into that part of the room where the table is laid. She is a pretty, intelligent woman, and the white in her hair is premature. She does not seem to notice the fracas. "Hello, darling," she says serenely to Francis. "Wash your hands, everyone.

Dinner is ready." She strikes a match and lights the six candles in this vale of tears.

This simple announcement, like the war cries of the Scottish chieftains, only refreshes the ferocity of the combatants. Louisa gives Henry a blow on the shoulder. Henry, although he seldom cries, has pitched nine innings and is tired. He bursts into tears. Little Toby discovers a splinter in his hand and begins to howl. Francis says loudly that he has been in a plane crash and that he is tired. Julia appears again, from the kitchen, and, still ignoring the chaos, asks Francis to go upstairs and tell Helen that everything is ready. Francis is happy to go; it is like getting back to headquarters company. He is planning to tell his oldest daughter about the airplane crash, but Helen is lying on her bed reading a *True Romance* magazine, and the first thing Francis does is to take the magazine from her hand and remind Helen that he has forbidden her to buy it. She did not buy it, Helen replies. It was given to her by her best friend, Bessie Black. Everybody reads *True Romance.* Bessie Black's father reads *True Romance.* There isn't a girl in Helen's class who doesn't read *True Romance.* Francis expresses his detestation of the magazine and then tells her that dinner is ready—although from the sounds downstairs it doesn't seem so. Helen follows him down the stairs. Julia has seated herself in the candlelight and spread a napkin over her lap. Neither Louisa nor Henry has come to the table. Little Toby is still howling, lying face down on the floor. Francis speaks to him gently: "Daddy was in a plane crash this afternoon, Toby. Don't you want to hear about it?" Toby goes on crying. "If you don't come to the table now, Toby," Francis says, "I'll have to send you to bed without any supper." The little boy rises, gives him a cutting look, flies up the stairs to his bedroom, and slams the door. "Oh dear," Julia says, and starts to go after him. Francis says that she will spoil him. Julia says that Toby is ten pounds underweight and has to be encouraged to eat. Winter is coming, and he will spend the cold months in bed unless he has his dinner. Julia goes upstairs. Francis sits down at the table with Helen. Helen is suffering from the dismal feeling of having read too intently on a fine day, and she gives her father and the room a jaded look. She doesn't understand about the plane crash, because there wasn't a drop of rain in Shady Hill.

Julia returns with Toby, and they all sit down and are served. "Do I have to look at that big, fat slob?" Henry says, of Louisa. Everybody but Toby enters into this skirmish, and it rages up and down the table for five minutes. Toward the end, Henry puts his napkin over his head and, trying to eat that way, spills spinach all over his shirt. Francis asks Julia if the children couldn't have their dinner earlier. Julia's guns are loaded for this. She can't cook two dinners and lay two tables. She paints with lightning strokes that panorama of drudgery in which her youth, her beauty, and her wit have been lost. Francis says that he must be understood; he was nearly killed in an airplane crash, and he doesn't like to come home every night to a battlefield. Now Julia is deeply committed. Her voice trembles. He doesn't come home every night to a battlefield. The accusation is stupid and mean. Everything was tranquil until he arrived. She stops speaking, puts down her knife and fork, and looks into her plate as if it is a gulf. She begins to cry. "Poor Mummy!" Toby says, and when Julia gets up from the table, drying her tears with a napkin, Toby goes to her side. "Poor Mummy," he says. "Poor Mummy!" And they climb the stairs together. The other children drift away from the battlefield, and Francis goes into the back garden for a cigarette and some air.

It was a pleasant garden, with walks and flower beds and places to sit. The sunset had nearly burned out, but there was still plenty of light. Put into a thoughtful mood by the crash and the battle, Francis listened to the evening sounds of Shady Hill. "Varmints! Rascals!" old Mr. Nixon shouted to the squirrels in his bird-feeding station. "Avaunt and quit my sight!" A door slammed. Someone was playing tennis on the Babcocks' court; someone was cutting grass. Then Donald Goslin, who lived at the corner, began to play the "Moonlight Sonata." He did this nearly every night. He threw the tempo out the window and played it *rubato* from beginning to end, like an outpouring of tearful petulance, lonesomeness, and self-pity—of everything it was Beethoven's greatness not to know. The music rang up and down the street beneath the trees like an appeal for love, for tenderness, aimed at some lonely housemaid—some fresh-faced, homesick girl from Galway, looking at old snapshots in her third-floor room. "Here, Jupiter, here, Jupiter," Francis called to the Mercers' retriever. Jupiter crashed through the tomato vines with the remains of a felt hat in his mouth.

Jupiter was an anomaly. His retrieving instincts and his high spirits were out of place in Shady Hill. He was as black as coal, with a long, alert, intelligent, rakehell face. His eyes gleamed with mischief, and he held his head high. It was the fierce, heavily collared dog's head that appears in heraldry, in tapestry, and that used to appear on umbrella handles and walking sticks. Jupiter went where he pleased, ransacking wastebaskets, clotheslines, garbage pails, and shoe bags. He broke up garden parties and tennis matches, and got mixed up in the processional at Christ Church on Sunday, barking at the men in red dresses. He crashed through old Mr. Nixon's rose garden two or three times a day, cutting a wide swath through the Condesa de Sastagos, and as soon as Donald Goslin lighted his barbecue fire on Thursday nights, Jupiter would get the scent. Nothing the Goslins did could drive him away. Sticks and stones and rude commands only moved him to the edge of the terrace, where he remained, with his gallant and heraldic muzzle, waiting for Donald Goslin to turn his back and reach for the salt. Then he would spring onto the terrace, lift the steak lightly off the fire, and run away with the Goslins' dinner. Jupiter's days were numbered. The Wrightsons' German gardener or the Farquarsons' cook would soon poison him. Even old Mr. Nixon might put some arsenic in the garbage that Jupiter loved. "Here, Jupiter, Jupiter!" Francis called, but the dog pranced off, shaking the hat in his white teeth. Looking in at the windows of his house, Francis saw that Julia had come down and was blowing out the candles.

Julia and Francis Weed went out a great deal. Julia was well liked and gregarious, and her love of parties sprang from a most natural dread of chaos and loneliness. She went through her morning mail with real anxiety, looking for invitations, and she usually found some, but she was insatiable, and if she had gone out seven nights a week, it would not have cured her of a reflective look—the look of someone who hears distant music—for she would always suppose that there was a more brilliant party somewhere else. Francis limited her to two weeknight parties, putting a flexible interpretation on Friday, and rode through the weekend like a dory in a gale. The day after the airplane crash, the Weeds were to have dinner with the Farquarsons.

Francis got home late from town, and Julia got the sitter while he dressed, and then hurried him out of the house. The party was small and pleasant, and Francis settled down to enjoy himself. A new maid passed the drinks. Her hair was dark, and her face was round and pale and seemed familiar to Francis. He had not developed his memory as a sentimental faculty. Wood smoke, lilac, and other such perfumes did not stir him, and his memory was something like his appendix—a vestigial repository. It was not his limitation at all to be unable to escape the past; it was perhaps his limitation that he had escaped it so successfully. He might have seen the maid at other parties, he might have seen her taking a walk on Sunday afternoons, but in either case he would not be searching his memory now. Her face was, in a wonderful way, a moon face—Norman or Irish—but it was not beautiful enough to account for his feeling that he had seen her before, in circumstances that he ought to be able to remember. He asked Nellie Farquarson who she was. Nellie said that the maid had come through an agency, and that her home was Trénon, in Normandy—a small place with a church and a restaurant that Nellie had once visited. While Nellie talked on about her travels abroad, Francis realized where he had seen the woman before. It had been at the end of the war. He had left a replacement depot with some other men and taken a three-day pass in Trénon. On their second day, they had walked out to a crossroads to see the public chastisement of a young woman who had lived with the German commandant during the Occupation.

It was a cool morning in the fall. The sky was overcast, and poured down onto the dirt crossroads a very discouraging light. They were on high land and could see how like one another the shapes of the clouds and the hills were as they stretched off toward the sea. The prisoner arrived sitting on a three-legged stool in a farm cart. She stood by the cart while the mayor read the accusation and the sentence. Her head was bent and her face was set in that empty half smile behind which the whipped soul is suspended. When the mayor was finished, she undid her hair and let it fall across her back. A little man with a gray mustache cut off her hair with shears and dropped it on the ground. Then, with a bowl of soapy water and a straight razor, he shaved her skull clean. A woman approached and began to undo the fastenings of her clothes, but the prisoner pushed her aside and undressed herself. When she pulled her chemise over her head and threw it on the ground, she was naked. The women jeered; the men were still. There was no change in the falseness or the plaintiveness of the prisoner's smile. The cold wind made her white skin rough and hardened the nipples of her breasts. The jeering ended gradually, put down by the recognition of their common humanity. One woman spat on her, but some inviolable grandeur in her nakedness lasted through the ordeal. When the crowd was quiet, she turned—she had begun to cry—and, with nothing on but a pair of worn black shoes and stockings, walked down the dirt road alone away from the village. The round white face had aged a little, but there was no question but that the maid who passed his cocktails and later served Francis his dinner was the woman who had been punished at the crossroads.

The war seemed now so distant and that world where the cost of partisanship had been death or torture so long ago. Francis had lost track of the men who had been with him in Vésey. He could not count on Julia's discretion. He could not tell anyone. And if he had told the story now, at the dinner table, it would have been a social as well as a human error. The people in the Farquarsons' living room seemed united in their tacit claim that there had been no past, no war—that there was no danger or trouble in the world. In the recorded history of human arrangements, this extraordinary meeting would have fallen into place, but the atmosphere of Shady Hill made the memory unseemly and impolite. The prisoner withdrew after passing the coffee, but the encounter left Francis feeling languid; it had opened his memory and his senses, and left them dilated. He and Julia drove home when the party ended, and Julia went into the house. Francis stayed in the car to take the sitter home.

Expecting to see Mrs. Henlein, the old lady who usually stayed with the children, he was surprised when a young girl opened the door and came out onto the lighted stoop. She stayed in the light to count her textbooks. She was frowning and beautiful. Now, the world is full of beautiful young girls, but Francis saw here the difference between beauty and perfection. All those endearing flaws, moles, birthmarks, and healed wounds were missing, and he experienced in his consciousness that moment when music breaks glass, and felt a pang of recognition as strange, deep, and wonderful as anything in his life. It hung from her frown, from an impalpable darkness in her face—a look that impressed him as a direct appeal for love. When she had counted her books, she came down the steps and opened the car door. In the light, he saw that her cheeks were wet. She got in and shut the door.

"You're new," Francis said.

"Yes. Mrs. Henlein is sick. I'm Anne Murchison."

"Did the children give you any trouble?"

"Oh, no, no." She turned and smiled at him unhappily in the dim dashboard light. Her light hair caught on the collar of her jacket, and she shook her head to set it loose.

"You've been crying."

"Yes."

"I hope it was nothing that happened in our house."

"No, no, it was nothing that happened in your house." Her voice was bleak. "It's no secret. Everybody in the village knows. Daddy's an alcoholic, and he just called me from some saloon and gave me a piece of his mind. He thinks I'm immoral. He called just before Mrs. Weed came back."

"I'm sorry."

"Oh, *Lord!*" She gasped and began to cry. She turned toward Francis, and he took her in his arms and let her cry on his shoulder. She shook in his embrace, and this movement accentuated his sense of the fineness of her flesh and bone. The layers of their clothing felt thin, and when her shuddering began to diminish, it was so much like a paroxysm of love that Francis lost his head and pulled her roughly against him. She drew away. "I live on Belleview Avenue," she said. "You go down Lansing Street to the railroad bridge."

"All right." He started the car.

"You turn left at that traffic light. . . . Now you turn right here and go straight on toward the tracks."

The road Francis took brought him out of his own neighborhood, across the tracks, and toward the river, to a street where the near-poor lived, in houses whose peaked gables and trimmings of wooden lace conveyed the purest feelings of pride and romance, although the houses themselves could not have offered much privacy or comfort, they were all so small. The street was dark, and, stirred by the grace and beauty of the troubled girl, he seemed, in turning in to it, to have come into the deepest part of some submerged memory. In the distance, he saw a porch light burning. It was the only one, and she said that the house with the light was where she lived.

When he stopped the car, he could see beyond the porch light into a dimly lighted hallway with an old-fashioned clothes tree. "Well, here we are," he said, conscious that a young man would have said something different.

She did not move her hands from the books, where they were folded, and she turned and faced him. There were tears of lust in his eyes. Determinedly—not sadly—he opened the door on his side and walked around to open hers. He took her free hand, letting his fingers in between hers, climbed at her side the two concrete steps, and went up a narrow walk through a front garden where dahlias, marigolds, and roses—things that had withstood the light frosts—still bloomed, and made a bittersweet smell in the night air. At the steps, she freed her hand and then turned and kissed him swiftly. Then she crossed the porch and shut the door. The porch light went out, then the light in the hall. A second later, a light went on upstairs at the side of the house, shining into a tree that was still covered with leaves. It took her only a few minutes to undress and get into bed, and then the house was dark.

Julia was asleep when Francis got home. He opened a second window and got into bed to shut his eyes on that night, but as soon as they were shut—as soon as he had dropped off to sleep—the girl entered his mind, moving with perfect freedom through its shut doors and filling chamber after chamber with her light, her perfume, and the music of her voice. He was crossing the Atlantic with her on the old *Mauretania* and, later, living with her in Paris. When he woke from his dream, he got up and smoked a cigarette at the open window. Getting back into bed, he cast around in his mind for something he desired to do that would injure no one, and he thought of skiing. Up through the dimness in his mind rose the image of a mountain deep in snow. It was late in the day. Wherever his eyes looked, he saw broad and heartening things. Over his shoulder, there was a snow-filled valley, rising into wooded hills where the trees dimmed the whiteness like a sparse coat of hair. The cold deadened all sound but the loud, iron clanking of the lift machinery. The light on the trails was blue, and it was harder than it had been a minute or two earlier to pick the turns, harder to judge—now that the snow was all deep blue—the crust, the ice, the bare spots, and the deep piles of dry powder. Down the mountain he swung, matching his speed against the contours of a slope that had been formed in the first ice age, seeking with ardor some simplicity of feeling and circumstance. Night fell then, and he drank a Martini with some old friend in a dirty country bar.

In the morning, Francis' snow-covered mountain was gone, and he was left with his vivid memories of Paris and the *Mauretania.* He had been bitten gravely. He washed his body, shaved his jaws, drank his coffee, and missed the seven-thirty-one. The train pulled out just as he brought his car to the station, and the longing he felt for the coaches as they drew stubbornly away from him reminded him of the humors of love. He waited for the eight-two, on what was now an empty platform. It was a clear morning; the morning seemed thrown like a gleaming bridge of light over his mixed affairs. His spirits were feverish and high. The image of the girl seemed to put him into a relationship to the world that was mysterious and enthralling. Cars were beginning to fill up the parking lot, and he noticed that those that had driven down from the high land above Shady Hill were white with hoarfrost. This first clear sign of autumn thrilled him. An express train—a night train from Buffalo or Albany—came down the tracks between the platforms, and he saw that the roofs of the foremost cars were covered with a skin of ice. Struck by the miraculous physicalness of everything, he smiled at the passengers in the dining car, who could be seen eating eggs and wiping their mouths with napkins as they traveled. The sleeping-car compartments, with their soiled bed linen, trailed through the fresh morning like a string of rooming-house windows. Then he saw an extraordinary thing; at one of the bedroom windows sat an unclothed woman of exceptional beauty, combining her golden hair. She passed like an apparition through Shady Hill, combing and combing her hair, and Francis followed her with his eyes until she was out of sight. Then old Mrs. Wrightson joined him on the platform and began to talk.

"Well, I guess you must be surprised to see me here the third morning in a row," she said, "but because of my window curtains I'm becoming a regular commuter. The curtains I bought on Monday I returned on Tuesday, and the curtains I bought Tuesday I'm returning today. On Monday, I got exactly what I wanted—it's a wool tapestry with roses and birds—but when I got them home, I found they were the wrong length. Well, I exchanged them yesterday, and when I got them home, I found they were still the wrong length. Now I'm praying to high Heaven that the decorator will have them in the right length, because you know my house, you *know* my living-room windows, and you can imagine what a problem they present. I don't know what to do with them."

"I know what to do with them," Francis said.

"What?"

"Paint them black on the inside, and shut up."

There was a gasp from Mrs. Wrightson, and Francis looked down at her to be sure that she knew he meant to be rude. She turned and walked away from him, so damaged in spirit that she limped. A wonderful feeling enveloped him, as if light were being shaken about him, and he thought again of Venus combing and combing her hair as she drifted through the Bronx. The realization of how many years had passed since he had enjoyed being deliberately impolite sobered him. Among his friends and neighbors, there were brilliant and gifted people—he saw that—but many of them, also, were bores and fools, and he had made the mistake of listening to them all with equal attention. He had confused a lack of discrimination with Christian love, and the confusion seemed general and destructive. He was grateful to the girl for this bracing sensation of independence. Birds were singing—cardinals and the last of the robins. The sky shone like enamel. Even the smell of ink from his morning paper honed his appetite for life, and the world that was spread out around him was plainly a paradise.

If Francis had believed in some hierarchy of love—in spirits armed with hunting bows, in the capriciousness of Venus and Eros—or even in magical potions, philters, and stews, in scapulae and quarters of the moon, it might have explained his susceptibility and his feverish high spirits. The autumnal loves of middle age are well publicized, and he guessed that he was face to face with one of these, but there was not a trace of autumn in what he felt. He wanted to sport in the green woods, scratch where he itched, and drink from the same cup.

His secretary, Miss Rainey, was late that morning—she went to a psychiatrist three mornings a week—and when she came in, Francis wondered what advice a psychiatrist would have for him. But the girl promised to bring back into his life something like the sound of music. The realization that this music might lead him straight to a trial for statutory rape at the county courthouse collapsed his happiness. The photograph of his four children laughing into the camera on the beach at Gay Head reproached him. On the letterhead of his firm there was a drawing of the Laocoön and the figure of the priest and his sons in the coils of the snake appeared to him to have the deepest meaning.

He had lunch with Pinky Trabert. At a conversational level, the mores of his friends were robust and elastic, but he knew that the moral card house would come down on them all—on Julia and the children as well—if he got caught taking advantage of a babysitter. Looking back over the recent history of Shady Hill for some precedent, he found there was none. There was no turpitude; there had not been a divorce since he lived there; there had not even been a breath of scandal. Things seemed arranged with more propriety even than in the Kingdom of Heaven. After leaving Pinky, Francis went to a jeweler's and bought the girl a bracelet. How happy this clandestine purchase made him, how stuffy and comical the jeweler's clerks seemed, how sweet the women who passed at his back smelled! On Fifth Avenue, passing Atlas with his shoulders bent under the weight of the world, Francis thought of the strenuousness of containing his physicalness within the patterns he had chosen.

He did not know when he would see the girl next. He had the bracelet in his inside pocket when he got home. Opening the door of his house, he found her in the hall. Her back was to him, and she turned when she heard the door close. Her smile was open and loving. Her perfection stunned him like a fine day—a day after a thunderstorm. He seized her and covered her lips with his, and she struggled but she did not have to struggle for long, because just then little Gertrude Flannery appeared from somewhere and said, "Oh, Mr. Weed . . ."

Gertrude was a stray. She had been born with a taste for exploration, and she did not have it in her to center her life with her affectionate parents. People who did not know the Flannerys concluded from Gertrude's behavior that she was the child of a bitterly divided family, where drunken quarrels were the rule. This was not true. The fact that little Gertrude's clothing was ragged and thin was her own triumph over her mother's struggle to dress her warmly and neatly. Garrulous, skinny, and unwashed, she drifted from house to house around the Blenhollow neighborhood, forming and breaking alliances based on an attachment to babies, animals, children her own age, adolescents, and sometimes adults. Opening your front door in the morning, you would find Gertrude sitting on your stoop. Going into the bathroom to shave, you would find Gertrude using the toilet. Looking into your son's crib, you would find it empty, and, looking further, you would find that Gertrude had pushed him in his baby carriage into the next village. She was helpful, pervasive, honest, hungry, and loyal. She never went home of her own choice. When the time to go arrived, she was indifferent to all its signs: "Go home, Gertrude," people could be heard saying in one house or another, night after night. "Go home, Gertrude. It's time for you to go home now, Gertrude." "You had better go home and get your supper, Gertrude." "I told you to go home twenty minutes ago, Gertrude." "Your mother will be worrying about you, Gertrude." "Go home, Gertrude, go home."

There are times when the lines around the human eye seem like shelves of eroded stone and when the staring eye itself strikes us with such a wilderness of animal feeling that we are at a loss. The look Francis gave the little girl was ugly and queer, and it frightened her. He reached into his pocket—his hands were shaking—and took out a quarter. "Go home, Gertrude, go home, and don't tell anyone, Gertrude. Don't—" He choked and ran into the living room as Julia called down to him from upstairs to hurry and dress.

The thought that he would drive Anne Murchison home later that night ran like a golden thread through the events of the party that Francis and Julia went to, and he laughed uproariously at dull jokes, dried a tear when Mabel Mercer told him about the death of her kitten, and stretched, yawned, sighed, and grunted like any other man with a rendezvous at the back of his mind. The bracelet was in his pocket. As he sat talking, the smell of grass was in his nose, and he was wondering where he would park the car. Nobody lived in the old Parker mansion, and the driveway was used as a lovers' lane. Townsend Street was a dead end, and he could park there, beyond the last house. The old lane that used to connect Elm Street to the riverbanks was overgrown, but he had walked there with his children, and he could drive his car deep enough into the brushwoods to be concealed.

The Weeds were the last to leave the party, and their host and hostess spoke of their own married happiness while they all four stood in the hallway saying good night. "She's my girl," their host said, squeezing his wife. "She's my blue sky. After sixteen years, I still bite her shoulders. She makes me feel like Hannibal crossing the Alps."

The Weeds drove home in silence. Francis brought the car up the driveway and sat still, with the motor running. "You can put the car in the garage," Julia said as she got out. "I told the Murchison girl she could leave at eleven. Someone drove her home." She shut the door, and Francis sat in the dark. He would be spared nothing then, it seemed, that a fool was not spared: ravening lewdness, jealousy, this hurt to his feelings that put tears in his eyes, even scorn—for he could see clearly the image he now presented, his arms spread over the steering wheel and his head buried in them for love.

Francis had been a dedicated Boy Scout when he was young, and, remembering the precepts of his youth, he left his office early the next afternoon and played some round-robin squash, but, with his body toned up by exercise and a shower, he realized that he might better have stayed at his desk. It was a frosty night when he got home. The air smelled sharply of change. When he stepped into the house, he sensed an unusual stir. The children were in their best clothes, and when Julia came down, she was wearing a lavender dress and her diamond sunburst. She explained the stir: Mr. Hubber was coming at seven to take their photograph for the Christmas card. She had put out Francis' blue suit and a tie with some color in it, because the picture was going to be in color this year. Julia was lighthearted at the thought of being photographed for Christmas. It was the kind of ceremony she enjoyed.

Francis went upstairs to change his clothes. He was tired from the day's work and tired with longing, and sitting on the edge of the bed had the effect of deepening his weariness. He thought of Anne Murchison, and the physical need to express himself, instead of being restrained by the pink lamps on Julia's dressing table, engulfed him. He went to Julia's desk, took a piece of writing paper, and began to write on it. "Dear Anne, I love you, I love you, I love you . . ." No one would see the letter, and he used no restraint. He used phrases like "heavenly bliss," and "love nest." He salivated, sighed, and trembled. When Julia called him to come down, the abyss between his fantasy and the practical world opened so wide that he felt it affect the muscles of his heart.

Julia and the children were on the stoop, and the photographer and his assistant had set up a double battery of floodlights to show the family and the architectural beauty of the entrance to their house. People who had come home on a late train slowed their cars to see the Weeds being photographed for their Christmas card. A few waved and called to the family. It took half an hour of smiling and wetting their lips before Mr. Hubber was satisfied. The heat of the lights made an unfresh smell in the frosty air, and when they were turned off, they lingered on the retina of Francis' eyes.

Later that night, while Francis and Julia were drinking their coffee in the living room, the doorbell rang. Julia answered the door and let in Clayton Thomas. He had come to pay her for some theater tickets that she had given his mother some time ago, and that Helen Thomas had scrupulously insisted on paying for, though Julia had asked her not to. Julia invited him in to have a cup of coffee. "I won't have any coffee," Clayton said, "but I will come in for a minute." He followed her into the living room, said good evening to Francis, and sat awkwardly in a chair.

Clayton's father had been killed in the war, and the young man's fatherlessness surrounded him like an element. This may have been conspicuous in Shady Hill because the Thomases were the only family that lacked a piece; all the other marriages were intact and productive. Clayton was in his second or third year of college, and he and his mother lived alone in a large house, which she hoped to sell. Clayton had once made some trouble. Years ago, he had stolen some money and run away; he had got to California before they caught up with him. He was tall and homely, wore horn-rimmed glasses, and spoke in a deep voice.

"When do you go back to college, Clayton?" Francis asked.

"I'm not going back," Clayton said. "Mother doesn't have the money, and there's no sense in all this pretense. I'm going to get a job, and if we sell the house, we'll take an apartment in New York."

"Won't you miss Shady Hill?" Julia asked.

"No," Clayton said. "I don't like it."

"Why not?" Francis asked.

"Well, there's a lot here I don't approve of," Clayton said gravely.

"Things like the club dances. Last Saturday night, I looked in toward the end and saw Mr. Granner trying to put Mrs. Minot into the trophy case. They were both drunk. I disapprove of so much drinking."

"It was Saturday night," Francis said.

"And all the dovecotes are phony," Clayton said. "And the way people clutter up their lives. I've thought about it a lot, and what seems to me to be really wrong with Shady Hill is that it doesn't have any future. So much energy is spent in perpetuating the place—in keeping out undesirables, and so forth—that the only idea of the future anyone has is just more and more commuting trains and more parties. I don't think that's healthy. I think people ought to be able to dream big dreams about the future. I think people ought to be able to dream great dreams."

"It's too bad you couldn't continue with college," Julia said.

"I wanted to go to divinity school," Clayton said.

"What's your church?" Francis asked.

"Unitarian, Theosophist, Transcendentalist, Humanist," Clayton said.

"Wasn't Emerson a transcendentalist?" Julia asked.

"I mean the English transcendentalists," Clayton said. "All the American transcendentalists were goops."

"What kind of a job do you expect to get?" Francis asked.

"Well, I'd like to work for a publisher," Clayton said, "but everyone tells me there's nothing doing. But it's the kind of thing I'm interested in. I'm writing a long verse play about good and evil. Uncle Charlie might get me into a bank, and that would be good for me. I need the discipline. I have a long way to go in forming my character. I have some terrible habits. I talk too much. I think I ought to take vows of silence. I ought to try not to speak for a week, and discipline myself. I've thought of making a retreat at one of the Episcopalian monasteries, but I don't like the Trinitarianism."

"Do you have any girl friends?" Francis asked.

"I'm engaged to be married," Clayton said. "Of course, I'm not old enough or rich enough to have my engagement observed or respected or anything, but I bought a simulated emerald for Anne Murchison with the money I made cutting lawns this summer. We're going to be married as soon as she finishes school."

Francis recoiled at the mention of the girl's name. Then a dingy light seemed to emanate from his spirit, showing everything—Julia, the boy, the chairs—in their true colorlessness. It was like a bitter turn of the weather.

"We're going to have a large family," Clayton said. "Her father's a terrible rummy, and I've had my hard times, and we want to have lots of children. Oh, she's wonderful, Mr. and Mrs. Weed, and we have so much in common. We like all the same things. We sent out the same Christmas card last year without planning it, and we both have an allergy to tomatoes, and our eyebrows grow together in the middle. Well, good night."

Julia went to the door with him. When she returned, Francis said that Clayton was lazy, irresponsible, affected, and smelly. Julia said that Francis seemed to be getting intolerant; the Thomas boy was young and should be given a chance. Julia had noticed other cases where Francis had been short-tempered. "Mrs. Wrightson has asked everyone in Shady Hill to her anniversary party but us," she said.

"I'm sorry, Julia."

"Do you know why they didn't ask us?"

"Why?"

"Because you insulted Mrs. Wrightson."

"Then you know about it?"

"June Masterson told me. She was standing behind you."

Julia walked in front of the sofa with a small step that expressed, Francis knew, a feeling of anger.

"I did insult Mrs. Wrightson, Julia, and I meant to. I've never liked her parties, and I'm glad she's dropped us."

"What about Helen?"

"How does Helen come into this?"

"Mrs. Wrightson's the one who decides who goes to the assemblies."

"You mean she can keep Helen from going to the dances?"

"Yes."

"I hadn't thought of that."

"Oh, I knew you hadn't thought of it," Julia cried, thrusting hilt-deep into this chink of his armor. "And it makes me furious to see this kind of stupid thoughtlessness wreck everyone's happiness."

"I don't think I've wrecked anyone's happiness."

"Mrs. Wrightson runs Shady Hill and has run it for the last forty years. I don't know what makes you think that in a community like this you can indulge every impulse you have to be insulting, vulgar, and offensive."

"I have very good manners," Francis said, trying to give the evening a turn toward the light.

"Damn you, Francis Weed!" Julia cried, and the spit of her words struck him in the face. "I've worked hard for the social position we enjoy in this place, and I won't stand by and see you wreck it. You must have understood when you settled here that you couldn't expect to live like a bear in a cave."

"I've got to express my likes and dislikes."

"You can conceal your dislikes. You don't have to meet everything head-on, like a child. Unless you're anxious to be a social leper. It's no accident that we get asked out a great deal. It's no accident that Helen has so many friends. How would you like to spend your Saturday nights at the movies? How would you like to spend your Sundays raking up dead leaves? How would you like it if your daughter spent the assembly nights sitting at her window, listening to the music from the club? How would you like it—" He did something then that was, after all, not so unaccountable, since her words seemed to raise up between them a wall so deadening that he gagged: He struck her full in the face. She staggered and then, a moment later, seemed composed. She went up the stairs to their room. She didn't slam the door. When Francis followed, a few minutes later, he found her packing a suitcase.

"Julia, I'm very sorry."

"It doesn't matter," she said. She was crying.

"Where do you think you're going?"

"I don't know. I just looked at a timetable. There's an eleven-sixteen into New York. I'll take that."

"You can't go, Julia."

"I can't stay. I know that."

"I'm sorry about Mrs. Wrightson, Julia, and I'm—"

"It doesn't matter about Mrs. Wrightson. That isn't the trouble."

"What is the trouble?"

"You don't love me."

"I do love you, Julia."

"No, you don't."

"Julia, I do love you, and I would like to be as we were—sweet and bawdy and dark—but now there are so many people."

"You hate me."

"I don't hate you, Julia."

"You have no idea of how much you hate me. I think it's subconscious. You don't realize the cruel things you've done."

"What cruel things, Julia?"

"The cruel acts your subconscious drives you to in order to express your hatred of me."

"What, Julia?"

"I've never complained."

"Tell me."

"You don't know what you're doing."

"Tell me."

"Your clothes."

"What do you mean?"

"I mean the way you leave your dirty clothes around in order to express your subconscious hatred of me."

"I don't understand."

"I mean your dirty socks and your dirty pajamas and your dirty underwear and your dirty shirts!" She rose from kneeling by the suitcase and faced him, her eyes blazing and her voice ringing with emotion. "I'm talking about the fact that you've never learned to hang up anything. You just leave your clothes all over the floor where they drop, in order to humiliate me. You do it on purpose!" She fell on the bed, sobbing.

"Julia, darling!" he said, but when she felt his hand on her shoulder she got up.

"Leave me alone," she said. "I have to go." She brushed past him to the closet and came back with a dress. "I'm not taking any of the things you've given me," she said. "I'm leaving my pearls and the fur jacket."

"Oh, Julia!" Her figure, so helpless in its self-deceptions, bent over the suitcase made him nearly sick with pity. She did not understand how desolate her life would be without him. She didn't understand the hours that working women have to keep. She didn't understand that most of her friendships existed within the framework of their marriage, and that without this she would find herself alone. She didn't understand about travel, about hotels, about money. "Julia, I can't let you go! What you don't understand, Julia, is that you've come to be dependent on me."

She tossed her head back and covered her face with her hands. "Did you say that *I* was dependent on *you?*" she asked. "Is that what you said? And who is it that tells you what time to get up in the morning and when to go to bed at night? Who is it that prepares your meals and picks up your dirty clothes and invites your friends to dinner? If it weren't for me, your neckties would be greasy and your clothing would be full of moth holes. You were alone when I met you, Francis Weed, and you'll be alone when I leave. When Mother asked you for a list to send out invitations to our wedding, how many names did you have to give her? Fourteen!"

"Cleveland wasn't my home, Julia."

"And how many of your friends came to the church? Two!"

"Cleveland wasn't my home, Julia."

"Since I'm not taking the fur jacket," she said quietly, "you'd better put it back into storage. There's an insurance policy on the pearls that comes due in January. The name of the laundry and the maid's telephone number—all those things are in my desk. I hope you won't drink too much, Francis. I hope that nothing bad will happen to you. If you do get into serious trouble, you can call me."

"Oh, my darling, I can't let you go!" Francis said. "I can't let you go, Julia!" He took her in his arms.

"I guess I'd better stay and take care of you for a little while longer," she said.

Riding to work in the morning, Francis saw the girl walk down the aisle of the coach. He was surprised; he hadn't realized that the school she went to was in the city, but she was carrying books, she seemed to be going to school. His surprise delayed his reaction, but then he got up clumsily and stepped into the aisle. Several people had come between them, but he could see her ahead of him, waiting for someone to open the car door, and then, as the train swerved, putting out her hand to support herself as she crossed the platform into the next car. He followed her through that car and halfway through another before calling her name—"Anne! Anne!"—but she didn't turn. He followed her into still another car, and she sat down in an aisle seat. Coming up to her, all his feelings warm and bent in her direction, he put his hand on the back of her seat—even this touch warmed him—and, leaning down to speak to her, he saw that it was not Anne. It was an older woman wearing glasses. He went on deliberately into another car, his face red with embarrassment and the much deeper feeling of having his good sense challenged; for if he couldn't tell one person from another, what evidence was there that his life with Julia and the children had as much reality as his dreams of iniquity in Paris or the litter, the grass smell, and the cave-shaped trees in Lovers' Lane.

Late that afternoon, Julia called to remind Francis that they were going out for dinner. A few minutes later, Trace Bearden called. "Look, fellar," Trace said. "I'm calling for Mrs. Thomas. You know? Clayton, that boy of hers, doesn't seem able to get a job, and I wondered if you could help. If you'd call Charlie Bell—I know he's indebted to you—and say a good word for the kid, I think Charlie would—"

"Trace, I hate to say this," Francis said, "but I don't feel that I can do anything for that boy. The kid's worthless. I know it's a harsh thing to say, but it's a fact. Any kindness done for him would backfire in everybody's face. He's just a worthless kid, Trace, and there's nothing to be done about it. Even if we got him a job, he wouldn't be able to keep it for a week. I know that to be a fact. It's an awful thing, Trace, and I know it is, but instead of recommending that kid, I'd feel obliged to warn people against him—people who knew his father and would naturally want to step in and do something. I'd feel obliged to warn them. He's a thief . . ."

The moment this conversation was finished, Miss Rainey came in and stood by his desk. "I'm not going to be able to work for you any more, Mr. Weed," she said. "I can stay until the seventeenth if you need me, but I've been offered a whirlwind of a job, and I'd like to leave as soon as possible."

She went out, leaving him to face alone the wickedness of what he had done to the Thomas boy. His children in their photograph laughed and laughed, glazed with all the bright colors of summer, and he remembered that they had met a bagpiper on the beach that day and he had paid the piper a dollar to play them a battle song of the Black Watch. The girl would be at the house when he got home. He would spend another evening among his kind neighbors, picking and choosing dead-end streets, cart tracks, and the driveways of abandoned houses. There was nothing to mitigate his feeling—nothing that laughter or a game of softball with the children would change—and, thinking back over the plane crash, the Farquarsons' new maid, and Anne Murchison's difficulties with her drunken father, he wondered how he could have avoided arriving at just where he was. He was in trouble. He had been lost once in his life, coming back from a trout stream in the north woods, and he had now the same bleak realization that no amount of cheerfulness or hopefulness or valor or perseverance could help him find, in the gathering dark, the path that he'd lost. He smelled the forest. The feeling of bleakness was intolerable, and he saw clearly that he had reached the point where he would have to make a choice.

He could go to a psychiatrist, like Miss Rainey; he could go to church and confess his lusts; he could go to a Danish massage parlor in the West Seventies that had been recommended by a salesman; he could rape the girl or trust that he would somehow be prevented from doing this; or he could get drunk. It was his life, his boat, and, like every other man, he was made to be the father of thousands, and what harm could there be in a tryst that would make them both feel more kindly toward the world? This was the wrong train of thought, and he came back to the first, the psychiatrist. He had the telephone number of Miss Rainey's doctor, and he called and asked for an immediate appointment. He was insistent with the doctor's secretary—it was his manner in business—and when she said that the doctor's schedule was full for the next few weeks, Francis demanded an appointment that day and was told to come at five.

The psychiatrist's office was in a building that was used mostly by doctors and dentists, and the hallways were filled with the candy smell of mouthwash and memories of pain. Francis' character had been formed upon a series of private resolves—resolves about cleanliness, about going off the high diving board or repeating any other feat that challenged his courage, about punctuality, honesty, and virtue. To abdicate the perfect loneliness in which he had made his most vital decisions shattered his concept of character and left him now in a condition that felt like shock. He was stupefied. The scene for his *miserere mei Deus* was, like the waiting room of so many doctors' offices, a crude token gesture toward the sweets of domestic bliss: a place arranged with antiques, coffee tables, potted plants, and etchings of snow-covered bridges and geese in flight, although there were no children, no marriage bed, no stove, even, in this travesty of a house, where no one had ever spent the night and where the curtained windows looked straight onto a dark air shaft. Francis gave his name and address to a secretary and then saw, at the side of the room, a policeman moving toward him. "Hold it, hold it," the policeman said. "Don't move. Keep your hands where they are."

"I think it's all right, officer," the secretary began. "I think it will be—"

"Let's make sure," the policeman said, and he began to slap Francis' clothes, looking for what—pistols, knives, an icepick? Finding nothing, he went off, and the secretary began a nervous apology: "When you called on the telephone, Mr. Weed, you seemed very excited, and one of the doctor's patients has been threatening his life, and we have to be careful. If you want to go in now?" Francis pushed open a door connected to an electrical chime, and in the doctor's lair sat down heavily, blew his nose into a handkerchief, searched in his pockets for cigarettes, for matches, for something, and said hoarsely, with tears in his eyes, "I'm in love, Dr. Herzog."

It is a week or ten days later in Shady Hill. The seven-fourteen has come and gone, and here and there dinner is finished and the dishes are in the dish-washing machine. The village hangs, morally and economically, from a thread; but it hangs by its thread in the evening light. Donald Goslin has begun to worry the "Moonlight Sonata" again. *Marcato ma sempre pianissimo!* He seems to be wringing out a wet bath towel, but the housemaid does not heed him. She is writing a letter to Arthur Godfrey. In the cellar of his house, Francis Weed is building a coffee table. Dr. Herzog recommended woodwork as a therapy, and Francis finds some true consolation in the simple arithmetic involved and in the holy smell of new wood. Francis is happy. Upstairs, little Toby is crying, because he is tired. He puts off his cowboy hat, gloves, and fringed jacket, unbuckles the belt studded with gold and rubies, the silver bullets and holsters, slips off his suspenders, his checked shirt, and Levis, and sits on the edge of his bed to pull off his high boots. Leaving this equipment in a heap, he goes to the closet and takes his space suit off a nail. It is a struggle for him to get into the long tights, but he succeeds. He loops the magic cape over his shoulders and, climbing onto the footboard of his bed, he spreads his arms and flies the short distance to the floor, landing with a thump that is audible to everyone in the house but himself.

"Go home, Gertrude, go home," Mrs. Masterson says. "I told you to go home an hour ago, Gertrude. It's way past your suppertime, and your mother will be worried. Go home!" A door on the Babcocks' terrace flies open, and out comes Mrs. Babcock without any clothes on, pursued by her naked husband. (Their children are away at boarding school, and their terrace is screened by a hedge.) Over the terrace they go and in at the kitchen door, as passionate and handsome a nymph and satyr as you will find on any wall in Venice. Cutting the last of the roses in her garden, Julia hears old Mr. Nixon shouting at the squirrels in his bird-feeding station. "Rapscallions! Varmints! Avaunt and quit my sight!" A miserable cat wanders into the garden, sunk in spiritual and physical discomfort. Tied to its head is a small straw hat—a doll's hat—and it is securely buttoned into a doll's dress, from the skirts of which protrudes its long, hairy tail. As it walks, it shakes its feet, as if it had fallen into water.

"Here, pussy, pussy, pussy!" Julia calls.

"Here, pussy, here, poor pussy!" But the cat gives her a skeptical look and stumbles away in its skirts. The last to come is Jupiter. He prances through the tomato vines, holding in his generous mouth the remains of an evening slipper. Then it is dark; it is a night where kings in golden suits ride elephants over the mountains.

1954

I Stand Here Ironing

TILLIE OLSEN

[b. 1913]

I stand here ironing, and what you asked me moves tormented back and forth with the iron.

"I wish you would manage the time to come in and talk with me about your daughter. I'm sure you can help me understand her. She's a youngster who needs help and whom I'm deeply interested in helping."

"Who needs help." Even if I came, what good would it do? You think because I am her mother I have a key, or that in some way you could use me as a key? She has lived for nineteen years. There is all that life that has happened outside of me, beyond me.

And when is there time to remember, to sift, to weight, to estimate, to total? I will start and there will be an interruption and I will have to gather it all together again. Or I will become engulfed with all I did or did not do, with what should have been and what cannot be helped.

She was a beautiful baby. The first and only one of our five that was beautiful at birth. You do not guess how new and uneasy her tenancy in her now-loveliness. You did not know her all those years she was thought homely, or see her poring over her baby pictures, making me tell her over and over how beautiful she had been—and would be, I would tell her—and was now, to the seeing eye. But the seeing eyes were few or nonexistent. Including mine.

I nursed her. They feel that's important nowadays. I nursed all the children, but with her, with all the fierce rigidity of first motherhood, I did like the books then said. Though her cries battered me to trembling and my breasts ached with swollenness, I waited till the clock decreed.

Why do I put that first? I do not even know if it matters, or if it explains anything.

She was a beautiful baby. She blew shining bubbles of sound. She loved motion, loved light, loved color and music and textures. She would lie on the floor in her blue overalls patting the surface so hard in ecstasy her hands and feet would blur. She was a miracle to me, but when she was eight months old I had to leave her daytimes with the woman downstairs to whom she was no miracle at all, for I worked or looked for work and for Emily's father, who "could no longer endure" (he wrote in his good-bye note) "sharing want with us."

I was nineteen. It was the pre-relief, pre-WPA world of the depression. I would start running as soon as I got off the streetcar, running up the stairs, the place smelling sour, and awake or asleep to startle awake, when she saw me she would break into a clogged weeping that could not be comforted, a weeping I can hear yet.

After a while I found a job hashing at night so I could be with her days, and it was better. But it came to where I had to bring her to his family and leave her.

It took a long time to raise the money for her fare back. Then she got chicken pox and I had to wait longer. When she finally came, I hardly knew her, walking quick and nervous like her father, looking like her father, thin, and dressed in a shoddy red that yellowed her skin and glared at the pockmarks. All the baby loveliness gone.

She was two. Old enough for nursery school they said, and I did not know then what I know now—the fatigue of the long day, and the lacerations of group life in nurseries that are only parking places for children.

Except that it would have made no difference if I had known. It was the only place there was. It was the only way we could be together, the only way I could hold a job.

And even without knowing, I knew. I knew the teacher that was evil because all these years it has curdled into my memory, the little boy hunched in the corner, her rasp, "why aren't you outside, because Alvin hits you? that's no reason, go out, scaredy." I knew Emily hated it even if she did not clutch and implore "don't go Mommy" like the other children, mornings.

She always had a reason why we should stay home. Momma, you look sick. Momma, I feel sick. Momma, the teachers aren't there today, they're sick. Momma, we can't go, there was a fire there last night. Momma, it's a holiday today, no school, they told me.

But never a direct protest, never rebellion. I think of our others in their three-, four-year-oldness—the explosions, the tempers, the denunciations, the demands—and I feel suddenly ill. I put the iron down. What in me demanded that goodness in her? And what was the cost, the cost to her of such goodness?

The old man living in the back once said in his gentle way: "You should smile at Emily more when you look at her." What *was* in my face when I looked at her? I loved her. There were all the acts of love.

It was only with the others I remembered what he said, and it was the face of joy, and not of care or tightness or worry I turned to them—too late for Emily. She does not smile easily, let alone almost always as her brothers and sisters do. Her face is closed and sombre, but when she wants, how fluid. You must have seen it in her pantomimes, you spoke of her rare gift for comedy on the stage that rouses a laughter out of the audience so dear they applaud and applaud and do not want to let her go.

Where does it come from, that comedy? There was none of it in her when she came back to me that second time, after I had had to send her away again. She had a new daddy now to learn to love, and I think perhaps it was a better time.

Except when we left her alone nights, telling ourselves she was old enough.

"Can't you go some other time, Mommy, like tomorrow?" she would ask. "Will it be just a little while you'll be gone? Do you promise?"

The time we came back, the front door open, the clock on the floor in the hall. She rigid awake. "It wasn't just a little while. I didn't cry. Three times I called you, just three times, and then I ran downstairs to open the door so you could come faster. The clock talked loud. I threw it away, it scared me what it talked."

She said the clock talked loud again that night I went to the hospital to have Susan. She was delirious with the fever that comes before red measles, but she was fully conscious all the week I was gone and the week after we were home when she could not come near the new baby or me.

She did not get well. She stayed skeleton thin, not wanting to eat, and night after night she had nightmares. She would call for me, and I would rouse from exhaustion to sleepily call back: "You're all right, darling, go to sleep, it's just a dream," and if she still called, in a sterner voice, "now go to sleep, Emily, there's nothing to hurt you." Twice, only twice, when I had to get up for Susan anyhow, I went in to sit with her.

Now when it is too late (as if she would let me hold and comfort her like I do the others) I get up and go to her at once at her moan or restless stirring. "Are you awake, Emily? Can I get you something?" And the answer is always the same: "No, I'm all right, go back to sleep, Mother."

They persuaded me at the clinic to send her away to a convalescent home in the country where "she can have the kind of food and care you can't manage for her, and you'll be free to concentrate on the new baby." They still send children to that place. I see pictures on the society page of sleek young women planning affairs to raise money for it, or dancing at the affairs, or decorating Easter eggs or filling Christmas stockings for the children.

They never have a picture of the children so I do not know if the girls still wear those gigantic red bows and the ravaged looks on the every other Sunday when parents can come to visit "unless otherwise notified"—as we were notified the first six weeks.

Oh it is a handsome place, green lawns and tall trees and fluted flower beds. High up on the balconies of each cottage the children stand, the girls in their red bows and white dresses, the boys in white suits and giant red ties. The parents stand below shrieking up to be heard and the children shriek down to be heard, and between them the invisible wall "Not To Be Contaminated by Parental Germs or Physical Affection."

There was a tiny girl who always stood hand in hand with Emily. Her parents never came. One visit she was gone. "They moved her to Rose College," Emily shouted in explanation. "They don't like you to love anybody here."

She wrote once a week, the labored writing of a seven-year-old. "I am fine. How is the baby. If I write my leter nicly I will have a star. Love." There never was a star. We wrote every other day, letters she could never hold or keep but only hear read—once. "We simply do not have room for children to keep any personal possessions," they patiently explained when we pieced one Sunday's shrieking together to plead how much it would mean to Emily, who loved so to keep things, to be allowed to keep her letters and cards.

Each visit she looked frailer. "She isn't eating," they told us.

(They had runny eggs for breakfast or mush with lumps, Emily said later, I'd hold it in my mouth and not swallow. Nothing ever tasted good, just when they had chicken.)

It took us eight months to get her released home, and only the fact that she gained back so little of her seven lost pounds convinced the social worker.

I used to try to hold and love her after she came back, but her body would stay stiff, and after a while she'd push away. She ate little. Food sickened her, and I think much of life too. Oh she had physical lightness and brightness, twinkling by on skates, bouncing like a ball up and down up and down over the jump rope, skimming over the hill; but these were momentary.

She fretted about her appearance, thin and dark and foreign-looking at a time when every little girl was supposed to look or thought she should look a chubby blonde replica of Shirley Temple. The doorbell sometimes rang for her, but no one seemed to come and play in the house or be a best friend. Maybe because we moved so much.

There was a boy she loved painfully through two school semesters. Months later she told me how she had taken pennies from my purse to buy him candy. "Licorice was his favorite and I brought him some every day, but he still liked Jennifer better'n me. Why, Mommy?" The kind of question for which there is no answer.

School was a worry to her. She was not glib or quick in a world where glibness and quickness were easily confused with ability to learn. To her overworked and exasperated teachers she was an over-conscientious "slow learner" who kept trying to catch up and was absent entirely too often.

I let her be absent, though sometimes the illness was imaginary. How different from my now-strictness about attendance with the others. I wasn't working. We had a new baby, I was home anyhow. Sometimes, after Susan grew old enough, I would keep her home from school, too, to have them all together.

Mostly Emily had asthma, and her breathing, harsh and labored, would fill the house with a curiously tranquil sound. I would bring the two old dresser mirrors and her boxes of collections to her bed.

She would select beads and single earrings, bottle tops and shells, dried flowers and pebbles, old postcards and scraps, all sorts of oddments; then she and Susan would play Kingdom, setting up landscapes and furniture, peopling them with action.

Those were the only times of peaceful companionship between her and Susan. I have edged away from it, that poisonous feeling between them, that terrible balancing of hurts and needs I had to do between the two, and did so badly, those earlier years.

Oh there are conflicts between the others too, each one human, needing, demanding, hurting, taking—but only between Emily and Susan, no, Emily toward Susan that corroding resentment. It seems so obvious on the surface, yet it is not obvious. Susan, the second child, Susan, golden- and curly-haired and chubby, quick and articulate and assured, everything in appearance and manner Emily was not; Susan, not able to resist Emily's precious things, losing or sometimes clumsily breaking them; Susan telling jokes and riddles to company for applause while Emily sat silent (to say to me later: that was *my* riddle, Mother, I told it to Susan); Susan, who for all the five years' difference in age was just a year behind Emily in developing physically.

I am glad for that slow physical development that widened the difference between her and her contemporaries, though she suffered over it. She was too vulnerable for that terrible world of youthful competition, of preening and parading, of constant measuring of yourself against every other, of envy, "If I had that copper hair," "If I had that skin. . . ." She tormented herself enough about not looking like the others, there was enough of the unsureness, the having to be conscious of words before you speak, the constant caring—what are they thinking of me? without having it all magnified by the merciless physical drives.

Ronnie is calling. He is wet and I change him. It is rare there is such a cry now. That time of motherhood is almost behind me when the ear is not one's own but must always be racked and listening for the child cry, the child call. We sit for a while and I hold him, looking out over the city spread in charcoal with its soft aisles of light. *"Shoogily,"* he breathes and curls closer. I carry him back to bed, asleep. *Shoogily.* A funny word, a family word, inherited from Emily, invented by her to say: *comfort.*

In this and other ways she leaves her seal, I say aloud. And startle at my saying it. What do I mean? What did I start to gather together, to try and make coherent? I was at the terrible, growing years. War years. I do not remember them well. I was working, there were four smaller ones now, there was not time for her. She had to help be a mother, and housekeeper, and shopper. She had to set her seal. Mornings of crisis and near hysteria trying to get lunches packed, hair combed, coats and shoes found, everyone to school or Child Care on time, the baby ready for transportation. And always the paper scribbled on by a smaller one, the book looked at by Susan then mislaid, the homework not done. Running out to that huge school where she was one, she was lost, she was a drop; suffering over the unpreparedness, stammering and unsure in her classes.

There was so little time left at night after the kids were bedded down. She would struggle over books, always eating (it was in those years she developed her enormous appetite that is legendary in our family) and I would be ironing, or preparing food for the next day, or writing V-mail to Bill, or tending the baby. Sometimes, to make me laugh, or out of her despair, she would imitate happenings or types at school.

I think I said once: "Why don't you do something like this in the school amateur show?" One morning she phoned me at work, hardly understandable through the weeping: "Mother, I did it. I won, I won; they gave me first prize; they clapped and clapped and wouldn't let me go."

Now suddenly she was Somebody, and as imprisoned in her difference as she had been in anonymity.

She began to be asked to perform at other high schools, even in colleges, then at city and statewide affairs. The first one we went to, I only recognized her that first moment when thin, shy, she almost drowned herself into the curtains. Then: Was this Emily? The control, the command, the convulsing and deadly clowning, the spell, then the roaring, stamping audience, unwilling to let this rare and precious laughter out of their lives.

Afterwards: You ought to do something about her with a gift like that—but without money or knowing how, what does one do? We have left it all to her, and the gift has as often eddied inside, clogged and clotted, as been used and growing.

She is coming. She runs up the stairs two at a time with her light graceful step, and I know she is happy tonight. Whatever it was that occasioned your call did not happen today.

"Aren't you ever going to finish the ironing, Mother? Whistler painted his mother in a rocker. I'd have to paint mine standing over an ironing board." This is one of her communicative nights and she tells me everything and nothing as she fixes herself a plate of food out of the icebox.

She is so lovely. Why did you want me to come in at all? Why were you concerned? She will find her way.

She starts up the stairs to bed. "Don't get me up with the rest in the morning." "But I thought you were having midterms." "Oh, those," she comes back in, kisses me, and says quite lightly, "in a couple of years when we'll all be atom-dead they won't matter a bit."

She has said it before. She *believes* it. But because I have been dredging the past, and all that compounds a human being is so heavy and meaningful in me, I cannot endure it tonight.

I will never total it all. I will never come in to say: She was a child seldom smiled at. Her father left me before she was a year old. I had to work her first six years when there was work, or I sent her home and to his relatives. There were years she had care she hated. She was dark and thin and foreign-looking in a world where the prestige went to blondeness and curly hair and dimples, she was slow where glibness was prized. She was a child of anxious, not proud, love. We were poor and could not afford for her the soil of easy growth. I was a young mother, I was a distracted mother. There were the other children pushing up, demanding. Her younger sister seemed all that she was not. There were years she did not let me touch her. She kept too much in herself, her life was such she had to keep too much in herself. My wisdom came too late. She has much to her and probably little will come of it. She is a child of her age, of depression, of war, of fear.

Let her be. So all that is in her will not bloom—but in how many does it? There is still enough left to live by. Only help her to know—help make it so there is cause for her to know—that she is more than this dress on the ironing board, helpless before the iron.

1953–1954

King of the Bingo Game

RALPH ELLISON

[b. 1914]

The woman in front of him was eating roasted peanuts that smelled so good that he could barely contain his hunger. He could not even sleep and wished they'd hurry and begin the bingo game. There, on his right, two fellows were drinking wine out of a bottle wrapped in a paper bag, and he could hear soft gurgling in the dark. His stomach gave a low, gnawing growl. "If this was down South," he thought, "all I'd have to do is lean over and say, 'Lady, gimme a few of those peanuts, please ma'm,' and she'd pass me the bag and never think nothing of it." Or he could ask the fellows for a drink in the same way. Folks down South stuck together that way; they didn't even have to know you. But up here it was different. Ask somebody for something, and they'd think you were crazy. Well, I ain't crazy. I'm just broke, 'cause I got no birth certificate to get a job, and Laura 'bout to die 'cause we got no money for a doctor. But I ain't crazy. And yet a pinpoint of doubt was focused in his mind as he glanced toward the screen and saw the hero stealthily entering a dark room and sending the beam of a flashlight along a wall of bookcases. This is where he finds the trapdoor, he remembered. The man would pass abruptly through the wall and find the girl tied to a bed, her legs and arms spread wide, and her clothing torn to rags. He laughed softly to himself. He had seen the picture three times, and this was one of the best scenes.

On his right the fellow whispered wide-eyed to his companion. "Man, look a-yonder!"

"Damn!"

"Wouldn't I like to have her tied up like that . . ."

"Hey! That fool's letting her loose!"

"Aw, man, he loves her."

"Love or no love!"

The man moved impatiently beside him, and he tried to involve himself in the scene. But Laura was on his mind. Tiring quickly of watching the picture he looked back to where the white beam filtered from the projection room above the balcony. It started small and grew large, specks of dust dancing in its whiteness as it reached the screen. It was strange how the beam always landed right on the screen and didn't mess up and fall somewhere else. But they had it all fixed. Everything was fixed. Now suppose when they showed that girl with her dress torn the girl started taking off the rest of her clothes, and when the guy came in he didn't untie her but kept her there and went to taking off his own clothes? *That* would be something to see. If a picture got out of hand like that those guys up there would go nuts. Yeah, and there'd be so many folks in here you couldn't find a seat for nine months! A strange sensation played over his skin. He shuddered. Yesterday he'd seen a bedbug on a woman's neck as they walked out into the bright street. But exploring his thigh through a hole in his pocket he found only goose pimples and old scars.

The bottle gurgled again. He closed his eyes. Now a dreamy music was accompanying the film and train whistles were sounding in the distance, and he was a boy again walking along a railroad trestle down South, and seeing the train coming, and running back as fast as he could go, and hearing the whistle blowing, and getting off the trestle to solid ground just in time, with the earth trembling beneath his feet, and feeling relieved as he ran down the cinder-strewn embankment onto the highway, and looking back and seeing with terror that the train had left the track and was following him right down the middle of the street, and all the white people laughing as he ran screaming . . .

"Wake up there, buddy! What the hell do you mean hollering like that! Can't you see we trying to enjoy this here picture?"

He stared at the man with gratitude.

"I'm sorry, old man," he said. "I musta been dreaming."

"Well, here, have a drink. And don't be making no noise like that, damn!"

His hands trembled as he tilted his head. It was not wine, but whiskey. Cold rye whiskey. He took a deep swoller, decided it was better not to take another, and handed the bottle back to its owner.

"Thanks, old man," he said.

Now he felt the cold whiskey breaking a warm path straight through the middle of him, growing hotter and sharper as it moved. He had not eaten all day, and it made him light-headed. The smell of the peanuts stabbed him like a knife, and he got up and found a seat in the middle aisle. But no sooner did he sit than he saw a row of intense-faced young girls, and got up again, thinking, "You chicks musta been Lindy-hopping somewhere." He found a seat several rows ahead as the lights came on, and he saw the screen disappear behind a heavy red and gold curtain; then the curtain rising, and the man with the microphone and a uniformed attendant coming on the stage.

He felt for his bingo cards, smiling. The guy at the door wouldn't like it if he knew about his having *five* cards. Well, not everyone played the bingo game; and even with five cards he didn't have much of a chance. For Laura, though, he had to have faith. He studied the cards, each with its different numerals, punching the free center hole in each and spreading them neatly across his lap; and when the lights faded he sat slouched in his seat so that he could look from his cards to the bingo wheel with but a quick shifting of his eyes.

Ahead, at the end of the darkness, the man with the microphone was pressing a button attached to a long cord and spinning the bingo wheel and calling out the number each time the wheel came to rest. And each time the voice rang out his finger raced over the cards for the number. With five cards he had to move fast. He became nervous; there were too many cards, and the man went too fast with his grating voice. Perhaps he should just select one and throw the others away. But he was afraid. He became warm. Wonder how much Laura's doctor would cost? Damn that, watch the cards! And with despair he heard the man call three in a row which he missed on all five cards. This way he'd never win . . .

When he saw the row of holes punched across the third card, he sat paralyzed and heard the man call three more numbers before he stumbled forward, screaming.

"Bingo! Bingo!"

"Let that fool up there," someone called.

"Get up there, man!"

He stumbled down the aisle and up the steps to the stage into a light so sharp and bright that for a moment it blinded him, and he felt that he had moved into the spell of some strange, mysterious power. Yet it was as familiar as the sun, and he knew it was the perfectly familiar bingo.

The man with the microphone was saying something to the audience as he held out his card. A cold light flashed from the man's finger as the card left his hand. His knees trembled. The man stepped closer, checking the card against the numbers chalked on the board. Suppose he had made a mistake? The pomade on the man's hair made him feel faint, and he backed away. But the man was checking the card over the microphone now, and he had to stay. He stood tense, listening.

"Under the O, forty-four," the man chanted. "Under the I, seven. Under the G, three. Under the B, ninety-six. Under the N, thirteen!"

His breath came easier as the man smiled at the audience.

"Yessir, ladies and gentlemen, he's one of the chosen people!"

The audience rippled with laughter and applause.

"Step right up to the front of the stage."

He moved slowly forward, wishing that the light was not so bright.

"To win tonight's jackpot of $36.90 the wheel must stop between the double zero, understand?"

He nodded, knowing the ritual from the many days and nights he had watched the winners march across the stage to press the button that controlled the spinning wheel and receive the prizes. And now he followed the instructions as though he'd crossed the slippery stage a million prize-winning times.

The man was making some kind of a joke, and he nodded vacantly. So tense had he become that he felt a sudden desire to cry and shook it away. He felt vaguely that his whole life was determined by the bingo wheel; not only that which would happen now that he was at last before it, but all that had gone before, since his birth, and his mother's birth and the birth of his father It had always been there, even though he had not been aware of it, handing out the unlucky cards and numbers of his days. The feeling persisted, and he started quickly away. I better get down from here before I make a fool of myself, he thought.

"Here, boy," the man called. "You haven't started yet."

Someone laughed as he went hesitantly back.

"Are you all reet?"

He grinned at the man's jive talk, but no words would come, and he knew it was not a convincing grin. For suddenly he knew that he stood on the slippery brink of some terrible embarrassment.

"Where are you from, boy?" the man asked.

"Down South."

"He's from down South, ladies and gentlemen," the man said. "Where from? Speak right into the mike."

"Rocky Mont," he said. "Rock' Mont, North Car'lina."

"So you decided to come down off that mountain to the U.S.," the man laughed. He felt that the man was making a fool of him, but then something cold was placed in his hand, and the lights were no longer behind him.

Standing before the wheel he felt alone, but that was somehow right, and he remembered his plan. He would give the wheel a short quick twirl. Just a touch of the button. He had watched it many times, and always it came close to double zero when it was short and quick. He steeled himself; the fear had left, and he felt a profound sense of promise, as though he were about to be repaid for all the things he'd suffered all his life. Trembling, he pressed the button. There was a whirl of lights, and in a second he realized with finality that though he wanted to, he could not stop. It was as though he held a high-powered line in his naked hand. His nerves tightened. As the wheel increased its speed it seemed to draw him more and more into its power, as though it held his fate; and with it came a deep need to submit, to whirl, to lose himself in its swirl of color. He could not stop it now, he knew. So let it be.

The button rested snugly in his palm where the man had placed it. And now he became aware of the man beside him, advising him through the microphone, while behind the shadowy audience hummed with noisy voices. He shifted his feet. There was still that feeling of helplessness within him, making part of him desire to turn back, even now that the jackpot was right in his hand. He squeezed the button until his fist ached. Then, like the sudden shriek of a subway whistle, a doubt tore through his head. Suppose he did not spin the wheel long enough? What could he do, and how could he tell? And then he knew, even as he wondered, that as long as he pressed the button, he could control the jackpot. He and only he could determine whether or not it was to be his. Not even the man with the microphone could do anything about it now. He felt drunk. Then, as though he had come down from a high hill into a valley of people, he heard the audience yelling.

"Come down from there, you jerk!"

"Let somebody else have a chance . . ."

"Ole Jack thinks he done found the end of the rainbow . . ."

The last voice was not unfriendly, and he turned and smiled dreamily into the yelling mouths. Then he turned his back squarely on them.

"Don't take too long, boy," a voice said.

He nodded. They were yelling behind him. Those folks did not understand what had happened to him. They had been playing the bingo game day in and night out for years, trying to win rent money or hamburger change. But not one of those wise guys had discovered this wonderful thing. He watched the wheel whirling past the numbers and experienced a burst of exaltation: This is God! This is the really truly God! He said it aloud, "This is God!"

He said it with such absolute conviction that he feared he would fall fainting into the footlights. But the crowd yelled so loud that they could not hear. Those fools, he thought. I'm here trying to tell them the most wonderful secret in the world, and they're yelling like they gone crazy. A hand fell upon his shoulder.

"You'll have to make a choice now, boy. You've taken too long."

He brushed the hand violently away.

"Leave me alone, man. I know what I'm doing!"

The man looked surprised and held on to the microphone for support. And because he did not wish to hurt the man's feelings he smiled, realizing with a sudden pang that there was no way of explaining to the man just why he had to stand there pressing the button forever.

"Come here," he called tiredly.

The man approached, rolling the heavy microphone across the stage.

"Anybody can play this bingo game, right?" he said.

"Sure, but . . ."

He smiled, feeling inclined to be patient with this slick looking white man with his blue sport shirt and his sharp gabardine suit.

"That's what I thought," he said. "Anybody can win the jackpot as long as they get the lucky number, right?"

"That's the rule, but after all . . ."

"That's what I thought," he said. "And the big prize goes to the man who knows how to win it?"

The man nodded speechlessly.

"Well then, go on over there and watch me win like I want to. I ain't going to hurt nobody," he said, "and I'll show you how to win. I mean to show the whole world how it's got to be done."

And because he understood, he smiled again to let the man know that he held nothing against him for being white and impatient. Then he refused to see the man any longer and stood pressing the button, the voices of the crowd reaching him like sounds in distant streets. Let them yell. All the Negroes down there were just ashamed because he was black like them. He smiled inwardly, knowing how it was. Most of the time he was ashamed of what Negroes did himself. Well, let them be ashamed for something this time. Like him. He was like a long thin black wire that was being stretched and wound upon the bingo wheel; wound until he wanted to scream; wound, but this time himself controlling the winding and the sadness and the shame, and because he did, Laura would be all right. Suddenly the lights flickered. He staggered backwards. Had something gone wrong? All this noise. Didn't they know that although he controlled the wheel, it also controlled him, and unless he pressed the button forever and forever and ever it would stop, leaving him high and dry, dry and high on this hard high slippery hill and Laura dead? There was only one chance; he had to do whatever the wheel demanded. And gripping the button in despair, he discovered with surprise that it imparted a nervous energy. His spine tingled. He felt a certain power.

Now he faced the raging crowd with defiance, its screams penetrating his eardrums like trumpets shrieking from a jukebox. The vague faces glowing in the bingo lights gave him a sense of himself that he had never known before. He was running the show, by God! They had to react to him, for he was their luck. This is *me,* he thought. Let the bastards yell. Then someone was laughing inside him, and he realized that somehow he had forgotten his own name. It was a sad, lost feeling to lose your name, and a crazy thing to do.

That name had been given him by the white man who had owned his grandfather a long lost time ago down South. But maybe those wise guys knew his name.

"Who am I?" he screamed.

"Hurry up and bingo, you jerk!"

They didn't know either, he thought sadly. They didn't even know their own names, they were all poor nameless bastards. Well, he didn't need that old name; he was reborn. For as long as he pressed the button he was The-man-who-pressed-the-button-who-held-the-prize-who-was-the-King-of-Bingo. That was the way it was, and he'd have to press the button even if nobody understood, even though Laura did not understand.

"Live!" he shouted.

The audience quieted like the dying of a huge fan.

"Live, Laura, baby. I got holt of it now, sugar. Live!"

He screamed it, tears streaming down his face. "I got nobody but YOU!"

The screams tore from his very guts. He felt as though the rush of blood to his head would burst out in baseball seams of small red droplets, like a head beaten by police clubs. Bending over he saw a trickle of blood splashing the toe of his shoe. With his free hand he searched his head. It was his nose. God, suppose something has gone wrong? He felt that the whole audience had somehow entered him and was stamping its feet in his stomach, and he was unable to throw them out. They wanted the prize, that was it. They wanted the secret for themselves. But they'd never get it; he would keep the bingo wheel whirling forever, and Laura would be safe in the wheel. But would she? It had to be, because if she were not safe the wheel would cease to turn; it could not go on. He had to get away, *vomit* all, and his mind formed an image of himself running with Laura in his arms down the tracks of the subway just ahead of an A train, running desperately *vomit* with people screaming for him to come out but knowing no way of leaving the tracks because to stop would bring the train crushing down upon him and to attempt to leave across the other tracks would mean to run into a hot third rail as high as his waist which threw blue sparks that blinded his eyes until he could hardly see.

He heard singing and the audience was clapping its hands.

Shoot the liquor to him, Jim, boy!
Clap-clap-clap
Well a-calla the cop
He's blowing his top!
Shoot the liquor to him, Jim, boy!

Bitter anger grew within him at the singing. They think I'm crazy. Well let 'em laugh. I'll do what I got to do.

He was standing in an attitude of intense listening when he saw that they were watching something on the stage behind him. He felt weak. But when he turned he saw no one. If only his thumb did not ache so. Now they were applauding. And for a moment he thought that the wheel had stopped. But that was impossible, his thumb still pressed the button. Then he saw them. Two men in uniform beckoned from the end of the stage. They were coming toward him, walking in step, slowly, like a tap-dance team returning for a third encore. But their shoulders shot forward, and he backed away, looking wildly about. There was nothing to fight them with. He had only the long black cord which led to a plug somewhere back stage, and he couldn't use that because it operated the bingo wheel. He backed slowly, fixing the men with his eyes as his lips stretched over his teeth in a tight, fixed grin; moved toward the end of the stage and realizing that he couldn't go much further, for suddenly the cord became taut and he couldn't afford to break the cord. But he had to do something. The audience was howling. Suddenly he stopped dead, seeing the men halt, their legs lifted as in an interrupted step of a slow-motion dance. There was nothing to do but run in the other direction and he dashed forward, slipping and sliding. The men fell back, surprised. He struck out violently going past.

"Grab him!"

He ran, but all too quickly the cord tightened, resistingly, and he turned and ran back again. This time he slipped them, and discovered by running in a circle before the wheel he could keep the cord from tightening. But this way he had to flail his arms to keep the men away. Why couldn't they leave a man alone? He ran, circling.

"Ring down the curtain," someone yelled. But they couldn't do that. If they did the wheel flashing from the projection room would be cut off. But they had him before he could tell them so, trying to pry open his fist, and he was wrestling and trying to bring his knees into the fight and holding on to the button, for it was his life. And now he was down, seeing a foot coming down, crushing his wrist cruelly, down, as he saw the wheel whirling serenely above.

"I can't give it up," he screamed. Then quietly, in a confidential tone, "Boys, I really can't give it up."

It landed hard against his head. And in the blank moment they had it away from him, completely now. He fought them trying to pull him up from the stage as he watched the wheel spin slowly to a stop. Without surprise he saw it rest at double zero.

"You see," he pointed bitterly.

"Sure, boy, sure, it's O.K.," one of the men said smiling.

And seeing the man bow his head to someone he could not see, he felt very, very happy; he would receive what all the winners received.

But as he warmed in the justice of the man's tight smile he did not see the man's slow wink, nor see the bow-legged man behind him step clear of the swiftly descending curtain and set himself for a blow. He only felt the dull pain exploding in his skull, and he knew even as it slipped out of him that his luck had run out on the stage.

1944

The Magic Barrel

BERNARD MALAMUD

[b. 1914]

Not long ago there lived in uptown New York, in a small almost meager room, though crowded with books, Leo Finkle, a rabbinical student in the Yeshivah University. Finkle, after six years of study, was to be ordained in June and had been advised by an acquaintance that he might find it easier to win himself a congregation if he were married. Since he had no present prospects of marriage, after two tormented days of turning it over in his mind, he called in Pinye Salzman, a marriage broker whose two-line advertisement he had read in the *Forward.*

The matchmaker appeared one night out of the dark fourth-floor hallway of the graystone rooming house where Finkle lived, grasping a black, strapped portfolio that had been worn thin with use. Salzman, who had been long in the business, was of slight but dignified build, wearing an old hat, and an overcoat too short and tight for him. He smelled frankly of fish, which he loved to eat, and although he was missing a few teeth, his presence was not displeasing, because of an amiable manner curiously contrasted with mournful eyes. His voice, his lips, his wisp of beard, his bony fingers were animated, but give him a moment of repose and his mild blue eyes revealed a depth of sadness, a characteristic that put Leo a little at ease although the situation, for him, was inherently tense.

He at once informed Salzman why he had asked him to come, explaining that his home was in Cleveland, and that but for his parents, who had married comparatively late in life, he was alone in the world. He had for six years devoted himself almost entirely to his studies, as a result of which, understandably, he had found himself without time for a social life and the company of young women. Therefore he thought it the better part of trial and error—of embarrassing fumbling—to call in an experienced person to advise him on these matters. He remarked in passing that the function of the marriage broker was ancient and honorable, highly approved in the Jewish community, because it made practical the necessary without hindering joy. Moreover, his own parents had been brought together by a matchmaker. They had made, if not a financially profitable marriage—since neither had possessed any worldly goods to speak of—at least a successful one in the sense of their everlasting devotion to each other. Salzman listened in embarrassed surprise, sensing a sort of apology. Later, however, he experienced a glow of pride in his work, an emotion that had left him years ago, and he heartily approved of Finkle.

The two went to their business. Leo had led Salzman to the only clear place in the room, a table near a window that overlooked the lamp-lit city. He seated himself at the matchmaker's side but facing him, attempting by an act of will to suppress the unpleasant tickle in his throat. Salzman eagerly unstrapped his portfolio and removed a loose rubber band from a thin packet of much-handled cards. As he flipped through them, a gesture and sound that physically hurt Leo, the student pretended not to see and gazed steadfastly out the window. Although it was still February, winter was on its last legs, signs of which he had for the first time in years begun to notice. He now observed the round white moon, moving high in the sky through a cloud menagerie, and watched with half-open mouth as it penetrated a huge hen, and dropped out of her like an egg laying itself. Salzman, though pretending through eyeglasses he had just slipped on, to be engaged in scanning the writing on the cards, stole occasional glances at the young man's distinguished face, noting with pleasure the long, severe scholar's nose, brown eyes heavy with learning, sensitive yet ascetic lips, and a certain, almost hollow quality of the dark cheeks. He gazed around at shelves upon shelves of books and let out a soft, contented sigh.

When Leo's eyes fell upon the cards, he counted six spread out in Salzman's hand.

"So few?" he asked in disappointment.

"You wouldn't believe me how much cards I got in my office,"

Salzman replied. "The drawers are already filled to the top, so I keep them now in a barrel, but is every girl good for a new rabbi?"

Leo blushed at this, regretting all he had revealed of himself in a curriculum vitae he had sent to Salzman. He had thought it best to acquaint him with his strict standards and specifications, but in having done so, felt he had told the marriage broker more than was absolutely necessary.

He hesitantly inquired, "Do you keep photographs of your clients on file?"

"First comes family, amount of dowry, also what kind promises," Salzman replied, unbuttoning his tight coat and settling himself in the chair. "After comes pictures, rabbi."

"Call me Mr. Finkle. I'm not yet a rabbi."

Salzman said he would, but instead called him doctor, which he changed to rabbi when Leo was not listening too attentively.

Salzman adjusted his horn-rimmed spectacles, gently cleared his throat and read in an eager voice the contents of the top card:

"Sophie P. Twenty four years. Widow one year. No children. Educated high school and two years college. Father promises eight thousand dollars. Has wonderful wholesale business. Also real estate. On the mother's side comes teachers, also one actor. Well known on Second Avenue."

Leo gazed up in surprise. "Did you say a widow?"

"A widow don't mean spoiled, rabbi. She lived with her husband maybe four months. He was a sick boy she made a mistake to marry him."

"Marrying a widow has never entered my mind."

"This is because you have no experience. A widow, especially if she is young and healthy like this girl, is a wonderful person to marry. She will be thankful to you the rest of her life. Believe me, if I was looking now for a bride, I would marry a widow."

Leo reflected, then shook his head.

Salzman hunched his shoulders in an almost imperceptible gesture of disappointment. He placed the card down on the wooden table and began to read another:

"Lily H. High school teacher. Regular. Not a substitute. Has savings and new Dodge car. Lived in Paris one year. Father is successful dentist thirty-five years. Interested in professional man. Well Americanized family. Wonderful opportunity."

"I knew her personally," said Salzman. "I wish you could see this girl. She is a doll. Also very intelligent. All day you could talk to her about books and theyater and what not. She also knows current events."

"I don't believe you mentioned her age?"

"Her age?" Salzman said, raising his brows. "Her age is thirty-two years."

Leo said after a while, "I'm afraid that seems a little too old."

Salzman let out a laugh. "So how old are you, rabbi?"

"Twenty-seven."

"So what is the difference, tell me, between twenty-seven and thirty-two? My own wife is seven years older than me. So what did I suffer?—Nothing. If Rothschild's daughter wants to marry you, would you say on account her age, no?"

"Yes," Leo said dryly.

Salzman shook off the no in the yes. "Five years don't mean a thing. I give you my word that when you will live with her for one week you will forget her age. What does it mean five years—that she lived more and knows more than somebody who is younger? On this girl, God bless her, years are not wasted. Each one that it comes makes better the bargain."

"What subject does she teach in high school?"

"Languages. If you heard the way she speaks French, you will think it is music. I am in the business twenty-five years, and I recommend her with my whole heart. Believe me, I know what I'm talking, rabbi."

"What's on the next card?" Leo said abruptly.

Salzman reluctantly turned up the third card:

"Ruth K. Nineteen years. Honor student. Father offers thirteen thousand cash to the right bridegroom. He is a medical doctor. Stomach specialist with marvelous practice. Brother in law owns own garment business. Particular people."

Salzman looked as if he had read his trump card.

"Did you say nineteen?" Leo asked with interest.

"On the dot."

"Is she attractive?" He blushed. "Pretty?"

Salzman kissed his finger tips. "A little doll. On this I give you my word. Let me call the father tonight and you will see what means pretty."

But Leo was troubled. "You're sure she's that young?"

"This I am positive. The father will show you the birth certificate."

"Are you positive there isn't something wrong with her?" Leo insisted.

"Who says there is wrong?"

"I don't understand why an American girl her age should go to a marriage broker."

A smile spread over Salzman's face.

"So for the same reason you went, she comes."

Leo flushed. "I am pressed for time."

Salzman, realizing he had been tactless, quickly explained. "The father came, not her. He wants she should have the best, so he looks around himself. When we will locate the right boy he will introduce him and encourage. This makes a better marriage than if a young girl without experience takes for herself. I don't have to tell you this."

"But don't you think this young girl believes in love?" Leo spoke uneasily.

Salzman was about to guffaw but caught himself and said soberly, "Love comes with the right person, not before."

Leo parted dry lips but did not speak. Noticing that Salzman had snatched a glance at the next card, he cleverly asked, "How is her health?"

"Perfect," Salzman said, breathing with difficulty. "Of course, she is a little lame on her right foot from an auto accident that it happened to her when she was twelve years, but nobody notices on account she is so brilliant and also beautiful."

Leo got up heavily and went to the window. He felt curiously bitter and upbraided himself for having called in the marriage broker. Finally, he shook his head.

"Why not?" Salzman persisted, the pitch of his voice rising.

"Because I detest stomach specialists."

"So what do you care what is his business? After you marry her do you need him? Who says he must come every Friday night in your house?"

Ashamed of the way the talk was going, Leo dismissed Salzman, who went home with heavy, melancholy eyes.

Though he had felt only relief at the marriage broker's departure,

Leo was in low spirits the next day. He explained it as arising from Salzman's failure to produce a suitable bride for him. He did not care for his type of clientele. But when Leo found himself hesitating whether to seek out another matchmaker, one more polished than Pinye, he wondered if it could be—his protestations to the contrary, and although he honored his father and mother—that he did not, in essence, care for the matchmaking institution? This thought he quickly put out of mind yet found himself still upset. All day he ran around in the woods—missed an important appointment, forgot to give out his laundry, walked out of a Broadway cafeteria without paying and had to run back with the ticket in his hand; had even not recognized his landlady in the street when she passed with a friend and courteously called out, "A good evening to you, Doctor Finkle." By nightfall, however, he had regained sufficient calm to sink his nose into a book and there found peace from his thoughts.

Almost at once there came a knock on the door. Before Leo could say enter, Salzman, commercial cupid, was standing in the room. His face was gray and meager, his expression hungry, and he looked as if he would expire on his feet. Yet the marriage broker managed, by some trick of the muscles, to display a broad smile.

"So good evening. I am invited?"

Leo nodded, disturbed to see him again, yet unwilling to ask the man to leave.

Beaming still, Salzman laid his portfolio on the table, "Rabbi, I got for you tonight good news."

"I've asked you not to call me rabbi. I'm still a student."

"Your worries are finished. I have for you a first-class bride."

"Leave me in peace concerning this subject." Leo pretended lack of interest.

"The world will dance at your wedding."

"Please, Mr. Salzman, no more."

"But first must come back my strength," Salzman said weakly. He fumbled with the portfolio straps and took out of the leather case an oily paper bag, from which he extracted a hard, seeded roll and a small, smoked white fish. With a quick motion of his hand he stripped the fish out of its skin and began ravenously to chew. "All day in a rush," he muttered.

Leo watched him eat.

"A sliced tomato you have maybe?" Salzman hesitantly inquired.

"No."

The marriage broker shut his eyes and ate. When he had finished he carefully cleaned up the crumbs and rolled up the remains of the fish, in the paper bag. His spectacled eyes roamed the room until he discovered, amid some piles of books, a one-burner gas stove. Lifting his hat he humbly asked, "A glass tea you got, rabbi?"

Conscience-stricken, Leo rose and brewed the tea. He served it with a chunk of lemon and two cubes of lump sugar, delighting Salzman.

After he had drunk his tea, Salzman's strength and good spirits were restored.

"So tell me, rabbi," he said amiably, "you considered some more the three clients I mentioned yesterday?"

"There was no need to consider."

"Why not?"

"None of them suits me."

"What then suits you?"

Leo let it pass because he could give only a confused answer.

Without waiting for a reply, Salzman asked, "You remember this girl I talked to you—the high school teacher?"

"Age thirty-two?"

But, surprisingly, Salzman's face lit in a smile. "Age twenty-nine."

Leo shot him a look. "Reduced from thirty-two?"

"A mistake," Salzman avowed. "I talked today with the dentist. He took me to his safety deposit box and showed me the birth certificate. She was twenty-nine years last August. They made her a party in the mountains where she went for her vacation. When her father spoke to me the first time I forgot to write the age and I told you thirty-two, but now I remember this was a different client, a widow."

"The same one you told me about? I thought she was twenty-four?"

"A different. Am I responsible that the world is filled with widows?"

"No, but I'm not interested in them, nor for that matter, in school teachers."

Salzman pulled his clasped hands to his breast. Looking at the ceiling he devoutly exclaimed, "Yiddishe kinder, what can I say to somebody that he is not interested in high school teachers? So what then you are interested?"

Leo flushed but controlled himself.

"In what else will you be interested," Salzman went on, "if you not interested in this fine girl that speaks four languages and has personally in the bank ten thousand dollars? Also her father guarantees further twelve thousand. Also she has a new car, wonderful clothes, talks on all subjects, and she will give you a first-class home and children. How near do we come in our life to paradise?"

"If she's so wonderful, why hasn't she married ten years ago?"

"Why?" said Salzman with a heavy laugh. "—Why? Because she is *partikiler.* This is why. She wants the *best.*"

Leo was silent, amused at how he had entangled himself. But Salzman had aroused his interest in Lily H., and he began seriously to consider calling on her. When the marriage broker observed how intently Leo's mind was at work on the facts he had supplied, he felt certain they would soon come to an agreement.

Late Saturday afternoon, conscious of Salzman, Leo Finkle walked with Lily Hirschorn along Riverside Drive. He walked briskly and erectly, wearing with distinction the black fedora he had that morning taken with trepidation out of the dusty hat box on his closet shelf, and the heavy black Saturday coat he had thoroughly whisked clean. Leo also owned a walking stick, a present from a distant relative, but quickly put temptation aside and did not use it. Lily, petite and not unpretty, had on something signifying the approach of spring. She was au courant, animatedly, with all sorts of subjects, and he weighed her words and found her surprisingly sound—score another for Salzman, whom he uneasily sensed to be somewhere around, hiding perhaps high in a tree along the street, flashing the lady signals with a pocket mirror; or perhaps a cloven-hoofed Pan, piping nuptial ditties as he danced his invisible way before them, strewing wild buds on the walk and purple grapes in their path, symbolizing fruit of a union, though there was of course still none.

Lily startled Leo by remarking, "I was thinking of Mr. Salzman, a curious figure, wouldn't you say?"

Not certain what to answer, he nodded.

She bravely went on, blushing, "I for one am grateful for his introducing us. Aren't you?"

He courteously replied, "I am."

"I mean," she said with a little laugh—and it was all in good taste, or at least gave the effect of being not in bad—"do you mind that we came together so?"

He was not displeased with her honesty, recognizing that she meant to set the relationship aright, and understanding that it took a certain amount of experience in life, and courage, to want to do it quite that way. One had to have some sort of past to make that kind of beginning.

He said that he did not mind. Salzman's function was traditional and honorable—valuable for what it might achieve, which, he pointed out, was frequently nothing.

Lily agreed with a sigh. They walked on for a while and she said after a long silence, again with a nervous laugh, "Would you mind if I asked you something a little bit personal? Frankly, I find the subject fascinating." Although Leo shrugged, she went on half embarrassedly, "How was it that you came to your calling? I mean was it a sudden passionate inspiration?"

Leo, after a time, slowly replied, "I was always interested in the Law."

"You saw revealed in it the presence of the Highest?"

He nodded and changed the subject. "I understand that you spent a little time in Paris, Miss Hirschorn?"

"Oh, did Mr. Salzman tell you, Rabbi Finkle?" Leo winced but she went on, "It was ages ago and almost forgotten. I remember I had to return for my sister's wedding."

And Lily would not be put off. "When," she asked in a trembly voice, "did you become enamored of God?"

He stared at her. Then it came to him that she was talking not about Leo Finkle, but of a total stranger, some mystical figure, perhaps even passionate prophet that Salzman had dreamed up for her—no relation to the living or dead. Leo trembled with rage and weakness. The trickster had obviously sold her a bill of goods, just as he had him, who'd expected to become acquainted with a young lady of twenty-nine, only to behold, the moment he laid eyes upon her strained and anxious face, a woman past thirty-five and aging rapidly. Only his self control had kept him this long in her presence.

"I am not," he said gravely, "a talented religious person," and in seeking words to go on, found himself possessed by shame and fear. "I think," he said in a strained manner, "that I came to God not because I loved Him, but because I did not."

This confession he spoke harshly because its unexpectedness shook him.

Lily wilted. Leo saw a profusion of loaves of bread go flying like ducks high over his head, not unlike the winged loaves by which he had counted himself to sleep last night. Mercifully, then, it snowed, which he would not put past Salzman's machinations.

He was infuriated with the marriage broker and swore he would throw him out of the room the minute he reappeared. But Salzman did not come that night, and when Leo's anger had subsided, an unaccountable despair grew in its place. At first he thought this was caused by his disappointment in Lily, but before long it became evident that he had involved himself with Salzman without a true knowledge of his own intent. He gradually realized—with an emptiness that seized him with six hands—that he had called in the broker to find him a bride because he was incapable of doing it himself. This terrifying insight he had derived as a result of his meeting and conversation with Lily Hirschorn. Her probing questions had somehow irritated him into revealing—to himself more than her—the true nature of his relationship to God, and from that it had come upon him, with shocking force, that apart from his parents, he had never loved anyone. Or perhaps it went the other way, that he did not love God so well as he might, because he had not loved man. It seemed to Leo that his whole life stood starkly revealed and he saw himself for the first time as he truly was—unloved and loveless. This bitter but somehow not fully unexpected revelation brought him to a point of panic, controlled only by extraordinary effort. He covered his face with his hands and cried.

The week that followed was the worst of his life. He did not eat and lost weight. His beard darkened and grew ragged. He stopped attending seminars and almost never opened a book. He seriously considered leaving the Yeshivah, although he was deeply troubled at the thought of the loss of all his years of study—saw them like pages torn from a book, strewn over the city—and at the devastating effect of this decision upon his parents. But he had lived without knowledge of himself, and never in the Five Books and all the

Commentaries—mea culpa—had the truth been revealed to him. He did not know where to turn, and in all this desolating loneliness there was no *to whom,* although he often thought of Lily but not once could bring himself to go downstairs and make the call. He became touchy and irritable, especially with his landlady, who asked him all manner of personal questions; on the other hand, sensing his own disagreeableness, he waylaid her on the stairs and apologized abjectly, until mortified, she ran from him. Out of this, however, he drew the consolation that he was a Jew and that a Jew suffered. But gradually, as the long and terrible week drew to a close, he regained his composure and some idea of purpose in life: to go on as planned. Although he was imperfect, the ideal was not. As for his quest of a bride, the thought of continuing afflicted him with anxiety and heartburn, yet perhaps with this new knowledge of himself he would be more successful than in the past. Perhaps love would now come to him and a bride to that love. And for this sanctified seeking who needed a Salzman?

The marriage broker, a skeleton with haunted eyes, returned that very night. He looked, withal, the picture of frustrated expectancy —as if he had steadfastly waited the week at Miss Lily Hirschorn's side for a telephone call that never came.

Casually coughing, Salzman came immediately to the point: "So how did you like her?"

Leo's anger rose and he could not refrain from chiding the matchmaker: "Why did you lie to me, Salzman?"

Salzman's pale face went dead white, the world had snowed on him.

"Did you not state that she was twenty-nine?" Leo insisted.

"I give you my word—"

"She was thirty-five, if a day. *At least* thirty-five."

"Of this don't be too sure. Her father told me—"

"Never mind. The worst of it was that you lied to her."

"How did I lie to her, tell me?"

"You told her things about me that weren't true. You made me out to be more, consequently less than I am. She had in mind a totally different person, a sort of semimystical Wonder Rabbi."

"All I said, you was a religious man."

"I can imagine."

Salzman sighed. "This is my weakness that I have," he confessed.

"My wife says to me I shouldn't be a salesman, but when I have two fine people that they would be wonderful to be married, I am so happy that I talk too much." He smiled wanly. "This is why Salzman is a poor man."

Leo's anger left him. "Well, Salzman, I'm afraid that's all."

The marriage broker fastened hungry eyes on him.

"You don't want any more a bride?"

"I do," said Leo, "but I have decided to seek her in a different way. I am no longer interested in an arranged marriage. To be frank, I now admit the necessity of premarital love. That is, I want to be in love with the one I marry."

"Love?" said Salzman, astounded. After a moment he remarked. "For us, our love is our life, not for the ladies. In the ghetto they —"

"I know, I know," said Leo. "I've thought of it often. Love, I have said to myself, should be a by-product of living and worship rather than its own end. Yet for myself I find it necessary to establish the level of my need and fulfill it."

Salzman shrugged but answered, "Listen, rabbi, if you want love, this I can find for you also. I have such beautiful clients that you will love them the minute your eyes will see them."

Leo smiled unhappily. "I'm afraid you don't understand."

But Salzman hastily unstrapped his portfolio and withdrew a manila packet from it.

"Pictures," he said, quickly laying the envelope on the table.

Leo called after him to take the pictures away, but as if on the wings of the wind, Salzman had disappeared.

March came. Leo had returned to his regular routine. Although he felt not quite himself yet—lacked energy—he was making plans for a more active social life. Of course it would cost something, but he was an expert in cutting corners; and when there were no corners left he would make circles rounder. All the while Salzman's pictures had lain on the table, gathering dust. Occasionally as Leo sat studying, or enjoying a cup of tea, his eyes fell on the manila envelope, but he never opened it.

The days went by and no social life to speak of developed with a member of the opposite sex—it was difficult, given the circumstances of his situation. One morning Leo toiled up the stairs to his room and stared out the window at the city. Although the day was bright his view of it was dark. For some time he watched the people in the street below hurrying along and then turned with a heavy heart to his little room. On the table was the packet. With a sudden relentless gesture he tore it open. For a half-hour he stood by the table in a state of excitement, examining the photographs of the ladies Salzman had included. Finally, with a deep sigh he put them down. There were six, of varying degrees of attractiveness, but look at them long enough and they all became Lily Hirschorn: all past their prime, all starved behind bright smiles, not a true personality in the lot. Life, despite their frantic yoohooings, had passed them by; they were pictures in a brief case that stank of fish. After a while, however, as Leo attempted to return the photographs into the envelope, he found in it another, a snapshot of the type taken by a machine for a quarter. He gazed at it a moment and let out a cry.

Her face deeply moved him. Why, he could at first not say. It gave him the impression of youth—spring flowers, yet age—a sense of having been used to the bone, wasted: this came from the eyes which were hauntingly familiar, yet absolutely strange. He had a vivid impression that he had met her before, but try as he might he could not place her although he could almost recall her name, as if he had read it in her own handwriting. No, this couldn't be; he would have remembered her. It was not, he affirmed, that she had an extraordinary beauty—no, though her face was attractive enough; it was that *something* about her moved him. Feature for feature, even some of the ladies of the photographs could do better; but she leaped forth to his heart—had *lived,* or wanted to—more than just wanted, perhaps regretted how she had lived—had somehow deeply suffered: it could be seen in the depths of those reluctant eyes, and from the way the light enclosed and shone from her, and within her, opening realms of possibility: this was her own. Her he desired. His head ached and eyes narrowed with the intensity of his gazing, then as if an obscure fog had blown up in the mind, he experienced fear of her and was aware that he had received an impression, somehow, of evil. He shuddered, saying softly, it is thus with us all. Leo brewed some tea in a small pot and sat sipping it without sugar, to calm himself. But before he had finished drinking, again with excitement he examined the face and found it good: good for Leo Finkle. Only such a one could understand him and help him seek whatever he was seeking. She might, perhaps, love him. How she had happened to be among the discards in Salzman's barrel he could never guess, but he knew he must urgently go find her.

Leo rushed downstairs, grabbed up the Bronx telephone book, and searched for Salzman's home address. He was not listed, nor was his office. Neither was he in the Manhattan book. But Leo remembered having written down the address on a slip of paper after he had read Salzman's advertisement in the "personals" column of the *Forward.* He ran up to his room and tore through his papers, without luck. It was exasperating. Just when he needed the matchmaker he was nowhere to be found. Fortunately Leo remembered to look in his wallet. There on a card he found his name written and a Bronx address. No phone number was listed, the reason—Leo now recalled—he had originally communicated with Salzman by letter. He got on his coat, put a hat on over his skull cap and hurried to the subway station. All the way to the far end of the Bronx he sat on the edge of his seat. He was more than once tempted to take out the picture and see if the girl's face was as he remembered it, but he refrained, allowing the snapshot to remain in his inside coat pocket, content to have her so close. When the train pulled into the station he was waiting at the door and bolted out. He quickly located the street Salzman had advertised.

The building he sought was less than a block from the subway, but it was not an office building, nor even a loft, nor a store in which one could rent office space. It was a very old tenement house. Leo found Salzman's name in pencil on a soiled tag under the bell and climbed three dark flights to his apartment. When he knocked, the door was opened by a thin, asthmatic, gray-haired woman, in felt slippers.

"Yes?" she said, expecting nothing. She listened without listening. He could have sworn he had seen her, too, before but knew it was an illusion.

"Salzman—does he live here? Pinye Salzman," he said, "the matchmaker?"

She stared at him a long minute. "Of course."

He felt embarrassed. "Is he in?"

"No." Her mouth, though left open, offered nothing more.

"The matter is urgent. Can you tell me where his office is?"

"In the air." She pointed upward.

"You mean he has no office?" Leo asked.

"In his socks."

He peered into the apartment. It was sunless and dingy, one large room divided by a half-open curtain, beyond which he could see a sagging metal bed. The near side of a room was crowded with rickety chairs, old bureaus, a three-legged table, racks of cooking utensils, and all the apparatus of a kitchen. But there was no sign of Salzman or his magic barrel, probably also a figment of the imagination. An odor of frying fish made Leo weak to the knees.

"Where is he?" he insisted. "I've got to see your husband."

At length she answered, "So who knows where he is? Every time he thinks a new thought he runs to a different place. Go home, he will find you."

"Tell him Leo Finkle."

She gave no sign she had heard.

He walked downstairs, depressed.

But Salzman, breathless, stood waiting at his door.

Leo was astounded and overjoyed. "How did you get here before me?"

"I rushed."

"Come inside."

They entered. Leo fixed tea, and a sardine sandwich for Salzman. As they were drinking he reached behind him for the packet of pictures and handed them to the marriage broker.

Salzman put down his glass and said expectantly, "You found somebody you like?"

"Not among these."

The marriage broker turned away.

"Here is the one I want." Leo held forth the snapshot.

Salzman slipped on his glasses and took the picture into his trembling hand. He turned ghastly and let out a groan.

"What's the matter?" cried Leo.

"Excuse me. Was an accident this picture. She isn't for you."

Salzman frantically shoved the manila packet into his portfolio. He thrust the snapshot into his pocket and fled down the stairs.

Leo, after momentary paralysis, gave chase and cornered the marriage broker in the vestibule. The landlady made hysterical outcries but neither of them listened.

"Give me back the picture, Salzman."

"No." The pain in his eyes was terrible.

"Tell me who she is then."

"This I can't tell you. Excuse me."

He made to depart, but Leo, forgetting himself, seized the matchmaker by his tight coat and shook him frenziedly.

"Please," sighed Salzman. *"Please."*

Leo ashamedly let him go. "Tell me who she is," he begged. "It's very important for me to know."

"She is not for you. She is a wild one—wild, without shame. This is not a bride for a rabbi."

"What do you mean wild?"

"Like an animal. Like a dog. For her to be poor was a sin. This is why to me she is dead now."

"In God's name, what do you mean?"

"Her I can't introduce to you," Salzman cried.

"Why are you so excited?"

"Why, he asks," Salzman said, bursting into tears. "This is my baby, my Stella, she should burn in hell."

Leo hurried up to bed and hid under the covers. Under the covers he thought his life through. Although he soon fell asleep he could not sleep her out of his mind. He woke, beating his breast. Though he prayed to be rid of her, his prayers went unanswered. Through days of torment he endlessly struggled not to love her; fearing success, he escaped it. He then concluded to convert her to goodness, himself to God. The idea alternately nauseated and exalted him.

He perhaps did not know that he had come to a final decision until he encountered Salzman in a Broadway cafeteria. He was sitting alone at a rear table, sucking the bony remains of a fish. The marriage broker appeared haggard, and transparent to the point of vanishing.

Salzman looked up at first without recognizing him. Leo had grown a pointed beard and his eyes were weighted with wisdom.

"Salzman," he said, "love has at last come to my heart."

"Who can love from a picture?" mocked the marriage broker.

"It is not impossible."

"If you can love her, then you can love anybody. Let me show you some new clients that they just sent me their photographs. One is a little doll."

"Just her I want," Leo murmured.

"Don't be a fool, doctor. Don't bother with her."

"Put me in touch with her, Salzman," Leo said humbly. "Perhaps I can be of service."

Salzman had stopped eating and Leo understood with emotion that it was now arranged.

Leaving the cafeteria, he was, however, afflicted by a tormenting suspicion that Salzman had planned it all to happen this way.

Leo was informed by letter that she would meet him on a certain corner, and she was there one spring night, waiting under a street lamp. He appeared, carrying a small bouquet of violets and rosebuds. Stella stood by the lamp post, smoking. She wore white with red shoes, which fitted his expectations, although in a troubled moment he had imagined the dress red, and only the shoes white. She waited uneasily and shyly. From afar he saw that her eyes—clearly her father's—were filled with desperate innocence. He pictured, in her, his own redemption. Violins and lit candles revolved in the sky. Leo ran forward with flowers outthrust.

Around the corner, Salzman, leaning against a wall, chanted prayers for the dead.

1954

A Tree • A Rock • A Cloud

CARSON McCULLERS

[1917–1967]

It was raining that morning, and still very dark. When the boy reached the streetcar café he had almost finished his route and he went in for a cup of coffee. The place was an all-night café owned by a bitter and stingy man called Leo. After the raw, empty street, the café seemed friendly and bright: along the counter there were a couple of soldiers, three spinners from the cotton mill, and in a corner a man who sat hunched over with his nose and half his face down in a beer mug. The boy wore a helmet such as aviators wear. When he went into the café he unbuckled the chin strap and raised the right flap up over his pink little ear; often as he drank his coffee someone would speak to him in a friendly way. But this morning Leo did not look into his face and none of the men were talking. He paid and was leaving the café when a voice called out to him:

"Son! Hey Son!"

He turned back and the man in the corner was crooking his finger and nodding to him. He had brought his face out of the beer mug and he seemed suddenly very happy. The man was long and pale, with a big nose and faded orange hair.

"Hey Son!"

The boy went toward him. He was an undersized boy of about twelve, with one shoulder drawn higher than the other because of the weight of the paper sack. His face was shallow, freckled, and his eyes were round child eyes.

"Yeah Mister?"

The man laid one hand on the paper boy's shoulders, then

grasped the boy's chin and turned his face slowly from one side to the other. The boy shrank back uneasily.

"Say! What's the big idea?"

The boy's voice was shrill; inside the café it was suddenly very quiet.

The man said slowly: "I love you."

All along the counter the men laughed. The boy, who had scowled and sidled away, did not know what to do. He looked over the counter at Leo, and Leo watched him with a weary, brittle jeer. The boy tried to laugh also. But the man was serious and sad.

"I did not mean to tease you, Son," he said. "Sit down and have a beer with me. There is something I have to explain."

Cautiously, out of the corner of his eye, the paper boy questioned the men along the counter to see what he should do. But they had gone back to their beer or their breakfast and did not notice him. Leo put a cup of coffee on the counter and a little jug of cream.

"He is a minor," Leo said.

The paper boy slid himself up onto the stool. His ear beneath the upturned flap of the helmet was very small and red. The man was nodding at him soberly. "It is important," he said. Then he reached in his hip pocket and brought out something which he held up in the palm of his hand for the boy to see.

"Look very carefully," he said.

The boy stared, but there was nothing to look at very carefully. The man held in his big, grimy palm a photograph. It was the face of a woman, but blurred, so that only the hat and the dress she was wearing stood out clearly.

"See?" the man asked.

The boy nodded and the man placed another picture in his palm. The woman was standing on a beach in a bathing suit. The suit made her stomach very big, and that was the main thing you noticed.

"Got a good look?" He leaned over closer and finally asked: "You ever seen her before?"

The boy sat motionless, staring slantwise at the man. "Not so I know of."

"Very well." The man blew on the photographs and put them back into his pocket. "That was my wife."

"Dead?" the boy asked.

Slowly the man shook his head. He pursed his lips as though

about to whistle and answered in a long-drawn way; "Nuuu—" he said. "I will explain."

The beer on the counter before the man was in a large brown mug. He did not pick it up to drink. Instead he bent down and, putting his face over the rim, he rested there for a moment. Then with both hands he tilted the mug and sipped.

"Some night you'll go to sleep with your nose in a mug and drown," said Leo. "Prominent transient drowns in beer. That would be a cute death."

The paper boy tried to signal to Leo. While the man was not looking he screwed up his face and worked his mouth to question soundlessly: "Drunk?" But Leo only raised his eyebrows and turned away to put some pink strips of bacon on the grill. The man pushed the mug away from him, straightened himself, and folded his loose crooked hands on the counter. His face was sad as he looked at the paper boy. He did not blink, but from time to time the lids closed down with delicate gravity over his pale green eyes. It was nearing dawn and the boy shifted the weight of the paper sack.

"I am talking about love," the man said. "With me it is a science."

The boy half slid down from the stool. But the man raised his forefinger, and there was something about him that held the boy and would not let him go away.

"Twelve years ago I married the woman in the photograph. She was my wife for one year, nine months, three days, and two nights. I loved her. Yes . . ." He tightened his blurred, rambling voice and said again: "I loved her. I thought also that she loved me. I was a railroad engineer. She had all home comforts and luxuries. It never crept into my brain that she was not satisfied. But do you know what happened?"

"Mgneeow!" said Leo.

The man did not take his eyes from the boy's face. "She left me. I came in one night and the house was empty and she was gone. She left me."

"With a fellow?" the boy asked.

Gently the man placed his palm down on the counter. "Why naturally, Son. A woman does not run off like that alone."

The café was quiet, the soft rain black and endless in the street outside. Leo pressed down the frying bacon with the prongs of his long fork. "So you have been chasing the floozie for eleven years. You frazzled old rascal!"

For the first time the man glanced at Leo. "Please don't be vulgar. Besides, I was not speaking to you." He turned back to the boy and said in a trusting and secretive undertone: "Let's not pay any attention to him. O.K.?"

The paper boy nodded doubtfully.

"It was like this," the man continued. "I am a person who feels many things. All my life one thing after another has impressed me. Moonlight. The leg of a pretty girl. One thing after another. But the point is that when I had enjoyed anything there was a peculiar sensation as though it was laying around loose in me. Nothing seemed to finish itself up or fit in with the other things. Women? I had my portion of them. The same. Afterwards laying around loose in me. I was a man who had never loved."

Very slowly he closed his eyelids, and the gesture was like a curtain drawn at the end of a scene in a play. When he spoke again his voice was excited and the words came fast—the lobes of his large, loose ears seemed to tremble.

"Then I met this woman. I was fifty-one years old and she always said she was thirty. I met her at a filling station and we were married within three days. And do you know what it was like? I just can't tell you. All I had ever felt was gathered together around this woman. Nothing lay around loose in me any more but was finished up by her."

The man stopped suddenly and stroked his long nose. His voice sank down to a steady and reproachful undertone: "I'm not explaining this right. What happened was this. There were these beautiful feelings and loose little pleasures inside me. And this woman was something like an assembly line for my soul. I run these little pieces of myself through her and I come out complete. Now do you follow me?"

"What was her name?" the boy asked.

"Oh," he said. "I called her Dodo. But that is immaterial."

"Did you try to make her come back?"

The man did not seem to hear. "Under the circumstances you can imagine how I felt when she left me."

Leo took the bacon from the grill and folded two strips of it between a bun. He had a gray face, with slitted eyes, and a pinched nose saddled by faint blue shadows. One of the mill workers signaled for more coffee and Leo poured it. He did not give refills on coffee free. The spinner ate breakfast there every morning, but the better Leo knew his customers the stingier he treated them. He nibbled his own bun as though he grudged it to himself.

"And you never got hold of her again?"

The boy did not know what to think of the man, and his child's face was uncertain with mingled curiosity and doubt. He was new on the paper route; it was still strange to him to be out in the town in the black, queer early morning.

"Yes," the man said. "I took a number of steps to get her back. I went around trying to locate her. I went to Tulsa where she had folks. And to Mobile. I went to every town she had ever mentioned to me, and I hunted down every man she had formerly been connected with. Tulsa, Atlanta, Chicago, Cheehaw, Memphis. . . . For the better part of two years I chased around the country trying to lay hold of her."

"But the pair of them had vanished from the face of the earth!" said Leo.

"Don't listen to him," the man said confidentially. "And also just forget those two years. They are not important. What matters is that around the third year a curious thing begun to happen to me."

"What?" the boy asked.

The man leaned down and tilted his mug to take a sip of beer. But as he hovered over the mug his nostrils fluttered slightly; he sniffed the staleness of the beer and did not drink. "Love is a curious thing to begin with. At first I thought only of getting her back. It was a kind of mania. But then as time went on I tried to remember her. But do you know what happened?"

"No," the boy said.

"When I laid myself down on a bed and tried to think about her my mind became a blank. I couldn't see her. I would take out her pictures and look. No good. Nothing doing. A blank. Can you imagine it?"

"Say Mac!" Leo called down the counter. "Can you imagine this bozo's mind a blank!"

Slowly, as though fanning away flies, the man waved his hand. His green eyes were concentrated and fixed on the shallow little face of the paper boy.

"But a sudden piece of glass on a sidewalk. Or a nickel tune in a music box. A shadow on a wall at night. And I would remember.

It might happen in a street and I would cry or bang my head against a lamppost. You follow me?"

"A piece of glass . . ." the boy said.

"Anything. I would walk around and I had no power of how and when to remember her. You think you can put up a kind of shield. But remembering don't come to a man face forward—it corners around sideways. I was at the mercy of everything I saw and heard. Suddenly instead of me combing the countryside to find her she begun to chase me around in my very soul. *She* chasing *me,* mind you! And in my soul."

The boy asked finally: "What part of the country were you in then?"

"Ooh," the man groaned. "I was a sick mortal. It was like smallpox. I confess, Son, that I boozed. I fornicated. I committed any sin that suddenly appealed to me. I am loath to confess it but I will do so. When I recall that period it is all curdled in my mind, it was so terrible."

The man leaned his head down and tapped his forehead on the counter. For a few seconds he stayed bowed over in this position, the back of his stringy neck covered with orange furze, his hands with their long warped fingers held palm to palm in an attitude of prayer. Then the man straightened himself; he was smiling and suddenly his face was bright and tremulous and old.

"It was in the fifth year that it happened," he said. "And with it I started my science."

Leo's mouth jerked with a pale, quick grin. "Well none of we boys are getting any younger," he said. Then with sudden anger he balled up a dishcloth he was holding and threw it down hard on the floor. "You draggle-tailed old Romeo!"

"What happened?" the boy asked.

The old man's voice was high and clear: "Peace," he answered.

"Huh?"

"It is hard to explain scientifically, Son," he said. "I guess the logical explanation is that she and I had fleed around from each other for so long that finally we just got tangled up together and lay down and quit. Peace. A queer and beautiful blankness. It was spring in Portland and the rain came every afternoon. All evening I just stayed there on my bed in the dark. And that is how the science come to me."

The windows in the streetcar were pale blue with light. The two soldiers paid for their beers and opened the door—one of the soldiers combed his hair and wiped off his muddy puttees before they went outside. The three mill workers bent silently over their breakfasts. Leo's clock was ticking on the wall.

"It is this. And listen carefully. I meditated on love and reasoned it out. I realized what is wrong with us. Men fall in love for the first time. And what do they fall in love with?"

The boy's soft mouth was partly open and he did not answer.

"A woman," the old man said. "Without science, with nothing to go by, they undertake the most dangerous and sacred experience in God's earth. They fall in love with a woman. Is that correct, Son?"

"Yeah," the boy said faintly.

"They start at the wrong end of love. They begin at the climax. Can you wonder it is so miserable? Do you know how men should love?"

The old man reached over and grasped the boy by the collar of his leather jacket. He gave him a gentle little shake and his green eyes gazed down unblinking and grave.

"Son, do you know how love should be begun?"

The boy sat small and listening and still. Slowly he shook his head. The old man leaned closer and whispered:

"A tree. A rock. A cloud."

It was still raining outside in the street: a mild, gray, endless rain. The mill whistle blew for the six o'clock shift and the three spinners paid and went away. There was no one in the café but Leo, the old man, and the little paper boy.

"The weather was like this in Portland," he said. "At the time my science was begun. I meditated and I started very cautious. I would pick up something from the street and take it home with me. I bought a goldfish and I concentrated on the goldfish and I loved it. I graduated from one thing to another. Day by day I was getting this technique. On the road from Portland to San Diego—"

"Aw shut up!" screamed Leo suddenly. "Shut up! Shut up!"

The old man still held the collar of the boy's jacket; he was trembling and his face was earnest and bright and wild. "For six years now I have gone around by myself and built up my science. And now I am a master. Son. I can love anything. No longer do I have to think about it even. I see a street full of people and a beautiful light comes in me. I watch a bird in the sky. Or I meet a traveler on the road. Everything, Son. And anybody. All strangers and all loved! Do you realize what a science like mine can mean?"

The boy held himself stiffly, his hands curled tight around the counter edge. Finally he asked: "Did you ever really find that lady?"

"What? What say, Son?"

"I mean," the boy asked timidly. "Have you fallen in love with a woman again?"

The old man loosened his grasp on the boy's collar. He turned away and for the first time his green eyes had a vague and scattered look. He lifted the mug from the counter, drank down the yellow beer. His head was shaking slowly from side to side. Then finally he answered: "No, Son. You see that is the last step in my science. I go cautious. And I am not quite ready yet."

"Well!" said Leo. "Well well well!"

The old man stood in the open doorway. "Remember," he said. Framed there in the gray damp light of the early morning he looked shrunken and seedy and frail. But his smile was bright. "Remember I love you," he said with a last nod. And the door closed quietly behind him.

The boy did not speak for a long time. He pulled down the bangs on his forehead and slid his grimy little forefinger around the rim of his empty cup. Then without looking at Leo he finally asked:

"Was he drunk?"

"No," said Leo shortly.

The boy raised his clear voice higher. "Then was he a dope fiend?"

"No."

The boy looked up at Leo, and his flat little face was desperate, his voice urgent and shrill. "Was he crazy? Do you think he was a lunatic?" The paper boy's voice dropped suddenly with doubt. "Leo? Or not?"

But Leo would not answer him. Leo had run a night café for fourteen years, and he held himself to be a critic of craziness. There were the town characters and also the transients who roamed in from the night. He knew the manias of all of them. But he did not want to satisfy the questions of the waiting child. He tightened his pale face and was silent.

So the boy pulled down the right flap of his helmet and as he turned to leave he made the only comment that seemed safe to him, the only remark that could not be laughed down and despised:

"He sure has done a lot of traveling."

1942

The Lottery

SHIRLEY JACKSON

[1919–1965]

The morning of June 27th was clear and sunny, with the fresh warmth of a full-summer day; the flowers were blossoming profusely and the grass was richly green. The people of the village began to gather in the square, between the post office and the bank, around ten o'clock; in some towns there were so many people that the lottery took two days and had to be started on June 26th, but in this village, where there were only about three hundred people, the whole lottery took less than two hours, so it could begin at ten o'clock in the morning and still be through in time to allow the villagers to get home for noon dinner.

The children assembled first, of course. School was recently over for the summer, and the feeling of liberty sat uneasily on most of them; they tended to gather together quietly for a while before they broke into boisterous play, and their talk was still of the classroom and the teacher, of books and reprimands. Bobby Martin had already stuffed his pockets full of stones, and the other boys soon followed his example, selecting the smoothest and roundest stones; Bobby and Harry Jones and Dickie Delacroix—the villagers pronounced his name "Dellacroy"—eventually made a great pile of stones in one corner of the square and guarded it against the raids of the other boys. The girls stood aside, talking among themselves, looking over their shoulders at the boys, and the very small children rolled in the dust or clung to the hands of their older brothers or sisters.

Soon the men began to gather, surveying their own children, speaking of planting and rain, tractors and taxes. They stood together, away from the pile of stones in the corner, and their jokes were quiet and they smiled rather than laughed. The women, wearing faded house dresses and sweaters, came shortly after their menfolk. They greeted one another and exchanged bits of gossip as they went to join their husbands. Soon the women, standing by their husbands, began to call to their children, and the children came reluctantly, having to be called four or five times. Bobby Martin ducked under his mother's grasping hand and ran, laughing, back to the pile of stones. His father spoke up sharply, and Bobby came quickly and took his place between his father and his oldest brother.

The lottery was conducted—as were the square dances, the teenage club, the Halloween program—by Mr. Summers, who had time and energy to devote to civic activities. He was a round-faced, jovial man and he ran the coal business, and people were sorry for him, because he had no children and his wife was a scold. When he arrived in the square, carrying the black wooden box, there was a murmur of conversation among the villagers, and he waved and called, "Little late today, folks." The postmaster, Mr. Graves, followed him, carrying a three-legged stool, and the stool was put in the center of the square and Mr. Summers set the black box down on it. The villagers kept their distance, leaving a space between themselves and the stool, and when Mr. Summers said, "Some of you fellows want to give me a hand?" there was a hesitation before two men, Mr. Martin and his oldest son, Baxter, came forward to hold the box steady on the stool while Mr. Summers stirred up the papers inside it.

The original paraphernalia for the lottery had been lost long ago, and the black box now resting on the stool had been put into use even before Old Man Warner, the oldest man in town, was born. Mr. Summers spoke frequently to the villagers about making a new box, but no one liked to upset even as much tradition as was represented by the black box. There was a story that the present box had been made with some pieces of the box that had preceded it, the one that had been constructed when the first people settled down to make a village here. Every year, after the lottery, Mr. Summers began talking again about a new box, but every year the subject was allowed to fade off without anything's being done. The black box grew shabbier each year; by now it was no longer completely black but splintered badly along one side to show the original wood color, and in some places faded or stained.

Mr. Martin and his oldest son, Baxter, held the black box securely on the stool until Mr. Summers had stirred the papers thoroughly with his hand. Because so much of the ritual had been forgotten or discarded, Mr. Summers had been successful in having slips of paper substituted for the chips of wood that had been used for generations. Chips of wood, Mr. Summers had argued, had been all very well when the village was tiny, but now that the population was more than three hundred and likely to keep on growing, it was necessary to use something that would fit more easily into the black box. The night before the lottery, Mr. Summers and Mr. Graves made up the slips of paper and put them in the box, and it was then taken to the safe of Mr. Summers' coal company and locked up until Mr. Summers was ready to take it to the square next morning. The rest of the year, the box was put away, sometimes one place, sometimes another; it had spent one year in Mr. Graves's barn and another year underfoot in the post office, and sometimes it was set on a shelf in the Martin grocery and left there.

There was a great deal of fussing to be done before Mr. Summers declared the lottery open. There were the lists to make up—of heads of families, heads of households in each family, members of each household in each family. There was the proper swearing-in of Mr. Summers by the postmaster, as the official of the lottery; at one time, some people remembered, there had been a recital of some sort, performed by the official of the lottery, a perfunctory, tuneless chant that had been rattled off duly each year; some people believed that the official of the lottery used to stand just so when he said or sang it, others believed that he was supposed to walk among the people, but years and years ago this part of the ritual had been allowed to lapse. There had been, also, a ritual salute, which the official of the lottery had had to use in addressing each person who came up to draw from the box, but this also had changed with time, until now it was felt necessary only for the official to speak to each person approaching. Mr. Summers was very good at all this; in his clean white shirt and blue jeans, with one hand resting carelessly on the black box, he seemed very proper and important as he talked interminably to Mr. Graves and the Martins.

Just as Mr. Summers finally left off talking and turned to the assembled villagers, Mrs. Hutchinson came hurriedly along the path to the square, her sweater thrown over her shoulders, and slid into place in the back of the crowd. "Clean forgot what day it was," she said to Mrs. Delacroix, who stood next to her, and they both laughed softly. "Thought my old man was out back stacking wood," Mrs. Hutchinson went on, "and then I looked out the window and the kids were gone, and then I remembered it was the twenty-seventh and came a-running." She dried her hands on her apron, and Mrs. Delacroix said, "You're in time, though. They're still talking away up there."

Mrs. Hutchinson craned her neck to see through the crowd and found her husband and children standing near the front. She tapped Mrs. Delacroix on the arm as a farewell and began to make her way through the crowd. The people separated good-humoredly to let her through; two or three people said, in voices just loud enough to be heard across the crowd, "Here comes your Missus, Hutchinson," and "Bill, she made it after all." Mrs. Hutchinson reached her husband, and Mr. Summers, who had been waiting, said cheerfully, "Thought we were going to have to get on without you, Tessie." Mrs. Hutchinson said, grinning, "Wouldn't have me leave m'dishes in the sink, now, would you, Joe?," and soft laughter ran through the crowd as the people stirred back into position after Mrs. Hutchinson's arrival.

"Well, now," Mr. Summers said soberly, "guess we better get started, get this over with, so's we can go back to work. Anybody ain't here?"

"Dunbar," several people said. "Dunbar, Dunbar."

Mr. Summers consulted his list. "Clyde Dunbar," he said. "That's right. He's broke his leg, hasn't he? Who's drawing for him?"

"Me, I guess," a woman said, and Mr. Summers turned to look at her. "Wife draws for her husband," Mr. Summers said. "Don't you have a grown boy to do it for you, Janey?" Although Mr. Summers and everyone else in the village knew the answer perfectly well, it was the business of the official of the lottery to ask such questions formally. Mr. Summers waited with an expression of polite interest while Mrs. Dunbar answered.

"Horace's not but sixteen yet," Mrs. Dunbar said regretfully. "Guess I gotta fill in for the old man this year."

"Right," Mr. Summers said. He made a note on the list he was holding. Then he asked, "Watson boy drawing this year?"

A tall boy in the crowd raised his hand. "Here," he said. "I'm drawing for m'mother and me." He blinked his eyes nervously and ducked his head as several voices in the crowd said things like "Good fellow, Jack," and "Glad to see your mother's got a man to do it."

"Well," Mr. Summers said, "guess that's everyone. Old Man Warner make it?"

"Here," a voice said, and Mr. Summers nodded.

A sudden hush fell on the crowd as Mr. Summers cleared his throat and looked at the list. "All ready?" he called. "Now, I'll read the names—heads of families first—and the men come up and take a paper out of the box. Keep the paper folded in your hand without looking at it until everyone has had a turn. Everything clear?"

The people had done it so many times that they only half listened to the directions; most of them were quiet, wetting their lips, not looking around. Then Mr. Summers raised one hand high and said, "Adams." A man disengaged himself from the crowd and came forward. "Hi, Steve," Mr. Summers said, and Mr. Adams said, "Hi, Joe." They grinned at one another humorlessly and nervously. Then Mr. Adams reached into the black box and took out a folded paper. He held it firmly by one corner as he turned and went hastily back to his place in the crowd, where he stood a little apart from his family, not looking down at his hand.

"Allen." Mr. Summers said. "Anderson. . . . Bentham."

"Seems like there's no time at all between lotteries any more," Mrs. Delacroix said to Mrs. Graves in the back row. "Seems like we got through with the last one only last week."

"Time sure goes fast," Mrs. Graves said.

"Clark. . . . Delacroix."

"There goes my old man," Mrs. Delacroix said. She held her breath while her husband went forward.

"Dunbar," Mr. Summers said, and Mrs. Dunbar went steadily to the box while one of the women said, "Go on, Janey," and another said, "There she goes."

"We're next," Mrs. Graves said. She watched while Mr. Graves came around from the side of the box, greeted Mr. Summers gravely, and selected a slip of paper from the box. By now, all through the crowd there were men holding the small folded papers in their large hands, turning them over and over nervously. Mrs.

Dunbar and her two sons stood together, Mrs. Dunbar holding the slip of paper.

"Harburt. . . . Hutchinson."

"Get up there, Bill," Mrs. Hutchinson said, and the people near her laughed.

"Jones."

"They do say," Mr. Adams said to Old Man Warner, who stood next to him, "that over in the north village they're talking of giving up the lottery."

Old Man Warner snorted. "Pack of crazy fools," he said. "Listening to the young folks, nothing's good enough for *them.* Next thing you know, they'll be wanting to go back to living in caves, nobody work any more, live *that* way for a while. Used to be a saying about 'Lottery in June, corn be heavy soon.' First thing you know, we'd all be eating stewed chickweed and acorns. There's *always* been a lottery," he added petulantly. "Bad enough to see young Joe Summers up there joking with everybody."

"Some places have already quit lotteries," Mrs. Adams said.

"Nothing but trouble in *that,*" Old Man Warner said stoutly. "Pack of young fools."

"Martin." And Bobby Martin watched his father go forward. "Overdyke. . . . Percy."

"I wish they'd hurry," Mrs. Dunbar said to her older son. "I wish they'd hurry."

"They're almost through," her son said.

"You get ready to run tell Dad," Mrs. Dunbar said.

Mr. Summers called his own name and then stepped forward precisely and selected a slip from the box. Then he called, "Warner."

"Seventy-seventh year I been in the lottery," Old Man Warner said as he went through the crowd. "Seventy-seventh time."

"Watson." The tall boy came awkwardly through the crowd. Someone said, "Don't be nervous, Jack," said Mr. Summers said, "Take your time, son."

"Zanini."

After that, there was a long pause, a breathless pause, until Mr. Summers, holding his slip of paper in the air, said, "All right, fellows." For a minute, no one moved, and then all the slips of paper were opened. Suddenly, all the women began to speak at once, saying, "Who is it," "Who's got it?," "Is it the Dunbars?," "Is it the Watsons?" Then the voices began to say, "It's Hutchinson. It's Bill," "Bill Hutchinson's got it."

"Go tell your father," Mrs. Dunbar said to her older son.

People began to look around to see the Hutchinsons. Bill Hutchinson was standing quiet, staring down at the paper in his hand. Suddenly, Tessie Hutchinson shouted to Mr. Summers, "You didn't give him time enough to take any paper he wanted. I saw you. It wasn't fair!"

"Be a good sport, Tessie," Mrs. Delacroix called, and Mrs. Graves said, "All of us took the same chance."

"Shut up, Tessie," Bill Hutchinson said.

"Well, everyone," Mr. Summers said, "that was done pretty fast, and now we've got to be hurrying a little more to get it done in time." He consulted his next list. "Bill," he said, "you draw for the Hutchinson family. You got any other households in the Hutchinsons?"

"There's Don and Eva," Mrs. Hutchinson yelled. "Make *them* take their chance!"

"Daughters draw with their husbands' families, Tessie," Mr. Summers said gently. "You know that as well as anyone else."

"It wasn't *fair,*" Tessie said.

"I guess not, Joe," Bill Hutchinson said regretfully. "My daughter draws with her husband's family, that's only fair. And I've got no other family except the kids."

"Then, as far as drawing for families is concerned, it's you," Mr. Summers said in explanation, "and as far as drawing for households is concerned, that's you, too. Right?"

"Right," Bill Hutchinson said.

"How many kids, Bill?" Mr. Summers asked formally.

"Three," Bill Hutchinson said. "There's Bill, Jr., and Nancy, and little Dave. And Tessie and me."

"All right, then," Mr. Summers said. "Harry, you got their tickets back?"

Mr. Graves nodded and held up the slips of paper. "Put them in the box, then," Mr. Summers directed. "Take Bill's and put it in."

"I think we ought to start over," Mrs. Hutchinson said, as quietly as she could. "I tell you it wasn't *fair.* You didn't give him time enough to choose. *Every*body saw that."

Mr. Graves had selected the five slips and put them in the box, and he dropped all the papers but those onto the ground, where the breeze caught them and lifted them off.

"Listen, everybody," Mrs. Hutchinson was saying to the people around her.

"Ready, Bill?" Mr. Summers asked, and Bill Hutchinson, with one quick glance around at his wife and children, nodded.

"Remember," Mr. Summers said, "take the slips and keep them folded until each person has taken one. Harry, you help little Dave." Mr. Graves took the hand of the little boy, who came willingly with him up to the box. "Take a paper out of the box, Davy," Mr. Summers said. Davy put his hand into the box and laughed. "Take just *one* paper," Mr. Summers said. "Harry, you hold it for him." Mr. Graves took the child's hand and removed the folded paper from the tight fist and held it while little Dave stood next to him and looked up at him wonderingly.

"Nancy next," Mr. Summers said. Nancy was twelve, and her school friends breathed heavily as she went forward, switching her skirt, and took a slip daintily from the box. "Bill, Jr.," Mr. Summers said, and Billy, his face red and his feet over-large, nearly knocked the box over as he got a paper out. "Tessie," Mr. Summers said. She hesitated for a minute, looking around defiantly, and then set her lips and went up to the box. She snatched a paper out and held it behind her.

"Bill," Mr. Summers said, and Bill Hutchinson reached into the box and felt around, bringing his hand out at last with the slip of paper in it.

The crowd was quiet. A girl whispered, "I hope it's not Nancy," and the sound of the whisper reached the edges of the crowd.

"It's not the way it used to be," Old Man Warner said clearly. "People ain't the way they used to be."

"All right," Mr. Summers said. "Open the papers. Harry, you open little Dave's."

Mr. Graves opened the slip of paper and there was a general sigh through the crowd as he held it up and everyone could see that it was blank. Nancy and Bill, Jr., opened theirs at the same time, and both beamed and laughed, turning around to the crowd and holding their slips of paper above their heads.

"Tessie," Mr. Summers said. There was a pause, and then Mr. Summers looked at Bill Hutchinson, and Bill unfolded his paper and showed it. It was blank.

"It's Tessie," Mr. Summers said, and his voice was hushed. "Show us her paper, Bill."

Bill Hutchinson went over to his wife and forced the slip of paper out of her hand. It had a black spot on it, the black spot Mr. Summers had made the night before with the heavy pencil in the coal-company office. Bill Hutchinson held it up, and there was a stir in the crowd.

"All right, folks," Mr. Summers said. "Let's finish quickly."

Although the villagers had forgotten the ritual and lost the original black box, they still remembered to use stones. The pile of stones the boys had made earlier was ready; there were stones on the ground with the blowing scraps of paper that had come out of the box. Mrs. Delacroix selected a stone so large she had to pick it up with both hands and turned to Mrs. Dunbar. "Come on," she said. "Hurry up."

Mrs. Dunbar had small stones in both hands, and she said, gasping for breath, "I can't run at all. You'll have to go ahead and I'll catch up with you."

The children had stones already, and someone gave little Davy Hutchinson a few pebbles.

Tessie Hutchinson was in the center of a cleared space by now, and she held her hands out desperately as the villagers moved in on her. "It isn't fair," she said. A stone hit her on the side of the head.

Old Man Warner was saying, "Come on, come on, everyone." Steve Adams was in the front of the crowd of villagers, with Mrs. Graves beside him.

"It isn't fair, it isn't right," Mrs. Hutchinson screamed, and then they were upon her.

1948

Our Friend Judith

DORIS LESSING

[b. 1919]

I stopped inviting Judith to meet people when a Canadian woman remarked, with the satisfied fervor of one who has at last pinned a label on a rare specimen: "She is, of course, one of your typical English spinsters."

This was a few weeks after an American sociologist, having elicited from Judith the facts that she was fortyish, unmarried, and living alone, had inquired of me: "I suppose she has given up?" "Given up what?" I asked; and the subsequent discussion was unrewarding.

Judith did not easily come to parties. She would come after pressure, not so much—one felt—to do one a favor, but in order to correct what she believed to be a defect in her character. "I really ought to enjoy meeting new people more than I do," she said once. We reverted to an earlier pattern of our friendship: odd evenings together, an occasional visit to the cinema, or she would telephone to say: "I'm on my way past you to the British Museum. Would you care for a cup of coffee with me? I have twenty minutes to spare."

It is characteristic of Judith that the word "spinster," used of her, provoked fascinated speculation about other people. There are my aunts, for instance: aged seventy-odd, both unmarried, one an ex-missionary from China, one a retired matron of a famous London hospital. These two old ladies live together under the shadow of the cathedral in a country town. They devote much time to the Church, to good causes, to letter writing with friends all over the world, to the grandchildren and the great-grandchildren of relatives. It would be a mistake, however, on entering a house in which nothing has been moved for fifty years, to diagnose a condition of fossilized late-Victorian integrity. They read every book reviewed in the *Observer* or the *Times,* so that I recently got a letter from Aunt Rose inquiring whether I did not think that the author of *On the Road* was not—perhaps?—exaggerating his difficulties. They know a good deal about music, and write letters of encouragement to young composers they feel are being neglected—"You must understand that anything new and original takes time to be understood." Well-informed and critical Tories, they are as likely to dispatch telegrams of protest to the Home Secretary as letters of support. These ladies, my aunts Emily and Rose, are surely what is meant by the phrase "English spinster." And yet, once the connection has been pointed out, there is no doubt that Judith and they are spiritual cousins, if not sisters. Therefore it follows that one's pitying admiration for women who have supported manless and uncomforted lives needs a certain modification?

One will, of course, never know; and I feel now that it is entirely my fault that I shall never know. I had been Judith's friend for upwards of five years before the incident occurred which I involuntarily thought of—stupidly enough—as the first time Judith's mask slipped.

A mutual friend, Betty, had been given a cast-off Dior dress. She was too short for it. Also she said: "It's not a dress for a married woman with three children and a talent for cooking. I don't know why not, but it isn't." Judith was the right build. Therefore one evening the three of us met by appointment in Judith's bedroom, with the dress. Neither Betty nor I was surprised at the renewed discovery that Judith was beautiful. We had both often caught each other, and ourselves, in moments of envy when Judith's calm and severe face, her undemonstratively perfect body, succeeded in making everyone else in a room or a street look cheap.

Judith is tall, small-breasted, slender. Her light brown hair is parted in the center and cut straight around her neck. A high straight forehead, straight nose, a full grave mouth are setting for her eyes, which are green, large and prominent. Her lids are very white, fringed with gold, and molded close over the eyeball, so that in profile she has the look of a staring gilded mask. The dress was of dark green glistening stuff, cut straight, with a sort of loose tunic. It opened simply at the throat. In it Judith could of course evoke nothing but classical images. Diana, perhaps, back from the hunt, in a relaxed moment? A rather intellectual wood nymph who had opted for an afternoon in the British Museum Reading Room? Something like that. Neither Betty nor I said a word, since Judith was examining herself in a long mirror, and must know she looked magnificent.

Slowly she drew off the dress and laid it aside. Slowly she put on the old cord skirt and woolen blouse she had taken off. She must have surprised a resigned glance between us, for she then remarked, with the smallest of mocking smiles: "One surely ought to stay in character, wouldn't you say?" She added, reading the words out of some invisible book, written not by her, since it was a very vulgar book, but perhaps by one of us: "It does everything *for* me, I must admit."

"After seeing you in it," Betty cried out, defying her, "I can't bear for anyone else to have it. I shall simply put it away." Judith shrugged, rather irritated. In the shapeless skirt and blouse, and without makeup, she stood smiling at us, a woman at whom forty-nine out of fifty people would not look twice.

A second revelatory incident occurred soon after. Betty telephoned me to say that Judith had a kitten. Did I know that Judith adored cats? "No, but of course she would," I said.

Betty lived in the same street as Judith and saw more of her than I did. I was kept posted about the growth and habits of the cat and its effect on Judith's life. She remarked for instance that she felt it was good for her to have a tie and some responsibility. But no sooner was the cat out of kittenhood than all the neighbors complained. It was a tomcat, ungelded, and making every night hideous. Finally the landlord said that either the cat or Judith must go, unless she was prepared to have the cat "fixed." Judith wore herself out trying to find some person, anywhere in Britain, who would be prepared to take the cat. This person would, however, have to sign a written statement not to have the cat "fixed." When Judith took the cat to the vet to be killed, Betty told me she cried for twenty-four hours.

"She didn't think of compromising? After all, perhaps the cat might have preferred to live, if given the choice?"

"Is it likely I'd have the nerve to say anything so sloppy to Judith?

It's the nature of a male cat to rampage lustfully about, and therefore it would be morally wrong for Judith to have the cat fixed, simply to suit her own convenience."

"She said that?"

"She wouldn't have to *say* it, surely?"

A third incident was when she allowed a visiting young American, living in Paris, the friend of a friend and scarcely known to her, to use her flat while she visited her parents over Christmas. The young man and his friends lived it up for ten days of alcohol and sex and marijuana, and when Judith came back it took a week to get the place clean again and the furniture mended. She telephoned twice to Paris, the first time to say that he was a disgusting young thug and if he knew what was good for him he would keep out of her way in the future; the second time to apologize for losing her temper. "I had a choice either to let someone use my flat, or to leave it empty. But having chosen that you should have it, it was clearly an unwarrantable infringement of your liberty to make any conditions at all. I do most sincerely ask your pardon." The moral aspects of the matter having been made clear, she was irritated rather than not to receive letters of apology from him—fulsome, embarrassed, but above all, baffled.

It was the note of curiosity in the letters—he even suggested coming over to get to know her better—that irritated her most. "What do you suppose he means?" she said to me. "He lived in my flat for ten days. One would have thought that should be enough, wouldn't you?"

The facts about Judith, then, are all in the open, unconcealed, and plain to anyone who cares to study them; or, as it became plain she feels, to anyone with the intelligence to interpret them.

She has lived for the last twenty years in a small two-room flat high over a busy West London street. The flat is shabby and badly heated. The furniture is old, was never anything but ugly, is now frankly rickety and fraying. She has an income of two hundred pounds a year from a dead uncle. She lives on this and what she earns from her poetry, and from lecturing on poetry to night classes and extramural university classes.

She does not smoke or drink, and eats very little, from preference, not self-discipline.

She studied poetry and biology at Oxford, with distinction.

She is a Castlewell. That is, she is a member of one of the academic upper-middle-class families, which have been producing for centuries a steady supply of brilliant but sound men and women who are the backbone of the arts and sciences in Britain. She is on cool good terms with her family, who respect her and leave her alone.

She goes on long walking tours, by herself, in such places as Exmoor or West Scotland.

Every three or four years she publishes a volume of poems.

The walls of her flat are completely lined with books. They are scientific, classical and historical; there is a great deal of poetry and some drama. There is not one novel. When Judith says: "Of course I don't read novels," this does not mean that novels have no place, or a small place, in literature; or that people should not read novels; but that it must be obvious she can't be expected to read novels.

I had been visiting her flat for years before I noticed two long shelves of books, under a window, each shelf filled with the works of a single writer. The two writers are not, to put it at the mildest, the kind one would associate with Judith. They are mild, reminiscent, vague and whimsical. Typical English *belles-lettres,* in fact, and by definition abhorrent to her. Not one of the books in the two shelves has been read; some of the pages are still uncut. Yet each book is inscribed or dedicated to her: gratefully, admiringly, sentimentally and, more than once, amorously. In short, it is open to anyone who cares to examine these two shelves, and to work out dates, to conclude that Judith from the age of fifteen to twenty-five had been the beloved young companion of one elderly literary gentleman, and from twenty-five to thirty-five the inspiration of another.

During all that time she had produced her own poetry, and the sort of poetry, it is quite safe to deduce, not at all likely to be admired by her two admirers. Her poems are always cool and intellectual; that is their form, which is contradicted or supported by a gravely sensuous texture. They are poems to read often; one has to, to understand them.

I did not ask Judith a direct question about these two eminent but rather fusty lovers. Not because she would not have answered, or because she would have found the question impertinent, but because such questions are clearly unnecessary. Having those two shelves of books where they are, and books she could not conceivably care for, for their own sake, is publicly giving credit where credit is due. I can imagine her thinking the thing over, and deciding it was only fair, or perhaps honest, to place the books there; and this despite the fact that she would not care at all for the same attention to be paid to her. There is something almost contemptuous in it. For she certainly despises people who feel they need attention.

For instance, more than once a new emerging wave of "modern" young poets have discovered her as the only "modern" poet among their despised and well-credited elders. This is because, since she began writing at fifteen, her poems have been full of scientific, mechanical and chemical imagery. This is how she thinks, or feels.

More than once has a young poet hastened to her flat, to claim her as an ally, only to find her totally and by instinct unmoved by words like "modern," "new," "contemporary." He has been outraged and wounded by her principle, so deeply rooted as to be unconscious, and to need no expression but a contemptuous shrug of the shoulders, that publicly seeking or to want critical attention is despicable. It goes without saying that there is perhaps one critic in the world she has any time for. He has sulked off, leaving her on her shelf, which she takes it for granted is her proper place, to be read by an appreciative minority.

Meanwhile she gives her lectures, walks alone through London, writes her poems, and is seen sometimes at a concert or a play with a middle-aged professor of Greek, who has a wife and two children.

Betty and I had speculated about this professor, with such remarks as: Surely she must sometimes be lonely? Hasn't she ever wanted to marry? What about that awful moment when one comes in from somewhere at night to an empty flat?

It happened recently that Betty's husband was on a business trip, her children visiting, and she was unable to stand the empty house. She asked Judith for a refuge until her own home filled again.

Afterwards Betty rang me up to report: "Four of the five nights Professor Adams came in about ten or so."

"Was Judith embarrassed?"

"Would you expect her to be?"

"Well, if not embarrassed, at least conscious there was a situation?"

"No, not at all. But I must say I don't think he's good enough for her. He can't possibly understand her. He calls her Judy."

"Good God."

"Yes. But I was wondering. Suppose the other two called her Judy—'little Judy'—imagine it! Isn't it awful? But it does rather throw a light on Judith?"

"It's rather touching."

"I suppose it's touching. But *I* was embarrassed—oh, not because of the situation. Because of how she was, with him. 'Judy, is there another cup of tea in that pot?' And she, rather daughterly and demure, pouring him one."

"Three of the nights he went to her bedroom with her—very casual about it, because she was being. But he was not there in the mornings. So I asked her. You know how it is when you ask her a question. As if you've been having long conversations on that very subject for years and years, and she is merely continuing where you left off last. So when she says something surprising, one feels such a fool to be surprised?"

"Yes. And then?"

"I asked her if she was sorry not to have children. She said yes, but one couldn't have everything."

"One can't have everything, she said?"

"Quite clearly feeling she *has* nearly everything. She said she thought it was a pity, because she would have brought up children very well."

"When you come to think of it, she would, too."

"I asked about marriage, but she said on the whole the role of a mistress suited her better."

"She used the word 'mistress'?"

"You must admit it's the accurate word."

"I suppose so."

"And then she said that while she liked intimacy and sex and everything, she enjoyed waking up in the morning alone and *her own person.*"

"Yes, *of course.*"

"Of course. But now she's bothered because the professor would like to marry her. Or he feels he ought. At least, he's getting all guilty and obsessive about it. She says she doesn't see the point of divorce, and anyway, surely it would be very hard on his poor old wife after all these years, particularly after bringing up two children so satisfactorily. She talks about his wife as if she's a kind of nice old charwoman, and it wouldn't be *fair* to sack her, you know. Anyway. What with one thing and another. Judith's going off to Italy soon in order *to collect herself.*"

"But how's she going to pay for it?"

"Luckily the Third Program's commissioning her to do some arty programs. They offered her a choice of The Cid—El Thid, you know—and the Borgias. Well, the Borghese, then. And Judith settled for the Borgias."

"The Borgias," I said, *"Judith?"*

"Yes, quite. I said that too, in that tone of voice. She saw my point. She says the epic is right up her street, whereas the Renaissance has never been on her wave length. Obviously it couldn't be, all the magnificence and cruelty and *dirt.* But of course chivalry and a high moral code and all those idiotically noble goings-on are right on her wave length."

"Is the money the same?"

"Yes. But is it likely Judith would let money decide? No, she said that one should always choose something new, that isn't up one's street. Well, because it's better for her character, and so on, to get herself unsettled by the Renaissance. She didn't say *that,* of course."

"Of course not."

Judith went to Florence; and for some months postcards informed us tersely of her doings. Then Betty decided she must go by herself for a holiday. She had been appalled by the discovery that if her husband was away for a night she couldn't sleep; and when he went to Australia for three weeks, she stopped living until he came back. She had discussed this with him, and he had agreed that if she really felt the situation to be serious, he would dispatch her by air, to Italy, in order to recover her self-respect. As she put it.

I got this letter from her: "It's no use, I'm coming home. I might have known. Better face it, once you're really married you're not fit for man nor beast. And if you remember what I used to be like! *Well!* I moped around Milan. I sunbathed in Venice, then I thought my tan was surely worth something, so I was on the point of starting an affair with another lonely soul, but I lost heart, and went to Florence to see Judith. She wasn't there. She'd gone to the Italian

Riviera. I had nothing better to do, so I followed her. When I saw the place I wanted to laugh, it's so much not Judith, you know, all those palms and umbrellas and gaiety at all costs and ever such an ornamental blue sea. Judith is in an enormous stone room up on the hillside above the sea, with grape vines all over the place. You should see her, she's got beautiful. It seems for the last fifteen years she's been going to Soho every Saturday morning to buy food at an Italian shop. I must have looked surprised, because she explained she liked Soho. I suppose because all that dreary vice and nudes and prostitutes and everything prove how right she is to be as she is? She told the people in the shop she was going to Italy, and the *signora* said, what a coincidence, she was going back to Italy too, and she did hope an old friend like Miss Castlewell would visit her there. Judith said to me: 'I felt lacking, when she used the word friend. Our relations have always been formal. Can you understand it?' she said to me. 'For fifteen years,' I said to her. She said: 'I think I must feel it's a kind of imposition, don't you know, expecting people to feel friendship for one.' *Well.* I said: 'You ought to understand it, because you're like that yourself.' 'Am I?' she said. 'Well, think about it,' I said. But I could see she didn't want to think about it. Anyway, she's here, and I've spent a week with her. The widow Maria Rineiri inherited her mother's house, so she came home, from Soho. On the ground floor is a tatty little *rosticceria* patronized by the neighbors. They are all working people. This isn't tourist country, up on the hill. The widow lives above the shop with her little boy, a nasty little brat of about ten. Say what you like, the English are the only people who know how to bring up children, I don't care if that's insular. Judith's room is at the back, with a balcony. Underneath her room is the barber's shop, and the barber is Luigi Rineiri, the widow's younger brother. Yes, I was keeping him until the last. He is about forty, tall dark handsome, a great *bull,* but rather a sweet fatherly bull. He has cut Judith's hair and made it lighter. Now it looks like a sort of gold helmet. Judith is all brown. The widow Rineiri has made her a white dress and a green dress. They fit, for a change. When Judith walks down the street to the lower town, all the Italian males take one look at the golden girl and melt in their own oil like ice cream. Judith takes all this in her stride. She sort of acknowledges the homage. Then she strolls into the sea and vanishes into the foam. She swims five miles every day.

Naturally. I haven't asked Judith whether she has collected herself, because you can see she hasn't. The widow Rineiri is matchmaking. When I noticed this I wanted to laugh, but luckily I didn't because Judith asked me, really wanting to know: 'Can you see me married to an Italian barber?' (Not being snobbish, but stating the position, so to speak.) 'Well yes,' I said, 'you're the only woman I know who I can see married to an Italian barber.' Because it wouldn't matter who she married, she'd always be her *own person.* 'At any rate, for a time,' I said. At which she said, asperously: 'You can use phrases like for a time in England but not in Italy.' Did you ever see England, at least London, as the home of license, liberty and free love? No, neither did I, but of course she's right. Married to Luigi it would be the family, the neighbors, the church and the *bambini.* All the same she's thinking about it, believe it or not. Here she's quite different, all relaxed and free. She's melting in the attention she gets. The widow mothers her and makes her coffee all the time, and listens to a lot of good advice about how to bring up that nasty brat of hers. Unluckily she doesn't take it. Luigi is crazy for her. At mealtimes she goes to the *trattoria* in the upper square and all the workmen treat her like a goddess. Well, a film star then. I said to her, you're mad to come home. For one thing her rent is ten bob a week, and you eat *pasta* and drink red wine till you bust for about one and sixpence. No, she said, it would be nothing but self-indulgence to stay. Why? I said. She said, she's got nothing to stay for. (Ho ho.) And besides, she's done her research on the Borghese, though so far she can't see her way to an honest presentation of the facts. What made these people tick? she wants to know. And so she's only staying because of the cat. I forgot to mention the cat. This is a town of cats. The Italians here love their cats. I wanted to feed a stray cat at the table, but the waiter said no; and after lunch, all the waiters came with trays crammed with leftover food and stray cats came from everywhere to eat. And at dark when the tourists go in to feed and the beach is empty—you know how empty and forlorn a beach is at dusk?—well cats appear from everywhere. The beach seems to move, then you see it's cats. They go stalking along the thin inch of gray water at the edge of the sea, shaking their paws crossly at each step, snatching at the dead little fish, and throwing them with their mouths up onto the dry sand. Then they scamper after them. You've never seen such a snarling and fighting. At dawn when the fishing boats come in to the empty beach, the cats are there in dozens. The fishermen throw them bits of fish. The cats snarl and fight over it. Judith gets up early and goes down to watch. Sometimes Luigi goes too, being tolerant. Because what he really likes is to join the evening promenade with Judith on his arm around and around the square of the upper town. Showing her off. Can you *see* Judith? But she does it. Being tolerant. But she smiles and enjoys the attention she gets, there's no doubt of it.

"She has a cat in her room. It's a kitten really, but it's pregnant. Judith says she can't leave until the kittens are born. The cat is too young to have kittens. Imagine Judith. She sits on her bed in that great stone room, with her bare feet on the stone floor, and watches the cat, and tries to work out why a healthy uninhibited Italian cat always fed on the best from the *rosticceria* should be neurotic. Because it is. When it sees Judith watching it gets nervous and starts licking at the roots of its tail. But Judith goes on watching, and says about Italy that the reason why the English love the Italians is because the Italians make the English feel superior. They have no discipline. And that's a despicable reason for one nation to love another. Then she talks about Luigi and says he has no sense of guilt, but a sense of sin; whereas she has no sense of sin but she has guilt. I haven't asked her if this has been an insuperable barrier, because judging from how she looks, it hasn't. She says she would rather have a sense of sin, because sin can be attoned for, and if she understood sin, perhaps she would be more at home with the Renaissance. Luigi is very healthy, she says, and not neurotic. He is a Catholic of course. He doesn't mind that she's an atheist. His mother has explained to him that the English are all pagans, but good people at heart. I suppose he thinks a few smart sessions with the local priest would set Judith on the right path for good and all. Meanwhile the cat walks nervously around the room, stopping to lick, and when it can't stand Judith watching it another second, it rolls over on the floor, with its paws tucked up, and rolls up its eyes, and Judith scratches its lumpy pregnant stomach and tells it to relax. It makes *me* nervous to see her, it's not like her. I don't know why. Then Luigi shouts up from the barber's shop, then he comes up and stands at the door laughing, and Judith laughs, and the widow says: Children, enjoy yourselves. And off they go, walking down to the town eating ice cream. The cat follows them. It won't let Judith out of its sight, like a dog. When she swims miles out to sea, the cat hides under a beach hut until she comes back. Then she carries it back up the hill, because that nasty little boy chases it. *Well.* I'm coming home tomorrow thank God, to my dear old Billy, I was mad ever to leave him. There is something about Judith and Italy that has upset me, I don't know what. The point is, what on earth can Judith and Luigi *talk* about? Nothing. How can they? And of course it doesn't matter. So I turn out to be a prude as well. See you next week."

It was my turn for a dose of the sun, so I didn't see Betty. On my way back from Rome I stopped off in Judith's resort and walked up through narrow streets to the upper town, where, in the square with the vine-covered *trattoria* at the corner, was a house with ROSTICCERIA written in black paint on a cracked wooden board over a low door. There was a door curtain of red beads, and flies settled on the beads. I opened the beads with my hands and looked into a small dark room with a stone counter. Loops of salami hung from metal hooks. A glass bell covered some plates of cooked meats. There were flies on the salami and on the glass bell. A few tins on the wooden shelves, a couple of pale loaves, some wine casks and an open case of sticky pale green grapes covered with fruit flies seemed to be the only stock. A single wooden table with two chairs stood in a corner, and two workmen sat there, eating lumps of sausage and bread. Through another bead curtain at the back came a short, smoothly fat, slender-limbed woman with graying hair. I asked for Miss Castlewell, and her face changed. She said in an offended, offhand way: "Miss Castlewell left last week." She took a white cloth from under the counter, and flicked at the flies on the glass bell. "I'm a friend of hers," I said, and she said: *"Si,"* and put her hands palm down on the counter and looked at me, expressionless. The workmen got up, gulped down the last of their wine, nodded and went. She *ciao*'d them; and looked back at me. Then, since I didn't go, she called: "Luigi!" A shout came from the back room, there was a rattle of beads, and in came first a wiry sharp-faced boy, and then Luigi. He was tall, heavy-shouldered, and his black rough hair was like a cap, pulled low over his brows. He looked good-natured, but at the moment uneasy. His sister said something, and he stood beside her, an ally, and confirmed: "Miss Castlewell went away." I was on the point of giving up, when through the bead curtain that screened off a dazzling light eased a thin tabby cat. It was ugly and it walked uncomfortably, with its back quarters bunched up. The child suddenly let out a "Ssssss" through his teeth, and the cat froze. Luigi said something sharp to the child, and something encouraging to the cat, which sat down, looked straight in front of it, then began frantically licking at its flanks. "Miss Castlewell was offended with us," said Mrs. Rineiri suddenly, and with dignity. "She left early one morning. We did not expect her to go." I said: "Perhaps she had to go home and finish some work."

Mrs. Rineiri shrugged, then sighed. Then she exchanged a hard look with her brother. Clearly the subject had been discussed, and closed forever.

"I've known Judith a long time," I said, trying to find the right note. "She's a remarkable woman. She's a poet." But there was no response to this at all. Meanwhile the child, with a fixed bared-teeth grin, was staring at the cat, narrowing his eyes. Suddenly he let out another "Sssssss" and added a short high yelp. The cat shot backwards, hit the wall, tried desperately to claw its way up the wall, came to its senses and again sat down and began its urgent, undirected licking at its fur. This time Luigi cuffed the child, who yelped in earnest, and then ran out into the street past the cat. Now that the way was clear the cat shot across the floor, up onto the counter, and bounded past Luigi's shoulder and straight through the bead curtain into the barber's shop, where it landed with a thud.

"Judith was sorry when she left us," said Mrs. Rineiri uncertainly. "She was crying."

"I'm sure she was."

"And so," said Mrs. Rineiri, with finality, laying her hands down again, and looking past me at the bead curtain. That was the end. Luigi nodded brusquely at me, and went into the back. I said goodbye to Mrs. Rineiri and walked back to the lower town. In the square I saw the child, sitting on the running board of a lorry parked outside the *trattoria,* drawing in the dust with his bare toes, and directing in front of him a blank, unhappy stare.

I had to go through Florence, so I went to the address Judith had been at. No, Miss Castlewell had not been back. Her papers and books were still here. Would I take them back with me to England? I made a great parcel and brought them back to England.

I telephoned Judith and she said she had already written for the papers to be sent, but it was kind of me to bring them. There had seemed to be no point, she said, in returning to Florence.

"Shall I bring them over?"

"I would be very grateful, of course."

Judith's flat was chilly, and she wore a bunchy sage-green woolen dress. Her hair was still a soft gold helmet, but she looked pale and rather pinched. She stood with her back to a single bar of electric fire—lit because I demanded it—with her legs apart and her arms folded. She contemplated me.

"I went to the Rineiris' house."

"Oh. Did you?"

"They seemed to miss you."

She said nothing.

"I saw the cat too."

"Oh. Oh, I suppose you and Betty discussed it?" This was with a small unfriendly smile.

"Well, Judith, you must see we were likely to?"

She gave this her consideration and said: "I don't understand why people discuss other people. Oh—I'm not criticizing you. But I don't see why you are so interested. I don't understand human behavior and I'm not particularly interested."

"I think you should write to the Rineiris."

"I wrote and thanked them, of course."

"I don't mean that."

"You and Betty have worked it out?"

"Yes, we talked about it. We thought we should talk to you, so you should write to the Rineiris."

"Why?"

"For one thing, they are both very fond of you."

"Fond," she said smiling.

"Judith, I've never in my life felt such an atmosphere of being let down."

Judith considered this. "When something happens that shows one there is really a complete gulf in understanding, what is there to say?"

"It could scarcely have been a complete gulf in understanding. I suppose you are going to say we are being interfering?"

Judith showed distaste. "That is a very stupid word. And it's a stupid idea. No one can interfere with me if I don't let them. No, it's that I don't understand people. I don't understand why you or Betty should care. Or why the Rineiris should, for that matter," she added with the small tight smile.

"Judith!"

"If you've behaved stupidly, there's no point in going on. You put an end to it."

"What happened? Was it the cat?"

"Yes, I suppose so. But it's not important." She looked at me, saw my ironical face, and said: "The cat was too young to have kittens. That is all there was to it."

"Have it your way. But that is obviously not all there is to it."

"What upsets me is that I don't understand at all why I was so upset then."

"What happened? Or don't you want to talk about it?"

"I don't give a damn whether I talk about it or not. You really do say the most extraordinary things, you and Betty. If you want to know, I'll tell you. What does it matter?"

"I would like to know, of course."

"Of course!" she said. "In your place I wouldn't care. Well, I think the essence of the thing was that I must have had the wrong attitude to that cat. Cats are supposed to be independent. They are supposed to go off by themselves to have their kittens. This one didn't. It was climbing up on to my bed all one night and crying for attention. I don't like cats on my bed. In the morning I saw she was in pain. I stayed with her all that day. Then Luigi—he's the brother, you know."

"Yes."

"Did Betty mention him? Luigi came up to say it was time I went for a swim. He said the cat should look after itself. I blame myself very much. That's what happens when you submerge yourself in somebody else."

Her look at me was now defiant; and her body showed both defensiveness and aggression. "Yes. It's true. I've always been afraid of it. And in the last few weeks I've behaved badly. It's because I let it happen."

"Well, go on."

"I left the cat and swam. It was late, so it was only for a few minutes. When I came out of the sea the cat had followed me and had had a kitten on the beach. That little beast Michele—the son, you know?—well, he always teased the poor thing, and now he had frightened her off the kitten. It was dead, though. He held it up by the tail and waved it at me as I came out of the sea. I told him to bury it. He scooped two inches of sand away and pushed the kitten in—on the beach, where people are all day. So I buried it properly. He had run off. He was chasing the poor cat. She was terrified and running up the town. I ran too. I caught Michele and I was so angry I hit him. I don't believe in hitting children. I've been feeling beastly about it ever since."

"You were angry."

"It's no excuse. I would never have believed myself capable of hitting a child. I hit him very hard. He went off, crying. The poor cat had got under a big lorry parked in the square. Then she screamed. And then a most remarkable thing happened. She screamed just once, and all at once cats just materialized. One minute there was just one cat, lying under a lorry, and the next, dozens of cats. They sat in a big circle around the lorry, all quite still, and watched my poor cat."

"Rather moving," I said.

"Why?"

"There is no evidence one way or the other," I said in inverted commas, "that the cats were there out of concern for a friend in trouble."

"No," she said energetically. "There isn't. It might have been curiosity. Or anything. How do we know? However, I crawled under the lorry. There were two paws sticking out of the cat's back end. The kitten was the wrong way round. It was stuck. I held the cat down with one hand and I pulled the kitten out with the other." She held out her long white hands. They were still covered with fading scars and scratches. "She bit and yelled, but the kitten was alive. She left the kitten and crawled across the square into the house. Then all the cats got up and walked away. It was the most extraordinary thing I've ever seen. They vanished again. One minute they were all there, and then they had vanished. I went after the cat, with the kitten. Poor little thing, it was covered with dust—being wet, don't you know. The cat was on my bed. There was another kitten coming, but it got stuck too. So when she screamed and screamed I just pulled it out. The kittens began to suck. One kitten was very big. It was a nice fat black kitten. It must have hurt her. But she suddenly bit out—snapped, don't you know, like a reflex action, at the back of the kitten's head. It died, just like that. Extraordinary, isn't it?" she said, blinking hard, her lips quivering. "She was its mother, but she killed it. Then she ran off the bed and went downstairs into the shop under the counter. I called to Luigi. You know, he's Mrs. Rineiri's brother."

"Yes, I know."

"He said she was too young, and she was badly frightened and very hurt. He took the alive kitten to her but she got up and walked away. She didn't want it. Then Luigi told me not to look. But I followed him. He held the kitten by the tail and he banged it against the wall twice. Then he dropped it into the rubbish heap. He moved aside some rubbish with his toe, and put the kitten there and pushed rubbish over it. Then Luigi said the cat should be destroyed. He said she was badly hurt and it would always hurt her to have kittens."

"He hasn't destroyed her. She's still alive. But it looks to me as if he were right."

"Yes, I expect he was."

"What upset you—that he killed the kitten?"

"Oh no, I expect the cat would if he hadn't. But that isn't the point, is it?"

"What is the point?"

"I don't think I really know." She had been speaking breathlessly, and fast. Now she said slowly: "It's not a question of right or wrong, is it? Why should it be? It's a question of what one is. That night Luigi wanted to go promenading with me. For him, that was *that.* Something had to be done, and he'd done it. But I felt ill. He was very nice to me. He's a very good person," she said, defiantly.

"Yes, he looks it."

"That night I couldn't sleep. I was blaming myself. I should never have left the cat to go swimming. Well, and then I decided to leave the next day. And I did. And that's all. The whole thing was a mistake from start to finish."

"Going to Italy at all?"

"Oh, to go for a holiday would have been all right."

"You've done all that work for nothing? You mean you aren't going to make use of all that research?"

"No. It was a mistake."

"Why don't you leave it a few weeks and see how things are then?"

"Why?"

"You might feel differently about it."

"What an extraordinary thing to say. Why should I? Oh, you mean, time passing, healing wounds—that sort of thing? What an extraordinary idea. It's always seemed to me an extraordinary idea. No, right from the beginning I've felt ill at ease with the whole business, not myself at all."

"Rather irrationally, I should have said."

Judith considered this, very seriously. She frowned while she thought it over. Then she said: "But if one cannot rely on what one feels, what can one rely on?"

"On what one thinks, I should have expected you to say."

"Should you? Why? Really, you people are all very strange. I don't understand you." She turned off the electric fire, and her face closed up. She smiled, friendly and distant, and said: "I don't really see any point at all in discussing it."

1963

A Conversation with My Father

GRACE PALEY

[b. 1922]

My father is eighty-six years old and in bed. His heart, that bloody motor, is equally old and will not do certain jobs any more. It still floods his head with brainy light. But it won't let his legs carry the weight of his body around the house. Despite my metaphors, this muscle failure is not due to his old heart, he says, but to a potassium shortage. Sitting on one pillow, leaning on three, he offers last-minute advice and makes a request.

"I would like you to write a simple story just once more," he says, "the kind de Maupassant wrote, or Chekhov, the kind you used to write. Just recognizable people and then write down what happened to them next."

I say, "Yes, why not? That's possible." I want to please him, though I don't remember writing that way. I *would* like to try to tell such a story, if he means the kind that begins: "There was a woman . . ." followed by plot, the absolute line between two points which I've always despised. Not for literary reasons, but because it takes all hope away. Everyone, real or invented, deserves the open destiny of life.

Finally I thought of a story that had been happening for a couple of years right across the street. I wrote it down, then read it aloud. "Pa," I said, "how about this? Do you mean something like this?"

Once in my time there was a woman and she had a son. They lived nicely, in a small apartment in Manhattan. This boy at about fifteen became a junkie, which is not unusual in our neighborhood. In order to maintain her close friendship with him, she became a junkie too. She said it was part of the youth culture, with which she felt very much at home. After a while, for a number of reasons, the boy gave it all up and left the city and his mother in disgust. Hopeless and alone, she grieved. We all visit her.

"O.K., Pa, that's it," I said, "an unadorned and miserable tale."

"But that's not what I mean," my father said. "You misunderstood me on purpose. You know there's a lot more to it. You know that. You left everything out. Turgenev wouldn't do that. Chekhov wouldn't do that. There are in fact Russian writers you never heard of, you don't have an inkling of, as good as anyone, who can write a plain ordinary story, who would not leave out what you have left out. I object not to facts but to people sitting in trees talking senselessly, voices from who knows where . . ."

"Forget that one, Pa, what have I left out now? In this one?"

"Her looks, for instance."

"Oh. Quite handsome, I think. Yes."

"Her hair?"

"Dark, with heavy braids, as though she were a girl or a foreigner."

"What were her parents like, her stock? That she became such a person. It's interesting, you know."

"From out of town. Professional people. The first to be divorced in their county. How's that? Enough?" I asked.

"With you, it's all a joke," he said. "What about the boy's father? Why didn't you mention him? Who was he? Or was the boy born out of wedlock?"

"Yes," I said. "He was born out of wedlock."

"For Godsakes, doesn't anyone in your stories get married? Doesn't anyone have the time to run down to City Hall before they jump into bed?"

"No," I said. "In real life, yes. But in my stories, no."

"Why do you answer me like that?"

"Oh, Pa, this is a simple story about a smart woman who came to N.Y.C. full of interest love trust excitement very up to date, and about her son, what a hard time she had in this world. Married or not, it's of small consequence."

"It is of great consequence," he said.

"O.K.," I said.

"O.K. O.K. yourself," he said, "but listen. I believe you that she's good-looking, but I don't think she was so smart."

"That's true," I said. "Actually that's the trouble with stories. People start out fantastic. You think they're extraordinary, but it turns out as the work goes along, they're just average with a good education. Sometimes the other way around, the person's a kind of dumb innocent, but he outwits you and you can't even think of an ending good enough."

"What do you do then?" he asked. He had been a doctor for a couple of decades and then an artist for a couple of decades and he's still interested in details, craft, technique.

"Well, you just have to let the story lie around till some agreement can be reached between you and the stubborn hero."

"Aren't you talking silly, now?" he asked. "Start again," he said. "It so happens I'm not going out this evening. Tell the story again. See what you can do this time."

"O.K.," I said. "But it's not a five-minute job." Second attempt:

Once, across the street from us, there was a fine handsome woman, our neighbor. She had a son whom she loved because she'd known him since birth (in helpless chubby infancy, and in the wrestling, hugging ages, seven to ten, as well as earlier and later). This boy, when he fell into the fist of adolescence, became a junkie. He was not a hopeless one. He was in fact hopeful, an ideologue and successful converter. With his busy brilliance, he wrote persuasive articles for his high-school newspaper. Seeking a wider audience, using important connections, he drummed into Lower Manhattan newsstand distribution a periodical called *Oh! Golden Horse!*

In order to keep him from feeling guilty (because guilt is the stony heart of nine tenths of all clinically diagnosed cancers in America today, she said), and because she had always believed in giving bad habits room at home where one could keep an eye on them, she too became a junkie. Her kitchen was famous for a while—a center for intellectual addicts who knew what they were doing. A few felt artistic like Coleridge and others were scientific and revolutionary like Leary. Although she was often high herself, certain good mothering reflexes remained, and she saw to it that there was lots of orange juice around and honey and milk and vitamin pills. However, she never cooked anything but chili, and that no more than once a week. She explained, when we talked to her, seriously, with neighborly concern, that it was her part in the youth culture and she would rather be with the young, it was an honor, than with her own generation.

One week, while nodding through an Antonioni film, this boy was severely jabbed by the elbow of a stern and proselytizing girl, sitting beside him. She offered immediate apricots and nuts for his sugar level, spoke to him sharply, and took him home.

She had heard of him and his work and she herself published, edited, and wrote a competitive journal called *Man Does Live By Bread Alone.* In the organic heat of her continuous presence he could not help but become interested once more in his muscles, his arteries, and nerve connections. In fact he began to love them, treasure them, praise them with funny little songs in *Man Does Live . . .*

the fingers of my flesh transcend
my transcendental soul
the tightness in my shoulders end
my teeth have made me whole

To the mouth of his head (that glory of will and determination) he brought hard apples, nuts, wheat germ, and soybean oil. He said to his old friends, From now on, I guess I'll keep my wits about me. I'm going on the natch. He said he was about to begin a spiritual deep-breathing journey. How about you too, Mom? he asked kindly.

His conversion was so radiant, splendid, that neighborhood kids his age began to say that he had never been a real addict at all, only a journalist along for the smell of the story. The mother tried several times to give up what had become without her son and his friends a lonely habit. This effort only brought it to supportable levels. The boy and his girl took their electronic mimeograph and moved to the bushy edge of another borough. They were very strict. They said they would not see her again until she had been off drugs for sixty days.

At home alone in the evening, weeping, the mother read and reread the seven issues of *Oh! Golden Horse!* They seemed to her as truthful as ever. We often crossed the street to visit and console. But if we mentioned any of our children who were at college or in the hospital or dropouts at home, she would cry out, My baby! My baby! and burst into terrible, face-scarring, time-consuming tears. The End.

First my father was silent, then he said, "Number One: You have a nice sense of humor. Number Two: I see you can't tell a plain story. So don't waste time." Then he said sadly, "Number Three: I suppose that means she was alone, she was left like that, his mother. Alone. Probably sick?"

I said, "Yes."

"Poor woman. Poor girl, to be born in a time of fools, to live among fools. The end. The end. You were right to put that down. The end."

I didn't want to argue, but I had to say, "Well, it is not necessarily the end, Pa."

"Yes," he said, "what a tragedy. The end of a person."

"No, Pa," I begged him. "It doesn't have to be. She's only about forty. She could be a hundred different things in this world as time goes on. A teacher or a social worker. An ex-junkie! Sometimes it's better than having a master's in education."

"Jokes," he said. "As a writer that's your main trouble. You don't want to recognize it. Tragedy! Plain tragedy! Historical tragedy! No hope. The end."

"Oh, Pa," I said. "She could change."

"In your own life, too, you have to look it in the face." He took a couple of nitroglycerin. "Turn to five," he said, pointing to the dial on the oxygen tank. He inserted the tubes into his nostrils and breathed deep. He closed his eyes and said, "No."

I had promised the family to always let him have the last word when arguing, but in this case I had a different responsibility. That woman lives across the street. She's my knowledge and my invention. I'm sorry for her. I'm not going to leave her there in that house crying. (Actually neither would Life, which unlike me has no pity.)

Therefore: She did change. Of course her son never came home again. But right now, she's the receptionist in a storefront community clinic in the East Village. Most of the customers are young people, some old friends. The head doctor has said to her, "If we only had three people in this clinic with your experiences . . ."

"The doctor said that?" My father took the oxygen tubes out of his nostrils and said, "Jokes. Jokes again."

"No, Pa, it could really happen that way, it's a funny world nowadays."

"No," he said. "Truth first. She will slide back. A person mus have character. She does not."

"No, Pa," I said. "That's it. She's got a job. Forget it. She's in tha storefront working."

"How long will it be?" he asked. "Tragedy! You too. When wil you look it in the face?"

197

Sonny's Blues

JAMES BALDWIN

[b. 1924]

I read about it in the paper, in the subway, on my way to work. I read it, and I couldn't believe it, and I read it again. Then perhaps I just stared at it, at the newsprint spelling out his name, spelling out the story. I stared at it in the swinging lights of the subway car, and in the faces and bodies of the people, and in my own face, trapped in the darkness which roared outside.

It was not to be believed and I kept telling myself that as I walked from the subway station to the high school. And at the same time I couldn't doubt it. I was scared, scared for Sonny. He became real to me again. A great block of ice got settled in my belly and kept melting there slowly all day long, while I taught my classes algebra. It was a special kind of ice. It kept melting, sending trickles of ice water all up and down my veins, but it never got less. Sometimes it hardened and seemed to expand until I felt my guts were going to come spilling out or that I was going to choke or scream. This would always be at a moment when I was remembering some specific thing Sonny had once said or done.

When he was about as old as the boys in my classes his face had been bright and open, there was a lot of copper in it; and he'd had wonderfully direct brown eyes, and great gentleness and privacy. I wondered what he looked like now. He had been picked up, the evening before, in a raid on an apartment downtown, for peddling and using heroin.

I couldn't believe it: but what I mean by that is that I couldn't find any room for it anywhere inside me. I had kept it outside me for a long time. I hadn't wanted to know. I had had suspicions, but I didn't name them, I kept putting them away. I told myself that

Sonny was wild, but he wasn't crazy. And he'd always been a good boy, he hadn't ever turned hard or evil or disrespectful, the way kids can, so quick, so quick, especially in Harlem. I didn't want to believe that I'd ever see my brother going down, coming to nothing, all that light in his face gone out, in the condition I'd already seen so many others. Yet it had happened and here I was, talking about algebra to a lot of boys who might, every one of them for all I knew, be popping off needles every time they went to the head. Maybe it did more for them than algebra could.

I was sure that the first time Sonny had ever had horse, he couldn't have been much older than these boys were now. These boys, now, were living as we'd been living then, they were growing up with a rush and their heads bumped abruptly against the low ceiling of their actual possibilities. They were filled with rage. All they really knew were two darknesses, the darkness of their lives, which was now closing in on them, and the darkness of the movies, which had blinded them to that other darkness, and in which they now, vindictively, dreamed, at once more together than they were at any other time, and more alone.

When the last bell rang, the last class ended, I let out my breath. It seemed I'd been holding it for all that time. My clothes were wet—I may have looked as though I'd been sitting in a steam bath, all dressed up, all afternoon. I sat alone in the classroom a long time. I listened to the boys outside, downstairs, shouting and cursing and laughing. Their laughter struck me for perhaps the first time. It was not the joyous laughter which—God knows why—one associates with children. It was mocking and insular, its intent was to denigrate. It was disenchanted, and in this, also, lay the authority of their curses. Perhaps I was listening to them because I was thinking about my brother and in them I heard my brother. And myself.

One boy was whistling a tune, at once very complicated and very simple, it seemed to be pouring out of him as though he were a bird, and it sounded very cool and moving through all that harsh, bright air, only just holding its own through all those other sounds.

I stood up and walked over to the window and looked down into the courtyard. It was the beginning of the spring and the sap was rising in the boys. A teacher passed through them every now and again, quickly, as though he or she couldn't wait to get out of that courtyard, to get those boys out of their sight and off their minds. I started collecting my stuff. I thought I'd better get home and talk to Isabel.

The courtyard was almost deserted by the time I got downstairs. I saw this boy standing in the shadow of a doorway, looking just like Sonny. I almost called his name. Then I saw that it wasn't Sonny, but somebody we used to know, a boy from around our block. He'd been Sonny's friend. He'd never been mine, having been too young for me, and, anyway, I'd never liked him. And now, even though he was a grown-up man, he still hung around that block, still spent hours on the street corner, was always high and raggy. I used to run into him from time to time and he'd often work around to asking me for a quarter or fifty cents. He always had some real good excuse, too, and I always gave it to him, I don't know why.

But now, abruptly, I hated him. I couldn't stand the way he looked at me, partly like a dog, partly like a cunning child. I wanted to ask him what the hell he was doing in the school courtyard.

He sort of shuffled over to me, and he said, "I see you got the papers. So you already know about it."

"You mean about Sonny? Yes, I already know about it. How come they didn't get you?"

He grinned. It made him repulsive and it also brought to mind what he'd looked like as a kid. "I wasn't there. I stay away from them people."

"Good for you." I offered him a cigarette and I watched him through the smoke. "You come all the way down here just to tell me about Sonny?"

"That's right." He was sort of shaking his head and his eyes looked strange, as though they were about to cross. The bright sun deadened his damp dark brown skin and it made his eyes look yellow and showed up the dirt in his conked hair. He smelled funky. I moved a little away from him and I said, "Well, thanks. But I already know about it and I got to get home."

"I'll walk you a little ways," he said. We started walking. There were a couple of kids still loitering in the courtyard and one of them said good night to me and looked strangely at the boy beside me.

"What're you going to do?" he asked me. "I mean, about Sonny?"

"Look. I haven't seen Sonny for over a year, I'm not sure I'm going to do anything. Anyway, what the hell *can* I do?"

"That's right," he said quickly, "ain't nothing you can do. Can't much help old Sonny no more, I guess."

It was what I was thinking and so it seemed to me he had no right to say it.

"I'm surprised at Sonny, though," he went on—he had a funny way of talking, he looked straight ahead as though he were talking to himself—"I thought Sonny was a smart boy, I thought he was too smart to get hung."

"I guess he thought so too," I said sharply, "and that's how he got hung. And how about you? You're pretty goddamn smart, I bet."

Then he looked directly at me, just for a minute. "I ain't smart," he said. "If I was smart, I'd have reached for a pistol a long time ago."

"Look. Don't tell *me* your sad story, if it was up to me, I'd give you one." Then I felt guilty—guilty, probably, for never having supposed that the poor bastard *had* a story of his own, much less a sad one, and I asked, quickly, "What's going to happen to him now?"

He didn't answer this. He was off by himself some place. "Funny thing," he said, and from his tone we might have been discussing the quickest way to get to Brooklyn, "when I saw the papers this morning, the first thing I asked myself was if I had anything to do with it. I felt sort of responsible."

I began to listen more carefully. The subway station was on the corner, just before us, and I stopped. He stopped, too. We were in front of a bar and he ducked slightly, peering in, but whoever he was looking for didn't seem to be there. The juke box was blasting away with something black and bouncy and I half watched the barmaid as she danced her way from the juke box to her place behind the bar. And I watched her face as she laughingly responded to something someone said to her, still keeping time to the music. When she smiled one saw the little girl, one sensed the doomed, still-struggling woman beneath the battered face of the semi-whore.

"I never *give* Sonny nothing," the boy said finally, "but a long time ago I come to school high and Sonny asked me how it felt." He paused, I couldn't bear to watch him, I watched the barmaid, and I listened to the music which seemed to be causing the pavement to shake. "I told him it felt great." The music stopped, the barmaid paused and watched the juke box until the music began again. "It did."

All this was carrying me some place I didn't want to go. I certainly didn't want to know how it felt. It filled everything, the people, the houses, the music, the dark, quicksilver barmaid, with menace; and this menace was their reality.

"What's going to happen to him now?" I asked again.

"They'll send him away some place and they'll try to cure him." He shook his head. "Maybe he'll even think he's kicked the habit. Then they'll let him loose"—he gestured, throwing his cigarette into the gutter. "That's all."

"What do you mean, that's *all?*"

But I knew what he meant.

"I *mean,* that's *all.*" He turned his head and looked at me, pulling down the corners of his mouth. "Don't you know what I mean?" he asked softly.

"How the hell *would* I know what you mean?" I almost whispered it, I don't know why.

"That's right," he said to the air, "how would *he* know what I mean?" He turned toward me again, patient and calm, and yet I somehow felt him shaking, shaking as though he were going to fall apart. I felt that ice in my guts again, the dread I'd felt all afternoon; and again I watched the barmaid, moving about the bar, washing glasses, and singing. "Listen. They'll let him out and then it'll just start all over again. That's what I mean."

"You mean—they'll let him out. And then he'll just start working his way back in again. You mean he'll never kick the habit. Is that what you mean?"

"That's right," he said, cheerfully. "*You* see what I mean."

"Tell me," I said at last, "why does he want to die? He must want to die, he's killing himself, why does he want to die?"

He looked at me in surprise. He licked his lips. "He don't want to die. He wants to live. Don't nobody want to die, ever."

Then I wanted to ask him—too many things. He could not have answered, or if he had, I could not have borne the answers. I started walking. "Well, I guess it's none of my business."

"It's going to be rough on old Sonny," he said. We reached the subway station. "This is your station?" he asked. I nodded. I took one step down. "Damn!" he said, suddenly. I looked up at him. He grinned again. "Damn if I didn't leave all my money home. You ain't got a dollar on you, have you? Just for a couple of days, is all."

All at once something inside gave and threatened to come pouring out of me. I didn't hate him any more. I felt that in another moment I'd start crying like a child.

"Sure," I said. "Don't sweat." I looked in my wallet and didn't have a dollar, I only had a five. "Here," I said. "That hold you?"

He didn't look at it—he didn't want to look at it. A terrible, closed look came over his face, as though he were keeping the number on the bill a secret from him and me. "Thanks," he said, and now he was dying to see me go. "Don't worry about Sonny. Maybe I'll write him or something."

"Sure," I said. "You do that. So long."

"Be seeing you," he said. I went on down the steps.

And I didn't write Sonny or send him anything for a long time. When I finally did, it was just after my little girl died, he wrote me back a letter which made me feel like a bastard.

Here's what he said:

Dear Brother,

You don't know how much I needed to hear from you. I wanted to write you many a time but I dug how much I must have hurt you and so I didn't write. But now I feel like a man who's been trying to climb up out of some deep, real deep and funky hole and just saw the sun up there, outside. I got to get outside.

I can't tell you much about how I got here. I mean I don't know how to tell you. I guess I was afraid of something or I was trying to escape from something and you know I have never been very strong in the head (smile). I'm glad Mama and Daddy are dead and can't see what's happened to their son and I swear if I'd known what I was doing I would never have hurt you so, you and a lot of other fine people who were nice to me and who believed in me.

I don't want you to think it had anything to do with me being a musician. It's more than that. Or maybe less than that. I can't get anything straight in my head down here and I try not to think about what's going to happen to me when I get outside again. Sometime I think I'm going to flip and *never* get outside and sometime I think I'll come straight back. I tell you one thing, though, I'd rather blow my brains out than go through this again. But that's what they all say, so they tell me. If I tell you when I'm coming to New York and if you could meet me, I sure would appreciate it. Give my love to Isabel and the kids and I was sorry to hear about little Gracie. I wish I could be like Mama and say the Lord's will be done, but I don't know it seems to me that trouble is the one thing that never does get stopped and I don't know what good it does to blame it on the Lord. But maybe it does some good if you believe it.

Your brother,
SONNY

Then I kept in constant touch with him and I sent him whatever I could and I went to meet him when he came back to New York. When I saw him many things I thought I had forgotten came flooding back to me. This was because I had begun, finally, to wonder about Sonny, about the life that Sonny lived inside. This life, whatever it was, had made him older and thinner and it had deepened the distant stillness in which he had always moved. He looked very unlike my baby brother. Yet, when he smiled, when we shook hands, the baby brother I'd never known looked out from the depths of his private life, like an animal waiting to be coaxed into the light.

"How you been keeping?" he asked me.

"All right. And you?"

"Just fine." He was smiling all over his face. "It's good to see you again."

"It's good to see you."

The seven years' difference in our ages lay between us like a chasm: I wondered if these years would ever operate between us as a bridge. I was remembering, and it made it hard to catch my breath, that I had been there when he was born; and I had heard the first words he had ever spoken. When he started to walk, he walked from our mother straight to me. I caught him just before he fell when he took the first steps he ever took in this world.

"How's Isabel?"

"Just fine. She's dying to see you."

"And the boys?"

"They're fine, too. They're anxious to see their uncle."

"Oh, come on. You know they don't remember me."

"Are you kidding? Of course they remember you."

He grinned again. We got into a taxi. We had a lot to say to each other, far too much to know how to begin.

As the taxi began to move, I asked, "You still want to go to India?"

He laughed. "You still remember that. Hell, no. This place is Indian enough for me."

"It used to belong to them," I said.

And he laughed again. "They damn sure knew what they were doing when they got rid of it."

Years ago, when he was around fourteen, he'd been all hipped on the idea of going to India. He read books about people sitting on rocks, naked, in all kinds of weather, but mostly bad, naturally, and walking barefoot through hot coals and arriving at wisdom. I used to say that it sounded to me as though they were getting away from wisdom as fast as they could. I think he sort of looked down on me for that.

"Do you mind," he asked, "if we have the driver drive alongside the park? On the west side—I haven't seen the city in so long."

"Of course not," I said. I was afraid that I might sound as though I were humoring him, but I hoped he wouldn't take it that way.

So we drove along, between the green of the park and the stony, lifeless elegance of hotels and apartment buildings, toward the vivid, killing streets of our childhood. These streets hadn't changed, though housing projects jutted up out of them now like rocks in the middle of a boiling sea. Most of the houses in which we had grown up had vanished, as had the stores from which we had stolen, the basements in which we had first tried sex, the rooftops from which we had hurled tin cans and bricks. But houses exactly like the houses of our past yet dominated the landscape, boys exactly like the boys we once had been found themselves smothering in these houses, came down into the streets for light and air and found themselves encircled by disaster. Some escaped the trap, most didn't. Those who got out always left something of themselves behind, as some animals amputate a leg and leave it in the trap. It might be said, perhaps, that I had escaped, after all, I was a school teacher; or that Sonny had, he hadn't lived in Harlem for years. Yet, as the cab moved uptown through streets which seemed, with a rush, to darken with dark people, and as I covertly studied Sonny's face, it came to me that what we both were seeking through our separate cab windows was that part of ourselves which had been left behind. It's always at the hour of trouble and confrontation that the missing member aches.

We hit 110th Street and started rolling up Lenox Avenue. And I'd known this avenue all my life, but it seemed to me again, as it had seemed on the day I'd first heard about Sonny's trouble, filled with a hidden menace which was its very breath of life.

"We almost there," said Sonny.

"Almost." We were both too nervous to say anything more.

We live in a housing project. It hasn't been up long. A few days after it was up it seemed uninhabitably new, now, of course, it's already run-down. It looks like a parody of the good, clean, faceless life—God knows the people who live in it do their best to make it a parody. The beat-looking grass lying around isn't enough to make their lives green, the hedges will never hold out the streets, and they know it. The big windows fool no one, they aren't big enough to make space out of no space. They don't bother with the windows, they watch the TV screen instead. The playground is most popular with the children who don't play at jacks, or skip rope, or roller skate, or swing, and they can be found in it after dark. We moved in partly because it's not too far from where I teach, and partly for the kids; but it's really just like the houses in which Sonny and I grew up. The same things happen, they'll have the same things to remember. The moment Sonny and I started into the house I had the feeling that I was simply bringing him back into the danger he had almost died trying to escape.

Sonny has never been talkative. So I don't know why I was sure he'd be dying to talk to me when supper was over the first night. Everything went fine, the oldest boy remembered him, and the youngest boy liked him, and Sonny had remembered to bring something for each of them; and Isabel, who is really much nicer than I am, more open and giving, had gone to a lot of trouble about dinner and was genuinely glad to see him. And she's always been able to tease Sonny in a way that I haven't. It was nice to see her face so vivid again and to hear her laugh and watch her make Sonny laugh. She wasn't, or, anyway, she didn't seem to be, at all uneasy or embarrassed. She chatted as though there were no subject which had to be avoided and she got Sonny past his first, faint stiffness. And thank God she was there, for I was filled with that icy dread again. Everything I did seemed awkward to me, and everything I said sounded freighted with hidden meaning. I was trying to remember everything I'd heard about dope addiction and I couldn't help watching Sonny for signs. I wasn't doing it out of malice. I was trying to find out something about my brother. I was dying to hear him tell me he was safe.

"Safe!" my father grunted, whenever Mama suggested trying to move to a neighborhood which might be safer for children. "Safe, hell! Ain't no place safe for kids, nor nobody."

He always went on like this, but he wasn't, ever, really as bad as he sounded, not even on weekends, when he got drunk. As a matter of fact, he was always on the lookout for "something a little better," but he died before he found it. He died suddenly, during a drunken weekend in the middle of the war, when Sonny was fifteen. He and Sonny hadn't ever got on too well. And this was partly because Sonny was the apple of his father's eye. It was because he loved Sonny so much and was frightened for him, that he was always fighting with him. It doesn't do any good to fight with Sonny. Sonny just moves back, inside himself, where he can't be reached. But the principal reason that they never hit it off is that they were so much alike. Daddy was big and rough and loud-talking, just the opposite of Sonny, but they both had—that same privacy.

Mama tried to tell me something about this, just after Daddy died. I was home on leave from the army.

This was the last time I ever saw my mother alive. Just the same, this picture gets all mixed up in my mind with pictures I had of her when she was younger. The way I always see her is the way she used to be on a Sunday afternoon, say, when the old folks were talking after the big Sunday dinner. I always see her wearing pale blue. She'd be sitting on the sofa. And my father would be sitting in the easy chair, not far from her. And the living room would be full of church folks and relatives. There they sit, in chairs all around the living room, and the night is creeping up outside, but nobody knows it yet. You can see the darkness growing against the window-panes and you hear the street noises every now and again, or maybe the jangling beat of a tambourine from one of the churches close by, but it's real quiet in the room. For a moment nobody's talking, but every face looks darkening, like the sky outside. And my mother rocks a little from the waist, and my father's eyes are closed. Everyone is looking at something a child can't see. For a minute they've forgotten the children. Maybe a kid is lying on the rug half asleep. Maybe somebody's got a kid on his lap and is absent-mindedly stroking the kid's head. Maybe there's a kid, quiet and big-eyed, curled up in a big chair in the corner. The silence, the darkness coming, and the darkness in the faces frightens the child obscurely. He hopes that the hand which strokes his forehead will never stop—will never die. He hopes that there will never come a time when the old folks won't be sitting around the living room, talking about where they've come from, and what they've seen, and what's happened to them and their kinfolk.

But something deep and watchful in the child knows that this is bound to end, is already ending. In a moment someone will get up and turn on the light. Then the old folks will remember the children and they won't talk any more that day. And when light fills the room, the child is filled with darkness. He knows that every time this happens he's moved just a little closer to that darkness outside. The darkness outside is what the old folks have been talking about. It's what they've come from. It's what they endure. The child knows that they won't talk any more because if he knows too much about what's happened to *them,* he'll know too much too soon, about what's going to happen to *him.*

The last time I talked to my mother, I remember I was restless. I wanted to get out and see Isabel. We weren't married then and we had a lot to straighten out between us.

There Mama sat, in black, by the window. She was humming an old church song, *Lord, you brought me from a long ways off.* Sonny was out somewhere. Mama kept watching the streets.

"I don't know," she said, "if I'll ever see you again, after you go off from here. But I hope you'll remember the things I tried to teach you."

"Don't talk like that," I said, and smiled. "You'll be here a long time yet."

She smiled, too, but she said nothing. She was quiet for a long time. And I said, "Mama, don't you worry about nothing. I'll be writing all the time, and you be getting the checks. . . ."

"I want to talk to you about your brother," she said, suddenly. "If anything happens to me he ain't going to have nobody to look out for him."

"Mama," I said, "ain't nothing going to happen to you *or* Sonny. Sonny's all right. He's a good boy and he's got good sense."

"It ain't a question of his being a good boy," Mama said, "nor of his having good sense. It ain't only the bad ones, nor yet the dumb ones that gets sucked under." She stopped, looking at me. "Your Daddy once had a brother," she said, and she smiled in a way that made me feel she was in pain. "You didn't never know that, did you?"

"No," I said, "I never knew that," and I watched her face.

"Oh, yes," she said, "your Daddy had a brother." She looked out of the window again. "I know you never saw your Daddy cry. But *I* did—many a time, through all these years."

I asked her, "What happened to his brother? How come nobody's ever talked about him?"

This was the first time I ever saw my mother look old.

"His brother got killed," she said, "when he was just a little younger than you are now. I knew him. He was a fine boy. He was maybe a little full of the devil, but he didn't mean nobody no harm."

Then she stopped and the room was silent, exactly as it had sometimes been on those Sunday afternoons. Mama kept looking out into the streets.

"He used to have a job in the mill," she said, "and, like all young folks, he just liked to perform on Saturday nights. Saturday nights, him and your father would drift around to different places, go to dances and things like that, or just sit around with people they knew, and your father's brother would sing, he had a fine voice, and play along with himself on his guitar. Well, this particular Saturday night, him and your father was coming home from some place, and they were both a little drunk and there was a moon that night, it was bright like day. Your father's brother was feeling kind of good, and he was whistling to himself, and he had his guitar slung over his shoulder. They was coming down a hill and beneath them was a road that turned off from the highway. Well, your father's brother, being always kind of frisky, decided to run down this hill, and he did, with that guitar banging and clanging behind him, and he ran across the road, and he was making water behind a tree. And your father was sort of amused at him and he was still coming down the hill, kind of slow. Then he heard a car motor and that same minute his brother stepped from behind the tree, into the road, in the moonlight. And he started to cross the road. And your father started to run down the hill, he says he don't know why. This car was full of white men. They was all drunk, and when they seen your father's brother they let out a great whoop and holler and they aimed the car straight at him. They was having fun, they just wanted to scare him, the way they do sometimes, you know. But they was drunk. And I guess the boy, being drunk, too, and scared, kind of lost his head. By the time he jumped it was too late. Your father says he heard his brother scream when the car rolled over him, and he heard the wood of that guitar when it give, and he heard them strings go flying, and he heard them white men shouting, and the car kept on a-going and it ain't stopped till this day. And, time your father got down the hill, his brother weren't nothing but blood and pulp."

Tears were gleaming on my mother's face. There wasn't anything I could say.

"He never mentioned it," she said, "because I never let him mention it before you children. Your Daddy was like a crazy man that night and for many a night thereafter. He says he never in his life seen anything as dark as that road after the lights of that car had gone away. Weren't nothing, weren't nobody on that road, just your Daddy and his brother and that busted guitar. Oh, yes. Your Daddy never did really get right again. Till the day he died he weren't sure but that every white man he saw was the man that killed his brother."

She stopped and took out her handkerchief and dried her eyes and looked at me.

"I ain't telling you all this," she said, "to make you scared or bitter or to make you hate nobody. I'm telling you this because you got a brother. And the world ain't changed."

I guess I didn't want to believe this. I guess she saw this in my face. She turned away from me, toward the window again, searching those streets.

"But I praise my Redeemer," she said at last, "that He called your Daddy home before me. I ain't saying it to throw no flowers at myself, but, I declare, it keeps me from feeling too cast down to know I helped your father get safely through this world. Your father always acted like he was the roughest, strongest man on earth. And everybody took him to be like that. But if he hadn't had *me* there—to see his tears!"

She was crying again. Still, I couldn't move. I said, "Lord, Lord, Mama, I didn't know it was like that."

"Oh, honey," she said, "there's a lot that you don't know. But you are going to find it out." She stood up from the window and came over to me. "You got to hold on to your brother," she said, "and don't let him fall, no matter what it looks like is happening to him and no matter how evil you gets with him. You going to be evil with him many a time. But don't you forget what I told you, you hear?"

"I won't forget," I said. "Don't you worry, I won't forget. I won't let nothing happen to Sonny."

My mother smiled as though she were amused at something she saw in my face. Then, "You may not be able to stop nothing from happening. But you got to let him know you's *there.*"

Two days later I was married, and then I was gone. And I had a lot of things on my mind and I pretty well forgot my promise to Mama until I got shipped home on a special furlough for her funeral.

And, after the funeral, with just Sonny and me alone in the empty kitchen, I tried to find out something about him.

"What do you want to do?" I asked him.

"I'm going to be a musician," he said.

For he had graduated, in the time I had been away, from dancing to the juke box to finding out who was playing what, and what they were doing with it, and he had bought himself a set of drums.

"You mean, you want to be a drummer?" I somehow had the feeling that being a drummer might be all right for other people but not for my brother Sonny.

"I don't think," he said, looking at me very gravely, "that I'll ever be a good drummer. But I think I can play a piano."

I frowned. I'd never played the role of the older brother quite so seriously before, had scarcely ever, in fact, *asked* Sonny a damn thing. I sensed myself in the presence of something I didn't really know how to handle, didn't understand. So I made my frown a little deeper as I asked: "What kind of musician do you want to be?"

He grinned. "How many kinds do you think there are?"

"Be *serious,*" I said.

He laughed, throwing his head back, and then looked at me. "I *am* serious."

"Well, then, for Christ's sake, stop kidding around and answer a serious question. I mean, do you want to be a concert pianist, you want to play classical music and all that, or—or what?" Long before I finished he was laughing again. "For Christ's *sake,* Sonny!"

He sobered, but with difficulty. "I'm sorry. But you sound so—*scared!*" and he was off again.

"Well, you may think it's funny now, baby, but it's not going to be so funny when you have to make your living at it, let me tell you *that.*" I was furious because I knew he was laughing at me and I didn't know why.

"No," he said, very sober now, and afraid, perhaps, that he'd hurt me, "I don't want to be a classical pianist. That isn't what interests me. I mean"—he paused, looking hard at me, as though his eyes would help me to understand, and then gestured helplessly, as though perhaps his hand would help—"I mean, I'll have a lot of studying to do, and I'll have to study *everything,* but I mean, I want to play *with*—jazz musicians." He stopped. "I want to play jazz," he said.

Well, the word had never before sounded as heavy, as real, as it sounded that afternoon in Sonny's mouth. I just looked at him and I was probably frowning a real frown by this time. I simply couldn't see why on earth he'd want to spend his time hanging around night clubs, clowning around on bandstands, while people pushed each other around a dance floor. It seemed—beneath him, somehow. I had never thought about it before, had never been forced to, but I suppose I had always put jazz musicians in a class with what Daddy called "good-time people."

"Are you *serious?*"

"Hell, *yes,* I'm serious."

He looked more helpless than ever, and annoyed, and deeply hurt.

I suggested, helpfully: "You mean—like Louis Armstrong?"

His face closed as though I'd struck him. "No. I'm not talking about none of that old-time, down home crap."

"Well, look, Sonny, I'm sorry, don't get mad. I just don't altogether get it, that's all. Name somebody—you know, a jazz musician you admire."

"Bird."

"Who?"

"Bird! Charlie Parker! Don't they teach you nothing in the goddamn army?"

I lit a cigarette. I was surprised and then a little amused to discover that I was trembling. "I've been out of touch," I said. "You'll have to be patient with me. Now. Who's this Parker character?"

"He's just one of the greatest jazz musicians alive," said Sonny, sullenly, his hands in his pockets, his back to me. "Maybe *the* greatest," he added, bitterly, "that's probably why *you* never heard of him."

"All right," I said, "I'm ignorant. I'm sorry. I'll go out and buy all the cat's records right away, all right?"

"It don't," said Sonny, with dignity, "make any difference to me. I don't care what you listen to. Don't do me no favors."

I was beginning to realize that I'd never seen him so upset before. With another part of my mind I was thinking that this would probably turn out to be one of those things kids go through and that I shouldn't make it seem important by pushing it too hard. Still, I didn't think it would do any harm to ask: "Doesn't all this take a lot of time? Can you make a living at it?"

He turned back to me and half leaned, half sat, on the kitchen table. "Everything takes time," he said, "and—well, yes, sure, I can make a living at it. But what I don't seem to be able to make you understand is that it's the only thing I want to do."

"Well Sonny," I said, gently, "you know people can't always do exactly what they *want* to do—"

"*No,* I don't know that," said Sonny, surprising me. "I think people *ought* to do what they want to do, what else are they alive for?"

"You getting to be a big boy," I said desperately, "it's time you started thinking about your future."

"I'm thinking about my future," said Sonny, grimly. "I think about it all the time."

I gave up. I decided, if he didn't change his mind, that we could always talk about it later. "In the meantime," I said, "you got to finish school." We had already decided that he'd have to move in with Isabel and her folks. I knew this wasn't the ideal arrangement because Isabel's folks are inclined to be dicty and they hadn't especially wanted Isabel to marry me. But I didn't know what else to do. "And we have to get you fixed up at Isabel's."

There was a long silence. He moved from the kitchen table to the window. "That's a terrible idea. You know it yourself."

"Do you have a *better* idea?"

He just walked up and down the kitchen for a minute. He was as tall as I was. He had started to shave. I suddenly had the feeling that I didn't know him at all.

He stopped at the kitchen table and picked up my cigarettes. Looking at me with a kind of mocking, amused defiance, he put one between his lips. "You mind?"

"You smoking already?"

He lit the cigarette and nodded, watching me through the smoke. "I just wanted to see if I'd have the courage to smoke in front of you." He grinned and blew a great cloud of smoke to the ceiling. "It was easy." He looked at my face. "Come on, now. I bet you was smoking at my age, tell the truth."

I didn't say anything but the truth was on my face, and he laughed. But now there was something very strained in his laugh. "Sure. And I bet that ain't all you was doing."

He was frightening me a little. "Cut the crap," I said. "We already decided that you was going to go and live at Isabel's. Now what's got into you all of a sudden?"

"*You* decided it," he pointed out. "*I* didn't decide nothing." He stopped in front of me, leaning against the stove, arms loosely folded. "Look, brother. I don't want to stay in Harlem no more, I really don't." He was very earnest. He looked at me, then over toward the kitchen window. There was something in his eyes I'd never seen before, some thoughtfulness, some worry all his own. He rubbed the muscle of one arm. "It's time I was getting out of here."

"Where do you want to *go,* Sonny?"

"I want to join the army. Or the navy, I don't care. If I say I'm old enough they'll believe me."

Then I got mad. It was because I was so scared. "You must be crazy. You goddamn fool, what the hell do you want to go and join the *army* for?"

"I just told you. To get out of Harlem."

"Sonny, you haven't even finished *school.* And if you really want to be a musician, how do you expect to study if you're in the *army?*"

He looked at me, trapped, and in anguish. "There's ways. I might be able to work out some kind of deal. Anyway, I'll have the G.I. Bill when I come out."

"*If* you come out." We stared at each other. "Sonny, please. Be reasonable. I know the setup is far from perfect. But we got to do the best we can."

"I ain't learning nothing in school," he said. "Even when I go." He turned away from me and opened the window and threw his cigarette out into the narrow alley. I watched his back. "At least, I ain't learning nothing you'd want me to learn." He slammed the window so hard I thought the glass would fly out, and turned back to me. "And I'm sick of the stink of these garbage cans!"

"Sonny," I said, "I know how you feel. But if you don't finish school now, you're going to be sorry later that you didn't." I grabbed him by the shoulders. "And you only got another year. It ain't so bad. And I'll come back and I swear I'll help you do *whatever* you want to do. Just try to put up with it till I come back. Will you please do that? For me?"

He didn't answer and he wouldn't look at me.

"Sonny. You hear me?"

He pulled away. "I hear you. But you never hear anything *I* say."

I didn't know what to say to that. He looked out of the window and then back at me. "OK," he said, and sighed. "I'll try."

Then I said, trying to cheer him up a little, "They got a piano at Isabel's. You can practice on it."

And as a matter of fact, it did cheer him up for a minute. "That's right," he said to himself. "I forgot that." His face relaxed a little. But the worry, the thoughtfulness, played on it still, the way shadows play on a face which is staring into the fire.

But I thought I'd never hear the end of that piano. At first, Isabel would write me, saying how nice it was that Sonny was so serious about his music and how, as soon as he came in from school, or wherever he had been when he was supposed to be at school, he went straight to that piano and stayed there until suppertime. And, after supper, he went back to that piano and stayed there until everybody went to bed. He was at the piano all day Saturday and all day Sunday. Then he bought a record player and started playing records. He'd play one record over and over again, all day long sometimes, and he'd improvise along with it on the piano. Or he'd play one section of the record, one chord, one change, one progression, then he'd do it on the piano. Then back to the record. Then back to the piano.

Well, I really don't know how they stood it. Isabel finally confessed that it wasn't like living with a person at all, it was like living with sound. And the sound didn't make any sense to her, didn't make any sense to any of them—naturally. They began, in a way, to be afflicted by this presence that was living in their home. It was as though Sonny were some sort of god, or monster. He moved in an atmosphere which wasn't like theirs at all. They fed him and he ate, he washed himself, he walked in and out of their door; he certainly wasn't nasty or unpleasant or rude, Sonny isn't any of those things; but it was as though he were all wrapped up in some cloud, some fire, some vision all his own; and there wasn't any way to reach him.

At the same time, he wasn't really a man yet, he was still a child, and they had to watch out for him in all kinds of ways. They certainly couldn't throw him out. Neither did they dare to make a great scene about that piano because even they dimly sensed, as I sensed, from so many thousands of miles away, that Sonny was at that piano playing for his life.

But he hadn't been going to school. One day a letter came from the school board and Isabel's mother got it—there had, apparently, been other letters but Sonny had torn them up. This day, when Sonny came in, Isabel's mother showed him the letter and asked where he'd been spending his time. And she finally got it out of him that he'd been down in Greenwich Village, with musicians and other characters, in a white girl's apartment. And this scared her and she started to scream at him and what came up, once she began—though she denies it to this day—was what sacrifices they were making to give Sonny a decent home and how little he appreciated it.

Sonny didn't play the piano that day. By evening, Isabel's mother had calmed down but then there was the old man to deal with, and Isabel herself. Isabel says she did her best to be calm but she broke down and started crying. She says she just watched Sonny's face. She could tell, by watching him, what was happening with him. And what was happening was that they penetrated his cloud, they had reached him. Even if their fingers had been a thousand times more gentle than human fingers ever are, he could hardly help feeling that they had stripped him naked and were spitting on that nakedness. For he also had to see that his presence, that music, which was life or death to him, had been torture for them and that they had endured it, not at all for his sake, but only for mine. And Sonny couldn't take that. He can take it a little better today than he could then but he's still not very good at it and, frankly, I don't know anybody who is.

The silence of the next few days must have been louder than the sound of all the music ever played since time began. One morning, before she went to work, Isabel was in his room for something and she suddenly realized that all of his records were gone. And she knew for certain that he was gone. And he was. He went as far as the navy would carry him. He finally sent me a postcard from some place in Greece and that was the first I knew that Sonny was still alive. I didn't see him any more until we were both back in New York and the war had long been over.

He was a man by then, of course, but I wasn't willing to see it. He came by the house from time to time, but we fought almost every time we met. I didn't like the way he carried himself, loose and dreamlike all the time, and I didn't like his friends, and his music seemed to be merely an excuse for the life he led. It sounded just that weird and disordered.

Then we had a fight, a pretty awful fight, and I didn't see him for months. By and by I looked him up, where he was living, in a furnished room in the Village, and I tried to make it up. But there were lots of other people in the room and Sonny just lay on his bed, and he wouldn't come downstairs with me, and he treated these other people as though they were his family and I weren't. So I got mad and then he got mad, and then I told him that he might just as well be dead as live the way he was living. Then he stood up and he told me not to worry about him any more in life, that he *was* dead as far as I was concerned. Then he pushed me to the door and the other people looked on as though nothing were happening, and he slammed the door behind me. I stood in the hallway, staring at the door. I heard somebody laugh in the room and then the tears came to my eyes. I started down the steps, whistling to keep from crying, I kept whistling to myself, *You going to need me, baby, one of these cold, rainy days.*

I read about Sonny's trouble in the spring. Little Grace died in the fall. She was a beautiful little girl. But she only lived a little over two years. She died of polio and she suffered. She had a slight fever for a couple of days, but it didn't seem like anything and we just kept her in bed. And we would certainly have called the doctor, but the fever dropped, she seemed to be all right. So we thought it had just been a cold. Then, one day, she was up, playing, Isabel was in the kitchen fixing lunch for the two boys when they'd come in from school, and she heard Grace fall down in the living room. When you have a lot of children you don't always start running when one of them falls, unless they start screaming or something. And, this time, Grace was quiet. Yet, Isabel says that when she heard that *thump* and then that silence, something happened in her to make her afraid. And she ran to the living room and there was little Grace on the floor, all twisted up and the reason she hadn't screamed was that she couldn't get her breath. And when she did scream, it was the worst sound, Isabel says, that she'd ever heard in all her life, and she still hears it sometimes in her dreams. Isabel will sometimes wake me up with a low, moaning, strangled sound and I have to be quick to awaken her and hold her to me and where Isabel is weeping against me seems a mortal wound.

I think I may have written Sonny the very day that little Grace was buried. I was sitting in the living room in the dark, by myself, and I suddenly thought of Sonny. My trouble made his real.

One Saturday afternoon, when Sonny had been living with us, or, anyway, been in our house, for nearly two weeks, I found myself wandering aimlessly about the living room, drinking from a can of beer, and trying to work up the courage to search Sonny's room. He was out, he was usually out whenever I was home, and Isabel had taken the children to see their grandparents. Suddenly I was standing still in front of the living room window, watching Seventh

Avenue. The idea of searching Sonny's room made me still. I scarcely dared to admit to myself what I'd be searching for. I didn't know what I'd do if I found it. Or if I didn't.

On the sidewalk across from me, near the entrance to a barbecue joint, some people were holding an old-fashioned revival meeting. The barbecue cook, wearing a dirty white apron, his conked hair reddish and metallic in the pale sun, and a cigarette between his lips, stood in the doorway, watching them. Kids and older people paused in their errands and stood there, along with some older men and a couple of very tough-looking women who watched everything that happened on the avenue, as though they owned it, or were maybe owned by it. Well, they were watching this, too. The revival was being carried on by three sisters in black, and a brother. All they had were their voices and their Bibles and a tambourine. The brother was testifying and while he testified two of the sisters stood together, seeming to say, Amen, and the third sister walked around with the tambourine outstretched and a couple of people dropped coins into it. Then the brother's testimony ended and the sister who had been taking up the collection dumped the coins into her palm and transferred them to the pocket of her long black robe. Then she raised both hands, striking the tambourine against the air, and then against one hand, and she started to sing. And the two other sisters and the brother joined in.

It was strange, suddenly, to watch, though I had been seeing these street meetings all my life. So, of course, had everybody else down there. Yet, they paused and watched and listened and I stood still at the window. *"Tis the old ship of Zion,"* they sang, and the sister with the tambourine kept a steady, jangling beat, *"It has rescued many a thousand!"* Not a soul under the sound of their voices was hearing this song for the first time, not one of them had been rescued. Nor had they seen much in the way of rescue work being done around them. Neither did they especially believe in the holiness of the three sisters and the brother, they knew too much about them, knew where they lived, and how. The woman with the tambourine, whose voice dominated the air, whose face was bright with joy, was divided by very little from the woman who stood watching her, a cigarette between her heavy, chapped lips, her hair a cuckoo's nest, her face scarred and swollen from many beatings, and her black eyes glittering like coal. Perhaps they both knew this, which was why, when, as rarely, they addressed each other, they addressed each other as Sister. As the singing filled the air the watching, listening faces underwent a change, the eyes focusing on something within; the music seemed to soothe a poison out of them; and time seemed, nearly, to fall away from the sullen, belligerent, battered faces, as though they were fleeing back to their first condition, while dreaming of their last. The barbecue cook half shook his head and smiled, and dropped his cigarette and disappeared into his joint. A man fumbled in his pockets for change and stood holding it in his hand impatiently, as though he had just remembered a pressing appointment further up the avenue. He looked furious. Then I saw Sonny, standing on the edge of the crowd. He was carrying a wide, flat notebook with a green cover, and it made him look, from where I was standing, almost like a schoolboy. The coppery sun brought out the copper in his skin, he was very faintly smiling, standing very still. Then the singing stopped, the tambourine turned into a collection plate again. The furious man dropped in his coins and vanished, so did a couple of the women, and Sonny dropped some change in the plate, looking directly at the woman with a little smile. He started across the avenue, toward the house. He has a slow, loping walk, something like the way Harlem hipsters walk, only he's imposed on this his own halfbeat. I had never really noticed it before.

I stayed at the window, both relieved and apprehensive. As Sonny disappeared from my sight, they began singing again. And they were still singing when his key turned in the lock.

"Hey," he said.

"Hey, yourself. You want some beer?"

"No. Well, maybe." But he came up to the window and stood beside me, looking out. "What a warm voice," he said.

They were singing *If I could only hear my mother pray again!*

"Yes," I said, "and she can sure beat that tambourine."

"But what a terrible song," he said, and laughed. He dropped his notebook on the sofa and disappeared into the kitchen. "Where's Isabel and the kids?"

"I think they went to see their grandparents. You hungry?"

"No." He came back into the living room with his can of beer. "You want to come some place with me tonight?"

I sensed, I don't know how, that I couldn't possibly say No. "Sure. Where?"

He sat down on the sofa and picked up his notebook and started leafing through it. "I'm going to sit in with some fellows in a joint in the Village."

"You mean, you're going to play, tonight?"

"That's right." He took a swallow of his beer and moved back to the window. He gave me a sidelong look. "If you can stand it."

"I'll try," I said.

He smiled to himself and we both watched as the meeting across the way broke up. The three sisters and the brother, heads bowed, were singing *God be with you till we meet again.* The faces around them were very quiet. Then the song ended. The small crowd dispersed. We watched the three women and the lone man walk slowly up the avenue.

"When she was singing before," said Sonny, abruptly, "her voice reminded me for a minute of what heroin feels like sometimes—when it's in your veins. It makes you feel sort of warm and cool at the same time. And distant. And—and sure." He sipped his beer, very deliberately not looking at me. I watched his face. "It makes you feel—in control. Sometimes you've got to have that feeling."

"Do you?" I sat down slowly in the easy chair.

"Sometimes." He went to the sofa and picked up his notebook again. "Some people do."

"In order," I asked, "to play?" And my voice was very ugly, full of contempt and anger.

"Well"—he looked at me with great, troubled eyes, as though, in fact, he hoped his eyes would tell me things he could never otherwise say—"they *think* so. And *if* they think so—!"

"And what do *you* think?" I asked.

He sat on the sofa and put his can of beer on the floor. "I don't know," he said, and I couldn't be sure if he were answering my question or pursuing his thoughts. His face didn't tell me. "It's not so much to *play.* It's to *stand* it, to be able to make it at all. On any level." He frowned and smiled: "In order to keep from shaking to pieces."

"But these friends of yours," I said, "they seem to shake themselves to pieces pretty goddamn fast."

"Maybe." He played with the notebook. And something told me that I should curb my tongue, that Sonny was doing his best to talk, that I should listen. "But of course you only know the ones that've gone to pieces. Some don't—or at least they haven't *yet* and that's just about all *any* of us can say." He paused. "And then there are some who just live, really, in hell, and they know it and they see what's happening and they go right on. I don't know." He sighed, dropped the notebook, folded his arms. "Some guys, you can tell from the way they play, they on something *all* the time. And you can see that, well, it makes something real for them. But of course," he picked up his beer from the floor and sipped it and put the can down again, "they *want* to, too, you've got to see that. Even some of them that say they don't—*some,* not all."

"And what about you?" I asked—I couldn't help it. "What about you? Do *you* want to?"

He stood up and walked to the window and remained silent for a long time. Then he sighed. "Me," he said. Then: "While I was downstairs before, on my way here, listening to that woman sing, it struck me all of a sudden how much suffering she must have had to go through—to sing like that. It's *repulsive* to think you have to suffer that much."

I said: "But there's no way not to suffer—is there, Sonny?"

"I believe not," he said, and smiled, "but that's never stopped anyone from trying." He looked at me. "Has it?" I realized, with this mocking look, that there stood between us, forever, beyond the power of time or forgiveness, the fact that I had held silence—so long!—when he had needed human speech to help him. He turned back to the window. "No, there's no way not to suffer. But you try all kinds of ways to keep from drowning in it, to keep on top of it, and to make it seem—well, like *you.* Like you did something, all right, and now you're suffering for it. You know?" I said nothing. "Well you know," he said, impatiently, "why *do* people suffer? Maybe it's better to do something to give it a reason, *any* reason."

"But we just agreed," I said, "that there's no way not to suffer. Isn't it better, then, just to—take it?"

"But nobody just takes it," Sonny cried, "that's what I'm telling you! *Everybody* tries not to. You're just hung up on the *way* some people try—it's not *your* way!"

The hair on my face began to itch, my face felt wet. "That's not true," I said, "that's not true. I don't give a damn what other people do, I don't even care how they suffer. I just care how *you* suffer." And he looked at me. "Please believe me," I said, "I don't want to see you—die—trying not to suffer."

"I won't," he said, flatly, "die trying not to suffer. At least, not any faster than anybody else."

"But there's no need," I said, trying to laugh, "is there? in killing yourself."

I wanted to say more, but I couldn't. I wanted to talk about will power and how life could be—well, beautiful. I wanted to say that it was all within; but was it? or, rather, wasn't that exactly the trouble? And I wanted to promise that I would never fail him again. But it would all have sounded—empty words and lies.

So I made the promise to myself and prayed that I would keep it.

"It's terrible sometimes, inside," he said, "that's what's the trouble. You walk these streets, black and funky and cold, and there's not really a living ass to talk to, and there's nothing shaking, and there's no way of getting it out—that storm inside. You can't talk it and you can't make love with it, and when you finally try to get with it and play it, you realize *nobody's* listening. So *you've* got to listen. You got to find a way to listen."

And then he walked away from the window and sat on the sofa again, as though all the wind had suddenly been knocked out of him. "Sometimes you'll do *anything* to play, even cut your mother's throat." He laughed and looked at me. "Or your brother's." Then he sobered. "Or your own." Then: "Don't worry. I'm all right now and I think I'll *be* all right. But I can't forget—where I've been. I don't mean just the physical place I've been, I mean where I've *been.* And *what* I've been."

"What have you been, Sonny?" I asked.

He smiled—but sat sideways on the sofa, his elbow resting on the back, his fingers playing with his mouth and chin, not looking at me. "I've been something I didn't recognize, didn't know I could be. Didn't know anybody could be." He stopped, looking inward, looking helplessly young, looking old. "I'm not talking about it now because I feel *guilty* or anything like that—maybe it would be better if I did, I don't know. Anyway, I can't really talk about it. Not to you, not to anybody," and now he turned and faced me. "Sometimes, you know, and it was actually when I was most *out* of the world, I felt that I was in it, and that I was *with* it, really, and I could play or I didn't really have to *play,* it just came out of me, it was there. And I don't know how I played, thinking about it now, but

I know I did awful things, those times, sometimes, to people. Or it wasn't that I *did* anything to them—it was that they weren't real." He picked up the beer can; it was empty; he rolled it between his palms: "And other times—well, I needed a fix, I needed to find a place to lean, I needed to clear a space to *listen*—and I couldn't find it, and I—went crazy, I did terrible things to *me,* I was terrible *for* me." He began pressing the beer can between his hands, I watched the metal begin to give. It glittered, as he played with it, like a knife, and I was afraid he would cut himself, but I said nothing. "Oh well. I can never tell you. I was all by myself at the bottom of something, stinking and sweating and crying and shaking, and I smelled it, you know? *my* stink, and I thought I'd die if I couldn't get away from it and yet, all the same, I knew that everything I was doing was just locking me in with it. And I didn't know," he paused, still flattening the beer can, "I didn't know, I still *don't* know, something kept telling me that maybe it was good to smell your own stink, but I didn't think that *that* was what I'd been trying to do—and—who can stand it?" and he abruptly dropped the ruined beer can, looking at me with a small, still smile, and then rose, walking to the window as though it were the lodestone rock. I watched his face, he watched the avenue. "I couldn't tell you when Mama died—but the reason I wanted to leave Harlem so bad was to get away from drugs. And then, when I ran away, that's what I was running from—really. When I came back, nothing had changed, *I* hadn't changed, I was just—older." And he stopped, drumming with his fingers on the windowpane. The sun had vanished, soon darkness would fall. I watched his face. "It can come again," he said, almost as though speaking to himself. Then he turned to me. "It can come again," he repeated. "I just want you to know that."

"All right," I said, at last. "So it can come again. All right."

He smiled, but the smile was sorrowful. "I had to try to tell you," he said.

"Yes," I said. "I understand that."

"You're my brother," he said, looking straight at me, and not smiling at all.

"Yes," I repeated, "yes. I understand that."

He turned back to the window, looking out. "All that hatred down there," he said, "all that hatred and misery and love. It's a wonder it doesn't blow the avenue apart."

We went to the only night club on a short, dark street, downtown. We squeezed through the narrow, chattering, jam-packed bar to the entrance of the big room, where the bandstand was. And we stood there for a moment, for the lights were very dim in this room and we couldn't see. Then, "Hello, boy," said a voice and an enormous black man, much older than Sonny or myself, erupted out of all that atmospheric lighting and put an arm around Sonny's shoulder. "I been sitting right here," he said, "waiting for you."

He had a big voice, too, and heads in the darkness turned toward us.

Sonny grinned and pulled a little away, and said, "Creole, this is my brother. I told you about him."

Creole shook my hand. "I'm glad to meet you, son," he said, and it was clear that he was glad to meet me *there,* for Sonny's sake. And he smiled, "You got a real musician in *your* family," and he took his arm from Sonny's shoulder and slapped him, lightly, affectionately, with the back of his hand.

"Well. Now I've heard it all," said a voice behind us. This was another musician, and a friend of Sonny's, a coal-black, cheerful-looking man, built close to the ground. He immediately began confiding to me, at the top of his lungs, the most terrible things about Sonny, his teeth gleaming like a lighthouse and his laugh coming up out of him like the beginning of an earthquake. And it turned out that everyone at the bar knew Sonny, or almost everyone; some were musicians, working there, or nearby, or not working, some were simply hangers-on, and some were there to hear Sonny play. I was introduced to all of them and they were all very polite to me. Yet, it was clear that, for them, I was only Sonny's brother. Here, I was in Sonny's world. Or, rather: his kingdom. Here, it was not even a question that his veins bore royal blood.

They were going to play soon and Creole installed me, by myself, at a table in a dark corner. Then I watched them, Creole, and the little black man, and Sonny, and the others, while they horsed around, standing just below the bandstand. The light from the bandstand spilled just a little short of them and, watching them laughing and gesturing and moving about, I had the feeling that they, nevertheless, were being most careful not to step into that circle of light too suddenly: that if they moved into the light too suddenly, without thinking, they would perish in flame. Then, while I watched, one of them, the small, black man, moved into the light and crossed the bandstand and started fooling around with his drums. Then—being funny and being, also, extremely ceremonious—Creole took Sonny by the arm and led him to the piano. A woman's voice called Sonny's name and a few hands started clapping. And Sonny, also being funny and being ceremonious, and so touched, I think, that he could have cried, but neither hiding it nor showing it, riding it like a man, grinned, and put both hands to his heart and bowed from the waist.

Creole then went to the bass fiddle and a lean, very bright-skinned brown man jumped up on the bandstand and picked up his horn. So there they were, and the atmosphere on the bandstand and in the room began to change and tighten. Someone stepped up to the microphone and announced them. Then there were all kinds of murmurs. Some people at the bar shushed others. The waitress ran around, frantically getting in the last orders, guys and chicks got closer to each other, and the lights on the bandstand, on the quartet, turned to a kind of indigo. Then they all looked different there. Creole looked about him for the last time, as though he were making certain that all his chickens were in the coop, and then he—jumped and struck the fiddle. And there they were.

All I know about music is that not many people ever really hear it. And even then, on the rare occasions when something opens within, and the music enters, what we mainly hear, or hear corroborated, are personal private, vanishing evocations. But the man who creates the music is hearing something else, is dealing with the roar rising from the void and imposing order on it as it hits the air. What is evoked in him, then, is of another order, more terrible because it has no words, and triumphant, too, for that same reason. And his triumph, when he triumphs, is ours. I just watched Sonny's face. His face was troubled, he was working hard, but he wasn't with it. And I had the feeling that, in a way, everyone on the bandstand was waiting for him, both waiting for him and pushing him along. But as I began to watch Creole, I realized that it was Creole who held them all back. He had them on a short rein. Up there, keeping the beat with his whole body, wailing on the fiddle, with his eyes half closed, he was listening to everything, but he was listening to Sonny. He was having a dialogue with Sonny. He wanted Sonny to leave the shore line and strike out for the deep water. He was Sonny's witness that deep water and drowning were not the same thing—he had been there, and he knew. And he wanted Sonny to know. He was waiting for Sonny to do the things on the keys which would let Creole know that Sonny was in the water.

And, while Creole listened, Sonny moved, deep within, exactly like someone in torment. I had never before thought of how awful the relationship must be between the musician and his instrument. He has to fill it, this instrument, with the breath of life, his own. He has to make it do what he wants it to do. And a piano is just a piano. It's made out of so much wood and wires and little hammers and big ones, and ivory. While there's only so much you can do with it, the only way to find this out is to try and make it do everything.

And Sonny hadn't been near a piano for over a year. And he wasn't on much better terms with his life, not the life that stretched before him now. He and the piano stammered, started one way, got scared, stopped; started another way, panicked, marked time, started again; then seemed to have found a direction, panicked again, got stuck. And the face I saw on Sonny I'd never seen before. Everything had been burned out of it, and, at the same time, things usually hidden were being burned in, by the fire and fury of the battle which was occurring in him up there.

Yet, watching Creole's face as they neared the end of the first set, I had the feeling that something had happened, something I hadn't heard. Then they finished, there was scattered applause, and then, without an instant's warning, Creole started into something else, it was almost sardonic, it was *Am I Blue.* And, as though he commanded, Sonny began to play. Something began to happen. And Creole let out the reins. The dry, low, black man said something awful on the drums, Creole answered, and the drums talked back. Then the horn insisted, sweet and high, slightly detached perhaps, and Creole listened, commenting now and then, dry, and driving, beautiful and calm and old. Then they all came together again, and Sonny was part of the family again. I could tell this from his face. He seemed to have found, right there beneath his fingers, a damn brand-new piano. It seemed that he couldn't get over it. Then, for awhile, just being happy with Sonny, they seemed to be agreeing with him that brand-new pianos certainly were a gas.

Then Creole stepped forward to remind them that what they were playing was the blues. He hit something in all of them, he hit something in me, myself, and the music tightened and deepened, apprehension began to beat the air. Creole began to tell us what the blues were all about. They were not about anything very new. He and his boys up there were keeping it new, at the risk of ruin, destruction, madness, and death, in order to find new ways to make us listen. For, while the tale of how we suffer, and how we are delighted, and how we may triumph is never new, it always must be heard. There isn't any other tale to tell, it's the only light we've got in all this darkness.

And this tale, according to that face, that body, those strong hands on those strings, has another aspect in every country, and a new depth in every generation. Listen, Creole seemed to be saying, listen. Now these are Sonny's blues. He made the little black man on the drums know it, and the bright, brown man on the horn. Creole wasn't trying any longer to get Sonny in the water. He was wishing him Godspeed. Then he stepped back, very slowly, filling the air with the immense suggestion that Sonny speak for himself.

Then they all gathered around Sonny and Sonny played. Every now and again one of them seemed to say, Amen. Sonny's fingers filled the air with life, his life. But that life contained so many others. And Sonny went all the way back, he really began with the spare, flat statement of the opening phrase of the song. Then he began to make it his. It was very beautiful because it wasn't hurried and it was no longer a lament. I seemed to hear with what burning he had made it his, with what burning we had yet to make it ours, how we could cease lamenting. Freedom lurked around us and I understood, at last, that he could help us to be free if we would listen, that he would never be free until we did. Yet, there was no battle in his face now. I heard what he had gone through, and would continue to go through until he came to rest in earth. He had made it his: that long line, of which we knew only Mama and Daddy. And he was giving it back, as everything must be given back, so that, passing through death, it can live forever. I saw my mother's face again, and felt, for the first time, how the stones of the road she had walked on must have bruised her feet. I saw the moonlit road where my father's brother died. And it brought something else back to me, and carried me past it, I saw my little girl again and felt Isabel's tears again, and I felt my own tears begin to rise. And I was yet aware that this was only a moment, that the world waited outside, as hungry as a tiger, and that trouble stretched above us, longer than the sky.

Then it was over. Creole and Sonny let out their breath, both soaking wet, and grinning. There was a lot of applause and some of it was real. In the dark, the girl came by and I asked her to take drinks to the bandstand. There was a long pause, while they talked up there in the indigo light and after awhile I saw the girl put a Scotch and milk on top of the piano for Sonny. He didn't seem to notice it, but just before they started playing again, he sipped from it and looked toward me, and nodded. Then he put it back on top of the piano. For me, then, as they began to play again, it glowed and shook above my brother's head like the very cup of trembling.

1965

Patriotism

YUKIO MISHIMA

[1925–1970]

In the twenty-eighth of February, 1936 (on the third day, that is, of the February Incident), Lieutenant Shinji Takeyama of the Konoe Transport Battalion—profoundly disturbed by the knowledge that his closest colleagues had been with the mutineers from the beginning, and indignant at the imminent prospect of Imperial troops attacking Imperial troops—took his officer's sword and ceremonially disemboweled himself in the eight-mat room of his private residence in the sixth block of Aoba-chō, in Yotsuya Ward. His wife, Reiko, followed him, stabbing herself to death. The lieutenant's farewell note consisted of one sentence: "Long live the Imperial Forces." His wife's, after apologies for her unfilial conduct in thus preceding her parents to the grave, concluded: "The day which, for a soldier's wife, had to come, has come. . . ." The last moments of this heroic and dedicated couple were such as to make the gods themselves weep. The lieutenant's age, it should be noted, was thirty-one, his wife's twenty-three; and it was not half a year since the celebration of their marriage.

2

Those who saw the bride and bridegroom in the commemorative photograph—perhaps no less than those actually present at the lieutenant's wedding—had exclaimed in wonder at the bearing of this handsome couple. The lieutenant, majestic in military uniform, stood protectively beside his bride, his right hand resting upon his

*Translated by Geoffrey W. Sargeant.

sword, his officer's cap held at his left side. His expression was severe, and his dark brows and wide-gazing eyes well conveyed the clear integrity of youth. For the beauty of the bride in her white over-robe no comparisons were adequate. In the eyes, round beneath soft brows, in the slender, finely shaped nose, and in the full lips, there was both sensuousness and refinement. One hand, emerging shyly from a sleeve of the over-robe, held a fan, and the tips of the fingers, clustering delicately, were like the bud of a moonflower.

After the suicide, people would take out this photograph and examine it, and sadly reflect that too often there was a curse on these seemingly flawless unions. Perhaps it was no more than imagination, but looking at the picture after the tragedy it almost seemed as if the two young people before the gold-lacquered screen were gazing, each with equal clarity, at the deaths which lay before them.

Thanks to the good offices of their go-between, Lieutenant General Ozeki, they had been able to set themselves up in a new home at Aoba-chō in Yotsuya. "New home" is perhaps misleading. It was an old three-room rented house backing onto a small garden. As neither the six- nor the four-and-a-half mat room downstairs was favored by the sun, they used the upstairs eight-mat room as both bedroom and guest room. There was no maid, so Reiko was left alone to guard the house in her husband's absence.

The honeymoon trip was dispensed with on the grounds that these were times of national emergency. The two of them had spent the first night of their marriage at this house. Before going to bed, Shinji, sitting erect on the floor with his sword laid before him, had bestowed upon his wife a soldierly lecture. A woman who had become the wife of a soldier should know and resolutely accept that her husband's death might come at any moment. It could be tomorrow. It could be the day after. But, no matter when it came—he asked—was she steadfast in her resolve to accept it? Reiko rose to her feet, pulled open a drawer of the cabinet, and took out what was the most prized of her new possessions, the dagger her mother had given her. Returning to her place, she laid the dagger without a word on the mat before her, just as her husband had laid his sword. A silent understanding was achieved at once and the lieutenant never again sought to test his wife's resolve.

In the first few months of her marriage Reiko's beauty grew daily more radiant, shining serene like the moon after rain.

As both were possessed of young, vigorous bodies, their relationship was passionate. Nor was this merely a matter of the night. On more than one occasion, returning home straight from maneuvers, and begrudging even the time it took to remove his mud-splashed uniform, the lieutenant had pushed his wife to the floor almost as soon as he had entered the house. Reiko was equally ardent in her response. For a little more or a little less than a month, from the first night of their marriage Reiko knew happiness, and the lieutenant, seeing this, was happy too.

Reiko's body was white and pure, and her swelling breasts conveyed a firm and chaste refusal; but, upon consent, those breasts were lavish with their intimate, welcoming warmth. Even in bed these two were frighteningly and awesomely serious. In the very midst of wild, intoxicating passions, their hearts were sober and serious.

By day the lieutenant would think of his wife in the brief rest periods between training; and all day long, at home, Reiko would recall the image of her husband. Even when apart, however, they had only to look at the wedding photograph for their happiness to be once more confirmed. Reiko felt not the slightest surprise that a man who had been a complete stranger until a few months ago should now have become the sun about which her whole world revolved.

All these things had a moral basis, and were in accordance with the Education Rescript's injunction that "husband and wife should be harmonious." Not once did Reiko contradict her husband, nor did the lieutenant ever find reason to scold his wife. On the god shelf below the stairway, alongside the tablet from the Great Ise Shrine, were set photographs of their Imperial Majesties, and regularly every morning, before leaving for duty, the lieutenant would stand with his wife at this hallowed place and together they would bow their heads low. The offering water was renewed each morning, and the sacred sprig of *sasaki* was always green and fresh. Their lives were lived beneath the solemn protection of the gods and were filled with an intense happiness which set every fiber in their bodies trembling.

3

Although Lord Privy Seal Saitō's house was in their neighborhood, neither of them heard any noise of gunfire on the morning of February 26. It was a bugle, sounding muster in the dim, snowy dawn, when the ten-minute tragedy had already ended, which first disrupted the lieutenant's slumbers. Leaping at once from his bed, and without speaking a word, the lieutenant donned his uniform, buckled on the sword held ready for him by his wife, and hurried swiftly out into the snow-covered streets of the still darkened morning. He did not return until the evening of the twenty-eighth.

Later, from the radio news, Reiko learned the full extent of this sudden eruption of violence. Her life throughout the subsequent two days was lived alone, in complete tranquillity, and behind locked doors.

In the lieutenant's face, as he hurried silently out into the snowy morning, Reiko had read the determination to die. If her husband did not return, her own decision was made: she too would die. Quietly she attended to the disposition of her personal possessions. She chose her sets of visiting kimonos as keepsakes for friends of her schooldays, and she wrote a name and address on the stiff paper wrapping in which each was folded. Constantly admonished by her husband never to think of the morrow, Reiko had not even kept a diary and was now denied the pleasure of assiduously rereading her record of the happiness of the past few months and consigning each page to the fire as she did so. Ranged across the top of the radio were a small china dog, a rabbit, a squirrel, a bear, and a fox. There were also a small vase and a water pitcher. These comprised Reiko's one and only collection. But it would hardly do, she imagined, to give such things as keepsakes. Nor again would it be quite proper to ask specifically for them to be included in the coffin. It seemed to Reiko, as these thoughts passed through her mind, that the expressions on the small animals' faces grew even more lost and forlorn.

Reiko took the squirrel in her hand and looked at it. And then, her thoughts turning to a realm far beyond these childlike affections, she gazed up in to the distance at the great sunlike principle which her husband embodied. She was ready, and happy, to be hurtled along to her destruction in that gleaming sun chariot—but now, for these few moments of solitude, she allowed herself to luxuriate in this innocent attachment to trifles. The time when she had genuinely loved these things, however, was long past. Now she merely loved the memory of having once loved them, and their place in her heart had been filled by more intense passions, by a more frenzied happiness. . . . For Reiko had never, even to herself, thought of those soaring joys of the flesh as a mere pleasure. The February cold, and the icy touch of the china squirrel, had numbed Reiko's slender fingers; yet, even so, in her lower limbs, beneath the ordered repetition of the pattern which crossed the skirt of her trim *meisen* kimono, she could feel now, as she thought of the lieutenant's powerful arms reaching out toward her, a hot moistness of the flesh which defied the snows.

She was not in the least afraid of the death hovering in her mind. Waiting alone at home, Reiko firmly believed that everything her husband was feeling or thinking now, his anguish and distress, was leading her—just as surely as the power in his flesh—to a welcome death. She felt as if her body could melt away with ease and be transformed to the merest fraction of her husband's thought.

Listening to the frequent announcements on the radio, she heard the names of several of her husband's colleagues mentioned among those of the insurgents. This was news of death. She followed the developments closely, wondering anxiously, as the situation became daily more irrevocable, why no Imperial ordinance was sent down, and watching what had at first been taken as a movement to restore the nation's honor come gradually to be branded with the infamous name of mutiny. There was no communication from the regiment. At any moment, it seemed, fighting might commence in the city streets where the remains of the snow still lay.

Toward sundown on the twenty-eighth Reiko was startled by a furious pounding on the front door. She hurried downstairs. As she pulled with fumbling fingers at the bolt, the shape dimly outlined beyond the frosted-glass panel made no sound, but she knew it was her husband. Reiko had never known the bolt on the sliding door to be so stiff. Still it resisted. The door just would not open.

In a moment, almost before she knew she had succeeded, the lieutenant was standing before her on the cement floor inside the porch, muffled in a khaki greatcoat, his top boots heavy with slush from the street. Closing the door behind him, he returned the bolt once more to its socket. With what significance, Reiko did not understand.

"Welcome home."

Reiko bowed deeply, but her husband made no response. As he had already unfastened his sword and was about to remove his greatcoat, Reiko moved around behind to assist. The coat, which was cold and damp and had lost the odor of horse dung it normally exuded when exposed to the sun, weighed heavily upon her arm. Draping it across a hanger, and cradling the sword and leather belt in her sleeves, she waited while her husband removed his top boots and then followed behind him into the "living room." This was the six-mat room downstairs.

Seen in the clear light from the lamp, her husband's face, covered with a heavy growth of bristle, was almost unrecognizably wasted and thin. The cheeks were hollow, their luster and resilience gone. In his normal good spirits he would have changed into old clothes as soon as he was home and have pressed her to get supper at once, but now he sat before the table still in his uniform, his head drooping dejectedly. Reiko refrained from asking whether she should prepare the supper.

After an interval the lieutenant spoke.

"I knew nothing. They hadn't asked me to join. Perhaps out of consideration, because I was newly married. Kanō, and Homma too, and Yamaguchi."

Reiko recalled momentarily the faces of high-spirited young officers, friends of her husband, who had come to the house occasionally as guests.

"There may be an Imperial ordinance sent down tomorrow. They'll be posted as rebels, I imagine. I shall be in command of a unit with orders to attack them. . . . I can't do it. It's impossible to do a thing like that."

He spoke again.

"They've taken me off guard duty, and I have permission to return home for one night. Tomorrow morning, without question, I must leave to join the attack. I can't do it, Reiko."

Reiko sat erect with lowered eyes. She understood clearly that her husband had spoken of his death. The lieutenant was resolved. Each word, being rooted in death, emerged sharply and with powerful significance against this dark, unmovable background. Although the lieutenant was speaking of his dilemma, already there was no room in his mind for vacillation.

However, there was a clarity, like the clarity of a stream fed from melting snows, in the silence which rested between them. Sitting in his own home after the long two-day ordeal, and looking across at the face of his beautiful wife, the lieutenant was for the first time experiencing true peace of mind. For he had at once known, though she said nothing, that his wife divined the resolve which lay beneath his words.

"Well, then . . ." The lieutenant's eyes opened wide. Despite his exhaustion they were strong and clear, and now for the first time they looked straight into the eyes of his wife. "Tonight I shall cut my stomach."

Reiko did not flinch.

Her round eyes showed tension, as taut as the clang of a bell.

"I am ready," she said. "I ask permission to accompany you."

The lieutenant felt almost mesmerized by the strength in those eyes. His words flowed swiftly and easily, like the utterances of a man in delirium, and it was beyond his understanding how permission in a matter of such weight could be expressed so casually.

"Good. We'll go together. But I want you as a witness, first, for my own suicide. Agreed?"

When this was said a sudden release of abundant happiness welled up in both their hearts. Reiko was deeply affected by the greatness of her husband's trust in her. It was vital for the lieutenant, whatever else might happen, that there should be no irregularity in his death. For that reason there had to be a witness. The fact that he had chosen his wife for this was the first mark of his trust. The second, and even greater mark, was that though he had pledged that they should die together he did not intend to kill his wife first—he had deferred her death to a time when he would no longer be there to verify it. If the lieutenant had been a suspicious husband, he would doubtless, as in the usual suicide pact, have chosen to kill his wife first.

When Reiko said, "I ask permission to accompany you," the lieutenant felt these words to be the final fruit of the education which he had himself given his wife, starting on the first night of their marriage, and which had schooled her, when the moment came, to say what had to be said without a shadow of hesitation. This flattered the lieutenant's opinion of himself as a self-reliant man. He was not so romantic or conceited as to imagine that the words were spoken spontaneously, out of love for her husband.

With happiness welling almost too abundantly in their hearts, they could not help smiling at each other. Reiko felt as if she had returned to her wedding night.

Before her eyes was neither pain nor death. She seemed to see only a free and limitless expanse opening out into vast distances.

"The water is hot. Will you take your bath now?"

"Ah yes, of course."

"And supper . . . ?"

The words were delivered in such level, domestic tones that the lieutenant came near to thinking, for the fraction of a second, that everything had been a hallucination.

"I don't think we'll need supper. But perhaps you could warm some sake?"

"As you wish."

As Reiko rose and took a *tanzen* gown from the cabinet for after the bath, she purposely directed her husband's attention to the opened drawer. The lieutenant rose, crossed to the cabinet, and looked inside. From the ordered array of paper wrapping she read, one by one, the addresses of the keepsakes. There was no grief in the lieutenant's response to this demonstration of heroic resolve. His heart was filled with tenderness. Like a husband who is proudly shown the childish purchases of a young wife, the lieutenant, overwhelmed by affection, lovingly embraced his wife from behind and implanted a kiss upon her neck.

Reiko felt the roughness of the lieutenant's unshaven skin against her neck. This sensation, more than being just a thing of this world, was for Reiko almost the world itself, but now—with the feeling that it was soon to be lost forever—it had freshness beyond all her experience. Each moment had its own vital strength, and the senses in every corner of her body were reawakened. Accepting her husband's caresses from behind, Reiko raised herself on the tips of her toes, letting the vitality seep through her entire body.

"First the bath, and then, after some sake . . . lay out the bedding upstairs, will you?"

The lieutenant whispered the words into his wife's ear. Reiko silently nodded.

Flinging off his uniform, the lieutenant went to the bath. To faint background noises of slopping water Reiko tended the charcoal brazier in the living room and began the preparations for warming the sake.

Taking the *tanzen,* a sash, and some underclothes, she went to the bathroom to ask how the water was. In the midst of a coiling cloud of steam the lieutenant was sitting cross-legged on the floor, shaving, and she could dimly discern the rippling movements of the muscles on his damp, powerful back as they responded to the movement of his arms.

There was nothing to suggest a time of any special significance. Reiko, going busily about her tasks, was preparing side dishes from odds and ends in stock. Her hands did not tremble. If anything, she managed even more efficiently and smoothly than usual. From time to time, it is true, there was a strange throbbing deep within her breast. Like distant lightning, it had a moment of sharp intensity and then vanished without trace. Apart from that, nothing was in any way out of the ordinary.

The lieutenant, shaving in the bathroom, felt his warmed body miraculously healed at last of the desperate tiredness of the days of indecision and filled—in spite of the death which lay ahead—with pleasurable anticipation. The sound of his wife going about her work came to him faintly. A healthy physical craving, submerged for two days, reasserted itself.

The lieutenant was confident there had been no impurity in that joy they had experienced when resolving upon death. They had both sensed at that moment—though not, of course, in any clear and conscious way—that those permissible pleasures which they shared in private were once more beneath the protection of Righteousness and Divine Power, and of a complete and unassailable morality. On looking into each other's eyes and discovering there an honorable death, they had felt themselves safe once more behind steel walls which none could destroy, encased in an impenetrable armor of Beauty and Truth. Thus, so far from seeing any inconsistency or conflict between the urges of his flesh and the sincerity of his patriotism, the lieutenant was even able to regard the two as parts of the same thing.

Thrusting his face close to the dark, cracked, misted wall mirror, the lieutenant shaved himself with great care. This would be his death face. There must be no unsightly blemishes. The clean-shaven face gleamed once more with a youthful luster, seeming to brighten the darkness of the mirror. There was a certain elegance, he even felt, in the association of death with this radiantly healthy face.

Just as it looked now, this would become his death face! Already, in fact, it had half departed from the lieutenant's personal possession and had become the bust above a dead soldier's memorial. As an experiment he closed his eyes tight. Everything was wrapped in blackness, and he was no longer a living, seeing creature.

Returning from the bath, the traces of the shave glowing faintly blue beneath his smooth cheeks, he seated himself beside the now well-kindled charcoal brazier. Busy though Reiko was, he noticed, she had found time lightly to touch up her face. Her cheeks were gay and her lips moist. There was no shadow of sadness to be seen. Truly, the lieutenant felt, as he saw this mark of his young wife's passionate nature, he had chosen the wife he ought to have chosen.

As soon as the lieutenant had drained his sake cup he offered it to Reiko. Reiko had never before tasted sake, but she accepted without hesitation and sipped timidly.

"Come here," the lieutenant said.

Reiko moved to her husband's side and was embraced as she leaned backward across his lap. Her breast was in violent commotion as if sadness, joy, and the potent sake were mingling and reacting within her. The lieutenant looked down into his wife's face. It was the last face he would see in this world, the last face he would see of his wife. The lieutenant scrutinized the face minutely, with the eyes of a traveler bidding farewell to splendid vistas which he will never revisit. It was a face he could not tire of looking at—the features regular yet not cold, the lips lightly closed with a soft strength. The lieutenant kissed those lips, unthinkingly. And suddenly, though there was not the slightest distortion of the face into the unsightliness of sobbing, he noticed that tears were welling slowly from beneath the long lashes of the closed eyes and brimming over into a glistening stream.

When, a little later, the lieutenant urged that they should move to the upstairs bedroom, his wife replied that she would follow after taking a bath. Climbing the stairs alone to the bedroom, where the air was already warmed by the gas heater, the lieutenant lay down on the bedding with arms outstretched and legs apart. Even the time at which he lay waiting for his wife to join him was no later and no earlier than usual.

He folded his hands beneath his head and gazed at the dark boards of the ceiling in the dimness beyond the range of the standard lamp. Was it death he was now waiting for? Or a wild ecstasy of the senses? The two seemed to overlap, almost as if the object of this bodily desire was death itself. But, however that might be, it was certain that never before had the lieutenant tasted such total freedom.

There was the sound of a car outside the window. He could hear the screech of its tires skidding in the snow piled at the side of the street. The sound of its horn re-echoed from near-by walls. . . . Listening to these noises he had the feeling that this house rose like a solitary island in the ocean of a society going as restlessly about its business as ever. All around, vastly and untidily, stretched the country for which he grieved. He was to give his life for it. But would that great country, with which he was prepared to remonstrate to the extent of destroying himself, take the slightest heed of his death? He did not know; and it did not matter. His was a battlefield without glory, a battlefield where none could display deeds of valor: it was the front line of the spirit.

Reiko's footsteps sounded on the stairway. The steep stairs in this old house creaked badly. There were fond memories in that creaking, and many a time, while waiting in bed, the lieutenant had listened to its welcome sound. At the thought that he would hear it no more he listened with intense concentration, striving for every corner of every moment of this precious time to be filled with the sound of those soft footfalls on the creaking stairway. The moments seemed transformed to jewels, sparkling with inner light.

Reiko wore a Nagoya sash about the waist of her *yukata,* but as the lieutenant reached toward it, its redness sobered by the dimness of the light, Reiko's hand moved to his assistance and the sash fell away, slithering swiftly to the floor. As she stood before him, still in her *yukata,* the lieutenant inserted his hands through the side slits beneath each sleeve, intending to embrace her as she was; but at the touch of his finger tips upon the warm naked flesh, and as the armpits closed gently about his hands, his whole body was suddenly aflame.

In a few moments the two lay naked before the glowing gas heater.

Neither spoke the thought, but their hearts, their bodies, and their pounding breasts blazed with the knowledge that this was the very last time. It was as if the words "The Last Time" were spelled out, in invisible brushstrokes, across every inch of their bodies.

The lieutenant drew his wife close and kissed her vehemently. As their tongues explored each other's mouths, reaching out into the smooth, moist interior, they felt as if the still unknown agonies of death had tempered their senses to the keenness of red-hot steel. The agonies they could not yet feel, the distant pains of death, had refined their awareness of pleasure.

"This is the last time I shall see your body," said the lieutenant. "Let me look at it closely." And, tilting the shade on the lampstand to one side, he directed the rays along the full length of Reiko's outstretched form.

Reiko lay still with her eyes closed. The light from the low lamp clearly revealed the majestic sweep of her white flesh. The lieutenant, not without a touch of egocentricity, rejoiced that he would never see this beauty crumble in death.

At his leisure, the lieutenant allowed the unforgettable spectacle to engrave itself upon his mind. With one hand he fondled the hair, with the other he softly stroked the magnificent face, implanting kisses here and there where his eyes lingered. The quiet coldness of the high, tapering forehead, the closed eyes with their long lashes beneath faintly etched brows, the set of the finely shaped nose, the gleam of teeth glimpsed between full, regular lips, the soft cheeks and the small, wise chin . . . these things conjured up in the lieutenant's mind the vision of a truly radiant death face, and again and again he pressed his lips tight against the white throat—where Reiko's own hand was soon to strike—and the throat reddened faintly beneath his kisses. Returning to the mouth he laid his lips against it with the gentlest of pressures, and moved them rhythmically over Reiko's with the light rolling motion of a small boat. If he closed his eyes, the world became a rocking cradle.

Wherever the lieutenant's eyes moved his lips faithfully followed. The high, swelling breasts, surmounted by nipples like the buds of a wild cherry, hardened as the lieutenant's lips closed about them. The arms flowed smoothly downward from each side of the breast, tapering toward the wrists, yet losing nothing of their roundness or symmetry, and at their tips were those delicate fingers which had held the fan at the wedding ceremony. One by one, as the lieutenant kissed them, the fingers withdrew behind their neighbor as if in shame. . . . The natural hollow curving between the bosom and the stomach carried in its lines a suggestion not only of softness but of resilient strength, and while it gave forewarning of the rich curves spreading outward from here to the hips it had, in itself, an appearance only of restraint and proper discipline. The whiteness and richness of the stomach and hips was like milk brimming in a great bowl, and the sharply shadowed dip of the navel could have been the fresh impress of a raindrop, fallen there that very moment. Where the shadows gathered more thickly, hair clustered, gentle and sensitive, and as the agitation mounted in the now no longer passive body there hung over this region a scent like the smoldering of fragrant blossoms, growing steadily more pervasive.

At length, in a tremulous voice, Reiko spoke.

"Show me. . . . Let me look too, for the last time."

Never before had he heard from his wife's lips so strong and unequivocal a request. It was as if something which her modesty had wished to keep hidden to the end had suddenly burst its bonds of constraint. The lieutenant obediently lay back and surrendered himself to his wife. Lithely she raised her white, trembling body, and—burning with an innocent desire to return to her husband what he had done for her—placed two white fingers on the lieutenant's eyes, which gazed fixedly up at her, and gently stroked them shut.

Suddenly overwhelmed by tenderness, her cheeks flushed by a dizzying uprush of emotion, Reiko threw her arms about the lieutenant's close-cropped head. The bristly hairs rubbed painfully against her breast, the prominent nose was cold as it dug into her flesh, and his breath was hot. Relaxing her embrace, she gazed down at her husband's masculine face. The severe brows, the closed eyes, the splendid bridge of the nose, the shapely lips drawn firmly together . . . the blue, cleanshaven cheeks reflecting the light and gleaming smoothly. Reiko kissed each of these. She kissed the broad nape of the neck, the strong, erect shoulders, the powerful chest with its twin circles like shields and its russet nipples. In the armpits, deeply shadowed by the ample flesh of the shoulders and chest, a sweet and melancholy odor emanated from the growth of hair, and in the sweetness of this odor was contained, somehow, the essence of young death. The lieutenant's naked skin glowed like a field of barley, and everywhere the muscles showed in sharp relief, converging on the lower abdomen about the small, unassuming navel. Gazing at the youthful, firm stomach, modestly covered by a vigorous growth of hair, Reiko thought of it as it was soon to be, cruelly cut by the sword, and she laid her head upon it, sobbing in pity, and bathed it with kisses.

At the touch of his wife's tears upon his stomach the lieutenant felt ready to endure with courage the cruelest agonies of his suicide.

What ecstasies they experienced after these tender exchanges may well be imagined. The lieutenant raised himself and enfolded his wife in a powerful embrace, her body now limp with exhaustion after her grief and tears. Passionately they held their faces close, rubbing cheek against cheek. Reiko's body was trembling. Their breasts, moist with sweat, were tightly joined, and every inch of the young and beautiful bodies had become so much one with the other that it seemed impossible there should ever again be a separation. Reiko cried out. From the heights they plunged into the abyss, and from the abyss they took wing and soared once more to dizzying heights. The lieutenant panted like the regimental standard-bearer on a route march. . . . As one cycle ended, almost immediately a new wave of passion would be generated, and together—with no trace of fatigue—they would climb again in a single breathless movement to the very summit.

4

When the lieutenant at last turned away, it was not from weariness. For one thing, he was anxious not to undermine the considerable strength he would need in carrying out his suicide. For another, he would have been sorry to mar the sweetness of these last memories by overindulgence.

Since the lieutenant had clearly desisted, Reiko too, with her usual compliance, followed his example. The two lay naked on their backs, with fingers interlaced, staring fixedly at the dark ceiling. The room was warm from the heater, and even when the sweat had ceased to pour from their bodies they felt no cold. Outside, in the hushed night, the sounds of passing traffic had ceased. Even the noises of the trains and streetcars around Yotsuya station did not penetrate this far. After echoing through the region bounded by the moat, they were lost in the heavily wooded park fronting the broad driveway before Akasaka Palace. It was hard to believe in the tension gripping this whole quarter, where the two factions of the bitterly divided Imperial Army now confronted each other, poised for battle.

Savoring the warmth glowing within themselves, they lay still and recalled the ecstasies they had just known. Each moment of the experience was relived. They remembered the taste of kisses which had never wearied, the touch of naked flesh, episode after episode of dizzying bliss. But already, from the dark boards of the ceiling, the face of death was peering down. These joys had been final, and their bodies would never know them again. Not that joy of this intensity—and the same thought had occurred to them both—was ever likely to be reexperienced, even if they should live on to old age.

The feel of their fingers intertwined—this too would soon be lost. Even the wood-grain patterns they now gazed at on the dark ceiling boards would be taken from them. They could feel death edging in, nearer and nearer. There could be no hesitation now. They must have the courage to reach out to death themselves, and to seize it.

"Well, let's make our preparations," said the lieutenant. The note of determination in the words was unmistakable, but at the same time Reiko had never heard her husband's voice so warm and tender.

After they had risen, a variety of tasks awaited them.

The lieutenant, who had never once before helped with the bedding, now cheerfully slid back the door of the closet, lifted the mattress across the room by himself, and stowed it away inside.

Reiko turned off the gas heater and put away the lamp standard. During the lieutenant's absence she had arranged this room carefully, sweeping and dusting it to a fresh cleanness, and now—if one overlooked the rosewood table drawn into one corner—the eight-mat room gave all the appearance of a reception room ready to welcome an important guest.

"We've seen some drinking here, haven't we? With Kanō and Homma and Noguchi."

"Yes, they were great drinkers, all of them."

"We'll be meeting them before long, in the other world. They'll tease us, I imagine, when they find I've brought you with me."

Descending the stairs, the lieutenant turned to look back into this calm clean room, now brightly illuminated by the ceiling lamp. There floated across his mind the faces of the young officers who had drunk there, and laughed, and innocently bragged. He had never dreamed then that he would one day cut open his stomach in this room.

In the two rooms downstairs husband and wife busied themselves smoothly and serenely with their respective preparations. The lieutenant went to the toilet, and then to the bathroom to wash. Meanwhile Reiko folded away her husband's padded robe, placed his uniform tunic, his trousers, and a newly cut bleached loincloth in the bathroom, and set out sheets of paper on the living-room table for the farewell notes. Then she removed the lid from the writing box and began rubbing ink from the ink tablet. She had already decided upon the wording of her own note.

Reiko's fingers pressed hard upon the cold gilt letters of the ink tablet, and the water in the shallow well at once darkened, as if a black cloud had spread across it. She stopped thinking that this repeated action, this pressure from her fingers, this rise and fall of faint sound, was all and solely for death. It was a routine domestic task, a simple paring away of time until death should finally stand before her. But somehow, in the increasingly smooth motion of the tablet rubbing on the stone, and in the scent from the thickening ink, there was unspeakable darkness.

Neat in his uniform, which he now wore next to his skin, the lieutenant emerged from the bathroom. Without a word he seated himself at the table, bolt upright, took a brush in his hand, and stared undecidedly at the paper before him.

Reiko took a white silk kimono with her and entered the bathroom. When she reappeared in the living room, clad in the white kimono and with her face lightly made up, the farewell note lay completed on the table beneath the lamp. The thick black brush-strokes said simply:

"Long Live the Imperial Forces—Army Lieutenant Takeyama Shinji."

While Reiko sat opposite him writing her own note, the lieutenant gazed in silence, intensely serious, at the controlled movement of his wife's pale fingers as they manipulated the brush.

With their respective notes in their hands—the lieutenant's sword strapped to his side, Reiko's small dagger thrust into the sash of her white kimono—the two of them stood before the god shelf and silently prayed. Then they put out all the downstairs lights. As he mounted the stairs the lieutenant turned his head and gazed back at the striking, white-clad figure of his wife, climbing behind him, with lowered eyes, from the darkness beneath.

The farewell notes were laid side by side in the alcove of the upstairs room. They wondered whether they ought not to remove the hanging scroll, but since it had been written by their go-between, Lieutenant General Ozeki, and consisted, moreover, of two Chinese characters signifying "Sincerity," they left it where it was. Even if it were to become stained with splashes of blood, they felt that the lieutenant general would understand.

The lieutenant sitting erect with his back to the alcove, laid his sword on the floor before him.

Reiko sat facing him, a mat's width away. With the rest of her so severely white the touch of rouge on her lips seemed remarkably seductive.

Across the dividing mat they gazed intently into each other's eyes. The lieutenant's sword lay before his knees. Seeing it, Reiko recalled their first night and was overwhelmed with sadness. The lieutenant spoke, in a hoarse voice:

"As I have no second to help me I shall cut deep. It may look unpleasant, but please do not panic. Death of any sort is a fearful thing to watch. You must not be discouraged by what you see. Is that all right?"

"Yes."

Reiko nodded deeply.

Looking at the slender white figure of his wife the lieutenant experienced a bizarre excitement. What he was about to perform was an act in his public capacity as a soldier, something he had never previously shown his wife. It called for a resolution equal to the courage to enter battle; it was a death of no less degree and quality than death in the front line. It was his conduct on the battlefield that he was now to display.

Momentarily the thought led the lieutenant to a strange fantasy. A lonely death on the battlefield, a death beneath the eyes of his beautiful wife . . . in the sensation that he was now to die in these two dimensions, realizing an impossible union of them both, there was sweetness beyond words. This must be the very pinnacle of good fortune, he thought. To have every moment of his death observed by those beautiful eyes—it was like being borne to death on a gentle, fragrant breeze. There was some special favor here. He did not understand precisely what it was, but it was a domain unknown to others: a dispensation granted to no one else had been permitted to himself. In the radiant, bridelike figure of his white-robed wife the lieutenant seemed to see a vision of all those things he had loved and for which he was to lay down his life—the Imperial Household, the Nation, the Army Flag. All these, no less than the wife who sat before him, were presences observing him closely with clear and never-faltering eyes.

Reiko too was gazing intently at her husband, so soon to die, and she thought that never in this world had she seen anything so beautiful. The lieutenant always looked well in uniform, but now, as he contemplated death with severe brows and firmly closed lips, he revealed what was perhaps masculine beauty at its most superb.

"It's time to go," the lieutenant said at last.

Reiko bent her body low to the mat in a deep bow. She could not raise her face. She did not wish to spoil her make-up with tears, but the tears could not be held back.

When at length she looked up she saw hazily through the tears that her husband had wound a white bandage around the blade of his now unsheathed sword, leaving five or six inches of naked steel showing at the point.

Resting the sword in its cloth wrapping on the mat before him, the lieutenant rose from his knees, resettled himself cross-legged, and unfastened the hooks of his uniform collar. His eyes no longer saw his wife. Slowly, one by one, he undid the flat brass buttons. The dusky brown chest was revealed, and then the stomach. He unclasped his belt and undid the buttons of his trousers. The pure whiteness of the thickly coiled loincloth showed itself. The lieutenant pushed the cloth down with both hands, further to ease his stomach, and then reached for the white-bandaged blade of his sword. With his left hand he massaged his abdomen, glancing downward as he did so.

To reassure himself on the sharpness of his sword's cutting edge the lieutenant folded back the left trouser flap, exposing a little of his thigh, and lightly drew the blade across the skin. Blood welled up in the wound at once, and several streaks of red trickled downward, glistening in the strong light.

It was the first time Reiko had ever seen her husband's blood, and she felt a violent throbbing in her chest. She looked at her husband's face. The lieutenant was looking at the blood with calm appraisal. For a moment—though thinking at the same time that it was hollow comfort—Reiko experienced a sense of relief.

The lieutenant's eyes fixed his wife with an intense, hawk-like stare. Moving the sword around to his front, he raised himself slightly on his hips and let the upper half of his body lean over the sword point. That he was mustering his whole strength was apparent from the angry tension of the uniform at his shoulders. The lieutenant aimed to strike deep into the left of his stomach. His sharp cry pierced the silence of the room.

Despite the effort he had himself put into the blow, the lieutenant had the impression that someone else had struck the side of his stomach agonizingly with a thick rod of iron. For a second or so his head reeled and he had no idea what had happened. The five or six inches of naked point had vanished completely into his flesh, and the white bandage, gripped in his clenched fist, pressed directly against his stomach.

He returned to consciousness. The blade had certainly pierced the wall of the stomach, he thought. His breathing was difficult, his chest thumped violently, and in some far deep region, which he could hardly believe was a part of himself, a fearful and excruciating pain came welling up as if the ground had split open to disgorge a boiling stream of molten rock. The pain came suddenly nearer, with terrifying speed. The lieutenant bit his lower lip and stifled an instinctive moan.

Was this *seppuku?*—he was thinking. It was a sensation of utter chaos, as if the sky had fallen on his head and the world was reeling drunkenly. His will power and courage, which had seemed so robust before he made the incision, had now dwindled to something like a single hairlike thread of steel, and he was assailed by the uneasy feeling that he must advance along this thread, clinging to it with desperation. His clenched fist had grown moist. Looking down, he saw that both his hand and the cloth were drenched in blood. His loincloth too was dyed a deep red. It struck him as incredible that, amidst this terrible agony, things which could be seen could still be seen, and existing things existed still.

The moment the lieutenant thrust the sword into his left side and she saw the deathly pallor fall across his face, like an abruptly lowered curtain, Reiko had to struggle to prevent herself from rushing to his side. Whatever happened, she must watch. She must be a witness. That was the duty her husband had lain upon her. Opposite her, a mat's space away, she could clearly see her husband biting his lip to stifle the pain. The pain was there, with absolute certainty, before her eyes. And Reiko had no means of rescuing him from it.

The sweat glistened on her husband's forehead. The lieutenant closed his eyes, and then opened them again, as if experimenting. The eyes had lost their luster, and seemed innocent and empty like the eyes of a small animal.

The agony before Reiko's eyes burned as strong as the summer sun, utterly remote from the grief which seemed to be tearing herself apart within. The pain grew steadily in stature, stretching upward. Reiko felt that her husband had already become a man in a separate world, a man whose whole being had been resolved into pain, a prisoner in a cage of pain where no hand could reach out to him. But Reiko felt no pain at all. Her grief was not pain. As she thought about this, Reiko began to feel as if someone had raised a cruel wall of glass high between herself and her husband.

Ever since her marriage her husband's existence had been her own existence, and every breath of his had been a breath drawn by herself. But now, while her husband's existence in pain was a vivid reality, Reiko could find in this grief of hers no certain proof at all of her own existence.

With only his right hand on the sword the lieutenant began to cut sideways across his stomach. But as the blade became entangled with the entrails it was pushed constantly outward by their soft resilience; and the lieutenant realized that it would be necessary, as he cut, to use both hands to keep the point pressed deep into his stomach. He pulled the blade across. It did not cut as easily as he had expected. He directed the strength of his whole body into his right hand and pulled again. There was a cut of three or four inches.

The pain spread slowly outward from the inner depths until the whole stomach reverberated. It was like the wild clanging of a bell. Or like a thousand bells which jangled simultaneously at every breath he breathed and every throb of his pulse, rocking his whole being. The lieutenant could no longer stop himself from moaning. But by now the blade had cut its way through to below the navel, and when he noticed this he felt a sense of satisfaction, and a renewal of courage.

The volume of blood had steadily increased, and now it spurted from the wound as if propelled by the beat of the pulse. The mat before the lieutenant was drenched red with splattered blood, and more blood overflowed onto it from pools which gathered in folds of the lieutenant's khaki trousers. A spot, like a bird, came flying across to Reiko and settled on the lap of her white silk kimono.

By the time the lieutenant had at last drawn the sword across to the right side of his stomach, the blade was already cutting shallow and had revealed its naked tip, slippery with blood and grease. But, suddenly stricken by a fit of vomiting, the lieutenant cried out hoarsely. The vomiting made the fierce pain fiercer still, and the stomach, which had thus far remained firm and compact, now abruptly heaved, opening wide its wound, and the entrails burst through, as if the wound too were vomiting. Seemingly ignorant of their master's suffering, the entrails gave an impression of robust health and almost disagreeable vitality as they slipped smoothly out and spilled over into the crotch. The lieutenant's head drooped, his shoulders heaved, his eyes opened to narrow slits, and a thin trickle of saliva dribbled from his mouth. The gold markings on his epaulettes caught the light and glinted.

Blood was scattered everywhere. The lieutenant was soaked in it to his knees, and he sat now in a crumpled and listless posture, one hand on the floor. A raw smell filled the room. The lieutenant, his head drooping, retched repeatedly, and the movement showed vividly in his shoulders. The blade of the sword, now pushed back by the entrails and exposed to its tip, was still in the lieutenant's right hand.

It would be difficult to imagine a more heroic sight than that of the lieutenant at this moment, as he mustered his strength and flung back his head. The movement was performed with sudden violence, and the back of his head struck with a sharp crack against the alcove pillar. Reiko had been sitting until now with her face lowered, gazing in fascination at the tide of blood advancing toward her knees, but the sound took her by surprise and she looked up.

The lieutenant's face was not the face of a living man. The eyes were hollow, the skin parched, the once so lustrous cheeks and lips the color of dried mud. The right hand alone was moving. Laboriously gripping the sword, it hovered shakily in the air like the hand of a marionette and strove to direct the point at the base of the lieutenant's throat. Reiko watched her husband make this last, most heart-rending, futile exertion. Glistening with blood and grease, the point was thrust at the throat again and again. And each time it missed its aim. The strength to guide it was no longer there. The straying point struck the collar and the collar badges. Although its hooks had been unfastened, the stiff military collar had closed together again and was protecting the throat.

Reiko could bear the sight no longer. She tried to go to her husband's help, but she could not stand. She moved through the blood on her knees, and her white skirts grew deep red. Moving to the rear of her husband, she helped no more than by loosening the collar. The quivering blade at last contacted the naked flesh of the throat. At that moment Reiko's impression was that she herself had propelled her husband forward; but that was not the case. It was a movement planned by the lieutenant himself, his last exertion of strength. Abruptly he threw his body at the blade, and the blade pierced his neck, emerging at the nape. There was a tremendous spurt of blood and the lieutenant lay still, cold blue-tinged steel protruding from his neck at the back.

5

Slowly, her socks slippery with blood, Reiko descended the stairway. The upstairs room was now completely still.

Switching on the ground-floor lights, she checked the gas jet and the main gas plug and poured water over the smoldering, half-buried charcoal in the brazier. She stood before the upright mirror in the four-and-a-half-mat room and held up her skirts. The bloodstains made it seem as if a bold, vivid pattern was printed across the lower half of her white kimono. When she sat down before the mirror, she was conscious of the dampness and coldness of her husband's blood in the region of her thighs, and she shivered. Then, for a long while, she lingered over her toilet preparations. She applied the rouge generously to her cheeks, and her lips too she painted heavily. This was no longer make-up to please her husband. It was make-up for the world which she would leave behind, and there was a touch of the magnificent and the spectacular in her brushwork. When she rose, the mat before the mirror was wet with blood. Reiko was not concerned about this.

Returning from the toilet, Reiko stood finally on the cement floor of the porchway. When her husband had bolted the door here last night it had been in preparation for death. For a while she stood immersed in the consideration of a simple problem. Should she now leave the bolt drawn? If she were to lock the door, it could be that the neighbors might not notice their suicide for several days. Reiko did not relish the thought of their two corpses putrifying before discovery. After all, it seemed, it would be best to leave it open. . . . She released the bolt, and also drew open the frosted-glass door a fraction. . . . At once a chill wind blew in. There was no sign of anyone in the midnight streets and stars glittered ice-cold through the trees in the large house opposite.

Leaving the door as it was, Reiko mounted the stairs. She had walked here and there for some time and her socks were no longer slippery. About halfway up, her nostrils were already assailed by a peculiar smell.

The lieutenant was lying on his face in a sea of blood. The point protruding from his neck seemed to have grown even more prominent than before. Reiko walked heedlessly across the blood. Sitting beside the lieutenant's corpse, she stared intently at the face, which lay on one cheek on the mat. The eyes were opened wide, as if the lieutenant's attention had been attracted by something. She raised the head, folding it in her sleeve, wiped the blood from the lips, and bestowed a last kiss.

Then she rose and took from the closet a new white blanket and a waist cord. To prevent any derangement of her skirts, she wrapped the blanket about her waist and bound it there firmly with the cord.

Reiko sat herself on a spot about one foot distant from the lieu tenant's body. Drawing the dagger from her sash, she examined it dully gleaming blade intently, and held it to her tongue. The tast of the polished steel was slightly sweet.

Reiko did not linger. When she thought how the pain which ha previously opened such a gulf between herself and her dying hus band was now to become a part of her own experience, she sav before her only the joy of herself entering a realm her husband ha already made his own. In her husband's agonized face there ha been something inexplicable which she was seeing for the first time Now she would solve that riddle. Reiko sensed that at last she to would be able to taste the true bitterness and sweetness of that grea moral principle in which her husband believed. What had until nov been tasted only faintly through her husband's example she wa about to savor directly with her own tongue.

Reiko rested the point of the blade against the base of her throat She thrust hard. The wound was only shallow. Her head blazed, an her hands shook uncontrollably. She gave the blade a strong pul sideways. A warm substance flooded into her mouth, and every thing before her eyes reddened, in a vision of spouting blood. Sh gathered her strength and plunged the point of the blade deep int her throat.

196

A Good Man Is Hard to Find

FLANNERY O'CONNOR

[1925–1964]

The grandmother didn't want to go to Florida. She wanted to visit some of her connections in east Tennessee and she was seizing at every chance to change Bailey's mind. Bailey was the son she lived with, her only boy. He was sitting on the edge of his chair at the table, bent over the orange sports section of the *Journal.* "Now look here, Bailey," she said, "see here, read this," and she stood with one hand on her thin hip and the other rattling the newspaper at his bald head. "Here this fellow that calls himself The Misfit is aloose from the Federal Pen and headed toward Florida and you read here what it says he did to these people. Just you read it. I wouldn't take my children in any direction with a criminal like that aloose in it. I couldn't answer to my conscience if I did."

Bailey didn't look up from his reading so she wheeled around then and faced the children's mother, a young woman in slacks, whose face was as broad and innocent as a cabbage and was tied round with a green head-kerchief that had two points on the top like rabbit's ears. She was sitting on the sofa, feeding the baby his apricots out of a jar. "The children have been to Florida before," the old lady said. "You all ought to take them somewhere else for a change so they would see different parts of the world and be broad. They never have been to east Tennessee."

The children's mother didn't seem to hear her but the eight-year-old boy, John Wesley, a stocky child with glasses, said, "If you don't want to go to Florida, why dontcha stay at home?" He and the little girl, June Star, were reading the funny papers on the floor.

"She wouldn't stay at home to be queen for a day," June Star said without raising her yellow head.

"Yes and what would you do if this fellow, The Misfit, caught you?" the grandmother asked.

"I'd smack his face," John Wesley said.

"She wouldn't stay at home for a million bucks," June Star said. "Afraid she'd miss something. She has to go everywhere we go."

"All right, Miss," the grandmother said. "Just remember that the next time you want me to curl your hair."

June Star said her hair was naturally curly.

The next morning the grandmother was the first one in the car, ready to go. She had her big black valise that looked like the head of a hippopotamus in one corner, and underneath it she was hiding a basket with Pitty Sing, the cat, in it. She didn't intend for the cat to be left alone in the house for three days because he would miss her too much and she was afraid he might brush against one of the gas burners and accidentally asphyxiate himself. Her son, Bailey, didn't like to arrive at a motel with a cat.

She sat in the middle of the back seat with John Wesley and June Star on either side of her. Bailey and the children's mother and the baby sat in the front and they left Atlanta at eight forty-five with the mileage on the car at 55890. The grandmother wrote this down because she thought it would be interesting to say how many miles they had been when they got back. It took them twenty minutes to reach the outskirts of the city.

The old lady settled herself comfortably, removing her white cotton gloves and putting them up with her purse on the shelf in front of the back window. The children's mother still had on slacks and still had her head tied up in a green kerchief, but the grandmother had on a navy blue straw sailor hat with a bunch of white violets on the brim and a navy blue dress with a small white dot in the print. Her collar and cuffs were white organdy trimmed with lace and at her neckline she had pinned a purple spray of cloth violets containing a sachet. In case of an accident, anyone seeing her dead on the highway would know at once that she was a lady.

She said she thought it was going to be a good day for driving, neither too hot nor too cold, and she cautioned Bailey that the speed limit was fifty-five miles an hour and that the patrolmen hid themselves behind billboards and small clumps of trees and sped out after you before you had a chance to slow down. She pointed out interesting details of the scenery: Stone Mountain; the blue granite that in some places came up to both sides of the highway; the brilliant red clay banks slightly streaked with purple; and the various crops that made rows of green lace-work on the ground. The trees were full of silver-white sunlight and the meanest of them sparkled. The children were reading comic magazines and their mother had gone back to sleep.

"Let's go through Georgia fast so we won't have to look at it much," John Wesley said.

"If I were a little boy," said the grandmother, "I wouldn't talk about my native state that way. Tennessee has the mountains and Georgia has the hills."

"Tennessee is just a hillbilly dumping ground," John Wesley said, "and Georgia is a lousy state too."

"You said it," June Star said.

"In my time," said the grandmother, folding her thin veined fingers, "children were more respectful of their native states and their parents and everything else. People did right then. Oh look at the cute little pickaninny!" she said and pointed to a Negro child standing in the door of a shack. "Wouldn't that make a picture, now?" she asked and they all turned and looked at the little Negro out of the back window. He waved.

"He didn't have any britches on," June said.

"He probably didn't have any," the grandmother explained. "Little niggers in the country don't have things like we do. If I could paint, I'd paint that picture," she said.

The children exchanged comic books.

The grandmother offered to hold the baby and the children's mother passed him over the front seat to her. She set him on her knee and bounced him and told him about the things they were passing. She rolled her eyes and screwed up her mouth and stuck her leathery thin face into his smooth bland one. Occasionally he gave her a faraway smile. They passed a large cotton field with five or six graves fenced in the middle of it, like a small island. "Look at the graveyard!" the grandmother said, pointing it out. "That was the old family burying ground. That belonged to the plantation."

"Where's the plantation?" John Wesley asked.

"Gone With the Wind," said the grandmother. "Ha. Ha."

When the children finished all the comic books they had brought, they opened the lunch and ate it. The grandmother ate a peanut butter sandwich and an olive and would not let the children throw the box and the paper napkins out the window. When there was nothing else to do they played a game by choosing a cloud and making the other two guess what shape it suggested. John Wesley took one the shape of a cow and June Star guessed a cow and John Wesley said, no, an automobile, and June Star said he didn't play fair, and they began to slap each other over the grandmother.

The grandmother said she would tell them a story if they would keep quiet. When she told a story, she rolled her eyes and waved her head and was very dramatic. She said once when she was a maiden lady she had been courted by a Mr. Edgar Atkins Teagarden from Jasper, Georgia. She said he was a very good-looking man and a gentleman and that he brought her a watermelon every Saturday afternoon with his initials cut in it, E. A. T. Well, one Saturday, she said, Mr. Teagarden brought the watermelon and there was nobody at home and he left it on the front porch and returned in his buggy to Jasper, but she never got the watermelon, she said, because a nigger boy ate it when he saw the initials, E. A. T.! This story tickled John Wesley's funny bone and he giggled and giggled but June Star didn't think it was any good. She said she wouldn't marry a man that just brought her a watermelon on Saturday. The grandmother said she would have done well to marry Mr. Teagarden because he was a gentleman and had bought Coca-Cola stock when it first came out and that he had died only a few years ago, a very wealthy man.

They stopped at The Tower for barbecued sandwiches. The Tower was a part stucco and part wood filling station and dance hall set in a clearing outside of Timothy. A fat man named Red Sammy Butts ran it and there were signs stuck here and there on the building and for miles up and down the highway saying, TRY RED SAMMY'S FAMOUS BARBECUE. NONE LIKE FAMOUS RED SAMMY'S! RED SAM! THE FAT BOY WITH THE HAPPY LAUGH. A VETERAN! SAMMY'S YOUR MAN!

Red Sammy was lying on the bare ground outside The Tower with his head under a truck while a gray monkey about a foot high, chained to a small chinaberry tree, chattered nearby. The monkey sprang back into the tree and got on the highest limb as soon as he saw the children jump out of the car and run toward him.

Inside, The Tower was a long dark room with a counter at one end and tables at the other and dancing space in the middle. They all sat down at a broad table next to the nickelodeon and Red Sam's wife, a tall burnt-brown woman with hair and eyes lighter than her skin, came and took their order. The children's mother put a dime in the machine and played "The Tennessee Waltz," and the grandmother said that tune always made her want to dance. She asked Bailey if he would like to dance but he only glared at her. He didn't have a naturally sunny disposition like she did and trips made him nervous. The grandmother's brown eyes were very bright. She swayed her head from side to side and pretended she was dancing in her chair. June Star said play something she could tap to so the children's mother put in another dime and played a fast number and June Star stepped out onto the dance floor and did her tap routine.

"Ain't she cute?" Red Sam's wife said, leaning over the counter. "Would you like to come be my little girl?"

"No I certainly wouldn't," June Star said. "I wouldn't live in a broken-down place like this for a million bucks!" and she ran back to the table.

"Ain't she cute?" the woman repeated, stretching her mouth politely.

"Aren't you ashamed?" hissed the grandmother.

Red Sam came in and told his wife to quit lounging on the counter and hurry with these people's order. His khaki trousers reached just to his hip bones and his stomach hung over them like a sack of meal swaying under his shirt. He came over and sat down at a table nearby and let out a combination sigh and yodel. "You can't win," he said. "You can't win," and he wiped his sweating red face off with a gray handkerchief. "These days you don't know who to trust," he said. "Ain't that the truth?"

"People are certainly not nice like they used to be," said the grandmother.

"Two fellers come in here last week," Red Sammy said, "driving a Chrysler. It was a old beat-up car but it was a good one and these boys looked all right to me. Said they worked at the mill and you know I let them fellers charge the gas they bought? Now why did I do that?"

"Because you're a good man!" the grandmother said at once.

"Yes'm, I suppose so," Red Sam said as if he were struck with th
answer.

His wife brought the orders, carrying the five plates all at onc
without a tray, two in each hand and one balanced on her arm. "I
isn't a soul in this green world of God's that you can trust," she said
"And I don't count anybody out of that, not nobody," she repeated
looking at Red Sammy.

"Did you read about that criminal, The Misfit, that's escaped?
asked the grandmother.

"I wouldn't be a bit surprised if he didn't attact this place righ
here," said the woman. "If he hears about it being here, I wouldn'
be none surprised to see him. If he hears it's two cent in the cas
register, I wouldn't be a tall surprised if he . . ."

"That'll do," Red Sam said. "Go bring these people their Co'
Colas," and the woman went off to get the rest of the order.

"A good man is hard to find," Red Sammy said. "Everything i
getting terrible. I remember the day you could go off and leave you
screen door unlatched. Not no more."

He and the grandmother discussed better times. The old lady sai
that in her opinion Europe was entirely to blame for the way thing
were now. She said the way Europe acted you would think we wer
made of money and Red Sam said it was no use talking about it, sh
was exactly right. The children ran outside into the white sunligh
and looked at the monkey in the lacy chinaberry tree. He was bus
catching fleas on himself and biting each one carefully between hi
teeth as if it were a delicacy.

They drove off again into the hot afternoon. The grandmothe
took cat naps and woke up every few minutes with her own snor
ing. Outside of Toombsboro she woke up and recalled an old plan
tation that she had visited in this neighborhood once when she wa
a young lady. She said the house had six white columns across th
front and that there was an avenue of oaks leading up to it and tw
little wooden trellis arbors on either side in front where you sa
down with your suitor after a stroll in the garden. She recalle
exactly which road to turn off to get to it. She knew that Baile
would not be willing to lose any time looking at an old house, bu
the more she talked about it, the more she wanted to see it onc
again and find out if the little twin arbors were still standing. "Ther
was a secret panel in this house," she said craftily, not telling th

truth but wishing that she were, "and the story went that all the family silver was hidden in it when Sherman came through but it was never found . . ."

"Hey!" John Wesley said. "Let's go see it! We'll find it! We'll poke all the woodwork and find it! Who lives there? Where do you turn off at? Hey Pop, can't we turn off there?"

"We never have seen a house with a secret panel!" June Star shrieked. "Let's go to the house with the secret panel! Hey, Pop, can't we go see the house with the secret panel!"

"It's not far from here, I know," the grandmother said. "It wouldn't take over twenty minutes."

Bailey was looking straight ahead. His jaw was as rigid as a horseshoe. "No," he said.

The children began to yell and scream that they wanted to see the house with the secret panel. John Wesley kicked the back of the front seat and June Star hung over her mother's shoulder and whined desperately into her ear that they never had any fun even on their vacation, and that they could never do what THEY wanted to do. The baby began to scream and John Wesley kicked the back of the seat so hard that his father could feel the blows in his kidney.

"All right!" he shouted, and drew the car to a stop at the side of the road. "Will you all shut up? Will you all just shut up for one second? If you don't shut up, we won't go anywhere."

"It would be very educational for them," the grandmother murmured.

"All right," Bailey said, "but get this: this is the only time we're going to stop for anything like this. This is the one and only time."

"The dirt road that you have to turn down is about a mile back," the grandmother directed. "I marked it when we passed."

"A dirt road," Bailey groaned.

After they had turned around and were headed toward the dirt road, the grandmother recalled other points about the house, the beautiful glass over the front doorway and the candle-lamp in the hall. John Wesley said that the secret panel was probably in the fireplace.

"You can't go inside this house," Bailey said. "You don't know who lives there."

"While you all talk to the people in front, I'll run around behind and get in a window," John Wesley suggested.

"We'll all stay in the car," his mother said.

They turned onto the dirt road and the car raced roughly along in a swirl of pink dust. The grandmother recalled the times when there were no paved roads and thirty miles was a day's journey. The dirt road was hilly and there were sudden washes in it and sharp curves on dangerous embankments. All at once they would be on a hill, looking down over the blue tops of trees for miles around, then the next minute, they would be in a red depression with the dust-coated trees looking down on them.

"This place had better turn up in a minute," Bailey said, "or I'm going to turn around."

The road looked as if no one had traveled on it in months.

"It's not much farther," the grandmother said and just as she said it, a horrible thought came to her. The thought was so embarrassing that she turned red in the face and her eyes dilated and her feet jumped up, upsetting her valise in the corner. The instant the valise moved, the newspaper top she had over the basket under it rose with a snarl and Pitty Sing, the cat, sprang onto Bailey's shoulder.

The children were thrown to the floor and their mother, clutching the baby, was thrown out the door onto the ground, the old lady was thrown into the front seat. The car turned over once and landed right-side-up in a gulch on the side of the road. Bailey remained in the driver's seat with the cat—gray-striped with a broad white face and an orange nose—clinging to his neck like a caterpillar.

As soon as the children saw they could move their arms and legs they scrambled out of the car, shouting. "We've had an ACCIDENT!" The grandmother was curled up under the dashboard, hoping she was injured so that Bailey's wrath would not come down on her all at once. The horrible thought she had had before the accident was that the house she had remembered so vividly was not in Georgia but in Tennessee.

Bailey removed the cat from his neck with both hands and flung it out the window against the side of a pine tree. Then he got out of the car and started looking for the children's mother. She was sitting against the side of the red gutted ditch, holding the screaming baby, but she only had a cut down her face and a broken shoulder. "We've had an ACCIDENT!" the children screamed in a frenzy of delight.

"But nobody's killed," June Star said with disappointment as the grandmother limped out of the car, her hat still pinned to her head but the broken front brim standing up at a jaunty angle and the violet spray hanging off the side. They all sat down in the ditch, except the children, to recover from the shock. They were all shaking.

"Maybe a car will come along," said the children's mother hoarsely.

"I believe I have injured an organ," said the grandmother, pressing her side, but no one answered her. Bailey's teeth were clattering. He had on a yellow sport shirt with bright blue parrots designed in it and his face was as yellow as the shirt. The grandmother decided that she would not mention that the house was in Tennessee.

The road was about ten feet above and they could see only the tops of the trees on the other side of it. Behind the ditch they were sitting in there were more woods, tall and dark and deep. In a few minutes they saw a car some distance away on top of a hill, coming slowly as if the occupants were watching them. The grandmother stood up and waved both arms dramatically to attract their attention. The car continued to come on slowly, disappeared around a bend and appeared again, moving even slower, on top of the hill they had gone over. It was a big black battered hearse-like automobile. There were three men in it.

It came to a stop just over them and for some minutes, the driver looked down with a steady expressionless gaze to where they were sitting, and didn't speak. Then he turned his head and muttered something to the other two and they got out. One was a fat boy in black trousers and a red sweat shirt with a silver stallion embossed on the front of it. He moved around on the right side of them and stood staring, his mouth partly open in a kind of loose grin. The other had on khaki pants and a blue striped coat and a gray hat pulled down very low, hiding most of his face. He came around slowly on the left side. Neither spoke.

The driver got out of the car and stood by the side of it, looking down at them. He was an older man than the other two. His hair was just beginning to gray and he wore silver-rimmed spectacles that gave him a scholarly look. He had a long creased face and didn't have on any shirt or undershirt. He had on blue jeans that were too tight for him and was holding a black hat and a gun. The two boys also had guns.

"We've had an ACCIDENT!" the children screamed.

The grandmother had the peculiar feeling that the bespectacled man was someone she knew. His face was as familiar to her as if she had known him all her life but she could not recall who he was. He moved away from the car and began to come down the embankment, placing his feet carefully so that he wouldn't slip. He had on tan and white shoes and no socks, and his ankles were red and thin. "Good afternoon," he said. "I see you all had you a little spill."

"We turned over twice!" said the grandmother.

"Oncet," he corrected. "We seen it happen. Try their car and see will it run, Hiram," he said quietly to the boy with the gray hat.

"What you got that gun for?" John Wesley asked. "Whatcha gonna do with that gun?"

"Lady," the man said to the children's mother, "would you mind calling them children to sit down by you? Children make me nervous. I want all you all to sit down right together there where you're at."

"What are you telling us what to do for?" June Star asked.

Behind them the line of woods gaped like a dark open mouth. "Come here," said their mother.

"Look here now," Bailey began suddenly, "we're in a predicament! We're in . . ."

The grandmother shrieked. She scrambled to her feet and stood staring. "You're The Misfit!" she said. "I recognized you at once."

"Yes'm," the man said, smiling slightly as if he were pleased in spite of himself to be known, "but it would have been better for all of you, lady, if you hadn't of reckernized me."

Bailey turned his head sharply and said something to his mother that shocked even the children. The old lady began to cry and The Misfit reddened.

"Lady," he said, "don't you get upset. Sometimes a man says things he don't mean. I don't reckon he meant to talk to you thataway."

"You wouldn't shoot a lady, would you?" the grandmother said and removed a clean handkerchief from her cuff and began to slap at her eyes with it.

The Misfit pointed the toe of his shoe into the ground and made a little hole and then covered it up again. "I would hate to have to," he said.

"Listen," the grandmother almost screamed, "I know you're a good man. You don't look a bit like you have common blood. I know you must come from nice people!"

"Yes mam," he said, "finest people in the world." When he smiled he showed a row of strong white teeth. "God never made a finer woman than my mother and my daddy's heart was pure gold," he said. The boy with the red sweat shirt had come around behind them and was standing with his gun at his hip. The Misfit squatted down on the ground. "Watch them children, Bobby Lee," he said. "You know they make me nervous." He looked at the six of them huddled together in front of him and he seemed to be embarrassed as if he couldn't think of anything to say. "Ain't a cloud in the sky," he remarked, looking up at it. "Don't see no sun but don't see no cloud neither."

"Yes, it's a beautiful day," said the grandmother. "Listen," she said, "you shouldn't call yourself The Misfit because I know you're a good man at heart. I can just look at you and tell."

"Hush!" Bailey yelled. "Hush! Everybody shut up and let me handle this!" He was squatting in the position of a runner about to sprint forward but he didn't move.

"I pre-chate that, lady," The Misfit said and drew a little circle in the ground with the butt of his gun.

"It'll take a half a hour to fix this here car," Hiram called, looking over the raised hood of it.

"Well, first you and Bobby Lee get him and that little boy to step over yonder with you," The Misfit said, pointing to Bailey and John Wesley. "The boys want to ask you something," he said to Bailey. "Would you mind stepping back in them woods there with them?"

"Listen," Bailey began, "we're in a terrible predicament. Nobody realizes what this is," and his voice cracked. His eyes were as blue and intense as the parrots in his shirt and he remained perfectly still.

The grandmother reached up to adjust her hat brim as if she were going to the woods with him but it came off in her hand. She stood staring at it and after a second she let it fall on the ground. Hiram pulled Bailey up by the arm as if he were assisting an old man. John Wesley caught hold of his father's hand and Bobby Lee followed. They went off toward the woods and just as they reached the dark edge, Bailey turned and supporting himself against a gray naked pine trunk, he shouted, "I'll be back in a minute, Mamma, wait on me!"

"Come back this instant!" his mother shrilled but they all disappeared into the woods.

"Bailey Boy!" the grandmother called in a tragic voice but she found she was looking at The Misfit squatting on the ground in front of her. "I just know you're a good man," she said desperately. "You're not a bit common!"

"Nome, I ain't a good man," The Misfit said after a second as if he had considered her statement carefully, "but I ain't the worst in the world neither. My daddy said I was different breed of dog from my brothers and sisters. 'You know,' Daddy said, 'it's some that can live their whole life out without asking about it and it's others has to know why it is, and this boy is one of the latters. He's going to be into everything!' " He put on his black hat and looked up suddenly and then away deep into the woods as if he were embarrassed again. "I'm sorry I don't have on a shirt before you ladies," he said, hunching his shoulders slightly. "We buried our clothes that we had on when we escaped and we're just making do until we can get better. We borrowed these from some folks we met," he explained.

"That's perfectly all right," the grandmother said. "Maybe Bailey has an extra shirt in his suitcase."

"I'll look and see terrectly," The Misfit said.

"Where are they taking him?" the children's mother screamed.

"Daddy was a card himself," the Misfit said. "You couldn't put anything over on him. He never got in trouble with the Authorities though. Just had the knack of handling them."

"You could be honest too if you'd only try," said the grandmother. "Think how wonderful it would be to settle down and live a comfortable life and not have to think about somebody chasing you all the time."

The Misfit kept scratching in the ground with the butt of his gun as if he were thinking about it. "Yes'm, somebody is always after you," he murmured.

The grandmother noticed how thin his shoulder blades were just behind his hat because she was standing up looking down on him. "Do you ever pray?" she asked.

He shook his head. All she saw was the black hat wiggle between his shoulder blades. "Nome," he said.

There was a pistol shot from the woods, followed closely by another. Then silence. The old lady's head jerked around. She could hear the wind move through the tree tops like a long satisfied insuck of breath. "Bailey Boy!" she called.

"I was a gospel singer for a while," The Misfit said. "I been most everything. Been in the arm service, both land and sea, at home and abroad, been twict married, been an undertaker, been with the railroads, plowed Mother Earth, been in a tornado, seen a man burnt alive oncet," and he looked up at the children's mother and the little girl who were sitting close together, their faces white and their eyes glassy; "I even seen a woman flogged," he said.

"Pray, pray," the grandmother began, "pray, pray . . ."

"I never was a bad boy that I remember of," The Misfit said in an almost dreamy voice, "but somewheres along the line I done something wrong and got sent to the penitentiary. I was buried alive," and he looked up and held her attention to him by a steady stare.

"That's when you should have started to pray," she said. "What did you do to get sent to the penitentiary that first time?"

"Turn to the right, it was a wall," The Misfit said, looking up again at the cloudless sky. "Turn to the left, it was a wall. Look up it was a ceiling, look down it was a floor. I forgot what I done, lady. I set there and set there, trying to remember what it was I done and I ain't recalled it to this day. Oncet in a while, I would think it was coming to me, but it never come."

"Maybe they put you in by mistake," the old lady said vaguely.

"Nome," he said. "It wasn't no mistake. They had the papers on me."

"You must have stolen something," she said.

The Misfit sneered slightly. "Nobody had nothing I wanted," he said. "It was a head-doctor at the penitentiary said what I had done was kill my daddy but I know that for a lie. My daddy died in nineteen ought nineteen of the epidemic flu and I never had a thing to do with it. He was buried in the Mount Hopewell Baptist churchyard and you can go there and see for yourself."

"If you would pray," the old lady said, "Jesus would help you."

"That's right," The Misfit said.

"Well then, why don't you pray?" she asked trembling with delight suddenly.

"I don't want no hep," he said. "I'm doing all right by myself."

Bobby Lee and Hiram came ambling back from the woods. Bobby Lee was dragging a yellow shirt with bright blue parrots in it.

"Throw me that shirt, Bobby Lee," The Misfit said. The shirt came flying at him and landed on his shoulder and he put it on. The grandmother couldn't name what the shirt reminded her of. "No, lady," The Misfit said while he was buttoning it up. "I found out the crime don't matter. You can do one thing or you can do another, kill a man or take a tire off his car, because sooner or later you're going to forget what it was you done and just be punished for it."

The children's mother had begun to make heaving noises as if she couldn't get her breath. "Lady," he asked, "would you and that little girl like to step off yonder with Bobby Lee and Hiram and join your husband?"

"Yes, thank you," the mother said faintly. Her left arm dangled helplessly and she was holding the baby, who had gone to sleep, in the other. "Hep that lady up, Hiram," The Misfit said as she struggled to climb out of the ditch, "and Bobby Lee, you hold onto that little girl's hand."

"I don't want to hold hands with him," June Star said. "He reminds me of a pig."

The fat boy blushed and laughed and caught her by the arm and pulled her off into the woods after Hiram and her mother.

Alone with The Misfit, the grandmother found that she had lost her voice. There was not a cloud in the sky nor any sun. There was nothing around her but woods. She wanted to tell him that he must pray. She opened and closed her mouth several times before anything came out. Finally she found herself saying, "Jesus, Jesus," meaning Jesus will help you, but the way she was saying it, it sounded as if she might be cursing.

"Yes'm," The Misfit said as if he agreed. "Jesus thown everything off balance. It was the same case with Him as with me except He hadn't committed any crime and they could prove I had committed one because they had the papers on me. Of course," he said, "they never shown me any papers. That's why I sign myself now. I said long ago, you get you a signature and sign everything you do and keep a copy of it. Then you'll know what you done and you can hold up the crime to the punishment and see do they match and in the end you'll have something to prove you ain't been treated right. I call myself The Misfit," he said, "because I can't make what all I done wrong fit what all I gone through in punishment."

There was a piercing scream from the woods, followed closely by a pistol report. "Does it seem right to you, lady, that one is punished a heap and another ain't punished at all?"

"Jesus!" the old lady cried. "You've got good blood! I know you wouldn't shoot a lady! I know you come from nice people! Pray! Jesus, you ought not to shoot a lady. I'll give you all the money I've got!"

"Lady," The Misfit said, looking beyond her far into the woods, "there never was a body that give the undertaker a tip."

There were two more pistol reports and the grandmother raised her head like a parched old turkey hen crying for water and called, "Bailey Boy, Bailey Boy!" as if her heart would break.

"Jesus was the only One that ever raised the dead," The Misfit continued, "and He shouldn't have done it. He thown everything off balance. If He did what He said, then it's nothing for you to do but thow away everything and follow Him, and if He didn't, then it's nothing for you to do but enjoy the few minutes you got left the best way you can—by killing somebody or burning down his house or doing some other meanness to him. No pleasure but meanness," he said and his voice had become almost a snarl.

"Maybe He didn't raise the dead," the old lady mumbled, not knowing what she was saying and feeling so dizzy that she sank down in the ditch with her legs twisted under her.

"I wasn't there so I can't say He didn't," The Misfit said. "I wisht I had of been there," he said, hitting the ground with his fist. "It ain't right I wasn't there because if I had of been there I would of known. Listen lady," he said in a high voice, "if I had of been there I would of known and I wouldn't be like I am now." His voice seemed about to crack and the grandmother's head cleared for an instant. She saw the man's face twisted close to her own as if he were going to cry and she murmured, "Why you're one of my babies. You're one of my own children!" She reached out and touched him on the shoulder. The Misfit sprang back as if a snake had bitten him and shot her three times through the chest. Then he put his gun down on the ground and took off his glasses and began to clean them.

Hiram and Bobby Lee returned from the woods and stood over the ditch, looking down at the grandmother who half sat and half lay in a puddle of blood with her legs crossed under her like a child's and her face smiling up at the cloudless sky.

Without his glasses, The Misfit's eyes were red-rimmed and pale and defenseless-looking. "Take her off and thow her where you down the others," he said, picking up the cat that was rubbing itself against his leg.

"She was a talker, wasn't she?" Bobby Lee said, sliding down the ditch with a yodel.

"She would of been a good woman," The Misfit said, "if it had been somebody there to shoot her every minute of her life."

"Some fun!" Bobby Lee said.

"Shut up, Bobby Lee," The Misfit said. "It's no real pleasure in life."

1953

A Very Old Man with Enormous Wings

A TALE FOR CHILDREN

GABRIEL GARCÍA MÁRQUEZ

[b. 1928]

On the third day of rain they had killed so many crabs inside the house that Pelayo had to cross his drenched courtyard and throw them into the sea, because the newborn child had a temperature all night and they thought it was due to the stench. The world had been sad since Tuesday. Sea and sky were a single ash-gray thing and the sands of the beach, which on March nights glimmered like powdered light, had become a stew of mud and rotten shellfish. The light was so weak at noon that when Pelayo was coming back to the house after throwing away the crabs, it was hard for him to see what it was that was moving and groaning in the rear of the courtyard. He had to go very close to see that it was an old man, a very old man, lying face down in the mud, who, in spite of his tremendous efforts, couldn't get up, impeded by his enormous wings.

Frightened by that nightmare, Pelayo ran to get Elisenda, his wife, who was putting compresses on the sick child, and he took her to the rear of the courtyard. They both looked at the fallen body with mute stupor. He was dressed like a ragpicker. There were only a few faded hairs left on his bald skull and very few teeth in his mouth, and his pitiful condition of a drenched great-grandfather had taken away any sense of grandeur he might have had. His huge buzzard wings, dirty and half-plucked, were forever entangled in the mud. They looked at him so long and so closely that Pelayo and Elisenda very soon overcame their surprise and in the end found him familiar. Then they dared speak to him, and he answered in an incomprehensible dialect with a strong sailor's voice. That was how they skipped over the inconvenience of the wings and quite intelligently concluded that he was a lonely castaway from some foreign ship wrecked by the storm. And yet, they called in a neighbor woman who knew everything about life and death to see him, and all she needed was one look to show them their mistake.

"He's an angel," she told them. "He must have been coming for the child, but the poor fellow is so old that the rain knocked him down."

On the following day everyone knew that a flesh-and-blood angel was held captive in Pelayo's house. Against the judgment of the wise neighbor woman, for whom angels in those times were the fugitive survivors of a celestial conspiracy, they did not have the heart to club him to death. Pelayo watched over him all afternoon from the kitchen, armed with his bailiff's club, and before going to bed he dragged him out of the mud and locked him up with the hens in the wire chicken coop. In the middle of the night, when the rain stopped, Pelayo and Elisenda were still killing crabs. A short time afterward the child woke up without a fever and with a desire to eat. Then they felt magnanimous and decided to put the angel on a raft with fresh water and provisions for three days and leave him to his fate on the high seas. But when they went out into the courtyard with the first light of dawn, they found the whole neighborhood in front of the chicken coop having fun with the angel, without the slightest reverence, tossing him things to eat through the openings in the wire as if he weren't a supernatural creature but a circus animal.

Father Gonzaga arrived before seven o'clock, alarmed at the strange news. By that time onlookers less frivolous than those at dawn had already arrived and they were making all kinds of conjectures concerning the captive's future. The simplest among them thought that he should be named mayor of the world. Others of sterner mind felt that he should be promoted to the rank of five-star general in order to win all wars. Some visionaries hoped that he could be put to stud in order to implant on earth a race of winged wise men who could take charge of the universe. But Father Gonzaga, before becoming a priest, had been a robust woodcutter. Standing by the wire, he reviewed his catechism in an instant and asked them to open the door so that he could take a close look at that pitiful man who looked more like a huge decrepit hen among the fascinated chickens. He was lying in a corner drying his open wings in the sunlight among the fruit peels and breakfast leftovers that the early risers had thrown him. Alien to the impertinences of the world, he only lifted his antiquarian eyes and murmured something in his dialect when Father Gonzaga went into the chicken coop and said good morning to him in Latin. The parish priest had his first suspicion of an imposter when he saw that he did not understand the language of God or know how to greet His ministers. Then he noticed that seen close up he was much too human: he had an unbearable smell of the outdoors, the back side of his wings was strewn with parasites and his main feathers had been mistreated by terrestrial winds, and nothing about him measured up to the proud dignity of angels. Then he came out of the chicken coop and in a brief sermon warned the curious against the risks of being ingenuous. He reminded them that the devil had the bad habit of making use of carnival tricks in order to confuse the unwary. He argued that if wings were not the essential element in determining the difference between a hawk and an airplane, they were even less so in the recognition of angels. Nevertheless, he promised to write a letter to his bishop so that the latter would write to his primate so that the latter would write to the Supreme Pontiff in order to get the final verdict from the highest courts.

His prudence fell on sterile hearts. The news of the captive angel spread with such rapidity that after a few hours the courtyard had the bustle of a marketplace and they had to call in troops with fixed bayonets to disperse the mob that was about to knock the house down. Elisenda, her spine all twisted from sweeping up so much marketplace trash, then got the idea of fencing in the yard and charging five cents admission to see the angel.

The curious came from far away. A traveling carnival arrived with a flying acrobat who buzzed over the crowd several times, but no one paid any attention to him because his wings were not those of an angel but, rather, those of a sidereal bat. The most unfortunate invalids on earth came in search of health: a poor woman who since childhood had been counting her heartbeats and had run out of numbers; a Portuguese man who couldn't sleep because the noise of the stars disturbed him; a sleepwalker who got up at night to undo the things he had done while awake; and many others with less serious ailments. In the midst of that shipwreck disorder that made the earth tremble, Pelayo and Elisenda were happy with fatigue, for in less than a week they had crammed their rooms with money and the line of pilgrims waiting their turn to enter still reached beyond the horizon.

The angel was the only one who took no part in his own act. He spent his time trying to get comfortable in his borrowed nest, befuddled by the hellish heat of the oil lamps and sacramental candles that had been placed along the wire. At first they tried to make him eat some mothballs, which, according to the wisdom of the wise neighbor woman, were the food prescribed for angels. But he turned them down, just as he turned down the papal lunches that the penitents brought him, and they never found out whether it was because he was an angel or because he was an old man that in the end he ate nothing but eggplant mush. His only supernatural virtue seemed to be patience. Especially during the first days, when the hens pecked at him, searching for the stellar parasites that proliferated in his wings, and the cripples pulled out feathers to touch their defective parts with, and even the most merciful threw stones at him, trying to get him to rise so they could see him standing. The only time they succeeded in arousing him was when they burned his side with an iron for branding steers, for he had been motionless for so many hours that they thought he was dead. He awoke with a start, ranting in his hermetic language and with tears in his eyes, and he flapped his wings a couple of times, which brought on a whirlwind of chicken dung and lunar dust and a gale of panic that did not seem to be of this world. Although many thought that his reaction had been one not of rage but of pain, from then on they were careful not to annoy him, because the majority understood that his passivity was not that of a hero taking his ease but that of a cataclysm in repose.

Father Gonzaga held back the crowd's frivolity with formulas of maidservant inspiration while awaiting the arrival of a final judgment on the nature of the captive. But the mail from Rome showed no sense of urgency. They spent their time finding out if the prisoner had a navel, if his dialect had any connection with Aramaic, how many times he could fit on the head of a pin, or whether he wasn't just a Norwegian with wings. Those meager letters might have come and gone until the end of time if a providential event had not put an end to the priest's tribulations.

It so happened that during those days, among so many other carnival attractions, there arrived in town the traveling show of the woman who had been changed into a spider for having disobeyed her parents. The admission to see her was not only less than the admission to see the angel, but people were permitted to ask her all manner of questions about her absurd state and to examine her up and down so that no one would ever doubt the truth of her horror. She was a frightful tarantula the size of a ram and with the head of a sad maiden. What was most heart-rending, however, was not her outlandish shape but the sincere affliction with which she recounted the details of her misfortune. While still practically a child she had sneaked out of her parents' house to go to a dance, and while she was coming back through the woods after having danced all night without permission, a fearful thunderclap rent the sky in two and through the crack came the lightning bolt of brimstone that changed her into a spider. Her only nourishment came from the meatballs that charitable souls chose to toss into her mouth. A spectacle like that, full of so much human truth and with such a fearful lesson, was bound to defeat without even trying that of a haughty angel who scarcely deigned to look at mortals. Besides, the few miracles attributed to the angel showed a certain mental disorder, like the blind man who didn't recover his sight but grew three new teeth, or the paralytic who didn't get to walk but almost won the lottery, and the leper whose sores sprouted sunflowers. Those consolation miracles, which were more like mocking fun, had already ruined the angel's reputation when the woman who had been changed into a spider finally crushed him completely. That was how Father Gonzaga was cured forever of his insomnia and Pelayo's courtyard went back to being as empty as during the time it had rained for three days and crabs walked through the bedrooms.

The owners of the house had no reason to lament. With the money they saved they built a two-story mansion with balconies and gardens and high netting so that crabs wouldn't get in during the winter, and with iron bars on the windows so that angels wouldn't get in. Pelayo also set up a rabbit warren close to town and gave up his job as bailiff for good, and Elisenda bought some satin pumps with high heels and many dresses of iridescent silk, the kind worn on Sunday by the most desirable women in those times. The chicken coop was the only thing that didn't receive any attention. If they washed it down with creolin and burned tears of myrrh inside it every so often, it was not in homage to the angel but to drive away the dungheap stench that still hung everywhere like a ghost and was turning the new house into an old one. At first, when the child learned to walk, they were careful that he not get too close to the chicken coop. But then they began to lose their fears and got used to the smell, and before the child got his second teeth he'd gone inside the chicken coop to play, where the wires were falling apart. The angel was no less standoffish with him than with other mortals, but he tolerated the most ingenious infamies with the patience of a dog who had no illusions. They both came down with chicken pox at the same time. The doctor who took care of the child couldn't resist the temptation to listen to the angel's heart, and he found so much whistling in the heart and so many sounds in his kidneys that it seemed impossible for him to be alive. What surprised him most, however, was the logic of his wings. They seemed so natural on that completely human organism that he couldn't understand why other men didn't have them too.

When the child began school it had been some time since the sun and rain had caused the collapse of the chicken coop. The angel went dragging himself about here and there like a stray dying man. They would drive him out of the bedroom with a broom and a moment later find him in the kitchen. He seemed to be in so many places at the same time that they grew to think that he'd been duplicated, that he was reproducing himself all through the house, and the exasperated and unhinged Elisenda shouted that it was awful living in that hell full of angels. He could scarcely eat and his antiquarian eyes had also become so foggy that he went about bumping into posts. All he had left were the bare cannulae of his last feathers. Pelayo threw a blanket over him and extended him the charity of letting him sleep in the shed, and only then did they notice that he had a temperature at night, and was delirious with the tongue twisters of an old Norwegian. That was one of the few times they became alarmed, for they thought he was going to die and not even the wise neighbor woman had been able to tell them what to do with dead angels.

And yet he not only survived his worst winter, but seemed improved with the first sunny days. He remained motionless for several days in the farthest corner of the courtyard, where no one would see him, and at the beginning of December some large, stiff feathers began to grow on his wings, the feathers of a scarecrow, which looked more like another misfortune of decrepitude. But he must have known the reason for those changes, for he was quite careful that no one should notice them, that no one should hear the sea chanteys that he sometimes sang under the stars. One morning Elisenda was cutting some bunches of onions for lunch when a wind that seemed to come from the high seas blew into the kitchen. Then she went to the window and caught the angel in his first attempts at flight. They were so clumsy that his fingernails opened a furrow in the vegetable patch and he was on the point of knocking the shed down with the ungainly flapping that slipped on the light and couldn't get a grip on the air. But he did manage to gain altitude. Elisenda let out a sigh of relief, for herself and for him, when she saw him pass over the last houses, holding himself up in some way with the risky flapping of a senile vulture. She kept watching him even when she was through cutting the onions and she kept on watching until it was no longer possible for her to see him, because then he was no longer an annoyance in her life but an imaginary dot on the horizon of the sea.

1972

The Ones Who Walk Away from Omelas

URSULA K. LE GUIN

[b. 1929]

With a clamor of bells that set the swallows soaring, the Festival of Summer came to the city Omelas, bright-towered by the sea. The rigging of the boats in harbor sparkled with flags. In the streets between houses with red roofs and painted walls, between old moss-grown gardens and under avenues of trees, past great parks and public buildings, processions moved. Some were decorous: old people in long stiff robes of mauve and gray, grave master workmen, quiet, merry women carrying their babies and chatting as they walked. In other streets the music beat faster, a shimmering of gong and tambourine, and the people went dancing, the procession was a dance. Children dodged in and out, their high calls rising like the swallows' crossing flights over the music and the singing. All the processions wound towards the north side of the city, where on the great water-meadow called the Green Fields boys and girls, naked in the bright air, with mud-stained feet and ankles and long, lithe arms, exercised their restive horses before the race. The horses wore no gear at all but a halter without bit. Their manes were braided with streamers of silver, gold, and green. They flared their nostrils and pranced and boasted to one another; they were vastly excited, the horse being the only animal who has adopted our ceremonies as his own. Far off to the north and west the mountains stood up half encircling Omelas on her bay. The air of morning was so clear that the snow still crowning the Eighteen Peaks burned with white-gold fire across the miles of sunlit air, under the dark blue of the sky. There was just enough wind to make the banners that marked the racecourse snap and flutter now and then. In the silence of the broad green meadows one could hear the music winding through the city streets, farther and nearer and ever approaching, a cheerful faint sweetness of the air that from time to time trembled and gathered together and broke out into the great joyous clanging of the bells.

Joyous! How is one to tell about joy? How describe the citizens of Omelas?

They were not simple folk, you see, though they were happy. But we do not say the words of cheer much any more. All smiles have become archaic. Given a description such as this one tends to make certain assumptions. Given a description such as this one tends to look next for the King, mounted on a splendid stallion and surrounded by his noble knights, or perhaps in a golden litter borne by great-muscled slaves. But there was no king. They did not use swords, or keep slaves. They were not barbarians. I do not know the rules and laws of their society, but I suspect that they were singularly few. As they did without monarchy and slavery, so they also got on without the stock exchange, the advertisement, the secret police, and the bomb. Yet I repeat that these were not simple folk, not dulcet shepherds, noble savages, bland utopians. They were not less complex than us. The trouble is that we have a bad habit, encouraged by pedants and sophisticates, of considering happiness as something rather stupid. Only pain is intellectual, only evil interesting. This is the treason of the artist: a refusal to admit the banality of evil and the terrible boredom of pain. If you can't lick 'em, join 'em. If it hurts, repeat it. But to praise despair is to condemn delight, to embrace violence is to lose hold of everything else. We have almost lost hold; we can no longer describe a happy man, nor make any celebration of joy. How can I tell you about the people of Omelas? They were not naïve and happy children—though their children were, in fact, happy. They were mature, intelligent, passionate adults whose lives were not wretched. O miracle! but I wish I could describe it better. I wish I could convince you. Omelas sounds in my words like a city in a fairy tale, long ago and far away, once upon a time. Perhaps it would be best if you imagined it as your own fancy bids, assuming it will rise to the occasion, for certainly I cannot suit you all. For instance, how about technology? I think that there would be no cars or helicopters in and above the streets; this follows from the fact that the people of Omelas are happy people. Happiness is based on a just discrimination of what is necessary, what is neither necessary nor destructive, and what is destructive. In the middle category, however—that of the unnecessary but undestructive, that of comfort, luxury, exuberance, etc.—they could perfectly well have central heating, subway trains, washing machines, and all kinds of marvelous devices not yet invented here, floating light-sources, fuelless power, a cure for the common cold. Or they could have none of that: it doesn't matter. As you like it. I incline to think that people from towns up and down the coast have been coming in to Omelas during the last days before the Festival on very fast little trains and double-decked trams, and that the train station of Omelas is actually the handsomest building in town, though plainer than the magnificent Farmers' Market. But even granted trains, I fear that Omelas so far strikes some of you as goody-goody. Smiles, bells, parades, horses, bleh. If so, please add an orgy. If an orgy would help, don't hesitate. Let us not, however, have temples from which issue beautiful nude priests and priestesses already half in ecstasy and ready to copulate with any man or woman, lover or stranger, who desires union with the deep godhead of the blood, although that was my first idea. But really it would be better not to have any temples in Omelas—at least, not manned temples. Religion yes, clergy no. Surely the beautiful nudes can just wander about, offering themselves like divine soufflés to the hunger of the needy and the rapture of the flesh. Let them join the processions. Let tambourines be struck above the copulations, and the glory of desire be proclaimed upon the gongs, and (a not unimportant point) let the offspring of these delightful rituals be beloved and looked after by all. One thing I know there is none of in Omelas is guilt. But what else should there be? I thought at first there were no drugs, but that is puritanical. For those who like it, the faint insistent sweetness of *drooz* may perfume the ways of the city, *drooz* which first brings a great lightness and brilliance to the mind and limbs, and then after some hours a dreamy languor, and wonderful visions at last of the very arcana and inmost secrets of the Universe, as well as exciting the pleasure of sex beyond all belief; and it is not habit-forming. For more modest tastes I think there ought to be beer. What else, what else belongs in the joyous city? The sense of victory, surely, the celebration of courage. But as we did without clergy, let us do without soldiers. The joy built upon successful slaughter is not the right kind of joy; it will not do; it is fearful and it is trivial. A boundless and generous contentment, a magnanimous triumph felt not against some outer enemy but in communion with the finest and fairest in the souls of all men everywhere and the splendor of the world's summer: this is what swells the hearts of the people of Omelas, and the victory they celebrate is that of life. I really don't think many of them need to take *drooz.*

Most of the processions have reached the Green Fields by now. A marvelous smell of cooking goes forth from the red and blue tents of the provisioners. The faces of small children are amiably sticky; in the benign gray beard of a man a couple of crumbs of rich pastry are entangled. The youths and girls have mounted their horses and are beginning to group around the starting line of the course. An old woman, small, fat, and laughing, is passing out flowers from a basket, and tall young men wear her flowers in their shining hair. A child of nine or ten sits at the edge of the crowd, alone, playing on a wooden flute. People pause to listen, and they smile, but they do not speak to him, for he never ceases playing and never sees them, his dark eyes wholly rapt in the sweet, thin magic of the tune.

He finishes, and slowly lowers his hands holding the wooden flute.

As if that little private silence were the signal, all at once a trumpet sounds from the pavilion near the starting line: imperious, melancholy, piercing. The horses rear on their slender legs, and some of them neigh in answer. Sober-faced, the young riders stroke the horses' necks and soothe them, whispering, "Quiet, quiet, there my beauty, my hope. . . ." They begin to form in rank along the starting line. The crowds along the racecourse are like a field of grass and flowers in the wind. The Festival of Summer has begun.

Do you believe? Do you accept the festival, the city, the joy? No? Then let me describe one more thing.

In a basement under one of the beautiful public buildings of Omelas, or perhaps in the cellar of one of its spacious private homes, there is a room. It has one locked door, and no window. A little light seeps in dustily between cracks in the boards, secondhand from a cobwebbed window somewhere across the cellar. In one corner of the little room a couple of mops, with stiff, clotted, foul-smelling heads, stand near a rusty bucket. The floor is dirt, a little damp to the touch, as cellar dirt usually is. The room is about three paces long and two wide: a mere broom closet or disused tool room. In the room a child is sitting. It could be a boy or a girl. It looks about six, but actually is nearly ten. It is feeble-minded. Perhaps it was born defective, or perhaps it has become imbecile through fear, malnutrition, and neglect. It picks its nose and occasionally fumbles vaguely with its toes or genitals, as it sits hunched in the corner farthest from the bucket and the two mops. It is afraid of the mops. It finds them horrible. It shuts its eyes, but it knows the mops are still standing there; and the door is locked; and nobody will come. The door is always locked; and nobody ever comes, except that sometimes—the child has no understanding of time or interval—sometimes the door rattles terribly and opens, and a person, or several people, are there. One of them may come in and kick the child to make it stand up. The others never come close, but peer in at it with frightened, disgusted eyes. The food bowl and the water jug are hastily filled, the door is locked, the eyes disappear. The people at the door never say anything, but the child, who has not always lived in the tool room, and can remember sunlight and its mother's voice, sometimes speaks. "I will be good," it says. "Please let me out. I will be good!" They never answer. The child used to scream for help at night, and cry a good deal, but now it only makes a kind of whining, "eh-haa, eh-haa," and it speaks less and less often. It is so thin there are no calves to its legs; its belly protrudes; it lives on a half-bowl of corn meal and grease a day. It is naked. Its buttocks and thighs are a mass of festered sores, as it sits in its own excrement continually.

They all know it is there, all the people of Omelas. Some of them have come to see it, others are content merely to know it is there. They all know that it has to be there. Some of them understand why, and some do not, but they all understand that their happiness, the beauty of their city, the tenderness of their friendships, the health of their children, the wisdom of their scholars, the skill of their makers, even the abundance of their harvest and the kindly weathers of their skies, depend wholly on this child's abominable misery.

This is usually explained to children when they are between eight and twelve, whenever they seem capable of understanding; and most of those who come to see the child are young people, though often enough an adult comes, or comes back, to see the child. No matter how well the matter has been explained to them, these young spectators are always shocked and sickened at the sight. They feel disgust, which they had thought themselves superior to. They feel anger, outrage, impotence, despite all the explanations. They would like to do something for the child. But there is nothing they can do. If the child were brought up into the sunlight out of that vile place, if it were cleaned and fed and comforted, that would be a good thing, indeed; but if it were done, in that day and hour all the prosperity and beauty and delight of Omelas would wither and be destroyed. Those are the terms. To exchange all the goodness and grace of every life in Omelas for that single, small improvement: to throw away the happiness of thousands for the chance of the happiness of one: that would be to let guilt within the walls indeed.

The terms are strict and absolute; there may not even be a kind word spoken to the child.

Often the young people go home in tears, or in a tearless rage, when they have seen the child and faced this terrible paradox. They may brood over it for weeks or years. But as time goes on they begin to realize that even if the child could be released, it would not get much good of its freedom: a little vague pleasure of warmth and food, no doubt, but little more. It is too degraded and imbecile to know any real joy. It has been afraid too long ever to be free of fear. Its habits are too uncouth for it to respond to humane treatment. Indeed, after so long it would probably be wretched without walls about it to protect it, and darkness for its eyes, and its own excrement to sit in. Their tears at the bitter injustice dry when they begin to perceive the terrible justice of reality, and to accept it. Yet it is their tears and anger, the trying of their generosity and the acceptance of their helplessness, which are perhaps the true source of the splendor of their lives. Theirs is no vapid, irresponsible happiness. They know that they, like the child, are not free. They know compassion. It is the existence of the child, and their knowledge of its existence, that makes possible the nobility of their architecture, the poignancy of their music, the profundity of their science. It is because of the child that they are so gentle with children. They know that if the wretched one were not there sniveling in the dark, the other one, the flute-player, could make no joyful music as the young riders line up in their beauty for the race in the sunlight of the first morning of summer.

Now do you believe in them? Are they not more credible? But there is one more thing to tell, and this is quite incredible.

At times one of the adolescent girls or boys who go to see the child does not go home to weep or rage, does not, in fact, go home at all. Sometimes also a man or woman much older falls silent for a day or two, and then leaves home. These people go out into the street, and walk down the street alone. They keep walking, and walk straight out of the city of Omelas, through the beautiful gates. They keep walking across the farmlands of Omelas. Each one goes alone, youth or girl, man or woman. Night falls; the traveler must pass down village streets, between the houses with yellow-lit windows, and on out into the darkness of the fields. Each alone, they go west or north, towards the mountains. They go on. They leave Omelas, they walk ahead into the darkness, and they do not come back. The place they go towards is a place even less imaginable to most of us than the city of happiness. I cannot describe it at all. It is possible that it does not exist. But they seem to know where they are going, the ones who walk away from Omelas.

1975

Lost in the Funhouse

JOHN BARTH

[b. 1930]

For whom is the funhouse fun? Perhaps for lovers. For Ambrose it is *a place of fear and confusion.* He has come to the seashore with his family for the holiday, *the occasion of their visit is Independence Day, the most important secular holiday of the United States of America.* A single straight underline is the manuscript mark for italic type, *which in turn* is the printed equivalent to oral emphasis of words and phrases as well as the customary type for titles of complete works, not to mention. Italics are also employed, in fiction stories especially, for "outside," intrusive, or artificial voices, such as radio announcements, the texts of telegrams and newspaper articles, et cetera. They should be used *sparingly.* If passages originally in roman type are italicized by someone repeating them, it's customary to acknowledge the fact. *Italics mine.*

Ambrose was "at that awkward age." His voice came out high-pitched as a child's if he let himself get carried away; to be on the safe side, therefore, he moved and spoke with *deliberate calm* and *adult gravity.* Talking soberly of unimportant or irrelevant matters and listening consciously to the sound of your own voice are useful habits for maintaining control in this difficult interval. *En route* to Ocean City he sat in the back seat of the family car with his brother Peter, age fifteen, and Magda G——, age fourteen, a pretty girl an exquisite young lady, who lived not far from them on B—— Street in the town of D——, Maryland. Initials, blanks, or both were often substituted for proper names in nineteenth-century fiction to enhance the illusion of reality. It is as if the author felt it necessary to delete the names for reasons of tact or legal liability. Interestingly, as with other aspects of realism, it is an *illusion* that is being enhanced, by purely artificial means. Is it likely, does it violate the principle of verisimilitude, that a thirteen-year-old boy could make such a sophisticated observation? A girl of fourteen is *the psychological coeval* of a boy of fifteen or sixteen; a thirteen-year-old boy, therefore, even one precocious in some other respects, might be three years *her emotional junior.*

Thrice a year—on Memorial, Independence, and Labor Days—the family visits Ocean City for the afternoon and evening. When Ambrose and Peter's father was their age, the excursion was made by train, as mentioned in the novel *The 42nd Parallel* by John Dos Passos. Many families from the same neighborhood used to travel together, with dependent relatives and often with Negro servants; schoolfuls of children swarmed through the railway cars; everyone shared everyone else's Maryland fried chicken, Virginia ham, deviled eggs, potato salad, beaten biscuits, iced tea. Nowadays (that is, in 19—, the year of our story) the journey is made by automobile—more comfortably and quickly though without the extra fun though without the *camaraderie* of a general excursion. It's all part of the deterioration of American life, their father declares. Uncle Karl supposes that when the boys take *their* families to Ocean City for the holidays they'll fly in Autogiros. Their mother, sitting in the middle of the front seat like Magda in the second, only with her arms on the seat-back behind the men's shoulders, wouldn't want the good old days back again, the steaming trains and stuffy long dresses; on the other hand she can do without Autogiros, too, if she has to become a grandmother to fly in them.

Description of physical appearance and mannerisms is one of several standard methods of characterization used by writers of fiction. It is also important to "keep the senses operating"; when a detail from one of the five senses, say visual, is "crossed" with a detail from another, say auditory, the reader's imagination is oriented to the scene, perhaps unconsciously. This procedure may be compared to the way surveyors and navigators determine their positions by two or more compass bearings, a process known as triangulation. The brown hair on Ambrose's mother's forearms gleamed in the sun like. Though right-handed, she took her left arm from the seat-back to press the dashboard cigar lighter for Uncle Karl. When the glass bead in its handle glowed red, the lighter was ready for use. The smell of Uncle Karl's cigar smoke reminded one of. The fragrance of the ocean came strong to the picnic ground where they always stopped for lunch, two miles inland from Ocean City. Having to pause for a full hour almost within sound of the breakers was difficult for Peter and Ambrose when they were younger; even at their present age it was not easy to keep their anticipation, *stimulated by the briny spume,* from turning into short temper. The Irish author James Joyce, in his unusual novel entitled *Ulysses,* now available in this country, uses the adjectives *snot-green* and *scrotum-tightening* to describe the sea. Visual, auditory, tactile, olfactory, gustatory. Peter and Ambrose's father, while steering their black 1936 LaSalle sedan with one hand, could with the other remove the first cigarette from a white pack of Lucky Strikes and, more remarkably, light it with a match forefingered from its book and thumbed against the flint paper without being detached. The matchbook cover merely advertised U. S. War Bonds and Stamps. A fine metaphor, simile, or other figure of speech, in addition to its obvious "first-order" relevance to the thing it describes, will be seen upon reflection to have a second order of significance: it may be drawn from the *milieu* of the action, for example, or be particularly appropriate to the sensibility of the narrator, even hinting to the reader things of which the narrator is unaware; or it may cast further and subtler lights upon the thing it describes, sometimes ironically qualifying the more evident sense of the comparison.

To say that Ambrose's and Peter's mother was *pretty* is to accomplish nothing; the reader may acknowledge the proposition, but his imagination is not engaged. Besides, Magda was also pretty, yet in an altogether different way. Although she lived on B—— Street she had very good manners and did better than average in school. Her figure was very well developed for her age. Her right hand lay casually on the plush upholstery of the seat, very near Ambrose's left leg, on which his own hand rested. The space between their legs, between her right and his left leg, was out of the line of sight of anyone sitting on the other side of Magda, as well as anyone glancing into the rearview mirror. Uncle Karl's face resembled Peter's—rather, vice versa. Both had dark hair and eyes, short husky statures, deep voices. Magda's left hand was probably in a similar position on her left side. The boys' father is difficult to describe;

no particular feature of his appearance or manner stood out. He wore glasses and was principal of a T—— County grade school. Uncle Karl was a masonry contractor.

Although Peter must have known as well as Ambrose that the latter, because of his position in the car, would be the first to see the electrical towers of the power plant at V——, the halfway point of their trip, he leaned forward and slightly toward the center of the car and pretended to be looking for them through the flat pinewoods and tuckahoe creeks along the highway. For as long as the boys could remember, "looking for the Towers" had been a feature of the first half of their excursions to Ocean City, "looking for the standpipe" of the second. Though the game was childish, their mother preserved the tradition of rewarding the first to see the Towers with a candy-bar or piece of fruit. She insisted now that Magda play the game; the prize, she said, was "something hard to get nowadays." Ambrose decided not to join in; he sat far back in his seat. Magda, like Peter, leaned forward. Two sets of straps were discernible through the shoulders of her sun dress; the inside right one, a brassiere-strap, was fastened or shortened with a small safety pin. The right armpit of her dress, presumably the left as well, was damp with perspiration. The simple strategy for being first to espy the Towers, which Ambrose had understood by the age of four, was to sit on the right-hand side of the car. Whoever sat there, however, had also to put up with the worst of the sun, and so Ambrose, without mentioning the matter, chose sometimes the one and sometimes the other. Not impossibly Peter had never caught on to the trick, or thought that his brother hadn't simply because Ambrose on occasion preferred shade to a Baby Ruth or tangerine.

The shade-sun situation didn't apply to the front seat, owing to the windshield; if anything the driver got more sun, since the person on the passenger side not only was shaded below by the door and dashboard but might swing down his sunvisor all the way too.

"Is that them?" Magda asked. Ambrose's mother teased the boys for letting Magda win, insinuating that "somebody [had] a girlfriend." Peter and Ambrose's father reached a long thin arm across their mother to butt his cigarette in the dashboard ashtray, under the lighter. The prize this time for seeing the Towers first was a banana. Their mother bestowed it after chiding their father for wasting a half-smoked cigarette when everything was so scarce. Magda, to take the prize, moved her hand from so near Ambrose's that he could have touched it as though accidentally. She offered to share the prize, things like that were so hard to find; but everyone insisted it was hers alone. Ambrose's mother sang an iambic trimeter couplet from a popular song, femininely rhymed:

"What's good is in the Army;
What's left will never harm me."

Uncle Karl tapped his cigar ash out the ventilator window; some particles were sucked by the slipstream back into the car through the rear window on the passenger side. Magda demonstrated her ability to hold a banana in one hand and peel it with her teeth. She still sat forward; Ambrose pushed his glasses back onto the bridge of his nose with his left hand, which he then negligently let fall to the seat cushion immediately behind her. He even permitted the single hair, gold, on the second joint of his thumb to brush the fabric of her skirt. Should she have sat back at that instant, his hand would have been caught under her.

Plush upholstery prickles uncomfortably through gabardine slacks in the July sun. The function of the *beginning* of a story is to introduce the principal characters, establish their initial relationships, set the scene for the main action, expose the background of the situation if necessary, plant motifs and foreshadowings where appropriate, and initiate the first complication or whatever of the "rising action." Actually, if one imagines a story called "The Funhouse," or "Lost in the Funhouse," the details of the drive to Ocean City don't seem especially relevant. The *beginning* should recount the events between Ambrose's first sight of the funhouse early in the afternoon and his entering it with Magda and Peter in the evening. The *middle* would narrate all relevant events from the time he goes in to the time he loses his way; middles have the double and contradictory function of delaying the climax while at the same time preparing the reader for it and fetching him to it. Then the *ending* would tell what Ambrose does while he's lost, how he finally finds his way out, and what everybody makes of the experience. So far there's been no real dialogue, very little sensory detail, and nothing in the way of a *theme.* And a long time has gone by already without anything happening; it makes a person wonder. We haven't even reached Ocean City yet: we will never get out of the funhouse.

The more closely an author identifies with the narrator, literally or metaphorically, the less advisable it is, as a rule, to use the first-person narrative viewpoint. Once three years previously the young people *aforementioned* played Niggers and Masters in the backyard; when it was Ambrose's turn to be Master and theirs to be Niggers Peter had to go serve his evening papers; Ambrose was afraid to punish Magda alone, but she led him to the whitewashed Torture Chamber between the woodshed and the privy in the Slaves Quarters; there she knelt sweating among bamboo rakes and dusty Mason jars, pleadingly embraced his knees, and while bees droned in the lattice as if on an ordinary summer afternoon, purchased clemency at a surprising price set by herself. Doubtless she remembered nothing of this event; Ambrose on the other hand seemed unable to forget the least detail of his life. He even recalled how, standing beside himself with awed impersonality in the reeky heat, he'd stared the while at an empty cigar box in which Uncle Karl kept stone-cutting chisels: beneath the words *El Producto,* a laureled, loose-toga'd lady regarded the sea from a marble bench; beside her, forgotten or not yet turned to, was a five-stringed lyre. Her shin reposed on the back of her right hand; her left depended negligently from the bencharm. The lower half of scene and lady was peeled away; the words EXAMINED BY—— were inked there into the wood. Nowadays cigar boxes are made of pasteboard. Ambrose wondered what Magda would have done, Ambrose wondered what Magda would do when she sat back on his hand as he resolved she should. Be angry. Make a teasing joke of it. Give no sign at all. For a long time she leaned forward, playing cowpoker with Peter against Uncle Karl and Mother and watching for the first sign of Ocean City. At nearly the same instant, picnic ground and Ocean City standpipe hove into view; an Amoco filling station on their side of the road cost Mother and Uncle Karl fifty cows and the game; Magda bounced back, clapping her right hand on Mother's right arm; Ambrose moved clear "in the nick of time."

At this rate our hero, at this rate our protagonist will remain in the funhouse forever. Narrative ordinarily consists of alternating dramatization and summarization. One symptom of nervous tension, paradoxically, is repeated and violent yawning; neither Peter ıor Magda nor Uncle Karl nor Mother reacted in this manner. Although they were no longer small children, Peter and Ambrose were each given a dollar to spend on boardwalk amusements in addition o what money of their own they'd brought along. Magda too, hough she protested she had ample spending money. The boys' nother made a little scene out of distributing the bills; she pre-ended that her sons and Magda were small children and cautioned hem not to spend the sum too quickly or in one place. Magda promised with a merry laugh and, having both hands free, took the bill with her left. Peter laughed also and pledged in a falsetto to be a good boy. His imitation of a child was not clever. The boys' father was tall and thin, balding, fair-complexioned. Assertions of that sort are not effective; the reader may acknowledge the proposition, but. We should be much farther along than we are; something has gone wrong; not much of this preliminary rambling seems relevant. Yet everyone begins in the same place; how is it that most go along without difficulty but a few lose their way?

"Stay out from under the boardwalk," Uncle Karl growled from the side of his mouth. The boys' mother pushed his shoulder *in mock annoyance.* They were all standing before Fat May the Laughing Lady who advertised the funhouse. Larger than life, Fat May mechanically shook, rocked on her heels, slapped her thighs while recorded laughter—uproarious, female—came amplified from a hidden loudspeaker. It chuckled, wheezed, wept; tried in vain to catch its breath; tittered, groaned, exploded raucous and anew. You couldn't hear it without laughing yourself, no matter how you felt. Father came back from talking to a Coast-Guardsman on duty and reported that the surf was spoiled with crude oil from tankers recently torpedoed offshore. Lumps of it, difficult to remove, made tarry tidelines on the beach and stuck on swimmers. Many bathed in the surf nevertheless and came out speckled; others paid to use a municipal pool and only sunbathed on the beach. We would do the latter. We would do the latter. We would do the latter.

Under the boardwalk, matchbook covers, grainy other things. What is the story's theme? Ambrose is ill. He perspires in the dark passages; candied apples-on-a-stick, delicious-looking, disappointing to eat. Funhouses need men's and ladies' rooms at intervals. Others perhaps have also vomited in corners and corridors; may even have had bowel movements liable to be stepped in in the dark.

The word *fuck* suggests suction and/or and/or flatulence. Mothe and Father; grandmothers and grandfathers on both side great-grandmothers and great-grandfathers on four sides, et ceter Count a generation as thirty years: in approximately the year whe Lord Baltimore was granted charter to the province of Marylan by Charles I, five hundred twelve women—English, Welsh, Bavari an, Swiss—of every class and character, received into themselve the penises the intromittent organs of five hundred twelve me ditto, in every circumstance and posture, to conceive the five hun dred twelve ancestors of the two hundred fifty-six ancestors of th et cetera et cetera et cetera et cetera et cetera et cetera et cetera e cetera of the author, of the narrator, of this story, *Lost in the Funhous* In alleyways, ditches, canopy beds, pinewoods, bridal suites, ship cabins, coach-and-fours, coaches-and-four, sultry toolsheds; on th cold sand under boardwalks, littered with *El Producto* cigar butt treasured with Lucky Strike cigarette stubs, Coca-Cola caps, gritt turds, cardboard lollipop sticks, matchbook covers warning that Slip of the Lip Can Sink a Ship. The shluppish whisper, continuou as seawash round the globe, tidelike falls and rises with the circu of dawn and dusk.

Magda's teeth. She *was* left-handed. Perspiration. They've gon all the way, through, Magda and Peter, they've been waiting fo hours with Mother and Uncle Karl while Father searches for his lo son; they draw french-fried potatoes from a paper cup and shak their heads. They've named the children they'll one day have an bring to Ocean City on holidays. Can spermatozoa properly b thought of as male animalcules when there are no female spermato zoa? They grope through hot, dark windings, past Love's Tunnel fearsome obstacles. Some perhaps lose their way.

Peter suggested then and there that they do the funhouse; he ha been through it before, so had Magda, Ambrose hadn't and sugges ed, his voice cracking on account of Fat May's laughter, that the swim first. All were chuckling, couldn't help it; Ambrose's fathe Ambrose's and Peter's father came up grinning like a lunatic wit two boxes of syrup-coated popcorn, one for Mother, one fo Magda; the men were to help themselves. Ambrose walked o Magda's right; being by nature lefthanded, she carried the box i her left hand. Up front the situation was reversed.

"What are you limping for?" Magda inquired of Ambrose. H

upposed in a husky tone that his foot had gone to sleep in the car. Her teeth flashed. "Pins and needles?" It was the honeysuckle on he lattice of the former privy that drew the bees. Imagine being tung there. How long is this going to take?

The adults decided to forgo the pool; but Uncle Karl insisted they hange into swimsuits and do the beach. "He wants to watch the retty girls," Peter teased, and ducked behind Magda from Uncle .arl's pretended wrath. "You've got all the pretty girls you need ght here," Magda declared, and Mother said: "Now that's the gos-el truth." Magda scolded Peter, who reached over her shoulder to neak some popcorn. "Your brother and father aren't getting any." Jncle Karl wondered if they were going to have fireworks that ight, what with the shortages. It wasn't the shortages, Mr. M—— eplied; Ocean City had fireworks from prewar. But it was too risky n account of the enemy submarines, some people thought.

"Don't seem like Fourth of July without fireworks," said Uncle .arl. The inverted tag in dialogue writing is still considered permis-ble with proper names or epithets, but sounds old-fashioned with ersonal pronouns. "We'll have 'em again soon enough," predicted e boys' father. Their mother declared she could do without fire-orks: they reminded her too much of the real thing. Their father id all the more reason to shoot off a few now and again. Uncle .arl asked *rhetorically* who needed reminding, just look at people's air and skin.

"The oil, yes," said Mrs. M——.

Ambrose had a pain in his stomach and so didn't swim but en-yed watching the others. He and his father burned red easily. Magda's figure was exceedingly well developed for her age. She too eclined to swim, and got mad, and became angry when Peter at-empted to drag her into the pool. She always swam, he insisted; hat did she mean not swim? Why did a person come to Ocean ity?

"Maybe I want to lay here with Ambrose," Magda teased.

Nobody likes a pedant.

"Aha," said Mother. Peter grabbed Magda by one ankle and or-ered Ambrose to grab the other. She squealed and rolled over on e beach blanket. Ambrose pretended to help hold her back. Her n was darker than even Mother's and Peter's. "Help out, Uncle arl!" Peter cried. Uncle Karl went to seize the other ankle. Inside the top of her swimsuit, however, you could see the line where th sunburn ended and, when she hunched her shoulders and squeale again, one nipple's auburn edge. Mother made them behave them selves. "*You* should certainly know," she said to Uncle Karl. Archly "That when a lady says she doesn't feel like swimming, a gentlema doesn't ask questions." Uncle Karl said excuse *him;* Mother winke at Magda; Ambrose blushed; stupid Peter kept saying "Phooey o *feel like!*" and tugging at Magda's ankle; then even he got the poin and cannonballed with a holler into the pool.

"I swear," Magda said, in mock *in feigned* exasperation.

The diving would make a suitable literary symbol. To go off th high board you had to wait in a line along the poolside and up th ladder. Fellows tickled girls and goosed one another and shoute to the ones at the top to hurry up, or razzed them for bellyflopper Once on the springboard some took a great while posing or clown ing or deciding on a dive or getting up their nerve; others ran righ off. Especially among the younger fellows the idea was to strike th funniest pose or do the craziest stunt as you fell, a thing that go harder to do as you kept on and kept on. But whether you hollere *Geronimo!* or *Sieg heil!,* held your nose or "rode a bicycle," pretende to be shot or did a perfect jackknife or changed your mind halfwa down and ended up with nothing, it was over in two seconds, afte all that wait. Spring, pose, splash. Spring, neat-o, splash. Sprin aw fooey, splash.

The grown-ups had gone on; Ambrose wanted to converse wit Magda; she was remarkably well developed for her age; it was sa that that came from rubbing with a turkish towel, and there we other theories. Ambrose could think of nothing to say except ho good a diver Peter was, who was showing off for her benefit. Yo could pretty well tell by looking at their bathing suits and arm mus cles how far along the different fellows were. Ambrose was gla he hadn't gone in swimming, the cold water shrank you up s Magda pretended to be uninterested in the diving; she probabl weighed as much as he did. If you knew your way around in th funhouse like your own bedroom, you could wait until a girl cam along and then slip away without ever getting caught, even if he boyfriend was right with her. She'd think *he* did it! It would be be ter to be the boyfriend, and act outraged, and tear the funhous apart.

Not act; *be.*

"He's a master diver," Ambrose said. In feigned admiration. "You really have to slave away at it to get that good." What would it matter anyhow if he asked her right out whether she remembered, even teased her with it as Peter would have?

There's no point in going farther; this isn't getting anybody anywhere; they haven't even come to the funhouse yet. Ambrose is off the track, in some new or old part of the place that's not supposed to be used; he strayed into it by some one-in-a-million chance, like the time the roller-coaster car left the tracks in the nineteen-teens against all the laws of physics and sailed over the boardwalk in the dark. And they can't locate him because they don't know where to look. Even the designer and operator have forgotten this other part, that winds around on itself like a whelk shell. That winds around the right part like the snakes on Mercury's caduceus. Some people, perhaps, don't "hit their stride" until their twenties, when the growing-up business is over and women appreciate other things besides wisecracks and teasing and strutting. Peter didn't have one-tenth the imagination *he* had, not one-tenth. Peter did this naming-their-children thing as a joke, making up names like Aloysius and Murgatroyd, but Ambrose knew *exactly* how it would feel to be married and have children of your own, and be a loving husband and father, and go comfortably to work in the mornings and to bed with your wife at night, and wake up with her there. With a breeze coming through the sash and birds and mockingbirds singing in the Chinese-cigar trees. His eyes watered, there aren't enough ways to say that. He would be quite famous in his line of work. Whether Magda was his wife or not, one evening when he was wise-lined and gray at the temples he'd smile gravely, at a fashionable dinner party, and remind her of his youthful passion. The time they went with his family to Ocean City; the *erotic fantasies* he used to have about her. How long ago it seemed, and childish! Yet tender, too, *n'est-ce pas?* Would she have imagined that the world-famous whatever remembered how many strings were on the lyre on the bench beside the girl on the label of the cigar box he'd stared at in the toolshed at age ten while she, age eleven. Even then he had felt *wise beyond his years;* he'd stroked her hair and said in his deepest voice and correctest English, as to a dear child: "I shall never forget this moment."

But though he had breathed heavily, groaned as if ecstatic, what he'd really felt throughout was an odd detachment, as though someone else were Master. Strive as he might to be transported, he heard his mind take notes upon the scene: *This is what they call* passion. *I am experiencing it.* Many of the bigger machines were out of order in the penny arcades and could not be repaired or replaced for the duration. Moreover the prizes, made now in USA, were less interesting than formerly, pasteboard items for the most part, and some of the machines wouldn't work on white pennies. The gypsy fortune-teller machine might have provided a foreshadowing of the climax of this story if Ambrose had operated it. It was even dilapidateder than most: the silver coating was worn off the brown metal handles, the glass windows around the dummy were cracked and taped, her kerchiefs and silks long-faded. If a man lived by himself, he could take a department-store mannequin with flexible joints and modify her in certain ways. *However:* by the time he was that old he'd have a real woman. There was a machine that stamped your name around a white-metal coin with a star in the middle: *A*——. His son would be the second, and when the lad reached thirteen or so he would put a strong arm around his shoulder and tell him calmly: "It is perfectly normal. We have all been through it. It will not last forever." Nobody knew how to be what they were right. He'd smoke a pipe, teach his son how to fish and softcrab, assure him he needn't worry about himself. Magda would certainly give, Magda would certainly yield a great deal of milk, although guilty of occasional solecisms. It don't taste so bad. Suppose the lights came on now!

The day wore on. You think you're yourself, but there are other persons in you. Ambrose gets hard when Ambrose doesn't want to, *and obversely.* Ambrose watches them disagree; Ambrose watches him watch. In the funhouse mirror-room you can't see yourself go on forever, because no matter how you stand, your head gets in the way. Even if you had a glass periscope, the image of your eye would cover up the thing you really wanted to see. The police will come; there'll be a story in the papers. That must be where it happened. Unless he can find a surprise exit, an unofficial backdoor or escape hatch opening on an alley, say, and then stroll up to the family in front of the funhouse and ask where everybody's been; *he's* been out of the place for ages. That's just where it happened, in that last lighted room: Peter and Magda found the right exit; he found one that you weren't supposed to find and strayed off into the works somewhere. In a perfect funhouse you'd be able to go only one way, like the divers off the highboard; getting lost would be impossible; the doors and halls would work like minnow traps or the valves in veins.

On account of German U-boats, Ocean City was "browned out": streetlights were shaded on the seaward side; shop-windows and boardwalk amusement places were kept dim, not to silhouette tankers and Liberty-ships for torpedoing. In a short story about Ocean City, Maryland, during World War II, the author could make use of the image of sailors on leave in the penny arcades and shooting galleries, sighting through the crosshairs of toy machine guns at swastika'd subs, while out in the black Atlantic a U-boat skipper squints through his periscope at real ships outlined by the glow of penny arcades. After dinner the family strolled back to the amusement end of the boardwalk. The boys' father had burnt red as always and was masked with Noxzema, a minstrel in reverse. The grownups stood at the end of the boardwalk where the Hurricane of '33 had cut an inlet from the ocean to Assawoman Bay.

"Pronounced with a long *o,*" Uncle Karl reminded Magda with a wink. His shirt sleeves were rolled up; Mother punched his brown biceps with the arrowed heart on it and said his mind was naughty. Fat May's laugh came suddenly from the funhouse, as if she'd just got the joke; the family laughed too at the coincidence. Ambrose went under the boardwalk to search for out-of-town matchbook covers with the aid of his pocket flashlight; he looked out from the edge of the North American continent and wondered how far their laughter carried over the water. Spies in rubber rafts; survivors in lifeboats. If the joke had been beyond his understanding, he could have said: *"The laughter was over his head."* And let the reader see the serious wordplay on second reading.

He turned the flashlight on and then off at once even before the woman whooped. He sprang away, heart athud, dropping the light. What had the man grunted? Perspiration drenched and chilled him by the time he scrambled up to the family. "See anything?" his father asked. His voice wouldn't come; he shrugged and violently brushed sand from his pants legs.

"Let's ride the old flying horses!" Magda cried. I'll never be an author. It's been forever already, everybody's gone home, Ocean City's deserted, the ghost-crabs are tickling across the beach and down the littered cold streets. And the empty halls of clapboard hotels and abandoned funhouses. A tidal wave; an enemy air raid; a monster-crab swelling like an island from the sea. *The inhabitants fled in terror.* Magda clung to his trouser leg; he alone knew the maze's secret. "He gave his life that we might live," said Uncle Karl with a scowl of pain, as he. The fellow's hands had been tattooed; the woman's legs, the woman's fat white legs had. *An astonishing coincidence.* He yearned to tell Peter. He wanted to throw up for excitement. They hadn't even chased him. He wished he were dead.

One possible ending would be to have Ambrose come across another lost person in the dark. They'd match their wits together against the funhouse, struggle like Ulysses past obstacle after obstacle, help and encourage each other. Or a girl. By the time they found the exit they'd be closest friends, sweethearts if it were a girl; they'd know each other's inmost souls, be bound together *by the cement of shared adventure;* then they'd emerge into the light and it would turn out that his friend was a Negro. A blind girl. President Roosevelt's son. Ambrose's former archenemy.

Shortly after the mirror room he'd groped along a musty corridor, his heart already misgiving him at the absence of phosphorescent arrows and other signs. He'd found a crack of light—not a door, it turned out, but a seam between the plyboard wall panels—and squinting up to it, espied a small old man, *in appearance not unlike* the photographs at home of Ambrose's late grandfather, nodding upon a stool beneath a bare, speckled bulb. A crude panel of toggle- and knife-switches hung beside the open fuse box near his head; elsewhere in the little room were wooden levers and ropes belayed to boat cleats. At the time, Ambrose wasn't lost enough to rap or call; later he couldn't find that crack. Now it seemed to him that he'd possibly dozed off for a few minutes somewhere along the way; certainly he was exhausted from the afternoon's sunshine and the evening's problems; he couldn't be sure he hadn't dreamed part or all of the sight. Had an old black wall fan droned like bees and shimmied two flypaper streamers? Had the funhouse operator—gentle, somewhat sad and tired-appearing, in expression not unlike the photographs at home of Ambrose's late Uncle Konrad—murmured

his sleep? Is there really such a person as Ambrose, or is he a fig-
ent of the author's imagination? Was it Assawoman Bay or
nepuxent? Are there other errors of fact in this fiction? Was there
other sound besides the little slap slap of thigh on ham, like water
cking at the chine-boards of a skiff?

When you're lost, the smartest thing to do is stay put till you're
und, hollering if necessary. But to holler guarantees humiliation
well as rescue; keeping silent permits some saving of face—you
n act surprised at the fuss when your rescuers find you and swear
u weren't lost, if they do. What's more you might find your own
ay yet, *however belatedly.*

"Don't tell me your foot's still asleep!" Magda exclaimed as the
ree young people walked from the inlet to the area set aside for
ris wheels, carrousels, and other carnival rides, they having de-
led in favor of the vast and ancient merry-go-round instead of
e funhouse. What a sentence, everything was wrong from the
tset. People don't know what to make of him, he doesn't know
at to make of himself, he's only thirteen, *athletically and socially*
vt, not astonishingly bright, but there are antennae; he has . . .
me sort of receivers in his head; things speak to him, he under-
nds more than he should, the world winks at him through its
jects, grabs grinning at his coat. Everybody else is in on some se-
t he doesn't know; they've forgotten to tell him. Through simple
crastination his mother put off his baptism until this year. Every-
e else had it done as a baby; he'd assumed the same of himself,
had his mother, so she claimed, until it was time for him to join
ace Methodist-Protestant and the oversight came out. He was
rtified, but pitched sleepless through his private catechizing, in-
idated by the ancient mysteries, a thirteen year old would never
that, resolved to experience conversion like St. Augustine.
hen the water touched his brow and Adam's sin left him, he con-
ved by a strain like defecation to bring tears into his eyes—but
t nothing. There was some simple, radical difference about him;
hoped it was genius, feared it was madness, devoted himself to
iability and inconspicuousness. Alone on the seawall near his
use he was seized by the terrifying transports he'd thought to
d in toolshed, in Communion-cup. The grass was alive! The
vn, the river, himself, were not imaginary; time roared in his ears

like wind; the world was *going on!* This part ought to be dramatize The Irish author James Joyce once wrote. Ambrose M—— is goir to scream.

There is no *texture of rendered sensory detail,* for one thing. The fade distorting mirrors beside Fat May; the impossibility of choosing mount when one had but a single ride on the great carrousel; tl *vertigo attendant on his recognition* that Ocean City was worn out, tl place of fathers and grandfathers, straw-boatered men and par soled ladies survived by their amusements. Money spent, the thr paused at Peter's insistence beside Fat May to watch the girls g their skirts blown up. The object was to tease Magda, who said: swear, Peter M——, you've got a one-track mind! Amby and n aren't *interested* in such things." In the tumbling-barrel, too, just i side the Devil's-mouth entrance to the funhouse, the girls were u ended and their boyfriends and others could see up their dress if they cared to. Which was the whole point, Ambrose realized. C the entire funhouse! If you looked around, you noticed that almo all the people on the boardwalk were paired off into couples exce the small children; in a way, that was the whole point of Oce City! If you had X-ray eyes and could see everything going on that instant under the boardwalk and in all the hotel rooms and ca and alley-ways, you'd realize that all that normally *showed,* like re taurants and dance halls and clothing and test-your-strength m chines, was merely preparation and intermission. Fat May screame

Because he watched the goings-on from the corner of his eye, was Ambrose who spied the half-dollar on the boardwalk near tl tumbling-barrel. Losers weepers. The first time he'd heard son people moving through a corridor not far away, just after he'd lo sight of the crack of light, he'd decided not to call to them, for fe they'd guess he was scared and poke fun; it sounded like roug necks; he'd hoped they'd come by and he could follow in the da without their knowing. Another time he'd heard just one perso unless he imagined it, bumping along as if on the other side of t plywood; perhaps Peter coming back for him, or Father, or Mag lost too. Or the owner and operator of the funhouse. He'd call out once, as though merrily: "Anybody know where the heck v are?" But the query was too stiff, his voice cracked, when tl sounds stopped he was terrified: maybe it was a queer who wait for fellows to get lost, or a longhaired filthy monster that lived

ome cranny of the funhouse. He stood rigid for hours it seemed
ke, scarcely respiring. His future was shockingly clear, in outline.
e tried holding his breath to the point of unconsciousness. There
ught to be a button you could push to end your life absolutely
ithout pain; disappear in a flick, like turning out a light. He would
ush it instantly! He despised Uncle Karl. But he despised his father
oo, for not being what he was suppsoed to be. Perhaps his father
ated *his* father, and so on, and his son would hate him, and so on.
stantly!

Naturally he didn't have nerve enough to ask Magda to go
rough the funhouse with him. With incredible nerve and to ev-
yone's surprise he invited Magda, quietly and politely, to go
rough the funhouse with him. "I warn you, I've never been
rough it before," he added, *laughing easily;* "but I reckon we can
anage somehow. The important thing to remember, after all, is
at it's meant to be a *fun*house; that is, a place of amusement. If
eople really got lost or injured or too badly frightened in it, the
wner'd go out of business. There'd even be lawsuits. No character
a work of fiction can make a speech this long without interrup-
on or acknowledgment from the other characters."

Mother teased Uncle Karl: "Three's a crowd, I always heard." But
tually Ambrose was relieved that Peter now had a quarter too.
othing was what it looked like. Every instant, under the surface
f the Atlantic Ocean, millicns of living animals devoured one an-
ther. Pilots were falling in flames over Europe; women were being
rcibly raped in the South Pacific. His father should have taken
im aside and said: "There is a simple secret to getting through the
nhouse, as simple as being first to see the Towers. Here it is. Peter
oes not know it; neither does your Uncle Karl. You and I are differ-
nt. Not surprisingly, you've often wished you weren't. Don't think
haven't noticed how unhappy your childhood has been! But you'll
nderstand, when I tell you, why it had to be kept secret until now.
nd you won't regret not being like your brother and your uncle.
n the contrary!" If you knew all the stories behind all the people
n the boardwalk, you'd see that *nothing* was what it looked like.
usbands and wives often hated each other; parents didn't neces-
rily love their children; et cetera. A child took things for granted
ecause he had nothing to compare his life to and everybody acted
s if things were as they should be. Therefore each saw himself as

the hero of the story, when the truth might turn out to be that he the villain, or the coward. And there wasn't one thing you cou do about it!

Hunchbacks, fat ladies, fools—that no one chose what he w was unbearable. In the movies he'd meet a beautiful young girl the funhouse; they'd have hairs-breadth escapes from real danger he'd do and say the right things; she also; in the end they'd be lo ers; their dialogue lines would match up; he'd be perfectly at eas she'd not only like him well enough, she'd think he was *marvelou* she'd lie awake thinking about *him,* instead of vice versa—the wa *his* face looked in different lights and how he stood and exact what he'd said—and yet that would be only one small episode his wonderful life, among many many others. Not a *turning point* all. What had happened in the toolshed was nothing. He hated, h loathed his parents! One reason for not writing a lost-in-the funhouse story is that either everybody's felt what Ambrose feel in which case it goes without saying, or else no normal person fee such things, in which case Ambrose is a freak. "Is anything mo tiresome, in fiction, than the problems of sensitive adolescents? And it's all too long and rambling, as if the author. For all a perso knows the first time through, the end could be just around any co ner; perhaps, *not impossibly* it's been within reach any number times. On the other hand he may be scarcely past the start, wit everything yet to get through, an intolerable idea.

Fill in: His father's raised eyebrows when he announced his dec sion to do the funhouse with Magda. Ambrose understands now but didn't then, that his father was wondering whether he kne what the funhouse was *for*—especially since he didn't object, as h should have, when Peter decided to come along too. The tick et-woman, witchlike, mortifying him when inadvertently he ga her his name-coin instead of the half-dollar, then unkindly callin Magda's attention to the birthmark on his temple: "Watch out fo him, girlie, he's a marked man!" She wasn't even cruel, he unde stood, only vulgar and insensitive. Somewhere in the world the was a young woman with such splendid understanding that she see him entire, like a poem or story, and find his words so valuab after all that when he confessed his apprehensions she would ex plain why they were in fact the very things that made him precio to her . . . and to Western Civilization! There was no such girl, th simple truth being. Violent yawns as they approached the mouth. Whispered advice from an old-timer on a bench near the barrel: "Go crabwise and ye'll get an eyeful without upsetting!" Composure vanished at the first pitch: Peter hollered joyously, Magda tumbled, shrieked, clutched her skirt; Ambrose scrambled crabwise, tight-lipped with terror, was soon out, watched his dropped name-coin slide among the couples. Shamefaced he saw that to get through expeditiously was not the point; Peter feigned assistance in order to trip Magda up, shouted "I see Christmas!" when her legs went flying. The old man, his latest betrayer, cackled approval. A dim hall then of black-thread cobwebs and recorded gibber: he took Magda's elbow to steady her against revolving discs set in the slanted floor to throw your feet out from under, and explained to her in a calm, deep voice his theory that each phase of the funhouse was triggered either automatically, by a series of photoelectric devices, or else manually by operators stationed at peepholes. But he lost his voice thrice as the discs unbalanced him; Magda was anyhow squealing; but at one point she clutched him about the waist to keep from falling, and her right cheek pressed for a moment against his belt-buckle. Heroically he drew her up, it was his chance to clutch her close as if for support and say: "I love you." He even put an arm lightly about the small of her back before a sailor-and-girl pitched into them from behind, sorely treading his left big toe and knocking Magda asprawl with them. The sailor's girl was a string-haired hussy with a loud laugh and light blue drawers; Ambrose realized that he wouldn't have said "I love you" anyhow, and was smitten with self-contempt. How much better it would be to be that common sailor! A wiry little Seaman 3rd, the fellow squeezed a girl to each side and stumbled hilarious into the mirror room, closer to Magda in thirty seconds than Ambrose had got in thirteen years. She giggled at something the fellow said to Peter; she drew her hair from her eyes with a movement so womanly it struck Ambrose's heart; Peter's smacking her backside then seemed particularly coarse. But Magda made a pleased indignant face and cried, "All right for *you,* mister!" and pursued Peter into the maze without a backward glance. The sailor followed after, leisurely, drawing his girl against his hip; Ambrose understood not only that they were all so relieved to be rid of his burdensome company that they didn't even notice his absence, but that he himself shared their relief. Stepping from the treacherous passage at last into the mirror-maze, he saw once again, more clearly than ever, how readily he deceived himself into supposing he was a person. He even foresaw, wincing at his dreadful self-knowledge, that he would repeat the deception, at ever-rarer intervals, all his wretched life, so fearful were the alternatives. Fame, madness, suicide; perhaps all three. It's not believable that so young a boy could articulate that reflection, and in fiction the merely true must always yield to the plausible. Moreover, the symbolism is in places heavy-footed. Yet Ambrose M—— understood, as few adults do, that the famous loneliness of the great was no popular myth but a general truth—furthermore, that it was as much cause as effect.

All the preceding except the last few sentences is exposition that should've been done earlier or interspersed with the present action instead of lumped together. No reader would put up with so much with such *prolixity.* It's interesting that Ambrose's father, though presumably an intelligent man (as indicated by his role as grade-school principal), neither encouraged nor discouraged his sons at all in any way—as if he either didn't care about them or cared all right but didn't know how to act. If this fact should contribute to one of them's becoming a celebrated but wretchedly unhappy scientist, was it a good thing or not? He too might someday face the question; it would be useful to know whether it had tortured his father for years, for example, or never once crossed his mind.

In the maze two important things happened. First, our hero found a name-coin someone else had lost or discarded: *AMBROSE*, suggestive of the famous lightship and of his late grandfather's favorite dessert, which his mother used to prepare on special occasions out of coconut, oranges, grapes, and what else. Second, as he wondered at the endless replication of his image in the mirrors, second, as he *lost himself in the reflection* that the necessity for an observer makes perfect observation impossible, better make him eighteen at least, yet that would render other things unlikely, he heard Peter and Magda chuckling somewhere together in the maze. "Here!" "No, here!" they shouted to each other; Peter said, "Where's Amby?" Magda murmured. "Amb?" Peter called. In a pleased, friendly voice. He didn't reply. The truth was, his brother was a *happy-go-lucky youngster* who'd've been better off with a regular brother of his own, but who seldom complained of his lot and was generally cordial. Ambrose's throat ached; there aren't enough different ways to say that. He stood quietly while the two young people giggled and thumped through the glittering maze, hurrah'd their discovery of its exit, cried out in joyful alarm at what next beset them. Then he set his mouth and followed after, as he supposed, took a wrong turn, strayed into the pass *wherein he lingers yet.*

The action of conventional dramatic narrative may be represented by a diagram called Freitag's Triangle:

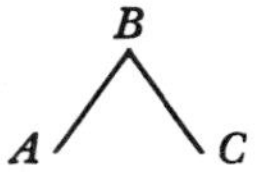

or more accurately by a variant of that diagram:

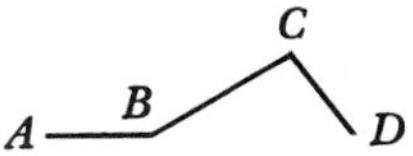

in which *AB* represents the exposition, *B* the introduction of conflict, *BC* the "rising action," complication, or development of the conflict, *C* the climax, or turn of the action, *CD* the dénouement, or resolution of the conflict. While there is no reason to regard this pattern as an absolute necessity, like many other conventions it became conventional because great numbers of people over many years learned by trial and error that it was effective; one ought not to forsake it, therefore, unless one wishes to forsake as well the effect of drama or has clear cause to feel that deliberate violation of the "normal" pattern can better can better effect that effect. This can't go on much longer; it can go on forever. He died telling stories to himself in the dark; years later, when that vast unsuspected area of the funhouse came to light, the first expedition found his skeleton in one of its labyrinthine corridors and mistook it for part of the entertainment. He died of starvation telling himself stories in the dark; but unbeknownst unbeknownst to him, an assistant operator of the funhouse, happening to overhear him, crouched just behind the plyboard partition and wrote down his every word. The operator's daughter, an exquisite young woman with a figure unusually well developed for her age, crouched just behind the partition and transcribed his every word. Though she had never laid eyes on him, she recognized that here was one of Western Culture's truly great imaginations, the eloquence of whose suffering would be an inspiration to unnumbered. And her heart was torn between her love for the misfortunte young man (yes, she loved him, though she had never laid though she knew him only—but how well!—through his words, and the deep, calm voice in which he spoke them) between her love et cetera and her womanly intuition that only in suffering and isolation could he give voice et cetera. Lone dark dying. Quietly she kissed the rough plyboard, and a tear fell upon the page. Where she had written in shorthand *Where she had written in shorthand* Where she had written in shorthand *Where she* et cetera. A long time ago we should have passed the apex of Freitag's Triangle and made brief work of the *dénouement;* the plot doesn't rise by meaningful steps but winds upon itself, digresses, retreats, hesitates, sighs, collapses, expires. The climax of the story must be its protagonist's discovery of a way to get through the funhouse. But he has found none, may have ceased to search.

What relevance does the war have to the story? Should there be fireworks outside or not?

Ambrose wandered, languished, dozed. Now and then he fell into his habit of rehearsing to himself the unadventurous story of his life, narrated from the third-person point of view, from his earliest memory parenthesis of maple leaves stirring in the summer breath of tidewater Maryland end of parenthesis to the present moment. Its principal events, on this telling, would appear to have been *A, B, C,* and *D.*

He imagined himself years hence, successful, married, at ease in the world, the trials of his adolescence far behind him. He has come to the seashore with his family for the holiday: how Ocean City has changed! But at one seldom at one ill-frequented end of the boardwalk a few derelict amusements survive from times gone by: the great carrousel from the turn of the century, with its monstrous griffins and mechanical concert band; the roller coaster rumored since 1916 to have been condemned; the mechanical shooting gallery in which only the image of our enemies changed. His own son laughs with Fat May and wants to know what a funhouse is; Ambrose hugs the sturdy lad close and smiles around his pipestem at his wife.

The family's going home. Mother sits between Father and Uncle Karl, who teases him good-naturedly who chuckles over the fact that the comrade with whom he'd fought his way shoulder to shoulder through the funhouse had turned out to be a blind Negro girl—to their mutual discomfort, as they'd opened their souls. But such are the walls of custom, which even. Whose arm is where? How must it feel. He dreams of a funhouse vaster by far than any yet constructed; but by then they may be out of fashion, like steamboats and excursion trains. Already quaint and seedy: the draperied ladies on the frieze of the carrousel are his father's father's moon-cheeked dreams; if he thinks of it more he will vomit his apple-on-a-stick.

He wonders: will he become a regular person? Something has gone wrong; his vaccination didn't take; at the Boy-Scout initiation campfire he only pretended to be deeply moved, as he pretends to this hour that it is not so bad after all in the funhouse, and that he has a little limp. How long will it last? He envisions a truly astonishing funhouse, incredibly complex yet utterly controlled from a great central switchboard like the console of a pipe organ. Nobody had enough imagination. He could design such a place himself, wiring and all, and he's only thirteen years old. He would be its operator: panel lights would show what was up in every cranny of its cunning of its multifarious vastness; a switch-flick would ease this fellow's way, complicate that's, to balance things out; if anyone seemed lost or frightened, all the operator had to do was.

He wishes he had never entered the funhouse. But he has. Then he wishes he were dead. But he's not. Therefore he will construct funhouses for others and be their secret operator—though he would rather be among the lovers for whom funhouses are designed.

1967

Report

DONALD BARTHELME

[b. 1931]

Our group is against the war. But the war goes on. I was sent to Cleveland to talk to the engineers. The engineers were meeting in Cleveland. I was supposed to persuade them not to do what they are going to do. I took United's 4:45 from LaGuardia arriving in Cleveland at 6:13. Cleveland is dark blue at that hour. I went directly to the motel, where the engineers were meeting. Hundreds of engineers attended the Cleveland meeting. I noticed many fractures among the engineers, bandages, traction. I noticed what appeared to be fracture of the carpal scaphoid in six examples. I noticed numerous fractures of the humeral shaft, of the os calcis, of the pelvic girdle. I noticed a high incidence of clay-shoveller's fracture. I could not account for these fractures. The engineers were making calculations, taking measurements, sketching on the blackboard, drinking beer, throwing bread, buttonholing employers, hurling glasses into the fireplace. They were friendly.

They were friendly. They were full of love and information. The chief engineer wore shades. Patella in Monk's traction, clamshell fracture by the look of it. He was standing in a slum of beer bottles and microphone cable. "Have some of this chicken à la Isambard Kingdom Brunel the Great Ingineer," he said. "And declare who you are and what we can do for you. What is your line, distinguished guest?"

"Software," I said. "In every sense. I am here representing a small group of interested parties. We are interested in your thing, which seems to be functioning. In the midst of so much dysfunction, function is interesting. Other people's things don't seem to be working. The State Department's thing doesn't seem to be working. The

U.N.'s thing doesn't seem to be working. The democratic left's thing doesn't seem to be working. Buddha's thing—"

"Ask us anything about our thing, which seems to be working," the chief engineer said. "We will open our hearts and heads to you, Software Man, because we want to be understood and loved by the great lay public, and have our marvels appreciated by that public, for which we daily unsung produced tons of new marvels each more life-enhancing than the last. Ask us anything. Do you want to know about evaporated thin-film metallurgy? Monolithic and hybrid integrated-circuit processes? The algebra of inequalities? Optimization theory? Complex high-speed micro-miniature closed and open loop systems? Fixed variable mathematical cost searches? Epitaxial deposition of semi-conductor materials? Gross interfaced space gropes? We also have specialists in the cuckoo-flower, the doctor-fish, and the dumdum bullet as these relate to aspects of today's expanding technology, and they do in the damnedest ways."

I spoke to him then about the war. I said the same things people always say when they speak against the war. I said that the war was wrong. I said that large countries should not burn down small countries. I said that the government had made a series of errors. I said that these errors once small and forgivable were now immense and unforgivable. I said that the government was attempting to conceal its original errors under layers of new errors. I said that the government was sick with error, giddy with it. I said that ten thousand of our soldiers had already been killed in pursuit of the government's errors. I said that tens of thousands of the enemy's soldiers and civilians had been killed because of various errors, ours and theirs. I said that we are responsible for errors made in our name. I said that the government should not be allowed to make additional errors.

"Yes, yes," the chief engineer said, "there is doubtless much truth in what you say, but we can't possibly *lose* the war, can we? And stopping is losing, isn't it? The war regarded as a process, stopping regarded as an abort? We don't know *how* to lose a war. That skill is not among our skills. Our array smashes their array, that is what we know. That is the process. That is what is.

"But let's not have any more of this dispiriting downbeat counterproductive talk. I have a few new marvels here I'd like to discuss with you just briefly. A few new marvels that are just about ready to be gaped at by the admiring layman. Consider for instance the area of realtime online computer-controlled wish evaporation. Wish evaporation is going to be crucial in meeting the rising expectations of the world's peoples, which are as you know rising entirely too fast."

I noticed then distributed about the room a great many transverse fractures of the ulna. "The development of the pseudo-ruminant stomach for underdeveloped peoples," he went on, "is one of our interesting things you should be interested in. With the pseudo-ruminant stomach they can chew cuds, that is to say, eat grass. Blue is the most popular color worldwide and for that reason we are working with certain strains of your native Kentucky *Poa pratensis,* or bluegrass, as the staple input for the p/r stomach cycle, which would also give a shot in the arm to our balance-of-payments thing don't you know. . . ." I noticed about me then a great number of metatarsal fractures in banjo splints. "The kangaroo initiative . . . eight hundred thousand harvested last year . . . highest percentage of edible protein of any herbivore yet studied. . . ."

"Have new kangaroos been planted?"

The engineer looked at me.

"I intuit your hatred and jealousy of our thing," he said. "The ineffectual always hate our thing and speak of it as anti-human, which is not at all a meaningful way to speak of our thing. Nothing mechanical is alien to me," he said (amber spots making bursts of light in his shades), "because I am human, in a sense, and if I think it up, then 'it' is human too, whatever 'it' may be. Let me tell you, Software Man, we have been damned forbearing in the matter of this little war you declare yourself to be interested in. Function is the cry, and our thing is functioning like crazy. There are things we could do that we have not done. Steps we could take that we have not taken. These steps are, regarded in a certain light, the light of our enlightened self-interest, quite justifiable steps. We could, of course, get irritated. We could, of course, *lose patience.*

"We could, of course, release thousands upon thousands of self-powered crawling-along-the-ground lengths of titanium wire eighteen inches long with a diameter of .0005 centimetres (that is to say, invisible) which, scenting an enemy, climb up his trouser leg and wrap themselves around his neck. We have developed those. They are within our capabilities. We could, of course, release n the arena of the upper air our new improved pufferfish toxin vhich precipitates an identity crisis. No special technical problems here. That is almost laughably easy. We could, of course, place up o two million maggots in their rice within twenty-four hours. The naggots are ready, massed in secret staging areas in Alabama. We ıave hypodermic darts capable of piebalding the enemy's pigmen-ation. We have rots, blights, and rusts capable of attacking his al-›habet. Those are dandies. We have a hut-shrinking chemical vhich penetrates the fibres of the bamboo, causing it, the hut, to trangle its occupants. This operates only after 10 P.M., when people re sleeping. Their mathematics are at the mercy of a suppurating urd we have invented. We have a family of fishes trained to attack heir fishes. We have the deadly testicle-destroying telegram. The able companies are cooperating. We have a green substance that, vell, I'd rather not talk about. We have a secret word that, if pro-ıounced, produces multiple fractures in all living things in an area he size of four football fields."

"That's why—"

"Yes. Some damned fool couldn't keep his mouth shut. The point ; that the whole structure of enemy life is within our power to *rend, itiate, devour,* and *crush.* But that's not the interesting thing."

"You recount these possibilities with uncommon relish."

"Yes I realize that there is too much relish here. But *you* must real-ze that these capabilities represent in and of themselves highly echnical and complex and interesting problems and hurdles on vhich our boys have expended many thousands of hours of hard vork and brilliance. And that the effects are often grossly exagger-ted by irresponsible victims. And that the whole thing represents fantastic series of triumphs for the multi-disciplined prob-em-solving team concept."

"I appreciate that."

"We *could* unleash all this technology at once. You can imagine vhat would happen then. But that's not the interesting thing."

"What is the interesting thing?"

"The interesting thing is that we have *a moral sense.* It is on unched cards, perhaps the most advanced and sensitive moral ense the world has ever known."

"Because it is on punched cards?"

"It considers all considerations in endless and subtle detail," he said. "It even quibbles. With this great new moral tool, how can we go wrong? I confidently predict that, although we *could* employ all this splendid new weaponry I've been telling you about, *we're not going to do it.*"

"We're not going to do it?"

I took United's 5:44 from Cleveland arriving at Newark at 7:19. New Jersey is bright pink at that hour. Living things move about the surface of New Jersey at that hour molesting each other only in traditional ways. I made my report to the group. I stressed the friendliness of the engineers. I said, It's all right. I said, We have a moral sense. I said, *We're not going to do it.* They didn't believe me.

1967

A & P

JOHN UPDIKE

[b. 1932]

In walks these three girls in nothing but bathing suits. I'm in the third checkout slot, with my back to the door, so I don't see them until they're over by the bread. The one that caught my eye first was the one in the plaid green two-piece. She was a chunky kid, with a good tan and a sweet broad soft-looking can with those two crescents of white just under it, where the sun never seems to hit, at the top of the backs of her legs. I stood there with my hand on a box of HiHo crackers trying to remember if I rang it up or not. I ring it up again and the customer starts giving me hell. She's one of these cash-register-watchers, a witch about fifty with rouge on her cheekbones and no eyebrows, and I know it made her day to trip me up. She'd been watching cash registers for fifty years and probably never seen a mistake before.

By the time I got her feathers smoothed and her goodies into a bag—she gives me a little snort in passing, if she'd been born at the right time they would have burned her over in Salem—by the time I get her on her way the girls had circled around the bread and were coming back, without a pushcart, back my way along the counters, in the aisle between the checkouts and the Special bins. They didn't even have shoes on. There was this chunky one, with the two-piece—it was bright green and the seams on the bra were still sharp and her belly was still pretty pale so I guessed she just got it (the suit)—there was this one, with one of those chubby berry-faces, the lips all bunched together under her nose, this one, and a tall one, with black hair that hadn't quite frizzed right, and one of these sunburns right across under the eyes, and a chin that was too long—you know, the kind of girl other girls think is very "striking" and "attractive" but never quite makes it, as they very well know, which is why they like her so much—and then the third one that wasn't quite so tall. She was the queen. She kind of led them the other two peeking around and making their shoulders round She didn't look around, not this queen, she just walked straight on slowly, on these long white prima-donna legs. She came down a little hard on her heels, as if she didn't walk in her bare feet that much, putting down her heels and then letting the weight move along to her toes as if she was testing the floor with every step, putting a little deliberate extra action into it. You never know for sure how girls' minds work (do you really think it's a mind in there or just a little buzz like a bee in a glass jar?) but you got the idea she had talked the other two into coming in here with her, and now she was showing them how to do it, walk slow and hold yourself straight.

She had on a kind of dirty-pink—beige maybe, I don't know—bathing suit with a little nubble all over it, and what got me, the straps were down. They were off her shoulders looped loose around the cool tops of her arms, and I guess as a result the suit had slipped a little on her, so all around the top of the cloth there was this shining rim. If it hadn't been there you wouldn't have known there could have been anything whiter than those shoulders. With the straps pushed off, there was nothing between the top of the suit and the top of her head except just *her,* this clean bare plane of the top of her chest down from the shoulder bones like a dented sheet of metal tilted in the light. I mean, it was more than pretty.

She had sort of oaky hair that the sun and salt had bleached, done up in a bun that was unravelling, and a kind of prim face. Walking into the A & P with your straps down, I suppose it's the only kind of face you *can* have. She held her head so high her neck, coming up out of those white shoulders, looked kind of stretched, but I didn't mind. The longer her neck was, the more of her there was.

She must have felt in the corner of her eye me and over my shoulder Stokesie in the second slot watching, but she didn't tip. Not this queen. She kept her eyes moving across the racks, and stopped, and turned so slow it made my stomach rub the inside of my apron, and buzzed to the other two, who kind of huddled against her for relief, and then they all three of them went up the cat-and-dog-food-breakfast-cereal-macaroni-rice-raisins-seasonings-spreads-spaghetti-soft-drinks-crackers-and-cookies aisle. From the third slot I look straight up this aisle to the meat counter, and I watched them all the way. The fat one with the tan sort of fumbled with the cookies, but on second thought she put the package back. The sheep pushing their carts down the aisle—the girls were walking against the usual traffic (not that we have one-way signs or anything)—were pretty hilarious. You could see them, when Queenie's white shoulders dawned on them, kind of jerk, or hop, or hiccup, but their eyes snapped back to their own baskets and on they pushed. I bet you could set off dynamite in an A & P and the people would by and large keep reaching and checking oatmeal off their lists and muttering "Let me see, there was a third thing, began with A, asparagus, no, ah, yes, applesauce!" or whatever it is they do mutter. But there was no doubt, this jiggled them. A few house-slaves in pin curlers even looked around after pushing their carts past to make sure what they had seen was correct.

You know, it's one thing to have a girl in a bathing suit down on the beach, where what with the glare nobody can look at each other much anyway, and another thing in the cool of the A & P, under the fluorescent lights, against all those stacked packages, with her feet paddling along naked over our checkerboard green-and-cream rubber-tile floor.

"Oh Daddy," Stokesie said beside me. "I feel so faint."

"Darling," I said. "Hold me tight." Stokesie's married, with two babies chalked up on his fuselage already, but as far as I can tell that's the only difference. He's twenty-two, and I was nineteen this April.

"Is it done?" he asks, the responsible married man finding his voice. I forgot to say he thinks he's going to be manager some sunny day, maybe in 1990 when it's called the Great Alexandrov and Petrooshki Tea Company or something.

What he meant was, our town is five miles from a beach, with a big summer colony out on the Point, but we're right in the middle of town, and the women generally put on a shirt or shorts or something before they get out of the car into the street. And anyway these are usually women with six children and varicose veins mapping their legs and nobody, including them, could care less. As I say, we're right in the middle of town, and if you stand at our front doors you can see two banks and the Congregational church and the newspaper store and three real-estate offices and about twenty-seven old freeloaders tearing up Central Street because the sewer broke again. It's not as if we're on the Cape; we're north of Boston and there's people in this town haven't seen the ocean for twenty years.

The girls had reached the meat counter and were asking McMahon something. He pointed, they pointed, and they shuffled out of sight behind a pyramid of Diet Delight peaches. All that was left for us to see was old McMahon patting his mouth and looking after them sizing up their joints. Poor kids, I began to feel sorry for them, they couldn't help it.

Now here comes the sad part of the story, at least my family says it's sad, but I don't think it's so sad myself. The store's pretty empty, it being Thursday afternoon, so there was nothing much to do except lean on the register and wait for the girls to show up again. The whole store was like a pinball machine and I didn't know which tunnel they'd come out of. After a while they came around out of the far aisle, around the light bulbs, records at discount of the Caribbean Six or Tony Martin Sings or some such gunk you wonder they waste the wax on, sixpacks of candy bars, and plastic toys done up in cellophane that fall apart when a kid looks at them anyway. Around they come, Queenie still leading the way, and holding a little gray jar in her hand. Slots Three through Seven are unmanned and I could see her wondering between Stokes and me, but Stokesie with his usual luck draws an old party in baggy gray pants who stumbles up with four giant cans of pineapple juice (what do these bums *do* with all that pineapple juice? I've often asked myself) so the girls come to me. Queenie puts down the jar and I take it into my fingers icy cold. Kingfish Fancy Herring Snacks in Pure Sour Cream: 49¢. Now her hands are empty, not a ring or a bracelet, bare as God made them, and I wonder where the money's coming from. Still with that prim look she lifts a folded dollar bill out of the hollow at the center of her nubbled pink top. The jar went heavy in my hand. Really, I thought that was so cute.

Then everybody's luck begins to run out. Lengel comes in from haggling with a truck full of cabbages on the lot and is about to scuttle into that door marked MANAGER behind which he hides all day when the girls touch his eye. Lengel's pretty dreary, teaches

Sunday school and the rest, but he doesn't miss that much. He comes over and says, "Girls, this isn't the beach."

Queenie blushes, though maybe it's just a brush of sunburn I was noticing for the first time, now that she was so close. "My mother asked me to pick up a jar of herring snacks." Her voice kind of startled me, the way voices do when you see the people first, coming out so flat and dumb yet kind of tony, too, the way it ticked over "pick up" and "snacks." All of a sudden I slid right down her voice into her living room. Her father and the other men were standing around in ice-cream coats and bow ties and the women were in sandals picking up herring snacks on toothpicks off a big glass plate and they were all holding drinks the color of water with olives and sprigs of mint in them. When my parents have somebody over they get lemonade and if it's a real racy affair Schlitz in tall glasses with "They'll Do It Every Time" cartoons stencilled on.

"That's all right," Lengel said. "But this isn't the beach." His repeating this struck me as funny, as if it had just occurred to him, and he had been thinking all these years the A & P was a great big sand dune and he was the head lifeguard. He didn't like my smiling—as I say he doesn't miss much—but he concentrates on giving the girls that sad Sunday-school-superintendent stare.

Queenie's blush is no sunburn now, and the plump one in plaid, that I liked better from the back—a really sweet can—pipes up, "We weren't doing any shopping. We just came in for the one thing."

"That makes no difference," Lengel tells her, and I could see from the way his eyes went that he hadn't noticed she was wearing a two-piece before. "We want you decently dressed when you come in here."

"We *are* decent," Queenie says suddenly, her lower lip pushing, getting sore now that she remembers her place, a place from which the crowd that runs the A & P must look pretty crummy. Fancy Herring Snacks flashed in her very blue eyes.

"Girls, I don't want to argue with you. After this come in here with your shoulders covered. It's our policy." He turns his back. That's policy for you. Policy is what the kingpins want. What the others want is juvenile delinquency.

All this while, the customers had been showing up with their carts but, you know, sheep, seeing a scene, they had all bunched up on Stokesie, who shook open a paper bag as gently as peeling a peach, not wanting to miss a word. I could feel in the silence everybody getting nervous, most of all Lengel, who asks me, "Sammy, have you rung up their purchase?"

I thought and said "No" but it wasn't about that I was thinking. I go through the punches, 4, 9, GROC, TOT—it's more complicated than you think, and after you do it often enough, it begins to make a little song, that you hear words to, in my case "Hello *(bing)* there, you *(gung)* hap-py *pee-* pul *(splat)*!"—the *splat* being the drawer flying out. I uncrease the bill, tenderly as you may imagine, it just having come from between the two smoothest scoops of vanilla I had ever known were there, and pass a half and a penny into her narrow pink palm, and nestle the herrings in a bag and twist its neck and hand it over, all the time thinking.

The girls, and who'd blame them, are in a hurry to get out, so I say "I quit" to Lengel quick enough for them to hear, hoping they'll stop and watch me, their unsuspected hero. They keep right on going, into the electric eye; the door flies open and they flicker across the lot to their car, Queenie and Plaid and Big Tall Goony-Goony (not that as raw material she was so bad), leaving me with Lengel and a kink in his eyebrow.

"Did you say something, Sammy?"

"I said I quit."

"I thought you did."

"You didn't have to embarrass them."

"It was they who were embarrassing us."

I started to say something that came out "Fiddle-de-doo." It's a saying of my grandmother's, and I know she would have been pleased.

"I don't think you know what you're saying," Lengel said.

"I know you don't," I said. "But I do." I pull the bow at the back of my apron and start shrugging it off my shoulders. A couple customers that had been heading for my slot begin to knock against each other, like scared pigs in a chute.

Lengel sighs and begins to look very patient and old and gray. He's been a friend of my parents for years. "Sammy, you don't want to do this to your Mom and Dad," he tells me. It's true, I don't. But it seems to me that once you begin a gesture it's fatal not to go through with it. I fold the apron, "Sammy" stitched in red on the pocket, and put it on the counter, and drop the bow tie on top of it. The bow tie is theirs, if you've ever wondered. "You'll feel this for the rest of your life," Lengel says, and I know that's true, too, but remembering how he made that pretty girl blush makes me so scrunchy inside I punch the No Sale tab and the machine whirs "pee-pul" and the drawer splats out. One advantage to this scene taking place in summer, I can follow this up with a clean exit, there's no fumbling around getting your coat and galoshes, I just saunter into the electric eye in my white shirt that my mother ironed the night before, and the door heaves itself open, and outside the sunshine is skating around on the asphalt.

I look around for my girls, but they're gone, of course. There wasn't anybody but some young married screaming with her children about some candy they didn't get by the door of a powder-blue Falcon station wagon. Looking back in the big windows, over the bags of peat moss and aluminum lawn furniture stacked on the pavement, I could see Lengel in my place in the slot, checking the sheep through. His face was dark gray and his back stiff, as if he'd just had an injection of iron, and my stomach kind of fell as I felt how hard the world was going to be to me hereafter.

1961

How I Contemplated the World from the Detroit House of Correction and Began My Life Over Again

Notes for an essay for an English class at Baldwin Country Day School; poking around in debris; disgust and curiosity; a revelation of the meaning of life; a happy ending . . .

JOYCE CAROL OATES

[b. 1938]

I Events

1. The girl (myself) is walking through Branden's, that excellent store. Suburb of a large famous city that is a symbol for large famous American cities. The event sneaks up on the girl, who believes she is herding it along with a small fixed smile, a girl of fifteen, innocently experienced. She dawdles in a certain style by a counter of costume jewelry. Rings, earrings, necklaces. Prices from $5 to $50, all within reach. All ugly. She eases over to the glove counter, where everything is ugly too. In her close-fitted coat with its black fur collar she contemplates the luxury of Branden's, which she has known for many years: its many mild pale lights, easy on the eye and the soul, its elaborate tinkly decorations, its women shoppers with their excellent shoes and coats and hairdos, all dawdling gracefully, in no hurry.

Who was ever in a hurry here?

2. The girl seated at home. A small library, paneled walls of oak. Someone is talking to me. An earnest, husky, female voice drives itself against my ears, nervous, frightened, groping around my heart, saying, "If you wanted gloves, why didn't you say so? Why didn't you ask for them?" That store, Branden's, is owned by Raymond Forrest who lives on Du Maurier Drive. We live on Sioux Drive. Raymond Forrest. A handsome man? An ugly man? A man of fifty or sixty, with gray hair, or a man of forty with earnest, courteous eyes, a good golf game; who is Raymond Forrest, this man who is my salvation? Father has been talking to him. Father is not his physician; Dr. Berg is his physician. Father and Dr. Berg refer patients to each other. There is a connection. Mother plays bridge with . . . On Mondays and Wednesdays our maid Billie works at . . . The strings draw together in a cat's cradle, making a net to save you when you fall . . .

3. *Harriet Arnold's.* A small shop, better than Branden's. Mother in her black coat, I in my close-fitted blue coat. Shopping. Now look at this, isn't this cute, do you want this, why don't you want this, try this on, take this with you to the fitting room, take this also, what's wrong with you, what can I do for you, why are you so strange . . . ? "I wanted to steal but not to buy," I don't tell her. The girl droops along in her coat and gloves and leather boots, her eyes scan the horizon, which is pastel pink and decorated like Branden's, tasteful walls and modern ceilings with graceful glimmering lights.

4. Weeks later, the girl at a bus stop. Two o'clock in the afternoon, a Tuesday; obviously she has walked out of school.

5. The girl stepping down from a bus. Afternoon, weather changing to colder. Detroit. Pavement and closed-up stores; grillwork over the windows of a pawnshop. What is a pawnshop, exactly?

II Characters

1. The girl stands five feet five inches tall. An ordinary height. Baldwin Country Day School draws them up to that height. She dreams along the corridors and presses her face against the Thermoplex glass. No frost or steam can ever form on that glass. A

smudge of grease from her forehead . . . could she be boiled down to grease? She wears her hair loose and long and straight in suburban teen-age style, 1968. Eyes smudged with pencil, dark brown. Brown hair. Vague green eyes. A pretty girl? An ugly girl? She sings to herself under her breath, idling in the corridor, thinking of her many secrets (the thirty dollars she once took from the purse of a friend's mother, just for fun, the basement window she smashed in her own house just for fun) and thinking of her brother who is at Susquehanna Boys' Academy, an excellent preparatory school in Maine, remembering him unclearly . . . he has long manic hair and a squeaking voice and he looks like one of the popular teen-age singers of 1968, one of those in a group, *The Certain Forces, The Way Out, The Maniacs Responsible.* The girl in her turn looks like one of those fieldsful of girls who listen to the boys' singing, dreaming and mooning restlessly, breaking into high sullen laughter, innocently experienced.

2. The mother. A Midwestern woman of Detroit and suburbs. Belongs to the Detroit Athletic Club. Also the Detroit Golf Club. Also the Bloomfield Hills Country Club. The Village Women's Club at which lectures are given each winter on Genet and Sartre and James Baldwin, by the Director of the Adult Education Program at Wayne State University. . . . The Bloomfield Art Association. Also the Founders Society of the Detroit Institute of Arts. Also . . . Oh, she is in perpetual motion, this lady, hair like blown-up gold and finer than gold, hair and fingers and body of inestimable grace. Heavy weighs the gold on the back of her hairbrush and hand mirror. Heavy heavy the candlesticks in the dining room. Very heavy is the big car, a Lincoln, long and black, that on one cool autumn day split a squirrel's body in two unequal parts.

3. The father. Dr.   . He belongs to the same clubs as #2. A player of squash and golf; he has a golfer's umbrella of stripes. Candy stripes. In his mouth nothing turns to sugar, however; saliva works no miracles here. His doctoring is of the slightly sick. The sick are sent elsewhere (to Dr. Berg?), the deathly sick are sent back for more tests and their bills are sent to their homes, the unsick are sent to Dr. Coronet (Isabel, a lady), an excellent psychiatrist for unsick people who angrily believe they are sick and want to do some-

thing about it. If they demand a male psychiatrist, the unsick are sent by Dr.   (my father) to Dr. Lowenstein, a male psychiatrist, excellent and expensive, with a limited practice.

4. Clarita. She is twenty, twenty-five, she is thirty or more? Pretty, ugly, what? She is a woman lounging by the side of a road, in jeans and a sweater, hitchhiking, or she is slouched on a stool at a counter in some roadside diner. A hard line of jaw. Curious eyes. Amused eyes. Behind her eyes processions move, funeral pageants, cartoons. She says, "I never can figure out why girls like you bum around down here. What are you looking for anyway?" An odor of tobacco about her. Unwashed underclothes, or no underclothes, unwashed skin, gritty toes, hair long and falling into strands, not recently washed.

5. Simon. In this city the weather changes abruptly, so Simon's weather changes abruptly. He sleeps through the afternoon. He sleeps through the morning. Rising, he gropes around for something to get him going, for a cigarette or a pill to drive him out to the street, where the temperature is hovering around 35°. Why doesn't it drop? Why, why doesn't the cold clean air come down from Canada; will he have to go up into Canada to get it? will he have to leave the Country of his Birth and sink into Canada's frosty fields . . . ? Will the F.B.I. (which he dreams about constantly) chase him over the Canadian border on foot, hounded out in a blizzard of broken glass and horns . . . ?

"Once I was Huckleberry Finn," Simon says, "but now I am Roderick Usher." Beset by frenzies and fears, this man who makes my spine go cold, he takes green pills, yellow pills, pills of white and capsules of dark blue and green . . . he takes other things I may not mention, for what if Simon seeks me out and climbs into my girl's bedroom here in Bloomfield Hills and strangles me, what then . . . ? (As I write this I begin to shiver. Why do I shiver? I am now sixteen and sixteen is not an age for shivering.) It comes from Simon, who is always cold.

III World Events

Nothing.

IV People & Circumstances Contributing to This Delinquency

Nothing.

V Sioux Drive

George, Clyde G. 240 Sioux. A manufacturer's representative; children, a dog, a wife. Georgian with the usual columns. You think of the White House, then of Thomas Jefferson, then your mind goes blank on the white pillars and you think of nothing. Norris, Ralph W. 246 Sioux. Public relations. Colonial. Bay window, brick, stone, concrete, wood, green shutters, sidewalk, lantern, grass, trees, blacktop drive, two children, one of them my classmate Esther (Esther Norris) at Baldwin. Wife, cars. Ramsey, Michael D. 250 Sioux. Colonial. Big living room, thirty by twenty-five, fireplaces in living room, library, recreation room, paneled walls wet bar five bathrooms five bedrooms two lavatories central air conditioning automatic sprinkler automatic garage door three children one wife two cars a breakfast room a patio a large fenced lot fourteen trees a front door with a brass knocker never knocked. Next is our house. Classic contemporary. Traditional modern. Attached garage, attached Florida room, attached patio, attached pool and cabana, attached roof. A front door mail slot through which pour *Time Magazine, Fortune, Life, Business Week,* the *Wall Street Journal,* the *New York Times,* the *New Yorker,* the *Saturday Review, M.D., Modern Medicine, Disease of the Month* . . . and also. . . . And in addition to all this, a quiet sealed letter from Baldwin saying: *Your daughter is not doing work compatible with her performance on the Stanford Binet. . . .* And your son is not doing well, not well at all, very sad. Where is your son anyway? Once he stole trick-and-treat candy from some six-year-old kids, he himself being a robust ten. The beginning. Now your daughter steals. In the Village Pharmacy she made off with, yes she did, don't deny it, she made off with a copy of *Pageant Magazine* for no reason, she swiped a roll of Life Savers in a green wrapper and was in no need of saving her life or even in need of sucking candy; when she was no more than eight years old she stole, don't blush, she stole a package of Tums only because it was out on the counter and available, and the nice lady behind the counter (now dead) said nothing. . . . Sioux Drive. Maples, oaks, elms. Diseased elms cut down. Sioux Drive runs into Roosevelt Drive. Slow, turning lanes, not streets, all drives and lanes and ways and passes. A private police force. Quiet private police, in unmarked cars. Cruising on Saturday evenings with paternal smiles for the residents who are streaming in and out of houses, going to and from parties, a thousand parties, slightly staggering, the women in their furs alighting from automobiles bought of Ford and General Motors and Chrysler, very heavy automobiles. No foreign cars. Detroit. In 275 Sioux, down the block in that magnificent French-Normandy mansion, lives   himself, who has the C   account itself, imagine that! Look at where he lives and look at the enormous trees and chimneys, imagine his many fireplaces, imagine his wife and children, imagine his wife's hair, imagine her fingernails, imagine her bathtub of smooth clean glowing pink, imagine their embraces, his trouser pockets filled with odd coins and keys and dust and peanuts, imagine their ecstasy on Sioux Drive, imagine their income tax returns, imagine their little boy's pride in his experimental car, a scaled-down C   as he roars around the neighborhood on the sidewalks frightening dogs and Negro maids, oh imagine all these things, imagine everything, let your mind roar out all over Sioux Drive and Du Maurier Drive and Roosevelt Drive and Ticonderoga Pass and Burning Bush Way and Lincolnshire Pass and Lois Lane.

When spring comes, its winds blow nothing to Sioux Drive, no odors of hollyhocks or forsythia, nothing Sioux Drive doesn't already possess, everything is planted and performing. The weather vanes, had they weather vanes, don't have to turn with the wind, don't have to contend with the weather. There is no weather.

VI Detroit

There is always weather in Detroit. Detroit's temperature is always 32°. Fast-falling temperatures. Slow-rising temperatures. Wind from the north-northeast four to forty miles an hour, small-craft warnings, partly cloudy today and Wednesday changing to partly sunny through Thursday . . . small warnings of frost, soot warnings, traffic warnings, hazardous lake conditions for small craft and swimmers, restless Negro gangs, restless cloud formations, restless temperatures aching to fall out the very bottom of the thermometer or shoot up over the top and boil everything over in red mercury.

Detroit's temperature is 32°. Fast-falling temperatures. Slow- rising temperatures. Wind from the north-northeast four to forty miles an hour. . . .

VII Events

1. The girl's heart is pounding. In her pocket is a pair of gloves! In a plastic bag! Airproof breathproof plastic bag, gloves selling for twenty-five dollars on Branden's counter! In her pocket! Shoplifted! . . . In her purse is a blue comb, not very clean. In her purse is a leather billfold (a birthday present from her grandmother in Philadelphia) with snapshots of the family in clean plastic windows, in the billfold are bills, she doesn't know how many bills. . . . In her purse is an ominous note from her friend Tykie *What's this about Joe H. and the kids hanging around at Louise's Sat. night? You heard anything?* . . . passed in French class. In her purse is a lot of dirty yellow Kleenex, her mother's heart would break to see such very dirty Kleenex, and at the bottom of her purse are brown hairpins and safety pins and a broken pencil and a ballpoint pen (blue) stolen from somewhere forgotten and a purse-size compact of Cover Girl Make-Up, Ivory Rose. . . . Her lipstick is Broken Heart, a corrupt pink; her fingers are trembling like crazy; her teeth are beginning to chatter; her insides are alive; her eyes glow in her head; she is saying to her mother's astonished face *I want to steal but not to buy.*

2. At Clarita's. Day or night? What room is this? A bed, a regular bed, and a mattress on the floor nearby. Wallpaper hanging in strips. Clarita says she tore it like that with her teeth. She was fighting a barbaric tribe that night, high from some pills; she was battling for her life with men wearing helmets of heavy iron and their faces no more than Christian crosses to breathe through, every one of those bastards looking like her lover Simon, who seems to breathe with great difficulty through the slits of mouth and nostrils in his face. Clarita has never heard of Sioux Drive. Raymond Forrest cuts no ice with her, nor does the C   account and its millions; Harvard Business School could be at the corner of Vernor and 12th Street for all she cares, and Vietnam might have sunk by now into

the Dead Sea under its tons of debris, for all the amazement she could show . . . her face is overworked, overwrought, at the age of twenty (thirty?) it is already exhausted but fanciful and ready for a laugh. Clarita says mournfully to me *Honey somebody is going to turn you out let me give you warning.* In a movie shown on late television Clarita is not a mess like this but a nurse, with short neat hair and a dedicated look, in love with her doctor and her doctor's patients and their diseases, enamored of needles and sponges and rubbing alcohol. . . . Or no: she is a private secretary. Robert Cummings is her boss. She helps him with fantastic plots, the canned audience laughs, no, the audience doesn't laugh because nothing is funny, instead her boss is Robert Taylor and they are not boss and secretary but husband and wife, she is threatened by a young starlet, she is grim, handsome, wifely, a good companion for a good man. . . . She is Claudette Colbert. Her sister too is Claudette Colbert. They are twins, identical. Her husband Charles Boyer is a very rich handsome man and her sister, Claudette Colbert, is plotting her death in order to take her place as the rich man's wife, no one will know because they are *twins.* . . . All these marvelous lives Clarita might have lived, but she fell out the bottom at the age of thirteen. At the age when I was packing my overnight case for a slumber party at Toni Deshield's she was tearing filthy sheets off a bed and scratching up a rash on her arms. . . . Thirteen is uncommonly young for a white girl in Detroit, Miss Brock of the Detroit House of Correction said in a sad newspaper interview for the *Detroit News;* fifteen and sixteen are more likely. Eleven, twelve, thirteen are not surprising in colored . . . they are more precocious. What can we do? Taxes are rising and the tax base is falling. The temperature rises slowly but falls rapidly. Everything is falling out the bottom, Woodward Avenue is filthy, Livernois Avenue is filthy! Scraps of paper flutter in the air like pigeons, dirt flies up and hits you right in the eye, oh Detroit is breaking up into dangerous bits of newspaper and dirt, watch out. . . .

Clarita's apartment is over a restaurant. Simon her lover emerges from the cracks at dark. Mrs. Olesko, a neighbor of Clarita's, an aged white wisp of a woman, doesn't complain but sniffs with contentment at Clarita's noisy life and doesn't tell the cops, hating cops, when the cops arrive. I should give more fake names, more blanks, instead of telling all these secrets. I myself am a secret; I am a minor.

3. My father reads a paper at a medical convention in Los Angeles. There he is, on the edge of the North American continent, when the unmarked detective put his hand so gently on my arm in the aisle of Branden's and said, "Miss, would you like to step over here for a minute?"

And where was he when Clarita put her hand on my arm, that wintry dark sulphurous aching day in Detroit, in the company of closed-down barber shops, closed-down diners, closed-down movie houses, homes, windows, basements, faces . . . she put her hand on my arm and said, "Honey, are you looking for somebody down here?"

And was he home worrying about me, gone for two weeks solid, when they carried me off . . . ? It took three of them to get me in the police cruiser, so they said, and they put more than their hands on my arm.

4. I work on this lesson. My English teacher is Mr. Forest, who is from Michigan State. Not handsome, Mr. Forest, and his name is plain, unlike Raymond Forrest's, but he is sweet and rodentlike, he has conferred with the principal and my parents, and everything is fixed . . . treat her as if nothing has happened, a new start, begin again, only sixteen years old, what a shame, how did it happen?—nothing happened, nothing could have happened, a slight physiological modification known only to a gynecologist or to Dr. Coronet. I work on my lesson. I sit in my pink room. I look around the room with my sad pink eyes. I sigh, I dawdle, I pause, I eat up time, I am limp and happy to be home, I am sixteen years old suddenly, my head hangs heavy as a pumpkin on my shoulders, and my hair has just been cut by Mr. Faye at the Crystal Salon and is said to be very becoming.

(Simon too put his hand on my arm and said, "Honey, you have got to come with me," and in his six-by-six room we got to know each other. Would I go back to Simon again? Would I lie down with him in all that filth and craziness? Over and over again.

a Clarita is being betrayed as in front of a Cunningham Drug Store she is nervously eying a colored man who may or may not have money, or a nervous white boy of twenty with sideburns and an Appalachian look, who may or may not have a knife hidden in his jacket pocket, or a husky red-faced man of friendly countenance who may or may not be a member of the Vice Squad out for an early twilight walk.)

I work on my lesson for Mr. Forest. I have filled up eleven pages. Words pour out of me and won't stop. I want to tell everything . . . what was the song Simon was always humming, and who was Simon's friend in a very new trench coat with an old high school graduation ring on his finger . . . ? Simon's bearded friend? When I was down too low for him, Simon kicked me out and gave me to him for three days, I think, on Fourteenth Street in Detroit, an airy room of cold cruel drafts with newspapers on the floor. . . . Do I really remember that or am I piecing it together from what they told me? Did they tell the truth? Did they know much of the truth?

VIII Characters

1. Wednesdays after school, at four; Saturday mornings at ten. Mother drives me to Dr. Coronet. Ferns in the office, plastic or real, they look the same. Dr. Coronet is queenly, an elegant nicotine-stained lady who would have studied with Freud had circumstances not prevented it, a bit of a Catholic, ready to offer you some mystery if your teeth will ache too much without it. Highly recommended by Father! Forty dollars an hour, Father's forty dollars! Progress! Looking up! Looking better! That new haircut is so becoming, says Dr. Coronet herself, showing how normal she is for a woman with an I.Q. of 180 and many advanced degrees.

2. Mother. A lady in a brown suede coat. Boots of shiny black material, black gloves, a black fur hat. She would be humiliated could she know that of all the people in the world it is my ex-lover Simon who walks most like her . . . self-conscious and unreal, listening to distant music, a little bowlegged with craftiness. . . .

3. Father. Tying a necktie. In a hurry. On my first evening home he put his hand on my arm and said, "Honey, we're going to forget all about this."

4. Simon. Outside, a plane is crossing the sky, in here we're in a hurry. Morning. It must be morning. The girl is half out of her

mind, whimpering and vague; Simon her dear friend is wretched this morning . . . he is wretched with morning itself . . . he forces her to give him an injection with that needle she knows is filthy, she has a dread of needles and surgical instruments and the odor of things that are to be sent into the blood, thinking somehow of her father. . . . This is a bad morning, Simon says that his mind is being twisted out of shape, and so he submits to the needle that he usually scorns and bites his lip with his yellowish teeth, his face going very pale. *Ah baby!* he says in his soft mocking voice, which with all women is a mockery of love, *do it like this—Slowly—* And the girl, terrified, almost drops the precious needle but manages to turn it up to the light from the window . . . is it an extension of herself then? She can give him this gift then? *I wish you wouldn't do this to me,* she says, wise in her terror, because it seems to her that Simon's danger—in a few minutes he may be dead—is a way of pressing her against him that is more powerful than any other embrace. She has to work over his arm, the knotted corded veins of his arm, her forehead wet with perspiration as she pushes and releases the needle, staring at that mixture of liquid now stained with Simon's bright blood. . . . When the drug hits him she can feel it herself, she feels that magic that is more than any woman can give him, striking the back of his head and making his face stretch as if with the impact of a terrible sun. . . . She tries to embrace him but he pushes her aside and stumbles to his feet. *Jesus Christ,* he says. . . .

5. Princess, a Negro girl of eighteen. What is her charge? She is closed-mouthed about it, shrewd and silent, you know that no one had to wrestle her to the sidewalk to get her in here; she came with dignity. In the recreation room she sits reading *Nancy Drew and the Jewel Box Mystery,* which inspires in her face tiny wrinkles of alarm and interest: what a face! Light brown skin, heavy shaded eyes, heavy eyelashes, a serious sinister dark brow, graceful fingers, graceful wristbones, graceful legs, lips, tongue, a sugar-sweet voice, a leggy stride more masculine than Simon's and my mother's, decked out in a dirty white blouse and dirty white slacks; vaguely nautical is Princess' style. . . . At breakfast she is in charge of clearing the table and leans over me, saying, *Honey you sure you ate enough?*

6. The girl lies sleepless, wondering. Why here, why not there? Why Bloomfield Hills and not jail? Why jail and not her pink room? Why downtown Detroit and not Sioux Drive? What is the difference? Is Simon all the difference? The girl's head is a parade of wonders. She is nearly sixteen, her breath is marvelous with wonders, not long ago she was coloring with crayons and now she is smearing the landscape with paints that won't come off and won't come off her fingers either. She says to the matron *I am not talking about anything,* not because everyone has warned her not to talk but because, because she will not talk; because she won't say anything about Simon, who is her secret. And she says to the matron, *I won't go home,* up until that night in the lavatory when everything was changed. . . . "No, I won't go home I want to stay here," she says, listening to her own words with amazement, thinking that weeds might climb everywhere over that marvelous $180,000 house and dinosaurs might return to muddy the beige carpeting, but never never will she reconcile four o'clock in the morning in Detroit with eight o'clock breakfasts in Bloomfield Hills. . . . oh, she aches still for Simon's hands and his caressing breath, though he gave her little pleasure, he took everything from her (five-dollar bills, ten-dollar bills, passed into her numb hands by men and taken out of her hands by Simon) until she herself was passed into the hands of other men, police, when Simon evidently got tired of her and her hysteria. . . . *No, I won't go home, I don't want to be bailed out.* The girl thinks as a *Stubborn and Wayward Child* (one of several charges lodged against her), and the matron understands her crazy white-rimmed eyes that are seeking out some new violence that will keep her in jail, should someone threaten to let her out. Such children try to strangle the matrons, the attendants, or one another . . . they want the locks locked forever, the doors nailed shut . . . and this girl is no different up until that night her mind is changed for her. . . .

IX That Night

Princess and Dolly, a little white girl of maybe fifteen, hardy however as a sergeant and in the House of Correction for armed robbery, corner her in the lavatory at the farthest sink and the other girls look away and file out to bed, leaving her. God, how she is beaten up! Why is she beaten up? Why do they pound her, why such hatred? Princess vents all the hatred of a thousand silent Detroit win ters on her body, this girl whose body belongs to me, fiercely sh rides across the Midwestern plains on this girl's tender bruised bod . . . revenge on the oppressed minorities of America! revenge on th slaughtered Indians! revenge on the female sex, on the male sex revenge on Bloomfield Hills, revenge revenge. . . .

X Detroit

In Detroit, weather weighs heavily upon everyone. The sky looms large. The horizon shimmers in smoke. Downtown the buildings are imprecise in the haze. Perpetual haze. Perpetual motion inside the haze. Across the choppy river is the city of Windsor, in Canada Part of the continent has bunched up here and is bulging outward at the tip of Detroit; a cold hard rain is forever falling on the expressways. . . . Shoppers shop grimly, their cars are not parked in safe places, their windshields may be smashed and graceful ebony hands may drag them out through their shatterproof smashed windshields, crying, *Revenge for the Indians!* Ah, they all fear leaving Hudson's and being dragged to the very tip of the city and thrown off the parking roof of Cobo Hall, that expensive tomb, into the river. . . .

XI Characters We Are Forever Entwined With

1. Simon drew me into his tender rotting arms and breathed gravity into me. Then I came to earth, weighed down. He said, *You are such a little girl,* and he weighed me down with his delight. In the palms of his hands were teeth marks from his previous life experiences. He was thirty-five, they said. Imagine Simon in this room, in my pink room: he is about six feet tall and stoops slightly, in a feline cautious way, always thinking, always on guard, with his scuffed light suede shoes and his clothes that are anyone's clothes, slightly rumpled ordinary clothes that ordinary men might wear to not-bad jobs. Simon has fair long hair, curly hair, spent languid curls that are like . . . exactly like the curls of wood shavings to the touch, I am trying to be exact . . . and he smells of unheated mornings and coffee and too many pills coating his tongue with a faint green-white scum. . . . Dear Simon, who would be panicked in this

›om and in this house (right now Billie is vacuuming next door ı my parents' room; a vacuum cleaner's roar is a sign of all good ıings), Simon who is said to have come from a home not much ifferent from this, years ago, fleeing all the carpeting and the polhed banisters . . . Simon has a deathly face, only desperate people ıll in love with it. His face is bony and cautious, the bones of his ıeeks prominent as if with the rigidity of his ceaseless thinking, lotting, for he has to make money out of girls to whom money ıeans nothing, they're so far gone they can hardly count it, and ı a sense money means nothing to him either except as a way of eeping on with his life. *Each Day's Proud Struggle,* the title of a novel 'e could read at jail. . . . Each day he needs a certain amount of ıoney. He devours it. It wasn't love he uncoiled in me with his hol›wed-out eyes and his courteous smile, that remnant of a prosperus past, but a dark terror that needed to press itself flat against im, or against another man . . . but he was the first, he came over › me and took my arm, a claim. We struggled on the stairs and said, *Let me loose, you're hurting my neck, my face,* it was such a surprise ıat my skin hurt where he rubbed it, and afterward we lay face › face and he breathed everything into me. In the end I think he ırned me in.

2. Raymond Forrest. I just read this morning that Raymond For:st's father, the chairman of the board at , died of a heart :tack on a plane bound for London. I would like to write Raymond ɔrrest a note of sympathy. I would like to thank him for not pressıg charges against me one hundred years ago, saving me, being so :nerous . . . well, men like Raymond Forrest are generous men, ɔt like Simon. I would like to write him a letter telling of my love, : of some other emotion that is positive and healthy. Not like imon and his poetry, which he scrawled down when he was high ıd never changed a word . . . but when I try to think of something › say, it is Simon's language that comes back to me, caught in my ead like a bad song, it is always Simon's language:

There is no reality only dreams
Your neck may get snapped when you wake
My love is drawn to some violent end
She keeps wanting to get away

My love is heading downward
And I am heading upward
She is going to crash on the sidewalk
And I am going to dissolve into the clouds

XII Events

1. Out of the hospital, bruised and saddened and converted, wit Princess' grunts still tangled in my hair . . . and Father in his over coat looking like a prince himself, come to carry me off. Up the ex pressway and out north to home. Jesus Christ, but the air is thinne and cleaner here. Monumental houses. Heartbreaking sidewalks, s clean.

2. Weeping in the living room. The ceiling is two stories high an two chandeliers hang from it. Weeping, weeping, though Billie th maid is *probably listening.* I will never leave home again. Never. Neve leave home. Never leave this home again, never.

3. Sugar doughnuts for breakfast. The toaster is very shiny an my face is distorted in it. Is that my face?

4. The car is turning in the driveway. Father brings me hom Mother embraces me. Sunlight breaks in movieland patches on th roof of our traditional-contemporary home, which was designed fc the famous automotive stylist whose identity, if I told you the nam of the famous car he designed, you would all know, so I can't te you because my teeth chatter at the thought of being sued . . . c having someone climb into my bedroom window with a rope t strangle me. . . . The car turns up the blacktop drive. The hous opens to me like a doll's house, so lovely in the sunlight, the bi living room beckons to me with its walls falling away in a deliriur of joy at my return, Billie the maid is *no doubt* listening from th kitchen as I burst into tears and the hysteria Simon got so sick o Convulsed in Father's arms, I say I will never leave again, neve why did I leave, where did I go, what happened, my mind is gon wrong, my body is one big bruise, my backbone was sucked dry it wasn't the men who hurt me and Simon never hurt me but onl those girls . . . my God, how they hurt me . . . I will never leav

home again. . . . The car is perpetually turning up the drive and I am perpetually breaking down in the living room and we are perpetually taking the right exit from the expressway (Lahser Road) and the wall of the rest room is perpetually banging against my head and perpetually are Simon's hands moving across my body and adding everything up and so too are Father's hands on my shaking bruised back, far from the surface of my skin on the surface of my good blue cashmere coat (dry-cleaned for my release). . . . I weep for all the money here, for God in gold and beige carpeting, for the beauty of chandeliers and the miracle of a clean polished gleaming toaster and faucets that run both hot and cold water, and I tell them, *I will never leave home, this is my home, I love everything here, I am in love with everything here. . . .*

I am home.

1969

Biographical Notes on the Authors

[Arranged alphabetically]

SHERWOOD ANDERSON [1876–1941]

Sherwood Anderson was born on September 13, 1876, in Camden, Ohio, the son of a former cavalryman and harnessmaker. The young Anderson was not well educated but was considered enterprising and ambitious. After serving in the army during the Spanish-American War, Anderson became an advertising salesman and then a copywriter in Chicago. His earliest literary efforts, often in praise of the business ethic, appeared at this time, primarily in trade journals. Anderson achieved success as the head of a paint manufacturing company in Ohio, but suffered a nervous breakdown and returned to Chicago to begin a new life among artists and writers. His first novel, *Windy McPherson's Son,* was published in 1916. *Winesburg, Ohio,* his best-known work, appeared in 1919 and made him famous. During the 1920s he traveled to Europe, where he met Gertrude Stein, James Joyce, and other expatriate artists and writers; he lived in New Orleans, where he befriended and encouraged William Faulkner; and in the late 1920s he moved to Marion, Virginia, where he bought and ran a country newspaper. Anderson continued to write for the rest of his life, but none of his later works were as successful as his earlier ones. He died on March 8, 1941, in Colon, Panama, while on a tour for the State Department. Among his other novels are *Poor White* (1920), *Many Marriages* (1922), and *Dark Laughter* (1925). In addition to *Winesburg, Ohio,* he published three collections of short stories.

ISAAC BABEL [1894–1941?]

Born in the Moldovanka, the Jewish ghetto of Odessa, Russia, Isaac Babel left there as a young man to seek a fuller life after the narrowness of his upbringing and his strict religious education. In 1915, at the age of 21, he settled in St. Petersburg, then the commercial and cultural center of Russia, and in 1920 enlisted in the army, joining the regiment of Kuban Cossacks. His first two collections of stories brought him immediate fame: *Odessa Tales* (1923–1924), written in a Russo-Jewish jargon, reflects his early experiences in the ghetto; *Red Cavalry* (1926), which employs the slang of the Cossacks, draws on his military experiences. Later in his career Babel turned to writing drama and published several plays. During the Stalin era he was denounced, arrested (1938), and imprisoned in a concentration camp, where he died a few years later. Several of Babel's works were reissued in the Soviet Union after Stalin's death (1953), but in censored versions.

JAMES BALDWIN [b. 1924]

Born in New York City on August 2, 1924, the son of a revivalist minister, James Baldwin was raised in poverty in Harlem. At the age of fourteen he followed in his father's footsteps and became a preacher in the Fireside Pentecostal Church. After graduation from high school, he decided to become a writer, and, with the help of the black American expatriate writer Richard Wright, won a grant which enabled him to live in Paris. There Baldwin worked on his first novel, *Go Tell It on the Mountain,* based on his experiences as a storefront preacher. The novel was published in 1953 and was well received. His other novels include *Giovanni's Room* (1956), *Another Country* (1962), *Tell Me How Long the Train's Been Gone* (1968), and *If Beale Street Could Talk* (1974). He has also published several volumes of essays, a collection of short stories, and two plays.

JOHN BARTH [b. 1930]

John Barth was born in Cambridge, Maryland, a locale he draws on frequently as a setting for his fictional work. For a brief time he studied music at the Juilliard School of Music, after which he went on to receive his B.A. (1951) and M.A. (1952) degrees at Johns Hopkins University. Barth has spent most of his life in the academic world, teaching first at Pennsylvania State University, then at the State University of New York at Buffalo. In 1972 he returned to Johns Hopkins, where he is now a professor of English and writer-in-residence. His first novel, *The Floating Opera,* was published in 1956 and has been followed by four others: *The End of the Road* (1958), *The Sot-Weed Factor* (1960), *Giles Goatboy* (1966), and *Letters* (1979). His short fiction appears regularly in magazines such as *Esquire, Atlantic Monthly,* and *New American Review,* and has been collected in two volumes, *Lost in the Funhouse* (1968) and *Chimera* (1972), which won the National Book Award.

DONALD BARTHELME [b. 1931]

Donald Barthelme was born in Philadelphia and grew up in Houston, Texas, where he attended the University of Houston. He has worked in a variety of jobs—as a newspaper reporter and editor of a literary review, a museum director, and a professor of creative writing. In 1966 Barthelme was the recipient of a Guggenheim Fellowship. Since the early 1960s his short stories have appeared regularly in *The New Yorker* and have been collected in five volumes, including *Come Back, Dr. Caligari* (1964), *Unspeakable Practices, Unnatural Acts* (1968), and *Amateurs* (1976). In addition, he has published two novels, *Snow White* (1967) and *The Dead Father* (1975); a collection of nonfiction pieces, *Guilty Pleasures* (1974); and a children's book, *The Slightly Irregular Fire Engine,* which won the National Book Award for Children's Literature in 1971. In recent years Barthelme has resided in New York City.

AMBROSE BIERCE [1842–1914?]

The son of a poor farm family, Ambrose Bierce was born in a religious camp in Meigs County, Ohio, and received little formal education as a child. At age 19 he enlisted in the Indiana infantry, serving four years in the Civil War. Twice wounded, Bierce experienced some of the bloodiest fighting of the war and began writing to describe the horrors he had seen. After his military service he moved to San Francisco to pursue a career in journalism writing for the *News-Letter,* of which he became editor in 1868. Between 1872 and 1875 Bierce lived in London, where he was on the staff of the magazine *Fun.* During this period he completed three books, including *Cobwebs from an Empty Skull* (1874), a collection of sketches and witty pieces. On his return to San Francisco he wrote a column for Hearst's *Sunday Examiner* nd soon became the most powerful literary influence on the West Coast. ı 1897 he went to Washington as a correspondent for the Hearst newspa-ers. Unhappiness and disillusionment, exacerbated by a series of domestic ·agedies, overshadowed Bierce's later life. In 1913 he left America and ent to Mexico, where all trace of him was lost. It is believed he died there ie following year. Bierce's best short stories are collected in two volumes, *ales of Soldiers and Civilians* (1891) and *Can Such Things Be?* (1893). Among his ther well known works is *The Devil's Dictionary* (1911), a collection of sar-onic definitions first published in 1906 as *The Cynic's Word Book.*

JORGE LUIS BORGES [b. 1899]

orn in Buenos Aires, Argentina, Borges from an early age could read and rite fluently in both Spanish and English. When he was 15 his family ioved to Switzerland, where he was educated at the Collège de Genève, tudying French, German, and Italian. Later he attended Cambridge Uni-ersity in England. After university Borges spent three years in Spain, here he became acquainted with many of the young avant-garde writers f the time, and then returned to Buenos Aires in 1921. A poet, essayist, nd film critic early in his literary career, Borges turned to the short story n the 1930s, the form which has been his primary genre ever since. He as also translated the works of a number of writers into Spanish, among hem Gide, Melville, Faulkner, and Kafka. Borges fell into official disfavor uring the Perón dictatorship in the 1940s and early 1950s, but after Perón's verthrow in 1955 he was appointed Director of the National Library of rgentina. He was also given a position as a professor of literature at the Jniversity of Buenos Aires. Among his many books available in English re *Labyrinths* (1962), *Dreamtigers* (1964), *The Book of Imaginary Beings* (1969), nd *The Book of Sand* (1979).

WILLA CATHER [1873–1947]

Born in Winchester, Virginia, of Anglo-Irish parents, Willa Cather moved vith her family to Red Cloud, Nebraska, in 1883 and grew up there among he pioneer farmers and immigrant families of the plains. This frontier set-ing and its people provide the focus for much of her fiction. At the Univer-sity of Nebraska Cather studied English and the classics and graduated in 1895. Shortly thereafter she moved to Pittsburgh, where she taught high school and worked as a journalist on a daily newspaper. In 1904 she settle in Greenwich Village in New York City, which became her home for th rest of her life. The first volume of Cather's stories, *The Troll Garden,* wa published in 1905. This led to her appointment a year later as an edito of *McClure's Magazine,* where she worked until 1912, eventually becomin managing editor. With the publication in 1912 of *Alexander's Bridge,* her firs novel, she was able to leave *McClure's* and devote herself full time to writ ing. In all Cather published sixteen novels. *One of Ours* (1922) was awarde the Pulitzer Prize; *My Ántonia* (1918) and *Death Comes for the Archbishop* (192 are regarded by many as her masterpieces. Later collections of her sho fiction include *Youth and the Bright Medusa* (1920), *My Mortal Enemy* (1926 and *The Old Beauty and Others* (1948).

JOHN CHEEVER [1912–1982]

John Cheever was born in Quincy, Massachusetts, and attended the exclu sive Thayer Academy, from which he was expelled at age 17. This exper ence became the subject of his first published short story, "Expelled which appeared in *New Republic* in 1930. With his expulsion from Thay Cheever's formal education ended and he devoted himself to writing. H short stories appeared regularly in magazines such as *Yale Review* and *Atlan Monthly,* and more than a hundred were published in *The New Yorker.* H first major success was the publication in 1953 of *The Enormous Radio,* a co lection of his short fiction. *The Stories of John Cheever* (1978), the largest colle tion of his work, containing 61 stories, was awarded the Pulitzer Prize. I addition to short stories, Cheever also wrote four novels, among them *T Wapshot Chronicle* (1957), which won the National Book Award, and *Bull Park* (1969), as well as several television scripts. During his career Cheev taught at Barnard College and the University of Iowa and lived and worke at the Yaddo writer's colony in Saratoga Springs, New York. He was se lected as a member of the American Academy of Arts and Letters in 197

ANTON CHEKHOV [1860–1904]

Born in Taganrog, a seacoast town in southern Russia, Chekhov was th son of a grocer and the grandson of a serf. He studied medicine at Mosco University and began writing humorous tales to support himself. In 188 he received his medical degree and published his first volume of short sto es. Throughout his life Chekhov was an active humanitarian and social former. Perhaps his best-known work in this vein was *The Island of Sakhalin* 890), a moving study of the lives of convicts. In addition to being a pro-ic writer of short stories—he wrote more than five hundred in all, many which have never been translated into English—Chekhov is probably e greatest of the Russian dramatists. In 1898 the Moscow Art Theatre oduced his play *The Seagull,* soon followed by superb productions of his asterpieces *Uncle Vanya* (1899), *The Three Sisters* (1901), and *The Cherry Or-ard* (1904). In 1901 he married the young actress Olga Knipper, but they d only three years together before he died of tuberculosis in a German ealth resort at the age of 44.

SAMUEL LANGHORNE CLEMENS [1835–1910]

muel Langhorne Clemens, better known by his pseudonym, Mark vain, was born in rural Florida, Missouri, the son of a Virginian who had ne west to seek his fortune on the frontier. In 1839 the family settled Hannibal, Missouri. Influenced by his father's restless spirit, Clemens d an adventurous boyhood which he later recreated in his two most idely known works, *The Adventures of Tom Sawyer* (1876) and *The Adventures Huckleberry Finn* (1884). After his father's death in 1847 Clemens was ap-enticed to a local printer and at that time began writing pieces for his other's newspaper. In 1853 and 1854 he worked as a printer in several ies in the East and Midwest. This was followed by a period of several ars as a river boat pilot on the Mississippi, the experience from which derived his pseudonym. "Mark Twain" in the jargon of the river meant o fathoms deep and was a phrase used by pilots in making soundings the river depth. When the river traffic stopped at the outbreak of the vil War, Clemens joined the war briefly with a group of Confederate my volunteers. In 1862 he went to Nevada with his brother, took a posi-on with the Virginia City *Examiner,* and began in earnest his career as a urnalist and writer of humorous tales and anecdotes. It was at this time at he began to use the pseudonym Mark Twain, the name by which he ould be known henceforth. Clemens subsequently went to work in San ancisco as a newspaperman and became very popular there as a lecturer. he Celebrated Jumping Frog of Calaveras County" was published in 65 in the New York *Saturday Press* and later became the centerpiece for e first collection of his short pieces, which was published in 1867 and ought him wide recognition. His travels in Europe and the Holy Land the late 1860s are humorously described in *Innocents Abroad* (1869). In 1870

he married Olivia Langdon and settled first in Buffalo then in Hartford
where he led a respectable, well-to-do life previously unknown to him
When a publishing and printing operation in which Clemens had investe
heavily failed in 1894, he found himself bankrupt. An extended lecture tou
of the world succeeded in paying off his debts, but the series of person
tragedies that followed—the death of his favorite daughter in 1896, h
wife's long illness and death in 1904, and the death of a second daught
in 1909—cast a permanent shadow over his life. His later writings took c
a deeply pessimistic and somber tone very different from the humorou
and exuberant early work. Clemens died in April 1910 at Stormfield,
house near Redding, Connecticut, and is buried in Elmira, New York.

JOSEPH CONRAD [1857–1924]

Conrad was born in Poland of an affluent family and christened Josef Teo
dor Konrad Walecz Korzeniowski. His parents died when he was sti
young, and Josef was raised by an uncle. In preparation for a gentleman
career, he was educated at the University of Cracow, but Conrad was dete
mined to go to sea. Beginning in 1874 he worked out of Marseilles for th
French navy and in 1878 joined the English merchant fleet, rising eventu
ally to the rank of master mariner (captain) and becoming a British subjec
After twenty years at sea he retired to begin a full-time career as a novelis
Among his friends in England were such well-known writers as H. G
Wells, Henry James, Stephen Crane, and Ford Madox Ford, with who
he collaborated on two novels. All of Conrad's novels and shorter work
were written in English, actually his third language after Polish and Frenc
and many of them draw on his adventures at sea for their themes. Begin
ning with the first novel, *Almayer's Folly,* published in 1895, his works we
critically acclaimed, but it was not until the appearance of *Chance,* in 191
that he had his first popular and financial success. All told, Conrad pro
duced some twenty-seven volumes, including *The Nigger of the Narcissu*
(1897), *Lord Jim* (1900), *Nostromo* (1904), *The Secret Agent* (1907), and *Victo*
(1915). He died on August 3, 1924, when his literary reputation was at i
highest.

STEPHEN CRANE [1871–1900]

Crane was born on November 1, 1871, in Newark, New Jersey, into an o
family that had gained distinction in the church, in government, and c

the battlefield. His father, a Methodist minister, and his mother, the daughter of a minister, raised their son strictly. At an early age he rebelled against his parents' puritanical existence and turned to a dissolute life, smoking, gambling, drinking, and spending his time in brothels. After failing at both Lafayette College and Syracuse University, he worked as a journalist for the New York *Tribune* and for an older brother who ran a news agency in Asbury Park, New Jersey. At this time he was also writing the first draft of *Maggie: A Girl of the Streets,* his brutally realistic novel about life in the New York slums. Because of its shocking content, the book had to be published with borrowed money under the pseudonym Johnston Smith. The work came to the attention of the respected New England writer William Dean Howells, and two years later, in 1895, *Maggie* was published in a proper edition, over Crane's own name, and with a preface by Howells. That same year saw the publication of a volume of his poems and his most famous work, *The Red Badge of Courage.* This novel was enthusiastically received; Crane, at the age of twenty-four, had gained wide recognition. During this period, in an attempt to improve his financial position, he also returned to journalism; serving as a war correspondent in the Greco-Turkish and the Spanish-American wars. He spent most of his later years living, rather extravagantly, in England, where he met Joseph Conrad, Henry James, and other literary figures. In the late 1890s Crane's health, which for many years had not been strong, deteriorated rapidly; he died of tuberculosis on June 5, 1900, in Germany.

RALPH ELLISON [b. 1914]

Ralph Ellison, born in Oklahoma City on March 1, 1914, was educated at Tuskegee Institute, where he studied music. He went to New York City, there met and was influenced by Richard Wright, and turned to a career as a writer. His novel, *The Invisible Man* (1952), has become a classic in American fiction and has received numerous accolades, including the 1953 National Book Award. Ellison has taught literature and writing at Bard College, the University of Chicago, Rutgers University, and New York University. His other works include many short stories, as yet not published in a collected edition, and *Shadow and Act,* a collection of essays published in 1964.

WILLIAM FAULKNER [1897–1962]

Born in New Albany, Mississippi, on September 25, 1897, William Faulkner moved as a young boy to Oxford, Mississippi, the place he was to call home all his life. His formal education was spotty at best; he completed only two years of high school and just over a year at the University of Mississippi. After a brief stint with the Royal Canadian Air Force during World War I, Faulkner worked at a variety of jobs—in his grandfather's bank in Oxford, at an arms plant in Connecticut, in a bookstore in New York City, and as the postmaster of the university post office in Oxford. His literary career began in New Orleans in 1925, when he met Sherwood Anderson. Encouraged by the older writer, Faulkner began work on his first novel, *Soldier's Pay,* which was published in 1926 to favorable reviews. *Sartoris,* published in 1929, was his third novel and the first set in Yoknapatawpha County, a fictional re-creation of the area around Oxford and a setting that appears again and again in his works. The next decade was a period of great productivity as Faulkner published a volume of poetry, two collections of short stories, and ten novels. Because his novels were not great financial successes, he spent periods of time in Hollywood writing film scripts to supplement his income. Only after he received the Nobel Prize in Literature, in 1949, did his books begin to sell in large quantities. Faulkner was also the recipient of two National Book Awards and two Pulitzer Prizes. Among his best-known novels are *The Sound and the Fury* (1929), *As I Lay Dying* (1930), *Sanctuary* (1931), *Light in August* (1932), and *Absalom! Absalom!* (1936). He died in Oxford, Mississippi, on July 6, 1962.

F. SCOTT FITZGERALD [1896–1940]

Born on September 24, 1896, in St. Paul, Minnesota, Fitzgerald was a spoiled, undisciplined child and a failure at school. He began writing at an early age and while attending the Newman School had one of his plays produced in an amateur performance. At Princeton University he worked on musical productions for the Triangle Club and wrote stories and poems, some of which were published by his friend and collaborator Edmund Wilson in the *Nassau Literary Magazine,* which Wilson edited. At the beginning of his senior year he left Princeton to report for officer's training at Fort Leavenworth, Kansas. After basic training he was stationed at Camp Sheridan, Alabama, and there met and fell in love with the beautiful Southern belle, Zelda Sayre. In 1920 his first novel, *This Side of Paradise,* was published;

t brought Fitzgerald fame and financial success. As a result of his new-found wealth, he and Zelda were able to marry and lead a glamourous, extravagant life, traveling back and forth between New York and Europe. *The Great Gatsby,* published in 1925 to critical acclaim, was probably his greatest novel, but it was a financial disappointment. His life at this time was in disorder: he was plagued by increasing alcoholism and Zelda's deterioration into madness, as well as by severe financial difficulties. After 1930 Zelda was intermittently institutionalized. In 1932 she published *Save Me the Waltz,* a novel describing the Fitzgeralds' life together as seen through her eyes. Fitzgerald's final years were spent in Hollywood trying to support himself by writing film scripts. There he met and had a love affair with the English journalist and columnist Sheilah Graham. He died in her apartment of a heart attack on December 21, 1940. His other novels include *Tender Is the Night* (1934) and *The Last Tycoon,* unfinished at the time of his death but edited by his friend Edmund Wilson and published posthumously in 1941. In addition, several collections of his short stories have been published.

NATHANIEL HAWTHORNE [1804–1864]

Nathaniel Hawthorne was born on July 4, 1804, in Salem, Massachusetts, into a once-prominent New England family. After his father died in 1808, the family relied on relatives for support. Hawthorne attended Bowdoin College in Maine, where he graduated in 1825. For the next thirteen years he lived in Salem in relative seclusion, reading, writing, and observing the New England landscape and people. His first novel, *Fanshawe,* was published in 1829. After years of discipline and dedication to his craft, he published *Twice-Told Tales,* a collection of stories, in 1837. In order to support himself he took a job in the Boston customs house but quit in 1841 to live at Brook Farm, an experimental utopian community. The following year he left Brook Farm, married Sophia Peabody, and moved to Concord. He returned to Salem in 1845, took a position as a customs inspector, and in 1849 began work full time on what was to be his most important novel, *The Scarlet Letter.* Published in 1850, the novel was a great success and was soon followed by *The House of the Seven Gables* (1851) and *The Blithedale Romance* (1852), based on his Brook Farm experience. In 1852 he also wrote a campaign biography of Franklin Pierce, who had been a college friend at Bowdoin. After Pierce became president (1853) he appointed Hawthorne consul to Liverpool. Hawthorne and his family traveled widely in Europe, finally returning to the United States in 1860. He died in his sleep on May 18, 1864, in Plymouth, New Hampshire.

ERNEST HEMINGWAY [1899–1961]

Born July 21, 1899, in Oak Park, Illinois, Hemingway from his early years led an active, vigorous life, spending summers in the wilds of northern Michigan with his physician father and in school playing football and boxing. His first employment as a writer was as a reporter for the Kansas City *Star;* later he worked on the Toronto *Star* and the Chicago *Tribune.* In 1918 he served as an ambulance driver in the war in Italy, was severely wounded, and was decorated by the Italian government. Three years later Hemingway was on his way back to Europe, this time to Paris, where he would meet Gertrude Stein, Ezra Pound, F. Scott Fitzgerald, and other artists and writers, many of whom, through their support and encouragement, had a significant influence on his work. His first book, *Three Stories and Ten Poems,* was published in Paris in 1923, followed soon after by *In Our Time,* a collection of short stories. With the publication in 1926 of *The Sun Also Rises* came success and acclamation as the spokesman for the "lost generation." *A Farewell to Arms* (1929), drawn from his war experiences in Italy, further increased his audience and his reputation. In 1936 Hemingway went to Spain as a war correspondent covering the Civil War. Out of this experience came perhaps his greatest novel, *For Whom The Bell Tolls* (1940). During the Second World War he served as a war correspondent for the American Army in Europe and received a Bronze Star. Throughout his life Hemingway continually pursued sport and adventure. His frequent travels took him to Spain for the bullfights, on fishing trips in the Caribbean, and on big-game hunting expeditions to the American West and Africa. During his later years his health, and with it his physical powers, deteriorated, and he suffered from periods of extreme depression, leading finally to suicide at his home in Ketchum, Idaho, on July 2, 1961. Among his other works are the novels *To Have and Have Not* (1937), *The Old Man and the Sea* (1952), and a memoir, *A Moveable Feast,* published posthumously in 1964. He was awarded the Nobel Prize in Literature in 1954.

SHIRLEY JACKSON [1919–1965]

Shirley Jackson was born in San Francisco and brought up in Rochester, New York. She received her undergraduate degree from Syracuse University, where she was the founder and editor of the campus literary magazine. After graduation she married the literary critic Stanley Edgar Hyman and settled with him in Bennington, Vermont. She is best known for her stories and novels of Gothic horror and the occult. Among her novels are *Hangsaman* (1951), *We Have Always Lived in the Castle* (1953), *The Bird's Nest* (1954), and *The Haunting of Hill House* (1959). Her short stories are collected in *The Lottery* (1944) and *The Magic of Shirley Jackson,* published posthumously by her husband in 1966.

HENRY JAMES [1843–1916]

Henry James was born in New York City on April 15, 1843, into a well-to-do, intellectual family. James's father was a writer and philosopher; his older brother, William, was to become perhaps the most influential philosopher of his day. From infancy James spent long periods of time in Europe, primarily London and Paris, receiving most of his early education from a variety of tutors there. Beginning at age nine James developed a love for the theater and a fondness for reading, especially the novels of Dickens. In 1862 he enrolled in Harvard Law School, studying there for one year. His literary career began shortly after that, with the publication of stories in the *Continental Monthly* and the *Atlantic Monthly.* On his frequent trips to Europe he became acquainted with many prominent literary figures—George Eliot, John Ruskin, Turgenev, Flaubert, Zola, and de Maupassant—and by 1876 he had decided to make England his home. He lived in London from 1876 to 1897, with only occasional visits to the United States. Out of financial necessity James turned, in the early 1890s, to writing plays, but with little success. The disastrous reception of one of his plays, the death of his sister, and the suicide of a long-time friend marked a turning point in his life. In 1896 he left London to settle in Rye, Sussex, where in the greater peace and solitude of the countryside he embarked on the most productive and creative period of his career. Between 1907 and 1909 he undertook a complete reconsideration and revision of every novel and tale he had written, an effort which resulted in the publication of the now famous New York edition of *The Novels and Tales of Henry James* in twenty-four volumes, each with a new preface by James. After the outbreak of World War I, James renounced his American citizenship and became a British subject as a gesture of support for the Allied cause. A series of strokes suffered in 1915 and early 1916 caused his death on February 28. The most important of his many novels are *The American* (1877), *Daisy Miller* (1879), *The Portrait of a Lady* (1881), *The Princess Casamassima* (1886), *The Turn of the Screw* (1898), *The Wings of the Dove* (1902), *The Ambassadors* (1903), and *The Golden Bowl* (1904).

JAMES JOYCE [1882–1941]

Born in Dublin, Ireland, on February 2, 1882, Joyce was educated at Jesuit schools in preparation for the priesthood. At an early age he abandoned Catholicism and in 1904 left Dublin for the broader horizons of the continent. Living in Paris, Zurich, and Trieste over the next twenty-five years, he tried to support himself and his family by teaching foreign languages and at one time almost became a professional singer. He returned to Dublin briefly in 1912 to arrange for publication of his short stories, *Dubliners,* but because of fear of censorship the book was burned by the printers and was not published until 1914, in England. During World War I he lived in Zurich, where he wrote *A Portrait of the Artist as a Young Man,* a partially autobiographical novel of his adolescent years. The book was published, with the help of Ezra Pound, in 1916. At about this time Joyce fell victim to glaucoma; for the remainder of his life he suffered periods of intense pain and near blindness. His masterpiece, the novel *Ulysses,* was written between 1914 and 1921, parts of it being published during that time in literary periodicals. There was strenuous opposition to publication of the work in book form because of obscenity charges, but it was finally published in Paris in 1922 by Shakespeare and Company, a bookstore owned and operated by an expatriate American, Sylvia Beach. Publication in the United States was banned until 1933. Because of the censorship and suppression of his books throughout the world and the many pirated editions that appeared, Joyce earned little in royalties and often had to rely upon his friends for support. He died after surgery in Zurich on January 13, 1941.

FRANZ KAFKA [1883–1924]

Kafka was born in Prague, Czechoslovakia, the son of middle-class Jewish parents. He was educated at the German University in Prague, where he studied law; after receiving his degree he was employed in the workmen's compensation division of the Austrian government, a position he held for many years. Because his method of writing was painstakingly slow, it was not possible for him to earn a living by his pen. Indeed, at the time of his death from tuberculosis he had published very little and had asked his friend Max Brod to burn all the uncompleted manuscripts Kafka had left. Fortunately Brod ignored this request and was responsible for the posthumous publication of Kafka's major long works—*The Trial* (1925), *The Castle* (1926), and *Amerika* (1927)—as well as a large number of his short stories.

RING LARDNER [1885–1933]

Born in Niles, Michigan, Ringgold Lardner was one of nine children of a wealthy and prominent family. He worked for many years as a newspaperman and sports writer in Chicago, St. Louis, Boston, and New York before he became successful as a short story writer. When he moved east in 1919, he became a friend of F. Scott Fitzgerald and other aspiring writers. Many of Lardner's stories grew out of his experiences as a sports writer and were published originally in popular magazines such as the *Saturday Evening Post.* The first collection of his short fiction, *You Know Me, Al; A Busher's Letters,* was published in 1916. A subsequent collection, *How to Write Short Stories (with Samples)* (1924) established his reputation as a biting satirist. This same cynical humor continued to appear in his later collections, *What of It?* (1925), *Round Up* (1929), and *First and Last* (1934). In addition to the stories, Lardner also wrote two successful plays.

D. H. LAWRENCE [1885–1930]

Born David Herbert Lawrence on September 11, 1885, he was the son of a coal miner in Nottinghamshire, England. His early years were overshadowed by poverty and by a fiercely ambitious, domineering mother who insisted on his bettering himself. After graduation from University College in Nottingham, he took a position as a schoolmaster in a suburb of London. While teaching he wrote both fiction and poetry. The first of his poems appeared in 1909 in the *English Review,* whose editor at that time was Ford Madox Ford. In 1911 his first novel, *The White Peacock,* was published, also with the assistance of Ford. He was forced by illness to return to Nottingham and there fell in love with Frieda von Richthofen Weekley, the German wife of a professor at the college. They eloped to the continent and subsequently were married, but spent the years of World War I in England, where, because of his wife's origins and his outspoken opposition to the war, they were suspected of being spies. The Lawrences left England in 1919 and thereafter resided at various times in Ceylon, Australia, the United States, Italy, Tahiti, Mexico, and France. In 1929 a London exhibition of his paintings was raided by the police and several were either banned or confiscated. His fiction fared just as poorly with the censors, three of his novels having been suppressed. Perhaps the most famous of these, *Lady Chatterley's Lover,* was privately printed in Italy but was banned in both England and the United States until 1959. The Grove Press edition, brought out that year, was immediately banned, but in a now-famous court case the ban was ruled unconstitutional. A victim of tuberculosis for many years, Lawrence succumbed to the disease on March 2, 1930, at the age of 44. His reputation declined after his death, but the eventual legal publication of *Lady Chatterley's Lover* revived his popularity. Among his other well-known novels are *Sons and Lovers* (1913), *The Rainbow* (1915), and *Women in Love* (1921).

URSULA K. LE GUIN [b. 1929]

Born Ursula Kroeber in Berkeley, California, she is the daughter of the respected anthropologist and writer Alfred L. Kroeber. After receiving her B.A. at Radcliffe College in 1951 and an M.A. from Columbia University in 1952, she went to Paris as a Fulbright scholar. While there she married the historian Charles Le Guin. *Rocannon's World,* her first novel, was published in 1964, and since then she has written more than a dozen novels. Having won several prizes for her work, including the Nebula and Hugo awards, Le Guin is one of the outstanding contemporary writers of science fiction and fantasy. Her short works have been collected in *The Wind's Twelve Quarters* (1975) and *Orsinian Tales* (1976). She now lives in Portland, Oregon.

DORIS LESSING [b. 1919]

Born Doris Taylor in Kermanshah, Persia, she is the daughter of an English bank manager who early in her life moved the family to a farm in Southern Rhodesia in Africa. Raised in this lonely rural environment, she was educated at a convent school and a girls' high school. At the age of 18 she moved to Salisbury, the capital of Rhodesia, where she became involved in politics and joined the Communist party in 1942. She left the party when she became disillusioned with it during the post-World War II Stalin regime. Lessing was married twice while in Africa. After the break-up of her second marriage in 1949, she moved to England with her son. Her first novel, *The Grass is Singing,* was published there in 1950. Since then she has published several novels, among them *The Children of Violence,* an autobiographical series of five novels published over 17 years beginning in 1952, and *The Golden Notebook* (1962), perhaps her best-known work. Several collections of her short stories have appeared, including *The Habit of Loving* (1957), *A Man and Two Women* (1963), *The Black Madonna* (1966), *A Small Per-*

onal Voice (1974), and *The Memoirs of a Survivor* (1975). Lessing now resides in London.

CARSON McCULLERS [1917–1967]

Born Carson Smith on February 19, 1917, in Columbus, Georgia, she left Georgia for New York after graduating from high school. McCullers soon abandoned her original plan to enroll in the Juilliard music school and decided instead to pursue a literary career; she studied writing first at Columbia University and then at New York University. In 1940, at the age of twenty-two, her first novel, *The Heart Is a Lonely Hunter,* was published and received favorable attention from the critics. Her most popular novel, *The Member of the Wedding,* was published in 1946, successfully produced as a Broadway play in 1951, and adapted as a musical in 1971. While still in her twenties she suffered a series of strokes that left her partially crippled for the rest of her life. She died of a cerebral hemorrhage on September 29, 1967. In addition to her novels, a collection of short stories, *The Ballad of the Sad Cafe,* was published in 1951.

BERNARD MALAMUD [b. 1914]

Born on April 26, 1914, in Brooklyn, New York, Malamud graduated from City College of New York in 1936 and received a master's degree from Columbia in 1942. He taught English at New York City high schools, Oregon State University, and Harvard University, and at Bennington College. Among his many awards are the Pulitzer Prize and two National Book Awards—for *The Magic Barrel* (1958), a collection of stories, and *The Fixer* (1966), a novel. His other works include the novels *The Natural* (1952), *The Assistant* (1957), *A New Life* (1961), and *The Tenant* (1971), and collections of stories, including *Idiots First* (1963) and *Rembrandt's Hat* (1973).

THOMAS MANN [1875–1955]

Thomas Mann was born in the northern German city of Lübeck, the son of a distinguished and well-to-do family. His father was a grain merchant and a government figure; his mother was a musician. At 19 Mann left home to settle in Munich. There he worked briefly in an insurance office, then studied art and literature at the University of Munich. After a year in Rome, Mann turned his attention full time to writing. His first novel, *Buddenbrooks,* was published in 1901 and became an immediate success. *The Magic Mountain,* perhaps his best-known novel, appeared in 1924. He was awarded the Nobel Prize in Literature in 1929. Mann was vehemently opposed to the Nazi regime, and, as a result, was forced to leave Germany in 1933. Hitler ordered his books burned and revoked Mann's German citizenship in 1936. After seeking refuge for a brief time in Switzerland, Mann came to the United States where he lived until the end of World War II; in 1944 he became a U.S. citizen. In 1953, during the McCarthy era, Mann returned to Switzerland and settled in Zurich, where he spent the last years of his life. His short fiction is collected in *Stories of Three Decades* (1936).

KATHERINE MANSFIELD [1888–1923]

Born in Wellington, New Zealand, as Kathleen Mansfield Beauchamp, she left there in 1902 to study music for four years at Queens College in London. Visiting home briefly after her schooling, she persuaded her parents to allow her to return to London in 1908 to pursue a career as a writer. After working for a short time as a journalist, Mansfield devoted herself full time to short-story writing. Following an unhappy first marriage, she met the critic and editor John Middleton Murry in 1912 and married him in 1918. Through him she met D. H. Lawrence and his wife Frieda. Mansfield's first collection of stories, *In a German Pension,* was published in 1911 when she was just 23, but it received little critical attention. It was not until the publication of two later collections, *Bliss* in 1920 and *The Garden Party* in 1922, that her reputation as a major writer was established. Throughout most of her adult life she suffered from ill health and at the age of 35 died of tuberculosis in an institute near Fontainebleau in France. Later volumes of her short stories are *The Dove's Nest* (1923) and *Something Childish,* published posthumously in 1924.

GABRIEL GARCÍA MÁRQUEZ [b. 1928]

Gabriel García Márquez was born in Aracataca, a small village in Colombia and attended the University of Bogotá. In his early years he gave up the study of the law to pursue a career as a writer, working as a journalist and film critic for *El Espectador,* a Colombian newspaper. His first novel was written when he was 19, and his first collection of short stories, *Leaf Storm,* was published in 1955. The novel *One Hundred Years of Solitude,* published in 1967, is his best known work. A politically active leftist, García Márquez moved to Mexico in 1954 and has been a resident of Barcelona, Spain, since 1967. He was awarded the Nobel Prize in Literature in 1982. The award cited him for novels and short stories "in which the fantastic and the realistic are combined in a richly composed world of imagination, reflecting a continent's life and conflicts."

GUY DE MAUPASSANT [1850–1893]

Born near Dieppe in France, Maupassant was the son of an old and well-to-do Norman family. Early in his life he became the protégé of Gustave Flaubert, a friend of the family. Difficult and unmanageable in school, he was eventually expelled and served with the French army during the Franco-Prussian War. Afterward he settled in Paris, where, through Flaubert, he became acquainted with Turgenev, Goncourt, Zola, and Daudet. For the next seven years he wrote steadily, under the tutelage of Flaubert, but the master would allow nothing to be published. Finally, in 1880, the short story "Boule de Suif" (Ball of Fat) was published in an anthology edited by Zola, and Maupassant became instantly famous. Over the next decade his output was prodigious, including plays, travel sketches, novels, and short stories, of which he produced nearly three hundred and which are considered his finest accomplishment. His work provided him with a comfortable income, but unfortunately the syphilis he had contracted in his youth drove him to madness; he died at the age of forty-three in a sanitarium. Among his novels are *Une Vie* (A Life) (1883), *Bel Ami* (Handsome Friend) (1885), and *Pierre et Jean* (1888). Several collections of his short stories have been published.

HERMAN MELVILLE [1819–1891]

Born August 1, 1819, in New York City, Melville was the second son of Alan and Maria Melville, both of whom came from affluent and well-established families. His early years were spent comfortably until, in 1830, his father went bankrupt and the family was forced to move to Albany, where they were helped by relatives. After his father's death, in 1832, the young Melville spent long periods of time at his uncle's farm near Pittsfield, Massachusetts, and taught school there briefly. Melville ran away to sea in 1839 and over the next five years made two tours through the South Pacific, jumped ship at one point, and found himself living among cannibals in the Marquesas Islands. On his return to the United States he began immediately to write, his adventures at sea providing the material for much of his work. The speed at which he wrote was extraordinary: he produced seven novels in six years, beginning with *Typee* in 1846 and including *Moby-Dick* in 1851 and *Pierre* in 1852. Of these, the early novels were well received and became quite popular with the public. However, *Moby-Dick,* now regarded as one of the masterpieces of American fiction, was misunderstood, and *Pierre* was a complete failure. During this period Melville had married Elizabeth Shaw, the daughter of a Massachusetts judge. At first they lived in New York City, then in 1850 moved to Massachusetts, where later that year he met Nathaniel Hawthorne; the two became intimate friends. The 1850s were a difficult time in Melville's life: his reputation with readers and critics was declining and he was troubled with severe financial problems. By 1856, on the edge of a nervous breakdown, he scraped together enough money to set forth on a long journey to Europe and Palestine. Three more works of fiction were published in the latter half of the 1850s—*Israel Potter* (1855), *The Piazza Tales* (1856), and *The Confidence Man* (1857)—and from then on Melville devoted his creative energies to writing poetry. Back in New York with his family in 1866, he was finally forced to take a government job as a customs inspector in order to support himself, a position he was to hold for twenty years, until his wife received a small inheritance and he was able to retire. In the final years of his life Melville began his last work, *Billy Budd,* the first work of fiction he had written in nearly three decades. This masterpiece was published posthumously in 1924. Melville died in poverty and obscurity on September 28, 1891.

YUKIO MISHIMA [1925–1970]

Yukio Mishima, a pseudonym for Kimitake Hiraoka, was born in Tokyo, Japan, the son of a samurai family (the descendants of the aristocratic warrior class of feudal Japan). During World War II he worked in an aircraft factory, then graduated in 1947 from Tokyo Imperial University and served briefly in the finance ministry. From that time on he devoted himself to writing and to a variety of other pursuits—performing on the stage and in movies, directing films, and organizing political activities. In 1968 he founded and led the Shield Society, a group of young men dedicated to restoring the ideals of the samurai to modern Japan. After an unsuccessful demonstration against Japan's weak military position, he committed ritual suicide—a public disembowelment and decapitation. At the time of his death, in 1970, he ranked as Japan's foremost writer, having produced an impressive array of novels, stories, poems, plays, and essays. His best-known novels that have been translated into English include *Temple of the Golden Pavilion* (1956), *After the Banquet* (1960), *The Sailor Who Fell from Grace with the Sea* (1963), and *Forbidden Colors* (1968).

VLADIMIR NABOKOV [1899–1977]

Nabokov was born in St. Petersburg, Russia, the son of a wealthy and cultured family. He was raised in a privileged environment until his family lost all of its property when they left Russia in 1919 following the Bolshevik Revolution. Nabokov attended Trinity College of Cambridge University in England, receiving his degree in modern languages in 1922. That same year, his father, a liberal, was assassinated in Berlin by fascist gunmen. After graduation from the university, Nabokov lived in Europe—first in Berlin and then in Paris—and supported himself by working as a tennis coach and giving language lessons. Multilingual since childhood, he wrote novels during this time in Russian, German, and French. Nabokov was living in France with his wife and son at the time of the Nazi invasion; they escaped to the United States in 1940, where he became a citizen in 1945. From that time Nabokov wrote in English and translated many of his earlier works into English. *The Real Life of Sebastian Knight,* his first novel in English, was published in 1938. In the United States he taught literature at Wellesley College from 1941 to 1948 and at Cornell University from 1948 to 1959. The enormous world-wide success of his novel *Lolita,* published in Paris in 1955 and in the United States in 1958, enabled him to retire from teaching and spend all his time writing. Among his other novels are *Pnin* (1957), *Pale Fire* (1962), and *Ada* (1969). Five volumes of his short stories have appeared in English, including *Nine Stories* (1947), *Nabokov's Dozen* (1958), and *A Russian Beauty and Other Stories* (1973). Nabokov resided in Montreux, Switzerland, from 1960 until his death in 1977.

JOYCE CAROL OATES [b. 1938]

Born in Lockport in upstate New York, Joyce Carol Oates earned her B.A. degree in English at Syracuse University and an M.A. at the University of Wisconsin. She began writing in high school and was first published at the age of 21. After teaching for several years at the University of Windsor in Canada, she was appointed to the faculty of Princeton University. One of America's most versatile and productive contemporary writers, Oates has published 14 novels, the first of which was *With Shuddering Fall* in 1964, followed by *Expensive People* (1968), *them* (1969; winner of the National Book Award), *Wonderland* (1971) and *Bellefleur* (1980), to name just a few. In addition, she has published several volumes of poetry, literary criticism, two plays, and 12 collections of short fiction. Her stories are regularly included in the O. Henry Prize Stories collection; she has received the O. Henry Special Award for Continuing Achievement. Among the most notable collections of her short stories are *The Wheel of Love* (1970), *Marriages and Infidelities* (1972), *The Goddess and Other Women* (1974), and *A Sentimental Education* (1980).

FLANNERY O'CONNOR [1925–1964]

Flannery O'Connor was born in Savannah, Georgia, on March 25, 1925, and in her early youth moved with her family to a farm in Milledgeville, Georgia. After graduating from Georgia State College for Women in 1945, she attended the Writer's Workshop at the University of Iowa, from which she received an M.F.A. in 1947. From Iowa she moved to New York City to begin her writing career but, after little more than two years, illness forced her to return to her mother's farm in Georgia. Confined to invalidism because of lupus, Flannery O'Connor spent the remaining fourteen years of her life in Milledgeville raising peacocks and writing. Only occasionally during that period was she able to travel away from home to lecture and give readings from her works. She died in 1964 at the age of thirty-nine. Among her numerous honors and prizes was a posthumous National Book Award for *The Complete Stories,* published in 1971.

FRANK O'CONNOR [1903–1966]

Frank O'Connor, the pseudonym of Michael John O'Donovan, was born into a poor family in Cork, Ireland. He was educated by the Christian Brothers but left school at the age of 14, and, with no money for university, was self-educated thereafter. In the early 1920s O'Connor fought with the Irish Republican Army in the Irish struggle for independence, serving a year in a British prison camp. He later worked as a librarian in Cork and Dublin and from 1936 to 1939 served as the director of Dublin's Abbey Theater. In the late 1920s O'Connor's stories began to appear in Irish magazines such as the *Irish Statesman.* After publication of his first collection of stories, *Guest of the Nation,* in 1931, he began to be published regularly in American magazines. O'Connor was a prolific writer, producing nearly three dozen books during his lifetime, including more than twenty collections of short stories, two novels, five plays, several critical works, poems, and two autobiographical volumes, *An Only Child* and *My Father's Son.* Collections of his stories include *Crabapple Jelly* (1944), *The Stories of Frank O'Connor* (1952), and *More Stories by Frank O'Connor* (1954). In his later years O'Connor spent much of his time in the United States lecturing and teaching at Harvard, Northwestern, and Stanford universities. He died in Dublin in 1966.

TILLIE OLSEN [b. 1913]

Tillie Olsen was born in Omaha, Nebraska, and lived there until she was in her twenties. At 19 she began work on a novel focusing on a poor family during the Depression years. (It was left unfinished then but was finally completed and published in 1974 under the title *Yonnondio.*) Olsen married and settled in the San Francisco Bay area of California and until the 1950s was engaged mainly in raising her children. During the 1950s she resumed her writing career and published four widely acclaimed stories. These have been collected in *Tell Me a Riddle* (1961). The title story of that volume won the O. Henry Prize for the best short story of 1961. Olsen now devotes herself full time to writing and to teaching in creative writing workshops at several colleges and universities.

GRACE PALEY [b. 1922]

Born and raised in New York City and still residing there, Grace Paley attended Hunter College and New York University. She has taught at Columbia and Syracuse universities and is currently in the Department of Literature and Writing at Sarah Lawrence College. Her work has been collected in two books of short stories, *The Little Disturbances of Man* (1959) and *Enormous Changes at the Last Minute* (1974), the latter volume establishing her reputation and securing a wide audience for her writing.

EDGAR ALLAN POE [1809–1849]

Born in Boston on January 19, 1809, Poe was the son of itinerant actors. His father abandoned the family when the child was only a year old, his mother died soon after, and young Edgar became the ward of a well-to-do Virginia family, Mr. and Mrs. John Allan, whose name he took as a middle name. When the family fortunes declined, the Allans moved to England; Poe was educated there and at the University of Virginia after their return to Richmond. Although he was a scholar of distinction, his gambling and drinking made him a disgrace in the eyes of Mr. Allan and he was withdrawn from the university after one year. Poe made his way to Boston, enlisted in the army, and eventually took an appointment at West Point. After further dissipation ended his military career, he set out to support himself by writing. His first volume of poetry, *Tamerlane and Other Poems,* appeared in 1827; two more volumes followed in 1829 and 1831. Poe reaped little financial reward from his poetry, however, and soon turned to magazine writing as an editor for the *Southern Literary Messenger,* the first of a number of such jobs he held and then lost as a result of his chronic alcoholism. In 1836 he married Virginia Clemm, his thirteen-year-old cousin, and took on the support of her mother as well, making his financial difficulties even more acute. In his early stories he imitated current literary fashions in the hope that the works would become popular and financially successful, but his writing was never able to lift him out of poverty. After the death of his wife, in 1847, Poe became engaged to a wealthy widow. Celebrating this reversal of his fortunes with friends in Baltimore, he disappeared on a five-day binge, was found unconscious in the street, and died a short time afterward, on October 7, 1849. Long admired abroad, particularly in France, his poetry and stories took much longer to be appreciated by his compatriots. His work is available in a number of collected editions.

KATHERINE ANNE PORTER [1890–1980]

Katherine Anne Porter was born on May 15, 1890, in Indian Creek, Texas, and was educated at convent and private schools in Louisiana and Texas. She had a number of different occupations—newspaper reporter, ghost writer, editor, critic, book reviewer, and free-lance journalist. Although the quantity of her work is small and she did not publish until after she was thirty years old, Porter is acknowledged to be one of the masters of the short story. Her first collection of stories, *Flowering Judas,* appeared in 1930 and brought her immediate critical acclaim and public recognition. She received both the Pulitzer Prize and, in 1966, the National Book Award for her *Collected Stories.* Among her other works are the novel *Ship of Fools* (1962) and several collections of shorter pieces. Katherine Anne Porter died in 1980 at the age of 90.

JOHN STEINBECK [1902–1968]

Born in Salinas, California, Steinbeck was first introduced to literature by his mother, a former school teacher who encouraged him to read widely. He attended Stanford University and left in 1925 to go to New York in pursuit of a career as a writer. He stayed there for a short time, working as a reporter and a bricklayer. In 1927 he returned to California where he moved through a variety of odd jobs, became involved in the plight of migrant workers, and all the while continued to write. His first novel, *Cup of Gold,* was published in 1929, but it was not until publication of his fourth novel, *Tortilla Flat,* in 1935 that he began to attract critical attention and wide popular acclaim. His subsequent novels, *Of Mice and Men* (1937) and his masterpiece, *The Grapes of Wrath* (1939; Pulitzer Prize, 1940) were also popular successes. During World War II Steinbeck served as a war correspondent for the New York *Herald Tribune,* covering the action in Italy and Africa. In addition to his novels, Steinbeck published several nonfiction pieces and collections of short stories, including *The Long Valley* (1938) and *The Red Pony* (1945), and wrote screenplays for motion pictures. In 1962 he received the Nobel Prize in Literature. During 1966 he lived in South Vietnam and wrote a column about his experiences. He died on December 20, 1968.

JAMES THURBER [1894–1961]

Born and raised in Columbus, Ohio, Thurber attended Ohio State University but did not receive a degree. Early in his life he suffered a serious eye injury that was to impair his vision permanently and lead eventually to blindness. He worked briefly as a code clerk for the State Department in Washington and Paris, then returned to Ohio to take a job as a reporter on the Columbus *Dispatch.* During this time he also pursued another interest, the theater, writing and directing musicals for an Ohio State University theater group. In 1927 Thurber began his long association with *The New Yorker,* the magazine in which so many of his essays, fables, satires, stories, and cartoons were published over the next three decades. His book *The Years with Ross* describes the early, turbulent years at *The New Yorker* and his relationship with the magazine's founder and editor Harold Ross. Among his many other works are *Is Sex Necessary?* (1929), in collaboration with E. B. White; *The Thurber Carnival* (1945); *The Beast In Me and Other Animals* (1948); and a play, *The Male Animal* (1940).

LEO TOLSTOY [1828–1910]

Tolstoy was born at Yasnaya Polyana, his family's estate near Tula in Russia. His parents, members of the Russian aristocracy, died when Tolstoy was only nine, and he was brought up by his aunts. At age sixteen he went to study languages and law at the University of Kazan. More interested in gambling than in his studies, Tolstoy found school tedious and left without receiving a degree. He led a vain, aimless, and dissolute life until, in 1851, he joined the army, serving as an officer in the Caucasus. During this time Tolstoy became interested in writing, initially producing several portraits of military life and an autobiographical trilogy, *Childhood* (1852), *Boyhood* (1854), and *Youth* (1857). After leaving the army in 1855 he traveled in Western Europe, then divided his time between the family estate and St. Petersburg, where he had become acquainted with the leading literary and cultural figures of mid-nineteenth-century Russia. In 1862 he married Sophia Andreyevna Bers, a well-educated aristocratic woman, and they had thirteen children. Tolstoy's two greatest novels—*War and Peace* and *Anna Karenina*—were published in 1869 and 1877, respectively. After 1876 he experienced a profound personal crisis and was converted to a simple life in which nonviolence and Christian love became his guiding principles. In his later years Tolstoy's writing took on a more moralistic tone, exemplied in the novel *Resurrection* (1899). His commitment to giving up all worldly possessions eventually led to an estrangement from most of his family. At the age of 83, in a state of mental turmoil, and accompanied by his youngest daughter Alexandra, he left home, became ill, and died at a railway station in Astapovo.

JOHN UPDIKE [b. 1932]

Updike was born in Shillington, Pennsylvania, an only child. His mother was a writer and his father taught high school. While attending Harvard University, Updike was a cartoonist on the Harvard *Lampoon.* After graduation he went to England for a year to study drawing at the Ruskin School of Drawing and Fine Art. On his return, he joined the staff of *The New Yorker,* where he worked from 1955 to 1957. In addition to four volumes of poetry, a play, and a volume of essays and speeches, Updike has published ten novels and several collections of short fiction. Among his best-known novels are *The Poorhouse Fair* (1959), *Rabbit, Run* (1960), *The Centaur* (1963), which received the National Book Award, *Couples* (1968), *A Month of Sundays* (1975), and *Rabbit Returns* (1981). His collections of short stories include *Pigeon Feathers* (1962), *The Music School* (1966), and *Problems* (1979). Since the early 1960s Updike has resided in Ipswich, Massachusetts.

EUDORA WELTY [b. 1909]

Eudora Welty was born in Jackson, Mississippi, on April 13, 1909, and was educated at Mississippi State College for Women and the University of Wisconsin, from which she received a B.A. in 1929. She studied advertising for a short time at Columbia University before returning to Jackson to begin a literary career. Most of her life has been spent in Mississippi, an area that, with only occasional exceptions, provides the setting for her fictional works. A first collection of short stories, *A Curtain of Green,* was published in 1941. Subsequently she has produced five novels—*The Robber Bridegroom* (1942), *Delta Wedding* (1946), *The Ponder Heart* (1954), *Losing Battles* (1970), and *The Optimist's Daughter* (1972)—and three more volumes of stories.

WILLIAM CARLOS WILLIAMS [1883–1963]

The son of an English father and a Puerto Rican mother, Williams was born in Rutherford, New Jersey, where he lived for most of his life. After attending schools in Europe as a youth, Williams studied medicine at the University of Pennsylvania, received a degree in pediatrics from the University of Leipzig, and opened his medical practice in 1910 in Rutherford. During this period Williams became acquainted with Ezra Pound, H.D., and many of the other avant garde writers of the time. He began his writing career as an Imagist poet, contributing poems to various anthologies and publishing his first volume of poems in 1909. *Paterson,* a five-volume impressionistic poem published between 1946 and 1958, is widely regarded as his major poetic work. *Pictures from Breughel and Other Poems* (1962) was awarded the Pulitzer Prize in 1963. In addition to his poetry Williams wrote novels, including *White Mule* (1937) and *In the Money* (1940); several plays, collected in *Many Loves* (1961); several collections of essays; and many short stories. His short fiction has been collected in *The Knife of the Times* (1932) and *Making Light of It* (1950). After suffering a stroke in 1951 Williams retired from his medical practice. He died in Rutherford on March 4, 1963.

VIRGINIA WOOLF [1882–1941]

The daughter of Sir Leslie Stephen, a leading scholar in Victorian England, Virginia Woolf was born in London and was educated entirely by her father. Shortly after their father's death in 1904, Virginia, her brothers, and sister moved to a new home in Bloomsbury, then a bohemian section of London. Their residence soon became the center of a group of artists, writers, and intellectuals, known collectively as the Bloomsbury Group, and including among them the novelist E.M. Forster and the economist John Maynard Keynes. In 1912 Virginia married Leonard Woolf, a journalist and critic, and a few years later they founded the Hogarth Press, which published much of her writing. Her fine novels, among them *Mrs. Dalloway* (1925), *To the Lighthouse* (1927), and the experimental *The Waves* (1931), along with her short stories, have clearly distinguished Virginia Woolf as one of the most innovative and significant writers of the 20th century. Her stories are collected in *A Haunted House and Other Stories* (1943). Woolf was also a master of the essay; her nonfiction pieces are collected in several volumes, including *The Common Reader* (1925) and *The Death of the Moth and Other Essays* (1942). As a staunch supporter of feminism, Woolf wrote many works advocating women's rights, perhaps the best known of which is *A Room of One's*

wn. Throughout much of her life Woolf had been plagued by deep de-
ressions and emotional instability, suffering mental breakdowns in 1895
nd again in 1915. Probably driven by the fear of suffering another such
ɔllapse, she committed suicide in 1941 by drowning herself.

RICHARD WRIGHT [1908–1960]

ichard Wright was born on a cotton plantation east of Natchez, Mississip-
i, the son of a sharecropper father and a schoolteacher mother, and the
randchild of slaves. While Wright was still a young boy, the family moved
) Memphis, and shortly afterward his father deserted them. Because of
is mother's poor health and their abject poverty, he spent most of his
outh moving from place to place with his mother while she looked for
ork; at times he lived in foster homes and orphanages and with his grand-
ıother in Jackson, Mississippi. His formal education ended when he grad-
ated from the ninth grade as class valedictorian. In 1927 he settled in Chi-
ıgo, where he soon became a member of the Communist party and also
egan writing. In the early 1930s Wright joined the Federal Writer's Project
ı Chicago, and while part of this group directed a Negro theater. During
ıese years he wrote *Uncle Tom's Children* (1938), a collection of four long
ːories that was his first success. By the late 1930s, with his reputation as
writer increasing, Wright moved to New York and was appointed Harlem
ditor of the *Daily Worker.* His first novel, *Native Son* (1940), is considered
y many critics his most important work and established him as a major
riter and the spokesman for black Americans. *Black Boy,* published in 1945,
ividly describes his childhood and youth. Wright broke with the Commu-
ist party in 1942, having become disillusioned with it over differences on
ıcial questions. In 1947 he left the United States and settled in Paris, where
e became acquainted with many noted writers and intellectuals, including
ïide, Gertrude Stein, Jean Paul Sartre, and Simone de Beauvoir. He spent
ıe rest of his life as an expatriate in Paris and died there on November
8, 1960. His short stories are collected in *Eight Men,* published posthu-
ıously in 1961.

James Baldwin: "Sonny's Blues" excerpted from the book *Going To Meet th Man* by James Baldwin. Originally published in *Mademoiselle.* Reprinte by permission of The Dial Press. Copyright © 1968 by James Baldwi

John Barth: "Lost in the Funhouse" copyright © 1967 by *The Atlant Monthly Company* from the book *Lost in the Funhouse* by John Barth. Re printed by permission of Doubleday & Company, Inc.

Donald Barthelme: "Report" reprinted by permission of Farrar, Straus an Giroux, Inc. from *Unspeakable Practices, Unnatural Acts* by Donald Ba thelme. Copyright © 1967, 1968 by Donald Barthelme.

Jorge Luis Borges: "The Secret Miracle" reprinted by permission of Ne Directions Publishing Corporation from *Labyrinths and Other Stories* b Jorge Luis Borges, translated by Harriet de Onis. Copyright © 1962, 196 by New Directions Publishing Corporation.

Willa Cather: "Paul's Case" from *Youth and the Bright Medusa* by Wil Cather. Copyright 1920 by Willa Cather and renewed 1948 by the Execu tors of the Estate of Willa Cather. Reprinted by permission of Alfred A Knopf, Inc.

John Cheever: "The Country Husband" copyright 1954 by John Cheeve Reprinted from *The Stories of John Cheever,* by John Cheever, by permissio of Alfred A. Knopf, Inc.

Anton Chekhov: "The Lady with the Dog" from *Short Novels and Stories* b A. P. Chekhov, translated by Ivy Litvinov (Moscow: Foreign Language n. d.). "A Visit to Friends," from *The Unknown Chekhov,* translated b Avrahm Yarmolinsky. Copyright 1954 by Avrahm Yarmolinsky. Copy right renewed © 1982 by Babette Deutsch Yarmolinsky. Reprinted b permission of Farrar, Straus & Giroux, Inc. "Dushechka," from *Best Rus sian Short Stories,* translated by Rosa Graham (New York: Boni & Liveright 1917).

Joseph Conrad: "The Secret Sharer" copyright 1910 by Harper & Bro. fror the book *Twixt Land and Sea* by Joseph Conrad. Reprinted by permissio of Doubleday & Company, Inc. and the Trustees of the Joseph Conra Estate.

Ralph Ellison: "King of the Bingo Game" reprinted by permission of Wil liam Morris Agency on behalf of the author. Copyright © 1944 by Ralpl Ellison.

Doris Lessing: "Our Friend Judith" from *A Man and Two Women* copyrig © 1958, 1962, 1963 by Doris Lessing. Reprinted by permission of Sim & Schuster, a Division of Gulf & Western Corporation. Copyright 1963 by Doris Lessing. Reprinted by permission of Curtis Brown Lt London, on behalf of Doris Lessing.

Bernard Malamud: "The Magic Barrel" reprinted by permission of Farra Straus and Giroux, Inc. from *The Magic Barrel* by Bernard Malamu Copyright © 1954, 1958, 1982 by Bernard Malamud.

Thomas Mann: "Disorder and Early Sorrow" copyright 1936 and renewe 1964 by Alfred A. Knopf, Inc. Reprinted from *Stories of Three Decades,* b Thomas Mann, translated by H. T. Lowe-Porter, by permission of th publisher.

Katherine Mansfield: "A Dill Pickle" copyright 1920 by Alfred A. Knop Inc. and renewed 1948 by J. Middleton Murry. Reprinted from *The Sho Stories of Katherine Mansfield,* by Katherine Mansfield, by permission of A fred A. Knopf, Inc.

Gabriel García Márquez: "A Very Old Man with Enormous Wings" fror *Leaf Storm and Other Stories* by Gabriel García Márquez, translated by Greg ory Rabassa. Copyright © 1971 by Gabriel García Márquez. Reprinte by permission of Harper & Row, Publishers, Inc.

Guy de Maupassant: "The Necklace" reprinted with permission of T. Wer ner Laurie Ltd. at The Bodley Head from *Boule de Suif and Other Short Storie* by Guy de Maupassant, translated by Marjorie Laurie.

Carson McCullers: "A Tree • A Rock • A Cloud" from *Ballad of the Sad Caf and Collected Short Stories* by Carson McCullers. Copyright © 1955 by Car- son McCullers. Reprinted by permission of Houghton Mifflin Company

Yukio Mishima: "Patriotism" translated by Geoffrey W. Sargent in *Deat in Midsummer and Other Stories.* Copyright © 1966 by New Directions Pub- lishing Corporation. Reprinted by permission of New Directions Pub- lishing Corporation.

Vladimir Nabokov: "The Vane Sisters" from *Tyrants Destroyed and Other Stories* by Vladimir Nabokov. Copyright © 1975. Published by and reprinted with permission of the McGraw-Hill Book Company.

Joyce Carol Oates: "How I Contemplated the World from the Detroit House of Correction and Began My Life Over Again" reprinted from *The Wheel of Love and Other Stories* by Joyce Carol Oates by permission of the publisher, Vanguard Press Inc. Copyright © 1970, 1969, 1968, 1967, 1966, 1965 by Joyce Carol Oates.

Flannery O'Connor: "A Good Man Is Hard To Find" copyright 1953 by Flannery O'Connor; renewed 1981 by Mrs. Regina O'Connor. Reprinted from *A Good Man Is Hard To Find and Other Stories* by Flannery O'Connor by permission of Harcourt Brace Jovanovich, Inc.

Frank O'Connor: "First Confession" copyright 1951 by Frank O'Connor. Reprinted from *Collected Stories,* by Frank O'Connor, by permission of Alfred A. Knopf, Inc. and Joan Daves.

Tillie Olsen: "I Stand Here Ironing" excerpted from the book *Tell Me A Riddle* by Tillie Olsen. Copyright © 1956 by Tillie Olsen. Reprinted by permission of Delacorte Press/Seymour Lawrence.

Grace Paley: "A Conversation With My Father" from *Enormous Changes at the Last Minute* by Grace Paley. Copyright © 1972, 1974 by Grace Paley. Reprinted by permission of Farrar, Straus and Giroux, Inc.

Katherine Anne Porter: "The Grave" from *The Leaning Tower and Other Stories,* copyright 1944, 1972 by Katherine Anne Porter. Reprinted by permission of Harcourt Brace Jovanovich, Inc.

John Steinbeck: "The Chrysanthemums" from *The Long Valley* by John Steinbeck. Copyright 1938 by John Steinbeck. Copyright renewed 1966 by John Steinbeck. Reprinted by permission of Viking Penguin Inc.

James Thurber: "The Secret Life of Walter Mitty" copyright © 1942 by James Thurber. Copyright © 1970 by Helen W. Thurber and Rosemary T. Sauers. *From My World—And Welcome to It,* published by Harcourt Brace Jovanovich, Inc.

Leo Tolstoy: "The Death of Ivan Ilych" from *The Death of Ivan Ilych and Other Stories* by Leo Tolstoy translated by Louis and Aylmer Maude (1935). Reprinted by permission of Oxford University Press.

John Updike: "A & P" copyright © 1962. Reprinted from *Pigeon Feathers,* by John Updike, by permission of Alfred A. Knopf, Inc.

Eudora Welty: "A Worn Path" copyright 1941, 1969 by Eudora Welty. Re printed from her volume *A Curtain of Green and Other Stories* by permissio of Harcourt Brace Jovanovich, Inc.

William Carlos Williams: "The Use of Force" from *The Farmer's Daughters* Copyright 1938 by William Carlos Williams. Reprinted by permissio of New Directions Publishing Corporation.

Virginia Woolf: "Kew Gardens" from *A Haunted House and Other Stories* b Virginia Woolf, copyright 1944, 1972 by Harcourt Brace Jovanovich, Inc Reprinted by permission of the publisher and the Author's Literary Es tate and The Hogarth Press.

Richard Wright: "The Man Who Was Almost a Man" from *Eight Men* by Richard Wright (The World Publishing Company). Copyright 1940, © 1961 by Richard Wright. Reprinted by permission of Harper & Row Publishers, Inc.